PEAK CASTLE, DERBYSHIRE

PEVERIL OF THE PEAK

BY

SIR WALTER SCOTT, Bart.

If my readers should at any time remark that I am particularly
dull, they may be assured there is a design under it.

BRITISH ESSAYIST

WITH THIRTY ILLUSTRATIONS

HENRY FROWDE
OXFORD UNIVERSITY PRESS
LONDON, NEW YORK, TORONTO AND MELBOURNE
1911

CONTENTS

	PAGE
LIST OF ILLUSTRATIONS	iii
LIST OF CHARACTERS	iv
INTRODUCTION	vii
TEXT	1
NOTES	621
GLOSSARY	655

LIST OF ILLUSTRATIONS

	PAGE
PEAK CASTLE, DERBYSHIRE	Frontispiece
TITLE. FACSIMILE OF SIR WALTER SCOTT'S HANDWRITING	1
LADY PEVERIL PRESENTING THE INFANT ALICE TO MAJOR BRIDGENORTH	9
ALICE INTRODUCED TO HER FATHER	17
THE CAVALIERS DINING AT MARTINDALE CASTLE	43
THE COUNTESS OF DERBY	53
THE EARL OF DERBY	56
THE CHALLENGE	107
ALICE DANCING BEFORE HER FATHER	141
ALICE BRIDGENORTH	151
FENELLA	193
ALICE AND JULIAN SURPRISED BY BRIDGENORTH	200
JULIAN AND FENELLA	222
THE TRAVELLERS LEAVING THE INN	263
CHIFFINCH	342
GEORGE VILLIERS, DUKE OF BUCKINGHAM	355
HENRY BENNETT, EARL OF ARLINGTON	365
THE DUKE OF ORMOND	383
NEWGATE, AS BUILT BY SIR RICHARD WHITTINGTON	428
JULIAN BEFORE THE WARDEN OF NEWGATE	430
WILLIAM EVANS, PORTER TO CHARLES I, AND SIR G. HUDSON, HIS DWARF	436
SIR GEOFFREY HUDSON	438
JULIAN PEVERIL AND SIR GEOFFREY HUDSON IN NEWGATE	452
COLONEL BLOOD	486
THE DUKE OF BUCKINGHAM AND ZARAH	498
CATHERINE OF BRAGANZA, QUEEN OF CHARLES II	511
TITUS OATES	527
SIR GEOFFREY AND JULIAN PEVERIL ATTACKED BY THE MOB	539
CHARLES II	601
THE BEACON OF MARTINDALE-MOULTRASSIE	620

CHARACTERS

ALDRICK, a Jesuit, confessor to the Countess of Derby.
ARLINGTON; HENRY BENNET, EARL OF, Lord Chamberlain.
BAJAZET, black page at the palace.
BARSTON, CAPTAIN, Jesuit; correspondent of Countess of Derby.
BEACON, TOM, groom to Chiffinch.
BLOOD, COLONEL THOMAS, agent to Duke of Buckingham.
BRAKEL, ADRIAN, a gipsy mountebank.
BREWER, SAM, a follower of Peveril.
BRIDGENORTH, RALPH, Edward Christian's brother-in-law.
BRIDLESLY, JOE, a horse-dealer.
BUCKINGHAM; GEORGE VILLIERS, DUKE OF.
CAPTAIN OF NEWGATE, chief jailer.
CARLETON, CAPTAIN, of the Guards.
CHAMBERLAIN, MATTHEW, of the 'Peveril Arms'.
CHARLES THE SECOND.
CHAUBERT, MONSIEUR, Chiffinch's cook.
CHIFFINCH, THOMAS, the King's private emissary.
CHOLMONDLEY OF VALE ROYAL, friend of Peveril.
CHRISTAL, MARTIN, Julian's landlord at the Savoy.
CHRISTIAN, EDWARD, brother to Colonel Christian.
CHRISTIAN, COLONEL WILLIAM, shot for insurrection.
CLEGG, HOLDFAST, a Puritan mill-wright.
CLINK, JEM, turnkey at Newgate.
COLEBY, MAJOR, warder at the Tower.
CRANBOURNE, SIR JASPER, friend of Sir Geoffrey Peveril.
CROFTS, MASTER, a gallant.
DANGERFIELD, CAPTAIN, a hired witness to the Popish Plot.
DERBY; PHILIP, EARL OF; AND KING OF MAN.
DITCHLEY, GAFFER, a miner.
DOUBLEFEE, JACOB, a money-lender.
DUMMERAR, DOCTOR, an episcopal parson.
EMPSON, the King's flageolet-player.
ETHEREGE, SIR GEORGE, a courtier.
EVANS, the giant porter of Charles I.
EVERETT, a hired witness to the Popish Plot.
GATHERAL, steward to the Duke of Buckingham.
GATHERILL, bailiff to Sir Geoffrey Peveril.
GREENHALGH, the Earl of Derby's messenger.
GRIFFITHS, his steward.

HANSON, ADRIAN, a Dutch merchant.
HODGESON, GAFFER, a Puritan.
HOWLAGLASS, MASTER, a preacher.
HUDSON, SIR GEOFFREY, Charles I's dwarf.
JAMES, DUKE OF YORK, the King's brother.
JENKINS, JACK, a fencer in the Duke of Buckingham's service.
JEREMY, MASTER, Lord Savile's chief domestic.
JERNINGHAM, THOMAS, gentleman to the Duke of Buckingham.
JONATHAN, attendant on Lord Savile.
LAMINGTON, follower of Sir Geoffrey Peveril.
MAULSTATUTE, MASTER, a magistrate.
MORRIS, servant to the Earl of Derby.
NORTH, LORD, Chief Justice of the Common Pleas.
OATES, TITUS, discoverer of the Popish Plot.
ORMOND, DUKE OF, a privy councillor.
OUTRAM, LANCE, park-keeper at Martindale Castle.
PEVERIL OF THE PEAK, SIR GEOFFREY, a Cavalier.
PEVERIL, JULIAN, son of Sir Geoffrey.
PIGAL, MONSIEUR DE, a dancing-master.
QUODLING, REV. MR., chaplain to the Duke of Buckingham.
RAINE, ROGER, landlord of the 'Peveril Arms'.
RALF, ROUGH, Lance Outram's helper.
RIMEGAP, JOE, a miner.
ROCHESTER ; JOHN WILMOT, EARL OF, the disgraced minister.
RUPERT, PRINCE, the king's cousin.
SAUNDERS, a groom.
SAVILE, LORD, a young nobleman.
SCROGGS, SIR WILLIAM, Lord Chief Justice.
SEDLEY, SIR CHARLES, a courtier.
SELBY, CAPTAIN, of the Guards.
SETTLE, ELKANA, the poet.
SHAFTESBURY ; ANTHONY ASHLEY COOPER, EARL OF, one of the king's ministers.
SHARPER, MASTER, a cutler in the Strand.
SHORTELL, MASTER, a mercer at Liverpool.
SOLSGRACE, NEHEMIAH, a Presbyterian pastor.
TOPHAM, CHARLES, Usher of the Black Rod.
WAKEMAN, SIR GEORGE, the Queen's physician.
WEEVER, OLD, a preacher.
WHALLEY, RICHARD, the regicide.
WHITAKER, RICHARD, steward at Martindale Castle.
WHITECRAFT, JOHN, innkeeper at Altringham.
WILDBLOOD OF THE VALE, DICK, a friend of Peveril.
WIN-THE-FIGHT, JOACHIM, Major Bridgenorth's attorney.

ALICE, servant-girl at Altringham.
ANNE, LADY, daughter of the Duke of York, afterwards Queen Anne.

BRIDGENORTH, ALICE, daughter of Ralph Bridgenorth.
BRIDGENORTH, MRS., her mother.
BUCKINGHAM, DUCHESS OF.
CATHARINE OF BRAGANZA, wife of Charles II.
CHIFFINCH, KATE, Chiffinch's mistress.
CLEVELAND, DUCHESS OF, one of the King's mistresses.
DEBBITCH, DEBORAH, servant at Martindale Castle.
DERBY; CHARLOTTE DE LA TREMOUILLE, COUNTESS OF; AND QUEEN
    OF MAN.
DOWLAS, DAME, the Duke of Buckingham's housekeeper.
ELLESMERE, MRS., head domestic at Martindale Castle.
FENELLA, a deaf and dumb girl, in the service of the Countess of
    Derby.
GWYN, NELL, one of the King's mistresses.
MARTHA, DAME, Major Bridgenorth's housekeeper.
NEWCASTLE, DUCHESS OF, an old noblewoman.
PEVERIL; MARGARET, LADY, Sir Geoffrey's wife.
PORTSMOUTH; LOUISE DE LA QUEROUAILLE, DUCHESS OF, one of the
    King's mistresses.
RACHAEL, a servant-girl.
RAINE, DAME, of the 'Peveril Arms'.
SELLOK, CISLY, a servant-girl at Martindale Castle.
WHITECRAFT, DAME, innkeeper's wife at Altringham.

INTRODUCTION

IF I had valued my own reputation, as it is said I ought in prudence to have done, I might have now drawn a line, and remained for life, or (who knows ?) perhaps for some years after death, the ' ingenious author of Waverley '. I was not, however, more desirous of this sort of immortality, which might have lasted some twenty or thirty years, than Falstaff of the embowelling which was promised him after the field of Shrewsbury by his patron the Prince of Wales. ' Embowelled ? If you embowel me to-day, you may powder and eat me to-morrow ! '

If my occupation as a romancer were taken from me, I felt I should have at a late hour in life to find me out another ; when I could hardly expect to acquire those new tricks which are proverbially said not to be learned by those dogs who are getting old. Besides, I had yet to learn from the public that my intrusions were disagreeable ; and while I was endured with some patience, I felt I had all the reputation which I greatly coveted. My memory was well stored, both with historical, local, and traditional notices, and I had become almost as licensed a plague to the public as the well-remembered beggar of the ward, whom men distinguish by their favour, perhaps for no better reason than that they had been in the habit of giving him alms, as a part of the business of their daily promenade. The general fact is undeniable—all men grow old, all men must wear out ; but men of ordinary wisdom, however aware of the general fact, are unwilling to admit in their own case any special instances of failure. Indeed, they can hardly be expected themselves to distinguish the effects of the Archbishop of Granada's apoplexy, and are not unwilling to pass over in their composition, as instances of mere carelessness or bad luck, what others may consider as symptoms of mortal decay. I had no choice save that of absolutely laying aside the pen, the use of which at my time of life was become a habit, or to continue its vagaries, until the public should let me plainly understand they would no more of me ; a hint which I was not unlikely to meet with, and which I was determined to take without waiting for a repetition. This hint, that the reader may plainly understand me, I was determined to take, when the publication of a new Waverley novel should not be the subject of some attention in the literary world.

An accidental circumstance decided my choice of a subject for the present work. It was now several years since my immediate younger brother, Thomas Scott, already mentioned in these notes, had resided for two or three seasons in the Isle of Man, and, having access to the registers of that singular territory, had copied many of them, which he subjected to my perusal. These papers were put into my hands while my brother had thoughts of making some literary use of them, I do not well remember what ; but he never came to any decision on that head, and grew tired of the task of transcription. The papers, I suppose, were lost in the course of a military man's life. The tenor of them, that is, of the most remarkable, remained engraved on the memory of the author.

The interesting and romantic story of William Christian especially struck my fancy. I found the same individual, as well as his father, particularly noticed in some memorials of the island, preserved by the Earl of Derby, and published in Dr. Peck's *Desiderata Curiosa*. This gentleman was the son of Edward, formerly governor of the island ; and William himself was afterwards one of its two Dempsters, or supreme judges. Both father and son embraced the party of the islanders, and contested some feudal rights claimed by the Earl of Derby as king of the island. When the earl had suffered death at Bolton-le-Moors, Captain Christian placed himself at the head of the Roundheads, if they might be so called, and found the means of holding communication with a fleet sent by the parliament. The island was surrendered to the parliament by the insurgent Manxmen. The high-spirited countess and her son were arrested, and cast into prison, where they were long detained, and very indifferently treated. When the Restoration took place, the countess, or by title the queen-dowager of the island, seized upon William Dhône, or Fair-haired William, as William Christian was termed, and caused him to be tried and executed, according to the laws of the island, for having dethroned his liege mistress, and imprisoned her and her family. Romancers, and readers of romance, will generally allow, that the fate of Christian, and the contrast of his character with that of the high-minded but vindictive Countess of Derby, famous during the civil wars for her valiant defence of Latham House, contained the essence of an interesting tale. I have, however, dwelt little either on the death of William Christian, or on the manner in which Charles II viewed that stretch of feudal power, and the heavy fine which he imposed upon the Derby estates for that extent of jurisdiction of which the countess had been guilty. Far less have I given any opinion on the justice or guilt of that action, which is to this day judged of by the people of the island as they happen to be connected with the sufferer, or perhaps as they may look back with the eyes of favour upon the Cavaliers or Roundheads of those contentious days. I do not conceive that I have done injury to the memory of this gentleman, or any of his descendants in his person ; at the same time, I have most willingly given his representative an opportunity of stating in this edition of the novel what he thinks necessary for the vindication of his ancestor, and the reader will find the exposition in the notices, for which Mr. Christian desires admission.[1] I could do no less, considering the polite and gentlemanlike manner in which he stated feelings concerning his ancestry, to which a Scotsman can hardly be supposed to be indifferent.

In another respect, Mr. Christian with justice complains, that Edward Christian, described in the romance as the brother of the gentleman executed in consequence of the countess's arbitrary act of authority, is portrayed as a wretch of unbounded depravity, having only ingenuity and courage to rescue him from abhorrence, as well as hatred. Any personal allusion was entirely undesigned on the part of the author. The Edward Christian of the tale is a mere creature of the imagination. Commentators have naturally enough identified him with a brother of William Christian, named Edward, who died in prison after being confined

[1] See Appendix, No. I, p. xiii.

seven or eight years in Peel Castle, in the year 1650. Of him I had no access to know anything ; and as I was not aware that such a person had existed, I could hardly be said to have traduced his character. It is sufficient for my justification, that there lived at the period of my story a person named Edward Christian, ' with whom connected, or by whom begot,' I am a perfect stranger, but who we know to have been engaged in such actions as may imply his having been guilty of anything bad. The fact is, that upon the 5th June, 1680, Thomas Blood (the famous crown-stealer), *Edward Christian*, Arthur O'Brian, and others, were found guilty of being concerned in a conspiracy for taking away the life and character of the celebrated Duke of Buckingham ; but that this Edward was the same with the brother of William Christian is impossible, since that brother died in 1650 ; nor would I have used his christened name of Edward, had I supposed there was a chance of its being connected with any existing family. These genealogical matters are fully illustrated in the notes to the Appendix.

I ought to have mentioned in the former editions of this romance, that Charlotte de la Tremouille, Countess of Derby, represented as a Catholic, was, in fact, a French Protestant. For misrepresenting the noble dame in this manner, I have only Lucio's excuse—' I spoke according to the trick.' In a story, where the greater part is avowedly fiction, the author is at liberty to introduce such variations from actual fact as his plot requires, or which are calculated to enhance it ; in which predicament the religion of the Countess of Derby, during the Popish Plot, appeared to fall. If I have over-estimated a romancer's privileges and immunities, I am afraid this is not the only nor most important case in which I have done so. To speak big words, the heroic countess has far less grounds for an action of scandal than the memory of Virgil might be liable to for his posthumous scandal of Dido.

The character of Fenella, which, from its peculiarity, made a favourable impression on the public, was far from being original. The fine sketch of Mignon, in *Wilhelm Meister's Lehrjahre*, a celebrated work from the pen of Goethe, gave the idea of such a being. But the copy will be found greatly different from my great prototype ; nor can I be accused of borrowing anything, save the general idea, from an author, the honour of his own country, and an example to the authors of other kingdoms, to whom all must be proud to own an obligation.

Family tradition supplied me with two circumstances which are somewhat analogous to that in question. The first is an account of a lawsuit, taken from a Scottish report of adjudged cases, quoted in note to Chapter XX.

The other, of which the editor has no reason to doubt, having often heard it from those who were witnesses of the fact, relates to the power of a female in keeping a secret (sarcastically said to be impossible), even when that secret refers to the exercise of her tongue.

In the middle of the eighteenth century, a female wanderer came to the door of Mr. Robert Scott, grandfather of the present author, an opulent farmer in Roxburghshire, and made signs that she desired shelter for the night, which, according to the custom of the times, was readily granted. The next day the country was covered with snow, and the departure of the wanderer was rendered impossible. She remained for many days, her maintenance adding little to the expense of a considerable household ; and by the time that the weather grew milder, she had learned to hold intercourse by signs with the household around her, and could intimate to them that she was desirous of staying where she was, and working at the wheel and other employ-ment to compensate for her food. This was a compact not unfrequent at that time, and the dumb woman entered upon her thrift, and proved a useful member of the patri-archal household. She was a good spinner, knitter, carder, and so forth, but her excellence lay in attending to the feed-ing and bringing up the domestic poultry. Her mode of whistling to call them together was so peculiarly elfish and shrill, that it was thought, by those who heard it, more like that of a fairy than a human being.

In this manner she lived three or four years, nor was there the slightest idea entertained in the family that she was other than the mute and deprived person she had always appeared. But in a moment of surprise she dropped the mask which she had worn so long.

It chanced upon a Sunday that the whole inhabitants of the household were at church excepting Dumb Lizzie, whose infirmity was supposed to render her incapable of profiting by divine service, and who therefore stayed at home to take charge of the house. It happened that, as she was sitting in the kitchen, a mischievous shepherd boy, instead of looking after his flock on the lea, as was his duty, slunk into the house to see what he could pick up, or perhaps out of mere curiosity. Being tempted by something which was in his eyes a nicety, he put forth his hand, unseen, as he conceived, to appropriate it. The dumb woman came suddenly upon him, and, in the surprise, forgot her part, and exclaimed in loud Scotch, and with distinct articulation, ' Ah, you little devil's limb ! ' The boy, terrified more by the character of the person who rebuked him, than by the mere circumstance of having been taken in the insignificant offence, fled in great dismay to the church, to carry the miraculous news that the dumb woman had found her tongue.

The family returned home in great surprise, but found that their inmate had relapsed into her usual mute condition, would communicate with them only by signs, and in that manner denied positively what the boy affirmed.

From this time confidence was broken betwixt the other inmates of the family and their dumb, or rather silent, guest. Traps were laid for the supposed imposter, all of which she skilfully eluded ; firearms were often suddenly discharged near her, but never on such occasions was she seen to start. It seems probable, however, that Lizzie grew tired of all this mistrust, for she one morning disappeared as she came, without any ceremony of leavetaking.

She was seen, it is said, upon the other side of the English border, in perfect possession of her speech. Whether this was exactly the case or not, my informers were no way anxious in inquiring, nor am I able to authenticate the fact. The shepherd boy lived to be a man, and always averred that she had spoken distinctly to him. What could be the woman's reason for persevering so long in a disguise as unnecessary as it was severe, could never be guessed, and was perhaps the consequence of a certain aberration of the mind. I can only add, that I have every reason to believe the tale to be perfectly authentic, so far as it is here given, and it may serve to parallel the supposed case of Fenella.

ABBOTSFORD,
1st July 1831.

APPENDIX TO INTRODUCTION

No. I

THE following notices were recommended to my attention, in the politest manner possible, by John Christian, Esq., of Milntown, in the Isle of Man, and Unrigg, in Cumberland, Dempster at present of the Isle of Man. This gentleman is naturally interested in the facts which are stated, as representative of the respectable family of Christian, and lineally descended from William Dhône, put to death by the Countess of Derby. I can be no way interested in refusing Mr. Christian this justice, and willingly lend my aid to extend the exculpation of the family.

HISTORICAL NOTICES OF EDWARD AND WILLIAM CHRISTIAN;

TWO CHARACTERS IN 'PEVERIL OF THE PEAK.'

THE venerable Dr. Dryasdust, in a preparatory dialogue, apprises the Eidolon, or apparition of the author, that he stood 'much accused for adulterating the pure sources of historical knowledge;' and is answered by that emanation of genius, 'that he has done some service to the public if he can present to them a lively fictitious picture, for which the original anecdote or circumstance which he made free to press into his service, only furnished a slight sketch;' 'that by introducing to the busy and the youthful,

Truths severe in fairy fiction dress'd,

and by creating an interest in fictitious adventures ascribed to an historical period and characters, the reader begins next to be anxious *to learn what the facts really were,* and how far the novelist has justly represented them.'

The adventures ascribed to 'historical characters' would, however, fail in their moral aim, if fiction were placed at variance with truth; if Hampden or Sydney, for example, were painted as

swindlers ; or Lady Jane Grey, or Rachel Russell, as abandoned
women.

' Odzooks ! must one swear to the truth of a song ? ' although
an excellent joke, were a bad palliation in such a case. Fancy may
be fairly indulged in the illustration, but not in the perversion of
fact; and if the fictitious picture should have no general resemblance
to the original, the flourish of

Truths severe in fairy fiction dress'd,

were but an aggravation of the wrong.

The family of CHRISTIAN is indebted to this splendid luminary of
the North for abundant notoriety.

The William Christian represented on one part as an ungrateful
traitor, on the other as the victim of a judicial murder, and his
brother (or relative) Edward, one of the suite of a Duke [1] of Buckingham, were so far real historical persons. Whether the talents and
skill of Edward in imposing on Fenella a feigned silence of several
years, be among the legitimate or supernatural wonders of this
fertile genius, his fair readers do not seem to be agreed. Whether
the residue of the canvas, filled up with a masterly picture of the
most consummate hypocrite and satanic villain ever presented to
the imagination, be consistent with the historical character of this
individual, is among the subjects of research to which the novelist
has given a direct invitation in his prefatory chapter.

English history furnishes few materials to aid the investigation
of transactions chiefly confined to the Isle of Man. Circumstances
led me, many years ago, to visit this ancient Lilliput ; whether as
one of those ' smart fellows worth talking to,' ' in consequence of
a tumble from my barouche,' ' as a ruined miner,' or as ' a disappointed speculator,' is of no material import. It may be that
temporary embarrassment drove me into seclusion, without any of
the irresistible inducements alluded to ; and want of employment,
added to the acquaintance and aid of a zealous local antiquary,
gradually led to an examination of all accessible authorities on this
very subject among others. So it happened, that I had not landed
many hours before I found the mournful ditty of ' William Dhône '
(brown or fair-haired William, this very identical William Christian)
twanged through the demi-nasal, demi-guttural trumpet of the car-
man, and warbled by the landlady's pretty daughter; in short, making
as great a figure in its little sphere as did once the more important
ballad of Chevy Chase in its wider range : the burden of the song
purporting that William Dhône was the mirror of virtue and patriotism, and that envy, hatred, and malice, and all uncharitableness,
operate the destruction of the wisest and the best.

Themes of popular feeling naturally attract the earliest notice

[1] Not the duke described in *Peveril*, but the companion of Charles I
in his Spanish romance.

of a stranger; and I found the story of this individual, though
abundantly garbled and discoloured on the insular records, full of
circumstances to excite the deepest interest, but which, to be rendered
intelligible, must be approached by a circuitous route, in which
neither elfin page, nor maiden fair, can be the companion of our walk.

The loyal and celebrated James, seventh Earl of Derby, was
induced, by the circumstances of the times, to fix his chief residence
in the Isle of Man from 1643 to 1651 [1].   During this period he composed, in the form of a letter [2] to his son Charles (Lord Strange),
an historical account of that island, with a statement of his own
proceedings there; interspersed with much political advice for the
guidance of his successor; full of acute observation, and evincing
an intimate acquaintance with the works of Machiavelli, which it
appears, by a quotation [3], that he had studied in a Latin edition.
The work, although formally divided into chapters and numbered
paragraphs, is professedly desultory,[4] and furnishes few means of
determining the relative dates of his facts, which must accordingly
be supplied by internal evidence, and in some cases by conjecture.

He appears to have been drawn thither, in 1643, by letters [5]
intimating the danger of a revolt : the ' people had begun the fashion
of England in murmuring '; assembled in a tumultuous manner;
desiring new laws, they would have no bishops, pay no tithes to
the clergie, despised authority, rescued people committed by the
governor,' &c. &c.

The earl's first care was to apply himself to the consideration of
these insurrectionary movements ; and as he found some interrrup-
tion to his proceedings in the conduct of *Edward Christian* [6], an

[1] His countess resided at Latham House (her heroic defence of which
is well known) until 1644 or 5, when she also retired to the Isle of Man.
A contemporary publication, the *Mercurius Aulicus*, by John Birkenhead,
says, 'the Countesse, it seems, stole the Earl's breeches, when he fled
long since into the Isle of Man, and hath in his absence played the man
at Latham.'   This insinuation is certainly unjust ; but the earl seems to
consider some explanation necessary ' why he left the land, when every
gallant spirit had engaged himself for king and country.'   Danger of
revolt and invasion of the island constitute the substance of this explanation.   There is reason, however, to conjecture that he had been
disappointed of the command he had a right to expect, when he brought
a considerable levy to join the king at York.   Any explanation, in short,
might be listened to, except a doubt of his loyalty and ardent military
spirit, which were above all impeachment.

[2] Published in Peck's *Desiderata Curiosa*, in 1779.

[3] Peck, p. 446,—*fortiter calumniari aliquid adhaerebit.*

[4] Peck, p. 446.   ' Loath to dwell too long on one subject,' skip over
to some other matter.

[5] Peck, 434.

[6] For a history of this family, established in the Isle of Man so early
as 1422, see Hutchinson's *History of Cumberland*, vol. iii, p. 146.   They
had previously been established in Wigtonshire.

attempt shall be made, so far as our limits will admit, to extract the earl's own account of this person. 'I was newly [1] got acquainted with Captain Christian, whom I perceived to have abilities enough to do me service. I was told he had made a good fortune in the Indies; that he was a Mankesman borne.'. . . 'He is excellent good companie; as rude as a sea captain should be; but refined as one that had civilized himself half a year at court, where he served the Duke of Buckingham.' . . . 'While he governed here some few years he pleased me very well,' &c. &c. 'But such is the condition of man, that most will have some fault or other to blurr all their best vertues; and his was of that condition which is reckoned with drunkenness, viz. *covetousness*, both marked *with age* to increase and grow in man.' . . . 'When a Prince has given all, and the favourite can desire no more, they both grow weary of one another.' [2]

An account of the Earl's successive public meetings, short, from the limits of our sketch, is extracted in a note [3] from the headings

[1] This is an example of the difficulty of arranging the relative dates; the word *newly*, thus employed at the earliest in 1643, refers to 1628, the date of the appointment of E. Christian to be governor of the Isle of Man, which office he had till 1635 (Sacheverill's *Account of the Isle of Man*, published in 1702, p. 100), the earl being then Lord Strange, but apparently taking the lead in public business during his father's lifetime.

[2] Peck, p. 444. There is apparently some error in Hutchinson's genealogy of the family in his *History of Cumberland*; 1st brother, John, born 1602; 2nd, died young; 3rd, William, born 1608; 4th, Edward, Lieut.-Governor of the Isle of Man, 1629 (according to Sacheverill, p. 100, 1628). This Edward's birth cannot be placed earlier than 1609, and he could not well have made a fortune in the Indies, have frequented the court of Charles I, and be selected as a fit person to be a governor, at the age of 19 or 20. The person mentioned in the text was obviously of *mature age*; and *Edward the governor* appears to have been the younger brother of *William Christian*, a branch of the same family, possessing the estate of Knockrushen, near Castle Rushen, who, as well as Edward, was imprisoned in Peel Castle in 1643.

[3] Peck, 338, et seq. 'Chap. viii. The earl appoints a meeting of the natives, every man to give in his grievances; upon which some think to outwit him, which he winks at, being not ready for them, therefore cajoles and divides them; on the appointed day he appears with a good guard; the people give in their complaints quietly and retire. Chap. ix. Another meeting appointed, when he also appears with a good guard. Many busy men speak only Mankes, which a more designing person (probably Captain Christian, a late governor) would hinder, but the earl forbids it; advice about it appearing in public; the Mankesmen great talkers and wranglers; the earl's spies get in with them and wheedle them. Chap. x. The night before the meeting the earl consults with his officers what to answer; but tells them nothing of his spies; compares both reports, and keeps back his own opinion; sends some of the officers, who he knew would be troublesome, out of the way, about other matters; the (present) governor afresh commended; what counsellors the proper-

of the chapters (apparently composed by Peck). In the last of these meetings it appears that Edward Christian attempted at its close to recapitulate the business of the day : ' Asked if we did not agree thus and thus,' mentioning some things (says the earl) ' he had instructed the people to aske ; which happily they had forgot.' The earl accordingly rose in wrath, and, after a short speech, ' bade the court to rise, and no man to speak more.'— ' Some (he adds) were *committed to prison*, and there abided, until upon *submission* and assurance of *being very good* and *quiet*, they were released, and others were put into their rooms.—I thought fit to make them be *deeply fined* ; since this they all come in most submisse and *loving manner*.' [1] Pretty efficient means of producing *quiet*, if the despot be strong enough, and with it such *love* as suits a despot's fancy ! Among the prisoners were *Edward Christian* and his brother William of Knockrushen ; the latter was released in 1644, on giving bond, among other conditions, *not to depart the island without licence*.

Of Edward, the earl says, ' I will return unto Captain Christian, whose business must be heard next week ' (either in 1644, or early in 1645). ' *He is still in prison*, and I believe many wonder thereat, as savoring of injustice, and that his trial should be deferred so long.' ' Also his business is of that condition that it *concerns not himself alone*.' ' If a Jurie of the people do passe upon him (being he had so cajoled them to believe he suffers for their sakes), it is likely they should quit him, and then might he laugh at us, whom I had rather he had betrayed.' ' I remember one said it was much safer to take men's lives than their estates ; for their children will sooner much forget the death of their father than the loss of their patrimonie.' [2] Edward *died in custody* in Peel Castle in 1650,[3] after an imprisonment of between seven and eight years ; and so far, at least, no ground can be discovered for that gratitude which is afterwards said to have been violated by this family, unless indeed we transplant ourselves to those countries where it is the fashion to flog a public officer one day and replace him in authority the next.

est.   Chap. xi.   The earl's carriage to the people at his first going over ; his carriage at the meeting to modest petitioners, to impudent, to the most confident, and to the most dangerous, viz. them who stood behind and prompted others. All things being agreed, Captain Christian cunningly begins disturbance ; the earl's reply and speech to the people ; Christian is stroke blank ; several people committed to prison and fined, which quiets them.'

[1] Peck, 442.   [2] Peck, 448-9.

[3] Feltham's *Tour*, p. 161, places this event (while a prisoner in Peel Castle), on the authority of a tombstone, in 1660, ' John Greenhalgh being governor.' Now John Greenhalgh ceased to be governor in 1651 ; the date is probably an error in the press for 1650.

The insular records detail with minuteness the complaints of the people relative to the exactions of the Church, and their adjustment by a sort of public arbitration in October, 1643. But it is singular, that neither in these records, nor in the earl's very studied narrative of the modes of discussion, the offences, and the punishments, is one word to be found regarding the more important points actually at issue between himself and the people. The fact, however, is fully developed, as if by accident, in one of the chapters (xvi) of this very desultory but sagacious performance. 'There comes this very instant an occasion to me to acquaint you with a special matter, which, if by reason of these troublesome and dangerous times, I cannot bring to passe my intents therein, you may in your better leisure consider thereof, and make some use hereafter of my present labors, in the matter of a certain holding in this country, called the tenure of the straw ; [1] whereby *men thinke their dwellings are their own auntient inheritances*, and that they may passe the same to any, and dispose thereof *without licence* from the lord, but paying him a bare small rent like unto a fee-farme in England : wherein they are much deceived.'

William the Conqueror, among his plans *for the benefit of his English subjects*, adopted that of inducing or compelling them to surrender their allodial lands, and receive them back to hold by feudal tenure. The Earl of Derby projected the surrender of a similar right, in order to create tenures more profitable to himself—a simple lease for three lives, or twenty-one years. The measure was entirely novel, although the attempt to prevent [2] alienation without licence from the lord, for purposes of a less profitable exaction, may be traced, together with the scenes of violence it produced, through many

---

[1] In the transfer of real estates both parties came into the common law court, and the granter, in the face of the court, transferred his title to the purchaser by the delivery of a straw ; which being recorded, was his title. The same practice prevailed in the transfer of personal property. Sir Edward Coke, iv. 69, when speaking of the Isle of Man, says, ' upon the sale of a horse, or any contract for any other thing, they make the stipulation perfect *per traditionem stipulae* ' (by the delivery of a straw). Perhaps a more feasible etymology of *stipulation*, than the usual derivation from stipes (a stake or land-mark), or stips (a piece of money or wages).

[2] Among those instances in which ' the commands of the lord proprietor have (in the emphatic words of the commissioners of 1791, p. 67) been *obtruded* on the people as laws,' we find, in 1583, the prohibition to dispose of lands without licence of the lord, is prefaced by the broad admission, that, ' contrary to good and laudable order, and diverse and sundry general restraints made, the inhabitants *have*, and *daily do*, notwithstanding the said restraints, *buy, sell, give, grant, chop*, and *exchange* their farms, *lands, tenements*, &c., *at their liberties and pleasures*.' Alienation fines were first exacted in 1643. Report of Commissioners of 1791. App. A, No. 71, Rep. of Law Officers.

passages in the ancient records, which would be inexplicable without this clue.

The earl proceeded certainly with sufficient energy and considerable skill to the accomplishment of his object. In the very year of his arrival, Dec. 1643, he appointed commissioners [1] to compound for leases, consisting of some of his principal officers (members of council), who had themselves been prevailed on by adequate considerations to surrender their estates, and are by general tradition accused of having conspired to delude their simple countrymen into the persuasion that, having no title-deeds, their estates were insecure ; that leases were title-deeds ; and although nominally for limited terms, declared the lands to be descendible to their eldest sons. It is remarkable that the names of *Ewan* and *William Christian,* two of the council, are alone excluded from this commission.

We have already seen two of the name committed to prison. The following notices, which abundantly unfold the ground of the earl's hostility to the name of Christian, relate to Ewan Christian, the father of William Dhône, and one of the Deemsters excluded from the commission. ' One presented me a petition against Deemster [2] Christian on the behalf of an infant who is conceived to have a right unto his Farme Rainsway (Ronaldsway), one of the principal holdings in this country, who, by reason of his eminencie here, and that he holdeth much of the same tenure of the straw in other places, he is soe observed, that certainly as I temper the matter with him in this, soe shall I prevail with others.' [3] . . . ' By policie [4] they (the Christians) are crept into the principal places of power, and they be seated round about the country, and in the heart of it ; they are matched with the best families,' &c.

' The prayer of the petition [5] formerly mentioned was to this effect, that there might be a fair tryal, and *when the right was recovered, that I would graunt them a lease thereof—this being in the tenure of the straw.'* . . . ' Upon some conference with the petitioner, I find a motion heretofore was made by my commissioners, that the Deemster should give this fellow a summe of money. But he would part with none, neverthelesse now it may be he will, and I hope be so wise as to assure unto himself his holding, by compounding with me for the lease of the same, to which, if they two agree, I shall grant it him on easy terms. For if he break the ice, I may haply catch some fish.' [6]

---

[1] The governor-comptroller, receiver ; and John Cannel, deemster.

[2] Deemster, evidently Anglicized, the person who deems the law ; a designation anciently unknown among the natives, who continue to call this officer *Brehon,* identical with the name of those judges and laws so often mentioned in the Histories of Ireland.

[3] Peck, 447.   [4] Ibid. 448.

[5] I have ascertained the date of this petition to be 1643.

[6] *Covetousness* is not attributed to the head of this family ; but the earl makes himself merry with his gallantry. Natural children, it seems,

The issue of this piscatory project was but too successful. Ewan bent to the *reign of terror*, and gave up Ronaldsway to his son William, who accepted the lease, and named his own descendants for the lives. Still the objects attained were unsubstantial, as being contrary to all law, written or oral; and the system was incomplete, until sanctioned by the semblance of legislative confirmation.

We have seen that the earl had in the island a considerable military force, and we know from other sources,[1] that they lived in a great measure at free quarters. We have his own testimony for stating, that he achieved his objects by imprisoning, until his prisoners '*promised to be good*'; and successively filling their places with others, until they also *conformed to his theory of public virtue*. And the reader will be prepared to hear, without surprise, that the same means enabled him, in 1645, to arrange a legislature [2] capable of yielding a forced assent to this notable system of submission and loving-kindness.

This is perhaps the most convenient place for stating, that in the subsequent surrender of the island to the troops of the Parliament, the only stipulation made by the islanders was, 'that they might enjoy their lands and liberties as they formerly had.' In what manner this stipulation was performed, my notes do not enable me to state. The restoration of Charles II, propitious in other respects, inflicted on the Isle of Man the revival of its feudal government; and the affair of the tenures continued to be a theme of perpetual contest and unavailing complaint, until finally adjusted in 1703, through the mediation of the excellent Bishop Wilson, in a legislative compromise, known by the name of the Act of Settlement, whereby the people obtained a full recognition of their ancient rights, on condition of doubling the actual quit-rents, and consenting to alienation fines, first exacted by the Earl James in 1643.[3]

In 1648, William Dhône was appointed receiver-general; and in the same year we find his elder brother, John (assistant Deemster to his father Ewan), committed to Peel Castle on one of these occasions, which strongly marks the character of the person and the times, and affords also a glimpse at the feeling of the people,

took the name of their father, and not of their mother, as elsewhere, and 'the deemster did not get soe many for lust's sake, as to make the name of Christian flourish.' Of him, or a successor of the same name, it is related, that he 'won £500 at play from the Bishop of Sodor and Man, with which he purchased the manor of *Ewanrigg* in Cumberland, still possessed by that family.'

[1] Evidence on the mock trial of William Dhône.

[2] We shall see, by and by, a very simple method of packing a judicial and legislative body, by removing and replacing *seven individuals* by one and the same mandate.

[3] Report of 1791, App. A, No. 71.

and at the condition of the devoted family of Christian. The inquisitive will find it in a note ; [1] other readers will pass on.

The circumstances are familiarly known, to the reader of English history, of the march of the Earl of Derby, in 1651, with a corps from the Isle of Man for the service of the king ; his joining the royal army on the eve of the battle of Worcester ; his flight and imprisonment at Chester, after that signal defeat ; and his trial and execution at Bolton in Lancashire, by the officers of the Parliament, on the 15th October of that year.

Immediately afterwards, Colonel Duckenfield, who commanded at Chester on behalf of the Parliament, proceeded with an armament of ten ships, and a considerable military force, for the reduction of the Isle of Man.

William Christian was condemned and executed in 1662-3, for acts connected with its surrender, twelve years before, which are still involved in obscurity ; and it will be most acceptable to the general reader that we should pass over the intermediate period, [2]

[1] A person named Charles Vaughan is brought to lodge an information, that, being in England, he fell into company with a young man named Christian, who said he had lately left the Isle of Man, and was in search of a brother, who was clerk to a parliament officer ; that in answer to some questions, he said, ‘ The earl did use the inhabitants of that isle very hardly ; had estreated great fines from the inhabitants ; had changed the ancient tenures, and *forced* them to take leases. That he had taken away one hundred pounds a-year from his father, and had kept his uncle in prison four or five years. But if ever the earl came to England, (he had used the inhabitants so hardly) that he was sure they would never suffer him to land in that island again.’ An order is given to imprison John Christian (probably the reputed head of the family, his father being advanced in years) in Peel Castle, until he entered into bonds to be of good behaviour, and *not to depart the isle without licence.*— (Insular Records.) The young man in question is said to have been the son of William Christian of Knockrushen.

[2] Some readers may desire an outline of this period. The lordship of the island was given to Lord Fairfax, who deputed commissioners to regulate its affairs ; one of them (Chaloner) published an account of the island in 1656. He puts down William Christian as receiver-general in 1653. We find his name, as governor, from 1656 to 1658 (Sacheverill, p. 101), in which year he was succeeded by Chaloner himself. Among the anomalies of those times, it would seem that he had retained the office of receiver while officiating as governor ; and episcopacy having been abolished, and the receipts of the see added to those of the exchequer, he had large accounts to settle, for which Chaloner sequestered his estates in his absence, and imprisoned and held to bail his brother John, for aiding what he calls his escape ; his son George returned from England, by permission of Lord Fairfax, to settle his father's accounts. Chaloner informs us, that the revenues of the suppressed see were *not appropriated* to the private use of Lord Fairfax, who, ‘ for the better encouragement and support of the ministers of the Gospel and for the promoting of

and leave the facts regarding this individual, all of them extra-ordinary, and some of peculiar interest, to be developed by the record of the trial, and documents derived from other sources.

A mandate by Charles, eighth Earl of Derby, dated at Latham in September, 1662, after descanting on the heinous sin of rebellion, ' aggravated by its being instrumental [1] in the death of the lord ; and stating that he is himself concerned to revenge a father's blood ', orders William Christian to be proceeded against forthwith, for all his illegal actions at, before, or after, the year 1651 (a pretty sweeping range). The indictment charges him with ' being the head of an insurrection against the Countess of Derby in 1651, assuming the power unto himself, and depriving her ladyship, his lordship, and heirs thereof.'

A series of depositions appear on record from the 3rd to the 13th October, and a reference by the precious depositaries of justice of that day, to the twenty-four Keys,[2] ' Whether upon the examination taken and read before, you find Mr. W. Christian, of Ronaldsway, within compass of the statute of the year 1422,—that is, to receive a sentence *without quest*, or to be tried in the ordinary course of law.' This body, designated on the record ' so many of the Keys as were then present ', were in number seventeen ; but not being yet suffi-ciently select to approve of *sentence without trial*, made their return, To be tried by course of law.

On the 26th November, it is recorded, that the Governor and Attorney-General having proceeded to the jail ' with a guard of soldiers, to require him (Christian) to the bar to receive his trial, he refused, and denied to come, and abide the same '—(admirable courtesy to invite, instead of bringing him to the bar !) Whereupon the Governor demanded the law of Deemster Norris, who then sat in judication. Deemster John Christian having not appeared, and Mr. Edward Christian,[3] his son, and assistant, having also *forborne*

learning, hath conferred all this revenue upon the ministers, and also for maintaining free schools, i. e. at Castletown, Peel, Douglass, and Ramsay.' Chaloner pays a liberal tribute to the talents of the clergy, and the learn-ing and piety of the late bishops.

[1] See the remark in Christian's dying speech, that the late earl had been executed eight days before the insurrection.

[2] The court for criminal trials was composed of the governor and council (including the deemsters) and the keys, who also, with the lord, composed the three branches of the legislative body ; and it was the practice in cases of doubt to refer points of customary law to the deemsters and keys.

[3] The grandson of *Ewan*. It appears by the proceedings of the king in council, 1663, that ' *he did, when the court refused to admit of the deceased William Christian's plea* of the Act of Indemnity, *make his protestation* against their *illegal proceedings*, and did withdraw himself, and came to England to solicit his Majesty, and implore his justice.'

to sit in this Court, he the said Deemster Norris craved the advice and assistance of the twenty-four Keys, and the said Deemster and Keys deemed the law therein, to wit, that he is at the mercy of the lord for life and goods.

It will be observed that seven of the Keys were formerly absent, on what account we shall presently see. All this was very cleverly arranged by the following recorded order, 29th December—'*These of the twenty-four Keys are removed of that Company, in reference to my Honourable Lord's order in that behalf*'; enumerating seven names, not of the seventeen before mentioned, and naming seven others who ' are sworn [1] in their places.' The judicature is further improved by transferring an eighth individual of the first seventeen to the council, and filling his place with another proper person. These facts have been related with some minuteness of detail for two reasons ; 1st, Although nearly equalled by some of the subsequent proceedings, they would not be credited on common authority ; and 2nd, They render all comment unnecessary, and prepare the reader for any judgement, however extraordinary, to be expected from such a tribunal.

Then come the proceedings of the 29th December—The Proposals, as they are named, to the Deemsters,[2] and twenty-four Keys now assembled, ' to be answered in point of law.' 1st, Any malefactor, &c., being indicted, &c., and denying to abide the law of his country in that course (notwithstanding any argument or plea he may offer for himself), and thereupon deemed to forfeit body and goods, &c., whether he may afterwards obtain the same benefit, &c. &c. ; to which, on the same day, they answered in the negative. It was found practicable, on the 31st, to *bring* the prisoner to the bar, to hear his sentence of being ' *shot to death, that thereupon his life may depart from his body* '; which sentence was executed on the 2nd of January, 1663.

That he made ' an excellent speech ' at the place of execution, is recorded, where we should little expect to find it, in the Parochial Register ; the accuracy of that which has been preserved as such in the family of a clergyman (and appears to have been printed on or before 1776),[3] rests chiefly on internal evidence ; and on its accordance, in some material points, with facts suppressed or distorted in the records, but established in the proceedings of the Privy Council. It is therefore given without abbreviation, and the

---

[1] The Commissioners of 1791 are in doubt regarding the time when, and the manner in which, the keys were first elected ; this notable precedent had, perhaps, not fallen under their observation.

[2] Hugh Cannel was now added as a second Deemster.

[3] One of the copies in my possession is stated to be transcribed in that year from the printed speech, the other as stated in the text.

material points of evidence in the voluminous depositions on both trials [1] are extracted for reference in a note.[2]

[1] Both trials : the first is for the same purposes as the English grand jury, with this most especial difference, that evidence is admitted *for the prisoner*, and it thus becomes what it is frequently called, the first trial ; the second, if the indictment be found, is in all respects like that by petty jury in England.

[2] This testimony will of course be received with due suspicion, and confronted with the only defence known, that of his dying speech. It goes to establish that Christian had placed himself at the head of an association, bound by a secret oath, to 'withstand the Lady of Derby in her designs until she had yielded or condescended to their aggriev- ances' : among which grievances, during the earl's residence, we find incidentally noticed, ' the troop that was in the isle and their free quarter- age' ; that he had represented her ladyship to have deceived him, by entering into negotiations with the Parliament, contrary to her promise to communicate with him in such a case ; that Christian and his associates declared that she was about to sell them for twopence or threepence a-piece ; that he told his associates that he had entered into correspon- dence with Major Fox and the Parliament, and received their authority to raise the country ; that in consequence of this insurrection her ladyship appointed commissioners to treat with others ' *on the part of the country*,' and articles of agreement were concluded (see the speech) which nowhere now appear ; that on the appearance of Duckenfield's ships, standing for Ramsay Bay, one of the insurgents boarded them off Douglass, ' to give intelligence of the condition of the country' ; the disposable troops marched under the governor, Sir Philip Musgrave, for Ramsay ; that when the shipping had anchored, a deputation of three persons, viz. John Christian, Ewan Curphey, and William Standish, proceeded on board, to negotiate for the surrender of the island (where William was does not appear). The destruction of the articles of agreement, and the silence of the records regarding the relative strength of the forces, leave us without the means of determining the degree of merit or demerit to be ascribed to these negotiators, or the precise authority under which they acted ; but the grievances to be redressed are cleared from every obscurity by the all-sufficient testimony of the terms demanded from the victors, ' *that they might enjoy their lands and liberties as formerly they had ;* and that it was demanded whether they asked any more, but nothing else was demanded that this examinant heard of.' The taking of Loyal Fort near Ramsay (commanded by a Major Duckenfield, who was made prisoner), and of Peel Castle, appear on record : but nothing could be found regarding the *surrender of Castle Rushen, or of the Countess of Derby's subsequent imprisonment*. Had the often repeated tale, of William Christian having ' treacherously seized upon the lady and her children, with the governors of both castles, in the middle of the night' (Rolt's *History of the Isle of Man*, published in 1773, p. 89) rested on the slightest semblance of truth, we should inevitably have found an attempt to prove it in the proceedings of this mock trial. In the absence of authentic details, the tradition may be adverted to, that her ladyship, on learning the proceedings at Ramsay, hastened to embark in a vessel

The last speech of William Christian, Esq., who was executed 2nd January, 1662-3 :

' Gentlemen, and the rest of you who have accompanied me this day to the gate of death, I know you expect I should say something at my departure ; and indeed I am in some measure willing to satisfy you, having not had the least liberty, since my imprisonment, to acquaint any with the sadness of my sufferings, which flesh and blood could not have endured, without the power and assistance of my most gracious and good God, into whose hands I do now commit my poor soul, not doubting but that I shall very quickly be in the arms of his mercy.

' I am, as you now see, hurried hither by the power of *a pretended court of justice,* the members whereof, or at least the greatest part of them, are by no means qualified, but very ill befitting their new places. The reasons you may give yourselves.

' The cause for which I am brought hither, as the *prompted* and *threatened* jury has delivered, is high treason against the Countess Dowager of Derby, for that I did, as they say, in the year fifty-one, raise a force against her for the suppressing and rooting out that family. How unjust the accusation is, very few of you that hear me this day but can witness ; and *that the then rising of the people,* in which afterwards I came to be engaged, did not at all, or in the least degree, intend the prejudice or ruin of that family ; *the chief whereof being, as you well remember, dead eight days, or thereabout, before that action happened.* But the true cause of that rising, as [1] *the jury did twice bring in,* was to present grievances to our honourable lady ; which was done by me, and afterwards approved by her ladyship, under the hand of her then secretary M. Trevach, who is yet living, *which agreement hath since, to my own ruin and my poor family's endless sorrow, been forced from me.* The Lord forgive them the injustice of their dealings with me, and I wish from my heart it may not be laid to their charge another day !

' You now see me here *a sacrifice ready to be offered up for that which was the preservation of your lives and fortunes, which were then in hazard, but that I stood between you and your* (then in all appear-

she had prepared, but was intercepted before she could reach it. The same uncertainty exists with regard to any negotiations on her part with the officers of the Parliament as affirmed by the insurgents; the earl's first letter, after his capture and before his trial, says, ' Truly, as matters go, it will be best for you to make conditions for yourself, children, and friends, in the manner as we have proposed, or as you can further agree with Col. Duckenfield ; who, being so much a gentleman born, will doubtless, for his own honor, deal fairly with you.' He seems also to have hoped at that time that it might influence his own fate : and the eloquent and affecting letter written immediately before his execution, repeats the same admonitions *to treat.* Rolt, pp. 74 and 84.

[1] This fact, as might be expected, is not to be traced on the record of the trial.

ance) *utter ruin.* I wish you still may, as hitherto, enjoy the sweet benefit and blessing of peace, though from that minute until now I have still been prosecuted and persecuted, nor have I ever since found a place to rest myself in. But my God be for ever blessed and praised, who hath given me so large a measure of patience !

'What services I have done for that noble family, by whose power I am now to take my latest breath, I dare appeal to themselves, whether I have not deserved better things from some of them, than the sentence of my bodily destruction, and seizure of the poor estate my son ought to enjoy, being purchased and left him by his grandfather. It might have been much better had I not spent it in the service of my honourable Lord of Derby and his family ; these things I need not mention to you, for that most of you are witnesses to it. I shall now beg your patience while I tell you here, in the presence of God, that I never in all my life acted anything with intention to prejudice my sovereign lord the king, nor the late Earl of Derby, nor the now earl ; yet notwithstanding, *being in England at the time* of his sacred Majesty's happy restoration, I went to London, with many others, to have a sight of my gracious king, whom God preserve, and whom until then I never had seen. But I was not long there when I was arrested upon an action of twenty thousand pounds, and clapped up in the Fleet ; unto which action, I, being a stranger, could give no bail, but was there kept nearly a whole year. How I suffered God he knows ; but at last having gained my liberty, I thought good to advise with several gentlemen concerning his Majesty's gracious Act of Indemnity, that was then set forth, in which I thought myself concerned ; unto which they told me, there was no doubt to be made but that all actions committed in the Isle of Man, relating in any kind to the war, were pardoned by the Act of Indemnity, and all other places within his Majesty's dominions and countries. Whereupon, and having been forced to absent myself from my poor wife and children near three years, being all that time under persecution, I did with great content and satisfaction return into this island, hoping then to receive the comfort and sweet enjoyment of my friends and poor family. But alas ! I have fallen into the snare of the fowler ; but my God shall ever be praised,—though he kill me, yet will I trust in him.

'I may justly say no man in this island knows better than myself the power the Lord Derby hath in this island, subordinate to his sacred Majesty, of which *I have given a full account in my declaration presented to my judges, which I much fear will never see light,*[1] *which is no small trouble to me.*

'It was his Majesty's most gracious Act of Indemnity gave me the confidence and assurance of my safety ; on which, and an appeal I made to his sacred Majesty and Privy Council, from the unjustness

---

[1] This apprehension was but too correct.

of the proceedings had against me, I did much rely, being his Majesty's subject here, and a denizen of England both by birth and fortune. And *in regard I have disobeyed the power of my Lord of Derby's Act of Indemnity, which you now look upon, and his Majesty's Act cast out as being of no force,* I have with greater violence been persecuted; yet nevertheless I do declare, that no subject whatever can or ought to take upon them Acts of Indemnity but his sacred Majesty only, with the confirmation of Parliament.

'It is very fit I should say something as to my education and religion.   I think I need not inform you, for you all know, I was brought up a son of the Church of England, which was at that time in her splendour and glory; and to my endless comfort I have ever since continued a faithful member, witness several of my actions in the late times of liberty.   And as for government, I never was against monarchy, which now, to my soul's great satisfaction, I have lived to see is settled and established.   I am well assured that men of upright life and conversation may have the favourable countenance of our gracious king, under whose happy government, God of his infinite mercy long continue these his kingdoms and dominions.   And now I do most heartily thank my good God that I have had so much liberty and time to disburden myself of several things that have laid heavy upon me all the time of my imprisonment, in which I have not had *time, or liberty, to speak or write* any of my thoughts; and from my soul I wish all animosity may after my death be quite laid aside, and my death by none be called in question, for I do freely forgive all that have had any hand in my persecution; and may our good God preserve you all in peace and quiet the remainder of your days.

'Be ye all of you his Majesty's liege people, loyal and faithful to his sacred Majesty; and, according to your oath of faith and fealty to my honourable Lord of Derby, *do you likewise, in all just and lawful ways, observe* his commands; and know that you must one day give an account of all your deeds.   And now the blessing of Almighty God be with you all, and preserve you from violent death, and keep you in peace of conscience all your days!

'I will now hasten, for my flesh is willing to be dissolved, and my spirit to be with God, who hath given me full assurance of his mercy and pardon for all my sins, of which his unspeakable goodness and loving-kindness my poor soul is exceedingly satisfied.'

Note.[1]   Here he fell upon his knees, and passed some time in prayer; then rising exceedingly cheerful, he addressed the soldiers appointed for his execution, saying—'Now for you, who are appointed by lot my executioners, I do freely forgive you.'   He requested them and all present to pray for him; adding, 'There is but a thin veil betwixt me and death; once more I request your prayers, for now I take my last farewell.'

[1] This note is annexed to all the copies of the speech.

The soldiers wished to bind him to the spot on which he stood. He said, 'Trouble not yourselves or me; for I that dare face death in whatever form he comes, will not start at your fire and bullets; nor can the power you have deprive me of my courage.' At his desire a piece of white paper was given him, which with the utmost composure he pinned to his breast, to direct them where to aim, and after a short prayer addressed the soldiers thus—'Hit this, and you do your own and my work.' And presently after, stretching forth his arms, which was the signal he gave them, he was shot through the heart and fell.

Edward Christian, the nephew, and George, the son, of the deceased, lost no time in appealing to his Majesty in Council against this judicial murder; and George was furnished with an order 'to pass and repass', &c., 'and bring with him such records and persons as he should desire, to make out the truth of his complaint.' Edward returned with him to the island for that purpose; for we find him, in April 1663, compelled, in the true spirit of the day, to give bond ' that he would at all times appear and answer to such charges as might be preferred against him, and *not depart the isle without licence.*' George was prevented, by various contrivances, from serving the king's order; but on presenting a second petition the Governor, Deemster, and Members of Council, were brought up to London by a serjeant-at-arms; and these six persons, together with the Earl of Derby, being compelled to appear, a full hearing took place before the king in person, the Chancellor, the Lord Chief Justice, Lord Chief Baron, and other Members of Council; judgement was extended on the 5th August, and that judgement was on the 14th of the same month ordered 'to be printed in folio, in such manner as Acts of Parliament are usually printed, and his Majesty's Arms prefixed.'

This *authentic document* designates the persons brought up as ' *Members of the pretended Court of Justice* '; declares ' that the general Act of Pardon and Amnesty did extend to the Isle of Man, and ought to have been taken notice of by the Judges in that island, *although it had not been pleaded*; that the Court *refused to admit* the deceased William Christian's *plea* of the Act of Indemnity ', &c. ' Full restitution is ordered to be made to his heirs of all his estates, real and personal.' Three[1] other persons ' who were by the same Court of Justice imprisoned, and their estates *seized and confiscated without any legal trial*,' are ordered, together with the Christians, ' to be restored to all their estates, real and personal, and to be fully repaired in all the charges and expenses which they have been at since their first imprisonment, as well in the prosecution of this business as in their journey hither, or in any other way thereunto relating.' The mode of raising funds for the purposes of this restitu-

---

[1] Ewan Curphey, Samuel Ratcliffe, and John Caesar, men of considerable landed property.

tion is equally peculiar and instructive : these ' sums of money are ordered to be furnished by the Deemsters, Members, and Assistants of the said Court of Justice ', who are directed ' to raise and make due payment thereof to the parties.'

' And to the end that the blood that has been unjustly spilt may in some sort be expiated,' &c., the Deemsters are ordered to be committed to the King's Bench to be proceeded against, &c. &c., and receive condign punishment. [It is believed that this part of the order was afterwards relaxed or rendered nugatory.] The three Members of Council were released on giving security to appear, if required, and to make the restitution ordered. ' And in regard that Edward Christian, being one of the Deemsters or Judges in the Isle of Man, *did, when the Court refused to admit of the deceased W. Christian's plea of the Act of Indemnity, make his protestation against their illegal proceedings, and did withdraw himself, and come to England to solicit his Majesty and implore his justice*, it is ordered that the Earl of Derby do forthwith, by commission, &c., restore and appoint him as Deemster, so to remain and continue, &c. [which order was disobeyed]. And lastly, that Henry Howell, Deputy Governor, whose fault hath been *the not complying with*, and *yielding due obedience to, the order* [1] *of his Majesty and this Board sent unto the island* [O most lame and impotent conclusion !], be permitted to return to the isle, and enforce the present Order of the King in Council.'

Of the Earl of Derby no further mention occurs in this document. The sacrifices made by this noble family in support of the royal cause, drew a large share of indulgence over the exceptionable parts of their conduct ; but the mortification necessarily consequent on this appeal, the incessant complaints of the people, and the difficulty subsequently experienced by them in obtaining access to a superior tribunal, receive a curious illustration in an Order of the King in Council, dated August 20, 1670, on a petition of the Earl of Derby, ' that the clerk of the council in waiting receive no petition, appeal, or complaint, *against the lord or government of the Isle of Man*, without having first good security from the complainant to answer costs, damages, and charges.'

The historical notices of this kingdom [2] of Lilliput are curious and instructive with reference to other times and different circumstances, and they have seemed to require little comment or antiquarian remark ; but to condense what may be collected with regard to

---

[1] Tradition, in accordance with the dirge of William Dhône, says, that the order to stop proceedings and suspend the sentence arrived on the day preceding that of his execution.

[2] Earl James, although studious of kingcraft, assigns good reasons for having never pretended to assume that title, and among others, ' Nor doth it please a king that any of his subjects should too much love that name, were it but to act in a play.'—Peck, 436.

Edward Christian, the accomplished villain of Peveril ; the insinua-tions of his accuser [1] constitute in themselves an abundant defence. When so little can be imputed by such an adversary, the character must indeed be invulnerable. Tradition ascribes to him nothing but what is amiable, patriotic, honourable, and good, in all the relations of public and private life. He died, after an imprisonment of seven or eight years, the victim of incorrigible obstinacy, according to one, of ruthless tyranny, according to another vocabulary; but resembling the character of the novel in nothing but unconquerable courage.

Treachery and ingratitude have been heaped on the memory of William Christian with sufficient profusion. Regarding the first of these crimes : if all that has been affirmed or insinuated in the mock trial, rested on a less questionable basis, posterity would scarcely pronounce a unanimous verdict of moral and political guilt against an association to subvert such a government as is described by its own author. The *peculiar* favours for which he or his family were ungrateful, are not to be discovered in these proceedings ; except, indeed, in the form of ' chastisements of the Almighty—blessings in disguise.' But if credit be given to the dying words of William Christian, his efforts were strictly limited to a redress of grievances, —a purpose always criminal in the eye of the oppressor. If he had lived and died on a larger scene, his memory would probably have survived among the patriots and the heroes. In some of the manu-script narratives he is designated as a *martyr* for the rights and liberties of his countrymen ; who add in their homely manner, that he was condemned without trial, and murdered without remorse.

We have purposely abstained from all attempt to enlist the passions in favour of the sufferings of a people, or in detestation of oppressions, which ought, perhaps, to be ascribed as much to the character of the times as to that of individuals. The naked facts of the case (unaided by the wild and plaintive notes in which the maidens of the isle were wont to bewail ' the [2] heart-rending death of fair-haired William ') are sufficient of themselves to awaken the sympathy of every generous mind ; and it were a more worthy exercise of that despotic power over the imagination, so eminently possessed by the Great Unknown, to embalm the remembrance of two such men in his immortal pages, than to load their memories with crimes, such as no human being ever committed.

I am enabled to add the translation of the lament over the fair-haired William Christian. It is originally composed in the Manx language, and consists of a series of imprecations of evil upon the enemies of Christian, and prophecies to the same purpose :—

---

[1] Peck, passim.
[2] The literal translation given to me by a young lady.

ON THE DEATH AND MURDER OF RECEIVER-GENERAL WILLIAM CHRISTIAN, OF RONALDSWAY, WHO WAS SHOT NEAR HANGO HILL, JANUARY 2, 1662.

1.

In so shifting a scene, who would confidence place
In family power, youth, or in personal grace?
No character's proof against enmity foul;
And thy fate, William Dhône, sickens our soul.

2.

You are Derby's receiver of patriot zeal,
Replete with good sense, and reputed genteel;
Your justice applauded by the young and the old;
    And thy fate, &c.

3.

A kind, able patron both to church and to state—
What roused their resentment but talents so great?
No character's proof against enmity foul;
    And thy fate, &c.

4.

Thy pardon, 'tis rumoured, came over the main,
Nor late, but concealed by a villain [1] in grain;
'Twas fear forced the jury to a sentence so foul;
    And thy fate, &c.

5.

Triumphant stood Colcott, he wished for no more,
When the pride of the Christians lay welt'ring in gore,
To malice a victim, though steady and bold;
    And thy fate, &c.

6.

With adultery stained, and polluted with gore,
He Ronaldsway eyed, as Loghuecolly before,
'Twas the land sought the culprit, as Ahab before;
    And thy fate, &c.

7.

Proceed to the once famed abode of the nuns,
Call the Colcotts aloud, till you torture your lungs,
Their short triumph's ended, extinct is the whole;
    And thy fate, &c.

[1] A person named in the next stanza is said to have intercepted a pardon sent from England for William Christian, found, it is alleged, in the foot of an old woman's stocking. The tradition is highly improbable. If Christian had been executed against the tenor of a pardon actually granted, it would not have failed to be charged as a high aggravation in the subsequent proceedings of the Privy Council.

8.

For years could Robert lay crippled in bed,
Nor knew the world peace while he held up his head,
The neighbourhood's scourge in iniquity bold;
       And thy fate, &c.

9.

Not one's heard to grieve, seek the country all through,
Nor lament for the name that Bemacan once knew;
The poor rather load it with curses untold;
       And thy fate, &c.

10.

Ballaclogh and the Criggans mark strongly their sin,
Not a soul of the name's there to welcome you in;
In the power of the strangers is centred the whole;
       And thy fate, &c.

11.

The opulent Scarlett on which the sea flows,
Is piecemeal disposed of to whom the Lord knows;
It is here without bread or defence from the cold;
       And thy fate, &c.

12.

They assert then in vain, that the law sought thy blood,
For all aiding the massacre never did good;
Like the rooted-up golding deprived of its gold,
They languished, were blasted, grew withered and old.

13.

When the shoots of a tree so corrupted remain,
Like the brier or thistle, they goad us with pain;
Deep, dark, undermining, they mimic the mole;
       And thy fate, &c.

14.

Round the infamous wretches who spilt Caesar's blood,
Dead spectres and conscience in sad array stood,
Not a man of the gang reached life's utmost goal;
       And thy fate, &c.

15.

Perdition, too, seized them who caused *thee* to bleed,
To decay fell their houses, their lands and their seed
Disappeared like the vapour when morn's tinged with gold;
       And thy fate, &c.

16.

From grief all corroding, to hope I'll repair,
That a branch of the Christians will soon grace the chair,
With royal instructions his foes to console:
       And thy fate, &c.

17.

With a book for my pillow, I dreamt as I lay,
That a branch of the Christians would hold Ronaldsway;
His conquests his topic with friends o'er a bowl,
And thy fate, &c.

18.

And now for a wish in concluding my song,—
May the Almighty withhold me from doing what's wrong;
Protect every mortal from enmity foul,
For thy fate, William Dhône, sickens our soul! [1]

No. II

*At the Court at Whitehall,
the 5th August, 1663.*

GEORGE CHRISTIAN, son and heir of William Christian, deceased, having exhibited his complaint to his Majesty in Council, that his father, being at a house of his in his Majesty's Isle of Man, was imprisoned by certain persons of that island, pretending themselves to be a Court of Justice; that he was by them accused of high treason, pretended to be committed against the Countess Dowager of Derby, in the year 1651; and that they thereupon proceeded to judgement, and caused him to be put to death, notwithstanding the Act of General Pardon and Indemnity, whereof he claimed the benefit: and his appeal to his Majesty, and humbly imploring his Majesty's princely compassion towards the distressed widow and seven fatherless children of the deceased: His Majesty was graciously pleased, with the advice of his Council, to order that Thomas Noris and Hugh Cannell, the two judges (by them in that island called Deemsters), and Richard Stevenson, Robert Calcot, and Richard Tyldesley, three of the members of the pretended Court of Justice, and Henry Howell, deputy of the said island, should be forthwith sent for, and brought up by a serjeant-at-arms here, before his Majesty in Council, to appear and answer to such accusations as should be exhibited against them; which said six persons being accordingly brought hither the fifteenth day of July last, appointed for a full hearing of the whole business, the Earl of Derby then also summoned to appear, and the Lord Chief Justice of the King's Bench, and the Lord Chief Baron of his Majesty's Exchequer, with the King's Council, learned in the laws, required to be present, and all the parties called in with their counsel and witnesses, after full hearing of the matter on both sides, and the parties withdrawn,

---

[1] It may be recollected that these verses are given through the medium of a meagre translation, and are deprived of the aid of the music, otherwise we would certainly think the memory of William Dhône little honoured by his native bard.

the said judges being desired to deliver their opinion, did, in presence of the King's Council, learned in the laws, declare that the Act of General Pardon and Indemnity did, and ought to be understood to, extend to the Isle of Mann, as well as into any other of his Majesty's dominions and plantations beyond the seas; and that, being a publique General Act of Parliament, it ought to have been taken notice of by the judges in the Isle of Mann, although it had not been pleaded, and although there were no proclamations made thereof. His Majesty being therefore deeply sensible of this violation of his Act of General Pardon, whereof his Majesty hath always been very tender, and doth expect and require that all his subjects in all his dominions and plantations shall enjoy the full benefit and advantage of the same; and having this day taken the business into further consideration, and all parties called in and heard, did, by and with the advice of the Council, order, and it is hereby ordered, that all persons any way concerned in the seizure of the estate of the said William Christian, deceased, or instrumental in the ejection of the widow and children out of their houses and fortune, do take care that entire restitution is to be made of all the said estate, as well real or personal, as also all damages sustained, with full satisfaction for all profits by them received since the said estate hath been in their hands; and that, whereas the said William Christian, deceased, was one of the two lives remaining in an estate in Lancashire, that the detriment accruing by the untimely death of the said William Christian therein, or in like cases, shall be estimated, and in like manner fully repaired. That in regard of the great trouble and charges the complainants have been at in pursuit of this business, ordered, that they do exhibit to this Board a true account, upon oath, of all expenses and damages by them sustained in the journies of themselves and witnesses, and of all other their charges in the following of this business.

And whereas Ewan Curghey, Sammual Radcliffe, and John Casar, were by the same Court of Justice imprisoned, and had their estates seized and confiscated, without any legal trial, it is ordered, that the said Ewan Curghey, Sammual Radcliffe, and John Casar, be likewise reinstated to all their estates, real and personall, and fully repaired in all the charges and expenses which they have been at since their first imprisment, as well in the prosecution of this business, as in their journey thither, or any other way whatsoever thereunto relating. The which satisfaction, expenses, and all the sums of money to be raised by virtue of this order, are to be furnished by the Deemsters, Members, and Assistants of the said Court of Justice, who are hereby ordered to raise all such the said sums, and thereof to make due payment, and give full satisfaction unto the parties respectively hereby appointed to receive it.

And to the end, the guilt of blood which hath been unjustly spilt, may in some sort be expiated, and his Majesty receive some kind of satisfaction for the untimely loss of a subject, it is ordered, that the said Thomas Norris and Hugh Cannell, who decreed this violent death, be committed, and remain prisoners in the King's Bench, to be proceeded against in the ordinary course of justice, so to receive condign punishment according to the merit of so heinous a fact.

That Richard Stevenson, Robert Calcott, and Richard Tyldesley, be discharged from further restraint, giving good security to appear at this Board whensoever summoned, and not depart this city until full satisfaction be given, and all orders of this Board whatsoever relating to this business fully executed in the island. And in regard, that upon the examination of this business, it doth appear that Edward Christian, being one of the Deemsters or Judges in the Isle of Mann, did, when the Court refused to admit of the deceased William Christian's plea of the Act of Indemnity, make his protestation against their illegal proceedings, and did withdraw himself, and come into England to solicit his Majesty, and implore his justice, it is ordered, that the Earl of Derby do forthwith, by commission, in due and accustomed manner, restore, constitute, and appoint the said Edward Christian, one of the Deemsters or Judges of the said island, so to remain and continue in the due execution of the said place.

And lastly, it is ordered that the said Henry Howell, Deputy-Governor, whose charge hath been the not complying with, and yielding due obedience to, the orders of his Majesty, and this Board sent into this island, giving good security to appear at this Board whensoever summoned, be forthwith discharged from all further restraint, and permitted to return into the island ; and he is hereby strictly commanded to employ the power and authority he hath, which by virtue of his commission he hath in that island, in performance of, and obedience to, all commands and orders of his Majesty and this Board in this whole business, or any way relating thereunto.

(Signed by)

LORD CHANCELLOR.	EARL OF CARBERRY.
LORD TREASURER.	LORD BISHOP OF LONDON.
LORD PRIVY SEAL.	LORD WENTWORTH.
DUKE OF ALBEMARLE.	LORD BERKELEY.
LORD CHAMBERLAIN.	LORD ASHLEY.
EARL OF BERKSHIRE.	SIR WILLIAM CROMPTON.
EARL OF ST. ALBAN.	MR. TREASURER.
EARL OF ANGLESEY.	MR. VICE CHAMBERLAIN.
EARL OF SANDWICH.	MR. SECRETARY MORICE.
EARL OF BATH.	MR. SECRETARY BENNETT.
EARL OF MIDDLETON.	

RICHARD BROWNE,
Clerk of the Council.

No. III

At the Court at Whitehall,
August 14th, 1663.

Present:

THE KING'S MOST EXCELLENT MAJESTY.

LORD CHANCELLOR.	EARL OF MIDDLETON.
LORD TREASURER.	EARL OF CARBERRY.
LORD PRIVY SEAL.	LORD BISHOP OF LONDON.
DUKE OF BUCKINGHAM.	LORD WENTWORTH.
DUKE OF ALBEMARLE.	LORD BERKELEY.
LORD CHAMBERLAIN.	LORD ASHLEY.
EARL OF BERKSHIRE.	SIR WILLIAM CROMPTON.
EARL OF ST. ALBAN.	MR. TREASURER.
EARL OF SANDWICH.	MR. VICE CHAMBERLAIN.
EARL OF ANGLESEY.	MR. SECRETARY MORICE.
EARL OF BATH.	MR. SECRETARY BENNETT.

To the end the world may the better take notice of his Majesty's royal intention, to observe the Act of Indemnity and General Pardon inviolably for the publique good and satisfaction of his subjects— it was this day ordered, that a copy of the order of this Board of the 5th inst., touching the illegal proceedings in the Isle of Mann against William Christian, and putting him to death contrary to the said Act of General Pardon, be sent unto his Majesty's printer, who is commanded forthwith to print the same in the English letters in folio, in such manner as Acts of Parliament are usually printed, and his Majesty's Arms prefixed.

RICHARD BROWNE.

PREFATORY LETTER

FROM THE REV. DR. DRYASDUST OF YORK, TO
CAPTAIN CLUTTERBUCK,

RESIDING AT FAIRYLODGE, NEAR KENNAQUHAIR, N.B.

VERY WORTHY AND DEAR SIR,

To your last letter I might have answered, with the classic, '*Haud equidem invideo, miror magis.*' For though my converse, from infancy, has been with things of antiquity, yet I love not ghosts or spectres to be commentators thereon ; and truly your account of the conversation you held with our great parent, in the crypt, or most intimate recess of the publishers at Edinburgh, had upon me much the effect of the apparition of Hector's phantom on the hero of the Aeneid—

> Obstupui, steteruntque comae.

And, as I said above, I repeat that I wondered at the Vision, without envying you the pleasure of seeing our great progenitor. But it seems that he is now permitted to show himself to his family more freely than formerly ; or that the old gentleman is turned somewhat garrulous in these latter days ; or, in short, not to exhaust your patience with conjectures of the cause, I also have seen the Vision of the Author of Waverley. I do not mean to take any undue state on myself, when I observe, that this interview was marked with circumstances in some degree more formally complaisant than those which attended your meeting with him in our worthy publisher's ; for yours had the appearance of a fortuitous rencontre, whereas mine was preceded by the communication of a large roll of papers, containing a new history, called PEVERIL OF THE PEAK.

I no sooner found that this manuscript consisted of a narrative, running to the length of perhaps three hundred and thirty pages in each volume, or thereabouts, than it instantly occurred to me from whom this boon came ; and having set myself to peruse the written sheets, I began to entertain strong expectations that I might, peradventure, next see the author himself.

Again, it seems to me a marked circumstance, that, whereas an inner apartment of Mr. Constable's shop was thought a place of sufficient solemnity for your audience, our venerable senior was pleased to afford mine in the recesses of my own lodgings, *intra parietes*, as it were, and without the chance of interruption. I must also remark, that the features, form, and dress of the *Eidolon*, as you well term the apparition of our parent, seemed to me more precisely distinct than was vouchsafed to you on the former occasion. Of this hereafter; but Heaven forbid I should glory or set up any claim of superiority over the other descendants of our common parent, from such decided marks of his preference—*Laus propria sordet*. I am well satisfied that the honour was bestowed not on my person, but my cloth—that the preference did not elevate Jonas Dryasdust over Clutterbuck, but the Doctor of Divinity over the Captain. *Cedant arma togae*—a maxim never to be forgotten at any time, but especially to be remembered when the soldier is upon half-pay.

But I bethink me that I am keeping you all this while in the porch, and wearying you with long inductions, when you would have me *properare in mediam rem*. As you will, it shall be done; for, as his Grace is wont to say of me wittily, ' No man tells a story so well as Dr. Dryasdust, when he has once got up to the starting-post.'—*Jocose hoc.* But to continue.

I had skimmed the cream of the narrative which I had received about a week before, and that with no small cost and pain; for the hand of our parent is become so small and so crabbed, that I was obliged to use strong magnifiers. Feeling my eyes a little exhausted towards the close of the second volume, I leaned back in my easy chair, and began to consider whether several of the objections which have been particularly urged against our father and patron, might not be considered as applying, in an especial manner, to the papers I had just perused. ' Here are figments enough,' said I to myself, ' to confuse the march of a whole history—anachronisms enough to overset all chronology !

The old gentleman hath broken all bounds—*abiit*—*evasit*
—*erupit.*'

As these thoughts passed through my mind, I fell into
a fit of musing, which is not uncommon with me after
dinner, when I am altogether alone, or have no one with me
but my curate. I was awake, however ; for I remember
seeing, in the embers of the fire, a representation of a mitre,
with the towers of a cathedral in the background ; moreover, I recollect gazing for a certain time on the comely
countenance of Dr. Whiterose, my uncle by the mother's
side—the same who is mentioned in *The Heart of Mid-
lothian*—whose portrait, graceful in wig and canonicals,
hangs above my mantelpiece. Further, I remember
marking the flowers in the frame of carved oak, and casting
my eye on the pistols which hang beneath, being the fire-
arms with which, in the eventful year 1746, my uncle meant
to have espoused the cause of Prince Charles Edward ;
for, indeed, so little did he esteem personal safety, in comparison of steady High-Church principle, that he waited
but the news of the Adventurer's reaching London to
hasten to join his standard.

Such a doze as I then enjoyed, I find compatible with
indulging the best and deepest cogitations which at any
time arise in my mind. I chew the cud of sweet and bitter
fancy, in a state betwixt sleeping and waking, which I
consider as so highly favourable to philosophy, that I have
no doubt some of its most distinguished systems have been
composed under its influence. My servant is, therefore,
instructed to tread as if upon down—my door-hinges are
carefully oiled—and all appliances used to prevent me from
being prematurely and harshly called back to the broad
waking-day of a laborious world. My custom, in this
particular, is so well known, that the very schoolboys cross
the alley on tiptoe, betwixt the hours of four and five.
My cell is the very dwelling of Morpheus. There is indeed
a bawling knave of a broom-man, *quem ego*—But this is
matter for the Quarter Sessions.

As my head sank back upon the easy chair in the philosophical mood which I have just described, and the eyes
of my body began to close, in order, doubtless, that those of
my understanding might be the more widely opened, I was

startled by a knock at the door, of a kind more authoritatively boisterous than is given at that hour by any visitor
acquainted with my habits. I started up in my seat, and
heard the step of my servant hurrying along the passage,
followed by a very heavy and measured pace, which shook
the long oak-floored gallery in such a manner, as forcibly
to arrest my attention. 'A stranger, sir, just arrived from
Edinburgh by the north mail, desires to speak with your
reverence.' Such were the words with which Jacob threw
the door to the wall ; and the startled tone in which he
pronounced them, although there was nothing particular in
the annunciation itself, prepared me for the approach of
a visitor of uncommon dignity and importance.

The Author of Waverley entered, a bulky and tall man,
in a travelling great-coat, which covered a suit of snuff-
brown, cut in imitation of that worn by the great Rambler.
His flapped hat, for he disdained the modern frivolities of
a travelling-cap, was bound over his head with a large silk
handkerchief, so as to protect his ears from cold at once,
and from the babble of his pleasant companions in the
public coach from which he had just alighted. There was
somewhat of a sarcastic shrewdness and sense, which sat
on the heavy penthouse of his shaggy grey eyebrow—his
features were in other respects largely shaped, and rather
heavy, than promising wit or genius ; but he had a notable
projection of the nose, similar to that line of the Latin poet—

immodicum surgit pro cuspide rostrum.

A stout walking-stick stayed his hand ; a double Barcelona
protected his neck ; his belly was something prominent,
'but that's not much'; his breeches were substantial
thickset ; and a pair of top-boots, which were slipped down
to ease his sturdy calves, did not conceal his comfortable
travelling stockings of lamb's wool, wrought, not on the
loom, but on wires, and after the venerable ancient fashion,
known in Scotland by the name of *ridge-and-furrow*. His
age seemed to be considerably above fifty, but could not
amount to threescore, which I observed with pleasure,
trusting there may be a good deal of work had out of him
yet ; especially as a general haleness of appearance, the
compass and strength of his voice, the steadiness of his

step, the rotundity of his calf, the depth of his hem, and the sonorous emphasis of his sneeze, were all signs of a constitution built for permanence.

It struck me forcibly, as I gazed on this portly person, that he realized, in my imagination, the Stout Gentleman in No. II who afforded such subject of varying speculation to our most amusing and elegant Utopian traveller, Master Geoffrey Crayon. Indeed, but for one little trait in the conduct of the said Stout Gentleman—I mean the gallantry towards his landlady, a thing which would greatly derogate from our Senior's character—I should be disposed to conclude that Master Crayon had, on that memorable occasion, actually passed his time in the vicinity of the Author of Waverley. But our worthy patriarch, be it spoken to his praise, far from cultivating the society of the fair sex, seems, in avoiding the company of womankind, rather to imitate the humour of our friend and relation, Master Jonathan Oldbuck, as I was led to conjecture, from a circumstance which occurred immediately after his entrance.

Having acknowledged his presence with fitting thanks and gratulations, I proposed to my venerated visitor, as a refreshment best suited to the hour of the day, to summon my cousin and housekeeper, Miss Catharine Whiterose, with the tea-equipage ; but he rejected my proposal with disdain, worthy of the Laird of Monkbarns. ' No scandal-broth,' he exclaimed ; ' no unidea'd woman's chatter for me. Fill the frothed tankard—slice the fatted rump— I desire no society but yours, and no refreshment but what the cask and the gridiron can supply.'

The beefsteak, and toast and tankard, were speedily got ready ; and, whether an apparition or a bodily presentation, my visitor displayed dexterity as a trencherman, which might have attracted the envy of a hungry hunter, after a fox-chase of forty miles. Neither did he fail to make some deep and solemn appeals, not only to the tankard aforesaid, but to two decanters of London particular Madeira and old Port ; the first of which I had extracted from its ripening place of deposition, within reach of the genial warmth of the oven ; the other, from a deep crypt in mine own ancient cellar, which whilom may have held the vintages of the victors of the world, the arch being

composed of Roman brick. I could not help admiring and
congratulating the old gentleman upon the vigorous appetite
which he displayed for the genial cheer of old England.
'Sir,' was his reply, 'I must eat as an Englishman, to
qualify myself for taking my place at one of the most select
companies of right English spirits, which ever girdled in,
and hewed asunder, a mountainous sirloin, and a generous
plum-pudding.'

I inquired, but with all deference and modesty, whither
he was bound, and to what distinguished Society he applied
a description so general. I shall proceed, in humble imitation of your example, to give the subsequent dialogue in a
dramatic form, unless when description becomes necessary.

Author of Waverley. To whom should I apply such
a description, save to the only Society to whom it can be
thoroughly applicable—those unerring judges of old books
and old wine—the Roxburghe Club of London ? Have
you not heard that I have been chosen a member of that
Society of select Bibliomaniacs ? [1]

Dryasdust (rummaging in his pocket). I did hear something
of it from Captain Clutterbuck, who wrote to me—aye,
here is his letter—that such a report was current among
the Scottish antiquaries, who were much alarmed lest you
should be seduced into the heresy of preferring English
beef to seven-year-old black-faced mutton, Maraschino to
whisky, and turtle-soup to cock-a-leekie ; in which case,
they must needs renounce you as a lost man.—' But,' adds
our friend (*looking at the letter*)—his hand is rather of
a military description, better used to handle the sword than
the pen—' Our friend is so much upon the SHUN '—the
shun, I think it is—' that it must be no light temptation
which will withdraw him from his incognito.'

Author. No light temptation, unquestionably ; but this
is a powerful one, to hob-or-nob with the lords of the literary
treasures of Althorpe and Hodnet, in Madeira negus,
brewed by the classical Dibdin—to share those profound

---

[1] The author has pride in recording, that he had the honour to be
elected a member of this distinguished association, merely as the Author
of *Waverley*, without any other designation ; and it was an additional
inducement to throw off the mask of an anonymous author, that it
gives him a right to occupy the vacant chair at that festive board.

debates which stamp accurately on each 'small volume, dark with tarnish'd gold,' its collar, not of S. S. but of R. R.—to toast the immortal memory of Caxton, Valdarar, Pynson, and the other fathers of that great art, which has made all, and each of us, what we are. These, my dear son, are temptations, to which you see me now in the act of resigning that quiet chimney-corner of life, in which, unknowing and unknown—save by means of the hopeful family to which I have given birth—I proposed to wear out the end of life's evening grey.

So saying, our venerable friend took another emphatic touch of the tankard, as if the very expression had suggested that specific remedy against the evils of life, recommended in the celebrated response of Johnson's anchorite—

'Come, my lad, and drink some beer.'

When he had placed on the table the silver tankard, and fetched a deep sigh to collect the respiration which the long draught had interrupted, I could not help echoing it, in a note so pathetically compassionate, that he fixed his eyes on me with surprise. 'How is this?' said he, somewhat angrily; 'do you, the creature of my will, grudge me my preferment? Have I dedicated to you, and your fellows, the best hours of my life for these seven years past; and do you presume to grumble or repine, because, in those which are to come, I seek for some enjoyments of life in society so congenial to my pursuits?' I humbled myself before the offended Senior, and professed my innocence in all that could possibly give him displeasure. He seemed partly appeased, but still bent on me an eye of suspicion, while he questioned me in the words of old Norton, in the ballad of the 'Rising in the North Country'.

> *Author.* What wouldst thou have, Francis Norton?
> Thou art my youngest son and heir;
> Something lies brooding at thy heart—
> Whate'er it be, to me declare.

Dryasdust. Craving, then, your paternal forgiveness for my presumption, I only sighed at the possibility of your venturing yourself amongst a body of critics, to whom, in the capacity of skilful antiquaries, the investigation of truth is an especial duty, and who may therefore visit with the more severe censure, those aberrations which it is so often your pleasure to make from the path of true history.

Author. I understand you. You mean to say these learned persons will have but little toleration for a romance, or a fictitious narrative, founded upon history ?

Dryasdust. Why, sir, I do rather apprehend, that their respect for the foundation will be such, that they may be apt to quarrel with the inconsistent nature of the super-structure ; just as every classical traveller pours forth expressions of sorrow and indignation, when, in travelling through Greece, he chances to see a Turkish kiosk rising on the ruins of an ancient temple.

Author. But since we cannot rebuild the temple, a kiosk may be a pretty thing, may it not ? Not quite correct in architecture, strictly and classically criticized ; but pre-senting something uncommon to the eye, and something fantastic to the imagination, on which the spectator gazes with pleasure of the same description which arises from the perusal of an Eastern tale.

Dryasdust. I am unable to dispute with you in metaphor, sir ; but I must say, in discharge of my conscience, that you stand much censured for adulterating the pure sources of historical knowledge. You approach them, men say, like the drunken yeoman, who, once upon a time, polluted the crystal spring which supplied the thirst of his family, with a score of sugar loaves and a hogshead of rum ; and thereby converted a simple and wholesome beverage into a stupefying, brutifying, and intoxicating fluid ; sweeter, indeed, to the taste than the natural lymph, but, for that very reason, more seductively dangerous.

Author. I allow your metaphor, Doctor ; but yet, though good punch cannot supply the want of spring water, it is, when modestly used, no *malum in se* ; and I should have thought it a shabby thing of the parson of the parish, had he helped to drink out the well on Saturday night, and preached against the honest hospitable yeoman on Sunday morning. I should have answered him, that the very flavour of the liquor should have put him at once upon his guard ; and that, if he had taken a drop over much, he ought to blame his own imprudence more than the hospitality of his entertainer.

Dryasdust. I profess I do not exactly see how this applies.

Author. No ; you are one of those numerous disputants, who will never follow their metaphors a step farther than it goes their own way. I will explain. A poor fellow, like myself, weary with ransacking his own barren and bounded imagination, looks out for some general subject in the huge and boundless field of history, which holds forth examples of every kind—lights on some personage, or some combination of circumstances, or some striking trait of manners, which he thinks may be advantageously used as the basis of a fictitious narrative—bedizens it with such colouring as his skill suggests—ornaments it with such romantic circumstances as may heighten the general effect—invests it with such shades of character, as will best contrast it with each other—and thinks, perhaps, he has done some service to the public, if he can present to them a lively fictitious picture, for which the original anecdote or circumstance which he made free to press into his service, only furnished a slight sketch. Now I cannot perceive any harm in this. The stores of history are accessible to every one ; and are no more exhausted or impoverished by the hints thus borrowed from them, than the fountain is drained by the water which we subtract for domestic purposes. And in reply to the sober charge of falsehood, against a narrative announced positively to be fictitious, one can only answer, by Prior's exclamation,

' Odzooks, must one swear to the truth of a song ? '

Dryasdust. Nay ; but I fear me that you are here eluding the charge. Men do not seriously accuse you of misrepresenting history ; although I assure you I have seen some grave treatises, in which it was thought necessary to contradict your assertions.

Author. That certainly was to point a discharge of artillery against a wreath of morning mist.

Dryasdust. But besides, and especially, it is said that you are in danger of causing history to be neglected—readers being contented with such frothy and superficial knowledge as they acquire from your works, to the effect of inducing them to neglect the severer and more accurate sources of information.

Author. I deny the consequence. On the contrary, I rather hope that I have turned the attention of the public on various points, which have received elucidation from writers of more learning and research, in consequence of my novels having attached some interest to them. I might give instances, but I hate vanity—I hate vanity. The history of the divining rod is well known—it is a slight valueless twig in itself, but indicates, by its motion, where veins of precious metal are concealed below the earth, which afterwards enrich the adventurers by whom they are laboriously and carefully wrought. I claim no more merit for my historical hints ; but this is something.

Dryasdust. We severer antiquaries, sir, may grant that this is true ; to wit, that your works may occasionally have put men of solid judgement upon researches which they would not perhaps have otherwise thought of undertaking. But this will leave you still accountable for misleading the young, the indolent, and the giddy, by thrusting into their hands works which, while they have so much the appearance of conveying information, as may prove perhaps a salve to their consciences for employing their leisure in the perusal, yet leave their giddy brains contented with the crude, uncertain, and often false statements, which your novels abound with.

Author. It would be very unbecoming in me, reverend sir, to accuse a gentleman of your cloth of cant ; but pray, is there not something like it in the pathos with which you enforce these dangers ? I aver, on the contrary, that by introducing the busy and the youthful to ' truths severe in fairy fiction dress'd,' [1] I am doing a real service to the more ingenious and the more apt among them ; for the love of knowledge wants but a beginning—the least spark

---

[1] The Doctor has denied the author's title to shelter himself under this quotation ; but the author continues to think himself entitled to all the shelter, which, threadbare as it is, it may yet be able to afford him. The *truth severe* applies not to the narrative itself, but to the moral it conveys, in which the author has not been thought deficient. The ' fairy fiction ' is the conduct of the story which the tale is invented to elucidate.

will give fire when the train is properly prepared ; and
having been interested in fictitious adventures, ascribed to
an historical period and characters, the reader begins next
to be anxious to learn what the facts really were, and how
far the novelist has justly represented them.

But even where the mind of the more careless reader
remains satisfied with the light perusal he has afforded to
a tale of fiction, he will still lay down the book with a degree
of knowledge, not perhaps of the most accurate kind, but
such as he might not otherwise have acquired. Nor is this
limited to minds of a low and incurious description ; but, on
the contrary, comprehends many persons otherwise of high
talents, who, nevertheless, either from lack of time, or of
perseverance, are willing to sit down contented with the
slight information which is acquired in such a manner.
The great Duke of Marlborough, for example, having quoted,
in conversation, some fact of English history rather in-
accurately, was requested to name his authority. ' Shakespeare's Historical Plays,' answered the conqueror of Blen-
heim ; ' the only English history I ever read in my life.'
And a hasty recollection will convince any of us how much
better we are acquainted with those parts of English history
which that immortal bard has dramatized, than with any
other portion of British story.

Dryasdust. And you, worthy sir, are ambitious to render
a similar service to posterity ?

Author. May the saints forefend I should be guilty of
such unfounded vanity ! I only show what has been done
when there were giants in the land. We pygmies of the
present day may at least, however, do something ; and it is
well to keep a pattern before our eyes, though that pattern
be inimitable.

Dryasdust. Well, sir, with me you must have your own
course ; and for reasons well known to you, it is impossible
for me to reply to you in argument. But I doubt if all you
have said will reconcile the public to the anachronisms of
your present volumes. Here you have a Countess of Derby
fetched out of her cold grave, and saddled with a set of
adventures dated twenty years after her death, besides
being given up as a Catholic, when she was in fact a zealous
Huguenot.

Author. She may sue me for damages, as in the case Dido *versus* Virgil.

Dryasdust. A worse fault is, that your manners are even more incorrect than usual. Your Puritan is faintly traced, in comparison to your Cameronian.

Author. I agree to the charge; but although I still consider hypocrisy and enthusiasm as fit food for ridicule and satire, yet I am sensible of the difficulty of holding fanaticism up to laughter or abhorrence, without using colouring which may give offence to the sincerely worthy and religious. Many things are lawful which we are taught are not convenient; and there are many tones of feeling which are too respectable to be insulted, though we do not altogether sympathize with them.

Dryasdust. Not to mention, my worthy sir, that perhaps you may think the subject exhausted.

Author. The devil take the men of this generation for putting the worst construction on their neighbour's conduct!

So saying, and flinging a testy sort of adieu towards me with his hand, he opened the door, and ran hastily down stairs. I started on my feet, and rang for my servant, who instantly came. I demanded what had become of the stranger—he denied that any such had been admitted—I pointed to the empty decanters, and he—he—he had the assurance to intimate that such vacancies were sometimes made when I had no better company than my own. I do not know what to make of this doubtful matter, but will certainly imitate your example, in placing this dialogue, with my present letter, at the head of PEVERIL OF THE PEAK. I am,

DEAR SIR,

Very much your faithful and

obedient servant,

JONAS DRYASDUST.

Michaelmas Day, 1822, YORK.

Peveril of the Peak

CHAPTER I

When civil dudgeon first grew high,
And men fell out, they knew not why;
When foul words, jealousies, and fears,
Set folk together by the ears—
                                    BUTLER.

WILLIAM, the Conqueror of England, was, or supposed himself to be, the father of a certain William Peveril, who attended him to the battle of Hastings, and there distinguished himself. The liberal-minded monarch, who assumed in his charters the veritable title of Gulielmus Bastardus, was not likely to let his son's illegitimacy be any bar to the course of his royal favour, when the laws of England were issued from the mouth of the Norman victor, and the lands of the Saxons were at his unlimited disposal. William Peveril obtained a liberal grant of property and lordships in Derbyshire, and became the erector of that Gothic fortress, which, hanging over the mouth of the Devil's Cavern, so well known to tourists, gives the name of Castleton to the adjacent village.

From this feudal baron, who chose his nest upon the principles on which an eagle selects her aerie, and built it in such a fashion as if he had intended it, as an Irishman said of the Martello towers, for the sole purpose of puzzling posterity, there was, or conceived themselves to be, descended (for their pedigree was rather hypothetical) an opulent family of knightly rank, in the same county of Derby. The great fief of Castleton, with its adjacent wastes and forests, and all the wonders which they contain, had been forfeited in King John's stormy days, by one William Peveril, and had been granted anew to the Lord Ferrers of that day. Yet this William's descendants, though no longer possessed of what they alleged to have been their original

PEVERIL   B

property, were long distinguished by the proud title of
Peverils of the Peak, which served to mark their high
descent and lofty pretensions.

In Charles the Second's time, the representative of this
ancient family was Sir Geoffrey Peveril, a man who had
many of the ordinary attributes of an old-fashioned country
gentleman, and very few individual traits to distinguish
him from the general portrait of that worthy class of mankind. He was proud of small advantages, angry at small
disappointments, incapable of forming any resolution or
opinion abstracted from his own prejudices—he was proud
of his birth, lavish in his housekeeping, convivial with those
kindred and acquaintances who would allow his superiority
in rank—contentious and quarrelsome with all that crossed
his pretensions—kind to the poor, except when they plundered his game—a royalist in his political opinions, and
one who detested alike a Roundhead, a poacher, and
a Presbyterian. In religion Sir Geoffrey was a high-church-
man, of so exalted a strain that many thought he still
nourished in private the Roman Catholic tenets, which his
family had only renounced in his father's time, and that
he had a dispensation for conforming in outward observances
to the Protestant faith. There was at least such a scandal
amongst the Puritans, and the influence which Sir Geoffrey
Peveril certainly appeared to possess amongst the Catholic
gentlemen of Derbyshire and Cheshire, seemed to give
countenance to the rumour.

Such was Sir Geoffrey, who might have passed to his
grave without further distinction than a brass plate in the
chancel, had he not lived in times which forced the most
inactive spirits into exertion, as a tempest influences the
sluggish waters of the deadest mere. When the Civil Wars
broke out, Peveril of the Peak, proud from pedigree, and
brave by constitution, raised a regiment for the king, and
showed upon several occasions more capacity for command
than men had heretofore given him credit for.

Even in the midst of the civil turmoil, he fell in love with,
and married, a beautiful and amiable young lady of the
noble house of Stanley ; and from that time had the more
merit in his loyalty, as it divorced him from her society,
unless at very brief intervals, when his duty permitted an

occasional visit to his home. Scorning to be allured from his military duty by domestic inducements, Peveril of the Peak fought on for several rough years of civil war, and performed his part with sufficient gallantry, until his regiment was surprised and cut to pieces by Poyntz, Cromwell's enterprising and successful general of cavalry. The defeated Cavalier escaped from the field of battle, and, like a true descendant of William the Conqueror, disdaining submission, threw himself into his own castellated mansion, which was attacked and defended in a siege of that irregular kind which caused the destruction of so many baronial residences during the course of those unhappy wars. Martindale Castle, after having suffered severely from the cannon which Cromwell himself brought against it, was at length surrendered when in the last extremity. Sir Geoffrey himself became a prisoner, and while his liberty was only restored upon a promise of remaining a peaceful subject to the Commonwealth in future, his former delinquencies, as they were termed by the ruling party, were severely punished by fine and sequestration.

But neither his forced promise, nor the fear of further unpleasant consequences to his person or property, could prevent Peveril of the Peak from joining the gallant Earl of Derby the night before the fatal engagement in Wiggan Lane, where the Earl's forces were dispersed. Sir Geoffrey having had his share in that action, escaped with the relics of the royalists after the defeat, to join Charles II. He witnessed also the final defeat of Worcester, where he was a second time made prisoner ; and as, in the opinion of Cromwell and the language of the times, he was regarded as an obstinate malignant, he was in great danger of having shared with the Earl of Derby his execution at Bolton-le-Moor, having partaken with him the dangers of two actions. But Sir Geoffrey's life was preserved by the interest of a friend, who possessed influence in the councils of Oliver. This was a Mr. Bridgenorth, a gentleman of middling quality, whose father had been successful in some commercial adventure during the peaceful reign of James I ; and who had bequeathed his son a considerable sum of money, in addition to the moderate patrimony which he inherited from his father.

The substantial, though small-sized brick building of Moultrassie Hall was but two miles distant from Martindale Castle, and the young Bridgenorth attended the same school with the heir of the Peverils. A sort of companionship, if not intimacy, took place betwixt them, which continued during their youthful sports—the rather that Bridgenorth, though he did not at heart admit Sir Geoffrey's claims of superiority to the extent which the other's vanity would have exacted, paid deference in a reasonable degree to the representative of a family so much more ancient and important than his own, without conceiving that he in any respect degraded himself by doing so.

Mr. Bridgenorth did not, however, carry his complaisance so far as to embrace Sir Geoffrey's side during the Civil War. On the contrary, as an active justice of the peace, he rendered much assistance in arraying the militia in the cause of the Parliament, and for some time held a military commission in that service. This was partly owing to his religious principles, for he was a zealous Presbyterian, partly to his political ideas, which, without being absolutely democratical, favoured the popular side of the great national question. Besides, he was a moneyed man, and to a certain extent had a shrewd eye to his worldly interest. He understood how to improve the opportunities which civil war afforded, of advancing his fortune, by a dexterous use of his capital ; and he was not at a loss to perceive that these were likely to be obtained in joining the Parliament ; while the king's cause, as it was managed, held out nothing to the wealthy but a course of exaction and compulsory loans. For these reasons, Bridgenorth became a decided Roundhead, and all friendly communication betwixt his neighbour and him was abruptly broken asunder. This was done with the less acrimony, that, during the Civil War, Sir Geoffrey was almost constantly in the field, following the vacillating and unhappy fortunes of his master ; while Major Bridgenorth, who soon renounced active military service, resided chiefly in London, and only occasionally visited the Hall.

Upon these visits, it was with great pleasure he received the intelligence that Lady Peveril had shown much kindness to Mrs. Bridgenorth, and had actually given her and her family shelter in Martindale Castle, when Moultrassie

Hall was threatened with pillage by a body of Prince
Rupert's ill-disciplined Cavaliers. This acquaintance had
been matured by frequent walks together, which the vicinity
of their places of residence suffered the Lady Peveril to
have with Mrs. Bridgenorth, who deemed herself much
honoured in being thus admitted into the society of so
distinguished a lady. Major Bridgenorth heard of this
growing intimacy with great pleasure, and he determined
to repay the obligation, as far as he could without much
hurt to himself, by interfering with all his influence in behalf
of her unfortunate husband. It was chiefly owing to Major
Bridgenorth's mediation, that Sir Geoffrey's life was saved
after the battle of Worcester. He obtained him permission
to compound for his estate on easier terms than many who
had been less obstinate in malignancy ; and, finally, when,
in order to raise the money to the composition, the knight
was obliged to sell a considerable portion of his patrimony,
Major Bridgenorth became the purchaser, and that at a
larger price than had been paid to any Cavalier under such
circumstances, by a member of the Committee for Sequestrations. It is true, the prudent committeeman did not, by
any means, lose sight of his own interest in the transaction,
for the price was, after all, very moderate, and the property
lay adjacent to Moultrassie Hall, the value of which was
at least trebled by the acquisition. But then it was also true
that the unfortunate owner must have submitted to much
worse conditions, had the committeeman used, as others
did, the full advantages which his situation gave him ; and
Bridgenorth took credit to himself, and received it from
others, for having, on this occasion, fairly sacrificed his
interest to his liberality.

Sir Geoffrey Peveril was of the same opinion, and the
rather that Mr. Bridgenorth seemed to bear his exaltation
with great moderation, and was disposed to show him
personally the same deference in his present sunshine of
prosperity, which he had exhibited formerly in their early
acquaintance. It is but justice to Major Bridgenorth to
observe, that in this conduct he paid respect as much to the
misfortunes as to the pretensions of his far-descended
neighbour, and that, with the frank generosity of a blunt
Englishman, he conceded points of ceremony, about which

he himself was indifferent, merely because he saw that his doing so gave pleasure to Sir Geoffrey.

Peveril of the Peak did justice to his neighbour's delicacy, in consideration of which he forgot many things. He forgot that Major Bridgenorth was already in possession of a fair third of his estate, and had various pecuniary claims affecting the remainder, to the extent of one-third more. He endeavoured even to forget, what it was still more difficult not to remember, the altered situation in which they and their mansions now stood to each other.

Before the Civil War, the superb battlements and turrets of Martindale Castle looked down on the red brick-built Hall, as it stole out from the green plantations, just as an oak in Martindale Chase would have looked beside one of the stunted and formal young beech-trees with which Bridgenorth had graced his avenue; but after the siege which we have commemorated, the enlarged and augmented Hall was as much predominant in the landscape over the shattered and blackened ruins of the Castle, of which only one wing was left habitable, as the youthful beech, in all its vigour of shoot and bud, would appear to the same aged oak stripped of its boughs, and rifted by lightning, one-half laid in shivers on the ground, and the other remaining a blackened and ungraceful trunk, rent and splintered, and without either life or leaves. Sir Geoffrey could not but feel that the situation and prospects were exchanged as disadvantageously for himself as the appearance of their mansions; and that though the authority of the man in office under the Parliament, the sequestrator, and the committeeman, had been only exerted for the protection of the Cavalier and the malignant, they would have been as effectual if applied to procure his utter ruin; and that he was become a client, while his neighbour was elevated into a patron.

There were two considerations, besides the necessity of the case and the constant advice of his lady, which enabled Peveril of the Peak to endure, with some patience, this state of degradation. The first was, that the politics of Major Bridgenorth began, on many points, to assimilate themselves to his own. As a Presbyterian, he was not an utter enemy to monarchy, and had been considerably shocked at the unexpected trial and execution of the king ; as a civilian and a man of property, he feared the domination of the military ; and though he wished not to see Charles restored by force of arms, yet he arrived at the conclusion that to bring back the heir of the royal family on such terms of composition as might ensure the protection of those popular immunities and privileges for which the Long Parliament had at first contended, would be the surest and most desirable termination to the mutations in state affairs which had agitated Britain. Indeed, the major's ideas on this point approached so nearly those of his neighbour, that he had wellnigh suffered Sir Geoffrey, who had a finger in almost all the conspiracies of the Royalists, to involve him in the unfortunate rising of Penruddock and Groves, in the west, in which many of the Presbyterian interest, as well as the Cavalier party, were engaged. And though his habitual prudence eventually kept him out of this and other dangers, Major Bridgenorth was considered during the last years of Cromwell's domination, and the interregnum which succeeded, as a disaffected person to the Commonwealth, and a favourer of Charles Stuart.

But besides this approximation to the same political opinions, another bond of intimacy united the families of the Castle and the Hall. Major Bridgenorth, fortunate, and eminently so, in all his worldly transactions, was visited by severe and reiterated misfortunes in his family, and became, in this particular, an object of compassion to his poorer and more decayed neighbour. Betwixt the breaking out of the Civil War and the Restoration, he lost successively a family of no less than six children, apparently through a delicacy of constitution, which cut off the little prattlers at the early age when they most wind themselves around the heart of the parents.

In the beginning of the year 1658, Major Bridgenorth was childless ; ere it ended, he had a daughter, indeed, but her birth was purchased by the death of an affectionate wife, whose constitution had been exhausted by maternal grief, and by the anxious and harrowing reflection, that from her the children they had lost derived that delicacy of health which proved unable to undergo the tear and wear of existence. The same voice which told Bridgenorth that he was father of a living child (it was the friendly voice of Lady Peveril), communicated to him the melancholy intelligence that he was no longer a husband. The feelings of Major Bridgenorth were strong and deep, rather than hasty and vehement ; and his grief assumed the form of a sullen stupor, from which neither the friendly remonstrances of Sir Geoffrey, who did not fail to be with his neighbour at this distressing conjuncture, even though he knew he must meet the Presbyterian pastor, nor the ghostly exhortations of this latter person, were able to rouse the unfortunate widower.

At length Lady Peveril, with the ready invention of a female sharpened by the sight of distress and the feelings of sympathy, tried on the sufferer one of those experiments by which grief is often awakened from despondency into tears. She placed in Bridgenorth's arms the infant whose birth had cost him so dear, and conjured him to remember that his Alice was not yet dead, since she survived in the helpless child she had left to his paternal care.

'Take her away—take her away !' said the unhappy man, and they were the first words he had spoken ; 'let me not look on her—it is but another blossom that has bloomed to fade, and the tree that bore it will never flourish more !'

He almost threw the child into Lady Peveril's arms, placed his hands before his face, and wept aloud. Lady Peveril did not say 'Be comforted', but she ventured to promise that the blossom should ripen to fruit.

'Never, never !' said Bridgenorth ; 'take the unhappy child away, and let me only know when I shall wear black for her—Wear black !' he exclaimed, interrupting himself, 'what other colour shall I wear during the remainder of my life ?'

'I will take the child for a season,' said Lady Peveril, 'since the sight of her is so painful to you ; and the little Alice shall share the nursery of our Julian, until it shall be pleasure and not pain for you to look on her.'

'That hour will never come,' said the unhappy father ; 'her doom is written—she will follow the rest—God's will be done. Lady, I thank you—I trust her to your care ; and I thank God that my eye shall not see her dying agonies.'

Without detaining the reader's attention longer on this painful theme, it is enough to say that the Lady Peveril did undertake the duties of a mother to the little orphan ; and

LADY PEVERIL PRESENTING THE INFANT ALICE TO MAJOR BRIDGENORTH

perhaps it was owing, in a great measure, to her judicious treatment of the infant, that its feeble hold of life was preserved, since the glimmering spark might probably have been altogether smothered, had it, like the major's former children, undergone the over-care and over-nursing of

a mother rendered nervously cautious and anxious by so
many successive losses. The lady was the more ready to
undertake this charge, that she herself had lost two infant
children ; and that she attributed the preservation of the
third, now a fine healthy child of three years old, to Julian's
being subjected to rather a different course of diet and
treatment than was then generally practised. She resolved
to follow the same regimen with the little orphan, which
she had observed in the case of her own boy ; and it was
equally successful. By a more sparing use of medicine, by
a bolder admission of fresh air, by a firm, yet cautious
attention to encourage rather than to supersede the exertions of nature, the puny infant, under the care of an
excellent nurse, gradually improved in strength and in
liveliness.

Sir Geoffrey, like most men of his frank and good-natured
disposition, was naturally fond of children, and so much
compassionated the sorrows of his neighbour, that he
entirely forgot his being a Presbyterian, until it became
necessary that the infant should be christened by a teacher
of that persuasion.

This was a trying case—the father seemed incapable of
giving direction ; and that the threshold of Martindale
Castle should be violated by the heretical step of a dissenting
clergyman was matter of horror to its orthodox owner. He
had seen the famous Hugh Peters, with a Bible in one hand
and a pistol in the other, ride in triumph through the court-
door when Martindale was surrendered ; and the bitterness
of that hour had entered like iron into his soul. Yet such
was Lady Peveril's influence over the prejudices of her
husband, that he was induced to connive at the ceremony
taking place in a remote garden-house, which was not
properly within the precincts of the castle-wall. The lady
even dared to be present while the ceremony was performed
by the Reverend Master Solsgrace, who had once preached
a sermon of three hours' length before the House of Commons, upon a thanksgiving occasion after the relief of
Exeter. Sir Geoffrey Peveril took care to be absent the
whole day from the castle, and it was only from the great
interest which he took in the washing, perfuming, and as it
were purification of the summer-house, that it could have

been guessed he knew anything of what had taken place in it.

But, whatever prejudices the good knight might entertain against his neighbour's form of religion, they did not in any way influence his feelings towards him as a sufferer under severe affliction. The mode in which he showed his sympathy was rather singular, but exactly suited the character of both, and the terms on which they stood with each other.

Morning after morning the good baronet made Moultrassie Hall the termination of his walk or ride, and said a single word of kindness as he passed. Sometimes he entered the old parlour where the proprietor sat in solitary wretchedness and despondency; but more frequently (for Sir Geoffrey did not pretend to great talents of conversation), he paused on the terrace, and stopping or halting his horse by the latticed window, said aloud to the melancholy inmate, ' How is it with you, Master Bridgenorth ? ' (the knight would never acknowledge his neighbour's military rank of major); ' I just looked in to bid you keep a good heart, man, and to tell you that Julian is well, and little Alice is well, and all are well at Martindale Castle.'

A deep sigh, sometimes coupled with ' I thank you, Sir Geoffrey; my grateful duty waits on Lady Peveril,' was generally Bridgenorth's only answer. But the news was received on the one part with the kindness which was designed upon the other; it gradually became less painful and more interesting; the lattice window was never closed, nor was the leathern easy chair which stood next to it ever empty, when the usual hour of the baronet's momentary visit approached. At length the expectation of that passing minute became the pivot upon which the thoughts of poor Bridgenorth turned during all the rest of the day. Most men have known the influence of such brief but ruling moments at some period of their lives. The moment when a lover passes the window of his mistress—the moment when the epicure hears the dinner-bell,—is that into which is crowded the whole interest of the day; the hours which precede it are spent in anticipation; the hours which follow, in reflection on what has passed; and fancy, dwelling on each brief circumstance, gives to seconds the duration of minutes, to minutes that of hours. Thus seated in his lonely

chair, Bridgenorth could catch at a distance the stately
step of Sir Geoffrey, or the heavy tramp of his war-horse,
Black Hastings, which had borne him in many an action ;
he could hear the hum of ' The King shall enjoy his own
again,' or the habitual whistle of ' Cuckolds and Roundheads ', die into reverential silence, as the knight approached
the mansion of affliction ; and then came the strong hale
voice of the huntsman soldier with its usual greeting.

By degrees the communication became something more
protracted, as Major Bridgenorth's grief, like all human
feelings, lost its overwhelming violence, and permitted him
to attend, in some degree, to what passed around him, to
discharge various duties which pressed upon him, and to
give a share of attention to the situation of the country,
distracted as it was by the contending factions, whose strife
only terminated in the Restoration. Still, however, though
slowly recovering from the effects of the shock which he
had sustained, Major Bridgenorth felt himself as yet unable
to make up his mind to the effort necessary to see his
infant ; and though separated by so short a distance from
the being in whose existence he was more interested than
in anything the world afforded, he only made himself
acquainted with the windows of the apartment where little
Alice was lodged, and was often observed to watch them
from the terrace, as they brightened in the evening under
the influence of the setting sun. In truth, though a strong-
minded man in most respects, he was unable to lay aside
the gloomy impression that this remaining pledge of affection was soon to be conveyed to that grave which had
already devoured all besides that was dear to him ; and he
awaited in miserable suspense the moment when he should
hear that symptoms of the fatal malady had begun to show
themselves.

The voice of Peveril continued to be that of a comforter,
until the month of April, 1660, when it suddenly assumed
a new and different tone. ' The King shall enjoy his own
again,' far from ceasing, as the hasty tread of Black Hastings
came up the avenue, bore burden to the clatter of his hoofs
on the paved court-yard, as Sir Geoffrey sprang from his
great war-saddle, now once more garnished with pistols of
two feet in length, and, armed with steel-cap, back and

breast, and a truncheon in his hand, he rushed into the apartment of the astonished major, with his eyes sparkling, and his cheek inflamed, while he called out, ' Up ! up, neighbour ! No time now to mope in the chimney-corner ! Where is your buff-coat and broadsword, man ? Take the true side once in your life, and mend past mistakes. The king is all lenity, man—all royal nature and mercy. I will get your full pardon.'

' What means all this ? ' said Bridgenorth—' Is all well with you—all well at Martindale Castle, Sir Geoffrey ? '

' Well as you could wish them, Alice, and Julian, and all. But I have news worth twenty of that—Monk has declared at London against those stinking scoundrels the Rump. Fairfax is up in Yorkshire—for the king—for the king, man ! Churchmen, Presbyterians, and all, are in buff and bandoleer for King Charles. I have a letter from Fairfax to secure Derby and Chesterfield with all the men I can make. D—n him, fine that I should take orders from him ! But never mind that—all are friends now, and you and I, good neighbour, will charge abreast, as good neighbours should. See there ! read—read—read—and then boot and saddle in an instant.

> Hey for cavaliers—ho for cavaliers,
> Pray for cavaliers.
> Dub-a-dub, dub-a-dub,
> Have at old Beelzebub,
> Oliver shakes in his bier ! '

After thundering forth this elegant effusion of loyal enthusiasm, the sturdy Cavalier's heart became too full. He threw himself on a seat, and exclaiming, ' Did ever I think to live to see this happy day ! ' he wept, to his own surprise, as much as to that of Bridgenorth.

Upon considering the crisis in which the country was placed, it appeared to Major Bridgenorth, as it had done to Fairfax, and other leaders of the Presbyterian party, that their frank embracing of the royal interest was the wisest and most patriotic measure which they could adopt in the circumstances, when all ranks and classes of men were seeking refuge from the uncertainty and varied oppression attending the repeated contests between the factions of Westminster Hall and of Wallingford House. Accordingly he joined with Sir Geoffrey, with less enthusiasm indeed, but with equal sincerity, taking such measures as seemed proper to secure their part of the country on the king's behalf, which was done as effectually and peaceably as in other parts of England. The neighbours were both at Chesterfield, when news arrived that the king had landed in England ; and Sir Geoffrey instantly announced his purpose of waiting upon his Majesty, even before his return to the Castle of Martindale.

' Who knows, neighbour,' he said, ' whether Sir Geoffrey Peveril will ever return to Martindale ? Titles must be going amongst them yonder, and I have deserved something among the rest. Lord Peveril would sound well—or stay, Earl of Martindale—no, not of Martindale—Earl of the Peak. Meanwhile, trust your affairs to me—I will see you secured —I would you had been no Presbyterian, neighbour— a knighthood,—I mean a knight-bachelor, not a knight-baronet,—would have served your turn well.'

' I leave these things to my betters, Sir Geoffrey,' said the major, ' and desire nothing so earnestly as to find all well at Martindale when I return.'

' You will—you will find them all well,' said the baronet ; ' Julian, Alice, Lady Peveril, and all of them—Bear my commendations to them, and kiss them all, neighbour, Lady Peveril and all—you may kiss a countess when I come back ; all will go well with you now you are turned honest man.'

' I always meant to be so, Sir Geoffrey,' said Bridgenorth, calmly.

' Well, well, well—no offence meant,' said the knight, ' all is well now—so you to Moultrassie Hall, and I to White-hall. Said I well, aha ! So ho, mine host, a stoup of canary to the king's health ere we get to horse—I forgot, neighbour —you drink no healths.'

' I wish the king's health, as sincerely as if I drank a gallon to it,' replied the major ; ' and I wish you, Sir Geoffrey, all success on your journey, and a safe return.'

CHAPTER II

Why then, we will have bellowing of beeves,
Broaching of barrels, brandishing of spigots;
Blood shall flow freely, but it shall be gore
Of herds and flocks, and venison and poultry,
Join'd to the brave heart's-blood of John-a-Barleycorn !
                                        Old Play.

WHATEVER rewards Charles might have condescended to bestow in acknowledgement of the sufferings and loyalty of Peveril of the Peak, he had none in his disposal equal to the pleasure which Providence had reserved for Bridgenorth on his return to Derbyshire. The exertion to which he had been summoned had had the usual effect of restoring to a certain extent the activity and energy of his character, and he felt it would be unbecoming to relapse into the state of lethargic melancholy from which it had roused him. Time also had its usual effect in mitigating the subjects of his regret ; and when he had passed one day at the Hall in regretting that he could not expect the indirect news of his daughter's health, which Sir Geoffrey used to communicate in his almost daily call, he reflected that it would be in every respect becoming that he should pay a personal visit at Martindale Castle, carry thither the remembrances of the knight to his lady, assure her of his health, and satisfy himself respecting that of his daughter. He armed himself for the worst—he called to recollection the thin cheeks, faded eye, wasted hand, pallid lip, which had marked the decaying health of all his former infants.

' I shall see,' he said, ' these signs of mortality once more—I shall once more see a beloved being to whom I have given birth, gliding to the grave which ought to enclose me long before her. No matter—it is unmanly so long to shrink from that which must be—God's will be done ! '

He went accordingly, on the subsequent morning, to Martindale Castle, and gave the lady the welcome assurances of her husband's safety, and of his hopes of preferment.

' For the first, may Almighty God be praised ! ' said the Lady Peveril ; ' and be the other as our gracious and restored sovereign may will it. We are great enough for our means, and have means sufficient for contentment, though not for splendour. And now I see, good Master Bridgenorth, the folly of putting faith in idle presentiments of evil. So often had Sir Geoffrey's repeated attempts in favour of the Stuarts led him into new misfortunes, that when, the other morning, I saw him once more dressed in his fatal armour, and heard the sound of his trumpet, which had been so long silent, it seemed to me as if I saw his shroud, and heard his death-knell. I say this to you, good neighbour, the rather because I fear your own mind has been harassed with anticipations of impending calamity, which it may please God to avert in your case as it has done in mine ; and here comes a sight which bears good assurance of it.'

The door of the apartment opened as she spoke, and two lovely children entered. The eldest, Julian Peveril, a fine boy betwixt four and five years old, led in his hand, with an air of dignified support and attention, a little girl of eighteen months, who rolled and tottered along, keeping herself with difficulty upright by the assistance of her elder, stronger, and masculine companion.

Bridgenorth cast a hasty and fearful glance upon the countenance of his daughter, and, even in that glimpse, perceived, with exquisite delight, that his fears were unfounded. He caught her in his arms, pressed her to his heart, and the child, though at first alarmed at the vehemence of his caresses, presently, as if prompted by Nature, smiled in reply to them. Again he held her at some distance from him, and examined her more attentively ; he satisfied himself that the complexion of the young cherub he had in his arms was not the hectic tinge of disease, but the clear hue of ruddy health ; and that though her little frame was slight, it was firm and springy.

' I did not think that it could have been thus,' he said, looking to Lady Peveril, who had sat observing the scene with great pleasure ; ' but praise be to God in the first instance, and next, thanks to you, madam, who have been His instrument.'

' Julian must lose his playfellow now, I suppose ?' said the lady ; ' but the Hall is not distant, and I will see my

little charge often. Dame Martha, the housekeeper at
Moultrassie, has sense, and is careful. I will tell her the
rules I have observed with little Alice, and '——

'God forbid my girl should ever come to Moultrassie,'
said Major Bridgenorth, hastily; 'it has been the grave
of her race. The air of the low grounds suited them not—
or there is perhaps a fate connected with the mansion.
I will seek for her some other place of abode.'

ALICE INTRODUCED TO HER FATHER

'That you shall not, under your favour be it spoken,
Major Bridgenorth,' answered the lady. 'If you do so,
we must suppose that you are undervaluing my qualities
as a nurse. If she goes not to her father's house, she shall
not quit mine. I will keep the little lady as a pledge of
her safety and my own skill; and since you are afraid of
the damp of the low grounds, I hope you will come here
frequently to visit her.'

This was a proposal which went to the heart of Major
Bridgenorth. It was precisely the point which he would

have given worlds to arrive at, but which he saw no chance
of attaining.

It is too well known, that those whose families are long
pursued by such a fatal disease as existed in his, become,
it may be said, superstitious respecting its fatal effects, and
ascribe to place, circumstance, and individual care, much
more perhaps than these can in any case contribute to
avert the fatality of constitutional distemper. Lady Peveril
was aware that this was peculiarly the impression of her
neighbour ; that the depression of his spirits, the excess
of his care, the feverishness of his apprehensions, the
restraint and gloom of the solitude in which he dwelt, were
really calculated to produce the evil which most of all he
dreaded. She pitied him, she felt for him, she was grateful
for former protection received at his hands—she had
become interested in the child itself. What female fails
to feel such interest in the helpless creature she has tended?
And to sum the whole up, the dame had a share of human
vanity ; and being a sort of Lady Bountiful in her way
(for the character was not then confined to the old and the
foolish), she was proud of the skill by which she had averted
the probable attacks of hereditary malady, so inveterate
in the family of Bridgenorth. It needed not, perhaps, in
other cases, that so many reasons should be assigned for
an act of neighbourly humanity ; but civil war had so
lately torn the country asunder, and broken all the usual
ties of vicinage and good neighbourhood, that it was unusual
to see them preserved among persons of different political
opinions.

Major Bridgenorth himself felt this ; and while the tear
of joy in his eye showed how gladly he would accept Lady
Peveril's proposal, he could not help stating the obvious
inconveniences attendant upon her scheme, though it was
in the tone of one who would gladly hear them overruled.
' Madam,' he said, ' your kindness makes me the happiest
and most thankful of men ; but can it be consistent with
your own convenience ? Sir Geoffrey has his opinions on
many points, which have differed, and probably do still
differ, from mine. He is high-born, and I of middling
parentage only. He uses the Church Service, and I the
Catechism of the Assembly of Divines at Westminster '——

'I hope you will find prescribed in neither of them,' said the Lady Peveril, 'that I may not be a mother to your motherless child. I trust, Master Bridgenorth, the joyful Restoration of his Majesty, a work wrought by the direct hand of Providence, may be the means of closing and healing all civil and religious dissensions among us, and that, instead of showing the superior purity of our faith by persecuting those who think otherwise from ourselves on doctrinal points, we shall endeavour to show its real Christian tendency, by emulating each other in actions of goodwill towards man, as the best way of showing our love to God.'

'Your ladyship speaks what your own kind heart dictates,' answered Bridgenorth, who had his own share of the narrow-mindedness of the time ; 'and sure am I, that if all who call themselves loyalists and cavaliers, thought like you—and like my friend Sir Geoffrey '—(this he added after a moment's pause, being perhaps rather complimentary than sincere)—'we, who thought it our duty in time past to take arms for freedom of conscience, and against arbitrary power, might now sit down in peace and contentment. But I wot not how it may fall. You have sharp and hot spirits amongst you ; I will not say our power was always moderately used, and revenge is sweet to the race of fallen Adam.'

'Come, Master Bridgenorth,' said the Lady Peveril gaily, 'these evil omenings do but point out conclusions, which, unless they were so anticipated, are most unlikely to come to pass. You know what Shakespeare says :—

> To fly the boar before the boar pursues,
> Were to incense the boar to follow us,
> And make pursuit when he did mean no chase.

But I crave your pardon—it is so long since we have met, that I forgot you love no play-books.'

'With reverence to your ladyship,' said Bridgenorth, 'I were much to blame did I need the idle words of a Warwickshire stroller to teach me my grateful duty to your ladyship on this occasion, which appoints me to be directed by you in all things which my conscience will permit.'

'Since you permit me such influence, then,' replied the Lady Peveril, 'I shall be moderate in exercising it, in order

that I may, in my domination at least, give you a favourable
impression of the new order of things. So, if you will be
a subject of mine for one day, neighbour, I am going, at
my lord and husband's command, to issue out my warrants
to invite the whole neighbourhood to a solemn feast at the
castle, on Thursday next ; and I not only pray you to be
personally present yourself, but to prevail on your worthy
pastor, and such neighbours and friends, high and low, as
may think in your own way, to meet with the rest of the
neighbourhood, to rejoice on this joyful occasion of the
king's Restoration, and thereby to show that we are to be
henceforward a united people.'

The Parliamentarian major was considerably embarrassed by this proposal. He looked upward, and downward,
and around, cast his eye first to the oak-carved ceiling,
and anon fixed it upon the floor ; then threw it around the
room till it lighted on his child, the sight of whom suggested
another and a better train of reflections than ceiling and
floor had been able to supply.

'Madam,' he said, 'I have long been a stranger to
festivity, perhaps from constitutional melancholy, perhaps
from the depression which is natural to a desolate and
deprived man, in whose ear mirth is marred, like a pleasant
air when performed on a mistuned instrument. But though
neither my thoughts nor temperament are jovial or
mercurial, it becomes me to be grateful to Heaven for the
good he has sent me by the means of your ladyship. David,
the man after God's own heart, did wash and eat bread
when his beloved child was removed—mine is restored to
me, and shall I not show gratitude under a blessing, when
he showed resignation under an affliction ? Madam, I will
wait on your gracious invitation with acceptance ; and
such of my friends with whom I may possess influence,
and whose presence your ladyship may desire, shall accompany me to the festivity, that our Israel may be as one
people.'

Having spoken these words with an aspect which belonged
more to a martyr than to a guest bidden to a festival, and
having kissed, and solemnly blessed his little girl, Major
Bridgenorth took his departure for Moultrassie Hall.

CHAPTER III

Here's neither want of appetite nor mouths;
Pray Heaven we be not scant of meat or mirth !
Old Play.

EVEN upon ordinary occasions, and where means were
ample, a great entertainment in those days was not such
a sinecure as in modern times, when the lady who presides
has but to intimate to her menials the day and hour when
she wills it to take place. At that simple period, the lady
was expected to enter deeply into the arrangement and
provision of the whole affair ; and from a little gallery,
which communicated with her own private apartment, and
looked down upon the kitchen, her shrill voice was to be
heard, from time to time, like that of the warning spirit
in a tempest, rising above the clash of pots and stewpans—
the creaking of spits—the clattering of marrow-bones and
cleavers—the scolding of cooks—and all the other various
kinds of din which form an accompaniment to dressing
a large dinner.

But all this toil and anxiety was more than doubled in
the case of the approaching feast at Martindale Castle,
where the presiding genius of the festivity was scarce
provided with adequate means to carry her hospitable
purpose into effect. The tyrannical conduct of husbands,
in such cases, is universal ; and I scarce know one house-
holder of my acquaintance who has not, on some ill-omened
and most inconvenient season, announced suddenly to his
innocent helpmate, that he had invited

Some odious Major Rock,
To drop in at six o'clock,

to the great discomposure of the lady, and the discredit,
perhaps, of her domestic arrangements.

Peveril of the Peak was still more thoughtless ; for he
had directed his lady to invite the whole honest men of
the neighbourhood to make good cheer at Martindale Castle,
in honour of the blessed Restoration of his most sacred
Majesty, without precisely explaining where the provisions
were to come from. The deer-park had lain waste ever

since the siege; the dovecot could do little to furnish
forth such an entertainment; the fish-ponds, it is true,
were well provided (which the neighbouring Presbyterians
noted as a suspicious circumstance); and game was to be
had for the shooting, upon the extensive heaths and hills
of Derbyshire. But these were but the secondary parts
of a banquet; and the house-steward and bailiff, Lady
Peveril's only coadjutors and counsellors, could not agree
how the butcher-meat—the most substantial part, or, as
it were, the main body of the entertainment—was to be
supplied. The house-steward threatened the sacrifice of a
fine yoke of young bullocks, which the bailiff, who pleaded
the necessity of their agricultural services, tenaciously
resisted; and Lady Peveril's good and dutiful nature did
not prevent her from making some impatient reflections
on the want of consideration of her absent knight, who had
thus thoughtlessly placed her in so embarrassing a situation.

These reflections were scarcely just, if a man is only
responsible for such resolutions as he adopts when he is
fully master of himself. Sir Geoffrey's loyalty, like that
of many persons in his situation, had, by dint of hopes and
fears, victories and defeats, struggles and sufferings, all
arising out of the same moving cause, and turning, as it
were, on the same pivot, acquired the character of an
intense and enthusiastic passion; and the singular and
surprising change of fortune, by which his highest wishes
were not only gratified, but far exceeded, occasioned for
some time a kind of intoxication of loyal rapture which
seemed to pervade the whole kingdom. Sir Geoffrey had
seen Charles and his brothers, and had been received by the
merry monarch with that graceful, and at the same time
frank urbanity, by which he conciliated all who approached
him; the knight's services and merits had been fully
acknowledged, and recompense had been hinted at, if not
expressly promised. Was it for Peveril of the Peak, in the
jubilee of his spirits, to consider how his wife was to find
beef and mutton to feast his neighbours?

Luckily, however, for the embarrassed lady, there existed
some one who had composure of mind sufficient to foresee
this difficulty. Just as she had made up her mind, very
reluctantly, to become debtor to Major Bridgenorth for

the sum necessary to carry her husband's commands into effect, and whilst she was bitterly regretting this departure from the strictness of her usual economy, the steward, who, by the by, had not been absolutely sober since the news of the king's landing at Dover, burst into the apartment, snapping his fingers, and showing more marks of delight than was quite consistent with the dignity of my lady's large parlour.

'What means this, Whitaker ? ' said the lady, somewhat peevishly ; for she was interrupted in the commencement of a letter to her neighbour on the unpleasant business of the proposed loan, ' Is it to be always thus with you ? Are you dreaming ? '

'A vision of good omen, I trust,' said the steward, with a triumphant flourish of the hand ; ' far better than Pharaoh's, though, like his, it be of fat kine.'

'I prithee be plain, man,' said the lady, ' or fetch some one who can speak to purpose.'

'Why, odds-my-life, madam,' said the steward, ' mine errand can speak for itself. Do you not hear them low ? Do you not hear them bleat ? A yoke of fat oxen, and half a score prime wethers. The castle is victualled for this bout, let them storm when they will ; and Gatherill may have his d—d mains ploughed to the boot.'

The lady, without further questioning her elated domestic, rose and went to the window, where she certainly beheld the oxen and sheep which had given rise to Whitaker's exultation. 'Whence come they ? ' said she, in some surprise.

'Let them construe that who can,' answered Whitaker ; ' the fellow who drove them was a west-country man, and only said they came from a friend to help to furnish out your ladyship's entertainment ; the man would not stay to drink—I am sorry he would not stay to drink—I crave your ladyship's pardon for not keeping him by the ears to drink—it was not my fault.'

'That I'll be sworn it was not,' said the lady.

'Nay, madam, by G—, I assure you it was not,' said the zealous steward ; ' for, rather than the castle should lose credit, I drank his health myself in double ale, though I had had my morning draught already. I tell you the naked truth, my lady, by G— ! '

'It was no great compulsion, I suppose,' said the lady ;
'but, Whitaker, suppose you should show your joy on such
occasions by drinking and swearing a little less, rather than
a little more, would it not be as well, think you ? '

'I crave your ladyship's pardon,' said Whitaker with
much reverence ; 'I hope I know my place. I am your
ladyship's poor servant ; and I know it does not become
me to drink and swear like your ladyship—that is, like his
honour, Sir Geoffrey, I would say. But I pray you, if I am
not to drink and swear after my degree, how are men to
know Peveril of the Peak's steward—and I may say butler
too, since I have had the keys of the cellar ever since old
Spigots was shot dead on the north-west turret, with
a black jack in his hand—I say, how is an old Cavalier
like me to be known from those cuckoldy Roundheads that
do nothing but fast and pray, if we are not to drink and
swear according to our degree ? '

The lady was silent, for she well knew speech availed
nothing ; and, after a moment's pause, proceeded to
intimate to the steward that she would have the persons,
whose names were marked in a written paper, which she
delivered to him, invited to the approaching banquet.

Whitaker, instead of receiving the list with the mute
acquiescence of a modern major-domo, carried it into the
recess of one of the windows, and, adjusting his spectacles,
began to read it to himself. The first names, being those
of distinguished Cavalier families in the neighbourhood, he
muttered over in a tone of approbation—paused and
pshawed at that of Bridgenorth—yet acquiesced, with the
observation, ' But he is a good neighbour, so it may pass
for once.' But when he read the name and surname of
Nehemiah Solsgrace, the Presbyterian parson, Whitaker's
patience altogether forsook him ; and he declared he would
as soon throw himself into Eldon-hole,[1] as consent that the
intrusive old Puritan howlet, who had usurped the pulpit
of a sound orthodox divine, should ever darken the gates
of Martindale Castle by any message or mediation of his.
'The false crop-eared hypocrites,' cried he, with a hearty
oath, ' have had their turn of the good weather. The sun

[1] A chasm in the earth supposed to be unfathomable, one of the
wonders of the Peak.

is on our side of the hedge now, and we will pay off old scores, as sure as my name is Richard Whitaker.'

' You presume on your long services, Whitaker, and on your master's absence, or you had not dared to use me thus,' said the lady.

The unwonted agitation of her voice attracted the attention of the refractory steward, notwithstanding his present state of elevation ; but he no sooner saw that her eye glistened, and her cheek reddened, than his obstinacy was at once subdued.

' A murrain on me,' he said, ' but I have made my lady angry in good earnest ! and that is an unwonted sight for to see. I crave your pardon, my lady ! It was not poor Dick Whitaker disputed your honourable commands, but only that second draught of double ale. We have put a double stroke of malt to it, as your ladyship well knows, ever since the happy Restoration. To be sure I hate a fanatic as I do the cloven foot of Satan ; but then your honourable ladyship hath a right to invite Satan himself, cloven foot and all, to Martindale Castle ; and to send me to hell's gate with a billet of invitation—and so your will shall be done.'

The invitations were sent round accordingly, in all due form ; and one of the bullocks was sent down to be roasted whole at the market-place of a little village called Martindale-Moultrassie, which stood considerably to the eastward both of the castle and hall, from which it took its double name, at about an equal distance from both ; so that, suppose a line drawn from the one manor-house to the other to be the base of a triangle, the village would have occupied the salient angle. As the said village, since the late transference of a part of Peveril's property, belonged to Sir Geoffrey and to Bridgenorth in nearly equal portions, the lady judged it not proper to dispute the right of the latter to add some hogsheads of beer to the popular festivity.

In the meanwhile, she could not but suspect the major of being the unknown friend who had relieved her from the dilemma arising from the want of provisions ; and she esteemed herself happy when a visit from him, on the day preceding the proposed entertainment, gave her, as she thought, an opportunity of expressing her gratitude.

CHAPTER IV

No, sir—I will not pledge—I'm one of those
Who think good wine needs neither bush nor preface
To make it welcome. If you doubt my word,
Fill the quart-cup, and see if I will choke on 't.
                                        Old Play.

THERE was a serious gravity of expression in the disclamation with which Major Bridgenorth replied to the
thanks tendered to him by Lady Peveril, for the supply
of provisions which had reached her castle so opportunely.
He seemed first not to be aware what she alluded to ;
and, when she explained the circumstance, he protested
so seriously that he had no share in the benefit conferred,
that Lady Peveril was compelled to believe him, the rather
that, being a man of plain downright character, affecting
no refined delicacy of sentiment, and practising almost a
quaker-like sincerity of expression, it would have been
much contrary to his general character to have made such
a disavowal, unless it were founded in truth.

'My present visit to you, madam,' said he, 'had indeed
some reference to the festivity of to-morrow.' Lady Peveril
listened, but as her visitor seemed to find some difficulty
in expressing himself, she was compelled to ask an explanation. 'Madam,' said the major, 'you are not perhaps
entirely ignorant that the more tender-conscienced among
us have scruples at certain practices, so general amongst
your people at times of rejoicing, that you may be said to
insist upon them as articles of faith, or at least greatly
to resent their omission.'

'I trust, Master Bridgenorth,' said the Lady Peveril, not
fully comprehending the drift of his discourse, 'that we
shall, as your entertainers, carefully avoid all allusions or
reproaches founded on past misunderstanding.'

'We would expect no less, madam, from your candour
and courtesy,' said Bridgenorth ; 'but I perceive you do
not fully understand me. To be plain, then, I allude to
the fashion of drinking healths, and pledging each other

in draughts of strong liquor, which most among us consider
as a superfluous and sinful provoking of each other to
debauchery, and the excessive use of strong drink ; and
which, besides, if derived, as learned divines have supposed,
from the custom of the blinded Pagans, who made libations
and invoked idols when they drank, may be justly said to
have something in it heathenish, and allied to demon-
worship.'

The lady had already hastily considered all the topics
which were likely to introduce discord into the proposed
festivity ; but this very ridiculous, yet fatal discrepancy,
betwixt the manners of the parties on convivial occasions,
had entirely escaped her. She endeavoured to soothe the
objecting party, whose brows were knit like one who had
fixed an opinion by which he was determined to abide.

' I grant,' she said, ' my good neighbour, that this custom
is at least idle, and may be prejudicial if it leads to excess
in the use of liquor, which is apt enough to take place
without such conversation. But I think, when it hath not
this consequence, it is a thing indifferent, affords a unanimous mode of expressing our good wishes to our friends,
and our loyal duty to our sovereign ; and, without meaning
to put any force upon the inclination of those who believe
otherwise, I cannot see how I can deny my guests and
friends the privilege of drinking a health to the king, or to
my husband, after the old English fashion.'

' My lady,' said the major, ' if the age of fashion were to
command it, Popery is one of the oldest English fashions
that I have heard of ; but it is our happiness that we are
not benighted like our fathers, and therefore we must act
according to the light that is in us, and not after their
darkness. I had myself the honour to attend the Lord-
Keeper Whitelocke, when, at the table of the chamberlain
of the kingdom of Sweden, he did positively refuse to pledge
the health of his queen, Christina, thereby giving great
offence, and putting in peril the whole purpose of that
voyage ; which it is not to be thought so wise a man would
have done, but that he held such compliance a thing not
merely indifferent, but rather sinful and damnable.'

' With all respect to Whitelocke,' said the Lady Peveril,
' I continue of my own opinion, though, Heaven knows,

I am no friend to riot or wassail. I would fain accommodate myself to your scruples, and will discourage all other pledges ; but surely those of the king and of Peveril of the Peak may be permitted ? '

' I dare not,' answered Bridgenorth, ' lay even the ninety-ninth part of a grain of incense upon an altar erected to Satan.'

' How, sir ! ' said the lady ; ' do you bring Satan into comparison with our master King Charles, and with my noble lord and husband ? '

' Pardon me, madam,' answered Bridgenorth, ' I have no such thoughts—indeed they would ill become me. I do wish the king's health and Sir Geoffrey's devoutly, and I will pray for both. But I see not what good it should do their health if I should prejudice my own by quaffing pledges out of quart-flagons.'

' Since we cannot agree upon this matter,' said Lady Peveril, ' we must find some resource by which to offend those of neither party. Suppose you winked at our friends drinking these pledges, and we should connive at your sitting still ? '

But neither would this composition satisfy Bridgenorth, who was of opinion, as he expressed himself, that it would be holding a candle to Beelzebub. In fact, his temper, naturally stubborn, was at present rendered much more so by a previous conference with his preacher, who, though a very good man in the main, was particularly and illiberally tenacious of the petty distinctions which his sect adopted ; and, while he thought with considerable apprehension on the accession of power which Popery, Prelacy, and Peveril of the Peak, were like to acquire by the late Revolution, became naturally anxious to put his flock on their guard, and prevent their being kidnapped by the wolf. He disliked extremely that Major Bridgenorth, indisputably the head of the Presbyterian interest in that neighbourhood, should have given his only daughter to be, as he termed it, nursed by a Canaanitish woman ; and he told him plainly that he liked not this going to feast in the high places with the uncircumcised in heart, and looked on the whole conviviality only as a making-merry in the house of Tirzah.

Upon receiving this rebuke from his pastor, Bridgenorth began to suspect he might have been partly wrong in the readiness which, in his first ardour of gratitude, he had shown to enter into intimate intercourse with the Castle of Martindale ; but he was too proud to avow this to the preacher, and it was not till after a considerable debate betwixt them, that it was mutually agreed their presence at the entertainment should depend upon the condition that no healths or pledges should be given in their presence. Bridgenorth, therefore, as the delegate and representative of his party, was bound to stand firm against all entreaty, and the lady became greatly embarrassed. She now regretted sincerely that her well-intended invitation had ever been given, for she foresaw that its rejection was to awaken all former subjects of quarrel, and perhaps to lead to new violences amongst people who had not many years since been engaged in civil war. To yield up the disputed point to the Presbyterians, would have been to offend the Cavalier party, and Sir Geoffrey in particular, in the most mortal degree ; for they made it as firm a point of honour to give healths, and compel others to pledge them, as the Puritans made it a deep article of religion to refuse both. At length the lady changed the discourse, introduced that of Major Bridgenorth's child, caused it to be sent for, and put into his arms. The mother's stratagem took effect ; for, though the Parliamentary major stood firm, the father, as in the case of the Governor of Tilbury, was softened, and he agreed that his friends should accept a compromise. This was, that the major himself, the reverend divine, and such of their friends as held strict Puritan tenets, should form a separate party in the large parlour, while the hall should be occupied by the jovial Cavaliers ; and that each party should regulate their potations after their own conscience, or after their own fashion.

Major Bridgenorth himself seemed greatly relieved after this important matter had been settled. He had held it matter of conscience to be stubborn in maintaining his own opinion, but was heartily glad when he escaped from the apparently inevitable necessity of affronting Lady Peveril by the refusal of her invitation. He remained longer than usual, and spoke and smiled more than was his custom.

His first care, on his return, was to announce to the clergyman and his congregation the compromise which he had made, and this not as a matter for deliberation, but one upon which he had already resolved ; and such was his authority among them, that though the preacher longed to pronounce a separation of the parties, and to exclaim ' To your tents, O Israel ! ' he did not see the chance of being seconded by so many as would make it worth while to disturb the unanimous acquiescence in their delegate's proposal.

Nevertheless, each party being put upon the alert by the consequences of Major Bridgenorth's embassy, so many points of doubt and delicate discussion were started in succession, that the Lady Peveril, the only person, perhaps, who was desirous of achieving an effectual reconciliation between them, incurred, in reward for her good intentions, the censure of both factions, and had much reason to regret her well-meant project of bringing the Capulets and Montagues of Derbyshire together on the same occasion of public festivity.

As it was now settled that the guests were to form two different parties, it became not only a subject of dispute betwixt themselves, which should be first admitted within the Castle of Martindale, but matter of serious apprehension to Lady Peveril and Major Bridgenorth, lest, if they were to approach by the same avenue and entrance, a quarrel might take place betwixt them, and proceed to extremities, even before they reached the place of entertainment. The lady believed she had discovered an admirable expedient for preventing the possibility of such interference, by directing that the Cavaliers should be admitted by the principal entrance, while the Roundheads should enter the castle through a great breach which had been made in the course of the siege, and across which there had been since made a sort of by-path to drive the cattle down to their pasture in the wood. By this contrivance the Lady Peveril imagined she had altogether avoided the various risks which might occur from two such parties encountering each other, and disputing for precedence. Several other circumstances of less importance were adjusted at the same time, and apparently so much to the satisfaction of the

Presbyterian teacher, that, in a long lecture on the subject of the marriage garment, he was at the pains to explain to his hearers, that outward apparel was not alone meant by that scriptural expression, but also a suitable frame of mind for enjoyment of peaceful festivity ; and therefore he exhorted the brethren, that whatever might be the errors of the poor blinded malignants, with whom they were in some sort to eat and drink upon the morrow, they ought not on this occasion to show any evil will against them, lest they should therein become troublers of the peace of Israel.

Honest Doctor Dummerar, the ejected episcopal Vicar of Martindale *cum* Moultrassie, preached to the Cavaliers on the same subject. He had served the cure before the breaking out of the Rebellion, and was in high favour with Sir Geoffrey, not merely on account of his sound orthodoxy and deep learning, but his exquisite skill in playing at bowls, and his facetious conversation over a pipe and tankard of October. For these latter accomplishments, the Doctor had the honour to be recorded by old Century White amongst the roll of lewd, incompetent, profligate clergymen of the Church of England, whom he denounced to God and man, on account chiefly of the heinous sin of playing at games of skill and chance, and of occasionally joining in the social meetings of their parishioners. When the king's party began to lose ground, Doctor Dummerar left his vicarage, and, betaking himself to the camp, showed upon several occasions, when acting as chaplain to Sir Geoffrey Peveril's regiment, that his portly bodily presence included a stout and masculine heart. When all was lost, and he himself, with most other loyal divines, was deprived of his living, he made such shift as he could ; now lurking in the garrets of old friends in the university, who shared with him, and such as him, the slender means of livelihood which the evil times had left them ; and now lying hid in the houses of the oppressed and sequestrated gentry, who respected at once his character and sufferings. When the Restoration took place, Doctor Dummerar emerged from some one of his hiding places, and hied him to Martindale Castle, to enjoy the triumph inseparable from this happy change.

His appearance at the castle in his full clerical dress,
and the warm reception which he received from the neighbouring gentry, added not a little to the alarm which was
gradually extending itself through the party which were
so lately the uppermost. It is true, Dr. Dummerar framed
(honest worthy man) no extravagant views of elevation or
preferment; but the probability of his being replaced in
the living, from which he had been expelled under very
flimsy pretences, inferred a severe blow to the Presbyterian
divine, who could not be considered otherwise than as an
intruder. The interest of the two preachers, therefore, as
well as the sentiments of their flocks, were at direct variance;
and here was another fatal objection in the way of Lady
Peveril's scheme of a general and comprehensive healing
ordinance.

Nevertheless, as we have already hinted, Doctor Dummerar behaved as handsomely upon the occasion as the
Presbyterian incumbent had done. It is true, that in
a sermon which he preached in the castle-hall to several
of the most distinguished Cavalier families, besides a world
of boys from the village, who went to see the novel circumstance of a parson in a cassock and surplice, he went at
great length into the foulness of the various crimes committed by the rebellious party during the late evil times,
and greatly magnified the merciful and peaceful nature of
the honourable lady of the manor, who condescended to
look upon, or receive into her house in the way of friendship
and hospitality, men holding the principles which had led
to the murder of the king—the slaying and despoiling his
loyal subjects—and the plundering and breaking down of
the Church of God. But then he wiped all this handsomely up again, with the observation, that since it was
the will of their gracious and newly restored sovereign, and
the pleasure of the worshipful Lady Peveril, that this
contumacious and rebellious race should be, for a time,
forborne by their faithful subjects, it would be highly
proper that all the loyal liegemen should, for the present,
eschew subjects of dissension or quarrel with these sons
of Shimei; which lesson of patience he enforced by the
comfortable assurance that they could not long abstain
from their old rebellious practices; in which case, the

CHAP. IV   PEVERIL OF THE PEAK   33

royalists would stand exculpated before God and man in extirpating them from the face of the earth.

The close observers of the remarkable passages of the times from which we draw the events of our history, have left it upon record, that these two several sermons, much contrary, doubtless, to the intention of the worthy divines by whom they were delivered, had a greater effect in exasperating, than in composing, the disputes betwixt the two factions. Under such evil auspices, and with corresponding forebodings on the mind of Lady Peveril, the day of festivity at length arrived.

By different routes, and forming each a sort of procession, as if the adherents of each party were desirous of exhibiting its strength and numbers, the two several factions approached Martindale Castle ; and so distinct did they appear in dress, aspect, and manners, that it seemed as if the revellers of a bridal party, and the sad attendants upon a funeral solemnity, were moving towards the same point from different quarters.

The Puritanical party was by far the fewer in numbers, for which two excellent reasons might be given. In the first place, they had enjoyed power for several years, and, of course, became unpopular among the common people, never at any time attached to those who, being in the immediate possession of authority, are often obliged to employ it in controlling their humours. Besides, the country people of England had, and still have, an animated attachment to field sports, and a natural unrestrained joviality of disposition, which rendered them impatient under the severe discipline of the fanatical preachers ; while they were not less naturally discontented with the military despotism of Cromwell's major-generals. Secondly, the people were fickle as usual, and the return of the king had novelty in it, and was therefore popular. The side of the Puritans was also deserted at this period by a numerous class of more thinking and prudential persons, who never forsook them till they became unfortunate. These sagacious personages were called in that age the Waiters upon Providence, and deemed it a high delinquency towards Heaven if they afforded countenance to any cause longer than it was favoured by fortune.

PEVERIL   D

But, though thus forsaken by the fickle and the selfish, a solemn enthusiasm, a stern and determined depth of principle, a confidence in the sincerity of their own motives, and the manly English pride which inclined them to cling to their former opinions, like the traveller in the fable to his cloak, the more strongly that the tempest blew around them, detained in the ranks of the Puritans many, who, if no longer formidable from numbers, were still so from their character. They consisted chiefly of the middling gentry, with others whom industry or successful speculations in commerce or in mining had raised into eminence— the persons who feel most umbrage from the overshadowing aristocracy, and are usually the most vehement in defence of what they hold to be their rights. Their dress was in general studiously simple and unostentatious, or only remarkable by the contradictory affectation of extreme simplicity or carelessness. The dark colour of their cloaks, varying from absolute black to what was called sad-coloured —their steeple-crowned hats, with their broad shadowy brims—their long swords, suspended by a simple strap around the loins, without shoulder-belt, sword-knot, plate, buckles, or any of the other decorations with which the Cavaliers loved to adorn their trusty rapiers—the shortness of their hair, which made their ears appear of disproportioned size—above all, the stern and gloomy gravity of their looks, announced their belonging to that class of enthusiasts, who, resolute and undismayed, had cast down the former fabric of government, and who now regarded with somewhat more than suspicion that which had been so unexpectedly substituted in its stead. There was gloom in their countenances ; but it was not that of dejection, far less of despair. They looked like veterans after a defeat, which may have checked their career and wounded their pride, but has left their courage undiminished.

The melancholy, now become habitual, which overcast Major Bridgenorth's countenance, well qualified him to act as the chief of the group who now advanced from the village. When they reached the point by which they were first to turn aside into the wood which surrounded the castle, they felt a momentary impression of degradation, as if they were yielding the high road to their old and oft-defeated enemies the Cavaliers. When they began to ascend the winding path, which had been the daily passage of the cattle, the opening of the wooded glade gave them a view of the castle-ditch, half choked with the rubbish of the breach, and of the breach itself, which was made at the angle of a large square flanking-tower, one-half of which had been battered into ruins, while the other fragment remained in a state strangely shattered and precarious, and seemed to be tottering above the huge aperture in the wall. A stern still smile was exchanged among the Puritans, as the sight reminded them of the victories of former days. Holdfast Clegg, a millwright of Derby, who had been himself active at the siege, pointed to the breach, and said with a grim smile to Mr. Solsgrace, ' I little thought that, when my own hand helped to level the cannon which Oliver pointed against yon tower, we should have been obliged to climb like foxes up the very walls which we won by our bow and by our spear. Methought these malignants had then enough of shutting their gates and making high their horn against us.'

' Be patient, my brother,' said Solsgrace ; ' be patient, and let not thy soul be disquieted. We enter not this high place dishonourably, seeing we ascend by the gate which the Lord opened to the godly.'

The words of the pastor were like a spark to gunpowder. The countenances of the mournful retinue suddenly expanded, and, accepting what had fallen from him as an omen and a light from heaven how they were to interpret their present situation, they uplifted, with one consent, one of the triumphant songs in which the Israelites celebrated the victories which had been vouchsafed to them over the heathen inhabitants of the Promised Land :

> Let God arise, and then his foes
>   Shall turn themselves to flight,
> His enemies for fear shall run,
>   And scatter out of sight ;
>
> And as wax melts before the fire,
>   And wind blows smoke away,
> So in the presence of the Lord,
>   The wicked shall decay.

God's army twenty thousand is,
   Of angels bright and strong,
The Lord also in Sinai
   Is present them among.

Thou didst, O Lord, ascend on high,
   And captive led'st them all,
Who, in times past, thy chosen flock
   In bondage did enthral.

These sounds of devotional triumph reached the joyous band of the Cavaliers, who, decked in whatever pomp their repeated misfortunes and impoverishment had left them, were moving towards the same point, though by a different road, and were filling the principal avenue to the castle with tiptoe mirth and revelry. The two parties were strongly contrasted ; for, during that period of civil dissension, the manners of the different factions distinguished them as completely as separate uniforms might have done. If the Puritan was affectedly plain in his dress, and ridiculously precise in his manners, the Cavalier often carried his love of ornament into tawdry finery, and his contempt of hypocrisy into licentious profligacy. Gay gallant fellows, young and old, thronged together towards the ancient castle, with general and joyous manifestation of those spirits, which, as they had been buoyant enough to support their owners during the worst of times, as they termed Oliver's usurpation, were now so inflated as to transport them nearly beyond the reach of sober reason. Feathers waved, lace glittered, spears jingled, steeds caracoled ; and here and there a petronel, or pistol, was fired off by some one who found his own natural talents for making a noise inadequate to the dignity of the occasion. Boys—for, as we said before, the rabble were with the uppermost party, as usual—halloed and whooped, ' Down with the Rump ! ' and ' Fie upon Oliver ! ' Musical instruments, of as many different fashions as were then in use, played all at once, and without any regard to each other's tune ; and the glee of the occasion, while it reconciled the pride of the high-born of the party to fraternize with the general rout, derived an additional zest from the conscious triumph, that their exultation was heard by their neighbours, the crestfallen Roundheads.

When the loud and sonorous swell of the psalm-tune, multiplied by all the echoes of the cliffs and ruinous halls, came full upon their ear, as if to warn them how little they were to reckon upon the depression of their adversaries, at first it was answered with a scornful laugh, raised to as much height as the scoffers' lungs would permit, in order that it might carry to the psalmodists the contempt of their auditors ; but this was a forced exertion of party spleen. There is something in melancholy feelings more natural to an imperfect and suffering state than in those of gaiety, and when they are brought into collision, the former seldom fail to triumph. If a funeral-train and wedding-procession were to meet unexpectedly, it will readily be allowed that the mirth of the last would be speedily merged in the gloom of the others. But the Cavaliers, moreover, had sympathies of a different kind. The psalm-tune, which now came rolling on their ear, had been heard too often, and upon too many occasions had preceded victory gained over the malignants, to permit them, even in their triumph, to hear it without emotion. There was a sort of pause, of which the party themselves seemed rather ashamed, until the silence was broken by the stout old knight, Sir Jasper Cranbourne, whose gallantry was so universally acknowledged, that he could afford, if we may use such an expression, to confess emotions, which men whose courage was in any respect liable to suspicion, would have thought it imprudent to acknowledge.

'Adad,' said the old knight, 'may I never taste claret again, if that is not the very tune with which the prick-eared villains began their onset at Wiggan Lane, where they trowled us down like so many ninepins ! Faith, neighbours, to say truth, and shame the devil, I did not like the sound of it above half.'

'If I thought the round-headed rogues did it in scorn of us,' said Dick Wildblood of the Dale, 'I would cudgel their psalmody out of their peasantly throats with this very truncheon ; ' a motion which, being seconded by old Roger Raine, the drunken tapster of the Peveril Arms in the village, might have brought on a general battle, but that Sir Jasper forbade the feud.

'We'll have no ranting, Dick,' said the old knight to the

young franklin ; ' adad, man, we'll have none, for three
reasons ; first, because it would be ungentle to Lady
Peveril ; then, because it is against the king's peace ; and,
lastly, Dick, because if we did set on the psalm-singing
knaves, thou mightest come by the worst, my boy, as has
chanced to thee before.'

' Who, I ! Sir Jasper ? ' answered Dick—' I come by the
worst !—I'll be d—d if it ever happened but in that
accursed lane, where we had no more flank, front, or rear,
than if we had been so many herrings in a barrel.'

' That was the reason, I fancy,' answered Sir Jasper,
' that you, to mend the matter, scrambled into the hedge,
and stuck there, horse and man, till I beat thee through it
with my leading-staff ; and then, instead of charging to
the front, you went right-about, and away as fast as your
feet would carry you.'

This reminiscence produced a laugh at Dick's expense,
who was known, or at least suspected, to have more tongue
in his head than mettle in his bosom. And this sort of
rallying on the part of the knight having fortunately abated
the resentment which had begun to awaken in the breasts
of the royalist cavalcade, further cause for offence was removed, by the sudden ceasing of the sounds which they had
been disposed to interpret into those of premeditated insult.

This was owing to the arrival of the Puritans at the
bottom of the large and wide breach, which had been
formerly made in the wall of the castle by their victorious
cannon. The sight of its gaping heaps of rubbish, and
disjointed masses of building, up which slowly winded
a narrow and steep path, such as is made amongst ancient
ruins by the rare passage of those who occasionally visit
them, was calculated, when contrasted with the grey and
solid massiveness of the towers and curtains which yet
stood uninjured, to remind them of their victory over the
stronghold of their enemies, and how they had bound
nobles and princes with fetters of iron.

But feelings more suitable to the purpose of their visit
to Martindale Castle were awakened in the bosoms even
of these stern sectaries, when the lady of the castle, still
in the very prime of beauty and of womanhood, appeared
at the top of the breach with her principal female attendants,

to receive her guests with the honour and courtesy becoming her invitation. She had laid aside the black dress which had been her sole attire for several years, and was arrayed with a splendour not unbecoming her high descent and quality. Jewels, indeed, she had none; but her long and dark hair was surmounted with a chaplet made of oak-leaves, interspersed with lilies; the former being the emblem of the king's preservation in the Royal Oak, and the latter, of his happy Restoration. What rendered her presence still more interesting to those who looked on her, was the presence of the two children whom she held in either hand; one of whom was well known to them all to be the child of their leader, Major Bridgenorth, who had been restored to life and health by the almost maternal care of the Lady Peveril.

If even the inferior persons of the party felt the healing influence of her presence, thus accompanied, poor Bridgenorth was almost overwhelmed with it. The strictness of his caste and manners permitted him not to sink on his knee, and kiss the hand which held his little orphan; but the deepness of his obeisance—the faltering tremor of his voice—and the glistening of his eye, showed a grateful respect for the lady whom he addressed, deeper and more reverential than could have been expressed even by Persian prostration. A few courteous and mild words, expressive of the pleasure she found in once more seeing her neighbours as her friends—a few kind inquiries, addressed to the principal individuals among her guests, concerning their families and connexions, completed her triumph over angry thoughts and dangerous recollections, and disposed men's bosoms to sympathize with the purposes of the meeting.

Even Solsgrace himself, although imagining himself bound by his office and duty to watch over and counteract the wiles of the 'Amalekitish woman,' did not escape the sympathetic infection; being so much struck with the marks of peace and goodwill exhibited by Lady Peveril, that he immediately raised the psalm,

> O what a happy thing it is,
> And joyful for to see,
> Brethren to dwell together in
> Friendship and unity!

Accepting this salutation as a mark of courtesy repaid, the Lady Peveril marshalled in person this party of her guests to the apartment, where ample good cheer was provided for them ; and had even the patience to remain while Master Nehemiah Solsgrace pronounced a benediction of portentous length, as an introduction to the banquet. Her presence was in some measure a restraint on the worthy divine, whose prolusion lasted the longer, and was the more intricate and embarrassed, that he felt himself debarred from rounding it off by his usual alliterative petition for deliverance from Popery, Prelacy, and Peveril of the Peak, which had become so habitual to him, that, after various attempts to conclude with some other form of words, he found himself at last obliged to pronounce the first words of his usual formula aloud, and mutter the rest in such a manner as not to be intelligible even by those who stood nearest to him.

The minister's silence was followed by all the various sounds which announce the onset of a hungry company on a well-furnished table ; and at the same time gave the lady an opportunity to leave the apartment, and look to the accommodation of her other company. She felt, indeed, that it was high time to do so ; and that the royalist guests might be disposed to misapprehend, or even to resent, the prior attentions which she had thought it prudent to offer to the Puritans.

These apprehensions were not altogether ill founded. It was in vain that the steward had displayed the royal standard, with its proud motto of *Tandem Triumphans*, on one of the great towers which flanked the main entrance of the castle ; while from the other floated the banner of Peveril of the Peak, under which many of those who now approached had fought during all the vicissitudes of civil war. It was in vain he repeated his clamorous ' Welcome, noble Cavaliers ! welcome, generous gentlemen ! ' There was a slight murmur amongst them, that their welcome ought to have come from the mouth of the colonel's lady— not from that of a menial. Sir Jasper Cranbourne, who had sense as well as spirit and courage, and who was aware of his fair cousin's motives, having been indeed consulted by her upon all the arrangements which she had adopted, saw matters were in such a state that no time ought to be lost in conducting the guests to the banqueting apartment, where a fortunate diversion from all these topics of rising discontent might be made, at the expense of the good cheer of all sorts, which the lady's care had so liberally provided.

The stratagem of the old soldier succeeded in its utmost extent. He assumed the great oaken chair usually occupied by the steward at his audits ; and Dr. Dummerar having pronounced a brief Latin benediction (which was not the less esteemed by the hearers that none of them understood it), Sir Jasper exhorted the company to whet their appetites to the dinner by a brimming cup to his Majesty's health, filled as high and as deep as their goblets would permit. In a moment all was bustle, with the clang of wine-cups and of flagons. In another moment the guests were on their feet like so many statues, all hushed as death, but with eyes glancing with expectation, and hands outstretched, which displayed their loyal brimmers. The voice of Sir Jasper, clear, sonorous, and emphatic, as the sound of his war-trumpet, announced the health of the restored monarch, hastily echoed back by the assemblage, impatient to render it due homage. Another brief pause was filled by the draining of their cups, and the mustering breath to join in a shout so loud, that not only the rafters of the old hall trembled while they echoed it back, but the garlands of oaken boughs and flowers with which they were decorated, waved wildly, and rustled as if agitated by a sudden whirlwind. This rite observed, the company proceeded to assail the good cheer with which the table groaned, animated as they were to the attack both by mirth and melody, for they were attended by all the minstrels of the district, who, like the Episcopal clergy, had been put to silence during the reign of the self-entitled saints of the Commonwealth. The social occupation of good eating and drinking, the exchange of pledges betwixt old neighbours who had been fellow soldiers in the moment of resistance— fellow sufferers in the time of depression and subjugation, and were now partners in the same general subject of congratulation, soon wiped from their memory the trifling cause of complaint, which in the minds of some had darkened the festivity of the day ; so that when the Lady Peveril walked into the hall, accompanied as before with the children and her female attendants, she was welcomed with the acclamations due to the mistress of the banquet and of the castle—the dame of the noble knight who had led most of them to battle with an undaunted and persevering valour, which was worthy of better success.

Her address to them was brief and matronly, yet spoken with so much feeling as found its way to every bosom. She apologized for the lateness of her personal welcome, by reminding them that there were then present in Martindale Castle that day, persons whom recent happy events had converted from enemies into friends, but on whom the latter character was so recently imposed, that she dared not neglect with them any point of ceremonial. But those whom she now addressed were the best, the dearest, the most faithful friends of her husband's house, to whom and to their valour Peveril had not only owed those successes, which had given them and him fame during the late unhappy times, but to whose courage she in particular had owed the preservation of their leader's life, even when it could not avert defeat. A word or two of heartfelt congratulation on the happy restoration of the royal line and authority, completed all which she had boldness to add, and, bowing gracefully round her, she lifted a cup to her lips as if to welcome her guests.

There still remained, and especially amongst the old Cavaliers of the period, some glimmering of that spirit which inspired Froissart when he declares that a knight hath double courage at need, when animated by the looks and words of a beautiful and virtuous woman. It was not until the reign which was commencing at the moment we are treating of, that the unbounded licence of the age, introducing a general course of profligacy, degraded the female sex into mere servants of pleasure, and, in so doing, deprived society of that noble tone of feeling towards the sex, which, considered as a spur to ' raise the clear spirit,' is superior to every other impulse, save those of religion and of patriotism. The beams of the ancient hall of Martindale Castle instantly rang with a shout louder and shriller than that at which they had so lately trembled, and the names of the Knight of the Peak and his lady were proclaimed

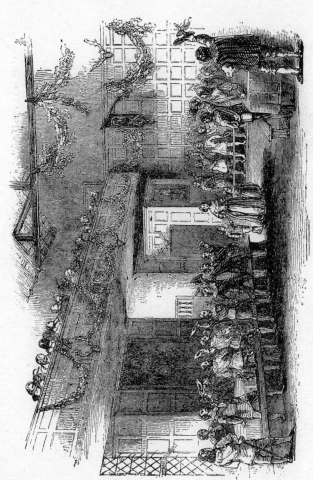

The Cavaliers dining at Martindale Castle

amid waving of caps and hats, and universal wishes for their health and happiness.

Under these auspices the Lady Peveril glided from the hall, and left free space for the revelry of the evening.

That of the Cavaliers may be easily conceived, since it had the usual accompaniments of singing, jesting, quaffing of healths, and playing of tunes, which have in almost every age and quarter of the world been the accompaniments of festive cheer. The enjoyments of the Puritans were of a different and less noisy character. They neither sung, jested, heard music, nor drank healths ; and yet they seemed not the less, in their own phrase, to enjoy the creature-comforts which the frailty of humanity rendered grateful to their outward man. Old Whitaker even protested, that, though much the smaller party in point of numbers, they discussed nearly as much sack and claret as his own more jovial associates. But those who considered the steward's prejudices, were inclined to think, that, in order to produce such a result, he must have thrown in his own by-drinkings—no inconsiderable item—to the sum total of the Presbyterian potations.

Without adopting such a partial and scandalous report, we shall only say, that on this occasion, as on most others, the rareness of indulgence promoted the sense of enjoyment, and that those who made abstinence, or at least moderation, a point of religious principle, enjoyed their social meeting the better that such opportunities rarely presented themselves. If they did not actually drink each other's healths, they at least showed, by looking and nodding to each other as they raised their glasses, that they all were sharing the same festive gratification of the appetite, and felt it enhanced, because it was at the same time enjoyed by their friends and neighbours. Religion, as it was the principal topic of their thoughts, became also the chief subject of their conversation, and as they sat together in small separate knots, they discussed doctrinal and metaphysical points of belief, balanced the merits of various preachers, compared the creeds of contending sects, and fortified by scriptural quotations those which they favoured. Some contests arose in the course of these debates, which might have proceeded further than was seemly, but for the cautious interference of Major Bridgenorth. He suppressed also, in the very bud, a dispute betwixt Gaffer Hodgeson of Charnelycot and the Reverend Mr. Solsgrace, upon the tender subject of lay-preaching and lay-ministering ; nor did he think it altogether prudent or decent to indulge the wishes of some of the warmer enthusiasts of the party, who felt disposed to make the rest partakers of their gifts in extemporaneous prayer and exposition. These were absurdities that belonged to the time, which, however, the major had sense enough to perceive were unfitted, whether the offspring of hypocrisy or enthusiasm, for the present time and place.

The major was also instrumental in breaking up the party at an early and decorous hour, so that they left the castle long before their rivals, the Cavaliers, had reached the springtide of their merriment ; an arrangement which afforded the greatest satisfaction to the lady, who dreaded the consequences which might not improbably have taken place, had both parties met at the same period and point of retreat.

It was near midnight ere the greater part of the Cavaliers, meaning such as were able to effect their departure without assistance, withdrew to the village of Martindale-Moultrassie, with the benefit of the broad moon to prevent the chance of accidents. Their shouts, and the burden of their roaring chorus of—

The King shall enjoy his own again !

were heard with no small pleasure by the lady, heartily glad that the riot of the day was over without the occurrence of any unpleasing accident. The rejoicing was not, however, entirely ended ; for the elevated Cavaliers, finding some of the villagers still on foot around a bonfire on the street, struck merrily in with them—sent to Roger Raine of the Peveril Arms, the loyal publican whom we have already mentioned, for two tubs of merry stingo (as it was termed), and lent their own powerful assistance at the *dusting* it off to the health of the king and the loyal General Monk. Their shouts for a long time disturbed, and even alarmed the little village ; but no enthusiasm is able to withstand for ever the natural consequences of late hours, and potations pottle-deep. The tumult of the exulting royalists at last sank into silence, and the moon and the owl were left in undisturbed sovereignty over the old tower of the village church, which, rising white above a circle of knotty oaks, was tenanted by the bird, and silvered by the planet.[n]

CHAPTER V

> 'Twas when they raised, 'mid sap and siege,
> The banners of their rightful liege,
>   At their she-captain's call,
> Who, miracle of womankind !
> Lent mettle to the meanest hind
>   That mann'd her castle wall.

WILLIAM S. ROSE.

ON the morning succeeding the feast, the Lady Peveril, fatigued with the exertions and the apprehensions of the former day, kept her apartment for two or three hours later than her own active habits, and the matutinal custom of the time, rendered usual. Meanwhile, Mistress Ellesmere, a person of great trust in the family, and who assumed much authority in her mistress's absence, laid her orders upon Deborah, the governante, immediately to carry the children to their airing in the park, and not to let any one enter the gilded chamber, which was usually their sporting-place. Deborah, who often rebelled, and sometimes successfully, against the deputed authority of Ellesmere, privately resolved that it was about to rain, and that the gilded chamber was a more suitable place for the children's exercise than the wet grass of the park on a raw morning.

But a woman's brain is sometimes as inconstant as a popular assembly ; and presently after she had voted the morning was like to be rainy, and that the gilded chamber was the fittest play-room for the children, Mistress Deborah came to the somewhat inconsistent resolution, that the park was the fittest place for her own morning walk. It is certain that, during the unrestrained joviality of the preceding evening, she had danced till midnight with Lance Outram, the park-keeper ; but how far the seeing him just pass the window in his woodland trim, with a feather in his hat, and a crossbow under his arm, influenced the discrepancy of the opinions Mrs. Deborah formed concerning the weather, we are far from presuming to guess. It is enough for us, that, so soon as Mistress Ellesmere's back was turned, Mistress Deborah carried the children into the gilded chamber, not without a strict charge (for we must do her justice) to Master Julian to take care of his little wife, Mistress Alice; and then, having taken so satisfactory a precaution, she herself glided into the park by the glass-door of the still-room, which was nearly opposite to the great breach.

The gilded chamber in which the children were, by this arrangement, left to amuse themselves, without better guardianship than what Julian's manhood afforded, was a large apartment, hung with stamped Spanish leather, curiously gilded, representing, in a manner now obsolete, but far from unpleasing, a series of tilts and combats betwixt the Saracens of Granada, and the Spaniards under the command of King Ferdinand and Queen Isabella, during that memorable siege, which was terminated by the overthrow of the last fragments of the Moorish empire in Spain.

The little Julian was careering about the room for the amusement of his infant friend, as well as his own, mimicking with a reed the menacing attitude of the Abencerrages and Zegris engaged in the Eastern sport of hurling the *jerid*, or javelin; and at times sitting down beside her, and caressing her into silence and good humour, when the petulant or timid child chose to become tired of remaining an inactive spectator of his boisterous sport; when, on a sudden, he observed one of the panelled compartments of the leather hangings slide apart, so as to show a fair hand, with its fingers resting upon its edge, prepared, it would seem, to push it still further back. Julian was much surprised, and somewhat frightened, at what he witnessed, for the tales of the nursery had strongly impressed on his mind the terrors of the invisible world. Yet, naturally bold and high-spirited, the little champion placed himself beside his defenceless sister, continuing to brandish his weapon in her defence, as boldly as he had himself been an Abencerrage of Granada.

The panel, on which his eye was fixed, gradually continued to slide back, and display more and more the form to which the hand appertained, until, in the dark aperture which was disclosed, the children saw the figure of a lady in a mourning dress, past the meridian of life, but whose countenance still retained traces of great beauty, although the predominant character both of her features and person was an air of almost royal dignity. After pausing a moment on the threshold of the portal which she had thus unexpectedly disclosed, and looking with some surprise at the children, whom she had not probably observed while engaged with the management of the panel, the stranger stepped into the apartment, and the panel, upon a touch of a spring, closed behind her so suddenly, that Julian almost doubted it had ever been open, and began to apprehend that the whole apparition had been a delusion.[n]

The stately lady, however, advanced to him, and said, ' Are not you the little Peveril ? '

' Yes,' said the boy, reddening, not altogether without a juvenile feeling of that rule of chivalry which forbade any one to disown his name, whatever danger might be annexed to the avowal of it.

' Then,' said the stately stranger, ' go to your mother's room, and tell her to come instantly to speak with me.'

' I wo'not,' said the little Julian.

' How ? ' said the lady,—' so young and so disobedient ? —but you do but follow the fashion of the time. Why will you not go, my pretty boy, when I ask it of you as a favour ? '

' I would go, madam,' said the boy, ' but '—and he stopped short, still drawing back as the lady advanced on him, but still holding by the hand Alice Bridgenorth, who, too young to understand the nature of the dialogue, clung, trembling, to her companion.

The stranger saw his embarrassment, smiled, and remained standing fast, while she asked the child once more, ' What are you afraid of, my brave boy—and why should you not go to your mother on my errand ? '

' Because,' answered Julian, firmly, ' if I go, little Alice must stay alone with you.'

' You are a gallant fellow,' said the lady, ' and will not

disgrace your blood, which never left the weak without
protection.'

The boy understood her not, and still gazed with anxious
apprehension, first on her who addressed him, and then
upon his little companion, whose eyes, with the vacant
glance of infancy, wandered from the figure of the lady to
that of her companion and protector, and at length, infected
by a portion of the fear which the latter's magnanimous
efforts could not entirely conceal, she flew into Julian's
arms, and, clinging to him, greatly augmented his alarm, and
by screaming aloud, rendered it very difficult for him to
avoid the sympathetic fear which impelled him to do the
same.

There was something in the manner and bearing of this
unexpected inmate which might justify awe at least, if not
fear, when joined to the singular and mysterious mode in
which she had made her appearance. Her dress was not
remarkable, being the hood and female riding attire of the
time, such as was worn by the inferior class of gentlewomen ;
but her black hair was very long, and, several locks having
escaped from under her hood, hung down dishevelled on
her neck and shoulders. Her eyes were deep black, keen,
and piercing, and her features had something of a foreign
expression. When she spoke, her language was marked by
a slight foreign accent, although, in construction, it was
pure English. Her slightest tone and gesture had the air of
one accustomed to command and to be obeyed ; the recollection of which probably suggested to Julian the apology
he afterwards made for being frightened, that he took the
stranger for an ' enchanted queen '.

While the stranger lady and the children thus confronted
each other, two persons entered almost at the same instant,
but from different doors, whose haste showed that they had
been alarmed by the screams of the latter.

The first was Major Bridgenorth, whose ears had been
alarmed with the cries of his child as he entered the hall,
which corresponded with what was called the gilded
chamber. His intention had been to remain in the more
public apartment, until the Lady Peveril should make her
appearance, with the good-natured purpose of assuring her
that the preceding day of tumult had passed in every

respect agreeably to his friends, and without any of those alarming consequences which might have been apprehended from a collision betwixt the parties. But when it is considered how severely he had been agitated by apprehensions for his child's safety and health, too well justified by the fate of those who had preceded her, it will not be thought surprising that the infantine screams of Alice induced him to break through the barriers of form, and intrude further into the interior of the house than a sense of strict propriety might have warranted.

He burst into the gilded chamber, therefore, by a side-door and narrow passage, which communicated betwixt that apartment and the hall, and, snatching the child up in his arms, endeavoured, by a thousand caresses, to stifle the screams which burst yet more violently from the little girl, on beholding herself in the arms of one to whose voice and manner she was, but for one brief interview, an entire stranger.

Of course, Alice's shrieks were redoubled, and seconded by those of Julian Peveril, who, on the appearance of this second intruder, was frightened into resignation of every more manly idea of rescue than that which consisted in invoking assistance at the very top of his lungs.

Alarmed by this noise, which in half a minute became very clamorous, Lady Peveril, with whose apartment the gilded chamber was connected by a private door of communication opening into her wardrobe, entered on the scene. The instant she appeared, the little Alice, extricating herself from the grasp of her father, ran towards *her* protectress, and when she had once taken hold of her skirts, not only became silent, but turned her large blue eyes, in which the tears were still glistening, with a look of wonder rather than alarm, towards the strange lady. Julian manfully brandished his reed, a weapon which he had never parted with during the whole alarm, and stood prepared to assist his mother if there should be danger in the encounter betwixt her and the stranger.

In fact, it might have puzzled an older person to account for the sudden and confused pause which the Lady Peveril made, as she gazed on her unexpected guest, as if dubious whether she did or did not recognize, in her still beautiful

though wasted and emaciated features, a countenance which
she had known well under far different circumstances.

The stranger seemed to understand her cause of hesitation,
for she said in that heart-thrilling voice which was peculiarly her own—

'Time and misfortune have changed me much, Margaret—
that every mirror tells me—yet methinks, Margaret Stanley
might still have known Charlotte de la Tremouille.'

The Lady Peveril was little in the custom of giving way
to sudden emotion, but in the present case she threw herself
on her knees in a rapture of mingled joy and grief, and,
half embracing those of the stranger, exclaimed, in broken
language—

'My kind, my noble benefactress—the princely Countess
of Derby—the royal Queen in Man—could I doubt your
voice, your features, for a moment—Oh, forgive, forgive
me ! '

The Countess raised the suppliant kinswoman of her
husband's house, with all the grace of one accustomed from
early birth to receive homage and to grant protection. She
kissed the Lady Peveril's forehead, and passed her hand in
a caressing manner over her face as she said—

'You too are changed, my fair cousin, but it is a change
becomes you, from a pretty and timid maiden to a sage and
comely matron. But my own memory, which I once held
a good one, has failed me strangely, if this gentleman be
Sir Geoffrey Peveril.'

'A kind and good neighbour. only, madam,' said Lady
Peveril ; 'Sir Geoffrey is at court.'

'I understood so much,' said the Countess of Derby,
'when I arrived here last night.'

'How, madam ! ' said Lady Peveril—'Did you arrive
at Martindale Castle—at the house of Margaret Stanley,
where you have such right to command, and did not
announce your presence to her ? '

'Oh, I know you are a dutiful subject, Margaret,' answered
the countess, 'though it be in these days a rare character—
but it was our pleasure,' she added with a smile, ' to travel
incognito—and finding you engaged in general hospitality,
we desired not to disturb you with our royal presence.'

'But how and where were you lodged, madam ? ' said

Lady Peveril ; ' or why should you have kept secret a visit which would, if made, have augmented tenfold the happiness of every true heart that rejoiced here yesterday ? '

'My lodging was well cared for by Ellesmere—your

The Countess of Derby

Ellesmere now, as she was formerly mine—she has acted as quartermaster ere now, you know, and on a broader scale ; you must excuse her—she had my positive order to lodge me in the most secret part of your castle '—(here she pointed to the sliding panel)—' she obeyed orders in that, and I suppose also in sending you now hither.'

'Indeed I have not yet seen her,' said the lady, 'and therefore was totally ignorant of a visit so joyful, so surprising.'

'And I,' said the countess, 'was equally surprised to find none but these beautiful children in the apartment where I thought I heard you moving. Our Ellesmere has become silly—your good-nature has spoiled her—she has forgotten the discipline she learned under me.'

'I saw her run through the wood,' said the Lady Peveril, after a moment's recollection, 'undoubtedly to seek the person who has charge of the children, in order to remove them.'

'Your own darlings, I doubt not,' said the countess, looking at the children. 'Margaret, Providence has blessed you.'

'That is my son,' said Lady Peveril, pointing to Julian, who stood devouring their discourse with greedy ear; 'the little girl—I may call mine too.' Major Bridgenorth, who had in the meantime again taken up his infant, and was engaged in caressing it, set it down as the Countess of Derby spoke, sighed deeply, and walked towards the oriel window. He was well aware that the ordinary rules of courtesy would have rendered it proper that he should withdraw entirely, or at least offer to do so; but he was not a man of ceremonious politeness, and he had a particular interest in the subjects on which the countess's discourse was likely to turn, which induced him to dispense with ceremony. The ladies seemed indeed scarce to notice his presence. The countess had now assumed a chair, and motioned to the Lady Peveril to sit upon a stool which was placed by her side. 'We will have old times once more, though there are here no roaring of rebel guns to drive you to take refuge at my side, and almost in my pocket.'

'I have a gun, madam,' said little Julian, 'and the park-keeper is to teach me how to fire it next year.'

'I will list you for my soldier, then,' said the countess.

'Ladies have no soldiers,' said the boy, looking wistfully at her.

'He has the true masculine contempt of our frail sex, I see,' said the countess; 'it is born with the insolent varlets of mankind, and shows itself so soon as they are out of their long clothes. Did Ellesmere never tell you of Latham House and Charlotte of Derby, my little master ? '

' A thousand thousand times,' said the boy, colouring ; ' and how the Queen of Man defended it six weeks against three thousand Roundheads, under Rogue Harrison the butcher.'

' It was your mother defended Latham House,' said the countess, ' not I, my little soldier—Hadst thou been there, thou hadst been the best captain of the three.'

' Do not say so, madam,' said the boy, ' for mamma would not touch a gun for all the universe.'

' Not I, indeed, Julian,' said his mother ; ' there I was for certain, but as useless a part of the garrison '——

' You forget,' said the countess, ' you nursed our hospital, and made lint for the soldiers' wounds.'

' But did not papa come to help you ? ' said Julian.

' Papa came at last,' said the countess, ' and so did Prince Rupert—but not, I think, till they were both heartily wished for. Do you remember that morning, Margaret, when the round-headed knaves, that kept us pent up so long, retreated without bag or baggage, at the first glance of the Prince's standards appearing on the hill—and how you took every high-crested captain you saw for Peveril of the Peak, that had been your partner three months before at the Queen's mask ? Nay, never blush for the thought of it— it was an honest affection—and though it was the music of trumpets that accompanied you both to the old chapel, which was almost entirely ruined by the enemy's bullets ; and though Prince Rupert, when he gave you away at the altar, was clad in buff and bandoleer, with pistols in his belt, yet I trust these warlike signs were no type of future discord ? '

' Heaven has been kind to me,' said Lady Peveril, ' in blessing me with an affectionate husband.'

' And in preserving him to you,' said the countess, with a deep sigh ; ' while mine, alas ! sealed with his blood his devotion to his king [1]—Oh, had he lived to see this day ! '

' Alas ! alas ! that he was not permitted ! ' answered

[1] The Earl of Derby and King in Man was beheaded at Bolton-on-the Moors, after having been made prisoner in a previous skirmish in Wiggin Lane.

Lady Peveril; ' how had that brave and noble earl rejoiced
in the unhoped-for redemption of our captivity ! '

The countess looked on Lady Peveril with an air of
surprise.

'Thou hast not then heard, cousin, how it stands with
our house ? How indeed had my noble lord wondered,

THE EARL OF DERBY

had he been told that the very monarch for whom he had
laid down his noble life on the scaffold at Bolton-le-Moor,
should make it his first act of restored monarchy to complete the destruction of our property, already wellnigh
ruined in the royal cause, and to persecute me his widow ! '

' You astonish me, madam ! ' said the Lady Peveril.
' It cannot be, that you—that you, the wife of the gallant,
the faithful, the murdered earl—you, Countess of Derby,

and Queen in Man—you, who took on you even the character of a soldier, and seemed a man when so many men proved women—that YOU should sustain evil from the event which has fulfilled—exceeded—the hopes of every faithful subject —it cannot be ! '

' Thou art as simple, I see, in this world's knowledge as ever, my fair cousin,' answered the countess. ' This restoration, which has given others security, has placed me in danger—this change which relieved other royalists, scarce less zealous, I presume to think, than I—has sent me here a fugitive, and in concealment, to beg shelter and assistance from you, fair cousin.'

' From me,' answered the Lady Peveril—' from me, whose youth your kindness sheltered—from the wife of Peveril, your gallant lord's companion in arms—you have a right to command everything ; but, alas ! that you should need such assistance as I can render—forgive me, but it seems like some ill-omened vision of the night—I listen to your words as if I hoped to be relieved from their painful import by awaking.'

' It is indeed a dream—a vision,' said the Countess of Derby ; ' but it needs no seer to read it—the explanation hath been long since given—Put not your faith in princes. I can soon remove your surprise. This gentleman, your friend, is doubtless *honest* ? '

The Lady Peveril well knew that the Cavaliers, like other factions, usurped to themselves the exclusive denomination of the *honest* party, and she felt some difficulty in explaining that her visitor was not honest in that sense of the word.

' Had we not better retire, madam,' she said to the countess, rising, as if in order to attend her. But the countess retained her seat.

' It was but a question of habit,' she said ; ' the gentleman's principles are nothing to me, for what I have to tell you is widely blazed, and I care not who hears my share of it. You remember—you must have heard, for I think Margaret Stanley would not be indifferent to my fate—that after my husband's murder at Bolton, I took up the standard which he never dropped until his death, and displayed it with my own hand in our sovereignty of Man.'

' I did indeed hear so, madam,' said the Lady Peveril ;

' and that you had bidden a bold defiance to the rebel
government, even after all other parts of Britain had submitted to them. My husband, Sir Geoffrey, designed at
one time to have gone to your assistance with some few
followers ; but we learned that the island was rendered to
the Parliament party, and that you, dearest lady, were
thrown into prison.'

' But you heard not,' said the countess, ' how that
disaster befell me. Margaret, I would have held out that
island against the knaves as long as the sea continued to
flow around it. Till the shoals which surround it had
become safe anchorage—till its precipices had melted
beneath the sunshine—till of all its strong abodes and
castles, not one stone remained upon another,—would
I have defended against these villanous hypocritical rebels,
my dear husband's hereditary dominion. The little kingdom of Man should have been yielded only when not an
arm was left to wield a sword, not a finger to draw a trigger
in its defence. But treachery did what force could never
have done. When we had foiled various attempts upon the
island by open force—treason accomplished what Blake
and Lawson, with their floating castles, had found too
hazardous an enterprise—a base rebel, whom we had
nursed in our own bosoms, betrayed us to the enemy. This
wretch was named Christian '——

Major Bridgenorth started and turned towards the speaker,
but instantly seemed to recollect himself, and again averted
his face. The countess proceeded, without noticing the
interruption which, however, rather surprised Lady Peveril,
who was acquainted with her neighbour's general habits of
indifference and apathy, and therefore the more surprised
at his testifying such sudden symptoms of interest. She
would once again have moved the countess to retire to
another apartment, but Lady Derby proceeded with too
much vehemence to endure interruption.

' This Christian,' she said, ' had ate of my lord his
sovereign's bread, and drunk of his cup, even from childhood
—for his fathers had been faithful servants to the House
of Man and Derby. He himself had fought bravely by my
husband's side, and enjoyed all his confidence ; and when
my princely earl was martyred by the rebels, he recommended

to me, amongst other instructions communicated in the last message I received from him, to continue my confidence in Christian's fidelity. I obeyed, although I never loved the man. He was cold and phlegmatic, and utterly devoid of that sacred fire which is the incentive to noble deeds ; suspected, too, of leaning to the cold metaphysics of Calvinistic subtlety. But he was brave, wise, and experienced, and, as the event proved, possessed but too much interest with the islanders. When these rude people saw themselves without hope of relief, and pressed by a blockade, which brought want and disease into their island, they began to fall off from the faith which they had hitherto shown.'

' What ! ' said the Lady Peveril, ' could they forget what was due to the widow of their benefactor—she who had shared with the generous Derby the task of bettering their condition ? '

' Do not blame them,' said the countess ; ' the rude herd acted but according to their kind—in present distress they forgot former benefits, and, nursed in their earthen hovels, with spirits suited to their dwellings, they were incapable of feeling the glory which is attached to constancy in suffering. But that Christian should have headed their revolt —that he, born a gentleman, and bred under my murdered Derby's own care in all that was chivalrous and noble—that *he* should have forgot a hundred benefits—why do I talk of benefits ?—that he should have forgotten that kindly intercourse which binds man to man far more than the reciprocity of obligation—that he should have headed the ruffians who broke suddenly into my apartment—immured me with my infants in one of my own castles, and assumed or usurped the tyranny of the island—that this should have been done by William Christian, my vassal, my servant, my friend, was a deed of ungrateful treachery, which even this age of treason will scarcely parallel ! '

' And you were then imprisoned,' said the Lady Peveril, ' and in your own sovereignty ? '

' For more than seven years I have endured strict captivity,' said the countess. ' I was indeed offered my liberty, and even some means of support, if I would have consented to leave the island, and pledge my word that I would not endeavour to repossess my son in his father's rights.

But they little knew the princely house from which I spring
—and as little the royal house of Stanley which I uphold,
who hoped to humble Charlotte of Tremouille into so base
a composition. I would rather have starved in the darkest
and lowest vault of Rushin Castle, than have consented to
aught which might diminish in one hair's breadth the right
of my son over his father's sovereignty ! '

'And could not your firmness, in a case where hope
seemed lost, induce them to be generous and dismiss you
without conditions ? '

'They knew me better than thou dost, wench,' answered
the countess ; ' once at liberty, I had not been long without
the means of disturbing their usurpation, and Christian
would have as soon uncaged a lioness to combat with, as
have given me the slightest power of returning to the
struggle with him. But time had liberty and revenge in store
—I had still friends and partisans in the island, though they
were compelled to give way to the storm. Even among the
islanders at large, most had been disappointed in the effects
which they expected from the change of power. They were
loaded with exactions by their new masters, their privileges
were abridged, and their immunities abolished, under the
pretext of reducing them to the same condition with the
other subjects of the pretended republic. When the news
arrived of the changes which were current in Britain, these
sentiments were privately communicated to me. Calcott
and others acted with great zeal and fidelity ; and a rising,
effected as suddenly and effectually as that which had made
me a captive, placed me at liberty and in possession of the
sovereignty of Man, as regent for my son, the youthful
Earl of Derby. Do you think I enjoyed that sovereignty
long without doing justice on that traitor Christian ? '

'How, madam,' said Lady Peveril, who, though she
knew the high and ambitious spirit of the countess, scarce
anticipated the extremities to which it was capable of
hurrying her—' Have you imprisoned Christian ? '

'Aye, wench—in that sure prison which felon never
breaks from,' answered the countess.

Bridgenorth, who had insensibly approached them, and
was listening with an agony of interest which he was unable
any longer to suppress, broke in with the stern exclamation—

' Lady, I trust you have not dared '——
The countess interrupted him in her turn.

' I know not who you are who question—and you know not me when you speak to me of that which I dare, or dare not, do. But you seem interested in the fate of this Christian, and you shall hear it. I was no sooner placed in possession of my rightful power, than I ordered the Dempster of the island to hold upon the traitor a high court of justice, with all the formalities of the isle, as prescribed in its oldest records. The court was held in the open air, before the Dempster and the Keys of the island, assembled under the vaulted cope of heaven, and seated on the terrace of the Zonwald Hill, where of old Druid and Scald held their courts of judgement. The criminal was heard at length in his own defence, which amounted to little more than those specious allegations of public consideration, which are ever used to colour the ugly front of treason. He was fully convicted of his crime, and he received the doom of a traitor.'

' But which, I trust, is not yet executed ? ' said Lady Peveril, not without an involuntary shudder.

' You are a fool, Margaret,' said the countess sharply ; ' think you I delayed such an act of justice, until some wretched intrigues of the new English court might have prompted their interference ? No, wench—he passed from the judgement-seat to the place of execution, with no further delay than might be necessary for his soul's sake. He was shot to death by a file of musketeers in the common place of execution, called Hangohill.' [11]

Bridgenorth clasped his hands together, wrung them, and groaned bitterly.

' As you seem interested for this criminal,' added the countess, addressing Bridgenorth, ' I do him but justice in repeating to you, that his death was firm and manly, becoming the general tenor of his life, which, but for that gross act of traitorous ingratitude, had been fair and honourable. But what of that ? The hypocrite is a saint, and the false traitor a man of honour, till opportunity, that faithful touchstone, proves their metal to be base.'

' It is false, woman—it is false ! ' said Bridgenorth, no longer suppressing his indignation.

' What means this bearing, Master Bridgenorth ? ' said

Lady Peveril, much surprised. 'What is this Christian to
you, that you should insult the Countess of Derby under
my roof?'

'Speak not to me of countesses and of ceremonies,' said
Bridgenorth; 'grief and anger leave me no leisure for idle
observances, to humour the vanity of overgrown children.
O Christian—worthy, well worthy, of the name thou didst
bear! My friend—my brother—the brother of my blessed
Alice—the only friend of my desolate estate! art thou then
cruelly murdered by a female fury, who, but for thee, had
deservedly paid with her own blood that of God's saints,
which she, as well as her tyrant husband, had spilled like
water! Yes, cruel murderess!' he continued, addressing
the countess, 'he whom thou hast butchered in thy insane
vengeance, sacrificed for many a year the dictates of his
own conscience to the interest of thy family, and did not
desert it till thy frantic zeal for royalty had wellnigh brought
to utter perdition the little community in which he was
born. Even in confining thee, he acted but as the friends
of the madman, who bind him with iron for his own preservation; and for thee, as I can bear witness, he was the
only barrier between thee and the wrath of the Commons
of England; and but for his earnest remonstrances, thou
hadst suffered the penalty of thy malignancy, even like the
wicked wife of Ahab.'

'Master Bridgenorth,' said Lady Peveril, 'I will allow
for your impatience upon hearing these unpleasing tidings;
but there is neither use nor propriety in further urging this
question. If in your grief you forget other restraints, I pray
you to remember that the countess is my guest and kinswoman, and is under such protection as I can afford her.
I beseech you, in simple courtesy, to withdraw, as what
must needs be the best and most becoming course in these
trying circumstances.'

'Nay, let him remain,' said the countess, regarding him
with composure, not unmingled with triumph; 'I would
not have it otherwise; I would not that my revenge should
be summed up in the stinted gratification which Christian's
death hath afforded. This man's rude and clamorous grief
only proves that the retribution I have dealt has been more
widely felt than by the wretched sufferer himself. I would

I knew that it had but made sore as many rebel hearts, as there were loyal breasts afflicted by the death of my princely Derby !'

'So please you, madam,' said Lady Peveril, 'since Master Bridgenorth hath not the manners to leave us upon my request, we will, if your ladyship lists, leave him, and retire to my apartment. Farewell, Master Bridgenorth ; we will meet hereafter on better terms.'

'Pardon me, madam,' said the major, who had been striding hastily through the room, but now stood fast, and drew himself up, as one who has taken a resolution ;—' to yourself I have nothing to say but what is respectful ; but to this woman I must speak as a magistrate. She has confessed a murder in my presence—the murder too of my brother-in-law—as a man, and as a magistrate, I cannot permit her to pass from hence, excepting under such custody as may prevent her further flight. She has already confessed that she is a fugitive, and in search of a place of concealment, until she should be able to escape into foreign parts. Charlotte, Countess of Derby, I attach thee of the crime of which thou hast but now made thy boast.'

'I shall not obey your arrest,' said the countess composedly, 'I was born to give, but not to receive such orders. What have your English laws to do with my acts of justice and of government, within my son's hereditary kingdom ? Am I not Queen in Man, as well as Countess of Derby ? A feudatory sovereign indeed ; but yet independent so long as my dues of homage are duly discharged. What right can you assert over me ?'

'That given by the precepts of Scripture,' answered Bridgenorth—' " Whoso spilleth man's blood, by man shall his blood be spilled." Think not the barbarous privileges of ancient feudal customs will avail to screen you from the punishment due for an Englishman murdered upon pretexts inconsistent with the Act of Indemnity.'

'Master Bridgenorth,' said Lady Peveril, 'if by fair terms you desist not from your present purpose, I tell you that I neither dare, nor will, permit any violence against this honourable lady, within the walls of my husband's castle.'

'You will find yourself unable to prevent me from executing my duty, madam,' said Bridgenorth, whose native

obstinacy now came in aid of his grief and desire of revenge ;
' I am a magistrate, and act by authority.'

' I know not that,' said Lady Peveril. ' That you *were*
a magistrate, Master Bridgenorth, under the late usurping
powers, I know well ; but till I hear of your having a commission in the name of the king, I now hesitate to obey you
as such.'

' I shall stand on small ceremony,' said Bridgenorth.
' Were I no magistrate, every man has title to arrest for
murder against the terms of the indemnities held out by the
king's proclamations, and I will make my point good.'

' What indemnities ? What proclamations ? ' said the
Countess of Derby indignantly. ' Charles Stuart may, if he
pleases (and it doth seem to please him), consort with those
whose hands have been red with the blood, and blackened
with the plunder, of his father and of his loyal subjects.
He may forgive them if he will, and count their deeds good
service. What has that to do with this Christian's offence
against me and mine ? Born a Manxman—bred and nursed
in the island—he broke the laws under which he lived, and
died for the breach of them, after the fair trial which they
allowed. Methinks, Margaret, we have enough of this
peevish and foolish magistrate—I attend you to your
apartment.'

Major Bridgenorth placed himself betwixt them and
the door, in a manner which showed him determined to
interrupt their passage ; when the Lady Peveril, who
thought she had already showed more deference to him in
this matter than her husband was likely to approve of,
raised her voice, and called loudly on her steward, Whitaker.
That alert person, who had heard high talking, and a female
voice with which he was unacquainted, had remained for
several minutes stationed in the anteroom, much afflicted
with the anxiety of his own curiosity. Of course he entered
in an instant.

' Let three of the men instantly take arms,' said his lady ;
' bring them into the ante-room, and wait my further orders.'

CHAPTER VI

You shall have no worse prison than my chamber,
Nor jailer than myself.   *The Captain.*

THE command which Lady Peveril laid on her domestics
to arm themselves, was so unlike the usual gentle acquiescence of her manners, that Major Bridgenorth was astonished.
' How mean you, madam ? ' said he ; ' I thought myself
under a friendly roof.'

' And you are so, Master Bridgenorth,' said the Lady
Peveril, without departing from the natural calmness of her
voice and manner ; ' but it is a roof which must not be
violated by the outrage of one friend against another.'

' It is well, madam,' said Bridgenorth, turning to the door
of the apartment. ' The worthy Master Solsgrace has
already foretold, that the time was returned when high
houses and proud names should be once more an excuse for
the crimes of those who inhabit the one and bear the other.
I believed him not, but now see he is wiser than I. Yet
think not I will endure this tamely. The blood of my brother—of the friend of my bosom—shall not long call from
the altar, " How long, O Lord, how long ! " If there is one
spark of justice left in this unhappy England, that proud
woman and I shall meet where she can have no partial friend
to protect her.'

So saying, he was about to leave the apartment, when
Lady Peveril said, ' You depart not from this place, Master
Bridgenorth, unless you give me your word to renounce all
purpose against the noble countess's liberty upon the
present occasion.'

' I would sooner,' answered he, ' subscribe to my own
dishonour, madam, written down in express words, than to
any such composition. If any man offers to interrupt me,
his blood be on his own head ! ' As Major Bridgenorth spoke,
Whitaker threw open the door, and showed that, with the
alertness of an old soldier, who was not displeased to see
things tend once more towards a state of warfare, he had

got with him four stout fellows in the Knight of the Peak's livery, well armed with swords and carabines, buff-coats, and pistols at their girdles.

' I will see,' said Major Bridgenorth, ' if any of these men be so desperate as to stop me, a freeborn Englishman, and a magistrate in the discharge of my duty.'

So saying, he advanced upon Whitaker and his armed assistants, with his hand on the hilt of his sword.

' Do not be so desperate, Master Bridgenorth,' exclaimed Lady Peveril ; and added, in the same moment, ' Lay hold upon, and disarm him, Whitaker ; but do him no injury.'

Her commands were obeyed. Bridgenorth, though a man of moral resolution, was not one of those who undertook to cope in person with odds of a description so formidable. He half drew his sword, and offered such show of resistance as made it necessary to secure him by actual force ; but then yielded up his weapon, and declared, that, submitting to force which one man was unable to resist, he made those who commanded, and who employed it, responsible for assailing his liberty without a legal warrant.

' Never mind a warrant on a pinch, Master Bridgenorth,' said old Whitaker ; ' sure enough you have often acted upon a worse yourself. My lady's word is as good a warrant, sure, as Old Noll's commission ; and you bore that many a day, Master Bridgenorth, and, moreover, you laid me in the stocks for drinking the King's health, Master Bridgenorth, and never cared a farthing about the laws of England.'

' Hold your saucy tongue, Whitaker,' said the Lady Peveril ; ' and do you, Master Bridgenorth, not take it to heart that you are detained prisoner for a few hours, until the Countess of Derby can have nothing to fear from your pursuit. I could easily send an escort with her that might bid defiance to any force you could muster ; but I wish, Heaven knows, to bury the remembrance of old civil dissensions, not to awaken new. Once more, will you think better on it—assume your sword again, and forget whom you have now seen at Martindale Castle ? '

' Never,' said Bridgenorth. ' The crime of this cruel woman will be the last of human injuries which I can forget. The last thought of earthly kind which will leave me, will be the desire that justice shall be done on her.'

'If such be your sentiments,' said Lady Peveril, 'though they are more allied to revenge than to justice, I must provide for my friend's safety by putting restraint upon your person. In this room you will be supplied with every necessary of life, and every convenience ; and a message shall relieve your domestics of the anxiety which your absence from the Hall is not unlikely to occasion. When a few hours, at most two days are over, I will myself relieve you from confinement, and demand your pardon for now acting as your obstinacy compels me to do.'

The major made no answer, but that he was in her hands, and must submit to her pleasure ; and then turned sullenly to the window, as if desirous to be rid of their presence.

The countess and the Lady Peveril left the apartment arm in arm ; and the lady issued forth her directions to Whitaker concerning the mode in which she was desirous that Bridgenorth should be guarded and treated during his temporary confinement ; at the same time explaining to him that the safety of the Countess of Derby required that he should be closely watched.

In all proposals for the prisoner's security, such as the regular relief of guards, and the like, Whitaker joyfully acquiesced, and undertook, body for body, that he should be detained in captivity for the necessary period. But the old steward was not half so docile when it came to be considered how the captive's bedding and table should be supplied ; and he thought Lady Peveril displayed a very undue degree of attention to her prisoner's comforts. 'I warrant,' he said, 'that the cuckoldy Roundhead ate enough of our fat beef yesterday to serve him for a month ; and a little fasting will do his health good. Marry, for drink, he shall have plenty of cold water to cool his hot liver, which I will be bound is still hissing with the strong liquors of yesterday. And as for bedding, there are the fine dry boards—more wholesome than the wet straw I lay upon when I was in the stocks, I trow.'

'Whitaker,' said the lady peremptorily, 'I desire you to provide Master Bridgenorth's bedding and food in the way I have signified to you ; and to behave yourself towards him in all civility.'

'Lack-a-day ! yes, my lady,' said Whitaker ; 'you shall

have all your directions punctually obeyed ; but as an old
servant, I cannot but speak my mind.'

The ladies retired after this conference with the steward
in the antechamber, and were soon seated in another
apartment, which was peculiarly dedicated to the use of the
mistress of the mansion—having, on the one side, access to
the family bedroom ; and, on the other, to the still-room
which communicated with the garden. There was also a
small door which, ascending a few steps, led to that balcony,
already mentioned, that overhung the kitchen ; and the
same passage, by a separate door, admitted to the principal
gallery in the chapel ; so that the spiritual and temporal
affairs of the castle were placed almost at once within the
reach of the same regulating and directing eye.[1]

In the tapestried room, from which issued these various
sallyports, the countess and Lady Peveril were speedily
seated ; and the former, smiling upon the latter, said, as
she took her hand, ' Two things have happened to-day,
which might have surprised me, if anything ought to surprise
me in such times :—the first is, that yonder roundheaded
fellow should have dared to use such insolence in the house
of Peveril of the Peak. If your husband is yet the same
honest and downright Cavalier whom I once knew, and had
chanced to be at home, he would have thrown the knave
out of window. But what I wonder at still more, Margaret,
is your generalship. I hardly thought you had courage
sufficient to have taken such decided measures, after keeping
on terms with the man so long. When he spoke of Justices
and warrants, you looked so overawed that I thought I felt
the clutch of the parish-beadles on my shoulder, to drag me
to prison as a vagrant.'

' We owe Master Bridgenorth some deference, my dearest
lady,' answered the Lady Peveril ; ' he has served us often,
and kindly, in these late times ; but neither he, nor any one
else, shall insult the Countess of Derby in the house of
Margaret Stanley.'

---

[1] This peculiar collocation of apartments may be seen at Haddon Hall,
Derbyshire, once a seat of the Vernons, where, in the lady's pew in the
chapel, there is a sort of scuttle, which opens into the kitchen, so that
the good lady could ever and anon, without much interruption of her
religious duties, give an eye that the roast-meat was not permitted to
burn, and that the turn-broche did his duty.

'Thou art become a perfect heroine, Margaret,' replied the countess.

'Two sieges, and alarms innumerable,' said Lady Peveril, 'may have taught me presence of mind. My courage is, I believe, as slender as ever.'

'Presence of mind *is* courage,' answered the countess. 'Real valour consists not in being insensible to danger, but in being prompt to confront and disarm it ;—and we may have present occasion for all that we possess,' she added, with some slight emotion, 'for I hear the trampling of horses' steps on the pavement of the court.'

In one moment, the boy Julian, breathless with joy, came flying into the room, to say that papa was returned, with Lamington and Sam Brewer ; and that he was himself to ride Black Hastings to the stable. In the second, the tramp of the honest knight's heavy jack-boots was heard, as, in his haste to see his lady, he ascended the staircase by two steps at a time. He burst into the room ; his manly countenance and disordered dress showing marks that he had been riding fast ; and without looking to any one else, caught his good lady in his arms, and kissed her a dozen of times. Blushing, and with some difficulty, Lady Peveril extricated herself from Sir Geoffrey's arms ; and in a voice of bashful and gentle rebuke, bid him, for shame, observe who was in the room.

'One,' said the countess, advancing to him, 'who is right glad to see that Sir Geoffrey Peveril, though turned courtier and favourite, still values the treasure which she had some share in bestowing upon him. You cannot have forgot the raising of the leaguer of Latham House !'

'The noble Countess of Derby !' said Sir Geoffrey, doffing his plumed hat with an air of deep deference, and kissing with much reverence the hand which she held out to him ; 'I am as glad to see your ladyship in my poor house, as I would be to hear that they had found a vein of lead in the Brown Tor. I rode hard, in the hope of being your escort through the country. I feared you might have fallen into bad hands, hearing there was a knave sent out with a warrant from the council.'

'When heard you so ? and from whom ? '

'It was from Cholmondeley of Vale-Royal,' said Sir

Geoffrey; 'he is come down to make provision for your safety through Cheshire; and I promised to bring you there in safety. Prince Rupert, Ormond, and other friends, do not doubt the matter will be driven to a fine ; but they say the Chancellor, and Harry Bennet, and some others of the over-sea counsellors, are furious at what they call a breach of the king's proclamation. Hang them, say I ! They left us to bear all the beating ; and now they are incensed that we should wish to clear scores with those who rode us like nightmares ! '

'What did they talk of for my chastisement ? ' said the countess.

'I wot not,' said Sir Geoffrey ; 'some friends, as I said, from our kind Cheshire, and others, tried to bring it to a fine ; but some, again, spoke of nothing but the Tower, and a long imprisonment.'

'I have suffered imprisonment long enough for King Charles's sake,' said the countess ; 'and have no mind to undergo it at his hand. Besides, if I am removed from the personal superintendence of my son's dominions in Man, I know not what new usurpation may be attempted there. I must be obliged to you, cousin, to contrive that I may get in security to Vale-Royal, and from thence I know I shall be guarded safely to Liverpool.'

'You may rely on my guidance and protection, noble lady,' answered her host, 'though you had come here at midnight, and with the rogue's head in your apron, like Judith in the Holy Apocrypha, which I joy to hear once more read in churches.'

'Do the gentry resort much to the court ? ' said the lady.

'Aye, madam,' replied Sir Geoffrey; 'and according to our saying, when miners do begin to bore in these parts, it is *for the grace of God, and what they there may find.*'

'Meet the old Cavaliers with much countenance ? ' continued the countess.

'Faith, madam, to speak truth,' replied the knight, 'the king hath so gracious a manner, that it makes every man's hopes blossom, though we have seen but few that have ripened into fruit.'

'You have not, yourself, my cousin,' answered the

countess, ' had room to complain of ingratitude, I trust ?
Few have less deserved it at the king's hand.'

Sir Geoffrey was unwilling, like most prudent persons, to
own the existence of expectations which had proved falla-
cious, yet had too little art in his character to conceal his
disappointment entirely. ' Who, I, madam ? ' he said ;
' Alas ! what should a poor country knight expect from the
king, besides the pleasure of seeing him in Whitehall once
more, and enjoying his own again ? And his Majesty was
very gracious when I was presented, and spoke to me of
Worcester, and of my horse, Black Hastings—he had forgot
his name, though—faith, and mine too, I believe, had not
Prince Rupert whispered it to him. And I saw some old
friends, such as his Grace of Ormond, Sir Marmaduke
Langdale, Sir Philip Musgrave, and so forth ; and had a jolly
rouse or two, to the tune of old times.'

' I should have thought so many wounds received—so
many dangers risked—such considerable losses—merited
something more than a few smooth words,' said the countess.

' Nay, my lady, there were other friends of mine who had
the same thought,' answered Peveril. ' Some were of
opinion that the loss of so many hundred acres of fair land
was worth some reward of honour at least ; and there were
who thought my descent from William the Conqueror—
craving your ladyship's pardon for boasting it in your
presence—would not have become a higher rank or title
worse than the pedigree of some who have been promoted.
But what said the witty Duke of Buckingham, forsooth ?
(whose grandsire was a Lei'stershire knight—rather poorer,
and scarcely so well-born as myself)—Why, he said, that if
all of my degree who deserved well of the king in the late
times were to be made peers, the House of Lords must meet
upon Salisbury Plain ! '

' And that bad jest passed for a good argument ! ' said the
countess ; ' and well it might, where good arguments pass for
bad jests. But here comes one I must be acquainted with.'

This was little Julian, who now re-entered the hall,
leading his little sister, as if he had brought her to bear
witness to the boastful tale which he told his father, of his
having manfully ridden Black Hastings to the stable-yard,
alone in the saddle ; and that Saunders, though he walked

by the horse's head, did not once put his hand upon the
rein, and Brewer, though he stood beside him, scarce held
him by the knee.   The father kissed the boy heartily ; and
the countess, calling him to her so soon as Sir Geoffrey had
set him down, kissed his forehead also, and then surveyed
all his features with a keen and penetrating eye.

'He is a true Peveril,' said she, ' mixed as he should be
with some touch of the Stanley.   Cousin, you must grant
me my boon, and when I am safely established, and have
my present affair arranged, you must let me have this little
Julian of yours some time hence, to be nurtured in my house,
held as my page, and the playfellow of the little Derby.
I trust in Heaven, they will be such friends as their fathers
have been, and may God send them more fortunate times!'[n]

'Marry, and I thank you for the proposal with all my
heart, madam,' said the knight.   ' There are so many noble
houses decayed, and so many more in which the exercise and
discipline for the training of noble youths is given up and
neglected, that I have often feared I must have kept Gil to
be young master at home ; and I have had too little nurture
myself to teach him much, and so he would have been a mere
hunting hawking knight of Derbyshi e.   But in your ladyship's household, and with the noble young earl, he will have
all, and more than all, the education which I could desire.'

'There shall be no distinction betwixt them, cousin,' said
the countess ; ' Margaret Stanley's son shall be as much the
object of care to me as my own, since you are kindly disposed to intrust him to my charge.   You look pale, Margaret,' she continued, ' and the tear stands in your eye !
Do not be so foolish, my love—what I ask is better than you
can desire for your boy ; for the house of my father, the
Duke de la Tremouille, was the most famous school of
chivalry in France ; nor have I degenerated from him, or
suffered any relaxation in that noble discipline which trained
young gentlemen to do honour to their race.   You can
promise your Julian no such advantages, if you train him up
a mere home-bred youth.'

'I acknowledge the importance of the favour, madam,'
said Lady Peveril, ' and must acquiesce in what your lady
ship honours us by proposing, and Sir Geoffrey approves of ;
but Julian is an only child, and '——

'An only son,' said the countess, ' but surely not an only child. You pay too high deference to our masters, the male sex, if you allow Julian to engross all your affection, and spare none for this beautiful girl.'

So saying, she set down Julian, and, taking Alice Bridgenorth on her lap, began to caress her ; and there was, notwithstanding her masculine character, something so sweet in the tone of her voice and in the cast of her features, that the child immediately smiled, and replied to her marks of fondness. This mistake embarrassed Lady Peveril exceedingly. Knowing the blunt impetuosity of her husband's character, his devotion to the memory of the deceased Earl of Derby, and his corresponding veneration for his widow, she was alarmed for the consequences of his hearing the conduct of Bridgenorth that morning, and was particularly desirous that he should not learn it save from herself in private, and after due preparation. But the countess's error led to a more precipitate disclosure.

'That pretty girl, madam,' answered Sir Geoffrey, ' is none of ours—I wish she were. She belongs to a neighbour hard by—a good man, and, to say truth, a good neighbour— though he was carried off from his allegiance in the late times by a d—d Presbyterian scoundrel, who calls himself a parson, and whom I hope to fetch down from his perch presently, with a wannion to him ! He has been cock of the roost long enough. There are rods in pickle to switch the Geneva cloak with, I can tell the sour-faced rogues that much. But this child is the daughter of Bridgenorth—neighbour Bridgenorth, of Moultrassie Hall.'

'Bridgenorth ? ' said the countess ; ' I thought I had known all the honourable names in Derbyshire—I remember nothing of Bridgenorth. But stay—was there not a sequestrator and committeeman of that name ? Sure, it cannot be he ? '

Peveril took some shame to himself as he replied, ' It is the very man whom your ladyship means, and you may conceive the reluctance with which I submitted to receive good offices from one of his kidney ; but had I not done so, I should have scarce known how to find a roof to cover Dame Margaret's head.'

The countess, as he spoke, raised the child gently from

her lap, and placed it upon the carpet, though little Alice
showed a disinclination to the change of place, which the
Lady of Derby and Man would certainly have indulged in
a child of patrician descent and loyal parentage.

'I blame you not,' she said ; ' no one knows what temptation will bring us down to.   Yet I *did* think Peveril of the
Peak would have resided in its deepest cavern, sooner than
owed an obligation to a regicide.'

'Nay, madam,' answered the knight, ' my neighbour is
bad enough, but not so bad as you would make him ; he is
but a Presbyterian—that I must confess—but not an
Independent.'

'A variety of the same monster,' said the countess, ' who
halloed while the others hunted, and bound the victim whom
the Independents massacred.   Betwixt such sects I prefer
the Independents.   They are at least bold, bare-faced,
merciless villains, have more of the tiger in them, and less
of the crocodile.   I have no doubt it was that worthy gentleman who took it upon him this morning '——

She stopped short, for she saw Lady Peveril was vexed
and embarrassed.

'I am,' she said, ' the most luckless of beings   I have
said something, I know not what, to distress you, Margaret
—Mystery is a bad thing, and betwixt us there should be
none.'

'There is none, madam,' said Lady Peveril, something
impatiently ;   'I waited but an opportunity to tell my
husband what had happened—Sir Geoffrey, Master Bridgenorth was unfortunately here when the Lady Derby and
I met ;   and he thought it part of his duty to speak
of '——

'To speak of what ? ' said the knight, bending his brows.
'You were ever something too fond, dame, of giving way to
the usurpation of such people.'

'I only mean,' said Lady Peveril, ' that as the person—
he to whom Lady Derby's story related,—was the brother
of his late lady, he threatened—but I cannot think that he
was serious.'

'Threaten ?—threaten the Lady of Derby and Man in
my house !—the widow of my friend—the noble Charlotte
of Latham House !—by Heaven, the prick-eared slave shall

answer it ! How comes it that my knaves threw him not
out of the window ? '

' Alas ! Sir Geoffrey, you forget how much we owe him,'
said the lady.

' Owe him ! ' said the knight, still more indignant ; for
in his singleness of apprehension he conceived that his wife
alluded to pecuniary obligations,—' if I do owe him some
money, hath he not security for it ? and must he have the
right, over and above, to domineer and play the magistrate
in Martindale Castle ? Where is he ?—what have you made
of him ? I will—I must speak with him.'

' Be patient, Sir Geoffrey,' said the countess, who now dis-
cerned the cause of her kinswoman's apprehension ; ' and be
assured I did not need your chivalry to defend me against
this discourteous faitour, as *Morte d'Arthur* would have
called him. I promise you my kinswoman hath fully
righted my wrong ; and I am so pleased to owe my
deliverance entirely to her gallantry, that I charge and
command you, as a true knight, not to mingle in the adventure of another.'

Lady Peveril, who knew her husband's blunt and impatient temper, and perceived that he was becoming angry,
now took up the story, and plainly and simply pointed out
the cause of Master Bridgenorth's interference.

' I am sorry for it,' said the knight ; ' I thought he had
more sense ; and that this happy change might have done
some good upon him. But you should have told me this
instantly—It consists not with my honour that he should
be kept prisoner in this house, as if I feared anything he
could do to annoy the noble countess, while she is under my
roof, or within twenty miles of this castle.'

So saying, and bowing to the countess, he went straight
to the gilded chamber, leaving Lady Peveril in great anxiety
for the event of an angry meeting between a temper hasty
as that of her husband, and stubborn like that of Bridgenorth. Her apprehensions were, however, unnecessary ;
for the meeting was not fated to take place.

When Sir Geoffrey Peveril, having dismissed Whitaker
and his sentinels, entered the gilded chamber, in which he
expected to find his captive, the prisoner had escaped, and
it was easy to see in what manner. The sliding panel had,

in the hurry of the moment, escaped the memory of Lady
Peveril, and of Whitaker, the only persons who knew anything of it.   It was probable that a chink had remained open,
sufficient to indicate its existence to Bridgenorth ; who,
withdrawing it altogether, had found his way into the secret
apartment with which it communicated, and from thence
to the postern of the castle by another secret passage, which
had been formed in the thickness of the wall, as is not uncommon in ancient mansions ; the lords of which were liable
to so many mutations of fortune, that they usually contrived
to secure some lurking place and secret mode of retreat from
their fortresses.   That Bridgenorth had discovered and
availed himself of this secret mode of retreat was evident ;
because the private doors communicating with the postern
and the sliding panel in the gilded chamber were both left
open.

Sir Geoffrey returned to the ladies with looks of perplexity.   While he deemed Bridgenorth within his reach,
he was apprehensive of nothing he could do ; for he felt
himself his superior in personal strength, and in that
species of courage which induces a man to rush, without
hesitation, upon personal danger.   But when at a distance,
he had been for many years accustomed to consider Bridgenorth's power and influence as something formidable ; and
notwithstanding the late change of affairs, his ideas so
naturally reverted to his neighbour as a powerful friend or
dangerous enemy, that he felt more apprehension on the
countess's score, than he was willing to acknowledge even to
himself.   The countess observed his downcast and anxious
brow, and requested to know if her stay there was likely to
involve him in any trouble or in any danger.

' The trouble should be welcome,' said Sir Geoffrey, ' and
more welcome the danger, which should come on such an
account.   My plan was, that your ladyship should have
honoured Martindale with a few days' residence, which
might have been kept private until the search after you was
ended.   Had I seen this fellow Bridgenorth, I have no
doubt I could have compelled him to act discreetly ; but
he is now at liberty, and will keep out of my reach ; and,
what is worse, he has the secret of the priest's chamber.'

Here the knight paused, and seemed much embarrassed.

' You can, then, neither conceal nor protect me ? ' said the countess.

' Pardon, my honoured lady,' answered the knight, ' and let me say out my say. The plain truth is, that this man hath many friends among the Presbyterians here, who are more numerous than I would wish them ; and if he falls in with the pursuivant fellow who carries the warrant of the Privy Council, it is likely he will back him with force sufficient to try to execute it. And I doubt whether any of our friends can be summoned together in haste, sufficient to resist such a power as they are like to bring together.'

' Nor would I wish any friends to take arms, in my name, against the king's warrant, Sir Geoffrey,' said the countess.

' Nay, for that matter,' replied the knight, ' an his Majesty will grant warrants against his best friends, he must look to have them resisted. But the best I can think of in this emergence is—though the proposal be something inhospitable —that your ladyship should take presently to horse, if your fatigue will permit. I will mount also, with some brisk fellows, who will lodge you safe at Vale-Royal, though the sheriff stopped the way with a whole *posse comitatus.*'

The Countess of Derby willingly acquiesced in this proposal. She had enjoyed a night's sound repose in the private chamber, to which Ellesmere had guided her on the preceding evening, and was quite ready to resume her route, or flight—' she scarce knew,' she said, ' which of the two she should term it.'

Lady Peveril wept at the necessity which seemed to hurry her earliest friend and protectress from under her roof, at the instant when the clouds of adversity were gathering around her ; but she saw no alternative equally safe. Nay, however strong her attachment to Lady Derby, she could not but be more readily reconciled to her hasty departure, when she considered the inconvenience, and even danger, in which her presence, at such a time, and in such circumstances, was likely to involve a man so bold and hot-tempered as her husband, Sir Geoffrey.

While Lady Peveril, therefore, made every arrangement which time permitted and circumstances required, for the countess prosecuting her journey, her husband, whose spirits always rose with the prospect of action, issued his

orders to Whitaker to get together a few stout fellows, with
back and breast pieces, and steep caps. 'There are the
two lackeys, and Outram and Saunders, besides the other
groom fellow, and Roger Raine, and his son ; but bid Roger
not come drunk again ;—thyself, young Dick of the Dale
and his servant, and a file or two of the tenants,—we shall
be enough for any force they can make. All these are
fellows that will strike hard, and ask no question why—
their hands are ever readier than their tongues, and their
mouths are more made for drinking than speaking.'

Whitaker, apprised of the necessity of the case, asked if he
should not warn Sir Jasper Cranbourne.

'Not a word to him, as you live,' said the knight ; 'this
may be an outlawry, as they call it, for what I know ; and
therefore I will bring no lands or tenements into peril, saving
mine own. Sir Jasper hath had a troublesome time of it
for many a year. By my will, he shall sit quiet for the rest
of 's days.'

CHAPTER VII

Fang. A rescue ! a rescue !
Mrs. Quickly. Good people, bring a rescue or two.
Henry IV, Part I.

THE followers of Peveril were so well accustomed to the
sound of 'boot and saddle', that they were soon mounted
and in order ; and in all the form, and with some of the
dignity of danger, proceeded to escort the Countess of Derby
through the hilly and desert track of country which connects
the frontier of the shire with the neighbouring county of
Cheshire. The cavalcade moved with considerable precaution, which they had been taught by the discipline of the
Civil Wars. One wary and well-mounted trooper rode about
two hundred yards in advance ; followed, at about half
that distance, by two more, with their carabines advanced,
as if ready for action. About one hundred yards behind
the advance came the main body ; where the Countess of
Derby, mounted on Lady Peveril's ambling palfrey (for her
own had been exhausted by the journey from London to

Martindale Castle), accompanied by one groom, of approved
fidelity, and one waiting-maid, was attended and guarded
by the Knight of the Peak, and three files of good and
practised horsemen. In the rear came Whitaker, with
Lance Outram, as men of especial trust, to whom the covering
the retreat was confided. They rode, as the Spanish proverb
expresses it, ' with the beard on the shoulder', looking
around, that is, from time to time, and using every precaution to have the speediest knowledge of any pursuit which
might take place.

But, however wise in discipline, Peveril and his followers
were somewhat remiss in civil policy. The knight had
communicated to Whitaker, though without any apparent
necessity, the precise nature of their present expedition ;
and Whitaker was equally communicative to his comrade
Lance, the keeper. 'It is strange enough, Master Whitaker,'
said the latter, when he had heard the case, ' and I wish you,
being a wise man, would expound it ;—why, when we have
been wishing for the king—and praying for the king—and
fighting for the king—and dying for the king, for these
twenty years, the first thing we find to do on his return, is
to get into harness to resist his warrant ? '

' Pooh ! you silly fellow,' said Whitaker, ' that is all you
know of the true bottom of our quarrel ! Why, man, we
fought for the king's person against his warrant, all along
from the very beginning ; for I remember the rogues' proclamations, and so forth, always ran in the name of the
king and Parliament.'

' Aye ! was it even so ? ' replied Lance. ' Nay, then, if
they begin the old game so soon again, and send out warrants
in the king's name against his loyal subjects, well fare our
stout knight, say I, who is ready to take them down in their
stocking-soles. And if Bridgenorth takes the chase after
us, I shall not be sorry to have a knock at him for one.'

' Why, the man, bating he is a pestilent Roundhead and
Puritan,' said Whitaker, ' is no bad neighbour. What has
he done to thee, man ? '

' He has poached on the manor,' answered the keeper.

' The devil he has ! ' replied Whitaker. ' Thou must be
jesting, Lance. Bridgenorth is neither hunter nor hawker ;
he hath not so much of honesty in him.'

' Aye, but he runs after game you little think of, with his sour, melancholy face, that would scare babes and curdle milk,' answered Lance.

' Thou canst not mean the wenches ? ' said Whitaker ; ' why, he hath been melancholy mad with moping for the death of his wife. Thou knowest our lady took the child, for fear he should strangle it for putting him in mind of its mother, in some of his tantrums. Under her favour, and among friends, there are many poor Cavaliers' children that care would be better bestowed upon—But to thy tale.'

' Why, thus it runs,' said Lance. ' I think you may have noticed, Master Whitaker, that a certain Mistress Deborah hath manifested a certain favour for a certain person in a certain household.'

' For thyself, to wit,' answered Whitaker ; ' Lance Outram, thou art the vainest coxcomb '——

' Coxcomb ? ' said Lance ; ' why, 'twas but last night the whole family saw her, as one would say, fling herself at my head.'

' I would she had been a brickbat, then, to have broken it, for thy impertinence and conceit,' said the steward.

' Well, but do but hearken. The next morning—that is, this very blessed morning—I thought of going to lodge a buck in the park, judging a bit of venison might be wanted in the larder, after yesterday's wassail ; and, as I passed under the nursery window, I did but just look up to see what madam governante was about ; and so I saw her, through the casement, whip on her hood and scarf as soon as she had a glimpse of me. Immediately after I saw the still-room door open, and made sure she was coming through the garden, and so over the breach and down to the park ; and so, thought I, " Aha, Mistress Deb, if you are so ready to dance after my pipe and tabor, I will give you a couranto before you shall come up with me." And so I went down Ivy-tod Dingle, where the copse is tangled, and the ground swampy, and round by Haxley Bottom, thinking all the while she was following, and laughing in my sleeve at the round I was giving her.'

' You deserved to be ducked for it,' said Whitaker, ' for a weather-headed puppy ; but what is all this Jack-a-lantern story to Bridgenorth ? '

'Why, it was all along of he, man,' continued Lance, 'that is, of Bridgenorth, that she did not follow me—Gad, I first walked slow, and then stopped, and then turned back a little, and then began to wonder what she had made of herself, and to think I had borne myself something like a jackass in the matter.'

'That I deny,' said Whitaker, 'never jackass but would have borne him better—but go on.'

'Why, turning my face towards the castle, I went back as if I had my nose bleeding, when just by the Copely thorn, which stands, you know, a flight-shot from the postern-gate, I saw Madam Deb in close conference with the enemy.'

'What enemy?' said the steward.

'What enemy! why, who but Bridgenorth? They kept out of sight, and among the copse; but, thought I, it is hard if I cannot stalk you, that have stalked so many bucks. If so, I had better give my shafts to be pudding-pins. So I cast round the thicket, to watch their waters; and may I never bend crossbow again, if I did not see him give her gold, and squeeze her by the hand!'

'And was that all you saw pass between them?' said the steward.

'Faith, and it was enough to dismount me from my hobby,' said Lance. 'What! when I thought I had the prettiest girl in the castle dancing after my whistle, to find that she gave me the bag to hold, and was smuggling in a corner with a rich old Puritan!'

'Credit me, Lance, it is not as thou thinkest,' said Whitaker. 'Bridgenorth cares not for these amorous toys, and thou thinkest of nothing else. But it is fitting our knight should know that he has met with Deborah in secret, and given her gold; for never Puritan gave gold yet, but it was earnest for some devil's work done, or to be done.'

'Nay, but,' said Lance, 'I would not be such a dog-bolt as to go and betray the girl to our master. She hath a right to follow her fancy, as the dame said who kissed her cow—only I do not much approve her choice, that is all. He cannot be six years short of fifty; and a verjuice countenance, under the penthouse of a slouched beaver, and bag of meagre dried bones, swaddled up in a black cloak, is no such temptation, methinks.'

' I tell you once more,' said Whitaker, ' you are mistaken ; and that there neither is, nor can be, any matter of love between them, but only some intrigue, concerning, perhaps, this same noble Countess of Derby. I tell thee, it behoves my master to know it, and I will presently tell it to him.'

So saying, and in spite of all the remonstrances which Lance continued to make on behalf of Mistress Deborah, the steward rode up to the main body of their little party, and mentioned to the knight, and the Countess of Derby, what he had just heard from the keeper, adding at the same time his own suspicions, that Master Bridgenorth of Moultrassie Hall was desirous to keep up some system of espial in the Castle of Martindale, either in order to secure his menaced vengeance on the Countess of Derby, as authoress of his brother-in-law's death, or for some unknown, but probably sinister purpose.

The Knight of the Peak was filled with high resentment at Whitaker's communication. According to his prejudices, those of the opposite faction were supposed to make up by wit and intrigue what they wanted in open force ; and he now hastily conceived that his neighbour, whose prudence he always respected, and sometimes even dreaded, was maintaining, for his private purposes, a clandestine correspondence with a member of his family. If this was for the betrayal of his noble guest, it argued at once treachery and presumption ; or, viewing the whole as Lance had done, a criminal intrigue with a woman so near the person of Lady Peveril, was in itself, he deemed, a piece of sovereign impertinence and disrespect on the part of such a person as Bridgenorth, against whom Sir Geoffrey's anger was kindled accordingly.

Whitaker had scarce regained his post in the rear, when he again quitted it, and galloped to the main body with more speed than before, with the unpleasing tidings that they were pursued by half a score of horsemen, and better.

' Ride on briskly to Hartley-nick,' said the knight, ' and there, with God to help, we will bide the knaves. Countess of Derby—one word and a short one—Farewell !—you must ride forward with Whitaker and another careful fellow, and let me alone to see that no one treads on your skirts.'

' I will abide with you and stand them,' said the countess ;
' you know of old, I fear not to look on man's work.'

' You *must* ride on, madam,' said the knight, ' for the sake
of the young earl, and the rest of my noble friend's family.
There is no manly work which can be worth your looking
upon ; it is but child's play that these fellows bring with
them.'

As she yielded a reluctant consent to continue her flight,
they reached the bottom of Hartley-nick, a pass very steep
and craggy, and where the road, or rather path, which had
hitherto passed over more open ground, became pent up
and confined, betwixt copsewood on the one side, and, on
the other, the precipitous bank of a mountain stream.

The Countess of Derby, after an affectionate adieu to Sir
Geoffrey, and having requested him to convey her kind
commendations to her little page-elect and his mother, proceeded up the pass at a round pace, and with her attendants
and escort, was soon out of sight. Immediately after she
had disappeared, the pursuers came up with Sir Geoffrey
Peveril, who had divided and drawn up his party so as completely to occupy the road at three different points.

The opposite party was led, as Sir Geoffrey had expected,
by Major Bridgenorth. At his side was a person in black,
with a silver greyhound on his arm ; and he was followed
by about eight or ten inhabitants of the village of Martindale
Moultrassie, two or three of whom were officers of the peace,
and others were personally known to Sir Geoffrey as favourers
of the subverted government.

As the party rode briskly up, Sir Geoffrey called to them
to halt ; and as they continued advancing, he ordered his
own people to present their pistols and carabines ; and after
assuming that menacing attitude, he repeated, with a voice
of thunder, ' Halt, or we fire ! '

The other party halted accordingly, and Major Bridgenorth advanced, as if to parley.

' Why, how now, neighbour,' said Sir Geoffrey, as if he
had at that moment recognized him for the first time,—
'what makes you ride so sharp this morning ? Are you not
afraid to harm your horse, or spoil your spurs ? '

' Sir Geoffrey,' said the major, ' I have no time for jesting
—I am on the king's affairs.'

' Are you sure it is not upon Old Noll's, neighbour ? You used to hold his the better errand,' said the knight, with a smile which gave occasion to a horse-laugh among his followers.

' Show him your warrant,' said Bridgenorth to the man in black formerly mentioned, who was a pursuivant. Then taking the warrant from the officer, he gave it to Sir Geoffrey —' To this, at least, you will pay regard.'

' The same regard which you would have paid to it a month back or so,' said the knight, tearing the warrant to shreds. ' What a plague do you stare at ? Do you think you have a monopoly of rebellion, and that we have not a right to show a trick of disobedience in our turn ? '

' Make way, Sir Geoffrey Peveril,' said Bridgenorth, ' or you will compel me to do that I may be sorry for. I am in this matter the avenger of the blood of one of the Lord's saints, and I will follow the chase while Heaven grants me an arm to make my way.'

' You shall make no way here, but at your peril,' said Sir Geoffrey ; ' this is my ground—I have been harassed enough for these twenty years by saints, as you call your-selves. I tell you, master, you shall neither violate the security of my house, nor pursue my friends over the grounds, nor tamper, as you have done, amongst my servants, with impunity. I have had you in respect for certain kind doings, which I will not either forget or deny, and you will find it difficult to make me draw a sword or bend a pistol against you ; but offer any hostile movement or presume to ad-vance a foot, and I will make sure of you presently. And for these rascals, who come hither to annoy a noble lady on my bounds, unless you draw them off, I will presently send some of them to the devil before their time.'

' Make room at your proper peril,' said Major Bridge-north ; and he put his right hand on his holster-pistol. Sir Geoffrey closed with him instantly, seized him by the collar, and spurred Black Hastings, checking him at the same time, so that the horse made a courbette, and brought the full weight of his chest against the counter of the other. A ready soldier might, in Bridgenorth's situation, have rid himself of his adversary with a bullet. But Bridgenorth's courage, notwithstanding his having served some time with the Parliament army, was rather of a civil than a military character; and he was inferior to his adversary, not only in strength and horsemanship, but also and especially in the daring and decisive resolution which made Sir Geoffrey thrust himself readily into personal contest. While, therefore, they tugged and grappled together upon terms which bore such little accordance with their long acquaintance and close neighbourhood, it was no wonder that Bridgenorth should be unhorsed with much violence. While Sir Geoffrey sprang from the saddle, the party of Bridgenorth advanced to rescue their leader, and that of the knight to oppose them. Swords were unsheathed, and pistols presented; but Sir Geoffrey, with the voice of a herald, commanded both parties to stand back, and to keep the peace.

The pursuivant took the hint, and easily found a reason for not prosecuting a dangerous duty. 'The warrant,' he said, ' was destroyed. They that did it must be answerable to the council; for his part, he could proceed no further without his commission.'

' Well said, and like a peaceable fellow!' said Sir Geoffrey. ' Let him have refreshment at the castle—his nag is sorely out of condition. Come, neighbour Bridgenorth, get up, man—I trust you have had no hurt in this mad affray? I was loath to lay hand on you, man, till you plucked out your petronel.'

As he spoke thus, he aided the major to rise. The pursuivant, meanwhile, drew aside; and with him the constable and headborough, who were not without some tacit suspicion, that though Peveril was interrupting the direct course of law in this matter, yet he was likely to have his offence considered by favourable judges; and therefore it might be as much for their interest and safety to give way as to oppose him. But the rest of the party, friends of Bridgenorth, and of his principles, kept their ground notwithstanding this defection, and seemed, from their looks, sternly determined to rule their conduct by that of their leader, whatever it might be.

But it was evident that Bridgenorth did not intend to renew the struggle. He shook himself rather roughly free from the hands of Sir Geoffrey Peveril; but it was not to

draw his sword. On the contrary, he mounted his horse
with a sullen and dejected air ; and, making a sign to his
followers, turned back the same road which he had come.
Sir Geoffrey looked after him for some minutes. ' Now,
there goes a man,' said he, ' who would have been a right
honest fellow had he not been a Presbyterian. But there
is no heartiness about them—they can never forgive a fair
fall upon the sod—they bear malice, and that I hate as I
do a black cloak, or a Geneva skull-cap, and a pair of long
ears rising on each side on't, like two chimneys at the
gable ends of a thatched cottage. They are as sly as the
devil to boot ; and, therefore, Lance Outram, take two with
you, and keep after them, that they may not turn our
flank, and get on the track of the countess again after all.'

' I had as soon they should course my lady's white tame
doe,' answered Lance, in the spirit of his calling. He proceeded to execute his master's orders by dogging Major
Bridgenorth at a distance, and observing his course from
such heights as commanded the country. But it was soon
evident that no manœuvre was intended, and that the
major was taking the direct road homeward. When this
was ascertained, Sir Geoffrey dismissed most of his followers ;
and retaining only his own domestics, rode hastily forward
to overtake the countess.

It is only necessary to say further. that he completed his
purpose of escorting the Countess of Derby to Vale-Royal,
without meeting any further hindrance by the way. The
lord of the mansion readily undertook to conduct the high-
minded lady to Liverpool, and the task of seeing her safely
embarked for her son's hereditary dominions, where there
was no doubt of her remaining in personal safety until the
accusation against her for breach of the royal indemnity,
by the execution of Christian, could be brought to some
compromise.

For a length of time this was no easy matter. Clarendon,
then at the head of Charles's administration, considered
her rash action, though dictated by motives which the
human breast must, in some respects, sympathize with, as
calculated to shake the restored tranquillity of England,
by exciting the doubts and jealousies of those who had
to apprehend the consequences of what is called, in our

own time, a *reaction*. At the same time, the high services
of this distinguished family—the merits of the countess
herself—the memory of her gallant husband—and the very
peculiar circumstances of jurisdiction which took the case
out of all common rules, pleaded strongly in her favour ;
and the death of Christian was at length only punished
by the imposition of a heavy fine, amounting, we believe,
to many thousand pounds ; which was levied, with great
difficulty, out of the shattered estates of the young Earl
of Derby.

CHAPTER VIII

My native land, good night !
                                    BYRON.

LADY PEVERIL remained in no small anxiety for several
hours after her husband and the countess had departed
from Martindale Castle ; more especially when she learned
that Major Bridgenorth, concerning whose motions she
made private inquiry, had taken horse with a party, and
was gone to the westward in the same direction with Sir
Geoffrey.

At length her immediate uneasiness in regard to the safety
of her husband and the countess was removed, by the
arrival of Whitaker, with her husband's commendations,
and an account of the scuffle betwixt himself and Major
Bridgenorth.

Lady Peveril shuddered to see how nearly they had
approached to renewal of the scenes of civil discord ; and
while she was thankful to Heaven for her husband's immediate preservation, she could not help feeling both regret
and apprehension for the consequences of his quarrel with
Major Bridgenorth. They had now lost an old friend, who
had showed himself such under those circumstances of
adversity by which friendship is most severely tried ;
and she could not disguise from herself, that Bridgenorth,
thus irritated, might be a troublesome, if not a dangerous
enemy. His rights as a creditor he had hitherto used
with gentleness ; but if he should employ rigour, Lady

Peveril, whose attention to domestic economy had made her much better acquainted with her husband's affairs than he was himself, foresaw considerable inconvenience from the measures which the law put in his power. She comforted herself with the recollection, however, that she had still a strong hold on Bridgenorth, through his paternal affection, and from the fixed opinion which he had hitherto manifested, that his daughter's health could only flourish while under her charge. But any expectations of reconciliation which Lady Peveril might probably have founded on this circumstance, were frustrated by an incident which took place in the course of the following morning.

The governante, Mistress Deborah, who has been already mentioned, went forth, as usual, with the children, to take their morning exercise in the park, attended by Rachael, a girl who acted occasionally as her assistant in attending upon them. But not as usual did she return. It was near the hour of breakfast, when Ellesmere, with an unwonted degree of primness in her mouth and manner, came to acquaint her lady that Mistress Deborah had not thought proper to come back from the park, though the breakfast hour approached so near.

'She will come, then, presently,' said Lady Peveril, with indifference.

Ellesmere gave a short and doubtful cough, and then proceeded to say, that Rachael had been sent home with little Master Julian, and that Mistress Deborah had been pleased to say, she would walk on with Miss Bridgenorth as far as Moultrassie Holt; which was a point at which the property of the major, as matters now stood, bounded that of Sir Geoffrey Peveril.

'Is the wench turned silly,' exclaimed the lady, something angrily, 'that she does not obey my orders, and return at regular hours ? '

'She may be turning silly,' said Ellesmere mysteriously; 'or she may be turning too sly; and I think it were as well your ladyship looked to it.'

'Looked to what, Ellesmere ? ' said the lady impatiently. 'You are strangely oracular this morning. If you know anything to the prejudice of this young woman, I pray you speak it out.'

' I prejudice ! ' said Ellesmere ; ' I scorn to prejudice man,
woman, or child, in the way of a fellow servant ; only I wish
your ladyship to look about you, and use your own eyes—
that is all.'

' You bid me use my own eyes, Ellesmere ; but I suspect,'
answered the lady, ' you would be better pleased were I
contented to see through your spectacles. I charge you—
and you know I will be obeyed—I charge you to tell me
what you know or suspect about this girl, Deborah Debbitch.'

' I see through spectacles ! ' exclaimed the indignant
abigail ; ' your ladyship will pardon me in that, for I never
use them, unless a pair that belonged to my poor mother,
which I put on when your ladyship wants your pinners
curiously wrought. No woman above sixteen ever did
white-seam without barnacles. And then as to suspecting,
I suspect nothing ; for as your ladyship hath taken Mistress
Deborah Debbitch from under my hand, to be sure it is
neither bread nor butter of mine. Only ' (here she began
to speak with her lips shut, so as scarce to permit a sound
to issue, and mincing her words as if she pinched off the ends
of them before she suffered them to escape),—' only, madam,
if Mistress Deborah goes so often of a morning to Moultrassie
Holt, why, I should not be surprised if she should never
find the way back again.'

' Once more, what do you mean, Ellesmere ? You were
wont to have some sense—let me know distinctly what the
matter is.'

' Only, madam,' pursued the abigail, ' that since Bridgenorth came back from Chesterfield, and saw you at the
castle-hall, Mistress Deborah has been pleased to carry
the children every morning to that place ; and it has so
happened that she has often met the major, as they call
him, there in his walks ; for he can walk about now like
other folks ; and I warrant you she hath not been the
worse of the meeting—one way at least, for she hath
bought a new hood might serve yourself, madam ; but
whether she hath had anything in hand besides a piece of
money, no doubt your ladyship is best judge.'

Lady Peveril, who readily adopted the more good-natured
construction of the governante's motives, could not help

laughing at the idea of a man of Bridgenorth's precise appearance, strict principles, and reserved habits, being suspected of a design of gallantry ; and readily concluded that Mistress Deborah had found her advantage in gratifying his parental affection by a frequent sight of his daughter during the few days which intervened betwixt his first seeing little Alice at the castle, and the events which had followed. But she was somewhat surprised, when, an hour after the usual breakfast hour, during which neither the child nor Mistress Deborah appeared, Major Bridgenorth's only man-servant arrived at the castle on horseback, dressed as for a journey ; and having delivered a letter addressed to herself, and another to Mistress Ellesmere, rode away without waiting any answer.

There would have been nothing remarkable in this, had any other person been concerned ; but Major Bridgenorth was so very quiet and orderly in all his proceedings—so little liable to act hastily or by impulse, that the least appearance of bustle where he was concerned excited surprise and curiosity.

Lady Peveril broke her letter hastily open, and found that it contained the following lines :—

' For the hands of the Honourable and Honoured
Lady Peveril—These :

' MADAM—Please it your ladyship, I write more to excuse myself to your ladyship, than to accuse either you or others, in respect that I am sensible it becomes our frail nature better to confess our own imperfections, than to complain of those of others. Neither do I mean to speak of past times, particularly in respect of your worthy ladyship, being sensible that if I have served you in that period when our Israel might be called triumphant, you have more than requited me, in giving to my arms a child, redeemed, as it were, from the vale of the shadow of death. And therefore, as I heartily forgive to your ladyship the unkind and violent measure which you dealt to me at our last meeting (seeing that the woman who was the cause of strife is accounted one of your kindred people), I do entreat you, in like manner, to pardon my enticing away from your service the young woman called Deborah Debbitch, whose nurture, instructed as she hath been under your ladyship's direction, is, it may be, indispensable to the health of my dearest child. I had purposed, madam, with your gracious permission, that Alice should have remained at Martindale Castle, under your kind charge, until she could so far discern betwixt good and evil that it should be matter of conscience to teach her the way in which she should go. For it is not unknown to your ladyship, and in no way do I speak it reproachfully, but rather sorrowfully, that a person so excellently gifted as yourself—I mean touching natural qualities—has not yet received that true light, which is a lamp to the paths, but are contented to stumble in darkness, and among the graves of dead men. It has been my prayer in the watches of the night, that your ladyship should cease from the doctrine which causeth to err ; but I grieve to say, that our candlestick being about to be removed, the land will most likely be involved in deeper darkness than ever ; and the return of the king, to which I and many looked forward as a manifestation of divine favour, seems to prove little else than a permitted triumph of the Prince of the Air, who setteth about to restore his Vanity Fair of bishops, deans, and such-like, extruding the peaceful ministers of the word, whose labours have proved faithful to many hungry souls. So, hearing from a sure hand that commission has gone forth to restore these dumb dogs, the followers of Laud and of Williams, who were cast forth by the late Parliament, and that an Act of Conformity, or rather of deformity, of worship, was to be expected, it is my purpose to flee from the wrath to come, and to seek some corner where I may dwell in peace, and enjoy liberty of conscience. For who would abide in the sanctuary, after the carved work thereof is broken down, and when it hath been made a place for owls, and satyrs of the wilderness ? And herein I blame myself, madam, that I went in the singleness of my heart too readily into that carousing in the house of feasting, wherein my love of union, and my desire to show respect to your ladyship, were made a snare to me. But I trust it will be an atonement, that I am now about to absent myself from the place of my birth, and the house of my fathers, as well as from the place which holdeth the dust of those pledges of my affection. I have also to remember, that in this land my honour (after the worldly estimation) hath been abated, and my utility circumscribed, by your husband, Sir Geoffrey Peveril ; and that without any chance of my obtaining reparation at his hand, whereby I may say the hand of a kinsman was lifted up against my credit and my life. These things are bitter to the taste of the old Adam ; wherefore, to prevent further bickerings, and, it may be, bloodshed, it is better that I leave this land for a time. The affairs which remain to be settled between Sir Geoffrey and myself, I shall place in the hand of the righteous Master Joachim Win-the-Fight, an attorney in Chesterfield, who will arrange them with such attention to Sir Geoffrey's convenience, as justice, and the due exercise of the law, will permit ; for, as I trust I shall have grace to resist the temptation to make the weapons of carnal warfare the instruments of my revenge, so I scorn to effect it through the means of Mammon. Wishing, madam, that the Lord may grant you every blessing, and, in especial, that which is over all others, namely, the true knowledge of His way,

' I remain,

' Your devoted servant to command,

' RALPH BRIDGENORTH.

' *Written at Moultrassie Hall, this tenth*
day of July, 1660.'

So soon as Lady Peveril had perused this long and singular homily, in which it seemed to her that her neighbour showed more spirit of religious fanaticism than she could have supposed him possessed of, she looked up and beheld Ellesmere,—with a countenance in which mortification, and an affected air of contempt, seemed to struggle together,—who, tired with watching the expression of her mistress's countenance, applied for confirmation of her suspicions in plain terms.

'I suppose, madam,' said the waiting-woman, ' the fanatic fool intends to marry the wench ? They say he goes to shift the country. Truly it 's time, indeed ; for, besides that the whole neighbourhood would laugh him to scorn, I should not be surprised if Lance Outram, the keeper, gave him a buck's head to bear ; for that is all in the way of his office.'

'There is no great occasion for your spite at present, Ellesmere,' replied her lady. 'My letter says nothing of marriage ; but it would appear that Master Bridgenorth, being to leave this country, has engaged Deborah to take care of his child ; and I am sure I am heartily glad of it, for the infant's sake.'

'And I am glad of it for my own,' said Ellesmere ; 'and, indeed, for the sake of the whole house. And your ladyship thinks she is not like to be married to him ? Troth, I could never see how he should be such an idiot ; but perhaps she is going to do worse, for she speaks here of coming to high preferment, and that scarce comes by honest servitude nowadays ; then she writes me about sending her things, as if I were mistress of the wardrobe to her ladyship—aye, and recommends Master Julian to the care of my age and experience, forsooth, as if she needed to recommend the dear little jewel to me ; and then, to speak of my age— But I will bundle away her rags to the Hall, with a witness !'

'Do it with all civility,' said the lady, 'and let Whitaker send her the wages for which she has served, and a broad-piece over and above ; for though a light-headed young woman, she was kind to the children.'

'I know who is kind to their servants, madam, and would spoil the best ever pinned a gown.'

'I spoiled a good one, Ellesmere, when I spoiled thee,' said the lady ; 'but tell Mrs. Deborah to kiss the little Alice for me, and to offer my good wishes to Major Bridgenorth for his temporal and future happiness.'

She permitted no observation or reply, but dismissed her attendant, without entering into further particulars.

When Ellesmere had withdrawn, Lady Peveril began to reflect, with much feeling of compassion, on the letter of Major Bridgenorth ; a person in whom there were certainly many excellent qualities, but whom a series of domestic misfortunes, and the increasing gloom of a sincere, yet stern feeling of devotion, rendered lonely and unhappy ; and she had more than one anxious thought for the happiness of the little Alice, brought up, as she was likely to be, under such a father. Still the removal of Bridgenorth was, on the whole, a desirable event ; for while he remained at the Hall, it was but too likely that some accidental collision with Sir Geoffrey might give rise to a rencontre betwixt them, more fatal than the last had been.

In the meanwhile, she could not help expressing to Doctor Dummerar her surprise and sorrow, that all which she had done and attempted, to establish peace and unanimity betwixt the contending factions, had been perversely fated to turn out the very reverse of what she had aimed at.

' But for my unhappy invitation,' she said, ' Bridgenorth would not have been at the castle on the morning which succeeded the feast, would not have seen the countess, and would not have incurred the resentment and opposition of my husband. And but for the king's return, an event which was so anxiously expected as the termination of all our calamities, neither the noble lady nor ourselves had been engaged in this new path of difficulty and danger.'

' Honoured madam,' said Doctor Dummerar, ' were the affairs of this world to be guided implicitly by human wisdom, or were they uniformly to fall out according to the conjectures of human foresight, events would no longer be under the domination of that time and chance which happen unto all men, since we should, in the one case, work out our own purposes to a certainty by our own skill, and in the other, regulate our conduct according to the views of unerring prescience. But man is, while in this vale of tears, like an uninstructed bowler, so to speak, who thinks to attain the jack by delivering his bowl straight forward upon it, being ignorant that there is a concealed bias within the spheroid, which will make it, in all probability, swerve away and lose the cast.'

Having spoken this with a sententious air, the doctor took his shovel-shaped hat, and went down to the castle green, to conclude a match of bowls with Whitaker, which had probably suggested this notable illustration of the uncertain course of human events.

Two days afterwards, Sir Geoffrey arrived. He had waited at Vale-Royal till he heard of the countess's being safely embarked for Man, and then had posted homeward to his

castle and Dame Margaret. On his way, he learned
from some of his attendants the mode in which his lady
had conducted the entertainment which she had given to
the neighbourhood at his order ; and notwithstanding the
great deference he usually showed in cases where Lady
Peveril was concerned, he heard of her liberality towards
the Presbyterian party with great indignation.

'I could have admitted Bridgenorth,' he said, 'for he
always bore him in neighbourly and kindly fashion till this
last career—I could have endured him, so he would have
drunk the king's health, like a true man—but to bring that
snuffling scoundrel Solsgrace, with all his beggarly, long-
eared congregation, to hold a conventicle in my father's
house—to let them domineer it as they listed—why, I
would not have permitted them such liberty, when they
held their head the highest ! They never, in the worst of
times, found any way into Martindale Castle but what
Noll's cannon made for them ; and, that they should come
and cant there, when good King Charles is returned—By
my hand, Dame Margaret shall hear of it !'

But, notwithstanding these ireful resolutions, resentment
altogether subsided in the honest knight's breast, when he
saw the fair features of his lady lightened with affectionate
joy at his return in safety. As he took her in his arms
and kissed her, he forgave her ere he mentioned her
offence.

'Thou hast played the knave with me, Meg,' he said,
shaking his head, and smiling at the same time, 'and
thou knowest in what manner : but I think thou art true
church-woman, and didst only act from some silly womanish
fancy of keeping fair with these roguish Roundheads. But
let me have no more of this. I had rather Martindale
Castle were again rent by their bullets, than receive any
of the knaves in the way of friendship—I always except
Ralph Bridgenorth of the Hall, if he should come to his
senses again.'

Lady Peveril was here under the necessity of explaining
what she had heard of Master Bridgenorth—the disappearance of the governante with his daughter, and placed
Bridgenorth's letter in his hand. Sir Geoffrey shook his
head at first, and then laughed extremely, at the idea

that there was some little love-intrigue between Bridge-north and Mistress Deborah.

' It is the true end of a dissenter,' he said, ' to marry his own maidservant, or some other person's. Deborah is a good likely wench, and on the merrier side of thirty, as I should think.'

' Nay, nay,' said the Lady Peveril, ' you are as un-charitable as Ellesmere—I believe it but to be affection to his child.'

' Pshaw! pshaw!' answered the knight, ' women are eternally thinking of children; but among men, dame, many one caresses the infant that he may kiss the child's maid; and where 's the wonder or the harm either, if Bridgenorth should marry the wench? Her father is a substantial yeoman; his family has had the same farm since Bosworth Field—as good a pedigree as that of the great-grandson of a Chesterfield brewer, I trow. But let us hear what he says for himself—I shall spell it out if there is any roguery in the letter about love and liking, though it might escape your innocence, Dame Margaret.'

The Knight of the Peak began to peruse the letter accordingly, but was much embarrassed by the peculiar language in which it was couched. ' What he means by moving of candlesticks, and breaking down of carved work in the church, I cannot guess; unless he means to bring back the large silver candlesticks which my grandsire gave to be placed on the altar at Martindale-Moultrassie; and which his crop-eared friends, like sacrilegious villains as they are, stole and melted down. And in like manner, the only breaking I know of, was when they pulled down the rails of the communion table (for which some of their fingers are hot enough by this time), and when the brass orna-ments were torn down from the Peveril monuments; and that was breaking and removing with a vengeance. How-ever, dame, the upshot is, that poor Bridgenorth is going to leave the neighbourhood. I am truly sorry for it, though I never saw him oftener than once a day, and never spoke to him above two words. But I see how it is—that little shake by the shoulder sticks in his stomach; and yet, Meg, I did but lift him out of the saddle as I might have lifted thee into it, Margaret—I was careful not to hurt him ; and I did not think him so tender in point of honour as to mind such a thing much ; but I see plainly where his sore lies ; and I warrant you I will manage that he stays at the Hall, and that you get back Julian's little companion. Faith, I am sorry myself at the thought of losing the baby, and of having to choose another ride when it is not hunting weather, than round by the Hall, with a word at the window.'

' I should be very glad, Sir Geoffrey,' said Lady Peveril, ' that you could come to a reconciliation with this worthy man, for such I must hold Master Bridgenorth to be.'

' But for his dissenting principles, as good a neighbour as ever lived,' said Sir Geoffrey.

' But I scarce see,' continued the lady, ' any possibility of bringing about a conclusion so desirable.'

' Tush, dame,' answered the knight, ' thou knowest little of such matters. I know the foot he halts upon, and you shall see him go as sound as ever.'

Lady Peveril had, from her sincere affection and sound sense, as good a right to claim the full confidence of her husband as any woman in Derbyshire ; and, upon this occasion, to confess the truth, she had more anxiety to know his purpose than her sense of their mutual and separate duties permitted her in general to entertain. She could not imagine what mode of reconciliation with his neighbour, Sir Geoffrey (no very acute judge of mankind or their peculiarities) could have devised, which might not be disclosed to her; and she felt some secret anxiety lest the means resorted to might be so ill chosen as to render the breach rather wider. But Sir Geoffrey would give no opening for further inquiry. He had been long enough colonel of a regiment abroad, to value himself on the right of absolute command at home ; and to all the hints which his lady's ingenuity could devise and throw out, he only answered, ' Patience, Dame Margaret, patience. This is no case for thy handling. Thou shalt know enough on't by and by, dame. Go, look to Julian. Will the boy never have done crying for lack of that little sprout of a Roundhead ? But we will have little Alice back with us in two or three days, and all will be well again.'

As the good knight spoke these words, a post winded his

horn in the court, and a large packet was brought in, addressed to the worshipful Sir Geoffrey Peveril, Justice of the Peace, and so forth; for he had been placed in authority as soon as the king's restoration was put upon a settled basis. Upon opening the packet, which he did with no small feeling of importance, he found that it contained the warrant which he had solicited for replacing Doctor Dummerar in the parish, from which he had been forcibly ejected during the usurpation.[n]

Few incidents could have given more delight to Sir Geoffrey. He could forgive a stout able-bodied sectary or nonconformist, who enforced his doctrines in the field by downright blows on the casques and cuirasses of himself and other Cavaliers. But he remembered, with most vindictive accuracy, the triumphant entrance of Hugh Peters through the breach of his castle; and for his sake, without nicely distinguishing betwixt sects or their teachers, he held all who mounted a pulpit without warrant from the Church of England—perhaps he might also in private except that of Rome—to be disturbers of the public tranquillity, seducers of the congregation from their lawful preachers, instigators of the late Civil War, and men well disposed to risk the fate of a new one.

Then, on the other hand, besides gratifying his dislike to Solsgrace, he saw much satisfaction in the task of replacing his old friend and associate in sport and in danger, the worthy Doctor Dummerar, in his legitimate rights, and in the ease and comforts of his vicarage. He communicated the contents of the packet, with great triumph, to the lady, who now perceived the sense of the mysterious paragraph in Major Bridgenorth's letter, concerning the removal of the candlestick, and the extinction of light and doctrine in the land. She pointed this out to Sir Geoffrey, and endeavoured to persuade him that a door was now opened to reconciliation with his neighbour, by executing the commission which he had received in an easy and moderate manner, after due delay, and with all respect to the feelings both of Solsgrace and his congregation, which circumstances admitted of. This, the lady argued, would be doing no injury whatever to Doctor Dummerar; nay, might be the means of reconciling many to his ministry, who might otherwise be disgusted with it for ever, by the premature expulsion of a favourite preacher.

There was much wisdom, as well as moderation, in this advice ; and, at another time, Sir Geoffrey would have had sense enough to have adopted it. But who can act composedly or prudently in the hour of triumph ? The ejection of Mr. Solsgrace was so hastily executed as to give it some appearance of persecution ; though, more justly considered, it was the restoring of his predecessor to his legal rights. Solsgrace himself seemed to be desirous to make his sufferings as manifest as possible. He held out to the last ; and on the Sabbath after he had received intimation of his ejection, attempted to make his way to the pulpit, as usual, supported by Master Bridgenorth's attorney, Win-the-Fight, and a few zealous followers.

Just as their party came into the churchyard on the one side, Dr. Dummerar, dressed in full pontificals, in a sort of triumphal procession, accompanied by Peveril of the Peak, Sir Jasper Cranbourne, and other Cavaliers of distinction, entered at the other.

To prevent an actual struggle in the church, the parish officers were sent to prevent the further approach of the Presbyterian minister ; which was effected without further damage than a broken head, inflicted by Roger Raine, the drunken innkeeper of the Peveril Arms, upon the Presbyterian attorney of Chesterfield.

Unsubdued in spirit, though compelled to retreat by superior force, the undaunted Mr. Solsgrace retired to the vicarage ; where under some legal pretext which had been started by Mr. Win-the-Fight (in that day unaptly named), he attempted to maintain himself—bolted gates—barred windows—and, as report said (though falsely), made provision of firearms to resist the officers. A scene of clamour and scandal accordingly took place, which being reported to Sir Geoffrey, he came in person, with some of his attendants carrying arms—forced the outer gate and inner doors of the house ; and proceeding to the study, found no other garrison save the Presbyterian parson, with the attorney, who gave up possession of the premises, after making protestation against the violence that had been used.

The rabble of the village being by this time all in motion,

Sir Geoffrey, both in prudence and good-nature, saw the propriety of escorting his prisoners, for so they might be termed, safely through the tumult ; and accordingly conveyed them in person, through much noise and clamour, as far as the avenue of Moultrassie Hall, which they chose for the place of their retreat.

But the absence of Sir Geoffrey gave the rein to some disorders, which, if present, he would assuredly have restrained. Some of the minister's books were torn and flung about as treasonable and seditious trash, by the zealous parish-officers or their assistants. A quantity of his ale was drunk up in healths to the king, and Peveril of the Peak. And, finally, the boys, who bore the ex-parson no good will for his tyrannical interference with their games at skittles, football, and so forth, and, moreover, remembered the unmerciful length of his sermons, dressed up an effigy with his Geneva gown and band, and his steeple-crowned hat, which they paraded through the village, and burnt on the spot whilom occupied by a stately Maypole, which Solsgrace had formerly hewed down with his own reverend hands.

Sir Geoffrey was vexed at all this, and sent to Mr. Solsgrace, offering satisfaction for the goods which he had lost ; but the Calvinistical divine replied, ' From a thread to a shoe-latchet, I will not take anything that is thine. Let the shame of the work of thy hands abide with thee.'

Considerable scandal, indeed, arose against Sir Geoffrey Peveril as having proceeded with indecent severity and haste upon this occasion ; and rumour took care to make the usual additions to the reality. It was currently reported, that the desperate Cavalier, Peveril of the Peak, had fallen on a Presbyterian congregation, while engaged in the peaceable exercise of religion, with a band of armed men— had slain some, desperately wounded many more, and finally pursued the preacher to his vicarage, which he burnt to the ground. Some alleged the clergyman had perished in the flames ; and the most mitigated report bore, that he had only been able to escape by disposing his gown, cap, and band, near a window, in such a manner as to deceive them with the idea of his person being still surrounded by flames, while he himself fled by the back part of the house.

And although few people believed in the extent of the atrocities thus imputed to our honest Cavalier, yet still enough of obloquy attached to him to infer very serious consequences, as the reader will learn at a future period of our history.

CHAPTER IX

Bessus. 'Tis a challenge, sir, is it not ?
Gentleman. 'Tis an inviting to the field.
King and No King.

FOR a day or two after this forcible expulsion from the vicarage, Mr. Solsgrace continued his residence at Moultrassie Hall, where the natural melancholy attendant on his situation added to the gloom of the owner of the mansion. In the morning, the ejected divine made excursions to different families in the neighbourhood, to whom his ministry had been acceptable in the days of his prosperity, and from whose grateful recollections of that period he now found sympathy and consolation. He did not require to be condoled with, because he was deprived of an easy and competent maintenance, and thrust out upon the common of life, after he had reason to suppose he would be no longer liable to such mutations of fortune. The piety of Mr. Solsgrace was sincere ; and if he had many of the uncharitable prejudices against other sects, which polemical controversy had generated, and the Civil War brought to a head, he had also that deep sense of duty, by which enthusiasm is so often dignified, and held his very life little, if called upon to lay it down in attestation of the doctrines in which he believed. But he was soon to prepare for leaving the district which Heaven, he conceived, had assigned to him as his corner of the vineyard ; he was to abandon his flock to the wolf—was to forsake those with whom he had held sweet counsel in religious communion—was to leave the recently converted to relapse into false doctrines, and forsake the wavering, whom his continued cares might have directed into the right path,—these were of themselves deep causes of sorrow, and were aggravated, doubtless, by those natural feelings with which all men, especially those whose duties or habits have confined them to a limited circle, regard the separation from wonted scenes, and their accustomed haunts of solitary musing, or social intercourse.

There was, indeed, a plan of placing Mr. Solsgrace at the head of a nonconforming congregation in his present parish, which his followers would have readily consented to endow with a sufficient revenue. But although the act for universal conformity was not yet passed, such a measure was understood to be impending, and there existed a general opinion among the Presbyterians, that in no hands was it likely to be more strictly enforced, than in those of Peveril of the Peak. Solsgrace himself considered not only his personal danger as being considerable,—for, assuming perhaps more consequence than was actually attached to him or his productions, he conceived the honest knight to be his mortal and determined enemy—but he also conceived, that he should serve the cause of his church by absenting himself from Derbyshire.

' Less known pastors,' he said, ' though perhaps more worthy of the name, may be permitted to assemble the scattered flocks in caverns or in secret wilds, and to them shall the gleaning of the grapes of Ephraim be better than the vintage of Abiezer. But I, that have so often carried the banner forth against the mighty—I, whose tongue hath testified, morning and evening, like the watchman upon the tower, against Popery, Prelacy, and the tyrant of the Peak—for me to abide here, were but to bring the sword of bloody vengeance amongst you, that the shepherd might be smitten, and the sheep scattered. The shedders of blood have already assailed me, even within that ground which they themselves call consecrated ; and yourselves have seen the scalp of the righteous broken, as he defended my cause. Therefore, I will put on my sandals, and gird my loins, and depart to a far country, and there do as my duty shall call upon me, whether it be to act or to suffer—to bear testimony at the stake or in the pulpit.'

Such were the sentiments which Mr. Solsgrace expressed to his desponding friends, and which he expatiated upon at more length with Major Bridgenorth ; not failing, with friendly zeal, to rebuke the haste which the latter had shown to thrust out the hand of fellowship to the Amalekite woman, whereby he reminded him, 'He had been rendered her slave and bondsman for a season, like Samson, betrayed by Delilah, and might have remained longer in the house of Dagon, had not Heaven pointed to him a way out of the snare. Also, it sprang originally from the major's going up to feast in the high place of Baal, that he who was the champion of the truth was stricken down, and put to shame by the enemy, even in the presence of the host.'

These objurgations seeming to give some offence to Major Bridgenorth, who liked, no better than any other man, to hear of his own mishaps, and at the same time to have them imputed to his own misconduct, the worthy divine proceeded to take shame to himself for his own sinful compliance in that matter ; for to the vengeance justly due for that unhappy dinner at Martindale Castle (which was, he said, a crying of peace when there was no peace, and a dwelling in the tents of sin), he imputed his ejection from his living, with the destruction of some of his most pithy and highly prized volumes of divinity, with the loss of his cap, gown, and band, and a double hogshead of choice Derby ale.

The mind of Major Bridgenorth was strongly tinged with devotional feeling, which his late misfortunes had rendered more deep and solemn ; and it is therefore no wonder, that, when he heard these arguments urged again and again, by a pastor whom he so much respected, and who was now a confessor in the cause of their joint faith, he began to look back with disapproval on his own conduct, and to suspect that he had permitted himself to be seduced by gratitude towards Lady Peveril, and by her special arguments in favour of a mutual and tolerating liberality of sentiments, into an action which had a tendency to compromise his religious and political principles.

One morning, as Major Bridgenorth had wearied himself with several details respecting the arrangement of his affairs, he was reposing in the leathern easy chair, beside the latticed window, a posture which, by natural associa-tion, recalled to him the memory of former times, and the feelings with which he was wont to expect the recurring visit of Sir Geoffrey, who brought him news of his child's welfare,—' Surely,' he said, thinking, as it were, aloud, ' there was no sin in the kindness with which I then regarded that man.'

Solsgrace, who was in the apartment, and guessed what passed through his friend's mind, acquainted as he was with every point of his history, replied—' When God caused Elijah to be fed by ravens, while hiding at the brook Cherith, we hear not of his fondling the unclean birds, whom, contrary to their ravening nature, a miracle compelled to minister to him.'

' It may be so,' answered Bridgenorth, ' yet the flap of their wings must have been gracious in the ear of the famished prophet, like the tread of his horse in mine. The ravens, doubtless, resumed their nature when the season was passed, and even so it has fared with him. Hark ! ' he exclaimed, starting, ' I hear his horse's hoof-tramp even now.'

It was seldom that the echoes of that silent house and courtyard were awakened by the trampling of horses, but such was now the case.

Both Bridgenorth and Solsgrace were surprised at the sound, and even disposed to anticipate some further oppression on the part of government, when the major's old servant introduced, with little ceremony (for his manners were nearly as plain as his master's), a tall gentleman, on the farther side of middle life, whose vest and cloak, long hair, slouched hat and drooping feather, announced him as a Cavalier. He bowed formally, but courteously, to both gentlemen, and said, that he was ' Sir Jasper Cranbourne, charged with an especial message to Master Ralph Bridgenorth of Moultrassie Hall, by his honourable friend Sir Geoffrey Peveril of the Peak, and that he requested to know whether Master Bridgenorth would be pleased to receive his acquittal of commission here or elsewhere.'

' Anything which Sir Geoffrey Peveril can have to say to me,' said Major Bridgenorth, ' may be told instantly, and before my friend, from whom I have no secrets.'

' The presence of any other friend were, instead of being objectionable, the thing in the world most to be desired,' said Sir Jasper, after a moment's hesitation, and looking at Mr. Solsgrace ; ' but this gentleman seems to be a sort of clergyman.'

'I am not conscious of any secrets,' answered Bridge-north, 'nor do I desire to have any, in which a clergyman is an unfitting confidant.'

'At your pleasure,' replied Sir Jasper. 'The confidence, for aught I know, may be well enough chosen, for your divines (always under your favour) have proved no enemies to such matters as I am to treat with you upon.'

'Proceed, sir,' answered Mr. Bridgenorth gravely ; 'and I pray you to be seated, unless it is rather your pleasure to stand.'

'I must, in the first place, deliver myself of my small commission,' answered Sir Jasper, drawing himself up ; 'and it will be after I have seen the reception thereof, that I shall know whether I am, or am not, to sit down at Moultrassie Hall. Sir Geoffrey Peveril, Master Bridgenorth, hath carefully considered with himself the unhappy circum-stances which at present separate you as neighbours. And he remembers many passages in former times—I speak his very words—which incline him to do all that can possibly consist with his honour, to wipe out unkindness between you ; and for this desirable object, he is willing to con-descend in a degree, which, as you could not have expected, it will no doubt give you great pleasure to learn.'

'Allow me to say, Sir Jasper,' said Bridgenorth, 'that this is unnecessary. I have made no complaints of Sir Geoffrey —I have required no submission from him—I am about to leave this country ; and what affairs we may have together, can be as well settled by others as by ourselves.'

'In a word,' said the divine, 'the worthy Major Bridge-north hath had enough of trafficking with the ungodly, and will no longer, on any terms, consort with them.'

'Gentlemen both,' said Sir Jasper, with imperturbable politeness, bowing, 'you greatly mistake the tenor of my commission, which you will do as well to hear out, before making any reply to it. I think, Master Bridgenorth, you cannot but remember your letter to the Lady Peveril, of which I have here a rough copy, in which you complain of the hard measure which you have received at Sir Geoffrey's hand, and in particular, when he pulled you from your horse at or near Hartley-nick. Now, Sir Geoffrey thinks so well of you as to believe that, were it not for the wide difference betwixt his descent and rank and your own, you would have sought to bring this matter to a gentlemanlike arbitrament, as the only mode whereby your stain may be honourably wiped away. Wherefore, in this slight note, he gives you, in his generosity, the offer of what you, in your modesty (for to nothing else does he impute your acquiescence), have declined to demand of him. And withal, I bring you the measure of his weapon; and when you have accepted the cartel which I now offer you, I shall be ready to settle the time, place, and other circumstances of your meeting.'

' And I,' said Solsgrace, with a solemn voice, ' should the Author of Evil tempt my friend to accept of so bloodthirsty a proposal, would be the first to pronounce against him sentence of the greater excommunication.'

' It is not you whom I address, reverend sir,' replied the envoy ; ' your interest, not unnaturally, may determine you to be more anxious about your patron's life than about his honour. I must know, from himself, to which *he* is disposed to give the preference.'

So saying, and with a graceful bow, he again tendered the challenge to Major Bridgenorth. There was obviously a struggle in that gentleman's bosom, between the suggestions of human honour and those of religious principle ; but the latter prevailed. He calmly waved receiving the paper which Sir Jasper offered to him, and spoke to the following purpose :—' It may not be known to you, Sir Jasper, that since the general pouring out of Christian light upon this kingdom, many solid men have been led to doubt whether the shedding human blood by the hand of a fellow creature be in *any* respect justifiable. And although this rule appears to me to be scarcely applicable to our state in this stage of trial, seeing that such non-resistance, if general, would surrender our civil and religious rights into the hands of whatsoever daring tyrants might usurp the same ; yet I am, and have been, inclined to limit the use of carnal arms to the case of necessary self-defence, whether such regards our own person, or the protection of our country against invasion ; or of our rights of property, and the freedom of our laws and of our conscience, against usurping power. And as I have never shown myself unwilling to draw my sword in any of the latter causes, so you shall excuse my suffering it now to remain in the scabbard, when, having sustained a grievous injury, the man who inflicted it summons me to combat, either upon an idle punctilio, or, as is more likely, in mere bravado.'

' I have heard you with patience,' said Sir Jasper ; ' and

THE CHALLENGE

now, Master Bridgenorth, take it not amiss, if I beseech you to bethink yourself better on this matter. I vow to Heaven, sir, that your honour lies a-bleeding ; and that in condescending to afford you this fair meeting, and thereby giving you some chance to stop its wounds, Sir Geoffrey has been moved by a tender sense of your condition, and an earnest wish to redeem your dishonour. And it will be but the

crossing of your blade with his honoured sword for the
space of some few minutes, and you will either live or die
a noble and honoured gentleman. Besides, that the knight's
exquisite skill of fence may enable him, as his good nature
will incline him, to disarm you with some flesh-wound, little
to the damage of your person, and greatly to the benefit of
your reputation.'

' The tender mercies of the wicked,' said Master Solsgrace,
emphatically, by way of commenting on this speech, which
Sir Jasper had uttered very pathetically, ' are cruel.'

' I pray to have no further interruption from your
reverence,' said Sir Jasper ; ' especially as I think this affair
very little concerns you ; and I entreat that you permit
me to discharge myself regularly of my commission from
my worthy friend.'

So saying, he took his sheathed rapier from his belt, and
passing the point through the silk thread which secured
the letter, he once more, and literally at sword-point, gracefully tendered it to Major Bridgenorth, who again waved
it aside, though colouring deeply at the same time, as if he
was putting a marked constraint upon himself—drew back,
and made Sir Jasper Cranbourne a deep bow.

' Since it is to be thus,' said Sir Jasper, ' I must myself
do violence to the seal of Sir Geoffrey's letter, and read it
to you, that I may fully acquit myself of the charge intrusted
to me, and make you, Master Bridgenorth, equally aware
of the generous intentions of Sir Geoffrey on your behalf.'

' If,' said Major Bridgenorth, ' the contents of the letter
be to no other purpose than you have intimated, methinks
further ceremony is unnecessary on this occasion, as I have
already taken my course.'

' Nevertheless,' said Sir Jasper, breaking open the letter,
' it is fitting that I read to you the letter of my worshipful
friend.' And he read accordingly as follows :—

' *For the worthy hands of Ralph Bridgenorth, Esquire, of
Moultrassie Hall—These :*

' By the honoured conveyance of the Worshipful Sir Jasper
Cranbourne, Knight, of Long Mallington.

' MASTER BRIDGENORTH,

' We have been given to understand by your letter to our

loving wife, Dame Margaret Peveril, that you hold hard
construction of certain passages betwixt you and I, of a late
date, as if your honour should have been, in some sort,
prejudiced by what then took place. And although you
have not thought it fit to have direct recourse to me, to
request such satisfaction as is due from one gentleman of
condition to another, yet I am fully minded that this pro-
ceeds only from modesty, arising out of the distinction of
our degree, and from no lack of that courage which you
have heretofore displayed, I would I could say in a good
cause. Wherefore I am purposed to give you, by my friend
Sir Jasper Cranbourne, a meeting, for the sake of doing
that which doubtless you entirely long for. Sir Jasper will
deliver you the length of my weapon, and appoint circumstances and an hour for our meeting ; which, whether early
or late—on foot or horseback—with rapier or backsword—
I refer to yourself, with all the other privileges of a challenged person ; only desiring, that if you decline to match
my weapon, you will send me forthwith the length and
breadth of your own. And nothing doubting that the issue
of this meeting must needs be to end, in one way or other,
all unkindness betwixt two near neighbours,

' I remain,

' Your humble servant to command,

' GEOFFREY PEVERIL OF THE PEAK.

' Given from my poor house of Martindale Castle, this
same —— of ——, sixteen hundred and sixty.'

' Bear back my respects to Sir Geoffrey Peveril,' said
Major Bridgenorth. ' According to his light, his meaning
may be fair towards me ; but tell him that our quarrel
had its rise in his own wilful aggression towards me ; and
that though I wish to be in charity with all mankind, I am
not so wedded to his friendship as to break the laws of
God, and run the risk of suffering or committing murder, in
order to regain it. And for you, sir, methinks your advanced
years and past misfortunes might teach you the folly of
coming on such idle errands.'

' I shall do your message, Master Ralph Bridgenorth,' said
Sir Jasper ; ' and shall then endeavour to forget your name,

as a sound unfit to be pronounced, or even remembered, by
a man of honour. In the meanwhile, in return for your
uncivil advice, be pleased to accept of mine ; namely, that
as your religion prevents your giving a gentleman satisfaction, it ought to make you very cautious of offering him
provocation.'

So saying, and with a look of haughty scorn, first at the
major and then at the divine, the envoy of Sir Geoffrey
put his hat on his head, replaced his rapier in its belt, and
left the apartment. In a few minutes afterwards, the tread
of his horse died away at a considerable distance.

Bridgenorth had held his hand upon his brow ever since
his departure, and a tear of anger and shame was on his
face as he raised it when the sound was heard no more.
' He carries this answer to Martindale Castle,' he said.
' Men will hereafter think of me as a whipped, beaten, dishonourable fellow, whom every one may baffle and insult
at their pleasure. It is well I am leaving the house of my
father.'

Master Solsgrace approached his friend with much
sympathy, and grasped him by the hand. ' Noble brother,'
he said, with unwonted kindness of manner, ' though a man
of peace, I can judge what this sacrifice hath cost to thy
manly spirit. But God will not have from us an imperfect
obedience. We must not, like Ananias and Sapphira,
reserve behind some darling lust, some favourite sin, while
we pretend to make sacrifice of our worldly affections.
What avails it to say that we have but secreted a little
matter, if the slightest remnant of the accursed thing
remain hidden in our tent ? Would it be a defence in thy
prayers to say, I have not murdered this man for the lucre
of gain, like a robber—nor for the acquisition of power, like
a tyrant,—nor for the gratification of revenge, like a
darkened savage ; but because the imperious voice of
worldly honour said, " Go forth—kill or be killed—is it not
I that have sent thee ? " Bethink thee, my worthy friend,
how thou couldst frame such a vindication in thy prayers ;
and if thou art forced to tremble at the blasphemy of such
an excuse, remember in thy prayers the thanks due to
Heaven, which enabled thee to resist the strong temptation.'

' Reverend and dear friend,' answered Bridgenorth,

'I feel that you speak the truth. Bitterer, indeed, and harder, to the old Adam, is the text which ordains him to suffer shame, than that which bids him to do valiantly for the truth. But happy am I that my path through the wilderness of this world will, for some space at least, be along with one whose zeal and friendship are so active to support me when I am fainting in the way.'

While the inhabitants of Moultrassie Hall thus communicated together upon the purport of Sir Jasper Cranbourne's visit, that worthy knight greatly excited the surprise of Sir Geoffrey Peveril, by reporting the manner in which his embassy had been received.

'I took him for a man of other metal,' said Sir Geoffrey ;— 'nay, I would have sworn it, had any one asked my testimony. But there is no making a silken purse out of a sow's ear. I have done a folly for him that I will never do for another : and that is, to think a Presbyterian would fight without his preacher's permission. Give them a two hours' sermon, and let them howl a psalm to a tune that is worse than the cries of a flogged hound, and the villains will lay on like threshers ; but for a calm, cool, gentleman-like turn upon the sod, hand to hand, in a neighbourly way, they have not honour enough to undertake it. But enough of our crop-eared cur of a neighbour. Sir Jasper, you will tarry with us to dine, and see how Dame Margaret's kitchen smokes ; and after dinner I will show you a long-winged falcon fly. She is not mine, but the countess's, who brought her from London on her fist almost the whole way, for all the haste she was in, and left her with me to keep the perch for a season.'

This match was soon arranged, and Dame Margaret overheard the good knight's resentment mutter itself off, with those feelings with which we listen to the last growling of the thunder-storm ; which, as the black cloud sinks beneath the hill, at once assures us that there has been danger, and that the peril is over. She could not, indeed, but marvel in her own mind at the singular path of reconciliation with his neighbour which her husband had, with so much confidence, and in the actual sincerity of his good-will to Mr. Bridgenorth, attempted to open ; and she blessed God internally that it had not terminated in bloodshed. But these reflections she locked carefully within her own bosom, well knowing that they referred to subjects in which the Knight of the Peak would neither permit his sagacity to be called in question, nor his will to be controlled.

The progress of the history hath hitherto been slow ; but after this period so little matter worthy of mark occurred at Martindale, that we must hurry over hastily the transactions of several years.

CHAPTER X

> *Cleopatra.* Give me to drink mandragora,
> That I may sleep away this gap of time.
> > *Antony and Cleopatra.*

THERE passed, as we hinted at the conclusion of the last chapter, four or five years after the period we have dilated upon ; the events of which scarcely require to be discussed, so far as our present purpose is concerned, in as many lines. The knight and his lady continued to reside at their castle—she, with prudence and with patience, endeavouring to repair the damages which the Civil Wars had inflicted upon their fortune ; and murmuring a little when her plans of economy were interrupted by the liberal hospitality which was her husband's principal expense, and to which he was attached, not only from his own English heartiness of disposition, but from ideas of maintaining the dignity of his ancestry—no less remarkable, according to the tradition of their buttery, kitchen, and cellar, for the fat beeves which they roasted, and the mighty ale which they brewed, than for their extensive estates, and the number of their retainers.

The world, however, upon the whole, went happily and easily with the worthy couple. Sir Geoffrey's debt to his neighbour Bridgenorth continued, it is true, unabated ; but he was the only creditor upon the Martindale estate—all others being paid off. It would have been most desirable that this encumbrance also should be cleared, and it was the great object of Dame Margaret's economy to effect the discharge ; for although interest was regularly settled with

Master Win-the-Fight, the Chesterfield attorney, yet the principal sum, which was a large one, might be called for at an inconvenient time. The man, too, was gloomy, important, and mysterious, and always seemed as if he was thinking upon his broken head in the churchyard of Martindale *cum* Moultrassie.

Dame Margaret sometimes transacted the necessary business with him in person ; and when he came to the castle on these occasions, she thought she saw a malicious and disobliging expression in his manner and countenance. Yet his actual conduct was not only fair, but liberal ; for indulgence was given, in the way of delay of payment, whenever circumstances rendered it necessary to the debtor to require it. It seemed to Lady Peveril, that the agent, in such cases, was acting under the strict orders of his absent employer, concerning whose welfare she could not help feeling a certain anxiety.

Shortly after the failure of the singular negotiation for attaining peace by combat, which Peveril had attempted to open with Major Bridgenorth, that gentleman left his seat of Moultrassie Hall in the care of his old housekeeper, and departed, no one knew whither, having in company with him his daughter Alice and Mrs. Deborah Debbitch, now formally installed in all the duties of a governante ; to these was added the Reverend Master Solsgrace. For some time public rumour persisted in asserting that Major Bridgenorth had only retreated to a distant part of the country for a season, to achieve his supposed purpose of marrying Mrs. Deborah, and of letting the news be cold, and the laugh of the neighbourhood be ended, ere he brought her down as mistress of Moultrassie Hall. This rumour died away ; and it was then affirmed that he had removed to foreign parts, to ensure the continuance of health in so delicate a constitution as that of little Alice. But when the major's dread of Popery was remembered, together with the still deeper antipathies of worthy Master Nehemiah Solsgrace, it was resolved unanimously that nothing less than what they might deem a fair chance of converting the Pope would have induced the parties to trust themselves within Catholic dominions. The most prevailing opinion was that they had gone to New England, the refuge then of many whom too intimate concern with the affairs of the late times, or the desire of enjoying uncontrolled freedom of conscience, had induced to emigrate from Britain.

Lady Peveril could not help entertaining a vague idea that Bridgenorth was not so distant. The extreme order in which everything was maintained at Moultrassie Hall seemed—no disparagement to the care of Dame Dickens the housekeeper, and the other persons engaged—to argue that the master's eye was not so very far off, but that its occasional inspection might be apprehended. It is true, that neither the domestics nor the attorney answered any questions respecting the residence of Master Bridgenorth ; but there was an air of mystery about them when interrogated that seemed to argue more than met the ear.

About five years after Master Bridgenorth had left the country, a singular incident took place. Sir Geoffrey was absent at the Chesterfield races, and Lady Peveril, who was in the habit of walking around every part of the neighbourhood unattended, or only accompanied by Ellesmere, or her little boy, had gone down one evening upon a charitable errand to a solitary hut, whose inhabitant lay sick of a fever which was supposed to be infectious. Lady Peveril never allowed apprehensions of this kind to stop ' devoted charitable deeds ' ; but she did not choose to expose either her son or her attendant to the risk which she herself, in some confidence that she knew precautions for escaping the danger, did not hesitate to incur.

Lady Peveril had set out at a late hour in the evening, and the way proved longer than she expected—several circumstances also occurred to detain her at the hut of her patient. It was a broad autumn moonlight when she prepared to return homeward through the broken glades and upland which divided her from the castle. This she considered as a matter of very little importance in so quiet and sequestered a country, where the road lay chiefly through her own domains, especially as she had a lad about fifteen years old, the son of her patient, to escort her on the way. The distance was better than two miles, but might be considerably abridged by passing through an avenue belonging to the estate of Moultrassie Hall, which she had avoided as she came, not from the ridiculous rumours which pronounced it to be haunted, but because her husband was much displeased when any attempt was made to render the walks of the castle and Hall common to the inhabitants of both. The good lady, in consideration, perhaps, of extensive latitude allowed to her in the more important concerns of the family, made a point of never interfering with her husband's whims or prejudices ; and it is a compromise which we would heartily recommend to all managing matrons of our acquaintance ; for it is surprising how much real power will be cheerfully resigned to the fair sex, for the pleasure of being allowed to ride one's hobby in peace and quiet.

Upon the present occasion, however, although the Dobby's Walk[1] was within the inhibited domains of the Hall, the Lady Peveril determined to avail herself of it, for the purpose of shortening her road home, and she directed her steps accordingly. But when the peasant-boy, her companion, who had hitherto followed her, whistling cheerily, with a hedge-bill in his hand, and his hat on one side, perceived that she turned to the stile which entered to the Dobby's Walk, he showed symptoms of great fear, and at length, coming to the lady's side, petitioned her, in a whimpering tone,—' Don't ye now—don't ye now, my lady, don't ye go yonder.'

Lady Peveril, observing that his teeth chattered in his head, and that his whole person exhibited great signs of terror, began to recollect the report, that the first Squire of Moultrassie, the brewer of Chesterfield, who had bought the estate, and then died of melancholy for lack of something to do (and, as was said, not without suspicions of suicide), was supposed to walk in this sequestered avenue, accompanied by a large headless mastiff, which, when he was alive, was a particular favourite of the ex-brewer. To have expected any protection from her escort, in the condition to which superstitious fear had reduced him, would have been truly a hopeless trust ; and Lady Peveril, who was not apprehensive of any danger, thought there would be great cruelty in dragging the cowardly boy into a scene which he regarded with so much apprehension. She gave him, therefore, a silver piece, and permitted him

[1] Dobby, an old English name for goblin.

to return. The latter boon seemed even more acceptable than the first ; for ere she could return the purse into her pocket she heard the wooden clogs of her bold convoy in full retreat, by the way from whence they came.

Smiling within herself at the fear she esteemed so ludicrous, Lady Peveril ascended the stile, and was soon hidden from the broad light of the moonbeams by the numerous and entangled boughs of the huge elms, which, meeting from either side, totally overarched the old avenue. The scene was calculated to excite solemn thoughts ; and the distant glimmer of a light from one of the numerous casements in the front of Moultrassie Hall, which lay at some distance, was calculated to make them even melancholy. She thought of the fate of that family—of the deceased Mrs. Bridgenorth, with whom she had often walked in this very avenue, and who, though a woman of no high parts or accomplishments, had always testified the deepest respect, and the most earnest gratitude, for such notice as she had shown to her. She thought of her blighted hopes— —her premature death—the despair of her self-banished husband—the uncertain fate of their orphan child, for whom she felt, even at this distance of time, some touch of a mother's affection.

Upon such sad subjects her thoughts were turned, when, just as she attained the middle of the avenue, the imperfect and chequered light which found its way through the sylvan archway showed her something which resembled the figure of a man. Lady Peveril paused a moment, but instantly advanced ;—her bosom, perhaps, gave one startled throb, as a debt to the superstitious belief of the times, but she instantly repelled the thought of supernatural appearances. From those that were merely mortal she had nothing to fear. A marauder on the game was the worst character whom she was likely to encounter ; and he would be sure to hide himself from her observation. She advanced, accordingly, steadily ; and, as she did so, had the satisfaction to observe, that the figure, as she expected, gave place to her, and glided away amongst the trees on the left-hand side of the avenue. As she passed the spot on which the form had been so lately visible, and bethought herself that this wanderer of the night might, nay, must, be in her vicinity, her resolution could not prevent her mending her pace, and that with so little precaution, that, stumbling over the limb of a tree, which, twisted off by a late tempest, still lay in the avenue, she fell, and, as she fell, screamed aloud. A strong hand in a moment afterwards added to her fears by assisting her to rise, and a voice, to whose accents she was not a stranger, though they had been long unheard, said, ' Is it not you, Lady Peveril ? '

' It is I,' said she, commanding her astonishment and fear ; ' and if my ear deceive me not, I speak to Master Bridgenorth.'

' I was that man,' said he, ' while oppression left me a name.'

He spoke nothing more, but continued to walk beside her for a minute or two in silence. She felt her situation embarrassing ; and, to divest it of that feeling, as well as out of real interest in the question, she asked him, ' How her god-daughter Alice now was ? '

' Of god-daughter, madam,' answered Major Bridgenorth, ' I know nothing ; that being one of the names which have been introduced to the corruption and pollution of God's ordinances. The infant who owed to your ladyship (so called) her escape from disease and death is a healthy and thriving girl, as I am given to understand by those in whose charge she is lodged, for I have not lately seen her. And it is even the recollection of these passages, which in a manner impelled me, alarmed also by your fall, to offer myself to you at this time and mode, which in other respects is no way consistent with my present safety.'

' With your safety, Master Bridgenorth ? ' said the Lady Peveril ; ' surely, I could never have thought that it was in danger ! '

' You have some news, then, yet to learn, madam,' said Major Bridgenorth ; ' but you will hear, in the course of to-morrow, reasons why I dare not appear openly in the neighbourhood of my own property, and wherefore there is small judgement in committing the knowledge of my present residence to any one connected with Martindale Castle.'

' Master Bridgenorth,' said the lady, ' you were in former times prudent and cautious—I hope you have been misled by no hasty impression—by no rash scheme—I hope '——

' Pardon my interrupting you, madam,' said Bridgenorth.
' I have indeed been changed—aye, my very heart within me
hath been changed. In the times to which your ladyship (so
called) thinks proper to refer, I was a man of this world—
bestowing on it all my thoughts—all my actions, save
formal observances—little deeming what was the duty of a
Christian man, and how far his self-denial ought to extend—
even unto his giving all as if he gave nothing. Hence
I thought chiefly on carnal things—on the adding of field
to field, and wealth to wealth—of balancing between party
and party—securing a friend here, without losing a friend
there—But Heaven smote me for my apostasy, the rather
that I abused the name of religion as a self-seeker and
a most blinded and carnal will-worshipper—But I thank
HIM who hath at length brought me out of Egypt.'

In our day—although we have many instances of enthusiasm among us—we might still suspect one who avowed
it thus suddenly and broadly, of hypocrisy, or of insanity ;
but, according to the fashion of the times, such opinions as
those which Bridgenorth expressed were openly pleaded
as the ruling motives of men's actions. The sagacious
Vane—the brave and skilful Harrison—were men who
acted avowedly under the influence of such. Lady Peveril,
therefore, was more grieved than surprised at the language
she heard Major Bridgenorth use, and reasonably concluded that the society and circumstances in which he might
lately have been engaged had blown into a flame the
spark of eccentricity which always smouldered in his
bosom. This was the more probable, considering that he
was melancholy by constitution and descent—that he had
been unfortunate in several particulars—and that no
passion is more easily nursed by indulgence than the
species of enthusiasm of which he now showed tokens.
She therefore answered him by calmly hoping, ' That the
expression of his sentiments had not involved him in
suspicion or in danger.'

' In suspicion, madam ? ' answered the major ;—' for
I cannot forbear giving to you, such is the strength of
habit, one of those idle titles by which we poor potsherds
are wont, in our pride, to denominate each other—I walk
not only in suspicion, but in that degree of danger, that,

were your husband to meet me at this instant—me, a native Englishman, treading on my own lands—I have no doubt he would do his best to offer me to the Moloch of Roman superstition who now rages abroad for victims among God's people.'

'You surprise me by your language, Major Bridgenorth,' said the lady, who now felt rather anxious to be relieved from his company, and with that purpose walked on somewhat hastily. He mended his pace, however, and kept close by her side.

'Know you not,' said he, 'that Satan hath come down upon earth with great wrath, because his time is short? The next heir to the crown is an avowed Papist; and who dare assert, save sycophants and time-servers, that he who wears it is not equally ready to stoop to Rome, were he not kept in awe by a few noble spirits in the Commons' House? You believe not this—yet in my solitary and midnight walks, when I thought on your kindness to the dead and to the living, it was my prayer that I might have the means granted to warn you—and lo! Heaven hath heard me.'

'Major Bridgenorth,' said Lady Peveril, 'you were wont to be moderate in these sentiments—comparatively moderate, at least, and to love your own religion without hating that of others.'

'What I was while in the gall of bitterness and in the bond of iniquity, it signifies not to recall,' answered he. 'I was then like to Gallio, who cared for none of these things. I doted on creature-comforts—I clung to worldly honour and repute—my thoughts were earthward—or those I turned to Heaven were cold, formal, pharisaical meditations—I brought nothing to the altar save straw and stubble. Heaven saw need to chastise me in love—I was stripped of all that I clung to on earth—my worldly honour was torn from me—I went forth an exile from the home of my fathers, a deprived and desolate man—a baffled, and beaten, and dishonoured man. But who shall find out the ways of Providence? Such were the means by which I was chosen forth as a champion for the truth—holding my life as nothing, if thereby that may be advanced. But this was not what I wished to speak of. Thou hast

saved the earthly life of my child—let me save the eternal
welfare of yours.'

Lady Peveril was silent. They were now approaching
the point where the avenue terminated in a communication
with a public road, or rather pathway, running through
an unenclosed common field ; this the lady had to prosecute
for a little way, until a turn of the path gave her admittance
into the park of Martindale. She now felt sincerely anxious
to be in the open moonshine, and avoided reply to Bridgenorth that she might make the more haste. But as they
reached the junction of the avenue and the public road,
he laid his hand on her arm, and commanded rather than
requested her to stop. She obeyed. He pointed to a huge
oak, of the largest size, which grew on the summit of a knoll
in the open ground which terminated the avenue, and was
exactly so placed as to serve for a termination to the vista.
The moonshine without the avenue was so strong, that,
amidst the flood of light which it poured on the venerable
tree, they could easily discover, from the shattered state of
the boughs on one side, that it had suffered damage from
lightning. ' Remember you,' he said, ' when we last looked
together on that tree ? I had ridden from London, and
brought with me a protection from the committee for
your husband ; and as I passed the spot—here on this spot
where we now stand, you stood with my lost Alice—two—
the last two—of my beloved infants gambolled before you.
I leaped from my horse—to her I was a husband—to those
a father—to you a welcome and revered protector. What
am I now to any one ? ' He pressed his hand on his
brow, and groaned in agony of spirit.

It was not in the Lady Peveril's nature to hear sorrow
without an attempt at consolation. ' Master Bridgenorth,'
she said, ' I blame no man's creed, while I believe and
follow my own ; and I rejoice that in yours you have
sought consolation for temporal afflictions. But does not
every Christian creed teach us alike that affliction should
soften our heart ? '

' Aye, woman,' said Bridgenorth sternly, ' as the lightning
which shattered yonder oak hath softened its trunk. No ;
the seared wood is the fitter for the use of the workmen—
the hardened and the dried-up heart is that which can best

bear the task imposed by these dismal times. God and
man will no longer endure the unbridled profligacy of the
dissolute—the scoffing of the profane—the contempt of the
divine laws—the infraction of human rights. The times
demand righters and avengers, and there will be no want of
them.'

'I deny not the existence of much evil,' said Lady
Peveril, compelling herself to answer, and beginning at the
same time to walk forward ; 'and from hearsay, though
not, I thank Heaven, from observation, I am convinced of
the wild debauchery of the times. But let us trust it may
be corrected without such violent remedies as you hint at.
Surely the ruin of a second civil war—though I trust your
thoughts go not that dreadful length—were at best a
desperate alternative.'

'Sharp, but sure,' replied Bridgenorth. 'The blood of
the Paschal lamb chased away the destroying angel—the
sacrifices offered on the threshing-floor of Araunah stayed
the pestilence. Fire and sword are severe remedies, but
they purge and purify.'

'Alas ! Major Bridgenorth,' said the lady, 'wise and
moderate in your youth, can you have adopted in your
advanced life the thoughts and language of those whom
you yourself beheld drive themselves and the nation to the
brink of ruin ? '

'I know not what I then was—you know not what I now
am,' he replied, and suddenly broke off ; for they even then
came forth into the open light, and it seemed as if, feeling
himself under the lady's eye, he was disposed to soften his
tone and his language.

At the first distinct view which she had of his person, she
was aware that he was armed with a short sword, a poniard,
and pistols at his belt—precautions very unusual for a man
who formerly had seldom, and only on days of ceremony,
carried a walking rapier, though such was the habitual
and constant practice of gentlemen of his station in life.
There seemed also something of more stern determination
than usual in his air, which indeed had always been rather
sullen than affable; and ere she could repress the sentiment,
she could not help saying, 'Master Bridgenorth, you are
indeed changed.'

'You see but the outward man,' he replied ; 'the change within is yet deeper. But it was not of myself that I desired to talk—I have already said, that as you have preserved my child from the darkness of the grave, I would willingly preserve yours from that more utter darkness, which, I fear, hath involved the path and walks of his father.'

'I must not hear this of Sir Geoffrey,' said the Lady Peveril ; 'I must bid you farewell for the present ; and when we again meet at a more suitable time, I will at least listen to your advice concerning Julian, although I should not perhaps incline to it.'

'That more suitable time may never come,' replied Bridgenorth. 'Time wanes, eternity draws nigh. Hearken ! it is said to be your purpose to send the young Julian to be bred up in yonder bloody island, under the hand of your kinswoman, that cruel murderess, by whom was done to death a man more worthy of vital existence than any that she can boast among her vaunted ancestry. These are current tidings—Are they true ? '

'I do not blame you, Master Bridgenorth, for thinking harshly of my cousin of Derby,' said Lady Peveril ; 'nor do I altogether vindicate the rash action of which she hath been guilty. Nevertheless, in her habitation, it is my husband's opinion and my own that Julian may be trained in the studies and accomplishments becoming his rank, along with the young Earl of Derby.'

'Under the curse of God, and the blessing of the Pope of Rome,' said Bridgenorth. 'You, lady, so quick-sighted in matters of earthly prudence, are you blind to the gigantic pace at which Rome is moving to regain this country, once the richest gem in her usurped tiara ? The old are seduced by gold, the youth by pleasure, the weak by flattery, cowards by fear, and the courageous by ambition. A thousand baits for each taste, and each bait concealing the same deadly hook.'

'I am well aware, Master Bridgenorth,' said Lady Peveril, 'that my kinswoman is a Catholic ;[1] but her son is educated

---

[1] I have elsewhere (p. x) noticed that this is a deviation from the truth—Charlotte, Countess of Derby, was a Huguenot.

in the Church of England's principles, agreeably to the command of her deceased husband.'

'Is it likely,' answered Bridgenorth, 'that she, who fears not shedding the blood of the righteous, whether on the field or scaffold, will regard the sanction of her promise when her religion bids her break it ? Or, if she does, what shall your son be the better, if he remain in the mire of his father ? What are your Episcopal tenets but mere Popery, save that ye have chosen a temporal tyrant for your Pope, and substitute a mangled mass in English for that which your predecessors pronounced in Latin. But why speak I of these things to one who hath ears, indeed, and eyes, yet cannot see, listen to, or understand what is alone worthy to be heard, seen, and known ? Pity that what hath been wrought so fair and exquisite in form and disposition, should be yet blind, deaf, and ignorant, like the things which perish ! '

'We shall not agree on these subjects, Master Bridgenorth,' said the lady, anxious still to escape from this strange conference, though scarce knowing what to apprehend ; 'once more, I must bid you farewell.'

'Stay yet an instant,' he said, again laying his hand on her arm ; 'I would stop you if I saw you rushing on the brink of an actual precipice—let me prevent you from a danger still greater. How shall I work upon your unbelieving mind ? Shall I tell you that the debt of bloodshed yet remains a debt to be paid by the bloody house of Derby ? And wilt thou send thy son to be among those from whom it shall be exacted ? '

'You wish to alarm me in vain, Master Bridgenorth,' answered the lady ; 'what penalty can be exacted from the countess, for an action which I have already called a rash one, has been long since levied.'

'You deceive yourself,' retorted he, sternly. 'Think you a paltry sum of money, given to be wasted on the debaucheries of Charles, can atone for the death of such a man as Christian—a man precious alike to heaven and to earth ? Not on such terms is the blood of the righteous to be poured forth ! Every hour's delay is numbered down as adding interest to the grievous debt which will one day be required from that bloodthirsty woman.'

At this moment the distant tread of horses was heard on the road on which they held this singular dialogue. Bridgenorth listened a moment, and then said, 'Forget that you have seen me—name not my name to your nearest or dearest—lock my counsel in your breast—profit by it, and it shall be well with you.'

So saying, he turned from her, and plunging through a gap in the fence, regained the cover of his own wood, along which the path still led.

The noise of horses advancing at full trot now came nearer; and Lady Peveril was aware of several riders, whose forms rose indistinctly on the summit of the rising ground behind her. She became also visible to them; and one or two of the foremost made towards her at increased speed, challenging her as they advanced with the cry of 'Stand! Who goes there?' The foremost who came up, however, exclaimed, 'Mercy on us, if it be not my lady!' and Lady Peveril, at the same moment, recognized one of her own servants. Her husband rode up immediately afterwards, with, 'How now, Dame Margaret? What makes you abroad so far from home and at an hour so late?'

Lady Peveril mentioned her visit at the cottage, but did not think it necessary to say aught of having seen Major Bridgenorth; afraid, it may be, that her husband might be displeased with that incident

'Charity is a fine thing and a fair,' answered Sir Geoffrey, 'but I must tell you, you do ill, dame, to wander about the country like a quack-salver, at the call of every old woman who has a colic-fit; and at this time of night especially, and when the land is so unsettled besides.'

'I am sorry to hear that it is so,' said the lady. 'I had heard no such news.'

'News?' repeated Sir Geoffrey; 'why, here has a new plot broken out among the Roundheads, worse than Venner's by a butt's length; [1] and who should be so deep in it as our old neighbour Bridgenorth? There is search for him everywhere; and I promise you, if he is found, he is like to pay old scores.'

[1] The celebrated insurrection of the Anabaptists and Fifth Monarchy men in London, in the year 1661.

' Then I am sure I trust he will not be found,' said Lady Peveril.

' Do you so ? ' replied Sir Geoffrey. ' Now I, on my part, hope that he will ; and it shall not be my fault if he be not, for which effect I will presently ride down to Moultrassie, and make strict search, according to my duty ; there shall neither rebel nor traitor earth so near Martindale Castle, that I will assure them. And you, my lady, be pleased for once to dispense with a pillion, and get up, as you have done before, behind Saunders, who shall convey you safe home.'

The lady obeyed in silence ; indeed, she did not dare to trust her voice in an attempt to reply, so much was she disconcerted with the intelligence she had just heard.

She rode behind the groom to the castle, where she awaited in great anxiety the return of her husband. He came back at length; but, to her great relief, without any prisoner. He then explained more fully than his haste had before permitted, that an express had come down to Chesterfield with news from court of a proposed insurrection amongst the old Commonwealth men, especially those who had served in the army ; and that Bridgenorth, said to be lurking in Derbyshire, was one of the principal conspirators.

After some time, this report of a conspiracy seemed to die away like many others of that period. The warrants were recalled, but nothing more was seen or heard of Major Bridgenorth ; although it is probable he might safely enough have shown himself as openly as many did who lay under the same circumstances of suspicion.[n]

About this time also, Lady Peveril, with many tears, took a temporary leave of her son Julian, who was sent, as had long been intended, for the purpose of sharing the education of the young Earl of Derby. Although the boding words of Bridgenorth sometimes occurred to Lady Peveril's mind, she did not suffer them to weigh with her in opposition to the advantages which the patronage of the Countess of Derby secured to her son.

The plan seemed to be in every respect successful ; and when, from time to time, Julian visited the house of his father, Lady Peveril had the satisfaction to see him, on every occasion, improved in person and in manner, as well as ardent in the pursuit of more solid acquirements. In process of time he became a gallant and accomplished youth, and travelled for some time upon the continent with the young earl. This was the more especially necessary for the enlarging of their acquaintance with the world; because the countess had never appeared in London, or at the court of King Charles, since her flight to the Isle of Man in 1660; but had resided in solitary and aristocratic state, alternately on her estates in England and in that island.

This had given to the education of both the young men, otherwise as excellent as the best teachers could render it, something of a narrow and restricted character; but though the disposition of the young earl was lighter and more volatile than that of Julian, both the one and the other had profited in a considerable degree by the opportunities afforded them. It was Lady Derby's strict injunction to her son, now returning from the continent, that he should not appear at the court of Charles. But having been for some time of age, he did not think it absolutely necessary to obey her in this particular; and had remained for some time in London, partaking the pleasures of the gay court there with all the ardour of a young man bred up in comparative seclusion.

In order to reconcile the countess to this transgression of her authority (for he continued to entertain for her the profound respect in which he had been educated), Lord Derby agreed to make a long sojourn with her in her favourite island, which he abandoned almost entirely to her management.

Julian Peveril had spent at Martindale Castle a good deal of the time which his friend had bestowed in London; and at the period to which, passing over many years, our story has arrived, as it were, *per saltum*, they were both living as the countess's guests, in the Castle of Rushin, in the venerable kingdom of Man.

CHAPTER XI

Mona—long hid from those who roam the main.
                                        COLLINS.

THE Isle of Man, in the middle of the seventeenth century, was very different, as a place of residence, from what it is now. Men had not then discovered its merit as a place of occasional refuge from the storms of life, and the society to be there met with was of a very uniform tenor. There were no smart fellows, whom fortune had tumbled from the seat of their barouches—no plucked pigeons or winged rooks—no disappointed speculators—no ruined miners—in short, no one worth talking to. The society of the island was limited to the natives themselves, and a few merchants, who lived by contraband trade. The amusements were rare and monotonous, and the mercurial young earl was soon heartily tired of his dominions. The islanders also, become too wise for happiness, had lost relish for the harmless and somewhat childish sports in which their simple ancestors had indulged themselves. May was no longer ushered in by the imaginary contest between the Queen of returning winter and advancing spring ; the listeners no longer sympathized with the lively music of the followers of the one, or the discordant sounds with which the other asserted a more noisy claim to attention. Christmas, too, closed, and the steeples no longer jangled forth a dissonant peal. The wren, to seek for which used to be the sport dedicated to the holytide, was left unpursued and unslain. Party spirit had come among these simple people, and destroyed their good humour, while it left them their ignorance. Even the races, a sport generally interesting to people of all ranks, were no longer performed, because they were no longer interesting. The gentlemen were divided by feuds hitherto unknown, and each seemed to hold it scorn to be pleased with the same diversions that amused those of the opposite faction. The hearts of both parties revolted from the recollection of former days, when all was peace among them, when the Earl of Derby, now slaughtered, used to bestow the prize, and Christian, since so vindictively executed, started horses to add to the amusement.[n]

Julian was seated in the deep recess which led to a latticed window of the old castle ; and, with his arms crossed, and an air of profound contemplation, was survey-ing the long perspective of ocean, which rolled its successive waves up to the foot of the rock on which the ancient pile is founded. The earl was suffering under the infliction of ennui—now looking into a volume of Homer—now whistling —now swinging on his chair—now traversing the room—till, at length, his attention became swallowed up in admiration of the tranquillity of his companion.

' King of Men ! ' he said, repeating the favourite epithet by which Homer describes Agamemnon,—' I trust, for the old Greek's sake, he had a merrier office than being King of Man—Most philosophical Julian, will nothing rouse thee —not even a bad pun on my own royal dignity ? '

' I wish you would be a little more the King in Man,' said Julian, starting from his reverie, ' and then you would find more amusement in your dominions.'

' What ! dethrone that royal Semiramis my mother,' said the young lord, ' who has as much pleasure in playing queen as if she were a real sovereign ? I wonder you can give me such counsel.'

' Your mother, as you well know, my dear Derby, would be delighted, did you take any interest in the affairs of the island.'

' Aye, truly, she would permit me to be king ; but she would choose to remain viceroy over me. Why, she would only gain a subject the more, by my converting my spare time, which is so very valuable to me, to the cares of royalty. No, no, Julian, she thinks it power to direct all the affairs of these poor Manxmen ; and, thinking it power, she finds it pleasure. I shall not interfere, unless she hold a high court of justice again. I cannot afford to pay another fine to my brother, King Charles—But I forget—this is a sore point with you.'

' With the countess, at least,' replied Julian ; ' and I wonder you will speak of it.'

' Why, I bear no malice against the poor man's memory any more than yourself, though I have not the same reasons

for holding it in veneration,' replied the Earl of Derby;
' and yet I have some respect for it too.   I remember their
bringing him out to die—It was the first holiday I ever had
in my life, and I heartily wish it had been on some other
account.'

' I would rather hear you speak of anything else, my
lord,' said Julian.

' Why, there it goes,' answered the earl; 'whenever I
talk of anything that puts you on your mettle, and warms
your blood, that runs as cold as a merman's—to use a
simile of this happy island—hey pass! you press me to
change the subject.   Well, what shall we talk of?   O
Julian, if you had not gone down to earth yourself among
the castles and caverns of Derbyshire, we should have had
enough of delicious topics—the playhouses, Julian—both
the king's house and the duke's—Louis's establishment is
a jest to them;—and the Ring in the Park, which beats
the Corso at Naples—and the beauties, who beat the whole
world!'

' I am very willing to hear you speak on the subject,
my lord,' answered Julian; ' the less I have seen of the
London world myself, the more I am likely to be amused
by your account of it.'

' Aye, my friend—but where to begin?—with the wit of
Buckingham, and Sedley, and Etherege, or with the grace
of Harry Jermyn—the courtesy of the Duke of Monmouth,
or with the loveliness of La Belle Hamilton—of the Duchess
of Richmond—of Lady ——, the person of Roxalana, the
smart humour of Mrs. Nelly '——

' Or what say you to the bewitching sorceries of Lady
Cynthia?' demanded his companion.

' Faith, I would have kept these to myself,' said the
earl, ' to follow your prudent example.   But since you ask
me, I fairly own I cannot tell what to say of them; only
I think of them twenty times as often as all the beauties
I have spoken of.   And yet she is neither the twentieth
part so beautiful as the plainest of these court beauties, nor
so witty as the dullest I have named, nor so modish—that is
the great matter—as the most obscure.   I cannot tell what
makes me dote on her, except that she is as capricious as
her whole sex put together.'

' That I should think a small recommendation,' answered his companion.

' Small, do you term it,' replied the earl, ' and write your-self a brother of the angle ? Why, which like you best ? to pull a dead strain on a miserable gudgeon, which you draw ashore by main force, as the fellows here tow in their fishing-boats—or a lively salmon, that makes your rod crack, and your line whistle—plays you ten thousand mischievous pranks—wearies your heart out with hopes and fears—and is only laid panting on the bank, after you have shown the most unmatchable display of skill, patience, and dexterity ? But I see you have a mind to go on angling after your own old fashion. Off laced coat, and on brown jerkin ;—lively colours scare fish in the sober waters of the Isle of Man ;—faith, in London you will catch few, unless the bait glistens a little. But you *are* going ?— well, good luck to you. I will take to the barge ;—the sea and wind are less inconstant than the tide you have embarked on.'

' You have learned to say all these smart things in London, my lord,' answered Julian ; ' but we shall have you a peni-tent for them, if Lady Cynthia be of my mind. Adieu, and pleasure till we meet.'

The young men parted accordingly ; and while the earl betook him to his pleasure voyage, Julian, as his friend had prophesied, assumed the dress of one who means to amuse himself with angling. The hat and feather were exchanged for a cap of grey cloth ; the deeply-laced cloak and doublet for a simple jacket of the same colour, with hose conform-ing ; and finally, with rod in hand, and pannier at his back, mounted upon a handsome Manx pony, young Peveril rode briskly over the country which divided him from one of those beautiful streams that descend to the sea from the Kirk Merlagh mountains.

Having reached the spot where he meant to commence his day's sport, Julian let his little steed graze, which, accustomed to the situation, followed him like a dog ; and now and then, when tired of picking herbage in the valley through which the stream winded, came near her master's side, and, as if she had been a curious amateur of the sport, gazed on the trouts as Julian brought them struggling to the

shore. But Fairy's master showed, on that day, little of
the patience of a real angler, and took no heed to old Isaac
Walton's recommendation to fish the streams inch by inch.
He chose, indeed, with an angler's eye, the most promising
casts, where the stream broke sparkling over a stone,
affording the wonted shelter to a trout ; or where, gliding
away from a rippling current to a still eddy, it streamed
under the projecting bank, or dashed from the pool of some
low cascade. By this judicious selection of spots whereon
to employ his art, the sportsman's basket was soon sufficiently heavy to show that his occupation was not a mere
pretext ; and so soon as this was the case, he walked briskly
up the glen, only making a cast from time to time, in case
of his being observed from any of the neighbouring heights.

It was a little green and rocky valley through which the
brook strayed, very lonely, although the slight track of an
unformed road showed that it was occasionally traversed,
and that it was not altogether void of inhabitants. As
Peveril advanced still farther, the right bank reached to
some distance from the stream, leaving a piece of meadow
ground, the lower part of which, being close to the brook,
was entirely covered with rich herbage, being possibly
occasionally irrigated by its overflow. The higher part of
the level ground afforded a stance for an old house, of a
singular structure, with a terraced garden, and a cultivated
field or two beside it. In former times, a Danish or Norwegian fastness had stood here, called the Black Fort, from
the colour of a huge heathy hill, which, rising behind the
building, appeared to be the boundary of the valley, and to
afford the source of the brook. But the original structure
had been long demolished, as, indeed, it probably only
consisted of dry stones, and its materials had been applied
to the construction of the present mansion—the work of
some churchman during the sixteenth century, as was
evident from the huge stone-work of its windows, which
scarce left room for light to pass through, as well as from
two or three heavy buttresses, which projected from the
front of the house, and exhibited on their surface little
niches for images. These had been carefully destroyed, and
pots of flowers were placed in the niches in their stead,
besides their being ornamented by creeping plants of

various kinds, fancifully twined around them. The garden was also in good order ; and though the spot was extremely solitary, there was about it altogether an air of comfort, accommodation, and even elegance, by no means generally characteristic of the habitations of the island at the time.

With much circumspection, Julian Peveril approached the low Gothic porch, which defended the entrance of the mansion from the tempests incident to its situation, and was, like the buttresses, overrun with ivy and other creeping plants. An iron ring, contrived so as when drawn up and down to rattle against the bar of notched iron through which it was suspended, served the purpose of a knocker ; and to this he applied himself, though with the greatest precaution.

He received no answer for some time, and indeed it seemed as if the house was totally uninhabited ; when, at length, his impatience getting the upper hand, he tried to open the door, and, as it was only upon the latch, very easily succeeded. He passed through a little low-arched hall, the upper end of which was occupied by a staircase, and turning to the left, opened the door of a summer parlour, wainscoted with black oak, and very simply furnished with chairs and tables of the same materials ; the former cushioned with leather. The apartment was gloomy —one of those stone-shafted windows which we have mentioned, with its small latticed panes, and thick garland of foliage, admitting but an imperfect light.

Over the chimneypiece (which was of the same massive materials with the panelling of the apartment) was the only ornament of the room ; a painting, namely, representing an officer in the military dress of the Civil Wars. It was a green jerkin, then the national and peculiar wear of the Manxmen ; his short band which hung down on the cuirass—the orange-coloured scarf, but, above all, the shortness of his close-cut hair, showing evidently to which of the great parties he had belonged. His right hand rested on the hilt of his sword ; and in the left he held a small Bible, bearing the inscription, ' *In hoc signo.*' The countenance was of a light complexion, with fair and almost effeminate blue eyes, and an oval form of face—one of those physiognomies to which, though not otherwise unpleasing, we naturally attach the idea of melancholy and of misfortune.[1] Apparently it was well known to Julian Peveril; for after having looked at it for a long time, he could not forbear muttering aloud, 'What would I give that that man had never been born, or that he still lived!'

'How now—how is this?' said a female, who entered the room as he uttered this reflection. '*You* here, Master Peveril, in spite of all the warnings you have had! You here in the possession of folk's house when they are abroad, and talking to yourself, as I shall warrant!'

'Yes, Mistress Deborah,' said Peveril, 'I am here once more, as you see, against every prohibition, and in defiance of all danger. Where is Alice?'

'Where you will never see her, Master Julian—you may satisfy yourself of that,' answered Mistress Deborah, for it was that respectable governante; and sinking down at the same time upon one of the large leathern chairs, she began to fan herself with her handkerchief, and complain of the heat in a most ladylike fashion.

In fact, Mistress Debbitch, while her exterior intimated a considerable change of condition for the better, and her countenance showed the less favourable effects of the twenty years which had passed over her head, was in mind and manners very much what she had been when she battled the opinions of Madam Ellesmere at Martindale Castle. In a word, she was self-willed, obstinate, and coquettish as ever, otherwise no ill-disposed person. Her present appearance was that of a woman of the better rank. From the sobriety of the fashion of her dress, and the uniformity of its colours, it was plain she belonged to some sect which condemned superfluous gaiety in attire; but no rules, not those of a nunnery or of a quaker's society, can prevent a little coquetry in that particular, where a woman

---

[1] I am told that a portrait of the unfortunate William Christian is still preserved in the family of Waterson of Ballnahow of Kirk Church, Rushin. William Dhône is dressed in a green coat without collar or cape, after the fashion of those puritanic times, with the head in a close cropt wig, resembling the bishop's peruke of the present day. The countenance is youthful and well-looking, very unlike the expression of foreboding melancholy. I have so far taken advantage of this criticism, as to bring my ideal portrait, in the present edition, nearer to the complexion at least of the fair-haired William Dhône.

is desirous of being supposed to retain some claim to personal attention. All Mistress Deborah's garments were so arranged as might best set off a good-looking woman, whose countenance indicated ease and good cheer—who called herself five-and-thirty, and was well entitled, if she had a mind, to call herself twelve or fifteen years older.

Julian was under the necessity of enduring all her tiresome and fantastic airs, and awaiting with patience till she had ' prinked herself and pinned herself '—flung her hoods back, and drawn them forward—snuffed at a little bottle of essences—closed her eyes like a dying fowl—turned them up like a duck in a thunder-storm ; when at length, having exhausted her round of *minauderies*, she condescended to open the conversation.

' These walks will be the death of me,' she said, ' and all on your account, Master Julian Peveril ; for if Dame Christian should learn that you have chosen to make your visits to her niece, I promise you Mistress Alice would be soon obliged to find other quarters, and so should I.'

' Come now, Mistress Deborah, be good-humoured,' said Julian ; ' consider, was not all this intimacy of ours of your own making ? Did you not make yourself known to me the very first time I strolled up this glen with my fishing-rod, and tell me that you were my former keeper, and that Alice had been my little playfellow ? And what could there be more natural, than that I should come back and see two such agreeable persons as often as I could ? '

' Yes,' said Dame Deborah ; ' but I did not bid you fall in love with us, though, or propose such a matter as marriage either to Alice or myself.'

' To do you justice, you never did, Deborah,' answered the youth ; ' but what of that ? Such things will come out before one is aware. I am sure you must have heard such proposals fifty times when you least expected them.'

' Fie, fie, fie, Master Julian Peveril,' said the governante ; ' I would have you to know that I have always so behaved myself, that the best of the land would have thought twice of it, and have very well considered both what he was going to say, and how he was going to say it, before he came out with such proposals to me.'

' True, true, Mistress Deborah,' continued Julian ; ' but

all the world hath not your discretion. Then Alice Bridgenorth is a child—a mere child ; and one always asks a baby to be one's little wife, you know. Come, I know you will forgive me. Thou wert ever the best-natured, kindest woman in the world ; and you know you have said twenty times we were made for each other.'

' Oh, no, Master Julian Peveril ; no, no, no ! ' ejaculated Deborah. ' I may indeed have said your estates were born to be united ; and to be sure it is natural for me, that come of the old stock of the yeomanry of Peveril of the Peak's estate, to wish that it was all within the ring fence again ; which sure enough it might be, were you to marry Alice Bridgenorth. But then there is the knight your father, and my lady your mother ; and there is her father, that is half crazy with his religion ; and her aunt that wears eternal black grogram for that unlucky Colonel Christian ; and there is the Countess of Derby, that would serve us all with the same sauce if we were thinking of anything that would displease her. And besides all that, you have broke your word with Mistress Alice, and everything is over between you ; and I am of opinion it is quite right it should be all over. And perhaps it may be, Master Julian, that I should have thought so a long time ago, before a child like Alice put it into my head ; but I am so good-natured.'

No flatterer like a lover, who wishes to carry his point.

' You are the best-natured, kindest creature in the world, Deborah. But you have never seen the ring I bought for you at Paris. Nay, I will put it on your finger myself ;— what ! your foster-son, whom you loved so well, and took such care of ? '

He easily succeeded in putting a pretty ring of gold, with a humorous affectation of gallantry, on the fat finger of Mistress Deborah Debbitch. Hers was a soul of a kind often to be met with, both among the lower and higher vulgar, who, without being, on a broad scale, accessible to bribes or corruption, are nevertheless much attached to perquisites, and considerably biased in their line of duty, though perhaps insensibly, by the love of petty observances, petty presents, and trivial compliments. Mistress Debbitch turned the ring round, and round, and round, and at length said, in a whisper, ' Well, Master Julian Peveril, it signifies nothing denying anything to such a young gentleman as you, for young gentlemen are always so obstinate! and so I may as well tell you, that Mistress Alice walked back from Kirk Truagh along with me, just now, and entered the house at the same time with myself.'

'Why did you not tell me so before?' said Julian, starting up; 'where—where is she?'

'You had better ask why I tell you so *now*, Master Julian,' said Dame Deborah; 'for, I promise you, it is against her express commands; and I would not have told you, had you not looked so pitiful;—but as for seeing you, that she will not—and she is in her own bedroom, with a good oak door shut and bolted upon her—that is one comfort. And so, as for any breach of trust on my part—I promise you the little saucy minx gives it no less name—it is quite impossible.'

'Do not say so, Deborah—only go—only try—tell her to hear me—tell her I have a hundred excuses for disobeying her commands—tell her I have no doubt to get over all obstacles at Martindale Castle.'

'Nay, I tell you it is all in vain,' replied the dame. 'When I saw your cap and rod lying in the hall, I did but say, "There he is again," and she ran up the stairs like a young deer; and I heard key turned, and bolt shot, ere I could say a single word to stop her—I marvel you heard her not.'

'It was because I am, as I ever was, an owl—a dreaming fool, who let all those golden minutes pass, which my luckless life holds out to me so rarely. Well—tell her I go—go for ever—go where she will hear no more of me—where no one shall hear more of me!'

'Oh, the Father!' said the dame, 'hear how he talks! What will become of Sir Geoffrey, and your mother, and of me, and of the countess, if you were to go so far as you talk of? And what would become of poor Alice too? for I will be sworn she likes you better than she says, and I know she used to sit and look the way that you used to come up the stream, and now and then ask me if the morning were good for fishing. And all the while you were on the continent, as they call it, she scarcely smiled once, unless it was when she got two beautiful long letters about foreign parts.'

' Friendship, Dame Deborah—only friendship—cold and calm remembrance of one who, by your kind permission, stole in on your solitude now and then, with news from the living world without—Once, indeed, I thought—but it is all over—farewell.'

So saying, he covered his face with one hand, and extended the other, in the act of bidding adieu to Dame Debbitch, whose kind heart became unable to withstand the sight of his affliction.

' Now, do not be in such haste,' she said ; ' I will go up again, and tell her how it stands with you, and bring her down, if it is in woman's power to do it.'

And so saying, she left the apartment and ran upstairs.

Julian Peveril, meanwhile, paced the apartment in great agitation, waiting the success of Deborah's intercession ; and she remained long enough absent to give us time to explain, in a short retrospect, the circumstances which had led to his present situation.

CHAPTER XII

Ah me ! for aught that ever I could read,
Could ever hear by tale or history,
The course of true love never did run smooth !
Midsummer-Night's Dream.

THE celebrated passage which we have prefixed to this chapter, has, like most observations of the same author, its foundation in real experience. The period at which love is formed for the first time, and felt most strongly, is seldom that at which there is much prospect of its being brought to a happy issue. The state of artificial society opposes many complicated obstructions to early marriages ; and the chance is very great that such obstacles prove insurmountable. In fine, there are few men who do not look back in secret to some period of their youth, at which a sincere and early affection was repulsed, or betrayed, or became abortive from opposing circumstances. It is these little passages of secret history which leave a tinge of

romance in every bosom, scarce permitting us, even in the
most busy or the most advanced period of life, to listen with
total indifference to a tale of true love.

Julian Peveril had so fixed his affections as to ensure the
fullest share of that opposition which early attachments are
so apt to encounter. Yet nothing so natural as that he
should have done so. In early youth, Dame Debbitch had
accidentally met with the son of her first patroness, and
who had himself been her earliest charge, fishing in the
little brook already noticed, which watered the valley in
which she resided with Alice Bridgenorth. The dame's
curiosity easily discovered who he was; and besides the
interest which persons in her condition usually take in the
young people who have been under their charge, she was
delighted with the opportunity to talk about former times
—about Martindale Castle, and friends there—about Sir
Geoffrey and his good lady—and, now and then, about
Lance Outram the park-keeper.

The mere pleasure of gratifying her inquiries would
scarce have had power enough to induce Julian to repeat his
visits to the lonely glen; but Deborah had a companion—
a lovely girl—bred in solitude, and in the quiet and unpretending tastes which solitude encourages—spirited, also,
and inquisitive, and listening, with laughing cheek, and an
eager eye, to every tale which the young angler brought
from the town and castle.

The visits of Julian to the Black Fort were only occasional
—so far Dame Deborah showed common sense—which was,
perhaps, inspired by the apprehension of losing her place,
in case of discovery. She had, indeed, great confidence in
the strong and rooted belief—amounting almost to superstition—which Major Bridgenorth entertained, that his
daughter's continued health could only be ensured by her
continuing under the charge of one who had acquired
Lady Peveril's supposed skill in treating those subject to
such ailments. This belief Dame Deborah had improved
to the utmost of her simple cunning—always speaking in
something of an oracular tone upon the subject of her
charge's health, and hinting at certain mysterious rules
necessary to maintain it in the present favourable state.
She had availed herself of this artifice to procure for herself

and Alice a separate establishment at the Black Fort ; for it was originally Major Bridgenorth's resolution, that his daughter and her governante should remain under the same roof with the sister-in-law of his deceased wife, the widow of the unfortunate Colonel Christian. But this lady was broken down with premature age, brought on by sorrow ; and, in a short visit which Major Bridgenorth made to the island, he was easily prevailed on to consider her house at Kirk Truagh as a very cheerless residence for his daughter. Dame Deborah, who longed for domestic independence, was careful to increase this impression by alarming her patron's fears on account of Alice's health. The mansion of Kirk Truagh stood, she said, much exposed to the Scottish winds, which could not but be cold, as they came from a country where, as she was assured, there was ice and snow at mid-summer. In short, she prevailed, and was put into full possession of the Black Fort, a house which, as well as Kirk Truagh, belonged formerly to Christian, and now to his widow.

Still, however, it was enjoined on the governante and her charge, to visit Kirk Truagh from time to time, and to consider themselves as under the management and guardian-ship of Mistress Christian—a state of subjection, the sense of which Deborah endeavoured to lessen, by assuming as much freedom of conduct as she possibly dared, under the influence, doubtless, of the same feelings of independence which induced her, at Martindale Hall, to spurn the advice of Mistress Ellesmere.

It was this generous disposition to defy control which induced her to procure for Alice, secretly, some means of education, which the stern genius of Puritanism would have proscribed. She ventured to have her charge taught music—nay, even dancing ; and the picture of the stern Colonel Christian trembled on the wainscot where it was suspended, while the sylph-like form of Alice, and the substantial person of Dame Deborah, executed French *chaussées* and *borées*, to the sound of a small kit, which screamed under the bow of Monsieur de Pigal, half smuggler, half dancing-master. This abomination reached the ears of the Colonel's widow, and by her was communicated to Bridgenorth, whose sudden appearance in the island showed the importance he attached to the communication. Had she been faithless to her own cause, that had been the latest hour of Mrs. Deborah's administration. But she retreated into her stronghold.

'Dancing,' she said, ' was exercise, regulated and timed by music ; and it stood to reason, that it must be the best of all exercise for a delicate person, especially as it could be taken within doors, and in all states of the weather.'

Bridgenorth listened, with a clouded and thoughtful brow, when, in exemplification of her doctrine, Mistress Deborah, who was no contemptible performer on the viol, began to jangle Sellenger's Round, and desired Alice to dance an old English measure to the tune. As the half-bashful, half-smiling girl, about fourteen—for such was her age—moved gracefully to the music, the father's eye unavoidably followed the light spring of her step, and marked with joy the rising colour in her cheek. When the dance was over, he folded her in his arms, smoothed her somewhat disordered locks with a father's affectionate hand, smiled, kissed her brow, and took his leave, without one single word further interdicting the exercise of dancing. He did not himself communicate the result of his visit at the Black Fort to Mrs. Christian, but she was not long of learning it, by the triumph of Dame Deborah on her next visit.

' It is well,' said the stern old lady ; ' my brother Bridgenorth hath permitted you to make a Herodias of Alice, and teach her dancing. You have only now to find her a partner for life—I shall neither meddle nor make more in their affairs.'

In fact, the triumph of Dame Deborah, or rather of Dame Nature, on this occasion, had more important effects than the former had ventured to anticipate ; for Mistress Christian, though she received with all formality the formal visits of the governante and her charge, seemed thenceforth so pettish with the issue of her remonstrance, upon the enormity of her niece dancing to a little fiddle, that she appeared to give up interference in her affairs, and left Dame Debbitch and Alice to manage both education and housekeeping—in which she had hitherto greatly concerned herself—much after their own pleasure.

It was in this independent state that they lived, when Julian first visited their habitation; and he was the rather encouraged to do so by Dame Deborah, that she believed him to be one of the last persons in the world with whom Mistress Christian would have desired her niece to be acquainted—the happy spirit of contradiction superseding, with Dame Deborah, on this, as on other occasions, all consideration of the fitness of things. She did not act altogether without precaution neither. She was aware she

ALICE DANCING BEFORE HER FATHER

had to guard not only against any reviving interest or curiosity on the part of Mistress Christian, but against the sudden arrival of Major Bridgenorth, who never failed once in the year to make his appearance at the Black Fort when least expected, and to remain there for a few days. Dame Debbitch, therefore, exacted of Julian, that his visits should be few and far between; that he should condescend to pass for a relation of her own, in the eyes of two ignorant Manx girls and a lad, who formed her establishment; and that he should always appear in his angler's dress made of the simple *Loughtan*, or buff-coloured wool of the island, which is not subjected to dyeing. By these cautions, she thought his intimacy at the Black Fort would be entirely unnoticed, or considered as immaterial, while, in the meantime, it furnished much amusement to her charge and herself.

This was accordingly the case during the earlier part of their intercourse, while Julian was a lad, and Alice a girl two or three years younger. But as the lad shot up to youth, and the girl to womanhood, even Dame Deborah Debbitch's judgement saw danger in their continued intimacy. She took an opportunity to communicate to Julian who Miss Bridgenorth actually was, and the peculiar circumstances which placed discord between their fathers. He heard the story of their quarrel with interest and surprise, for he had only resided occasionally at Martindale Castle, and the subject of Bridgenorth's quarrel with his father had never been mentioned in his presence. His imagination caught fire at the sparks afforded by this singular story ; and, far from complying with the prudent remonstrance of Dame Deborah, and gradually estranging himself from the Black Fort and its fair inmate, he frankly declared, he considered his intimacy there, so casually commenced, as intimating the will of Heaven, that Alice and he were designed for each other, in spite of every obstacle which passion or prejudice could raise up betwixt them. They had been companions in infancy ; and a little exertion of memory enabled him to recall his childish grief for the unexpected and sudden disappearance of his little companion, whom he was destined again to meet with in the early bloom of opening beauty, in a country which was foreign to them both.

Dame Deborah was confounded at the consequences of her communication, which had thus blown into a flame the passion which she hoped it would have either prevented or extinguished. She had not the sort of head which resists the masculine and energetic remonstrances of passionate attachment, whether addressed to her on her own account or on behalf of another. She lamented, and wondered, and ended her feeble opposition by weeping, and sympathizing, and consenting to allow the continuance of Julian's visits, provided he should only address himself to Alice as a friend ; to gain the world, she would consent to nothing more. She

was not, however, so simple, but that she also had her
forebodings of the designs of Providence on this youthful
couple ; for certainly they could not be more formed to be
united than the good estates of Martindale and Moultrassie.

Then came a long sequence of reflections. Martindale
Castle wanted but some repairs to be almost equal to Chatsworth. The Hall might be allowed to go to ruin ; or, what
would be better, when Sir Geoffrey's time came (for the
good knight had seen service, and must be breaking now),
the Hall would be a good dowery-house, to which my lady
and Ellesmere might retreat ; while (empress of the still-
room, and queen of the pantry) Mistress Deborah Debbitch
should reign housekeeper at the castle, and extend, perhaps,
the crown-matrimonial to Lance Outram, provided he was
not become too old, too fat, or too fond of ale.

Such were the soothing visions under the influence of
which the dame connived at an attachment, which lulled
also to pleasing dreams, though of a character so different,
her charge and her visitant.

The visits of the young angler became more and more
frequent ; and the embarrassed Deborah, though foreseeing
all the dangers of discovery, and the additional risk of an
explanation betwixt Alice and Julian, which must necessarily
render their relative situation so much more delicate, felt
completely overborne by the enthusiasm of the young
lover, and was compelled to let matters take their course.

The departure of Julian for the continent interrupted the
course of his intimacy at the Black Fort, and while it
relieved the elder of its inmates from much internal apprehension, spread an air of languor and dejection over the
countenance of the younger, which, at Bridgenorth's next
visit to the Isle of Man, renewed all his terrors for his
daughter's constitutional malady.

Deborah promised faithfully she should look better the
next morning, and she kept her word. She had retained
in her possession for some time a letter which Julian had,
by some private conveyance, sent to her charge, for his
youthful friend. Deborah had dreaded the consequences
of delivering it as a billet-doux, but, as in the case of the
dance, she thought there could be no harm in administering
it as a remedy.

It had complete effect ; and next day the cheeks of the maiden had a tinge of the rose, which so much delighted her father, that, as he mounted his horse, he flung his purse into Deborah's hand, with the desire she should spare nothing that could make herself and his daughter happy, and the assurance that she had his full confidence.

This expression of liberality and confidence from a man of Major Bridgenorth's reserved and cautious disposition, gave full plumage to Mistress Deborah's hopes ; and emboldened her not only to deliver another letter of Julian's to the young lady, but to encourage more boldly and freely than formerly the intercourse of the lovers when Peveril returned from abroad.

At length, in spite of all Julian's precaution, the young earl became suspicious of his frequent solitary fishing parties ; and he himself, now better acquainted with the world than formerly, became aware that his repeated visits and solitary walks with a person so young and beautiful as Alice, might not only betray prematurely the secret of his attachment, but be of essential prejudice to her who was its object.

Under the influence of this conviction, he abstained, for an unusual period, from visiting the Black Fort. But when he next indulged himself with spending an hour in the place where he would gladly have abode for ever, the altered manner of Alice—the tone in which she seemed to upbraid his neglect, penetrated his heart, and deprived him of that power of self-command which he had hitherto exercised in their interviews. It required but a few energetic words to explain to Alice at once his feelings, and to make her sensible of the real nature of her own. She wept plentifully, but her tears were not all of bitterness. She sat passively still, and without reply, while he explained to her, with many an interjection, the circumstances which had placed discord between their families ; for hitherto, all that she had known was, that Master Peveril, belonging to the household of the great Countess or Lady of Man, must observe some precautions in visiting a relative of the unhappy Colonel Christian. But, when Julian concluded his tale with the warmest protestations of eternal love, ' My poor father ! ' she burst forth, ' and was this to be the end of all thy precautions ? This, that the son of him that disgraced and banished thee should hold such language to your daughter ? '

' You err, Alice, you err,' cried Julian, eagerly. ' That I hold this language—that the son of Peveril addresses thus the daughter of your father—that he thus kneels to you for forgiveness of injuries which passed when we were both infants, shows the will of Heaven, that in our affection should be quenched the discord of our parents. What else could lead those who parted infants on the hills of Derbyshire, to meet thus in the valleys of Man ? '

Alice, however new such a scene, and, above all, her own emotions, might be, was highly endowed with that exquisite delicacy which is imprinted in the female heart, to give warning of the slightest approach to impropriety in a situation like hers.

' Rise, rise, Master Peveril,' she said ; ' do not do yourself and me this injustice—we have done both wrong—very wrong ; but my fault was done in ignorance. O God ! my poor father, who needs comfort so much—is it for me to add to his misfortunes ? Rise ! ' she added, more firmly ; ' if you retain this unbecoming posture any longer, I will leave the room, and you shall never see me more.'

The commanding tone of Alice overawed the impetuosity of her lover, who took in silence a seat removed to some distance from hers, and was again about to speak. ' Julian,' said she, in a milder tone, ' you have spoken enough, and more than enough. Would you had left me in the pleasing dream in which I could have listened to you for ever ! but the hour of wakening is arrived.' Peveril waited the prosecution of her speech as a criminal while he waits his doom ; for he was sufficiently sensible that an answer, delivered not certainly without emotion, but with firmness and resolution, was not to be interrupted. ' We have done wrong,' she repeated, ' very wrong ; and if we now separate for ever, the pain we may feel will be but a just penalty for our error. We should never have met : meeting, we should part as soon as possible. Our further intercourse can but double our pain at parting. Farewell, Julian ; and forget we ever have seen each other ! '

' Forget ! ' said Julian ; ' never, never. To *you*, it is easy to speak the word—to think the thought. To *me*, an approach to either can only be by utter destruction. Why should you doubt that the feud of our fathers, like so many of which we have heard, might be appeased by our friendship ? You are my only friend. I am the only one whom Heaven has assigned to you. Why should we separate for the fault of others, which befell when we were but children ?'

' You speak in vain, Julian,' said Alice ; ' I pity you—perhaps I pity myself—indeed, I should pity myself, perhaps, the most of the two ; for you will go forth to new scenes and new faces, and will soon forget me ; but I, remaining in this solitude, how shall *I* forget ?—that, however, is not now the question—I can bear my lot, and it commands us to part.'

' Hear me yet a moment,' said Peveril ; 'this evil is not, cannot be remediless. I will go to my father—I will use the intercession of my mother, to whom he can refuse nothing—I will gain their consent—they have no other child—and they must consent, or lose him for ever. Say, Alice, if I come to you with my parents' consent to my suit, will you again say, with that tone so touching and so sad, yet so incredibly determined—Julian, we must part ?' Alice was silent. ' Cruel girl, will you not even deign to answer me ? ' said her lover.

' We answer not those who speak in their dreams,' said Alice. ' You ask me what I would do were impossibilities performed. What right have you to make such suppositions, and ask such a question ? '

' Hope, Alice, Hope,' answered Julian, ' the last support of the wretched, which even you surely would not be cruel enough to deprive me of. In every difficulty, in every doubt, in every danger, Hope will fight even if he cannot conquer. Tell me once more, if I come to you in the name of my father—in the name of that mother, to whom you partly owe your life, what would you answer to me ? '

' I would refer you to my own father,' said Alice, blushing, and casting her eyes down ; but instantly raising them again, she repeated, in a firmer and a sadder tone, ' Yes, Julian, I would refer you to my father ; and you would find that your pilot, Hope, had deceived you ; and that you had but escaped the quicksands to fall upon the rocks.'

' I would that could be tried ! ' said Julian. ' Methinks
I could persuade your father that in ordinary eyes our
alliance is not undesirable. My family have fortune, rank,
long descent—all that fathers look for when they bestow
a daughter's hand.'

' All this would avail you nothing,' said Alice. ' The
spirit of my father is bent upon the things of another world ;
and if he listened to hear you out, it would be but to tell
you that he spurned your offers.'

' You know not—you know not, Alice,' said Julian. ' Fire
can soften iron—thy father's heart cannot be so hard, or his
prejudices so strong, but I shall find some means to melt him.
Forbid me not—Oh, forbid me not at least the experiment ! '

' I can but advise,' said Alice ; ' I can forbid you nothing ;
for, to forbid, implies power to command obedience. But
if you will be wise, and listen to me—Here, and on this
spot, we part for ever ! '

' Not so, by Heaven ! ' said Julian, whose bold and
sanguine temper scarce saw difficulty in attaining aught
which he desired. ' We now part, indeed, but it is
that I may return armed with my parents' consent. They
desire that I should marry—in their last letters they pressed
it more openly—they shall have their desire ; and such
a bride as I will present to them has not graced their house
since the Conqueror gave it origin. Farewell, Alice ! Farewell, for a brief space ! '

She replied, ' Farewell, Julian ! Farewell for ever ! '

Julian, within a week of this interview, was at Martindale
Castle, with the view of communicating his purpose. But
the task which seems easy at a distance, proves as difficult,
upon a nearer approach, as the fording of a river, which,
from afar, appeared only a brook. There lacked not opportunities of entering upon the subject ; for in the first ride
which he took with his father, the knight resumed the
subject of his son's marriage, and liberally left the lady to
his choice ; but under the strict proviso, that she was of
a loyal and an honourable family ;—if she had fortune, it
was good and well, or rather, it was better than well ; but
if she was poor, why, ' there is still some picking,' said
Sir Geoffrey, ' on the bones of the old estate ; and Dame
Margaret and I will be content with the less, that you young

folks may have your share of it. I am turned frugal already, Julian. You see what a north-country shambling bit of a Galloway nag I ride upon—a different beast, I wot, from my own old Black Hastings, who had but one fault, and that was his wish to turn down Moultrassie avenue.'

'Was that so great a fault?' said Julian, affecting indifference, while his heart was trembling, as it seemed to him, almost in his very throat.

'It used to remind me of that base, dishonourable Presbyterian fellow, Bridgenorth,' said Sir Geoffrey; 'and I would as lief think of a toad:—they say he has turned Independent, to accomplish the full degree of rascality. I tell you, Gill, I turned off the cow-boy for gathering nuts in his woods—I would hang a dog that would so much as kill a hare there. But what is the matter with you? You look pale.'

Julian made some indifferent answer, but too well understood, from the language and tone which his father used, that his prejudices against Alice's father were both deep and envenomed, as those of country gentlemen often become, who, having little to do or think of, are but too apt to spend their time in nursing and cherishing petty causes of wrath against their next neighbours.

In the course of the same day, he mentioned the Bridgenorths to his mother, as if in a casual manner. But the Lady Peveril instantly conjured him never to mention the name, especially in his father's presence.

'Was that Major Bridgenorth, of whom I have heard the name mentioned,' said Julian, 'so very bad a neighbour?'

'I do not say so,' said Lady Peveril; 'nay, we were more than once obliged to him, in the former unhappy times; but your father and he took some passages so ill at each other's hands, that the least allusion to him disturbs Sir Geoffrey's temper, in a manner quite unusual, and which, now that his health is somewhat impaired, is sometimes alarming to me. For Heaven's sake, then, my dear Julian, avoid upon all occasions the slightest allusion to Moultrassie, or any of its inhabitants.'

This warning was so seriously given, that Julian himself saw that mentioning his secret purpose would be the sure way to render it abortive, and therefore he returned disconsolate to the isle.

Peveril had the boldness, however, to make the best he could of what had happened, by requesting an interview with Alice, in order to inform her what had passed betwixt his parents and him on her account. It was with great difficulty that this boon was obtained; and Alice Bridgenorth showed no slight degree of displeasure, when she discovered, after much circumlocution, and many efforts to give an air of importance to what he had to communicate, that all amounted but to this, that Lady Peveril continued to retain a favourable opinion of her father, Major Bridgenorth, which Julian would fain have represented as an omen of their future more perfect reconciliation.

'I did not think you would thus have trifled with me, Master Peveril,' said Alice, assuming an air of dignity; 'but I will take care to avoid such intrusion in future— I request you will not again visit the Black Fort; and I entreat of you, good Mistress Debbitch, that you will no longer either encourage or permit this gentleman's visits, as the result of such persecution will be to compel me to appeal to my aunt and father for another place of residence, and perhaps also for another and more prudent companion.'

This last hint struck Mistress Deborah with so much terror that she joined her ward in requiring and demanding Julian's instant absence, and he was obliged to comply with their request. But the courage of a youthful lover is not easily subdued; and Julian, after having gone through the usual round of trying to forget his ungrateful mistress, and again entertaining his passion with augmented violence, ended by the visit to the Black Fort, the beginning of which we narrated in the last chapter.

We then left him anxious for, yet almost fearful of, an interview with Alice, which he had prevailed upon Deborah to solicit; and such was the tumult of his mind, that, while he traversed the parlour, it seemed to him that the dark melancholy eyes of the slaughtered Christian's portrait followed him wherever he went, with the fixed, chill, and ominous glance which announced to the enemy of his race mishap and misfortune.

The door of the apartment opened at length, and these visions were dissipated.

CHAPTER XIII

Parents have flinty hearts! No tears can move them.
                                                        OTWAY.

WHEN Alice Bridgenorth at length entered the parlour
where her anxious lover had so long expected her, it was
with a slow step, and a composed manner. Her dress was
arranged with an accurate attention to form, which at
once enhanced the appearance of its puritanic simplicity, and
struck Julian as a bad omen; for although the time bestowed
upon the toilet may, in many cases, intimate the wish to
appear advantageously at such an interview, yet a ceremonious arrangement of attire is very much allied with
formality, and a preconceived determination to treat a lover
with cold politeness.

The sad-coloured gown—the pinched and plaited cap,
which carefully obscured the profusion of long dark-brown
hair—the small ruff, and the long sleeves, would have
appeared to great disadvantage on a shape less graceful than
Alice Bridgenorth's; but an exquisite form, though not,
as yet, sufficiently rounded in the outlines to produce the
perfection of female beauty, was able to sustain and give
grace even to this unbecoming dress. Her countenance,
fair and delicate, with eyes of hazel, and a brow of alabaster,
had, notwithstanding, less regular beauty than her form,
and might have been justly subjected to criticism. There
was, however, a life and spirit in her gaiety, and a depth of
sentiment in her gravity, which made Alice, in conversation
with the very few persons with whom she associated, so
fascinating in her manners and expression, whether of
language or countenance—so touching, also, in her simplicity and purity of thought, that brighter beauties might
have been overlooked in her company. It was no wonder,
therefore, that an ardent character like Julian, influenced
by these charms, as well as by the secrecy and mystery
attending his intercourse with Alice, should prefer the
recluse of the Black Fort to all others with whom he had
become acquainted in general society.

ALICE BRIDGENORTH

His heart beat high as she came into the apartment, and it was almost without an attempt to speak that his profound obeisance acknowledged her entrance.

'This is a mockery, Master Peveril,' said Alice, with an effort to speak firmly, which yet was disconcerted by a slightly tremulous inflection of voice—'a mockery, and a cruel one. You come to this lone place, inhabited only by two women, too simple to command your absence—too weak to enforce it—you come, in spite of my earnest request—to the neglect of your own time—to the prejudice, I may fear, of my character—you abuse the influence you possess over the simple person to whom I am intrusted—All this you do, and think to make it up by low reverences and constrained courtesy! Is this honourable, or is it fair? Is it,' she added, after a moment's hesitation—'is it kind?'

The tremulous accent fell especially on the last word she uttered, and it was spoken in a low tone of gentle reproach, which went to Julian's heart.

'If,' said he, 'there was a mode by which, at the peril of my life, Alice, I could show my regard—my respect—my devoted tenderness—the danger would be dearer to me than ever was pleasure.'

'You have said such things often,' said Alice, 'and they are such as I ought not to hear, and do not desire to hear. I have no tasks to impose on you—no enemies to be destroyed—no need or desire of protection—no wish, Heaven knows, to expose you to danger—It is your visits here alone to which danger attaches. You have but to rule your own wilful temper—to turn your thoughts and your cares elsewhere, and I can have nothing to ask—nothing to wish for. Use your own reason—consider the injury you do yourself—the injustice you do us—and let me once more, in fair terms, entreat you to absent yourself from this place—till—till'——

She paused, and Julian eagerly interrupted her. 'Till when, Alice?—till when?—impose on me any length of absence which your severity can inflict, short of a final separation—Say, Begone for years, but return when these years are over; and, slow and wearily as they must pass away, still the thought that they must at length have their period will enable me to live through them. Let me, then,

conjure thee, Alice, to name a date—to fix a term—to say
till *when* ! '

' Till you can bear to think of me only as a friend and
sister.'

' That is a sentence of eternal banishment indeed ! ' said
Julian ; ' it is seeming, no doubt, to fix a term of exile, but
attaching to it an impossible condition.'

' And why impossible, Julian ? ' said Alice, in a tone of
persuasion ; ' were we not happier ere you threw the mask
from your own countenance, and tore the veil from my
foolish eyes ? Did we not meet with joy, spend our time
happily, and part cheerily, because we transgressed no
duty, and incurred no self-reproach ? Bring back that state
of happy ignorance, and you shall have no reason to call me
unkind. But while you form schemes which I know to be
visionary, and use language of such violence and passion,
you shall excuse me if I now, and once for all, declare, that
since Deborah shows herself unfit for the trust reposed in
her, and must needs expose me to persecutions of this
nature, I will write to my father, that he may fix me another
place of residence ; and in the meanwhile I will take shelter
with my aunt at Kirk Truagh.'

' Hear me, unpitying girl,' said Peveril, ' hear me, and you
shall see how devoted I am to obedience, in all that I can
do to oblige you ! You say you were happy when we spoke
not on such topics—well—at all expense of my own suppressed feelings, that happy period shall return. I will
meet you—walk with you—read with you—but only as a
brother would with his sister, or a friend with his friend ;
the thoughts I may nourish, be they of hope or of despair,
my tongue shall not give birth to, and therefore I cannot
offend ; Deborah shall be ever by your side, and her
presence shall prevent my even hinting at what might displease you—only do not make a crime to me of those
thoughts which are the dearest part of my existence ; for
believe me it were better and kinder to rob me of existence
itself.'

' This is the mere ecstasy of passion, Julian,' answered
Alice Bridgenorth ; ' that which is unpleasant, our selfish
and stubborn will represents as impossible. I have no
confidence in the plan you propose—no confidence in your

resolution, and less than none in the protection of Deborah. Till you can renounce, honestly and explicitly, the wishes you have lately expressed, we must be strangers ; and could you renounce them even at this moment, it were better that we should part for a long time ; and, for Heaven's sake, let it be as soon as possible—perhaps it is even now too late to prevent some unpleasant accident—I thought I heard a noise.'

'It was Deborah,' answered Julian. 'Be not afraid, Alice ; we are secure against surprise.'

'I know not,' said Alice, 'what you mean by such security—I have nothing to hide. I sought not this inter- view ; on the contrary, averted it as long as I could—and am now most desirous to break it off.'

'And wherefore, Alice, since you say it must be our last ? Why should you shake the sand which is passing so fast ? the very executioner hurries not the prayers of the wretches upon the scaffold. And see you not—I will argue as coldly as you can desire—see you not that you are breaking your own word, and recalling the hope which yourself held out to me ?'

'What hope have I suggested ? What word have I given, Julian ?' answered Alice. 'You yourself build wild hopes in the air, and accuse me of destroying what had never any earthly foundation. Spare yourself, Julian—spare me— and in mercy to us both depart, and return not again till you can be more reasonable.'

'Reasonable ?' replied Julian ; 'it is you, Alice, who will deprive me altogether of reason. Did you not say, that if our parents could be brought to consent to our union, you would no longer oppose my suit ?'

'No—no—no,' said Alice eagerly, and blushing deeply— 'I did not say so, Julian—it was your own wild imagination which put construction on my silence and my confusion.'

'You do *not* say so, then,' answered Julian ; 'and if all other obstacles were removed, I should find one in the cold flinty bosom of her who repays the most devoted and sincere affection, with contempt and dislike ? Is that,' he added, in a deep tone of feeling—'is that what Alice Bridgenorth says to Julian Peveril ?'

'Indeed—indeed, Julian,' said the almost weeping girl,

'I do not say so—I say nothing, and I ought not to say anything concerning what I might do, in a state of things which can never take place. Indeed, Julian, you ought not thus to press me. Unprotected as I am—wishing you well—very well—why should you urge me to say or do what would lessen me in my own eyes ? to own affection for one from whom fate has separated me for ever ? It is ungenerous —it is cruel—it is seeking a momentary and selfish gratification to yourself, at the expense of every feeling which I ought to entertain.'

'You have said enough, Alice,' said Julian, with sparkling eyes ; 'you have said enough in deprecating my urgency, and I will press you no further. But you overrate the impediments which lie betwixt us—they must and shall give way.'

'So you said before,' answered Alice, 'and with what probability, your own account may show. You dared not to mention the subject to your own father—how should you venture to mention it to mine ? '

'That I will soon enable you to decide upon. Major Bridgenorth, by my mother's account, is a worthy and an estimable man. I will remind him, that to my mother's care he owes the dearest treasure and comfort of his life ; and I will ask him if it is a just retribution to make that mother childless. Let me but know where to find him, Alice, and you shall soon hear if I have feared to plead my cause with him.'

'Alas ! ' answered Alice, 'you well know my uncertainty as to my dear father's residence. How often has it been my earnest request to him that he would let me share his solitary abode, or his obscure wanderings ! But the short and infrequent visits which he makes to this house are all that he permits me of his society. Something I might surely do, however little, to alleviate the melancholy by which he is oppressed.'

'Something we might both do,' said Peveril. 'How willingly would I aid you in so pleasing a task ! All old griefs should be forgotten—all old friendships revived. My father's prejudices are those of an Englishman—strong, indeed, but not insurmountable by reason. Tell me, then, where Major Bridgenorth is, and leave the rest to me ; or let me but know by what address your letters reach him, and I will forthwith essay to discover his dwelling.'

'Do not attempt it, I charge you,' said Alice. 'He is already a man of sorrows ; and what would he think were I capable of entertaining a suit so likely to add to them ? Besides, I could not tell you, if I would, where he is now to be found. My letters reach him from time to time, by means of my aunt Christian ; but of his address I am entirely ignorant.'

'Then, by Heaven,' answered Julian, 'I will watch his arrival in this island, and in this house ; and ere he has locked thee in his arms, he shall answer to me on the subject of my suit.'

'Then demand that answer now,' said a voice from without the door, which was at the same time slowly opened— 'Demand that answer now, for here stands Ralph Bridgenorth.'

As he spoke, he entered the apartment with his usual slow and sedate step—raised his flapped and steeple-crowned hat from his brows, and, standing in the midst of the room, eyed alternately his daughter and Julian Peveril with a fixed and penetrating glance.

'Father !' said Alice, utterly astonished, and terrified, besides, by his sudden appearance at such a conjuncture— 'Father, I am not to blame.'

'Of that anon, Alice,' said Bridgenorth ; 'meantime retire to your apartment—I have that to say to this youth which will not endure your presence.'

'Indeed—indeed, father,' said Alice, alarmed at what she supposed these words indicated, 'Julian is as little to be blamed as I ! It was chance, it was fortune, which caused our meeting together.' Then suddenly rushing forward, she threw her arms around her father, saying, 'Oh, do him no injury—he meant no wrong ! Father, you were wont to be a man of reason and of religious peace.'

'And wherefore should I not be so now, Alice ?' said Bridgenorth, raising his daughter from the ground, on which she had almost sunk in the earnestness of her supplication. 'Dost thou know aught, maiden, which should inflame my anger against this young man, more than reason or religion may bridle ? Go—go to thy chamber. Compose

thine own passions—learn to rule these—and leave it to me
to deal with this stubborn young man.'

Alice arose, and, with her eyes fixed on the ground, retired
slowly from the apartment.   Julian followed her steps with
his eyes till the last wave of her garment was visible at the
closing door ;   then turned his looks to Major Bridgenorth,
and then sank them on the ground.   The major continued
to regard him in profound silence ;   his looks were melancholy and even austere ;   but there was nothing which
indicated either agitation or keen resentment.   He motioned
to Julian to take a seat, and assumed one himself.   After
which, he opened the conversation in the following
manner :—

'You seemed but now, young gentleman, anxious to
learn where I was to be found.   Such I at least conjectured,
from the few expressions which I chanced to overhear ;   for
I made bold, though it may be contrary to the code of
modern courtesy, to listen a moment or two, in order to
gather upon what subject so young a man as you entertained
so young a woman as Alice in a private interview.'

'I trust, sir,' said Julian, rallying spirits in what he felt
to be a case of extremity, 'you have heard nothing on my
part which has given offence to a gentleman whom, though
unknown, I am bound to respect so highly.'

'On the contrary,' said Bridgenorth, with the same formal
gravity, 'I am pleased to find that your business is, or appears to be, with me, rather than with my daughter.   I only
think you had done better to have entrusted it to me in the
first instance, as my sole concern.'

The utmost sharpness of attention which Julian applied
could not discover if Bridgenorth spoke seriously or ironic-
ally to the above purpose.   He was, however, quick-witted
beyond his experience, and was internally determined to
endeavour to discover something of the character and the
temper of him with whom he spoke.   For that purpose,
regulating his reply in the same tone with Bridgenorth's
observation, he said, that not having the advantage to know
his place of residence, he had applied for information to his
daughter.

'Who is now known to you for the first time ?' said
Bridgenorth.   'Am I so to understand you ?'

'By no means,' answered Julian, looking down ; 'I have
been known to your daughter for many years ; and what
I wished to say respects both her happiness and my own.'

'I must understand you,' said Bridgenorth, 'even as
carnal men understand each other on the matters of this
world. You are attached to my daughter by the cords of
love ; I have long known this.'

'You, Master Bridgenorth ? ' exclaimed Peveril—' *You*
have long known it ? '

'Yes, young man. Think you, that as the father of an
only child, I could have suffered Alice Bridgenorth—the
only living pledge of her who is now an angel in heaven—
to have remained in this seclusion without the surest knowledge of all her material actions ? I have, in person, seen
more, both of her and of you, than you could be aware of ;
and when absent in the body, I had the means of maintaining the same superintendence. Young man, they say that
such love as you entertain for my daughter teaches much
subtilty ; but believe not that it can overreach the affection
which a widowed father bears to an only child.'

'If,' said Julian, his heart beating thick and joyfully, ' if
you have known this intercourse so long, may I not hope
that it has not met your disapprobation ? '

The major paused for an instant, and then answered,
'In some respects, certainly not. Had it done so—had
there seemed aught on your side, or on my daughter's, to
have rendered your visits here dangerous to her, or dis-
pleasing to me, she had not been long the inhabitant of this
solitude, or of this island. But be not so hasty as to
presume that all which you may desire in this matter can
be either easily or speedily accomplished.'

'I foresee, indeed, difficulties,' answered Julian ; ' but
with your kind acquiescence, they are such as I trust to
remove. My father is generous—my mother is candid and
liberal. They loved you once ; I trust they will love you
again. I will be the mediator betwixt you—peace and
harmony shall once more inhabit our neighbourhood,
and '——

Bridgenorth interrupted him with a grim smile ; for such
it seemed, as it passed over a face of deep melancholy.
'My daughter well said, but short while past, that you

were a dreamer of dreams—an architect of plans and hopes
fantastic as the visions of the night. It is a great thing
you ask of me ;—the hand of my only child—the sum of my
worldly substance, though that is but dross in comparison.
You ask the key of the only fountain from which I may yet
hope to drink one pleasant draught ; you ask to be the
sole and absolute keeper of my earthly happiness—and
what have you offered, or what have you to offer, in return,
of the surrender you require of me ? '

' I am but too sensible,' said Peveril, abashed at his own
hasty conclusions, ' how difficult it may be.'

' Nay, but interrupt me not,' replied Bridgenorth, ' till
I show you the amount of what you offer me in exchange
for a boon, which, whatever may be its intrinsic value, is
earnestly desired by you, and comprehends all that is
valuable on earth which I have it in my power to bestow.
You may have heard, that in the late times I was the
antagonist of your father's principles and his profane
faction, but not the enemy of his person.'

' I have ever heard,' replied Julian, ' much the contrary ;
and it was but now that I reminded you that you had been
his friend.'

' Aye. When he was in affliction and I in prosperity,
I was neither unwilling, nor altogether unable, to show
myself such. Well, the tables are turned—the times are
changed. A peaceful and unoffending man might have
expected from a neighbour, now powerful in his turn, such
protection, when walking in the paths of the law, as all
men, subjects of the same realm, have a right to expect even
from perfect strangers. What chances ? I pursue, with the
warrant of the king and law, a murderess, bearing on her
hand the blood of my near connexion, and I had, in such
a case, a right to call on every liege subject to render
assistance to the execution. My late friendly neighbour,
bound, as a man and a magistrate, to give ready assistance
to a legal action—bound, as a grateful and obliged friend,
to respect my rights and my person—thrusts himself
betwixt me—me, the avenger of blood—and my lawful
captive ; beats me to the earth, at once endangering my
life, and, in mere human eyes, sullying mine honour ; and
under his protection, the Midianitish woman reaches, like

a sea-eagle, the nest which she hath made in the wave-surrounded rocks, and remains there till gold, duly administered at court, wipes out all memory of her crime, and baffles the vengeance due to the memory of the best and bravest of men.—But,' he added, apostrophizing the portrait of Christian, ' thou art not yet forgotten, my fair-haired William ! The vengeance which dogs thy murderess is slow—but it is sure ! '

There was a pause of some moments, which Julian Peveril, willing to hear to what conclusion Major Bridgenorth was finally to arrive, did not care to interrupt. Accordingly, in a few minutes, the latter proceeded. ' These things,' he said, ' I recall not in bitterness, so far as they are personal to me—I recall them not in spite of heart, though they have been the means of banishing me from my place of residence, where my fathers dwelt, and where my earthly comforts lie interred. But the public cause sets further strife betwixt your father and me. Who so active as he to execute the fatal edict of black St. Bartholomew's Day, when so many hundreds of gospel-preachers were expelled from house and home—from hearth and altar—from church and parish, to make room for belly-gods and thieves ? Who, when a devoted few of the Lord's people were united to lift the fallen standard, and once more advance the good cause, was the readiest to break their purpose—to search for, persecute, and apprehend them ? Whose breath did I feel warm on my neck—whose naked sword was thrust within a foot of my body, whilst I lurked darkling, like a thief in concealment, in the house of my fathers ? It was Geoffrey Peveril's—it was your father's ! What can you answer to all this, or how can you reconcile it with your present wishes ? '

Julian, in reply, could only remark, ' That these injuries had been of long standing—that they had been done in heat of times, and heat of temper, and that Master Bridgenorth, in Christian kindness, should not entertain a keen resentment of them, when a door was opened for reconciliation.'

' Peace, young man,' said Bridgenorth, ' thou speakest of thou knowest not what. To forgive our human wrongs is Christian-like and commendable ; but we have no commission to forgive those which have been done to the cause

M

of religion and of liberty ; we have no right to grant im-
munity, or to shake hands with those who have poured forth
the blood of our brethren.' He looked at the picture of
Christian, and was silent for a few minutes, as if he feared to
give too violent way to his own impetuosity, and resumed
the discourse in a milder tone.

' These things I point out to you, Julian, that I may show
you how impossible, in the eyes of a merely worldly man,
would be the union which you are desirous of. But
Heaven hath at times opened a door, where man beholds no
means of issue. Julian, your mother, for one to whom the
truth is unknown, is, after the fashion of the world, one of
the best, and one of the wisest of women ; and Providence,
which gave her so fair a form, and tenanted that form with
a mind as pure as the original frailty of our vile nature will
permit, means not, I trust, that she shall continue to the end
to be a vessel of wrath and perdition. Of your father I say
nothing—he is what the times and example of others, and
the counsels of his lordly priest, have made him ; and of
him, once more, I say nothing, save that I have power over
him, which ere now he might have felt, but that there is one
within his chambers, who might have suffered in his suffering.
Nor do I wish to root up your ancient family. If I prize not
your boast of family honours and pedigree, I would not
willingly destroy them ; more than I would pull down a
moss-grown tower, or hew to the ground an ancient oak,
save for the straightening of the common path, and the
advantage of the public. I have, therefore, no resentment
against the humbled house of Peveril—nay, I have regard
to it in its depression.'

He here made a second pause, as if he expected Julian to
say something. But notwithstanding the ardour with which
the young man had pressed his suit, he was too much
trained in ideas of the importance of his family, and in the
better habit of respect for his parents, to hear, without displeasure, some part of Bridgenorth's discourse.

' The house of Peveril,' he replied, ' was never humbled.'

' Had you said the sons of that house had never been
humble,' answered Bridgenorth, ' you would have come
nearer the truth. Are *you* not humbled ? Live you not
here, the lackey of a haughty woman, the play-companion of

an empty youth ? If you leave this isle, and go to the court
of England, see what regard will there be paid to the old
pedigree that deduces your descent from kings and con-
querors. A scurril or obscene jest, an impudent carriage,
a laced cloak, a handful of gold, and the readiness to wager
it on a card, or a die, will better advance you at the court
of Charles than your father's ancient name, and slavish
devotion of blood and fortune to the cause of *his* father.'

   ' That is, indeed, but too probable,' said Peveril ; ' but
the court shall be no element of mine. I will live like my
fathers, among my people, care for their comforts, decide
their differences '——

   ' Build Maypoles, and dance around them,' said Bridgenorth, with another of those grim smiles which passed over
his features like the light of a sexton's torch, as it glares and
is reflected by the window of the church, when he comes
from locking a funeral vault. ' No, Julian, these are not
times in which, by the dreaming drudgery of a country
magistrate, and the petty cares of a country proprietor, a
man can serve his unhappy country. There are mighty
designs afloat, and men are called to make their choice
betwixt God and Baal. The ancient superstition—the
abomination of our fathers—is raising its head, and flinging
abroad its snares, under the protection of the princes of the
earth ; but she raises not her head unmarked or unwatched ;
the true English hearts are as thousands, which wait but a
signal to arise as one man, and show the kings of the earth
that they have combined in vain ! We will cast their cords
from us—the cup of their abominations we will not taste.'

   ' You speak in darkness, Master Bridgenorth,' said Peveril.
' Knowing so much of me, you may, perhaps, also be aware
that I at least have seen too much of the delusions of Rome
to desire that they should be propagated at home.'

   ' Else, wherefore do I speak to thee friendly and so free ? '
said Bridgenorth. ' Do I not know with what readiness of
early wit you baffled the wily attempts of the woman's
priest to seduce thee from the Protestant faith ? Do I not
know how thou wast beset when abroad, and that thou didst
both hold thine own faith and secure the wavering belief
of thy friend ? Said I not, this was done like the son of
Margaret Peveril ? Said I not, he holdeth, as yet, but the

dead letter—but the seed which is sown shall one day sprout and quicken ?   Enough, however, of this.   For to-day this is thy habitation.   I will see in thee neither the servant of that daughter of Eshbaal, nor the son of him who pursued my life, and blemished my honours ; but thou shalt be to me, for this day, as the child of her without whom my house had been extinct.'

So saying, he stretched out his thin, bony hand, and grasped that of Julian Peveril ; but there was such a look of mourning in his welcome, that whatever delight the youth anticipated, spending so long a time in the neighbourhood of Alice Bridgenorth, perhaps in her society, or however strongly he felt the prudence of conciliating her father's goodwill, he could not help feeling as if his heart was chilled in his company.

CHAPTER XIV

This day at least is friendship's—on the morrow
Let strife come an she will.
                                        OTWAY.

DEBORAH DEBBITCH, summoned by her master, now made her appearance, with her handkerchief at her eyes, and an appearance of great mental trouble.   ' It was not my fault, Major Bridgenorth,' she said ; ' how could I help it ? like will to like—the boy would come—the girl would see him.'

' Peace, foolish woman,' said Bridgenorth, ' and hear what I have got to say.'

' I know what your honour has to say well enough,' said Deborah.   ' Service, I wot, is no inheritance nowadays— some are wiser than other some—if I had not been wheedled away from Martindale, I might have had a house of mine own by this time.'

' Peace, idiot ! ' said Bridgenorth ; but so intent was Deborah on her vindication, that he could but thrust the interjection, as it were edgewise, between her exclamations, which followed as thick as is usual in cases, where folks endeavour to avert deserved censure by a clamorous justifi-cation ere the charge be brought.

'No wonder she was cheated,' she said, 'out of sight of her own interest, when it was to wait on pretty Miss Alice. All your honour's gold should never have tempted me, but that I knew she was but a dead castaway, poor innocent, if she were taken away from my lady or me.   And so this is the end on't !—up early, and down late—-and this is all my thanks! But your honour had better take care what you do —she has the short cough yet sometimes—and should take physic, spring and fall.'

'Peace, chattering fool !' said her master, so soon as her failing breath gave him an opportunity to strike in, 'thinkest thou I knew not of this young gentleman's visits to the Black Fort, and that, if they had displeased me, I would not have known how to stop them ?'

'Did I know that your honour knew of his visits !' exclaimed Deborah, in a triumphant tone,—for, like most of her condition, she never sought further for her defence than a lie, however inconsistent and improbable—'Did I know that your honour knew of it ! Why, how should I have permitted his visits else ? I wonder what your honour takes me for ! Had I not been sure it was the thing in this world that your honour most desired, would I have presumed to lend it a hand forward ? I trust I know my duty better. Hear if I ever asked another youngster into the house, save himself—for I knew your honour was wise, and quarrels cannot last for ever, and love begins where hatred ends ; and, to be sure, they love as if they were born one for the other—and then, the estates of Moultrassie and Martindale suit each other like sheath and knife.'

'Parrot of a woman, hold your tongue !' said Bridgenorth, his patience almost completely exhausted ; 'or, if you will prate, let it be to your playfellows in the kitchen, and bid them get ready some dinner presently, for Master Peveril is far from home.'

'That I will, and with all my heart,' said Deborah ; 'and if there are a pair of fatter fowls in Man than shall clap their wings on the table presently, your honour shall call me goose as well as parrot.' She then left the apartment.

'It is to such a woman as that,' said Bridgenorth, looking after her significantly, 'that you conceived me to have abandoned the charge of my only child ! But enough of this subject—we will walk abroad, if you will, while she is engaged in a province fitter for her understanding.'

So saying, he left the house, accompanied by Julian Peveril, and they were soon walking side by side, as if they had been old acquaintances.

It may have happened to many of our readers, as it has done to ourselves, to be thrown by accident into society with some individual whose claims to what is called a *serious* character stand considerably higher than our own, and with whom, therefore, we have conceived ourselves likely to spend our time in a very stiff and constrained manner ; while, on the other hand, our destined companion may have apprehended some disgust from the supposed levity and thoughtless gaiety of a disposition so different from his own.   Now it has frequently happened, that when we, with that urbanity and good humour which is our principal characteristic, have accommodated ourself to our companion, by throwing as much seriousness into our conversation as our habits will admit, he, on the other hand, moved by our liberal example, hath divested his manners of a part of their austerity ; and our conversation has, in consequence, been of that pleasant texture, betwixt the useful and agreeable, which best resembles 'the fairy-web of night and day', usually called in prose the twilight.   It is probable both parties may, on such occasions, have been the better for their encounter, even if it went no further than to establish for the time a community of feeling between men, who, separated more perhaps by temper than by principle, are too apt to charge each other with profane frivolity on the one hand, or fanaticism on the other.

It fared thus in Peveril's walk with Bridgenorth, and in the conversation which he held with him.

Carefully avoiding the subject on which he had already spoken, Major Bridgenorth turned his conversation chiefly on foreign travel, and on the wonders he had seen in distant countries, and which he appeared to have marked with a curious and observant eye.   This discourse made the time fly light away ; for although the anecdotes and observations thus communicated were all tinged with the serious and almost gloomy spirit of the narrator, they yet contained traits of interest and of wonder, such as are usually interesting to a youthful ear, and were particularly so to Julian, who had, in his disposition, some cast of the romantic and adventurous.

It appeared that Bridgenorth knew the south of France, and could tell many stories of the French Huguenots, who already began to sustain those vexations which a few years afterwards were summed up by the revocation of the Edict of Nantz. He had even been in Hungary, for he spoke as from personal knowledge of the character of several of the heads of the great Protestant insurrection, which at this time had taken place under the celebrated Tekeli ; and laid down solid reasons why they were entitled to make common cause with the Great Turk, rather than submit to the Pope of Rome. He talked also of Savoy, where those of the reformed religion still suffered a cruel persecution ; and he mentioned with a swelling spirit, the protection which Oliver had afforded to the oppressed Protestant Churches ; ' therein showing himself,' he added, ' more fit to wield the supreme power, than those who, claiming it by right of inheritance, use it only for their own vain and voluptuous pursuits.'

' I did not expect,' said Peveril modestly, ' to have heard Oliver's panegyric from you, Master Bridgenorth.'

' I do not panegyrize him,' answered Bridgenorth ; ' I speak but truth of that extraordinary man, now being dead, whom, when alive, I feared not to withstand to his face. It is the fault of the present unhappy king, if he make us look back with regret to the days when the nation was respected abroad, and when devotion and sobriety were practised at home. But I mean not to vex your spirit by controversy. You have lived amongst those who find it more easy and more pleasant to be the pensioners of France than her controllers—to spend the money which she doles out to themselves, than to check the tyranny with which she oppresses our poor brethren of the religion. When the scales shall fall from thine eyes, all this thou shalt see ; and seeing, shalt learn to detest and despise it.'

By this time they had completed their walk, and were returned to the Black Fort by a different path from that which had led them up the valley. The exercise and the general tone of conversation had removed, in some degree, the shyness and embarrassment which Peveril originally felt in Bridgenorth's presence, and which the tenor of his first remarks had rather increased than diminished. Deborah's promised banquet was soon on the board; and in simplicity, as well as neatness and good order, answered the character she had claimed for it. In one respect alone, there seemed some inconsistency, perhaps a little affectation. Most of the dishes were of silver, and the plates were of the same metal; instead of the trenchers and pewter which Peveril had usually seen employed on similar occasions at the Black Fort.

Presently, with the feeling of one who walks in a pleasant dream from which he fears to awake, and whose delight is mingled with wonder and with uncertainty, Julian Peveril found himself seated between Alice Bridgenorth and her father—the being he most loved on earth, and the person whom he had ever considered as the great obstacle to their intercourse. The confusion of his mind was such that he could scarcely reply to the importunate civilities of Dame Deborah; who, seated with them at table in her quality of governante, now dispensed the good things which had been prepared under her own eye.

As for Alice, she seemed to have formed a resolution to play the mute; for she answered not, excepting briefly, to the questions of Dame Debbitch; nay, even when her father, which happened once or twice, attempted to bring her forward in the conversation, she made no further reply than respect for him rendered absolutely necessary.

Upon Bridgenorth himself, then, devolved the task of entertaining the company; and, contrary to his ordinary habits, he did not seem to shrink from it. His discourse was not only easy, but almost cheerful, though ever and anon crossed by some expressions indicative of natural and habitual melancholy, or prophetic of future misfortune and woe. Flashes of enthusiasm, too, shot along his conversation, gleaming like the sheet-lightning of an autumn eve, which throws a strong, though momentary illumination, across the sober twilight, and all the surrounding objects, which, touched by it, assume a wilder and more striking character. In general, however, Bridgenorth's remarks were plain and sensible; and as he aimed at no graces of language, any ornament which they received arose out of the interest with which they were impressed on his hearers. For example, when Deborah, in the pride and vulgarity of her heart, called Julian's attention to the plate from which they had been eating, Bridgenorth seemed to think an apology necessary for such superfluous expense.

'It was a symptom,' he said, 'of approaching danger, when such men, as were not usually influenced by the vanities of life, employed much money in ornaments composed of the precious metals. It was a sign that the merchant could not obtain a profit for the capital, which, for the sake of security, he invested in this inert form. It was a proof that the noblemen or gentlemen feared the rapacity of power, when they put their wealth into forms the most portable and the most capable of being hidden; and it showed the uncertainty of credit, when a man of judgement preferred the actual possession of a mass of silver to the convenience of a goldsmith's or a banker's receipt. While a shadow of liberty remained,' he said, 'domestic rights were last invaded; and, therefore, men disposed upon their cupboards and tables the wealth which in these places would remain longest, though not perhaps finally, sacred from the grasp of a tyrannical government. But let there be a demand for capital to support a profitable commerce, and the mass is at once consigned to the furnace, and, ceasing to be a vain and cumbrous ornament of the banquet, becomes a potent and active agent for furthering the prosperity of the country.'

'In war, too,' said Peveril, 'plate has been found a ready resource.'

'But too much so,' answered Bridgenorth. 'In the late times, the plate of the nobles and gentry, with that of the colleges, and the sale of the crown-jewels, enabled the king to make his unhappy stand, which prevented matters returning to a state of peace and good order, until the sword had attained an undue superiority both over king and Parliament.'

He looked at Julian as he spoke, much as he who proves a horse offers some object suddenly to his eyes, then watches to see if he starts or blenches from it. But Julian's thoughts were too much bent on other topics to manifest any alarm.

His answer referred to a previous part of Bridgenorth's discourse, and was not returned till after a brief pause. ' War, then,' he said, ' war, the grand impoverisher, is also a creator of the wealth which it wastes and devours ? '

' Yes,' replied Bridgenorth, ' even as the sluice brings into action the sleeping waters of the lake, which it finally drains. Necessity invents arts and discovers means ; and what necessity is sterner than that of civil war ? Therefore, even war is not in itself unmixed evil, being the creator of impulses and energies which could not otherwise have existed in society.'

' Men should go to war, then,' said Peveril, ' that they may send their silver plate to the mint, and eat from pewter dishes and wooden platters ? '

' Not so, my son,' said Bridgenorth. Then checking himself as he observed the deep crimson in Julian's cheek and brow, he added, ' I crave your pardon for such familiarity ; but I meant not to limit what I said even now to such trifling consequences, although it may be something salutary to tear men from their pomps and luxuries, and teach those to be Romans who would otherwise be Sybarites. But I would say, that times of public danger, as they call into circulation the miser's hoard and the proud man's bullion, and so add to the circulating wealth of the country, do also call into action many a brave and noble spirit, which would otherwise lie torpid, give no example to the living, and bequeath no name to future ages. Society knows not, and cannot know, the mental treasures which slumber in her bosom, till necessity and opportunity call forth the statesman and the soldier from the shades of lowly life to the parts they are designed by Providence to perform, and the stations which nature had qualified them to hold.   So rose Oliver—so rose Milton—so rose many another name which cannot be forgotten—even as the tempest summons forth and displays the address of the mariner.'

' You speak,' said Peveril, ' as if national calamity might be, in some sort, an advantage.'

' And if it were not so,' replied Bridgenorth, ' it had not existed in this state of trial, where all temporal evil is alleviated by something good in its progress or result, and where all that is good is close coupled with that which is in itself evil.'

'It must be a noble sight,' said Julian, 'to behold the slumbering energies of a great mind awakened into energy, and to see it assume the authority which is its due over spirits more meanly endowed.'

'I once witnessed,' said Bridgenorth, 'something to the same effect ; and as the tale is brief, I will tell it you, if you will :—

'Amongst my wanderings, the Transatlantic settlements have not escaped me ; more especially the country of New England, into which our native land has shaken from her lap, as a drunkard flings from him his treasures, so much that is precious in the eyes of God and of his children. There thousands of our best and most godly men—such whose righteousness might come between the Almighty and his wrath, and prevent the ruin of cities—are content to be the inhabitants of the desert, rather encountering the unenlightened savages, than stooping to extinguish, under the oppression practised in Britain, the light that is within their own minds.   There I remained for a time, during the wars which the colony maintained with Philip, a great Indian chief, or sachem, as they were called, who seemed a messenger sent from Satan to buffet them.   His cruelty was great—his dissimulation profound ; and the skill and promptitude with which he maintained a destructive and desultory warfare, inflicted many dreadful calamities on the settlement.   I was, by chance, at a small village in the woods, more than thirty miles from Boston, and in its situation exceedingly lonely, and surrounded with thickets. Nevertheless, there was no idea of any danger from the Indians at that time, for men trusted to the protection of a considerable body of troops who had taken the field for protection of the frontiers, and who lay, or were supposed to lie, betwixt the hamlet and the enemy's country.   But they had to do with a foe, whom the devil himself had inspired at once with cunning and cruelty.   It was on a Sabbath morning, when we had assembled to take sweet counsel together in the Lord's house.   Our temple was but constructed of wooden logs ; but when shall the chant of trained hirelings, or the sounding of tin and brass tubes

amid the aisles of a minster, arise so sweetly to Heaven, as
did the psalm in which we united at once our voices and our
hearts! An excellent worthy, who now sleeps in the Lord,
Nehemiah Solsgrace, long the companion of my pilgrimage,
had just begun to wrestle in prayer, when a woman, with
disordered looks and dishevelled hair, entered our chapel in
a distracted manner, screaming incessantly, "The Indians!
The Indians!" In that land no man dares separate himself
from his means of defence; and whether in the city or in
the field, in the ploughed land or the forest, men keep beside
them their weapons, as did the Jews at the rebuilding of the
Temple. So we sallied forth with our guns and pikes, and
heard the whoop of these incarnate devils, already in possession of a part of the town, and exercising their cruelty on
the few whom weighty causes or indisposition had withheld
from public worship; and it was remarked as a judgement,
that, upon that bloody Sabbath, Adrian Hanson, a Dutch-
man, a man well enough disposed towards man, but whose
mind was altogether given to worldly gain, was shot and
scalped as he was summing his weekly gains in his warehouse.
In fine, there was much damage done; and although our
arrival and entrance into combat did in some sort put them
back, yet being surprised and confused, and having no
appointed leader of our band, the devilish enemy shot hard
at us, and had some advantage. It was pitiful to hear the
screams of women and children amid the report of guns and
the whistling of bullets, mixed with the ferocious yells of
these savages, which they term their war-whoop. Several
houses in the upper part of the village were soon on fire;
and the roaring of the flames, and crackling of the great
beams as they blazed, added to the horrible confusion;
while the smoke which the wind drove against us gave
further advantage to the enemy, who fought, as it were,
invisible, and under cover, whilst we fell fast by their
unerring fire. In this state of confusion, and while we were
about to adopt the desperate project of evacuating the
village, and, placing the women and children in the centre, of
attempting a retreat to the nearest settlement, it pleased
Heaven to send us unexpected assistance. A tall man, of
a reverend appearance, whom no one of us had ever seen
before, suddenly was in the midst of us, as we hastily

agitated the resolution of retreating. His garments were
of the skin of the elk, and he wore sword and carried gun ;
I never saw anything more august than his features, over-
shadowed by locks of grey hair, which mingled with a long
beard of the same colour. " Men and brethren," he said,
in a voice like that which turns back the flight, " why sink
your hearts ? and why are you thus disquieted ? Fear ye
that the God we serve will give you up to yonder heathen
dogs ? Follow me, and you shall see this day that there is
a captain in Israel ! " He uttered a few brief but distinct
orders, in the tone of one who was accustomed to command ;
and such was the influence of his appearance, his mien, his
language, and his presence of mind, that he was implicitly
obeyed by men who had never seen him until that moment.
We were hastily divided, by his orders, into two bodies ;
one of which maintained the defence of the village with
more courage than ever, convinced that the Unknown was
sent by God to our rescue. At his command they assumed
the best and most sheltered positions for exchanging their
deadly fire with the Indians ; while, under cover of the
smoke, the stranger sallied from the town, at the head of
the other division of the New England men, and, fetching
a circuit, attacked the Red Warriors in the rear. The
surprise, as is usual amongst savages, had complete effect ;
for they doubted not that they were assailed in their turn,
and placed betwixt two hostile parties by the return of
a detachment from the provincial army. The heathens fled
in confusion, abandoning the half-won village, and leaving
behind them such a number of their warriors, that the tribe
hath never recovered its loss. Never shall I forget the
figure of our venerable leader, when our men, and not they
only, but the women and children of the village, rescued
from the tomahawk and scalping-knife, stood crowded
around him, yet scarce venturing to approach his person
and more minded, perhaps, to worship him as a descended
angel, than to thank him as a fellow-mortal. " Not unto
me be the glory," he said ; " I am but an implement, frail
as yourselves, in the hand of Him who is strong to deliver.
Bring me a cup of water, that I may allay my parched
throat, ere I essay the task of offering thanks where they
are most due." I was nearest to him as he spoke, and I gave

into his hand the water he requested.   At that moment we exchanged glances, and it seemed to me that I recognized a noble friend whom I had long since deemed in glory ; but he gave me no time to speak, had speech been prudent. Sinking on his knees, and signing us to obey him, he poured forth a strong and energetic thanksgiving for the turning back of the battle, which, pronounced with a voice loud and clear as a war-trumpet, thrilled through the joints and marrow of the hearers.   I have heard many an act of devotion in my life, had Heaven vouchsafed me grace to profit by them ; but such a prayer as this, uttered amid the dead and the dying, with a rich tone of mingled triumph and adoration, was beyond them all—it was like the song of the inspired prophetess who dwelt beneath the palm-tree between Ramah and Bethel.   He was silent ; and for a brief space we remained with our faces bent to the earth—no man daring to lift his head.   At length we looked up, but our deliverer was no longer amongst us ; nor was he ever again seen in the land which he had rescued.'

Here Bridgenorth, who had told this singular story with an eloquence and vivacity of detail very contrary to the usual dryness of his conversation, paused for an instant, and then resumed—' Thou seest, young man, that men of valour and of discretion are called forth to command in circumstances of national exigence, though their very existence is unknown in the land which they are predestined to deliver.'

' But what thought the people of the mysterious stranger ? ' said Julian, who had listened with eagerness, for the story was of a kind interesting to the youthful and the brave.

' Many things,' answered Bridgenorth, ' and, as usual, little to the purpose.   The prevailing opinion was, notwithstanding his own disclamation, that the stranger was really a supernatural being ; others believed him an inspired champion, transported in the body from some distant climate, to show us the way to safety ; others, again, concluded that he was a recluse, who, either from motives of piety, or other cogent reasons, had become a dweller in the wilderness, and shunned the face of man.'

' And, if I may presume to ask,' said Julian, ' to which of these opinions were you disposed to adhere ? '

' The last suited best with the transient though close view
with which I had perused the stranger's features,' replied
Bridgenorth ; ' for although I dispute not that it may
please Heaven, on high occasions, even to raise one from
the dead in defence of his country, yet I doubted not then,
as I doubt not now, that I looked on the living form of one,
who had indeed powerful reasons to conceal him in the cleft
of the rock.'

' Are these reasons a secret ? ' asked Julian Peveril.

' Not properly a secret,' replied Bridgenorth ; ' for I fear
not thy betraying what I might tell thee in private discourse;
and besides, wert thou so base, the prey lies too distant for
any hunters to whom thou couldst point out its traces.   But
the name of this worthy will sound harsh in thy ear, on
account of one action of his life—being his accession to a
great measure, which made the extreme isles of the earth
to tremble.   Have you never heard of Richard Whalley ? '

' Of the regicide ? ' exclaimed Peveril, starting.

' Call his act what thou wilt,' said Bridgenorth ; ' he was
not less the rescuer of that devoted village, that, with other
leading spirits of the age, he sat in the judgement-seat
when Charles Stuart was arraigned at the bar, and subscribed the sentence that went forth upon him.'

' I have ever heard,' said Julian, in an altered voice,
and colouring deeply, ' that you, Master Bridgenorth, with
other Presbyterians, were totally averse to that detestable
crime, and were ready to have made joint cause with the
Cavaliers in preventing so horrible a parricide.'

' If it were so,' replied Bridgenorth, ' we have been
richly rewarded by his successor.'

' Rewarded ! ' exclaimed Julian ; ' does the distinction of
good and evil, and our obligation to do the one and forbear
the other, depend on the reward which may attach to our
actions ? '

' God forbid ! ' answered Bridgenorth ; ' yet those who
view the havoc which this house of Stuart have made in
the Church and State—the tyranny which they exercise
over men's persons and consciences—may well doubt
whether it be lawful to use weapons in their defence.   Yet
you hear me not praise, or even vindicate, the death of the
king, though so far deserved as he was false to his oath as

a prince and magistrate. I only tell you what you desired
to know, that Richard Whalley, one of the late king's judges,
was he of whom I have just been speaking. I knew his
lofty brow, though time had made it balder and higher ;
his grey eye retained all its lustre ; and though the grizzled
beard covered the lower part of his face, it prevented me
not from recognizing him. The scent was hot after him for
his blood ; but by the assistance of those friends whom
Heaven had raised up for his preservation, he was concealed
carefully, and emerged only to do the will of Providence in
the matter of that battle. Perhaps his voice may be heard
in the field once more, should England need one of her
noblest hearts.' n

'Now, God forbid !' said Julian.

'Amen,' returned Bridgenorth. 'May God avert civil
war, and pardon those whose madness would bring it on us !'

There was a long pause, during which Julian, who had
scarce lifted his eyes towards Alice, stole a glance in that
direction, and was struck by the deep cast of melancholy
which had stolen over features to which a cheerful, if not
gay, expression was most natural. So soon as she caught
his eye, she remarked, and, as Julian thought, with signi-
ficance, that the shadows were lengthening and evening
coming on.

He heard ; and although satisfied that she hinted at his
departure, he could not, upon the instant, find resolution
to break the spell which detained him. The language which
Bridgenorth held was not only new and alarming, but so
contrary to the maxims in which he was brought up, that,
as a son of Sir Geoffrey Peveril of the Peak, he would, in
another case, have thought himself called upon to dispute
its conclusions, even at the sword's point. But Bridgenorth's
opinions were delivered with so much calmness—seemed so
much the result of conviction—that they excited in Julian
rather a spirit of wonder, than of angry controversy. There
was a character of sober decision, and sedate melancholy,
in all that he said, which, even had he not been the father
of Alice (and perhaps Julian was not himself aware how
much he was influenced by that circumstance), would have
rendered it difficult to take personal offence. His language
and sentiments were of that quiet, yet decided kind, upon

which it is difficult either to fix controversy, or quarrel, although it be impossible to acquiesce in the conclusions to which they lead.

While Julian remained, as if spell-bound to his chair, scarce more surprised at the company in which he found himself, than at the opinions to which he was listening, another circumstance reminded him that the proper time of his stay at Black Fort had been expended. Little Fairy, the Manx pony, which, well accustomed to the vicinity of Black Fort, used to feed near the house while her master made his visits there, began to find his present stay rather too long. She had been the gift of the Countess to Julian, whilst a youth, and came of a high-spirited mountain breed, remarkable alike for hardiness, for longevity, and for a degree of sagacity approaching to that of the dog. Fairy showed the latter quality, by the way in which she chose to express her impatience to be moving homewards. At least such seemed the purpose of the shrill neigh with which she startled the female inmates of the parlour, who, the moment after-wards, could not forbear smiling to see the nose of the pony advanced through the opened casement.

'Fairy reminds me,' said Julian, looking to Alice, and rising, 'that the term of my stay here is exhausted.'

'Speak with me yet one moment,' said Bridgenorth, withdrawing him into a Gothic recess of the old-fashioned apartment, and speaking so low that he could not be over-heard by Alice and her governante, who, in the meantime, caressed and fed with fragments of bread the intruder Fairy.

'You have not, after all,' said Bridgenorth, 'told me the cause of your coming hither.' He stopped, as if to enjoy his embarrassment, and then added, 'And indeed it were most unnecessary that you should do so. I have not so far forgotten the days of my youth, or those affections which bind poor frail humanity but too much to the things of this world. Will you find no words to ask of me the great boon which you seek, and which, peradventure, you would not have hesitated to have made your own, without my knowledge, and against my consent ? Nay, never vindi-cate thyself, but mark me further. The patriarch bought his beloved by fourteen years' hard service to her father Laban, and they seemed to him but as a few days. But he that would wed my daughter must serve, in comparison, but a few days ; though in matters of such mighty import, that they shall seem as the service of many years. Reply not to me now, but go, and peace be with you.'

He retired so quickly, after speaking, that Peveril had literally not an instant to reply. He cast his eyes around the apartment, but Deborah and her charge had also disappeared. His gaze rested for a moment on the portrait of Christian, and his imagination suggested that his dark features were illuminated by a smile of haughty triumph. He stared, and looked more attentively—it was but the effect of the evening beam, which touched the picture at the instant. The effect was gone, and there remained but the fixed, grave, inflexible features of the republican soldier.

Julian left the apartment as one who walks in a dream ; he mounted Fairy, and, agitated by a variety of thoughts, which he was unable to reduce to order, he returned to Castle Rushin before the night sat down.

Here he found all in movement. The countess, with her son, had, upon some news received, or resolution formed, during his absence, removed, with a principal part of their family, to the yet stronger castle of Holm Peel, about eight miles' distance across the island ; and which had been suffered to fall into a much more dilapidated condition than that of Castletown ; so far as it could be considered as a place of residence. But as a fortress, Holm Peel was stronger than Castletown ; nay, unless assailed regularly, was almost impregnable ; and was always held by a garrison belonging to the Lords of Man. Here Peveril arrived at nightfall. He was told in the fishing-village that the night-bell of the castle had been rung earlier than usual, and the watch set with circumstances of unusual and jealous precaution.

Resolving, therefore, not to disturb the garrison by entering at that late hour, he obtained an indifferent lodging in the town for the night, and determined to go to the castle early on the succeeding morning. He was not sorry thus to gain a few hours of solitude, to think over the agitating events of the preceding day.

CHAPTER XV

What seem'd its head,
The likeness of a kingly crown had on.
                              Paradise Lost.

SODOR, or Holm Peel,[n] so is named the castle to which
our Julian directed his course early on the following morning, is one of those extraordinary monuments of antiquity
with which this singular and interesting island abounds.
It occupies the whole of a high rocky peninsula, or rather
an island, for it is surrounded by the sea at high water, and
scarcely accessible even when the tide is out, although
a stone causeway, of great solidity, erected for the express
purpose, connects the island with the mainland. The
whole space is surrounded by double walls of great strength
and thickness ; and the access to the interior, at the time
which we treat of, was only by two flights of steep and
narrow steps, divided from each other by a strong tower
and guard-house ; under the former of which there is an
entrance-arch. The open space within the walls extends
to two acres, and contains many objects worthy of antiquarian curiosity. There were, besides the castle itself,
two cathedral churches, dedicated, the earlier to Saint
Patrick, the latter to Saint Germain ; besides two smaller
churches ; all of which had become, even in that day, more
or less ruinous. Their decayed walls, exhibiting the rude
and massive architecture of the most remote period, were
composed of a ragged greystone, which formed a singular
contrast with the bright red freestone of which the window-
cases, corner-stones, arches, and other ornamental parts
of the building were composed.

Besides these four ruinous churches, the space of ground
enclosed by the massive exterior walls of Holm Peel exhibited many other vestiges of the olden time. There
was a square mound of earth, facing, with its angles to the
points of the compass, one of those motes, as they were
called, on which, in ancient times, the northern tribes
elected or recognized their chiefs, and held their solemn

popular assemblies, or *comitia*.   There was also one of those
singular towers, so common in Ireland as to have proved
the favourite theme of her antiquaries, but of which the
real use and meaning seems yet to be hidden in the mist
of ages.   This of Holm Peel had been converted to the
purpose of a watch-tower.   There were, besides, Runic
monuments, of which the legends could not be deciphered ;
and later inscriptions to the memory of champions, of whom
the names only were preserved from oblivion.   But tradition
and superstitious eld, still most busy where real history is
silent, had filled up the long blank of accurate information
with tales of sea-kings and pirates, Hebridean chiefs and
Norwegian Resolutes, who had formerly warred against,
and in defence of, this famous castle.   Superstition, too,
had her tales of fairies, ghosts, and spectres—her legends
of saints and demons, of fairies and of familiar spirits, which
in no corner of the British empire are told and received with
more absolute credulity than in the Isle of Man.

Amidst all these ruins of an older time arose the castle
itself—now   ruinous—but   in   Charles   II's   reign   well
garrisoned, and, in a military point of view, kept in complete order.   It was a venerable and very ancient building,
containing several apartments of sufficient size and height
to be termed noble.   But in the surrender of the island by
Christian, the furniture had been, in a great measure,
plundered or destroyed by the republican soldiers ; so that,
as we have before hinted, its present state was ill adapted
for the residence of the noble proprietor.   Yet it had been
often the abode, not only of the Lords of Man, but of
those state prisoners whom the Kings of Britain sometimes
committed to their charge.

In this castle of Holm Peel the great king-maker, Richard,
Earl of Warwick, was confined, during one period of his
eventful life, to ruminate at leisure on his further schemes
of ambition.   And here, too, Eleanor, the haughty wife of
the good Duke of Gloucester, pined out in seclusion the last
days of her banishment.   The sentinels pretended that her
discontented spectre was often visible at night, traversing
the battlements of the external walls, or standing motionless
beside a particular solitary turret of one of the watch-
towers with which they are flanked ; but dissolving into

air at cock-crow, or when the bell tolled from the yet remaining tower of Saint Germain's Church.

Such was Holm Peel, as records inform us, till towards tne end of the seventeenth century.

It was in one of the lofty but almost unfurnished apartments of this ancient castle that Julian Peveril found his friend the Earl of Derby, who had that moment sat down to a breakfast composed of various sorts of fish. ' Welcome, most imperial Julian,' he said ; ' welcome to our royal fortress ; in which, as yet, we are not like to be starved with hunger, though wellnigh dead for cold.'

Julian answered by inquiring the meaning of this sudden movement.

' Upon my word,' replied the earl, ' you know nearly as much of it as I do. My mother has told me nothing about it ; supposing, I believe, that I shall at length be tempted to inquire ; but she will find herself much mistaken. I shall give her credit for full wisdom in her proceedings, rather than put her to the trouble to render a reason, though no woman can render one better.'

' Come, come ; this is affectation, my good friend,' said Julian. ' You should inquire into these matters a little more curiously.'

' To what purpose ? ' said the earl. ' To hear old stories about the Tinwald laws, and the contending rights of the lords and the clergy, and all the rest of that Celtic barbarism, which, like Burgesse's thorough-paced doctrine, enters at one ear, paces through, and goes out at the other ? '

' Come, my lord,' said Julian, ' you are not so indifferent as you would represent yourself—you are dying of curiosity to know what this hurry is about ; only you think it the courtly humour to appear careless about your own affairs.'

' Why, what should it be about,' said the young earl, ' unless some factious dispute between our Majesty's minister, Governor Nowel, and our vassals ? or perhaps some dispute betwixt our Majesty and the ecclesiastical jurisdictions ? for all which our Majesty cares as little as any king in Christendom.'

' I rather suppose there is intelligence from England,' said Julian. ' I heard last night in Peel Town, that Greenhalgh is come over with unpleasant news.'

' He brought me nothing that was pleasant, I wot well,' said the earl. ' I expected something from St. Evremond or Hamilton—some new plays by Dryden or Lee, and some waggery or lampoons from the Rose Coffee-house ; and the fellow has brought me nothing but a parcel of tracts about Protestants and Papists, and a folio play-book, one of the conceptions, as she calls them, of that old madwoman the Duchess of Newcastle.'

' Hush, my lord, for Heaven's sake,' said Peveril ; ' here comes the countess ; and you know she takes fire at the least slight to her ancient friend.'

' Let her read her ancient friend's works herself, then,' said the earl, ' and think her as wise as she can ; but I would not give one of Waller's songs, or Denham's satires, for a whole cartload of her Grace's trash. But here comes our mother with care on her brow.'

The Countess of Derby entered the apartment accordingly, holding in her hand a number of papers. Her dress was a mourning habit, with a deep train of black velvet, which was borne by a little favourite attendant, a deaf and dumb girl, whom, in compassion to her misfortune, the countess had educated about her person for some years. Upon this unfortunate being, with the touch of romance which marked many of her proceedings, Lady Derby had conferred the name of Fenella, after some ancient princess of the island. The countess herself was not much changed since we last presented her to our readers. Age had rendered her step more slow, but not less majestic ; and while it traced some wrinkles on her brow, had failed to quench the sedate fire of her dark eye. The young men rose to receive her with the formal reverence which they knew she loved, and were greeted by her with equal kindness.

' Cousin Peveril,' she said (for so she always called Julian, in respect of his mother being a kinswoman of her husband), ' you were ill abroad last night, when we much needed your counsel.'

Julian answered with a blush which he could not prevent, ' That he had followed his sport among the mountains too far—had returned late—and finding her ladyship was removed from Castletown, had instantly followed the

family hither ; but as the night-bell was rung, and the watch
set, he had deemed it more respectful to lodge for the night
in the town.'

' It is well,' said the countess ; ' and, to do you justice,
Julian, you are seldom a truant neglecter of appointed hours,
though, like the rest of the youth of this age, you sometimes
suffer your sports to consume too much of time that should
be spent otherwise. But for your friend Philip, he is an
avowed contemner of good order, and seems to find pleasure
in wasting time, even when he does not enjoy it.'

' I have been enjoying my time just now at least,' said
the earl, rising from table, and picking his teeth carelessly.
' These fresh mullets are delicious, and so is the Lachrymae
Christi. I pray you to sit down to breakfast, Julian, and
partake the goods my royal foresight has provided. Never
was King of Man nearer being left to the mercy of the
execrable brandy of his dominions. Old Griffiths would
never, in the midst of our speedy retreat of last night, have
had sense enough to secure a few flasks, had I not given
him a hint on that important subject. But presence of
mind amid danger and tumult is a jewel I have always
possessed.'

' I wish, then, Philip, you would exert it to better purpose,'
said the countess, half smiling, half displeased ; for she
doted upon her son with all a mother's fondness, even when
she was most angry with him for being deficient in the
peculiar and chivalrous disposition which had distinguished
his father, and which was so analogous to her own romantic
and high-minded character. ' Lend me your signet,' she
added with a sigh ; ' for it were, I fear, vain to ask you to
read over these dispatches from England, and execute the
warrants which I have thought necessary to prepare in
consequence.'

' My signet you shall command with all my heart, madam,'
said Earl Philip ; ' but spare me the revision of what you
are much more capable to decide upon. I am, you know,
a most complete *Roi fainéant*, and never once interfered
with my *Maire de palais* in her proceedings.'

The countess made signs to her little train-bearer, who
immediately went to seek for wax and a light, with which
she presently returned.

In the meanwhile, the countess continued, addressing Peveril, ' Philip does himself less than justice. When you were absent, Julian (for if you had been here I would have given you the credit of prompting your friend), he had a spirited controversy with the bishop, for an attempt to enforce spiritual censures against a poor wretch, by con-fining her in the vault under the chapel.'[1]

' Do not think better of me than I deserve,' said the earl to Peveril ; ' my mother has omitted to tell you the culprit was pretty Peggy of Ramsey, and her crime what in Cupid's courts would have been called a peccadillo.'

' Do not make yourself worse than you are,' replied Peveril, who observed the countess's cheek redden—' you know you would have done as much for the oldest and poorest cripple in the island. Why, the vault is under the burial-ground of the chapel, and, for aught I know, under the ocean itself, such a roaring do the waves make in its vicinity. I think no one could remain there long, and retain his reason.'

' It is an infernal hole,' answered the earl, ' and I will have it built up one day—that is full certain. But hold—hold—for God's sake, madam—what are you going to do ? Look at the seal before you put it to the warrant—you will see it is a choice antique cameo Cupid, riding on a flying fish—I had it for twenty zechins, from Signor Furabosco at Rome—a most curious matter for an antiquary, but which will add little faith to a Manx warrant.'

' How can you trifle thus, you simple boy ? ' said the countess, with vexation in her tone and look. ' Let me have your signet, or rather, take these warrants, and sign them yourself.'

' My signet—my signet—Oh ! you mean that with the

[1] Beneath the only one of the four churches in Castle Rushin, which is or was kept a little in repair, is a prison or dungeon, for ecclesiastical offenders. ' This,' says Waldron, ' is certainly one of the most dreadful places that imagination can form ; the sea runs under it through the hollows of the rock with such a continual roar, that you would think it were every moment breaking in upon you, and over it are the vaults for burying the dead. The stairs descending to this place of terrors are not above thirty, but so steep and narrow, that they are very difficult to go down, a child of eight or nine years not being able to pass them but sideways.'—WALDRON'S Description of the Isle of Man, in his Works, p. 105, folio.

three monstrous legs, which I suppose was devised as the most preposterous device, to represent our most absurd Majesty of Man. The signet—I have not seen it since I gave it to Gibbon, my monkey, to play with. He did whine for it most piteously—I hope he has not gemmed the green breast of ocean with my symbol of sovereignty ! '

' Now, by Heaven,' said the countess, trembling, and colouring deeply with anger, ' it was your father's signet ! the last pledge which he sent, with his love to me, and his blessing to thee, the night before they murdered him at Bolton ! '

' Mother, dearest mother,' said the earl, startled out of his apathy, and taking her hand, which he kissed tenderly, ' I did but jest—the signet is safe—Peveril knows that it is so. Go fetch it, Julian, for Heaven's sake—here are my keys—it is in the left-hand drawer of my travelling cabinet—Nay, mother, forgive me—it was but a *mauvaise plaisanterie* ; only an ill-imagined jest, ungracious, and in bad taste, I allow—but only one of Philip's follies. Look at me, dearest mother, and forgive me.'

The countess turned her eyes towards him, from which the tears were fast falling.

' Philip,' she said, ' you try me too unkindly, and too severely. If times are changed, as I have heard you allege —if the dignity of rank, and the high feelings of honour and duty, are now drowned in giddy jests and trifling pursuits, let *me* at least, who live secluded from all others, die without perceiving the change which has happened, and, above all, without perceiving it in mine own son. Let me not learn the general prevalence of this levity, which laughs at every sense of dignity or duty, through your personal disrespect —Let me not think that when I die '——

' Speak nothing of it, mother,' said the earl, interrupting her affectionately. ' It is true, I cannot promise to be all my father and his fathers were ; for we wear silk vests for their steel coats, and feathered beavers for their crested helmets. But believe me, though to be an absolute Palmerin of England is not in my nature, no son ever loved a mother more dearly, or would do more to oblige her. And that you may own this, I will forthwith not only seal the warrants, to the great endangerment of my precious fingers, but also

read the same from end to end, as well as the dispatches
thereunto appertaining.'

A mother is easily appeased, even when most offended ;
and it was with an expanding heart that the countess saw
her son's very handsome features, while reading these
papers, settle into an expression of deep seriousness, such
as they seldom wore. It seemed to her as if the family
likeness to his gallant but unfortunate father increased,
when the expression of their countenances became similar
in gravity. The earl had no sooner perused the dispatches,
which he did with great attention, than he rose and said,
' Julian, come with me.'

The countess looked surprised. ' I was wont to share
your father's counsels, my son,' she said ; ' but do not think
that I wish to intrude myself upon yours. I am too well
pleased to see you assume the power and the duty of
thinking for yourself, which is what I have so long urged
you to do. Nevertheless, my experience, who have been
so long administrator of your authority in Man, might not,
I think, be superfluous to the matter in hand.'

' Hold me excused, dearest mother,' said the earl gravely.
' The interference was none of my seeking ; had you taken
your own course, without consulting me, it had been well ;
but since I have entered on the affair—and it appears
sufficiently important—I must transact it to the best of
my own ability.'

' Go, then, my son,' said the countess, ' and may Heaven
enlighten thee with its counsel, since thou wilt have none of
mine. I trust that you, Master Peveril, will remind him
of what is fit for his own honour ; and that only a coward
abandons his rights, and only a fool trusts his enemies.'

The earl answered not, but, taking Peveril by the arm,
led him up a winding stair to his own apartment, and from
thence into a projecting turret, where, amidst the roar of
waves and sea-mews' clang, he held with him the following
conversation.

' Peveril, it is well I looked into these warrants. My
mother queens it at such a rate as may cost me not only my
crown, which I care little for, but perhaps my head, which,
though others may think little of, I would feel it an inconvenience to be deprived of.'

' What on earth is the matter ? ' said Peveril, with considerable anxiety.

' It seems,' said the Earl of Derby, ' that Old England, who takes a frolicsome brain-fever once every two or three years, for the benefit of her doctors, and the purification of the torpid lethargy brought on by peace and prosperity, is now gone stark staring mad on the subject of a real or supposed Popish Plot. I read one programme on the subject, by a fellow called Oates, and thought it the most absurd foolery I ever perused. But that cunning fellow Shaftesbury, and some others amongst the great ones, have taken it up, and are driving on at such a rate as makes harness crack, and horses smoke for it. The king, who has sworn never to kiss the pillow his father went to sleep on, temporizes, and gives way to the current ; the Duke of York, suspected and hated on account of his religion, is about to be driven to the continent ; several principal Catholic nobles are in the Tower already ; and the nation, like a bull at Tutbury-running, is persecuted with so many inflammatory rumours and pestilent pamphlets, that she has cocked her tail, flung up her heels, taken the bit betwixt her teeth, and is as furiously unmanageable as in the year 1642.'

' All this you must have known already,' said Peveril ; ' I wonder you told me not of news so important.'

' It would have taken long to tell,' said the earl ; ' moreover, I desired to have you *solus* ; thirdly, I was about to speak when my mother entered ; and, to conclude, it was no business of mine. But these dispatches of my politic mother's private correspondent put a new face on the whole matter ; for it seems some of the informers—a trade which, having become a thriving one, is now pursued by many— have dared to glance at the countess herself as an agent in this same plot—aye, and have found those that are willing enough to believe their report.'

' On mine honour,' said Peveril, ' you both take it with great coolness. I think the countess the more composed of the two ; for, except her movement hither, she exhibited no mark of alarm, and, moreover, seemed no way more anxious to communicate the matter to your lordship than decency rendered necessary.'

'My good mother,' said the earl, 'loves power, though it has cost her dear. I wish I could truly say that my neglect of business is entirely assumed in order to leave it in her hands, but that better motive combines with natural indolence. But she seems to have feared I should not think exactly like her in this emergency, and she was right in supposing so.'

'How comes the emergency upon you?' said Julian; 'and what form does the danger assume?'

'Marry, thus it is,' said the earl: 'I need not bid you remember the affair of Colonel Christian. That man, besides his widow, who is possessed of large property—Dame Christian of Kirk Truagh, whom you have often heard of, and perhaps seen—left a brother called Edward Christian, whom you never saw at all. Now this brother—but I dare say you know all about it.'

'Not I, on my honour,' said Peveril; 'you know the countess seldom or never alludes to the subject.'

'Why,' replied the earl, 'I believe in her heart she is something ashamed of that gallant act of royalty and supreme jurisdiction, the consequences of which maimed my estate so cruelly. Well, cousin, this same Edward Christian was one of the dempsters at the time, and, naturally enough, was unwilling to concur in the sentence which adjudged his *aîné* to be shot like a dog. My mother, who was then in high force, and not to be controlled by any one, would have served the dempster with the same sauce with which she dressed his brother, had he not been wise enough to fly from the island. Since that time, the thing has slept on all hands; and though we knew that Dempster Christian made occasionally secret visits to his friends in the island, along with two or three other Puritans of the same stamp, and particularly a prick-eared rogue, called Bridgenorth, brother-in-law to the deceased, yet my mother, thank Heaven, has hitherto had the sense to connive at them, though, for some reason or other, she holds this Bridgenorth in especial disfavour.'

'And why,' said Peveril, forcing himself to speak, in order to conceal the very unpleasant surprise which he felt, 'why does the countess now depart from so prudent a line of conduct?'

'You must know the case is now different. The rogues are not satisfied with toleration—they would have supremacy. They have found friends in the present heat of the popular mind. My mother's name, and especially that of her confessor, Aldrick the Jesuit, have been mentioned in this beautiful maze of a plot, which, if any such at all exists, she knows as little of as you or I. However, she is a Catholic, and that is enough ; and I have little doubt that if the fellows could seize on our scrap of a kingdom here, and cut all our throats, they would have the thanks of the present House of Commons, as willingly as old Christian had those of the Rump, for a similar service.'

'From whence did you receive all this information ? ' said Peveril, again speaking, though by the same effort which a man makes who talks in his sleep.

'Aldrick has seen the Duke of York in secret, and his Royal Highness, who wept while he confessed his want of power to protect his friends—and it is no trifle will wring tears from him—told him to send us information that we should look to our safety, for that Dempster Christian and Bridgenorth were in the island, with secret and severe orders ; that they had formed a considerable party there, and were likely to be owned and protected in anything they might undertake against us. The people of Ramsey and Castletown are unluckily discontented about some new regulation of the imposts ; and to tell you the truth, though I thought yesterday's sudden remove a whim of my mother's, I am almost satisfied they would have blockaded us in Rushin Castle, where we could not have held out for lack of provisions. Here we are better supplied, and, as we are on our guard, it is likely the intended rising will not take place.'

'And what is to be done in this emergency ? ' said Peveril.

'That is the very question, my gentle coz,' answered the earl. 'My mother sees but one way of going to work, and that is by royal authority. Here are the warrants she had prepared, to search for, take, and apprehend the bodies of Edward Christian and Robert—no, Ralph Bridgenorth, and bring them to instant trial. No doubt, she would soon have had them in the castle court, with a dozen of the old match-

locks levelled against them—that is her way of solving all
sudden difficulties.'

' But in which, I trust, you do not acquiesce, my lord,'
answered Peveril, whose thoughts instantly reverted to
Alice, if they could ever be said to be absent from her.

' Truly, I acquiesce in no such matter,' said the earl.
' William Christian's death cost me a fair half of my inheritance. I have no fancy to fall under the displeasure of my
royal brother, King Charles, for a new escapade of the same
kind. But how to pacify my mother I know not. I wish
the insurrection would take place, and then, as we are
better provided than they can be, we might knock the knaves
on the head ; and yet, since they began the fray, we should
keep the law on our side.'

' Were it not better,' said Peveril, ' if by any means these
men could be induced to quit the island ? '

' Surely,' replied the earl ; ' but that will be no easy
matter—they are stubborn on principle, and empty threats
will not move them. This stormblast in London is wind in
their sails, and they will run their length, you may depend
on it. I have sent orders, however, to clap up the Manxmen upon whose assistance they depended, and if I can find
the two worthies themselves, here are sloops enough in the
harbour—I will take the freedom to send them on a pretty
distant voyage, and I hope matters will be settled before
they return to give an account of it.'

At this moment a soldier belonging to the garrison
approached the two young men, with many bows and tokens
of respect. ' How now, friend ? ' said the earl to him.
' Leave off thy courtesies, and tell thy business.'

The man, who was a native islander, answered in Manx
that he had a letter for his honour, Master Julian Peveril.
Julian snatched the billet hastily, and asked whence it
came.

' It was delivered to him by a young woman,' the soldier
replied, ' who had given him a piece of money to deliver it
into Master Peveril's own hand.'

' Thou art a lucky fellow, Julian,' said the earl. ' With
that grave brow of thine, and thy character for sobriety
and early wisdom, you set the girls a-wooing, without
waiting till they are asked ; whilst I, their drudge and

vassal, waste both language and leisure, without getting a kind word or look, far less a billet-doux.'

This the young earl said with a smile of conscious triumph, as in fact he valued himself not a little upon the interest which he supposed himself to possess with the fair sex.

Meanwhile the letter impressed on Peveril a different train of thoughts from what his companion apprehended. It was in Alice's hand, and contained these few words :—

'I fear what I am going to do is wrong ; but I must see you. Meet me at noon at Goddard Crovan's Stone, with as much secrecy as you may.'

The letter was signed only with the initials A. B. ; but Julian had no difficulty in recognizing the handwriting, which he had often seen, and which was remarkably beautiful. He stood suspended, for he saw the difficulty and impropriety of withdrawing himself from the countess and his friend at this moment of impending danger ; and yet to neglect this invitation was not to be thought of. He paused in the utmost perplexity.

'Shall I read your riddle ?' said the earl. 'Go where love calls you—I will make an excuse to my mother—only, most grave anchorite, be hereafter more indulgent to the failings of others than you have been hitherto, and blaspheme not the power of the little deity.'

'Nay, but, Cousin Derby'— said Peveril, and stopped short, for he really knew not what to say. Secured himself by a virtuous passion from the contagious influence of the time, he had seen with regret his noble kinsman mingle more in its irregularities than he approved of, and had sometimes played the part of a monitor. Circumstances seemed at present to give the earl a right of retaliation. He kept his eye fixed on his friend, as if he waited till he should complete his sentence, and at length exclaimed, 'What ! cousin, quite *à la mort* ! Oh, most judicious Julian ! Oh, most precise Peveril ! have you bestowed so much wisdom on me, that you have none left for yourself ? Come, be frank—tell me name and place—or say but the colour of the eyes of the most emphatic she—or do but let me have the pleasure to hear thee say, "I love ! "—confess one touch of human frailty—conjugate the verb *amo*, and I will be a gentle schoolmaster, and you shall have, as

Father Richards used to say, when we were under his ferule,
" *licentia exeundi.*" '

'Enjoy your pleasant humour at my expense, my lord,'
said Peveril ; ' I fairly will confess thus much, that I would
fain, if it consisted with my honour and your safety, have
two hours at my own disposal ; the more especially as the
manner in which I shall employ them may much concern
the safety of the island.'

'Very likely, I dare say,' answered the earl, still laughing.
'No doubt you are summoned out by some Lady Politic
Wouldbe of the isle, to talk over some of the breast-laws :
but never mind—go, and go speedily, that you may return
as quick as possible. I expect no immediate explosion of
this grand conspiracy. When the rogues see us on our
guard, they will be cautious how they break out. Only,
once more, make haste.'

Peveril thought this last advice was not to be neglected ;
and, glad to extricate himself from the raillery of his cousin,
walked down towards the gate of the castle, meaning to
cross over to the village, and there take horse at the earl's
stables for the place of rendezvous.

CHAPTER XVI

Acasto. Can she not speak ?
Oswald. If speech be only in accented sounds,
Framed by the tongue and lips, the maiden's dumb ;
But if by quick and apprehensive look,
By motion, sign, and glance, to give each meaning,
Express as clothed in language, be term'd speech,
She hath that wondrous faculty ; for her eyes,
Like the bright stars of heaven, can hold discourse,
Though it be mute and soundless.
                                              Old Play.

At the head of the first flight of steps which descended
towards the difficult and well-defended entrance of the
castle of Holm Peel, Peveril was met and stopped by the
countess's train-bearer. This little creature—for she was
of the least and slightest size of womankind—was exquisitely
well formed in all her limbs, which the dress she usually

wore (a green silk tunic, of a peculiar form) set off to the best advantage. Her face was darker than the usual hue of Europeans; and the profusion of long and silken hair,

FENELLA

which, when she undid the braids in which she commonly wore it, fell down almost to her ankles, was also rather a foreign attribute. Her countenance resembled a most beautiful miniature; and there was a quickness, decision and fire in Fenella's look, and especially in her eyes, which was probably rendered yet more alert and acute, because, through the imperfection of her other organs, it was only by sight that she could obtain information of what passed around her.

The pretty mute was mistress of many little accomplishments, which the countess had caused to be taught to her in compassion for her forlorn situation, and which she learned with the most surprising quickness. Thus, for example, she was exquisite in the use of the needle, and so ready and ingenious a draughtswoman, that, like the ancient Mexicans, she sometimes made a hasty sketch with her pencil the means of conveying her ideas, either by direct or emblematical representation. Above all, in the art of ornamental writing, much studied at that period, Fenella was so great a proficient, as to rival the fame of Messrs. Snow, Shelley, and other masters of the pen, whose copybooks, preserved in the libraries of the curious, still show the artists smiling on the frontispiece in all the honours of flowing gowns and full-bottomed wigs, to the eternal glory of caligraphy.

The little maiden had, besides these accomplishments, much ready wit and acuteness of intellect. With Lady Derby, and with the two young gentlemen, she was a great favourite, and used much freedom in conversing with them, by means of a system of signs which had been gradually established amongst them, and which served all ordinary purposes of communication.

But, though happy in the indulgence and favour of her mistress, from whom indeed she was seldom separated, Fenella was by no means a favourite with the rest of the household. In fact, it seemed that her temper, exasperated perhaps by a sense of her misfortune, was by no means equal to her abilities. She was very haughty in her demeanour, even towards the upper domestics, who in that establishment were of a much higher rank and better birth than in the families of the nobility in general. These often complained, not only of her pride and reserve, but of her high and irascible temper and vindictive disposition. Her passionate propensity had been indeed idly encouraged by the young men, and particularly by the earl, who sometimes amused himself with teazing her, that he might enjoy the various singular motions and murmurs by which she expressed her resentment.   Towards him, these were of course only petulant and whimsical indications of pettish anger.   But when she was angry with others of inferior degree—before whom she did not control herself—the expression of her passion, unable to display itself in language, had something even frightful, so singular were the tones, contortions, and gestures to which she had recourse.   The lower domestics, to whom she was liberal almost beyond her apparent means, observed her with much deference and respect, but much more from fear than from any real attachment; for the caprices of her temper displayed themselves even in her gifts; and those who most frequently shared her bounty, seemed by no means assured of the benevolence of the motives which dictated her liberality.

All these peculiarities led to a conclusion consonant with Manx superstition.   Devout believers in all the legends of fairies so dear to the Celtic tribes, the Manx people held it for certainty that the elves were in the habit of carrying off mortal children before baptism, and leaving in the cradle of the new-born babe one of their own brood, which was almost always imperfect in some one or other of the organs proper to humanity.   Such a being they conceived Fenella to be; and the smallness of her size, her dark complexion, her long locks of silken hair, the singularity of her manners and tones, as well as the caprices of her temper, were to their thinking all attributes of the irritable, fickle, and dangerous race from which they supposed her to be sprung. And it seemed that although no jest appeared to offend her more than when Lord Derby called her in sport the Elfin Queen, or otherwise alluded to her supposed connexion with ' the pygmy folk ', yet still her perpetually affecting to wear the colour of green, proper to the fairies, as well as some other peculiarities, seemed voluntarily assumed by her, in order to countenance the superstition, perhaps because it gave her more authority among the lower orders.

Many were the tales circulated respecting the countess's *Elf*, as Fenella was currently called in the island; and the malcontents of the stricter persuasion were convinced that no one but a Papist and a malignant would have kept near her person a creature of such doubtful origin. They conceived that Fenella's deafness and dumbness were only towards those of this world, and that she had been heard talking, and singing, and laughing most elvishly, with the invisibles of her own race. They alleged, also, that she had a *Double*, a sort of apparition resembling her, which slept in the countess's anteroom, or bore her train, or wrought in her cabinet, while the real Fenella joined the song of the mermaids on the moonlight sands, or the dance of the fairies in the haunted valley of Glenmoy, or on the heights of Snawfell and Barool. The sentinels, too, would have sworn they had seen the little maiden trip past them in their solitary night walks, without their having it in their power to challenge her, any more than if they had been as mute as herself. To all this mass of absurdities the better informed paid no more attention than to the usual idle exaggerations of the vulgar, which so frequently connect that which is unusual with what is supernatural.[n]

Such, in form and habits, was the little female who, holding in her hand a small old-fashioned ebony rod, which might have passed for a divining wand, confronted Julian on the top of the flight of steps which led down the rock from the castle-court. We ought to observe, that as Julian's manner to the unfortunate girl had been always gentle, and free from those teasing jests in which his gay friend indulged, with less regard to the peculiarity of her situation and feelings ; so Fenella, on her part, had usually shown much greater deference to him than to any of the household, her mistress, the countess, always excepted.

On the present occasion, planting herself in the very midst of the narrow descent, so as to make it impossible for Peveril to pass by her, she proceeded to put him to the question by a series of gestures, which we will endeavour to describe. She commenced by extending her hand slightly, accompanied with the sharp inquisitive look which served her as a note of interrogation. This was meant as an inquiry whether he was going to a distance. Julian, in reply, extended his arm more than half, to intimate that the distance was considerable. Fenella looked grave, shook her head, and pointed to the countess's window, which was visible from the spot where they stood. Peveril smiled, and nodded, to intimate there was no danger in quitting her mistress for a short space. The little maiden next touched an eagle's feather which she wore in her hair, a sign which she usually employed to designate the earl, and then looked inquisitively at Julian once more, as if to say, ' Goes he with you ? ' Peveril shook his head, and, somewhat wearied by these interrogatories, smiled, and made an effort to pass. Fenella frowned, struck the end of her ebony rod perpendicularly on the ground, and again shook her head, as if opposing his departure. But finding that Julian persevered in his purpose, she suddenly assumed another and a milder mood, held him by the skirt of his cloak with one hand, and raised the other in an imploring attitude, whilst every feature of her lively countenance was composed into the like expression of supplication ; and the fire of the large dark eyes, which seemed in general so keen and piercing as almost to over-animate the little sphere to which they belonged, seemed quenched, for the moment, in the large drops which hung on her long eyelashes, but without falling.

Julian Peveril was far from being void of sympathy towards the poor girl, whose motives in opposing his departure appeared to be her affectionate apprehension for her mistress's safety. He endeavoured to reassure her by smiles, and, at the same time, by such signs as he could devise, to intimate that there was no danger, and that he would return presently ; and having succeeded in extricating his cloak from her grasp, and in passing her on the stair, he began to descend the steps as speedily as he could in order to avoid further importunity.

But with activity much greater than his, the dumb maiden hastened to intercept him, and succeeded by throwing herself, at the imminent risk of life and limb, a second time into the pass which he was descending, so as to interrupt his purpose. In order to achieve this, she was obliged to let herself drop a considerable height from the wall of a small flanking battery, where two patereroes were placed to scour the pass, in case any enemy could have mounted so high. Julian had scarce time to shudder at her purpose, as he beheld her about to spring from the

parapet, ere, like a thing of gossamer, she stood light and
uninjured on the rocky platform below. He endeavoured,
by the gravity of his look and gesture, to make her understand how much he blamed her rashness ; but the reproof,
though obviously quite intelligible, was entirely thrown
away. A hasty wave of her hand intimated how she
contemned the danger and the remonstrance ; while, at the
same time, she instantly resumed, with more eagerness than
before, the earnest and impressive gestures by which she
endeavoured to detain him in the fortress.

Julian was somewhat staggered by her pertinacity. ' Is
it possible,' he thought, ' that any danger can approach the
countess, of which this poor maiden has, by the extreme
acuteness of her observation, obtained knowledge which
has escaped others ? '

He signed to Fenella hastily to give him the tablets and
the pencil which she usually carried with her, and wrote on
them the question, ' Is there danger near to your mistress,
that you thus stop me ? '

' There is danger around the countess,' was the answer
instantly written down ; ' but there is much more in your
own purpose.'

' How ?—what ?—what know you of my purpose ? ' said
Julian, forgetting, in his surprise, that the party he addressed had neither ear to comprehend, nor voice to reply,
to uttered language. She had regained her book in the
meantime, and sketched, with a rapid pencil, on one of the
leaves, a scene which she showed to Julian. To his infinite
surprise he recognized Goddard Crovan's Stone, a remarkable monument, of which she had given the outline with
sufficient accuracy ; together with a male and female figure,
which, though only indicated by a few slight touches of the
pencil, bore yet, he thought, some resemblance to himself
and Alice Bridgenorth.

When he had gazed on the sketch for an instant with
surprise, Fenella took the book from his hand, laid her finger
upon the drawing, and slowly and sternly shook her head,
with a frown which seemed to prohibit the meeting which
was there represented. Julian, however, though disconcerted, was in no shape disposed to submit to the authority
of his monitress. By whatever means she, who so seldom

stirred from the countess's apartment, had become acquainted with a secret which he thought entirely his own, he esteemed it the more necessary to keep the appointed rendezvous, that he might learn from Alice, if possible, how the secret had transpired. He had also formed the intention of seeking out Bridgenorth; entertaining an idea that a person so reasonable and calm as he had shown himself in their late conference, might be persuaded, when he understood that the countess was aware of his intrigues, to put an end to her danger and his own, by withdrawing from the island. And could he succeed in this point, he should at once, he thought, render a material benefit to the father of his beloved Alice—remove the earl from his state of anxiety —save the countess from a second time putting her feudal jurisdiction in opposition to that of the Crown of England —and secure quiet possession of the island to her and her family.

With this scheme of mediation in his mind, Peveril determined to rid himself of the opposition of Fenella to his departure, with less ceremony than he had hitherto observed towards her; and suddenly lifting up the damsel in his arms before she was aware of his purpose, he turned about, set her down on the steps above him, and began to descend the pass himself as speedily as possible. It was then that the dumb maiden gave full course to the vehemence of her disposition; and clapping her hands repeatedly, expressed her displeasure in a sound, or rather a shriek, so extremely dissonant, that it resembled more the cry of a wild creature than anything which could have been uttered by female organs. Peveril was so astounded at the scream as it rang through the living rocks, that he could not help stopping and looking back in alarm, to satisfy himself that she had not sustained some injury. He saw her, however, perfectly safe, though her face seemed inflamed and distorted with passion. She stamped at him with her foot, shook her clenched hand, and turning her back upon him, without further adieu, ran up the rude steps as lightly as a kid could have tripped up that rugged ascent, and paused for a moment at the summit of the first flight.

Julian could feel nothing but wonder and compassion for the impotent passion of a being so unfortunately circumstanced, cut off, as it were, from the rest of mankind, and incapable of receiving in childhood that moral discipline which teaches us mastery of our wayward passions, ere yet they have attained their meridian strength and violence. He waved his hand to her, in token of amicable farewell; but she only replied by once more menacing him with her little hand clenched; and then ascending the rocky staircase with almost preternatural speed, was soon out of sight.

Julian, on his part, gave no further consideration to her conduct or its motives, but hastening to the village on the mainland, where the stables of the castle were situated, he again took his palfrey from the stall, and was soon mounted and on his way to the appointed place of rendezvous, much marvelling, as he ambled forward with speed far greater than was promised by the diminutive size of the animal he was mounted on, what could have happened to produce so great a change in Alice's conduct towards him, that, in place of enjoining his absence as usual, or recommending his departure from the island, she should now voluntarily invite him to a meeting. Under impression of the various doubts which succeeded each other in his imagination, he sometimes pressed Fairy's sides with his legs; sometimes laid his holly rod lightly on her neck; sometimes incited her by his voice, for the mettled animal needed neither whip nor spur, and achieved the distance betwixt the castle of Holm Peel and the stone at Goddard Crovan at the rate of twelve miles within the hour.

The monumental stone, designed to commemorate some feat of an ancient King of Man, which had been long forgotten, was erected on the side of a narrow lonely valley, or rather glen, secluded from observation by the steepness of its banks, upon a projection of which stood the tall, shapeless, solitary rock, frowning, like a shrouded giant, over the brawling of the small rivulet which watered the ravine.

CHAPTER XVII

This a love-meeting ? See the maiden mourns,
And the sad suitor bends his looks on earth.
There's more hath pass'd between them than belongs
To Love's sweet sorrows.   *Old Play.*

As he approached the monument of Goddard Crovan,
Julian cast many an anxious glance to see whether any
object visible beside the huge grey stone should apprise
him whether he was anticipated, at the appointed place of
rendezvous, by her who had named it. Nor was it long
before the flutter of a mantle, which the breeze slightly
waved, and the motion necessary to replace it upon the
wearer's shoulders, made him aware that Alice had already
reached their place of meeting. One instant set the palfrey
at liberty, with slackened girths and loosened reins, to pick
its own way through the dell at will ; another placed Julian
Peveril by the side of Alice Bridgenorth.

That Alice should extend her hand to her lover, as with
the ardour of a young greyhound he bounded over the
obstacles of the rugged path, was as natural as that Julian,
seizing on the hand so kindly stretched out, should devour
it with kisses, and, for a moment or two, without reprehension ; while the other hand, which should have aided
in the liberation of its fellow, served to hide the blushes of
the fair owner. But Alice, young as she was, and attached
to Julian by such long habits of kindly intimacy, still knew
well how to subdue the tendency of her own treacherous
affections.

' This is not right,' she said, extricating her hand from
Julian's grasp, ' this is not right, Julian. If I have been
too rash in admitting such a meeting as the present, it is
not you that should make me sensible of my folly.'

Julian Peveril's mind had been early illuminated with
that touch of romantic fire which deprives passion of
selfishness, and confers on it the high and refined tone of
generous and disinterested devotion. He let go the hand
of Alice with as much respect as he could have paid to that

of a princess ; and when she seated herself upon a rocky fragment, over which nature had stretched a cushion of moss and lichen, interspersed with wild flowers, backed with a bush of copsewood, he took his place beside her, indeed, but at such distance as to intimate the duty of an attendant, who was there only to hear and to obey.   Alice Bridgenorth became more assured as she observed the power which she possessed over her lover ; and the self-command which Peveril exhibited, which other damsels in her situation might have judged inconsistent with intensity of passion, she appreciated more justly, as a proof of his respectful and disinterested sincerity.   She recovered, in addressing him, the tone of confidence which rather belonged to the scenes of their early acquaintance, than to those which had passed betwixt them since Peveril had disclosed his affection, and thereby had brought restraint upon their intercourse.

' Julian,' she said, ' your visit of yesterday—your most ill-timed visit, has distressed me much.   It has misled my father—it has endangered you.   At all risks, I resolved that you should know this, and blame me not if I have taken a bold and imprudent step in desiring this solitary interview, since you are aware how little poor Deborah is to be trusted.'

' Can you fear misconstruction from me, Alice ? ' replied Peveril warmly ; ' from me, whom you have thus highly favoured—thus deeply obliged ? '

' Cease your protestations, Julian,' answered the maiden, ' they do but make me the more sensible that I have acted over boldly.   But I did for the best.   I could not see you whom I have known so long—you, who say you regard me with partiality '——

' *Say* that I regard you with partiality ! ' interrupted Peveril in his turn.   ' Ah, Alice, what a cold and doubtful phrase you have used to express the most devoted, the most sincere affection ! '

' Well, then,' said Alice sadly, ' we will not quarrel about words ; but do not again interrupt me.   I could not, I say, see you, who, I believe, regard me with sincere though vain and fruitless attachment, rush blindfold into a snare, deceived and seduced by those very feelings towards me.'

' I understand you not, Alice,' said Peveril ; ' nor can

I see any danger to which I am at present exposed. The
sentiments which your father has expressed towards me
are of a nature irreconcilable with hostile purposes. If he
is not offended with the bold wishes I may have formed—
and his whole behaviour shows the contrary—I know not
a man on earth from whom I have less cause to apprehend
any danger or ill will.'

' My father,' said Alice, ' means well by his country, and
well by you ; yet I sometimes fear he may rather injure
than serve his good cause ; and still more do I dread that
in attempting to engage you as an auxiliary, he may forget
those ties which ought to bind you, and I am sure which
will bind you, to a different line of conduct from his own.'

' You lead me into still deeper darkness, Alice,' answered
Peveril. ' That your father's especial line of politics differs
widely from mine, I know well ; but how many instances
have occurred, even during the bloody scenes of civil
warfare, of good and worthy men laying the prejudice of
party affections aside, and regarding each other with respect,
and even with friendly attachment, without being false to
principle on either side ? '

' It may be so,' said Alice ; ' but such is not the league
which my father desires to form with you, and that to which
he hopes your misplaced partiality towards his daughter may
afford a motive for your forming with him.'

' And what is it,' said Peveril, ' which I would refuse,
with such a prospect before me ? '

' Treachery and dishonour ! ' replied Alice ; ' whatever
would render you unworthy of the poor boon at which you
aim—aye, were it more worthless than I confess it to be.'

' Would your father,' said Peveril, as he unwillingly
received the impression which Alice designed to convey,—
' would he, whose views of duty are so strict and severe—
would he wish to involve me in aught, to which such harsh
epithets as treachery and dishonour can be applied with the
slightest shadow of truth ? '

' Do not mistake me, Julian,' replied the maiden ; ' my
father is incapable of requesting aught of you that is not
to his thinking just and honourable ; nay, he conceives that
he only claims from you a debt, which is due as a creature
to the Creator, and as a man to your fellow men.'

' So guarded, where can be the danger of our intercourse ? '
replied Julian.   ' If he be resolved to require, and I determined to accede to, nothing save what flows from conviction,
what have I to fear, Alice ?   And how is my intercourse
with your father dangerous ?   Believe not so ; his speech
has already made impression on me in some particulars,
and he listened with candour and patience to the objections
which I made occasionally.   You do Master Bridgenorth
less than justice in confounding him with the unreasonable
bigots in policy and religion, who can listen to no argument
but what favours their own prepossessions.'

' Julian,' replied Alice, ' it is you who misjudge my
father's powers, and his purpose with respect to you, and
who overrate your own powers of resistance.   I am but
a girl, but I have been taught by circumstances to think for
myself, and to consider the character of those around me.
My father's views in ecclesiastical and civil policy are as
dear to him as the life which he cherishes only to advance
them.   They have been, with little alteration, his companions through life.   They brought him at one period into
prosperity, and when they suited not the times, he suffered
for having held them.   They have become not only a part,
but the very dearest part, of his existence.   If he shows
them not to you at first, in the flexible strength which they
have acquired over his mind, do not believe that they are
the less powerful.   He who desires to make converts, must
begin by degrees.   But that he should sacrifice to an
inexperienced young man, whose ruling motive he will term
a childish passion, any part of those treasured principles
which he has maintained through good repute and bad
repute—Oh, do not dream of such an impossibility !   If
you meet at all, you must be the wax, he the seal—you
must receive, he must bestow, an absolute impression.'

' That,' said Peveril, ' were unreasonable.   I will frankly
avow to you, Alice, that I am not a sworn bigot to the
opinions entertained by my father, much as I respect his
person.   I could wish that our Cavaliers, or whatsoever
they are pleased to call themselves, would have some more
charity towards those who differ from them in Church and
State.   But to hope that I would surrender the principles
in which I have lived, were to suppose me capable of

deserting my benefactress, and breaking the hearts of my parents.'

'Even so I judged of you,' answered Alice ; 'and therefore I asked this interview, to conjure that you will break off all intercourse with our family—return to your parents —or, what will be much safer, visit the continent once more, and abide till God sends better days to England, for these are black with many a storm.'

'And can you bid me go, Alice ? ' said the young man, taking her unresisting hand ; 'can you bid me go, and yet own an interest in my fate ? Can you bid me, for fear of dangers, which, as a man, as a gentleman, and a loyal one, I am bound to show my face to, meanly abandon my parents, my friends, my country—suffer the existence of evils which I might aid to prevent—forgo the prospect of doing such little good as might be in my power—fall from an active and honourable station into the condition of a fugitive and time-server—Can you bid me do all this, Alice ? Can you bid me do all this, and, in the same breath, bid farewell for ever to you and happiness? It is impossible—I cannot surrender at once my love and my honour.'

'There is no remedy,' said Alice, but she could not suppress a sigh while she said so—' there is no remedy— none whatever. What we might have been to each other, placed in more favourable circumstances, it avails not to think of now ; and, circumstanced as we are, with open war about to break out betwixt our parents and friends, we can be but well-wishers—cold and distant well-wishers, who must part on this spot, and at this hour, never to meet again.'

'No, by Heaven ! ' said Peveril, animated at the same time by his own feelings, and by the sight of the emotions which his companion in vain endeavoured to suppress,— 'No, by Heaven ! ' he exclaimed, ' we part not—Alice, we part not. If I am to leave my native land, you shall be my companion in my exile. What have you to lose ?—Whom have you to abandon ?—Your father ?—The good old cause, as it is termed, is dearer to him than a thousand daughters ; and setting him aside, what tie is there between you and this barren isle—between my Alice and any spot of the British dominions, where her Julian does not sit by her.'

' O Julian,' answered the maiden, ' why make my duty more painful by visionary projects, which you ought not to name, or I to listen to ?   Your parents—my father—it cannot be ! '

' Fear not for my parents, Alice,' replied Julian, and, pressing close to his companion's side, he ventured to throw his arm around her ; ' they love me, and they will soon learn to love, in Alice, the only being on earth who could have rendered their son happy.   And for your own father, when State and Church intrigues allow him to bestow a thought upon you, will he not think that your happiness, your security, is better cared for when you are my wife, than were you to continue under the mercenary charge of yonder foolish woman ?   What could his pride desire better for you than the establishment which will one day be mine ? Come then, Alice, and since you condemn me to banishment —since you deny me a share in those stirring achievements which are about to agitate England—come ! do you—for you only can—do you reconcile me to exile and inaction, and give happiness to one, who, for your sake, is willing to resign honour.'

' It cannot—it cannot be,' said Alice, faltering as she uttered her negative.   ' And yet,' she said, ' how many in my place—left alone and unprotected, as I am—But I must not—I must not—for your sake, Julian, I must not.'

' Say not for my sake you must not, Alice,' said Peveril eagerly ; ' this is adding insult to cruelty.   If you will do aught for my sake, you will say yes ; or you will suffer this dear head to drop on my shoulder—the slightest sign—the moving of an eyelid, shall signify consent.   All shall be prepared within an hour ; within another the priest shall unite us ; and within a third, we leave the isle behind us, and seek our fortunes on the continent.'   But while he spoke, in joyful anticipation of the consent which he implored, Alice found means to collect together her resolution, which, staggered by the eagerness of her lover, the impulse of her own affections, and the singularity of her situation—seeming, in her case, to justify what would have been most blameable in another—had more than half abandoned her.

The result of a moment's deliberation was fatal to Julian's

proposal. She extricated herself from the arm which had pressed her to his side—arose, and repelling his attempts to approach or detain her, said, with a simplicity not unmingled with dignity, 'Julian, I always knew I risked much in inviting you to this meeting; but I did not guess that I could have been so cruel both to you and to myself, as to suffer you to discover what you have to-day seen too plainly—that I love you better than you love me. But since you do know it, I will show you that Alice's love is disinterested—She will not bring an ignoble name into your ancient house. If hereafter, in your line, there should arise some who may think the claims of the hierarchy too exorbitant, the powers of the crown too extensive, men shall not say these ideas were derived from Alice Bridgenorth, their Whig granddame.'

'Can you speak thus, Alice?' said her lover. 'Can you use such expressions? and are you not sensible that they show plainly it is your own pride, not regard for me, that makes you resist the happiness of both?'

'Not so, Julian; not so,' answered Alice, with tears in her eyes; 'it is the command of duty to us both—of duty, which we cannot transgress, without risking our happiness here and hereafter. Think what I, the cause of all, should feel, when your father frowns, your mother weeps, your noble friends stand aloof, and you, even you yourself, shall have made the painful discovery, that you have incurred the contempt and resentment of all to satisfy a boyish passion; and that the poor beauty, once sufficient to mislead you, is gradually declining under the influence of grief and vexation. This I will not risk. I see distinctly it is best we should here break off and part; and I thank God, who gives me light enough to perceive, and strength enough to withstand, your folly as well as my own. Farewell, then, Julian; but first take the solemn advice which I called you hither to impart to you:—Shun my father—you cannot walk in his paths, and be true to gratitude and to honour. What he doth from pure and honourable motives, you cannot aid him in, except upon the suggestion of a silly and interested passion, at variance with all the engagements you have formed at coming into life.'

'Once more, Alice,' answered Julian, 'I understand you

not. If a course of action is good, it needs no vindication
from the actor's motives—if bad, it can derive none.'

'You cannot blind me with your sophistry, Julian,'
replied Alice Bridgenorth, 'any more than you can overpower me with your passion. Had the patriarch destined
his son to death upon any less ground than faith and humble
obedience to a divine commandment, he had meditated
a murder and not a sacrifice. In our late bloody and
lamentable wars, how many drew swords on either side,
from the purest and most honourable motives? How many
from the culpable suggestions of ambition, self-seeking,
and love of plunder? Yet while they marched in the same
ranks, and spurred their horses at the same trumpet-sound,
the memory of the former is dear to us as patriots or loyalists
—that of those who acted on mean or unworthy promptings
is either execrated or forgotten. Once more, I warn you,
avoid my father—leave this island, which will be soon
agitated by strange incidents—while you stay, be on your
guard—distrust everything—be jealous of every one, even
of those to whom it may seem almost impossible, from
circumstances, to attach a shadow of suspicion—trust not
the very stones of the most secret apartment in Holm Peel,
for that which hath wings shall carry the matter.'

Here Alice broke off suddenly, and with a faint shriek ;
for, stepping from behind the stunted copse, which had
concealed him, her father stood unexpectedly before them.

The reader cannot have forgotten that this was the second
time in which the stolen interviews of the lovers had been
interrupted by the unexpected apparition of Major Bridgenorth. On this second occasion his countenance exhibited
anger mixed with solemnity, like that of the spirit to a
ghost-seer, whom he upbraids with having neglected a charge
imposed at their first meeting. Even his anger, however,
produced no more violent emotion than a cold sternness
of manner in his speech and action. 'I thank you, Alice,'
he said to his daughter, 'for the pains you have taken to
traverse my designs towards this young man, and towards
yourself. I thank you for the hints you have thrown out
before my appearance, the suddenness of which alone has
prevented you from carrying your confidence to a pitch
which would have placed my life and that of others at the

discretion of a boy, who, when the cause of God and his country is laid before him, has not leisure to think of them, so much is he occupied with such a baby-face as thine.' Alice, pale as death, continued motionless, with her eyes

ALICE AND JULIAN SURPRISED BY BRIDGENORTH

fixed on the ground, without attempting the slightest reply to the ironical reproaches of her father.

'And you,' continued Major Bridgenorth, turning from his daughter to her lover,—' you, sir, have well repaid the liberal confidence which I placed in you with so little reserve. You I have to thank also for some lessons, which may teach me to rest satisfied with the churl's blood which nature has poured into my veins, and with the rude nurture which my father allotted to me.'

'I understand you not, sir,' replied Julian Peveril, who, feeling the necessity of saying something, could not, at the moment, find anything more fitting to say.

'Yes, sir, I thank you,' said Major Bridgenorth, in the same cold sarcastic tone, 'for having shown me, that breach of hospitality, infringement of good faith, and such like peccadilloes, are not utterly foreign to the mind and conduct of the heir of a knightly house of twenty descents. It is a great lesson to me, sir : for hitherto I had thought with the vulgar, that gentle manners went with gentle blood. But perhaps courtesy is too chivalrous a quality to be wasted in intercourse with a roundheaded fanatic like myself.'

'Major Bridgenorth,' said Julian, 'whatever has happened in this interview which may have displeased you, has been the result of feelings suddenly and strongly animated by the crisis of the moment—nothing was premeditated.'

'Not even your meeting, I suppose ? ' replied Bridgenorth, in the same cold tone. 'You, sir, wandered hither from Holm Peel—my daughter strolled forth from the Black Fort ; and chance, doubtless, assigned you a meeting by the stone of Goddard Crovan ? Young man, disgrace yourself by no more apologies—they are worse than useless. —And you, maiden, who, in your fear of losing your lover, could verge on betraying what might have cost a father his life—begone to your home. I will talk with you at more leisure, and teach you practically those duties which you seem to have forgotten.'

'On my honour, sir,' said Julian, 'your daughter is guiltless of all that can offend you ; she resisted every offer which the headstrong violence of my passion urged me to press upon her.'

'And, in brief,' said Bridgenorth, 'I am not to believe that you met in this remote place of rendezvous by Alice's special appointment ? '

Peveril knew not what to reply, and Bridgenorth again signed with his hand to his daughter to withdraw.

' I obey you, father,' said Alice, who had by this time recovered from the extremity of her surprise—' I obey you ; but Heaven is my witness that you do me more than injustice in suspecting me capable of betraying your secrets, even had it been necessary to save my own life or that of Julian. That you are walking in a dangerous path I well know ; but you do it with your eyes open, and are actuated by motives of which you can estimate the worth and value. My sole wish was, that this young man should not enter blindfold on the same perils ; and I had a right to warn him, since the feelings by which he is hoodwinked had a direct reference to me.'

' 'Tis well, minion,' said Bridgenorth, ' you have spoken your say. Retire, and let me complete the conference which you have so considerately commenced.'

' I go, sir,' said Alice.—' Julian, to you my last words are, and I would speak them with my last breath—Farewell, and caution ! '

She turned from them, disappeared among the underwood, and was seen no more.

' A true specimen of womankind,' said her father, looking after her, ' who would give the cause of nations up, rather than endanger a hair of her lover's head. You, Master Peveril, doubtless, hold her opinion, that the best love is a safe love ! '

' Were danger alone in my way,' said Peveril, much surprised at the softened tone in which Bridgenorth made this observation, ' there are few things which I would not face to—to—deserve your good opinion.'

' Or rather to win my daughter's hand,' said Bridgenorth. ' Well, young man, one thing has pleased me in your conduct, though of much I have my reasons to complain—one thing *has* pleased me. You have surmounted that bounding wall of aristocratical pride, in which your father, and, I suppose, his fathers, remained imprisoned, as in the precincts of a feudal fortress—you have leaped over this barrier, and shown yourself not unwilling to ally yourself with a family, whom your father spurns as low-born and ignoble.'

However favourable this speech sounded towards success in his suit, it so broadly stated the consequences of that success so far as his parents were concerned, that Julian felt it in the last degree difficult to reply. At length, perceiving that Major Bridgenorth seemed resolved quietly to await his answer, he mustered up courage to say, ' The feelings which I entertain towards your daughter, Master Bridgenorth, are of a nature to supersede many other considerations, to which, in any other case, I should feel it my duty to give the most reverential attention. I will not disguise from you, that my father's prejudices against such a match would be very strong ; but I devoutly believe they would disappear when he came to know the merit of Alice Bridgenorth, and to be sensible that she only could make his son happy.'

' In the meanwhile, you are desirous to complete the union which you propose without the knowledge of your parents, and take the chance of their being hereafter reconciled to it ? So I understand, from the proposal which you made but lately to my daughter.'

The turns of human nature, and of human passion, are so irregular and uncertain, that although Julian had but a few minutes before urged to Alice a private marriage, and an elopement to the continent, as a measure upon which the whole happiness of his life depended, the proposal seemed not to him half so delightful when stated by the calm, cold, dictatorial accents of her father. It sounded no longer like the dictates of ardent passion, throwing all other considerations aside, but as a distinct surrender of the dignity of his house to one who seemed to consider their relative situation as the triumph of Bridgenorth over Peveril. He was mute for a moment, in the vain attempt to shape his answer so as at once to intimate acquiescence in what Bridgenorth stated, and a vindication of his own regard for his parents and for the honour of his house.

This delay gave rise to suspicion, and Bridgenorth's eye gleamed, and his lip quivered while he gave vent to it. ' Hark ye, young man—deal openly with me in this matter, if you would not have me think you the execrable villain who would have seduced an unhappy girl, under promises which he never designed to fulfil. Let me but suspect this, and you shall see, on the spot, how far your pride and your pedigree will preserve you against the just vengeance of a father.'

'You do me wrong,' said Peveril—'you do me infinite wrong, Major Bridgenorth, I am incapable of the infamy which you allude to. The proposal I made to your daughter was as sincere as ever was offered by man to woman. I only hesitated, because you think it necessary to examine me so very closely ; and to possess yourself of all my purposes and sentiments, in their fullest extent, without explaining to me the tendency of your own.'

'Your proposal, then, shapes itself thus,' said Bridgenorth :—' You are willing to lead my only child into exile from her native country, to give her a claim to kindness and protection from your family, which you know will be disregarded, on condition I consent to bestow her hand on you, with a fortune sufficient to have matched that of your ancestors, when they had most reason to boast of their wealth. This, young man, seems no equal bargain. And yet,' he continued, after a momentary pause, ' so little do I value the goods of this world, that it might not be utterly beyond thy power to reconcile me to the match which you have proposed to me, however unequal it may appear.'

'Show me but the means which can propitiate your favour, Major Bridgenorth,' said Peveril,—' for I will not doubt that they will be consistent with my honour and duty —and you shall soon see how eagerly I will obey your directions, or submit to your conditions.'

'They are summed in few words,' answered Bridgenorth. ' Be an honest man, and the friend of your country.'

'No one has ever doubted,' replied Peveril, ' that I am both.'

'Pardon me,' replied the major ; ' no one has, as yet, seen you show yourself either. Interrupt me not—I question not your will to be both ; but you have hitherto neither had the light nor the opportunity necessary for the display of your principles, or the service of your country. You have lived when an apathy of mind, succeeding to the agitations of the Civil War, had made men indifferent to State affairs, and more willing to cultivate their own ease, than to stand in the gap when the Lord was pleading with Israel. But we are Englishmen ; and with us such unnatural lethargy cannot continue long. Already, many of those who most

desired the return of Charles Stuart, regard him as a king
whom Heaven, importuned by our entreaties, gave to us
in His anger. His unlimited licence—an example so readily
followed by the young and the gay around him—has disgusted the minds of all sober and thinking men. I had not
now held conference with you in this intimate fashion, were
I not aware that you, Master Julian, were free from such
stain of the times. Heaven, that rendered the king's course
of licence fruitful, had denied issue to his bed of wedlock ;
and in the gloomy and stern character of his bigoted successor, we already see what sort of monarch shall succeed
to the crown of England. This is a critical period, at which
it necessarily becomes the duty of all men to step forward,
each in his degree, and aid in rescuing the country which
gave us birth.' Peveril remembered the warning which he
had received from Alice, and bent his eyes on the ground,
without returning any reply. ' How is it, young man,' continued Bridgenorth, after a pause—' so young as thou art,
and bound by no ties of kindred profligacy with the enemies
of your country, you can be already hardened to the claims
she may form on you at this crisis ? '

' It were easy to answer you generally, Major Bridgenorth,' replied Peveril—' It were easy to say that my country cannot make a claim on me which I will not promptly
answer at the risk of lands and life. But in dealing thus
generally, we should but deceive each other. What is the
nature of this call ? By whom is it to be sounded ? And
what are to be the results ? for I think you have already seen
enough of the evils of civil war to be wary of again awakening
its terrors in a peaceful and happy country.'

' They that are drenched with poisonous narcotics,' said
the major, ' must be awakened by their physicians, though
it were with the sound of the trumpet. Better that men
should die bravely, with their arms in their hands, like free-
born Englishmen, than that they should slide into the blood-
less but dishonoured grave which slavery opens for its
vassals. But it is not of war that I was about to speak,' he
added, assuming a milder tone. ' The evils of which England now complains are such as can be remedied by the
wholesome administration of her own laws, even in the state
in which they are still suffered to exist. Have these laws not

a right to the support of every individual who lives under them ? Have they not a right to yours ? '

As he seemed to pause for an answer, Peveril replied, ' I have to learn, Major Bridgenorth, how the laws of England have become so far weakened as to require such support as mine. When that is made plain to me, no man will more willingly discharge the duty of a faithful liegeman to the law as well as the king. But the laws of England are under the guardianship of upright and learned judges, and of a gracious monarch.'

' And of a House of Commons,' interrupted Bridgenorth, ' no longer doting upon restored monarchy, but awakened, as with a peal of thunder, to the perilous state of our religion, and of our freedom. I appeal to your own con-science, Julian Peveril, whether this awakening hath not been in time, since you yourself know, and none better than you, the secret but rapid strides which Rome has made to erect her Dagon of idolatry within our Protestant land.'

Here Julian seeing, or thinking he saw, the drift of Bridge-north's suspicions, hastened to exculpate himself from the thought of favouring the Roman Catholic religion. ' It is true,' he said, ' I have been educated in a family where that faith is professed by one honoured individual, and that I have since travelled in Popish countries ; but even for these very reasons I have seen Popery too closely to be friendly to its tenets. The bigotry of the laymen—the persevering arts of the priesthood—the perpetual intrigue for the extension of the forms without the spirit of religion—the usurpation of that church over the consciences of men—and her impious pretensions to infallibility, are as incon-sistent to my mind as they can seem to yours, with common sense, rational liberty, freedom of conscience, and pure religion.'

' Spoken like the son of your excellent mother,' said Bridgenorth, grasping his hand ; ' for whose sake I have consented to endure so much from your house unrequited, even when the means of requital were in my own hand.'

' It was indeed from the instructions of that excellent parent,' said Peveril, ' that I was enabled, in my early youth, to resist and repel the insidious attacks made upon

my religious faith by the Catholic priests into whose company I was necessarily thrown. Like her, I trust to live and
die in the faith of the reformed Church of England.'

'The Church of England!' said Bridgenorth, dropping
his young friend's hand, but presently resuming it—' Alas!
that church, as now constituted, usurps scarcely less than
Rome herself upon men's consciences and liberties; yet,
out of the weakness of this half-reformed church, may God
be pleased to work out deliverance to England, and praise
to Himself. I must not forget, that one whose services have
been in the cause incalculable, wears the garb of an English
priest, and hath had episcopal ordination. It is not for us
to challenge the instrument, so that our escape is achieved
from the net of the fowler. Enough, that I find thee not
as yet enlightened with the purer doctrine, but prepared to
profit by it when the spark shall reach thee. Enough, in
especial, that I find thee willing to uplift thy testimony, to
cry aloud and spare not, against the errors and arts of the
Church of Rome. But remember, what thou hast now said,
thou wilt soon be called upon to justify, in a manner the
most solemn—the most awful.'

'What I have said,' replied Julian Peveril, 'being the
unbiassed sentiments of my heart, shall, upon no proper
occasion, want the support of my open avowal; and I think
it strange you should doubt me so far.'

'I doubt thee not, my young friend,' said Bridgenorth;
'and I trust to see that name rank high amongst those by
whom the prey shall be rent from the mighty. At present,
thy prejudices occupy thy mind like the strong keeper of
the house mentioned in Scripture. But there shall come
a stronger than he, and make forcible entry, displaying on
the battlements that sign of faith in which alone there is
found salvation. Watch, hope, and pray, that the hour
may come.'

There was a pause in the conversation, which was first
broken by Peveril. 'You have spoken to me in riddles,
Major Bridgenorth; and I have asked you for no explanation. Listen to a caution on my part, given with the most
sincere goodwill. Take a hint from me, and believe it,
though it is darkly expressed. You are here—at least are
believed to be here—on an errand dangerous to the lord of

the island. That danger will be retorted on yourself, if you make Man long your place of residence. Be warned, and depart in time.'

'And leave my daughter to the guardianship of Julian Peveril! Runs not your counsel so, young man?' answered Bridgenorth. 'Trust my safety, Julian, to my own prudence. I have been accustomed to guide myself through worse dangers than now environ me. But I thank you for your caution, which I am willing to believe was at least partly disinterested.'

'We do not, then, part in anger?' said Peveril.

'Not in anger, my son,' said Bridgenorth, 'but in love and strong affection. For my daughter, thou must forbear every thought of seeing her, save through me. I accept not thy suit, neither do I reject it; only this I intimate to you, that he who would be my son, must first show himself the true and loving child of his oppressed and deluded country. Farewell; do not answer me now, thou art yet in the gall of bitterness, and it may be that strife (which I desire not) should fall between us. Thou shalt hear of me sooner than thou thinkest for.'

He shook Peveril heartily by the hand, and again bade him farewell, leaving him under the confused and mingled impression of pleasure, doubt, and wonder. Not a little surprised to find himself so far in the good graces of Alice's father, that his suit was even favoured with a sort of negative encouragement, he could not help suspecting, as well from the language of the daughter as of the father, that Bridgenorth was desirous, as the price of his favour, that he should adopt some line of conduct inconsistent with the principles in which he had been educated.

'You need not fear, Alice,' he said in his heart; 'not even your hand would I purchase by aught which resembled unworthy or truckling compliance with tenets which my heart disowns; and well I know, were I mean enough to do so, even the authority of thy father were insufficient to compel thee to the ratification of so mean a bargain. But let me hope better things. Bridgenorth, though strong-minded and sagacious, is haunted by the fears of Popery, which are the bugbears of his sect. My residence in the family of the Countess of Derby is more than enough to inspire him with suspicions of my faith, from which, thank Heaven, I can vindicate myself with truth and a good conscience.'

So thinking, he again adjusted the girths of his palfrey, replaced the bit which he had slipped out of its mouth, that it might feed at liberty, and mounting, pursued his way back to the Castle of Holm Peel, where he could not help fearing that something extraordinary might have happened in his absence.

But the old pile soon rose before him, serene, and sternly still, amid the sleeping ocean. The banner, which indicated that the Lord of Man held residence within its ruinous precincts, hung motionless by the ensign-staff. The sentinels walked to and fro on their posts, and hummed or whistled their Manx airs. Leaving his faithful companion, Fairy, in the village as before, Julian entered the castle, and found all within in the same state of quietness and good order which external appearances had announced.

CHAPTER XVIII

Now rede me, rede me, brother dear,
  Throughout Merry England,
Where will I find a messenger,
  Betwixt us two to send.
      Ballad of King Estmere.

JULIAN's first rencontre, after re-entering the castle, was with its young lord, who received him with his usual kindness and lightness of humour.

'Thrice welcome, Sir Knight of Dames,' said the earl; 'here you rove gallantly, and at free will, through our dominions, fulfilling of appointments, and achieving amorous adventures; while we are condemned to sit in our royal halls, as dull and as immovable as if our Majesty was carved on the stern of some Manx smuggling dogger, and christened the King Arthur of Ramsey.'

'Nay, in that case you would take the sea,' said Julian, 'and so enjoy travel and adventure enough.'

'Oh, but suppose me wind-bound, or detained in harbour by a revenue pink, or ashore, if you like it, and lying high and dry upon the sand. Imagine the royal image in the dullest of all predicaments, and you have not equalled mine.'

'I am happy to hear, at least, that you have had no disagreeable employment,' said Julian; 'the morning's alarm has blown over, I suppose ?'

'In faith it has, Julian; and our close inquiries cannot find any cause for the apprehended insurrection. That Bridgenorth is in the island seems certain; but private affairs of consequence are alleged as the cause of his visit; and I am not desirous to have him arrested unless I could prove some malpractices against him and his companions. In fact, it would seem we had taken the alarm too soon. My mother speaks of consulting you on the subject, Julian; and I will not anticipate her solemn communication. It will be partly apologetical, I suppose; for we begin to think our retreat rather unroyal, and that, like the wicked, we have fled when no man pursued. This idea afflicts my mother, who, as a Queen Dowager, a Queen Regent, a heroine, and a woman in general, would be extremely mortified to think that her precipitate retreat hither had exposed her to the ridicule of the islanders; and she is disconcerted and out of humour accordingly. In the meanwhile, my sole amusement has been the grimaces and fantastic gestures of that ape Fenella, who is more out of humour, and more absurd, in consequence, than you ever saw her. Morris says it is because you pushed her downstairs, Julian—how is that ?'

'Nay, Morris has misreported me,' answered Julian; 'I did but lift her *up*stairs to be rid of her importunity; for she chose, in her way, to contest my going abroad in such an obstinate manner, that I had no other mode of getting rid of her.'

'She must have supposed your departure, at a moment so critical, was dangerous to the state of our garrison,' answered the earl; 'it shows how dearly she esteems my mother's safety, how highly she rates your prowess. But, thank Heaven, there sounds the dinner-bell. I would the philosophers, who find a sin and waste of time in good cheer, could devise us any pastime half so agreeable.'

The meal which the young earl had thus longed for, as a means of consuming a portion of the time which hung heavy on his hands, was soon over; as soon, at least, as

the habitual and stately formality of the countess's household permitted. She herself, accompanied by her gentlewomen and attendants, retired early after the tables were
drawn ; and the young gentlemen were left to their own
company. Wine had, for the moment, no charms for
either ; for the earl was out of spirits from ennui and
impatience of his monotonous and solitary course of life ;
and the events of the day had given Peveril too much
matter for reflection to permit his starting amusing or
interesting topics of conversation. After having passed
the flask in silence betwixt them once or twice, they withdrew each to a separate embrasure of the windows of the
dining apartment, which, such was the extreme thickness
of the wall, were deep enough to afford a solitary recess,
separated, as it were, from the chamber itself. In one of
these sat the Earl of Derby, busied in looking over some
of the new publications which had been forwarded from
London, and at intervals confessing how little power or
interest these had for him by yawning fearfully as he
looked out on the solitary expanse of waters, which, save
from the flight of a flock of sea-gulls, or of a solitary cor-
morant, offered so little of variety to engage his attention.

Peveril, on his part, held a pamphlet also in his hand,
without giving, or affecting to give it, even his occasional
attention. His whole soul turned upon the interview which
he had had that day with Alice Bridgenorth, and with her
father ; while he in vain endeavoured to form any hypothesis
which could explain to him why the daughter, to whom he
had no reason to think himself indifferent, should have been
so suddenly desirous of their eternal separation, while her
father, whose opposition he so much dreaded, seemed to be
at least tolerant of his addresses. He could only suppose,
in explanation, that Major Bridgenorth had some plan in
prospect, which it was in his own power to further or
to impede ; while, from the demeanour, and indeed the
language, of Alice, he had but too much reason to apprehend
that her father's favour could only be conciliated by something, on his own part, approaching to dereliction of principle. But by no conjecture which he could form could he
make the least guess concerning the nature of that compliance, of which Bridgenorth seemed desirous. He could

not imagine, notwithstanding Alice had spoken of treachery, that her father would dare to propose to him uniting in any plan by which the safety of the countess, or the security of her little kingdom of Man, was to be endangered. This carried such indelible disgrace in the front, that he could not suppose the scheme proposed to him by any who was not prepared to defend with his sword, upon the spot, so flagrant an insult offered to his honour. And such a proceeding was totally inconsistent with the conduct of Major Bridgenorth in every other respect, besides his being too calm and cold-blooded to permit of his putting a mortal affront upon the son of his old neighbour, to whose mother he confessed so much of obligation.

While Peveril in vain endeavoured to extract something like a probable theory out of the hints thrown out by the father and by the daughter—not without the additional and lover-like labour of endeavouring to reconcile his passion to his honour and conscience—he felt something gently pull him by the cloak. He unclasped his arms, which, in medita-tion, had been folded on his bosom ; and withdrawing his eyes from the vacant prospect of sea-coast and sea which they perused, without much consciousness upon what they rested, he beheld beside him the little dumb maiden, the elfin Fenella. She was seated on a low cushion or stool, with which she had nestled close to Peveril's side, and had remained there for a short space of time, expecting, no doubt, he would become conscious of her presence ; until, tired of remaining unnoticed, she at length solicited his attention in the manner which we have described. Startled out of his reverie by this intimation of her presence, he looked down, and could not, without interest, behold this singular and helpless being.

Her hair was unloosened, and streamed over her shoulders in such length, that much of it lay upon the ground, and in such quantity, that it formed a dark veil, or shadow, not only around her face, but over her whole slender and minute form. From the profusion of her tresses looked forth her small and dark, but well-formed features, together with the large and brilliant black eyes ; and her whole countenance was composed into the imploring look of one who is doubtful of the reception she is about to meet with from a valued friend, while she confesses a fault, pleads an apology, or solicits a reconciliation. In short, the whole face was so much alive with expression, that Julian, though her aspect

JULIAN AND FENELLA

was so familiar to him, could hardly persuade himself but that her countenance was entirely new. The wild, fantastic, elvish vivacity of the features seemed totally vanished, and had given place to a sorrowful, tender, and pathetic cast of countenance, aided by the expression of the large dark eyes, which, as they were turned up towards Julian, glistened with moisture, that, nevertheless, did not overflow the eyelids.

Conceiving that her unwonted manner arose from a recollection of the dispute which had taken place betwixt them in the morning, Peveril was anxious to restore the little maiden's gaiety, by making her sensible that there dwelt on his mind no unpleasing recollection of their quarrel. He smiled kindly, and shook her hand in one of his; while, with the familiarity of one who had known her from childhood, he stroked down her long dark tresses with the other. She stooped her head, as if ashamed, and, at the same time, gratified with his caresses—and he was thus induced to continue them, until, under the veil of her rich and abundant locks, he suddenly felt his other hand, which she still held fast in hers, slightly touched with her lips, and, at the same time, moistened with a tear.

At once, and for the first time in his life, the danger of being misinterpreted in his familiarity with a creature to whom the usual modes of explanation were a blank occurred to Julian's mind; and, hastily withdrawing his hand, and changing his posture, he asked of her, by a sign which custom had rendered familiar, whether she brought any message to him from the countess. In an instant Fenella's whole deportment was changed. She started up, and arranged herself in her seat with the rapidity of lightning; and, at the same moment, with one turn of her hand, braided her length of locks into a natural head-dress of the most beautiful kind. There was, indeed, when she looked up, a blush still visible on her dark features; but their melancholy and languid expression had given place to that of wild and restless vivacity, which was most common to them. Her eyes gleamed with more than their wonted fire, and her glances were more piercingly wild and unsettled than usual. To Julian's inquiry she answered by laying her hand on her heart—a motion by which she always indicated the countess—and rising, and taking the direction of her apartment, she made a sign to Julian to follow her.

The distance was not great betwixt the dining apartment and that to which Peveril now followed his mute guide; yet, in going thither, he had time enough to suffer cruelly from

the sudden suspicion that this unhappy girl had misinterpreted the uniform kindness with which he had treated her,
and hence come to regard him with feelings more tender
than those which belong to friendship. The misery which
such a passion was likely to occasion to a creature in her
helpless situation, and actuated by such lively feelings, was
great enough to make him refuse credit to the suspicion
which pressed itself upon his mind ; while, at the same time,
he formed the internal resolution so to conduct himself
towards Fenella as to check such misplaced sentiments, if
indeed she unhappily entertained them towards him.

When they reached the countess's apartment, they found
her with writing implements and many sealed letters before
her. She received Julian with her usual kindness ; and
having caused him to be seated, beckoned to the mute to
resume her needle. In an instant Fenella was seated at an
embroidering-frame, where, but for the movement of her
dexterous fingers, she might have seemed a statue, so little
did she move from her work, either head or eye. As her
infirmity rendered her presence no bar to the most confidential conversation, the countess proceeded to address
Peveril as if they had been literally alone together.

'Julian,' she said, 'I am not now about to complain to
you of the sentiments and conduct of Derby. He is your
friend—he is my son. He has kindness of heart and
vivacity of talent ; and yet ' ——

'Dearest lady,' said Peveril, 'why will you distress yourself with fixing your eye on deficiencies which arise rather
from a change of times and manners than any degeneracy
of my noble friend ? Let him be once engaged in his duty,
whether in peace or war, and let me pay the penalty if he
acquits not himself becoming his high station.'

'Aye,' replied the countess ; 'but when will the call of
duty prove superior to that of the most idle or trivial indulgence which can serve to drive over the lazy hour ? His
father was of another mould ; and how often was it my lot
to entreat that he would spare, from the rigid discharge of
those duties which his high station imposed, the relaxation
absolutely necessary to recruit his health and his spirits ! '

'Still, my dearest lady,' said Peveril, 'you must allow
that the duties to which the times summoned your late

honoured lord were of a more stirring, as well as a more peremptory cast, than those which await your son.'

'I know not that,' said the countess. 'The wheel appears to be again revolving ; and the present period is not unlikely to bring back such scenes as my younger years witnessed. Well, be it so ; they will not find Charlotte de la Tremouille broken in spirit, though depressed by years. It was even on this subject I would speak with you, my young friend. Since our first early acquaintance—when I saw your gallant behaviour as I issued forth to your childish eye, like an apparition, from my place of conceal-ment in your father's castle—it has pleased me to think you a true son of Stanley and Peveril. I trust your nurture in this family has been ever suited to the esteem in which I hold you. Nay, I desire no thanks. I have to require of you, in return, a piece of service, not perhaps entirely safe to yourself, but which, as times are circumstanced, no person is so well able to render to my house.'

'You have been ever my good and noble lady,' answered Peveril, 'as well as my kind, and I may say maternal, protectress. You have a right to command the blood of Stanley in the veins of every one—You have a thousand rights to command it in mine.' [1]

'My advices from England,' said the countess, 'resemble more the dreams of a sick man than the regular information which I might have expected from such correspondents as mine ;—their expressions are like those of men who walk in their sleep, and speak by snatches of what passes in their dreams. It is said a plot, real or fictitious, has been de-tected among the Catholics, which has spread far wider and more uncontrollable terror than that of the fifth of Novem-ber. Its outlines seem utterly incredible, and are only sup-ported by the evidence of wretches, the meanest and most worthless in the creation ; yet it is received by the credulous people of England with the most undoubting belief.'

'This is a singular delusion to rise without some real ground,' answered Julian.

'I am no bigot, cousin, though a Catholic,' replied the countess. 'I have long feared that the well-meant zeal of

---

[1] The reader cannot have forgotten that the Earl of Derby was head of the great house of Stanley.

our priests for increasing converts would draw on them the
suspicion of the English nation. These efforts have been
renewed with double energy since the Duke of York conformed to the Catholic faith ; and the same event has
doubled the hate and jealousy of the Protestants. So far,
I fear, there may be just cause for suspicion that the duke
is a better Catholic than an Englishman, and that bigotry
has involved him, as avarice, or the needy greed of a
prodigal, has engaged his brother, in relations with France,
whereof England may have too much reason to complain.
But the gross, thick, and palpable fabrications of conspiracy
and murder, blood and fire—the imaginary armies—the
intended massacres—form a collection of falsehoods, that
one would have thought indigestible, even by the coarse
appetite of the vulgar for the marvellous and horrible ; but
which are, nevertheless, received as truth by both Houses
of Parliament, and questioned by no one who is desirous to
escape the odious appellation of friend to the bloody Papists,
and favourer of their infernal schemes of cruelty.'

' But what say those who are most likely to be affected by
these wild reports ? ' said Julian. ' What say the English
Catholics themselves ?—a numerous and wealthy body com-
prising so many noble names ? '

' Their hearts are dead within them,' said the countess.
' They are like sheep penned up in the shambles, that the
butcher may take his choice among them. In the obscure
and brief communications which I have had by a secure
hand, they do but anticipate their own utter ruin, and ours
—so general is the depression, so universal the despair.'

' But the king,' said Peveril—' the king and the Protestant royalists—what say they to this growing tempest ? '

' Charles,' replied the countess, ' with his usual selfish
prudence, truckles to the storm ; and will let cord and axe
do their work on the most innocent men in his dominions,
rather than lose an hour of pleasure in attempting their
rescue. And, for the royalists, either they have caught the
general delirium which has seized on Protestants in general,
or they stand aloof and neutral, afraid to show any interest
in the unhappy Catholics, lest they be judged altogether
such as themselves, and abettors of the fearful conspiracy
in which they are alleged to be engaged. In fact, I cannot

blame them. It is hard to expect that mere compassion for a persecuted sect—or, what is yet more rare, an abstract love of justice—should be powerful enough to engage men to expose themselves to the awakened fury of a whole people ; for, in the present state of general agitation, whoever disbelieves the least tittle of the enormous improbabilities which have been accumulated by these wretched informers is instantly hunted down as one who would smother the discovery of the plot. It is indeed an awful tempest ; and, remote as we lie from its sphere, we must expect soon to feel its effects.'

'Lord Derby already told me something of this,' said Julian ; 'and that there were agents in this island whose object was to excite insurrection.'

'Yes,' answered the countess, and her eye flashed fire as she spoke ; 'and had my advice been listened to, they had been apprehended in the very fact ; and so dealt with as to be a warning to all others how they sought this independent principality on such an errand. But my son, who is generally so culpably negligent of his own affairs, was pleased to assume the management of them upon this crisis.'

'I am happy to learn, madam,' answered Peveril, 'that the measures of precaution which my kinsman has adopted have had the complete effect of disconcerting the conspiracy.'

'For the present, Julian ; but they should have been such as would have made the boldest tremble to think of such infringement of our rights in future. But Derby's present plan is fraught with greater danger ; and yet there is something in it of gallantry, which has my sympathy.'

'What is it, madam ? ' inquired Julian anxiously.; ' and in what can I aid it, or avert its dangers ? '

'He purposes,' said the countess, ' instantly to set forth for London. He is, he says, not merely the feudal chief of a small island, but one of the noble peers of England, who must not remain in the security of an obscure and distant castle, when his name, or that of his mother, is slandered before his prince and people. He will take his place, he says, in the House of Lords, and publicly demand justice for the insult thrown on his house by perjured and interested witnesses.'

'It is a generous resolution, and worthy of my friend,'

said Julian Peveril.   ' I will go with him and share his fate,
be it what it may.'

' Alas, foolish boy ! ' answered the countess, ' as well may
you ask a hungry lion to feel compassion, as a prejudiced
and furious people to do justice.   They are like the madman
at the height of frenzy, who murders without compunction
his best and dearest friend ; and only wonders and wails
over his own cruelty when he is recovered from his delirium.'

' Pardon me, dearest lady,' said Julian, ' this cannot be.
The noble and generous people of England cannot be thus
strangely misled.   Whatever prepossessions may be current
among the more vulgar, the Houses of Legislature cannot
be deeply infected by them—they will remember their own
dignity.'

' Alas ! cousin,' answered the countess, ' when did Englishmen, even of the highest degree, remember anything when
hurried away by the violence of party feeling ?   Even those
who have too much sense to believe in the incredible fictions
which gull the multitude will beware how they expose them,
if their own political party can gain a momentary advantage
by their being accredited.   It is amongst such, too, that
your kinsman has found friends and associates.   Neglecting
the old friends of his house, as too grave and formal companions for the humour of the times, his intercourse has
been with the versatile Shaftesbury, the mercurial Buckingham—men who would not hesitate to sacrifice to the popular
Moloch of the day whatsoever or whomsoever whose ruin
could propitiate the deity.   Forgive a mother's tears, kinsman ; but I see the scaffold at Bolton again erected.   If
Derby goes to London while these bloodhounds are in
full cry, obnoxious as he is, and I have made him by my
religious faith and my conduct in this island, he dies his
father's death.   And yet upon what other course to
resolve ! '——

' Let me go to London, madam,' said Peveril, much
moved by the distress of his patroness ; ' your ladyship was
wont to rely something on my judgement.   I will act for
the best—will communicate with those whom you point
out to me, and only with them ; and I trust soon to send
you information that this delusion, however strong it may
now be, is in the course of passing away ; at the worst,

I can apprise you of the danger, should it menace the earl or yourself ; and may be able also to point out the means by which it may be eluded.'

The countess listened with a countenance in which the anxiety of maternal affection, which prompted her to embrace Peveril's generous offer, struggled with her native disinterested and generous disposition. ' Think what you ask of me, Julian,' she replied, with a sigh. ' Would you have me expose the life of my friend's son to those perils to which I refuse my own ?   No, never ! '

' Nay, but, madam,' replied Julian, ' I do not run the same risk—my person is not known in London—my situation, though not obscure in my own country, is too little known to be noticed in that huge assemblage of all that is noble and wealthy. No whisper, I presume, however indirect, has connected my name with the alleged conspiracy. I am a Protestant, above all ; and can be accused of no intercourse, direct or indirect, with the Church of Rome. My connexions also lie amongst those who, if they do not, or cannot, befriend me, cannot at least be dangerous to me. In a word, I run no danger where the earl might incur great peril.'

' Alas ! ' said the Countess of Derby, ' all this generous reasoning may be true ; but it could only be listened to by a widowed mother. Selfish as I am, I cannot but reflect that my kinswoman has, in all events, the support of an affectionate husband—such is the interested reasoning to which we are not ashamed to subject our better feelings.'

' Do not call it so, madam,' answered Peveril ; ' think of me as the younger brother of my kinsman. You have ever done by me the duties of a mother ; and have a right to my filial service, were it at a risk ten times greater than a journey to London, to inquire into the temper of the times.   I will instantly go and announce my departure to the earl.'

' Stay, Julian,' said the countess ; ' if you must make this journey in our behalf—and, alas ! I have not generosity enough to refuse your noble proffer—you must go alone, and without communication with Derby.   I know him well ; his lightness of mind is free from selfish baseness ; and for the world would he not suffer you to leave Man without his company.   And if he went with you, your noble and disinterested kindness would be of no avail—you would but share his ruin, as the swimmer who attempts to save a drowning man is involved in his fate, if he permit the sufferer to grapple with him.'

'It shall be as you please, madam,' said Peveril. 'I am ready to depart upon half an hour's notice.'

'This night, then,' said the countess, after a moment's pause—'this night I will arrange the most secret means of carrying your generous project into effect; for I would not excite that prejudice against you, which will instantly arise, were it known you had so lately left this island and its Popish lady. You will do well, perhaps, to use a feigned name in London.'

'Pardon me, madam,' said Julian; 'I will do nothing that can draw on me unnecessary attention; but to bear a feigned name, or affect any disguise beyond living with extreme privacy, would, I think, be unwise as well as unworthy; and what, if challenged, I might find some difficulty in assigning a reason for, consistent with perfect fairness of intentions.'

'I believe you are right,' answered the countess, after a moment's consideration; and then added, 'You propose, doubtless, to pass through Derbyshire, and visit Martindale Castle?'

'I should wish it, madam, certainly,' replied Peveril, 'did time permit, and circumstances render it advisable.'

'Of that,' said the countess, 'you must yourself judge. Dispatch is, doubtless, desirable; on the other hand, arriving from your own family-seat, you will be less an object of doubt and suspicion than if you posted up from hence, without even visiting your parents. You must be guided in this—in all—by your own prudence. Go, my dearest son—for to me you should be dear as a son—go, and prepare for your journey. I will get ready some dispatches, and a supply of money—Nay, do not object. Am I not your mother; and are you not discharging a son's duty? Dispute not my right of defraying your expenses. Nor is this all; for, as I must trust your zeal and prudence to act in our behalf when occasion shall demand, I will furnish you with effectual recommendations to our friends and kindred, entreating and enjoining them to render whatever aid you may require, either for your own protection, or the advancement of what you may propose in our favour.' ----

Peveril made no further opposition to an arrangement, which in truth the moderate state of his own finances rendered almost indispensable, unless with his father's assistance ; and the countess put into his hand bills of exchange to the amount of two hundred pounds, upon a merchant in the city. She then dismissed Julian for the space of an hour ; after which, she said, she must again require his presence.

The preparations for his journey were not of a nature to divert the thoughts which speedily pressed on him. He found that half an hour's conversation had once more completely changed his immediate prospects and plans for the future. He had offered to the Countess of Derby a service which her uniform kindness had well deserved at his hand ; but, by her accepting it, he was upon the point of being separated from Alice Bridgenorth at a time when she was become dearer to him than ever by her avowal of mutual passion. Her image rose before him, such as he had that day pressed her to his bosom——her voice was in his ear, and seemed to ask whether he could desert her in the crisis which everything seemed to announce as impending. But Julian Peveril, his youth considered, was strict in judging his duty, and severely resolved in executing it. He trusted not his imagination to pursue the vision which presented itself ; but resolutely seizing his pen, wrote to Alice the following letter, explaining his situation, as far as justice to the countess permitted him to do so :—

' I leave you, dearest Alice,' thus ran the letter. ' I leave you ; and though, in doing so, I but obey the command you have laid on me, yet I can claim little merit for my compliance, since, without additional and most forcible reasons in aid of your orders, I fear I should have been unable to comply with them. But family affairs of importance compel me to absent myself from this island for, I fear, more than one week. My thoughts, hopes, and wishes will be on the moment that shall restore me to the Black Fort and its lovely valley. Let me hope that yours will sometimes rest on the lonely exile, whom nothing could render such but the command of honour and duty. Do not fear that I mean to involve you in a private correspondence, and let not your father fear it. I could not love you so much, but for the openness and candour of your nature ; and I would not that you concealed from Major Bridgenorth one syllable of what I now avow. Respecting other matters, he himself cannot desire the welfare of our common country with more zeal than I do. Differences may occur concerning the mode in which that is to be obtained ; but, in the principle, I am convinced there can be only one mind between us ; nor can I refuse to listen to his experience and wisdom, even where they may ultimately fail to convince me. Farewell— Alice, farewell ! Much might be added to that melancholy word, but nothing that could express the bitterness with which it is written. Yet I could transcribe it again and again, rather than conclude the last communication which I can have with you for some time. My sole comfort is, that my stay will scarce be so long as to permit you to forget one who never can forget you.'

He held the paper in his hand for a minute after he had folded, but before he had sealed it, while he hurriedly debated in his own mind whether he had not expressed himself towards Major Bridgenorth in so conciliating a manner as might excite hopes of proselytism, which his conscience told him he could not realize with honour. Yet, on the other hand, he had no right, from what Bridgenorth had said, to conclude that their principles were diametrically irreconcilable ; for though the son of a high Cavalier, and educated in the family of the Countess of Derby, he was himself, upon principle, an enemy of prerogative, and a friend to the liberty of the subject. And with such considerations, he silenced all internal objections on the point of honour ; although his conscience secretly whispered that these conciliatory expressions towards the father were chiefly dictated by the fear that, during his absence, Major Bridgenorth might be tempted to change the residence of his daughter, and perhaps to convey her altogether out of his reach.

Having sealed his letter, Julian called his servant, and directed him to carry it under cover of one addressed to Mrs. Debbitch, to a house in the town of Rushin, where packets and messages intended for the family at Black Fort were usually deposited ; and for that purpose to take horse immediately. He thus got rid of an attendant who might have been in some degree a spy on his motions. He then exchanged the dress he usually wore for one more suited to travelling ; and, having put a change or two of linen into a small cloak-bag, selected as arms a strong double-edged sword and an excellent pair of pistols, which last he carefully loaded with double bullets. Thus appointed, and with twenty pieces in his purse, and the bills we have mentioned secured in a private pocket-book, he was in readiness to depart as soon as he should receive the countess's commands.

The buoyant spirit of youth and hope, which had, for a moment, been chilled by the painful and dubious circumstances in which he was placed, as well as the deprivation which he was about to undergo, now revived in full vigour. Fancy, turning from more painful anticipations, suggested to him that he was now entering upon life at a crisis when resolution and talents were almost certain to make the fortune of their possessor. How could he make a more honourable entry on the bustling scene than sent by, and acting in behalf of, one of the noblest houses in England ; and should he perform what his charge might render incumbent with the resolution and the prudence necessary to secure success, how many occurrences might take place to render his mediation necessary to Bridgenorth ; and thus enable him, on the most equal and honourable terms, to establish a claim to his gratitude and to his daughter's hand.

Whilst he was dwelling on such pleasing, though imaginary prospects, he could not help exclaiming aloud—' Yes, Alice, I will win thee nobly ! ' The words had scarce escaped his lips, when he heard at the door of his apartment, which the servant had left ajar, a sound like a deep sigh, which was instantly succeeded by a gentle tap—' Come in,' replied Julian, somewhat ashamed of his exclamation, and not a little afraid that it had been caught up by some eavesdropper —' Come in,' he again repeated ; but his command was not obeyed ; on the contrary, the knock was repeated somewhat louder. He opened the door, and Fenella stood before him.

With eyes that seemed red with recent tears, and with a look of the deepest dejection, the little mute, first touching her bosom, and beckoning with her finger, made to him the usual sign that the countess desired to see him—then

turned, as if to usher him to her apartment.   As he followed
her through the long gloomy vaulted passages which
afforded communication betwixt the various apartments of
the castle, he could not but observe that her usual light trip
was exchanged for a tardy and mournful step, which she
accompanied with low inarticulate moaning (which she
was probably the less able to suppress, because she could not
judge how far it was audible), and also with wringing of the
hands, and other marks of extreme affliction.

At this moment a thought came across Peveril's mind,
which, in spite of his better reason, made him shudder involuntarily. As a Peaksman, and a long resident in the
Isle of Man, he was well acquainted with many a superstitious
legend, and particularly with a belief, which attached to
the powerful family of the Stanleys, for their peculiar
demon, a Banshee, or female spirit, who was wont to shriek
' foreboding evil times ' ; and who was generally seen
weeping and bemoaning herself before the death of any
person of distinction belonging to the family. For an
instant, Julian could scarcely divest himself of the belief
that the wailing, jibbering form, which glided before him,
with a lamp in her hand, was the genius of his mother's
race, come to announce to him his predestined doom.   It
instantly occurred to him as an analogous reflection, that if
the suspicion which had crossed his mind concerning Fenella
was a just one, her ill-fated attachment to him, like that of
the prophetic spirit to his family, could bode nothing but
disaster, and lamentation, and woe.

CHAPTER XIX

Now, hoist the anchor, mates—and let the sails
    Give their broad bosom to the buxom wind,
    Like lass that woos a lover.
                                ANONYMOUS.

THE presence of the countess dispelled the superstitious
feeling which, for an instant, had encroached on Julian's
imagination, and compelled him to give attention to the
matters of ordinary life. ' Here are your credentials,' she
said, giving him a small packet carefully packed up in

a sealskin cover ; ' you had better not open them till you come to London. You must not be surprised to find that there are one or two addressed to men of my own persuasion. These, for all our sakes, you will observe caution in delivering.'

'I go your messenger, madam,' said Peveril ; ' and whatever you desire me to charge myself with, of that I undertake the care. Yet allow me to doubt whether an intercourse with Catholics will at this moment forward the purposes of my mission.'

' You have caught the general suspicion of this wicked sect already,' said the countess, smiling, ' and are the fitter to go amongst Englishmen in their present mood. But, my cautious friend, these letters are so addressed, and the persons to whom they are addressed so disguised, that you will run no danger in conversing with them. Without their aid, indeed, you will not be able to obtain the accurate information you go in search of. None can tell so exactly how the wind sets, as the pilot whose vessel is exposed to the storm. Besides, though you Protestants deny our priesthood the harmlessness of the dove, you are ready enough to allow us a full share of the wisdom of the serpent ; in plain terms, their means of information are extensive, and they are not deficient in the power of applying it. I therefore wish you to have the benefit of their intelligence and advice, if possible.'

' Whatever you impose upon me as a part of my duty, madam, rely on its being discharged punctually,' answered Peveril. ' And now, as there is little use in deferring the execution of a purpose when once fixed, let me know your ladyship's wishes concerning my departure.'

' It must be sudden and secret,' said the countess ; ' the island is full of spies ; and I would not wish that any of them should have notice that an envoy of mine was about to leave Man for London. Can you be ready to go on board to-morrow ? '

' To-night—this instant if you will,' said Julian—' my little preparations are complete.'

' Be ready, then, in your chamber, at two hours after midnight. I will send one to summon you, for our secret must be communicated, for the present, to as few as possible.

A foreign sloop is engaged to carry you over ; then make
the best of your way to London, by Martindale Castle, or
otherwise, as you find most advisable.   When it is necessary
to announce your absence, I will say you are gone to see
your parents.   But stay—your journey will be on horseback,
of course, from Whitehaven.   You have bills of exchange,
it is true ; but are you provided with ready money to
furnish yourself with a good horse ? '

' I am sufficiently rich, madam,' answered Julian ; ' and
good nags are plenty in Cumberland.   There are those
among them who know how to come by them good and
cheap.'

' Trust not to that,' said the countess.   ' Here is what
will purchase for you the best horse on the Borders.   Can
you be simple enough to refuse it ? ' she added, as she
pressed on him a heavy purse, which he saw himself obliged
to accept.

' A good horse, Julian,' continued the countess, ' and
a good sword, next to a good heart and head, are the
accomplishments of a cavalier.'

' I kiss your hands, then, madam,' said Peveril, ' and
humbly beg you to believe, that whatever may fail in my
present undertaking, my purpose to serve you, my noble
kinswoman and benefactress, can at least never swerve or
falter.'

' I know it, my son, I know it ; and may God forgive me
if my anxiety for your friend has sent you on dangers which
should have been his !   Go—go—May saints and angels
bless you !   Fenella shall acquaint him that you sup in your
own apartment.   So indeed will I ; for to-night I should be
unable to face my son's looks.   Little will he thank me for
sending you on his errand ; and there will be many to ask,
whether it was like the Lady of Latham to trust her friend's
son on the danger which should have been braved by her
own.   But oh !   Julian, I am now a forlorn widow, whom
sorrow has made selfish ! '

' Tush, madam,' answered Peveril ; ' it is more unlike
the Lady of Latham to anticipate dangers which may not
exist at all, and to which, if they do indeed occur, I am less
obnoxious than my noble kinsman.   Farewell !   All blessings attend you, madam.   Commend me to Derby, and

make him my excuses. I shall expect a summons at two hours after midnight.'

They took an affectionate leave of each other ; the more affectionate, indeed, on the part of the countess, that she could not entirely reconcile her generous mind to exposing Peveril to danger on her son's behalf ; and Julian betook himself to his solitary apartment.

His servant soon afterwards brought him wine and refreshments ; to which, notwithstanding the various matters he had to occupy his mind, he contrived to do reasonable justice. But when this needful occupation was finished, his thoughts began to stream in upon him like a troubled tide—at once recalling the past, and anticipating the future. It was in vain that he wrapped himself in his riding cloak, and, lying down on his bed, endeavoured to compose himself to sleep. The uncertainty of the prospect before him—the doubt how Bridgenorth might dispose of his daughter during his absence—the fear that the major himself might fall into the power of the vindictive countess, besides a numerous train of vague and half-formed apprehensions, agitated his blood, and rendered slumber impossible. Alternately to recline in the old oaken easy chair, and listen to the dashing of the waves under the windows, mingled, as the sound was, with the scream of the sea-birds ; or to traverse the apartment with long and slow steps, pausing occasionally to look out on the sea, slumbering under the influence of a full moon, which tipped each wave with silver —such were the only pastimes he could invent, until midnight had passed for one hour ; the next was wasted in anxious expectation of the summons of departure.

At length it arrived—a tap at his door was followed by a low murmur, which made him suspect that the countess had again employed her mute attendant as the most secure minister of her pleasure on this occasion. He felt something like impropriety in this selection ; and it was with a feeling of impatience alien to the natural generosity of his temper, that, when he opened the door, he beheld the dumb maiden standing before him. The lamp which he held in his hand showed his features distinctly, and probably made Fenella aware of the expression which animated them. She cast her large dark eyes mournfully on the ground ; and,

without again looking him in the face, made him a signal
to follow her.   He delayed no longer than was necessary to
secure his pistols in his belt, wrap his cloak closer around
him, and take his small portmanteau under his arm.   Thus
accoutred, he followed her out of the keep, or inhabited
part of the castle, by a series of obscure passages leading
to a postern gate, which she unlocked with a key selected
from a bundle which she carried at her girdle.

They now stood in the castle-yard, in the open moonlight,
which glimmered white and ghastly on the variety of strange
and ruinous objects to which we have formerly alluded,
and which gave the scene rather the appearance of some
ancient cemetery, than of the interior of a fortification.
The round and elevated tower—the ancient mount, with
its quadrangular sides facing the ruinous edifices which
once boasted the name of cathedral—seemed of yet more
antique and anomalous form when seen by the pale light
which now displayed them.   To one of these churches
Fenella took the direct course, and was followed by Julian ;
although he at once divined, and was superstitious enough
to dislike, the path which she was about to adopt.   It was
by a secret passage through this church that in former times
the guard-room of the garrison, situated at the lower and
external defences, communicated with the keep of the
castle ; and through this passage were the keys of the castle
every night carried to the governor's apartment, so soon
as the gates were locked, and the watch set.   The custom
was given up in James the First's time, and the passage
abandoned, on account of the well-known legend of the
Mauthe Dog—a fiend, or demon, in the shape of a large,
shaggy, black mastiff, by which the church was said to be
haunted.   It was devoutly believed, that in former times
this spectre became so familiar with mankind, as to appear
almost nightly in the guard-room, issuing from the passage
which we have mentioned at night, and retiring to it at
daybreak.   The soldiers became partly familiarized to its
presence ;   yet not so much so as to use any licence of
language while the apparition was visible ;   until one fellow,
rendered daring by intoxication, swore he would know
whether it was dog or devil, and, with his drawn sword,
followed the spectre when it retreated by the usual passage.

The man returned in a few minutes, sobered by terror, his mouth gaping, and his hair standing on end, under which horror he died ; but, unhappily for the lovers of the mar- vellous, altogether unable to disclose the horrors which he had seen. Under the evil repute arising from this tale of wonder, the guard-room was abandoned, and a new one constructed. In like manner, the guards after that period held another and more circuitous communication with the governor or seneschal of the castle ; and that which lay through the ruinous church was entirely abandoned.[1]

In defiance of the legendary terrors which tradition had attached to the original communication, Fenella, followed by Peveril, now boldly traversed the ruinous vaults through which it lay—sometimes only guided over heaps of ruins by the precarious light of the lamp borne by the dumb maiden—sometimes having the advantage of a gleam of moonlight, darting into the dreary abyss through the shafted windows, or through breaches made by time. As the path was by no means a straight one, Peveril could not but admire the intimate acquaintance with the mazes which his singular companion displayed, as well as the boldness with which she traversed them. He himself was not so utterly void of the prejudices of the times, but that he contemplated, with some apprehension, the possibility of their intruding on the lair of the phantom hound, of which he had heard so often ; and in every remote sigh of the breeze among the ruins, he thought he heard him baying at the mortal footsteps which disturbed his gloomy realm. No such terrors, however, interrupted their journey ; and in the course of a few minutes, they attained the deserted and now ruinous guard-house. The broken walls of the little edifice served to conceal them from the sentinels, one of whom was keeping a drowsy watch at the lower gate of the castle ; whilst another, seated on the stone steps which communicated with the parapet of the bounding and exterior wall, was slumbering, in full security, with his musket peacefully grounded by his side. Fenella made a sign to Peveril to move with silence and caution, and then

---

This curious legend, and many others, in which the Isle of Man is perhaps richer than even Ireland, Wales, or the Highlands of Scotland, will be found in Note 9, pp. 628–31.

showed him, to his surprise, from the window of the deserted
guard-room, a boat, for it was now high water, with four
rowers, lurking under the cliff on which the castle was built ;
and made him further sensible, that he was to have access
to it by a ladder of considerable height placed at the window
of the ruin.

Julian was both displeased and alarmed by the security
and carelessness of the sentinels, who had suffered such
preparations to be made without observation or alarm
given ; and he hesitated whether he should not call the
officer of the guard, upbraid him with negligence, and show
him how easily Holm Peel, in spite of its natural strength,
and although reported impregnable, might be surprised
by a few resolute men.   Fenella seemed to guess his thoughts
with that extreme acuteness of observation which her
deprivations had occasioned her acquiring.   She laid one
hand on his arm, and a finger of the other on her own lips,
as if to enjoin forbearance ; and Julian, knowing that she
acted by the direct authority of the countess, obeyed her
accordingly ; but with the internal resolution to lose no
time in communicating his sentiments to the earl, concerning
the danger to which the castle was exposed on this point.

In the meantime he descended the ladder with some
precaution, for the steps were unequal, broken, wet, and
slippery ; and having placed himself in the stern of the boat,
made a signal to the men to push off, and turned to take
farewell of his guide.   To his utter astonishment, Fenella
rather slid down, than descended regularly, the perilous
ladder, and, the boat being already pushed off, made a
spring from the last step of it with incredible agility, and
seated herself beside Peveril, ere he could express either
remonstrance or surprise.   He commanded the men once
more to pull in to the precarious landing-place ; and
throwing into his countenance a part of the displeasure
which he really felt, endeavoured to make her comprehend
the necessity of returning to her mistress.   Fenella folded
her arms, and looked at him with a haughty smile, which
completely expressed the determination of her purpose.
Peveril was extremely embarrassed ; he was afraid of
offending the countess, and interfering with her plan, by
giving alarm, which otherwise he was much tempted to

have done. On Fenella, it was evident, no species of argument which he could employ was likely to make the least impression ; and the question remained, how, if she went on with him, he was to rid himself of so singular and inconvenient a companion, and provide, at the same time, sufficiently for her personal security.

The boatmen brought the matter to a decision ; for, after lying on their oars for a minute, and whispering among themselves in Low Dutch or German, they began to pull stoutly, and were soon at some distance from the castle. The possibility of the sentinels sending a musket-ball, or even a cannon-shot, after them, was one of the contingencies which gave Peveril momentary anxiety ; but they left the fortress, as they must have approached it, unnoticed, or at least unchallenged—a carelessness on the part of the garrison, which, notwithstanding that the oars were muffled, and that the men spoke little, and in whispers, argued, in Peveril's opinion, great negligence on the part of the sentinels. When they were a little way from the castle, the men began to row briskly towards a small vessel which lay at some distance. Peveril had, in the meantime, leisure to remark, that the boatmen spoke to each other doubtfully, and bent anxious looks on Fenella, as if uncertain whether they had acted properly in bringing her off.

After about a quarter of an hour's rowing, they reached the little sloop, where Peveril was received by the skipper, or captain, on the quarter-deck, with an offer of spirits or refreshments. A word or two among the seamen withdrew the captain from his hospitable cares, and he flew to the ship's side, apparently to prevent Fenella from entering the vessel. The men and he talked eagerly in Dutch, looking anxiously at Fenella as they spoke together ; and Peveril hoped the result would be that the poor young woman should be sent ashore again. But she baffled whatever opposition could be offered to her ; and when the accommodation-ladder, as it is called, was withdrawn, she snatched the end of a rope, and climbed on board with the dexterity of a sailor, leaving them no means of preventing her entrance, save by actual violence, to which apparently they did not choose to have recourse. Once on deck, she took the captain by the sleeve, and led him to the head of the vessel, where they seemed to hold inter-course in a manner intelligible to both.

Peveril soon forgot the presence of the mute, as he began to muse upon his own situation, and the probability that he was separated for some considerable time from the object of his affections. 'Constancy,' he repeated to himself—'Constancy.' And, as if in coincidence with the theme of his reflections, he fixed his eyes on the polar star, which that night twinkled with more than ordinary bril-liancy. Emblem of pure passion and steady purpose—the thoughts which arose as he viewed its clear and unchang-ing light were disinterested and noble. To seek his country's welfare, and secure the blessings of domestic peace—to dis-charge a bold and perilous duty to his friend and patron—to regard his passion for Alice Bridgenorth as the lodestar which was to guide him to noble deeds—were the resolutions which thronged upon his mind, and which exalted his spirits to that state of romantic melancholy, which perhaps is ill exchanged even for feelings of joyful rapture.

He was recalled from those contemplations by something which nestled itself softly and closely to his side—a woman's sigh sounded so near him as to disturb his reverie ; and as he turned his head, he saw Fenella seated beside him, with her eyes fixed on the same star which had just occupied his own. His first emotion was that of displeasure ; but it was impossible to persevere in it towards a being so helpless in many respects, so interesting in others ; whose large dark eyes were filled with dew which glistened in the moonlight ; and the source of whose emotions seemed to be in a partiality which might well claim indulgence, at least from him who was the object of it. At the same time, Julian resolved to seize the present opportunity for such expostulations with Fenella on the strangeness of her conduct, as the poor maiden might be able to comprehend. He took her hand with great kindness, but at the same time with much gravity, pointed to the boat, and to the castle, whose towers and extended walls were now scarce visible in the distance ; and thus intimated to her the necessity of her return to Holm Peel. She looked down, and shook her head, as if negativing his proposal with obstinate decision. Julian renewed his expostulation by look and gesture—

pointed to his own heart, to intimate the countess—and bent his brows to show the displeasure which she must entertain. To all which the maiden only answered by her tears.

At length, as if driven to explanation by his continued remonstrances, she suddenly seized him by the arm to arrest his attention—cast her eye hastily around, as if to see whether she was watched by any one—then drew the other hand, edgewise, across her slender throat—pointed to the boat, and to the castle, and nodded.

On this series of signs, Peveril could put no interpretation, excepting that he was menaced with some personal danger, from which Fenella seemed to conceive that her presence was a protection. Whatever was her meaning, her purpose seemed unalterably adopted ; at least it was plain he had no power to shake it. He must therefore wait till the end of their short voyage, to disembarrass himself of his companion ; and, in the meanwhile, acting on the idea of her having harboured a misplaced attachment to him, he thought he should best consult her interest, and his own character, in keeping at as great a distance from her as circumstances admitted. With this purpose, he made the sign she used for going to sleep, by leaning his head on his palm ; and having thus recommended to her to go to rest, he himself desired to be conducted to his berth.

The captain readily showed him a hammock, in the after-cabin, into which he threw himself, to seek that repose which the exercise and agitation of the preceding day, as well as the lateness of the hour, made him now feel desirable. Sleep, deep and heavy, sank down on him in a few minutes, but it did not endure long. In his sleep he was disturbed by female cries ; and at length, as he thought, distinctly heard the voice of Alice Bridgenorth call on his name.

He awoke, and, starting up to quit his bed, became sensible, from the motion of the vessel, and the swinging of the hammock, that his dream had deceived him. He was still startled by its extreme vivacity and liveliness. ' Julian Peveril, help ! Julian Peveril ! ' The sounds still rung in his ears—the accents were those of Alice—and he could scarce persuade himself that his imagination had deceived him. Could she be in the same vessel ? The thought was not altogether inconsistent with her father's character, and the intrigues in which he was engaged ; but then, if so, to what peril was she exposed, that she invoked his name so loudly ?

Determined to make instant inquiry, he jumped out of his hammock, half-dressed as he was, and stumbling about the little cabin, which was as dark as pitch, at length, with considerable difficulty, reached the door. The door, however, he was altogether unable to open; and was obliged to call loudly to the watch upon deck. The skipper, or captain, as he was called, being the only person aboard who could speak English, answered to the summons, and replied to Peveril's demand, what noise that was ?—that a boat was going off with the young woman—that she whimpered a little as she left the vessel—and ' dat vaas all '.

This explanation satisfied Julian, who thought it probable that some degree of violence might have been absolutely necessary to remove Fenella ; and although he rejoiced at not having witnessed it, he could not feel sorry that such had been employed. Her pertinacious desire to continue on board, and the difficulty of freeing himself, when he should come ashore, from so singular a companion, had given him a good deal of anxiety on the preceding night, which he now saw removed by this bold stroke of the captain.

His dream was thus fully explained. Fancy had caught up the inarticulate and vehement cries with which Fenella was wont to express resistance or displeasure—had coined them into language, and given them the accents of Alice Bridgenorth. Our imagination plays wilder tricks with us almost every night.

The captain now undid the door, and appeared with a lantern ; without the aid of which, Peveril could scarce have regained his couch, where he now slumbered, secure and sound, until day was far advanced, and the invitation of the captain called him up to breakfast.

CHAPTER XX

Now, what is this that haunts me like my shadow,
Frisking and mumming like an elf in moonlight ?
                                        BEN JONSON.

PEVERIL found the master of the vessel rather less rude
than those in his station of life usually are, and received
from him full satisfaction concerning the fate of Fenella,
upon whom the captain bestowed a hearty curse, for
obliging him to lay-to until he had sent his boat ashore,
and had her back again.

' I hope,' said Peveril, ' no violence was necessary to
reconcile her to go ashore ?   I trust she offered no foolish
resistance ? '

' Resist ! mein Gott,' said the captain, ' she did resist
like a troop of horse—she did cry, you might hear her at
Whitehaven—she did go up the rigging like a cat up a
chimney ; but dat vas ein trick of her old trade.'

' What trade do you mean ? ' said Peveril.

' Oh,' said the seaman, ' I vas know more about her than
you, Meinheer.   I vas know that she vas a little, very little
girl, and prentice to one seiltanzer, when my lady yonder
had the good luck to buy her.'

' A seiltanzer ! ' said Peveril ; ' what do you mean by
that ? '

' I mean a rope-danzer, a mountebank, a Hans pickel-
harring.   I vas know Adrian Brackel vell—he sell de
powders dat empty men's stomach, and fill him's own purse.
Not know Adrian Brackel, mein Gott ! I have smoked many
a pound of tabak with him.'

Peveril now remembered that Fenella had been brought
into the family when he and the young earl were in England,
and while the countess was absent on an expedition to
the continent.   Where the countess found her, she never
communicated to the young men ; but only intimated that
she had received her out of compassion, in order to relieve
her from a situation of extreme distress.

He hinted so much to the communicative seaman, who

replied, ' that for distress he knew nocht's on 't ; only, that
Adrian Brackel beat her when she would not dance on the
rope, and starved her when she did, to prevent her growth.'
The bargain between the countess and the mountebank,
he said, he had made himself ; because the countess had
hired his brig upon her expedition to the continent. None
else knew where she came from. The countess had seen
her on a public stage at Ostend—compassionated her
helpless situation, and the severe treatment she received—
and had employed him to purchase the poor creature from
her master, and charged him with silence towards all her
retinue.[n] 'And so I do keep silence,' continued the faithful
confidant, ' van I am in the havens of Man ; but when I am
on the broad seas, den my tongue is mine own, you know.
Die foolish beoples in the island, they say she is a wechsel-
balg—what you call a fairy-elf changeling. My faith, they
do not never have seen ein wechsel-balg ; for I saw one
myself at Cologne, and it was twice as big as yonder girl,
and did break the poor people, with eating them up, like
de great big cuckoo in the sparrow's nest ; but this Venella
eat no more than other girls—it was no wechsel-balg in the
world.'

By a different train of reasoning, Julian had arrived at
the same conclusion ; in which, therefore, he heartily acquiesced. During the seaman's prosing, he was reflecting
within himself, how much of the singular flexibility of her
limbs and movements the unfortunate girl must have
derived from the discipline and instructions of Adrian
Brackel ; and also how far the germs of her wilful and
capricious passions might have been sown during her
wandering and adventurous childhood. Aristocratic, also, as
his education had been, these anecdotes respecting Fenella's
original situation and education rather increased his pleasure
at having shaken off her company ; and yet he still felt
desirous to know any further particulars which the seaman
could communicate on the same subject. But he had
already told all he knew. Of her parents he knew nothing,
except that ' her father must have been a damned hundsfoot,
and a schelm, for selling his own flesh and blood to Adrian
Brackel ' ; for by such a transaction had the mountebank
become possessed of his pupil.

This conversation tended to remove any passing doubts which might have crept on Peveril's mind concerning the fidelity of the master of the vessel, who appeared from thence to have been a former acquaintance of the countess, and to have enjoyed some share of her confidence. The threatening motion used by Fenella, he no longer considered as worthy of any notice, excepting as a new mark of the irritability of her temper.

He amused himself with walking the deck, and musing on his past and future prospects, until his attention was forcibly arrested by the wind, which began to rise in gusts from the north-west, in a manner so unfavourable to the course they intended to hold, that the master, after many efforts to beat against it, declared his bark, which was by no means an excellent sea-boat, was unequal to making Whitehaven; and that he was compelled to make a fair wind of it, and run for Liverpool. To this course Peveril did not object. It saved him some land journey, in case he visited his father's castle; and the countess's commission would be discharged as effectually the one way as the other.

The vessel was put, accordingly, before the wind, and ran with great steadiness and velocity. The captain, notwithstanding, pleading some nautical hazards, chose to lie off, and did not attempt the mouth of the Mersey until morning, when Peveril had at length the satisfaction of being landed upon the quay of Liverpool, which even then showed symptoms of the commercial prosperity that has since been carried to such a height.

The master, who was well acquainted with the port, pointed out to Julian a decent place of entertainment, chiefly frequented by seafaring people; for, although he had been in the town formerly, he did not think it proper to go anywhere at present where he might have been unnecessarily recognized. Here he took leave of the seaman, after pressing upon him with difficulty a small present for his crew. As for his passage, the captain declined any recompense whatever; and they parted upon the most civil terms.

The inn to which he was recommended was full of strangers, seamen, and mercantile people, all intent upon their own affairs, and discussing them with noise and eagerness, peculiar to the business of a thriving seaport. But although the general clamour of the public room, in which the guests mixed with each other, related chiefly to their own commercial dealings, there was a general theme mingling with them, which was alike common and interesting to all ; so that, amidst disputes about freight, tonnage, demurrage, and such like, were heard the emphatic sounds of ' Deep, damnable, accursed plot,'—' Bloody Papist villains,'—' The king in danger—the gallows too good for them,' and so forth.

The fermentation excited in London had plainly reached even this remote seaport, and was received by the inhabitants with the peculiar stormy energy which invests men in their situation with the character of the winds and waves with which they are chiefly conversant. The commercial and nautical interests of England were indeed particularly anti-Catholic ; although it is not, perhaps, easy to give any distinct reason why they should be so, since theological disputes in general could scarce be considered as interesting to them. But zeal, amongst the lower orders at least, is often in an inverse ratio to knowledge ; and sailors were not probably the less earnest and devoted Protestants, that they did not understand the controversy between the churches. As for the merchants, they were almost necessarily inimical to the gentry of Lancashire and Cheshire ; many of whom still retained the faith of Rome, which was rendered ten times more odious to the men of commerce, as the badge of their haughty aristocratic neighbours.

From the little which Peveril heard of the sentiments of the people of Liverpool, he imagined he should act most prudently in leaving the place as soon as possible, and before any suspicion should arise of his having any connexion with the party which appeared to have become so obnoxious.

In order to accomplish his journey, it was first necessary that he should purchase a horse ; and for this purpose he resolved to have recourse to the stables of a dealer well known at the time, and who dwelt in the outskirts of the place ; and, having obtained directions to his dwelling, he went thither to provide himself.

Joe Bridlesley's stables exhibited a large choice of good horses : for that trade was in former days more active than

at present. It was an ordinary thing for a stranger to buy
a horse for the purpose of a single journey, and to sell him,
as well as he could, when he had reached the point of his
destination ; and hence there was a constant demand, and
a corresponding supply ; upon both of which, Bridlesley,
and those of his trade, contrived, doubtless, to make
handsome profits.

Julian, who was no despicable horse-jockey, selected for
his purpose a strong well-made horse, about sixteen hands
high, and had him led into the yard, to see whether his
paces corresponded with his appearance. As these also gave
perfect satisfaction to the customer, it remained only to
settle the price with Bridlesley ; who of course swore his
customer had pitched upon the best horse ever darkened the
stable-door since he had dealt that way ; that no such
horses were to be had nowadays, for that the mares were
dead that foaled them ; and having named a corresponding
price, the usual haggling commenced betwixt the seller and
purchaser, for adjustment of what the French dealers call
le prix juste.

The reader, if he be at all acquainted with this sort of
traffic, well knows it is generally a keen encounter of wits,
and attracts the notice of all the idlers within hearing,
who are usually very ready to offer their opinions, or their
evidence. Amongst these, upon the present occasion, was
a thin man, rather less than the ordinary size, and meanly
dressed ; but whose interference was in a confident tone,
and such as showed himself master of the subject on which
he spoke. The price of the horse being settled to about
fifteen pounds, which was very high for the period, that of
the saddle and bridle had next to be adjusted, and the thin
mean-looking person before-mentioned, found nearly as
much to say on this subject as on the other. As his remarks
had a conciliating and obliging tendency towards the
stranger, Peveril concluded he was one of those idle persons,
who, unable or unwilling to supply themselves with the means
of indulgence at their own cost, do not scruple to deserve them
at the hands of others, by a little officious complaisance ;
and considering that he might acquire some useful information from such a person, was just about to offer him the
courtesy of a morning draught, when he observed he had

suddenly left the yard. He had scarce remarked this circumstance, before a party of customers entered the place, whose haughty assumption of importance claimed the instant attention of Bridlesley, and all his militia of grooms and stable-boys.

'Three good horses,' said the leader of the party, a tall bulky man, whose breath was drawn full and high, under a consciousness of fat, and of importance—'three good and able-bodied horses for the service of the Commons of England.'

Bridlesley said he had some horses which might serve the Speaker himself at need; but that, to speak Christian truth, he had just sold the best in his stable to that gentleman present, who, doubtless, would give up the bargain if the horse was needed for the service of the State.

'You speak well, friend,' said the important personage; and advancing to Julian, demanded, in a very haughty tone, the surrender of the purchase which he had just made.

Peveril, with some difficulty, subdued the strong desire which he felt to return a round refusal to so unreasonable a request, but fortunately, recollecting that the situation in which he at present stood, required, on his part, much circumspection, he replied simply, that upon showing him any warrant to seize upon horses for the public service, he must of course submit to resign his purchase.

The man with an air of extreme dignity, pulled from his pocket, and thrust into Peveril's hands, a warrant, subscribed by the Speaker of the House of Commons, empowering Charles Topham, their officer of the Black Rod, to pursue and seize upon the persons of certain individuals named in the warrant; and of all other persons who are, or should be, accused by competent witnesses of being accessory to, or favourers of, the hellish and damnable Popish Plot, at present carried on within the bowels of the kingdom; and charging all men, as they loved their allegiance, to render the said Charles Topham their readiest and most effective assistance, in execution of the duty intrusted to his care.

On perusing a document of such weighty import, Julian had no hesitation to give up his horse to this formidable functionary; whom somebody compared to a lion, which, as the House of Commons was pleased to maintain such an animal, they were under the necessity of providing for by frequent commitments; until ' *Take him, Topham,*' became a proverb, and a formidable one, in the mouth of the public.

The acquiescence of Peveril procured him some grace in the sight of the emissary; who, before selecting two horses for his attendants, gave permission to the stranger to purchase a grey horse, much inferior, indeed, to that which he had resigned, both in form and in action, but very little lower in price, as Mr. Bridlesley, immediately on learning the demand for horses upon the part of the Commons of England, had passed a private resolution in his own mind, augmenting the price of his whole stud, by an imposition of at least twenty per cent, *ad valorem.*

Peveril adjusted and paid the price with much less argument than on the former occasion; for, to be plain with the reader, he had noticed in the warrant of Mr. Topham, the name of his father, Sir Geoffrey Peveril of Martindale Castle, engrossed at full length, as one of those subjected to arrest by that officer.

When aware of this material fact, it became Julian's business to leave Liverpool directly, and carry the alarm to Derbyshire, if, indeed, Mr. Topham had not already executed his charge in that country, which he thought unlikely, as it was probable they would commence by secur-ing those who lived nearest to the seaports. A word or two which he overheard, strengthened his hopes.

' And hark ye, friend,' said Mr. Topham; ' you will have the horses at the door of Mr. Shortell, the mercer, in two hours, as we shall refresh ourselves there with a cool tankard, and learn what folks live in the neighbourhood that may be concerned in my way. And you will please to have that saddle padded, for I am told the Derbyshire roads are rough. And you, Captain Dangerfield, and Master Everett, you must put on your Protestant spectacles, and show me where there is the shadow of a priest, or of a priest's favourer; for I am come down with a broom in my cap to sweep this north country of such-like cattle.'

One of the persons he thus addressed, who wore the garb

of a broken-down citizen, only answered, ' Aye, truly,
Master Topham, it is time to purge the garner.'

The other, who had a formidable pair of whiskers, a red
nose, and a tarnished laced coat, together with a hat of
Pistol's dimensions, was more loquacious. ' I take it on my
damnation,' said this zealous Protestant witness, 'that I
will discover the marks of the beast on every one of them
betwixt sixteen and seventy, as plainly as if they had
crossed themselves with ink, instead of holy water. Since
we have a king willing to do justice, and a House of Commons
to uphold prosecutions, why, damn me, the cause must not
stand still for lack of evidence.'

' Stick to that, noble captain,' answered the officer ;
' but, prithee, reserve thy oaths for the court of justice ; it
is but sheer waste to throw them away, as you do, in your
ordinary conversation.'

' Fear you nothing, Master Topham,' answered Dangerfield ; ' it is right to keep a man's gifts in use ; and were
I altogether to renounce oaths in my private discourse, how
should I know how to use one when I needed it ? But you
hear me use none of your Papist abjurations. I swear not
by the Mass, or before George, or by anything that belongs
to idolatry ; but such downright oaths as may serve a poor
Protestant gentleman, who would fain serve Heaven and
the king.'

' Bravely spoken, most noble Festus,' said his yokefellow.
' But do not suppose, that although I am not in the habit
of garnishing my words with oaths out of season, I shall be
wanting, when called upon, to declare the height and the
depth, the width and the length, of this hellish plot against
the king and the Protestant faith.'

Dizzy, and almost sick, with listening to the undisguised
brutality of these fellows, Peveril, having with difficulty
prevailed on Bridlesley to settle his purchase, at length
led forth his grey steed ; but was scarce out of the yard,
when he heard the following alarming conversation pass, of
which he seemed himself the object.

' Who is that youth ? ' said the slow soft voice of the
more precise of the two witnesses. ' Methinks I have seen
him somewhere before. Is he from these parts ? '

' Not that I know of,' said Bridlesley ; who, like all the

other inhabitants of England at the time, answered the interrogatories of these fellows with the deference which is paid in Spain to the questions of an inquisitor. ' A stranger —entirely a stranger—never saw him before—a wild young colt, I warrant him ; and knows a horse's mouth as well as I do.'

' I begin to bethink me I saw such a face as his at the Jesuits' consult, in the White Horse Tavern,' answered Everett.

' And I think I recollect,' said Captain Dangerfield——

' Come, come, master and captain,' said the authoritative voice of Topham, ' we will have none of your recollections at present. We all know what these are likely to end in. But I will have you know, you are not to run till the leash is slipped. The young man is a well-looking lad, and gave up his horse handsomely for the service of the House of Commons. He knows how to behave himself to his betters, I warrant you ; and I scarce think he has enough in his purse to pay the fees.' [n]

This speech concluded the dialogue, which Peveril, finding himself so much concerned in the issue, thought it best to hear to an end. Now, when it ceased, to get out of the town unobserved, and take the nearest way to his father's castle, seemed his wisest plan. He had settled his reckoning at the inn, and brought with him to Bridlesley's the small portmanteau which contained his few necessaries, so that he had no occasion to return thither. He resolved, therefore, to ride some miles before he stopped, even for the purpose of feeding his horse ; and being pretty well acquainted with the country, he hoped to be able to push forward to Martindale Castle sooner than the worshipful Master Topham ; whose saddle was, in the first place, to be padded, and who, when mounted, would, in all probability, ride with the precaution of those who require such security against the effects of a hard trot.

Under the influence of these feelings, Julian pushed for Warrington, a place with which he was well acquainted ; but, without halting in the town, he crossed the Mersey, by the bridge built by an ancestor of his friend the Earl of Derby, and continued his route towards Dishley, on the borders of Derbyshire. He might have reached this latter village easily, had his horse been fitter for a forced march ; but in the course of the journey, he had occasion, more than once, to curse the official dignity of the person who had robbed him of his better steed, while taking the best direction he could through a country with which he was only generally acquainted.

At length, near Altringham, a halt became unavoidable ; and Peveril had only to look for some quiet and sequestered place of refreshment. This presented itself, in the form of a small cluster of cottages ; the best of which united the characters of an alehouse and a mill, where the sign of the Cat (the landlord's faithful ally in defence of his meal-sacks), booted as high as Grimalkin in the fairy tale, and playing on the fiddle for the more grace, announced that John Whitecraft united the two honest occupations of landlord and miller ; and, doubtless, took toll from the public in both capacities.

Such a place promised a traveller who journeyed incognito safer, if not better accommodation, than he was like to meet with in more frequented inns ; and at the door of the Cat and Fiddle Julian halted accordingly.

CHAPTER XXI

In these distracted times, when each man dreads
The bloody stratagems of busy heads.

OTWAY.

At the door of the Cat and Fiddle, Julian received the usual attention paid to the customers of an inferior house of entertainment. His horse was carried by a ragged lad, who acted as ostler, into a paltry stable ; where, however, the nag was tolerably supplied with food and litter.

Having seen the animal on which his comfort, perhaps his safety, depended, properly provided for, Peveril entered the kitchen, which indeed was also the parlour and hall of the little hostelry, to try what refreshment he could obtain for himself. Much to his satisfaction, he found there was only one guest in the house besides himself ; but he was less

pleased when he found that he must either go without
dinner, or share with that single guest the only provisions
which chanced to be in the house, namely, a dish of trouts
and eels, which their host, the miller, had brought in from
his mill-stream.

At the particular request of Julian, the landlady undertook to add a substantial dish of eggs and bacon, which
perhaps she would not have undertaken for, had not the
sharp eye of Peveril discovered the flitch hanging in its
smoky retreat, when, as its presence could not be denied,
the hostess was compelled to bring it forward as a part of
her supplies.

She was a buxom dame about thirty, whose comely and
cheerful countenance did honour to the choice of the jolly
miller, her loving mate ; and was now stationed under the
shade of an old-fashioned huge projecting chimney, within
which it was her province to ' work i' the fire ', and provide,
for the wearied wayfaring man, the good things which
were to send him rejoicing on his course. Although, at first,
the honest woman seemed little disposed to give herself
much additional trouble on Julian's account, yet the good
looks, handsome figure, and easy civility of her new guest,
soon bespoke the principal part of her attention ; and
while busy in his service, she regarded him, from time to
time, with looks, where something like pity mingled with
complacency. The rich smoke of the rasher, and the eggs
with which it was flanked, already spread itself through the
apartment ; and the hissing of these savoury viands bore
chorus to the simmering of the pan, in which the fish were
undergoing a slower decoction. The table was covered with
a clean huckaback napkin, and all was in preparation for
the meal, which Julian began to expect with a good deal of
impatience, when the companion who was destined to share
it with him, entered the apartment.

At the first glance, Julian recognized, to his surprise, the
same indifferently-dressed, thin-looking person, who, during
the first bargain which he had made with Bridlesley, had
officiously interfered with his advice and opinion. Displeased at having the company of any stranger forced upon
him, Peveril was still less satisfied to find one who might
make some claim of acquaintance with him, however

slender, since the circumstances in which he stood compelled him to be as reserved as possible. He therefore turned his back upon his destined messmate, and pretended to amuse himself by looking out of the window, determined to avoid all intercourse until it should be inevitably forced upon him.

In the meanwhile, the other stranger went straight up to the landlady, where she toiled on household cares intent, and demanded of her, what she meant by preparing bacon and eggs, when he had positively charged her to get nothing ready but the fish.

The good woman, important as every cook in the discharge of her duty, deigned not for some time so much as to acknowledge that she heard the reproof of her guest; and when she did so, it was only to repel it in a magisterial and authoritative tone. 'If he did not like bacon—(bacon from their own hutch, well fed on pease and bran)—if he did not like bacon and eggs—(new-laid eggs, which she had brought in from the hen-roost with her own hands)—why so put case—it was the worse for his honour, and the better for those who did.'

'The better for those who like them?' answered the guest; 'that is as much as to say I am to have a companion, good woman.'

'Do not good woman me, sir,' replied the miller's wife, 'till I call you good man; and, I promise you, many would scruple to do that to one who does not love eggs and bacon of a Friday.'

'Nay, my good lady,' said her guest, 'do not fix any misconstruction upon me—I dare say the eggs and the bacon are excellent; only, they are rather a dish too heavy for my stomach.'

'Aye, or your conscience perhaps, sir,' answered the hostess. 'And now, I bethink me, you must needs have your fish fried with oil, instead of the good drippings I was going to put to them. I would I could spell the meaning of all this now; but I warrant John Bigstaff, the constable, could conjure something out of it.'

There was a pause here; but Julian, somewhat alarmed at the tone which the conversation assumed, became interested in watching the dumb-show which succeeded.

By bringing his head a little towards the left, but without turning round, or quitting the projecting latticed window where he had taken his station, he could observe that the stranger, secured, as he seemed to think himself, from observation, had sidled close up to the landlady, and, as he conceived, had put a piece of money into her hand. The altered tone of the miller's moiety corresponded very much with this supposition.

'Nay, indeed, and forsooth,' she said, 'her house was Liberty Hall; and so should every publican's be. What was it to her what gentlefolks ate or drank, providing they paid for it honestly? There were many honest gentlemen, whose stomachs could not abide bacon, grease, or dripping, especially on a Friday; and what was that to her, or any one in her line, so gentlefolks paid honestly for the trouble? Only, she would say, that her bacon and eggs could not be mended betwixt this and Liverpool; and that she would live and die upon.'

'I shall hardly dispute it,' said the stranger; and turning towards Julian, he added, 'I wish this gentleman, who I suppose is my trencher-companion, much joy of the dainties which I cannot assist him in consuming.'

'I assure you, sir,' answered Peveril, who now felt himself compelled to turn about, and reply with civility, 'that it was with difficulty I could prevail on my landlady to add my cover to yours, though she seems now such a zealot for the consumption of eggs and bacon.'

'I am zealous for nothing,' said the landlady, 'save that men would eat their victuals, and pay their score; and if there be enough in one dish to serve two guests, I see little purpose in dressing them two; however, they are ready now, and done to a nicety. Here, Alice! Alice!'

The sound of that well-known name made Julian start; but the Alice who replied to the call ill resembled the vision which his imagination connected with the accents, being a dowdy slipshod wench, the drudge of the low inn which afforded him shelter. She assisted her mistress in putting on the table the dishes which the latter had prepared; and a foaming jug of home-brewed ale being placed betwixt them, was warranted by Dame Whitecraft as excellent; 'for,' said she, 'we know by practice that too much water

drowns the miller, and we spare it on our malt as we would
in our mill-dam.'

' I drink to your health in it, dame,' said the elder stranger,
' and a cup of thanks for these excellent fish ; and to the
drowning of all unkindness between us.'

' I thank you, sir,' said the dame, ' and wish you the like;
but I dare not pledge you, for our Gaffer says, the ale is
brewed too strong for women ; so I only drink a glass of
canary at a time with a gossip, or any gentleman guest that
is so minded.'

' You shall drink one with me then, dame,' said Peveril,
' so you will let me have a flagon.'

' That you shall, sir, and as good as ever was broached ;
but I must to the mill, to get the key from the goodman.'

So saying, and tucking her clean gown through the pocket-
holes, that her steps might be the more alert, and her dress
escape dust, off she tripped to the mill, which lay close
adjoining. ' A dainty dame, and dangerous, is the miller's
wife,' said the stranger, looking at Peveril. ' Is not that
old Chaucer's phrase ? '

' I—I believe so,' said Peveril, not much read in Chaucer,
who was then even more neglected than at present ; and
much surprised at a literary quotation from one of the
mean appearance exhibited by the person before him.

' Yes,' answered the stranger, ' I see that you, like other
young gentlemen of the time, are better acquainted with
Cowley and Waller, than with the " well of English un-
defiled." I cannot help differing. There are touches of
nature about the old bard of Woodstock, that, to me, are
worth all the turns of laborious wit in Cowley, and all the
ornate and artificial simplicity of his courtly competitor.
The description, for instance, of his country coquette—

> Wincing she was, as is a wanton colt,
> Sweet as a flower, and upright as a bolt.

Then, again, for pathos, where will you mend the dying
scene of Arcite ?

> Alas, my heartis queen ! alas, my wife !
> Giver at once, and ender of my life.
> What is this world ?—What axen men to have ?
> Now with his love—now in his cold grave
> Alone, withouten other company.

But I tire you, sir ; and do injustice to the poet, whom I remember but by halves.'

'On the contrary, sir,' replied Peveril, ' you make him more intelligible to me in your recitation, than I have found him when I have tried to peruse him myself.'

'You were only frightened by the antiquated spelling, and " the letters black ",' said his companion. ' It is many a scholar's case, who mistakes a nut, which he could crack with a little exertion, for a bullet, which he must needs break his teeth on ; but yours are better employed. Shall I offer you some of this fish ? '

'Not so, sir,' replied Julian, willing to show himself a man of reading in his turn ; ' I hold with old Caius, and profess to fear judgement, to fight where I cannot choose, and to eat no fish.'

The stranger cast a startled look around him at this observation, which Julian had thrown out, on purpose to ascertain, if possible, the quality of his companion, whose present language was so different from the character he had assumed at Bridlesley's. His countenance, too, although the features were of an ordinary, not to say mean cast, had that character of intelligence which education gives to the most homely face ; and his manners were so easy and disembarrassed, as plainly showed a complete acquaintance with society, as well as the habit of mingling with it in the higher stages. The alarm which he had evidently shown at Peveril's answer, was but momentary ; for he almost instantly replied, with a smile, ' I promise you, sir, that you are in no dangerous company ; for notwithstanding my fish dinner, I am much disposed to trifle with some of your savoury mess, if you will indulge me so far.'

Peveril accordingly reinforced the stranger's trencher with what remained of the bacon and eggs, and saw him swallow a mouthful or two with apparent relish ; but presently after, he began to dally with his knife and fork, like one whose appetite was satiated ; and then took a long draught of the black jack, and handed his platter to the large mastiff dog, who, attracted by the smell of the dinner, had sat down before him for some time, licking his chops, and following with his eye every morsel which the guest raised to his head.

'Here, my poor fellow,' said he, 'thou hast had no fish, and needest this supernumerary trencher-load more than I do. I cannot withstand thy mute supplication any longer.'

The dog answered these courtesies by a civil shake of the tail, while he gobbled up what was assigned him by the stranger's benevolence, in the greater haste, that he heard his mistress's voice at the door.

'Here is the canary, gentlemen,' said the landlady; 'and the goodman has set off the mill, to come to wait on you himself. He always does so, when company drink wine.'

'That he may come in for the host's, that is, for the lion's share,' said the stranger, looking at Peveril.

'The shot is mine,' said Julian; 'and if mine host will share it, I will willingly bestow another quart on him, and on you, sir. I never break old customs.'

These sounds caught the ear of Gaffer Whitecraft, who had entered the room, a strapping specimen of his robust trade, prepared to play the civil or the surly host, as his company should be acceptable or otherwise. At Julian's invitation, he doffed his dusty bonnet—brushed from his sleeve the looser particles of his professional dust—and sitting down on the end of a bench, about a yard from the table, filled a glass of canary, and drank to his guests, and 'especially to this noble gentleman,' indicating Peveril, who had ordered the canary.

Julian returned the courtesy by drinking his health, and asking what news were about in the country.

'Naught, sir, I hears on naught, except this Plot, as they call it, that they are pursuing the Papishers about; but it brings water to my mill, as the saying is. Between expresses hurrying hither and thither, and guards and prisoners riding to and again, and the custom of the neighbours, that come to speak over the news of an evening, nightly, I may say, instead of once a week, why the spigot is in use, gentlemen, and your land thrives; and then I, serving as constable, and being a known Protestant, I have tapped, I may venture to say, it may be ten stands of ale extraordinary, besides a reasonable sale of wine for a country corner. Heaven make us thankful, and keep all good Protestants from Plot and Popery!'

'I can easily conceive, my friend,' said Julian, 'that

curiosity is a passion which runs naturally to the alehouse; and that anger, and jealousy, and fear, are all of them thirsty passions, and great consumers of home-brewed. But I am a perfect stranger in these parts ; and I would willingly learn, from a sensible man like you, a little of this same Plot, of which men speak so much, and appear to know so little.'

'Learn a little of it ?   Why, it is the most horrible—the most damnable, bloodthirsty beast of a Plot—But hold, hold, my good master ; I hope, in the first place, you believe there is a Plot ; for, otherwise, the justice must have a word with you, as sure as my name is John Whitecraft.'

'It shall not need,' said Peveril ; 'for I assure you, mine host, I believe in the Plot as freely and fully as a man can believe in anything he cannot understand.'

'God forbid that anybody should pretend to understand it,' said the implicit constable ; 'for his worship the justice says it is a mile beyond him ; and he be as deep as most of them.   But men may believe, though they do not understand ; and that is what the Romanists say themselves. But this I am sure of, it makes a rare stirring time for justices, and witnesses, and constables.   So here's to your health again, gentlemen, in a cup of neat canary.'

'Come, come, John Whitecraft,' said his wife, 'do not you demean yourself by naming witnesses along with justices and constables.   All the world knows how they come by their money.'

'Aye, but all the world knows that they *do* come by it, dame ; and that is a great comfort.   They rustle in their canonical silks, and swagger in their buff and scarlet, who but they ?   Aye, aye, the cursed fox thrives—and not so cursed neither.   Is there not Doctor Titus Oates, the saviour of the nation—does he not live at Whitehall, and eat off plate, and have a pension of thousands a year, for what I know ?   and is he not to be Bishop of Litchfield, so soon as Dr. Doddrum dies ? '

'Then I hope Dr. Doddrum's reverence will live these twenty years ; and I dare say I am the first that ever wished such a wish,' said the hostess.   'I do not understand these doings, not I ; and if a hundred Jesuits came to hold a consult at my house, as they did at the White Horse

Tavern, I should think it quite out of the line of business to bear witness against them, provided they drank well, and paid their score.'

'Very true, dame,' said her elder guest ; ' that is what I call keeping a good publican conscience ; and so I will pay my score presently, and be jogging on my way.'

Peveril, on his part, also demanded a reckoning, and discharged it so liberally, that the miller flourished his hat as he bowed, and the hostess curtsied down to the ground.

The horses of both guests were brought forth ; and they mounted, in order to depart in company. The host and hostess stood in the doorway, to see them depart. The landlord proffered a stirrup-cup to the elder guest, while the landlady offered Peveril a glass from her own peculiar bottle. For this purpose, she mounted on the horse-block with flask and glass in hand ; so that it was easy for the departing guest, although on horseback, to return the courtesy in the most approved manner, namely, by throwing his arm over his landlady's shoulder, and saluting her at parting.

Dame Whitecraft did not decline this familiarity ; for there is no room for traversing upon a horse-block, and the hands which might have served her for resistance, were occupied with glass and bottle—matters too precious to be thrown away in such a struggle. Apparently, however, she had something else in her head ; for, as, after a brief affectation of reluctance, she permitted Peveril's face to approach hers, she whispered in his ear, ' Beware of trepans ! '—an awful intimation, which, in those days of distrust, suspicion, and treachery, was as effectual in interdicting free and social intercourse as the advertisement of ' man-traps and spring-guns ' to protect an orchard. Pressing her hand in intimation that he comprehended her hint, she shook his warmly in return, and bade God speed him. There was a cloud on John Whitecraft's brow ; nor did his final farewell sound half so cordial as that which had been spoken within doors. But then Peveril reflected, that the same guest is not always equally acceptable to landlord and landlady ; and unconscious of having done anything to excite the miller's displeasure, he pursued his journey without thinking further of the matter.

Julian was a little surprised, and not altogether pleased, to find that his new acquaintance held the same road with him. He had many reasons for wishing to travel alone; and the hostess's caution still rang in his ears. If this man, possessed of so much shrewdness as his countenance and conversation intimated, versatile, as he had occasion to remark, and disguised beneath his condition, should

THE TRAVELLERS LEAVING THE INN

prove, as was likely, to be a concealed Jesuit or seminary-priest, travelling upon their great task of the conversion of England, and rooting out of the northern heresy—a more dangerous companion, for a person in his own circumstances, could hardly be imagined; since keeping society with him might seem to authorize whatever reports had been spread concerning the attachment of his family to the Catholic cause. At the same time, it was very difficult, without actual rudeness, to shake off the company of one who seemed determined, whether spoken to or not, to remain alongside of him.

Peveril tried the experiment of riding slow ; but his companion, determined not to drop him, slackened his pace, so as to keep close by him. Julian then spurred his horse to a full trot ; and was soon satisfied, that the stranger, notwithstanding the meanness of his appearance, was so much better mounted than himself, as to render vain any thoughts of outriding him. He pulled up his horse to a more reasonable pace, therefore, in a sort of despair. Upon his doing so, his companion, who had been hitherto silent, observed, that Peveril was not so well qualified to try speed upon the road as he would have been had he abode by his first bargain of horse-flesh that morning.

Peveril assented dryly, but observed that the animal would serve his immediate purpose, though he feared it would render him indifferent company for a person better mounted.

' By no means,' answered his civil companion ; ' I am one of those who have travelled so much as to be accustomed to make my journey at any rate of motion which may be most agreeable to my company.'

Peveril made no reply to this polite intimation, being too sincere to tender the thanks which, in courtesy, were the proper answer. A second pause ensued, which was broken by Julian asking the stranger whether their roads were likely to lie long together in the same direction.

' I cannot tell,' said the stranger, smiling, ' unless I knew which way you were travelling.'

' I am uncertain how far I shall go to-night,' said Julian, willingly misunderstanding the purport of the reply.

" And so am I,' replied the stranger ; ' but though my horse goes better than yours, I think it will be wise to spare him ; and in case our road continues to lie the same way, we are likely to sup, as we have dined, together.'

Julian made no answer whatever to this round intimation, but continued to ride on, turning, in his own mind, whether it would not be wisest to come to a distinct understanding with his pertinacious attendant, and to explain, in so many words, that it was his pleasure to travel alone. But, besides that the sort of acquaintance which they had formed during dinner rendered him unwilling to be directly uncivil towards a person of gentlemanlike manners, he had also to consider that he might very possibly be mistaken in this man's character and purpose ; in which case, the cynically refusing the society of a sound Protestant, would afford as pregnant matter of suspicion, as travelling in company with a disguised Jesuit.

After brief reflection, therefore, he resolved to endure the encumbrance of the stranger's society, until a fair opportunity should occur to rid himself of it ; and, in the meantime, to act with as much caution as he possibly could, in any communication that might take place between them ; for Dame Whitecraft's parting caution still rang anxiously in his ears, and the consequences of his own arrest upon suspicion, must deprive him of every opportunity of serving his father, or the countess, or Major Bridgenorth, upon whose interest, also, he had promised himself to keep an eye.

While he revolved these things in his mind, they had journeyed several miles without speaking ; and now entered upon a more waste country, and worse roads, than they had hitherto found, being, in fact, approaching the more hilly district of Derbyshire. In travelling on a very stony and uneven lane, Julian's horse repeatedly stumbled ; and, had he not been supported by the rider's judicious use of the bridle, must at length certainly have fallen under him.

'These are times which crave wary riding, sir,' said his companion ; 'and by your seat in the saddle, and your hand on the rein, you seem to understand it to be so.'

'I have been long a horseman, sir,' answered Peveril.

'And long a traveller, too, sir, I should suppose ; since, by the great caution you observe, you seem to think the human tongue requires a curb, as well as the horse's jaws.'

'Wiser men than I have been of opinion,' answered Peveril, 'that it were a part of prudence to be silent, when men have little or nothing to say.'

'I cannot approve of their opinion,' answered the stranger. 'All knowledge is gained by communication, either with the dead, through books, or, more pleasingly, through the conversation of the living. The *deaf and dumb*, alone, are excluded from improvement ; and surely their situation is not so enviable that we should imitate them.'

At this illustration, which awakened a startling echo in Peveril's bosom, the young man looked hard at his companion ; but in the composed countenance, and calm blue eye, he read no consciousness of a further meaning than the words immediately and directly implied. He paused a moment, and then answered, ' You seem to be a person, sir, of shrewd apprehension ; and I should have thought it might have occurred to you, that, in the present suspicious times, men may, without censure, avoid communication with strangers. You know not me ; and to me you are totally unknown. There is not room for much discourse between us, without trespassing on the general topics of the day, which carry in them seeds of quarrel between friends, much more betwixt strangers. At any other time, the society of an intelligent companion would have been most acceptable upon my solitary ride ; but at present '——

' At present ! ' said the other, interrupting him. ' You are like the old Romans, who held that *hostis* meant both a stranger and an enemy. I will therefore be no longer a stranger. My name is Ganlesse—by profession I am a Roman Catholic priest—I am travelling here in dread of my life—and I am very glad to have you for a companion.'

' I thank you for the information with all my heart,' said Peveril ; ' and to avail myself of it to the uttermost, I must beg of you to ride forward, or lag behind, or take a side-path, at your own pleasure ; for as I am no Catholic, and travel upon business of high concernment, I am exposed both to risk and delay, and even to danger, by keeping such suspicious company. And so, Master Ganlesse, keep your own pace, and I will keep the contrary ; for I beg leave to forbear your company.'

As Peveril spoke thus, he pulled up his horse, and made a full stop.

The stranger burst out a-laughing. ' What ! ' he said, ' you forbear my company for a trifle of danger ? Saint Anthony ! How the warm blood of the Cavaliers is chilled in the young men of the present day ! This young gallant, now, has a father, I warrant, who has endured as many adventures for hunting priests, as a knight-errant for distressed damsels.'

'This raillery avails nothing, sir,' said Peveril.   'I must request you will keep your own way.'

'My way is yours,' said the pertinacious Master Ganlesse, as he called himself ; 'and we will both travel the safer, that we journey in company. I have the receipt of fern-seed, man, and walk invisible. Besides, you would not have me quit you in this lane, where there is no turn to right or left ? '

Peveril moved on, desirous to avoid open violence—for which the indifferent tone of the traveller, indeed, afforded no apt pretext—yet highly disliking his company, and determined to take the first opportunity to rid himself of it.

The stranger proceeded at the same pace with him, keeping cautiously on his bridle hand, as if to secure that advantage in case of a struggle. But his language did not intimate the least apprehension. 'You do me wrong,' he said to Peveril, ' and you equally wrong yourself. You are uncertain where to lodge to-night—trust to my guidance. Here is an ancient hall, within four miles, with an old knightly pantaloon for its lord—an all-be-ruffed Dame Barbara for the lady gay,—a Jesuit, in a butler's habit, to say grace—an old tale of Edgehill and Worcester fights to relish a cold venison pasty, and a flask of claret mantled with cobwebs—a bed for you in the priest's hiding-hole— and, for aught I know, pretty Mistress Betty, the dairy-maid, to make it ready.'

'This has no charms for me, sir,' said Peveril, who, in spite of himself, could not but be amused with the ready sketch which the stranger gave of many an old mansion in Cheshire and Derbyshire, where the owners retained the ancient faith of Rome.

'Well, I see I cannot charm you in this way,' continued his companion ; 'I must strike another key. I am no longer Ganlesse, the seminary priest, but ' (changing his tone, and snuffling in the nose) 'Simon Canter, a poor preacher of the word, who travels this way to call sinners to repentance ; and to strengthen, and to edify, and to fructify among the scattered remnant who hold fast the truth. What say you to this, sir ? '

'I admire your versatility, sir, and could be entertained

with it at another time. At present sincerity is more in request.'

' Sincerity ! ' said the stranger ;—' a child's whistle, with but two notes in it—yea, yea, and nay, nay. Why, man, the very Quakers have renounced it, and have got in its stead a gallant recorder, called Hypocrisy, that is somewhat like Sincerity in form, but of much greater compass, and combines the whole gamut. Come, be ruled—be a disciple of Simon Canter for the evening, and we will leave the old tumble-down castle of the knight aforesaid, on the left hand, for a new brick-built mansion, erected by an eminent salt-boiler from Nantwich, who expects the said Simon to make a strong spiritual pickle for the preservation of a soul some-what corrupted by the evil communications of this wicked world. What say you ? He has two daughters—brighter eyes never beamed under a pinched hood ; and for myself, I think there is more fire in those who live only to love and to devotion, than in your court beauties, whose hearts are running on twenty follies besides. You know not the pleasure of being conscience-keeper to a pretty precisian, who in one breath repeats her foibles, and in the next confesses her passion. Perhaps, though, you may have known such in your day ? Come, sir, it grows too dark to see your blushes ; but I am sure they are burning on your cheek.'

' You take great freedom, sir,' said Peveril, as they now approached the end of the lane, where it opened on a broad common ; 'and you seem rather to count more on my forbearance than you have room to do with safety. We are now nearly free of the lane which has made us companions for this last half hour. To avoid your further company, I will take the turn to the left, upon that common ; and if you follow me, it shall be at your peril. Observe, I am well armed ; and you will fight at odds.'

' Not at odds,' returned the provoking stranger, ' while I have my brown jennet, with which I can ride round and round you at pleasure ; and this text, of a handful in length (showing a pistol which he drew from his bosom), which discharges very convincing doctrine on the pressure of a forefinger, and is apt to equalize all odds, as you call

them, of youth and strength. Let there be no strife
between us, however—the moor lies before us—choose your
path on it—I take the other.'

'I wish you good-night, sir,' said Peveril to the stranger.
'I ask your forgiveness, if I have misconstrued you in
anything ; but the times are perilous, and a man's life may
depend on the society in which he travels.'

'True,' said the stranger ; 'but in your case, the danger
is already undergone, and you should seek to counteract
it. You have travelled in my company long enough to
devise a handsome branch of the Popish Plot. How will
you look, when you see come forth, in comely folio form,
The Narrative of Simon Canter, otherwise called Richard
Ganlesse, concerning the horrid Popish Conspiracy for the
Murder of the King, and Massacre of all Protestants, as
given on oath to the Honourable House of Commons ;
setting forth, how far Julian Peveril, younger, of Martindale
Castle, is concerned in carrying on the same '——n

'How, sir ? What mean you ?' said Peveril, much
startled.

'Nay, sir,' replied his companion, 'do not interrupt my
title-page. Now that Oates and Bedloe have drawn the
great prizes, the subordinate discoverers get little but by the
sale of their Narrative ; and Janeway, Newman, Simmons,
and every bookseller of them, will tell you that the title is
half the narrative. Mine shall therefore set forth the
various schemes you have communicated to me, of landing
ten thousand soldiers from the Isle of Man upon the coast
of Lancashire ; and marching into Wales, to join the ten
thousand pilgrims who are to be shipped from Spain ; and
so completing the destruction of the Protestant religion,
and of the devoted city of London. Truly, I think such a
Narrative, well spiced with a few horrors, and published
cum privilegio parliamenti, might, though the market be
somewhat overstocked, be still worth some twenty or thirty
pieces.'

'You seem to know me, sir,' said Peveril ; 'and if so,
I think I may fairly ask you your purpose in thus bearing
me company, and the meaning of all this rhapsody. If it
be mere banter, I can endure it within proper limit ;
although it is uncivil on the part of a stranger. If you have

any further purpose, speak it out ; I am not to be trifled with.'

' Good, now,' said the stranger, laughing, ' into what an unprofitable chafe you have put yourself ! An Italian *fuoruscito*, when he desires a parley with you, takes aim from behind a wall, with his long gun, and prefaces his conference with *Posso tirare.* So does your man-of-war fire a gun across the bows of a Hansmogan Indiaman, just to bring her to ; and so do I show Master Julian Peveril, that, if I were one of the honourable society of witnesses and informers, with whom his imagination has associated me for these two hours past, he is as much within my danger now, as what he is ever likely to be.' Then, suddenly changing his tone to serious, which was in general ironical, he added, ' Young man, when the pestilence is diffused through the air of a city, it is in vain men would avoid the disease, by seeking solitude, and shunning the company of their fellow-sufferers.'

' In what, then, consists their safety ? ' said Peveril, willing to ascertain, if possible, the drift of his companion's purpose.

' In following the counsels of wise physicians ; ' such was the stranger's answer.

' And as such,' said Peveril, ' you offer me your advice ? '

' Pardon me, young man,' said the stranger haughtily, ' I see no reason I should do so. I am not,' he added, in his former tone, ' your fee'd physician—I offer no advice —I only say it would be wise that you sought it.'

' And from whom, or where, can I obtain it ? ' said Peveril ; ' I wander in this country, like one in a dream ; so much a few months have changed it. Men who formerly occupied themselves with their own affairs, are now swallowed up in matters of State policy ; and those tremble under the apprehension of some strange and sudden convulsion of empire, who were formerly only occupied by the fear of going to bed supperless. And to sum up the matter, I meet a stranger, apparently well acquainted with my name and concerns, who first attaches himself to me, whether I will or no ; and then refuses me an explanation of his business, while he menaces me with the strangest accusations.'

' Had I meant such infamy,' said the stranger, ' believe me, I had not given you the thread of my intrigue.   But be wise, and come on with me   There is, hard by, a small inn, where, if you can take a stranger's warrant for it, we shall sleep in perfect security.'

' Yet you yourself,' said Peveril, ' but now were anxious to avoid observation ; and in that case, how can you protect me ? '

' Pshaw ! I did but silence that tattling landlady, in the way in which such people are most readily hushed ; and for Topham, and his brace of night owls, they must hawk at other and lesser game than I should prove.'

Peveril could not help admiring the easy and confident indifference with which the stranger seemed to assume a superiority to all the circumstances of danger around him ; and after hastily considering the matter with himself, came to the resolution to keep company with him for this night, at least ; and to learn, if possible, who he really was, and to what party in the estate he was attached.   The boldness and freedom of his talk seemed almost inconsistent with his following the perilous, though at that time the gainful, trade of an informer.   No doubt, such persons assumed every appearance which could insinuate them into the confidence of their destined victims ; but Julian thought he discovered in this man's manner a wild and reckless frankness, which he could not but connect with the idea of sincerity in the present case.   He therefore answered, after a moment's recollection, ' I embrace your proposal, sir ; although, by doing so, I am reposing a sudden, and perhaps an unwary, confidence.'

' And what am I, then, reposing in you ? ' said the stranger.   ' Is not our confidence mutual ? '

' No ;   much the contrary.   I know nothing of you whatever—you have named me ; and, knowing me to be Julian Peveril, know you may travel with me in perfect security.'

' The devil I do ! ' answered his companion.   ' I travel in the same security as with a lighted petard, which I may expect to explode every moment.   Are you not the son of Peveril of the Peak, with whose name Prelacy and Popery are so closely allied, that no old woman of either sex in

Derbyshire concludes her prayer without a petition to be freed from all three ?   And do you not come from the Popish Countess of Derby, bringing, for aught I know, a whole army of Manxmen in your pocket, with full complement of arms, ammunition, baggage, and a train of field artillery ? '

' It is not very likely I should be so poorly mounted,' said Julian, laughing, ' if I had such a weight to carry.   But lead on, sir.   I see I must wait for your confidence, till you think proper to confer it ; for you are already so well acquainted with my affairs, that I have nothing to offer you in exchange for it.'

' Allons, then,' said his companion ; ' give your horse the spur, and raise the curb rein, lest he measure the ground with his nose, instead of his paces. We are not now more than a furlong or two from the place of entertainment.'

They mended their pace accordingly, and soon arrived at the small solitary inn which the traveller had mentioned. When its light began to twinkle before them, the stranger, as if recollecting something he had forgotten, ' By the way, you must have a name to pass by ; for it may be ill travelling under your own, as the fellow who keeps this house is an old Cromwellian. What will you call yourself ? My name is —for the present—Ganlesse.'

' There is no occasion to assume a name at all,' answered Julian. ' I do not incline to use a borrowed one, especially as I may meet with some one who knows my own.'

' I will call you Julian, then,' said Master Ganlesse ; ' for Peveril will smell, in the nostrils of mine host, of idolatry, conspiracy, Smithfield fagots, fish on Fridays, the murder of Sir Edmondsbury Godfrey, and the fire of purgatory.'

As he spoke thus, they alighted under the great broad-branched oak-tree, that served to canopy the ale-bench, which, at an earlier hour, had groaned under the weight of a frequent conclave of rustic politicians. Ganlesse, as he dismounted, whistled in a particularly shrill note, and was answered from within the house.[n]

CHAPTER XXII

He was a fellow in a peasant's garb ;
Yet one could censure you a woodcock's carving,
Like any courtier at the ordinary.
The Ordinary.

THE person who appeared at the door of the little inn to receive Ganlesse, as we mentioned in our last chapter, sang, as he came forward, this scrap of an old ballad,—

'Good even to you, Diccon ;
And how have you sped ;
Bring you the bonny bride
To banquet and bed ? '

To which Ganlesse answered, in the same tone and tune—

'Content thee, kind Robin ;
He need little care,
Who brings home a fat buck
Instead of a hare.'

'You have missed your blow, then ? ' said the other, in reply.

'I tell you I have not,' answered Ganlesse ; 'but you will think of naught but your own thriving occupation—May the plague that belongs to it stick to it ! though it hath been the making of thee.'

'A man must live, Diccon Ganlesse,' said the other.

'Well, well,' said Ganlesse, 'bid my friend welcome for my sake. Hast thou got any supper ? '

'Reeking like a sacrifice—Chaubert has done his best. That fellow is a treasure ! give him a farthing candle, and he will cook a good supper out of it. Come in, sir. My friend's friend is welcome, as we say in my country.'

'We must have our horses looked to first,' said Peveril, who began to be considerably uncertain about the character of his companions—'that done, I am for you.'

Ganlesse gave a second whistle ; a groom appeared, who took charge of both their horses, and they themselves entered the inn.

The ordinary room of a poor inn seemed to have undergone some alterations, to render it fit for company of a higher description. There were a beaufet, a couch, and one or two other pieces of furniture, of a style inconsistent with the appearance of the place. The tablecloth, which was already laid, was of the finest damask ; and the spoons, forks, &c., were of silver. Peveril looked at this apparatus with some surprise ; and again turning his eyes attentively upon his travelling companion, Ganlesse, he could not help discovering (by the aid of imagination, perhaps), that though insignificant in person, plain in features, and dressed like one in indigence, there lurked still about his person and manners that indefinable ease of manner which belongs only to men of birth and quality, or to those who are in the constant habit of frequenting the best company. His companion, whom he called Will Smith, although tall and rather good-looking, besides being much better dressed, had not, nevertheless, exactly the same ease of demeanour ; and was obliged to make up for the want, by an additional proportion of assurance. Who these two persons could be, Peveril could not attempt even to form a guess. There was nothing for it but to watch their manner and conversation.

After speaking a moment in whispers, Smith said to his companion, ' We must go look after our nags for ten minutes, and allow Chaubert to do his office.'

' Will not he appear, and minister before us, then ? ' said Ganlesse.

' What ! he ?—he shift a trencher—he hand a cup ? No, you forget whom you speak of. Such an order were enough to make him fall on his own sword—he is already on the borders of despair, because no craw-fish are to be had.'

' Alack-a-day ! ' replied Ganlesse. ' Heaven forbid I should add to such a calamity ! To stable, then, and see we how our steeds eat their provender, while ours is getting ready.'

They adjourned to the stable accordingly, which, though a poor one, had been hastily supplied with whatever was necessary for the accommodation of four excellent horses ; one of which, that from which Ganlesse was just dismounted, the groom we have mentioned was cleaning and dressing by the light of a huge wax-candle.

' I am still so far Catholic,' said Ganlesse, laughing, as he saw that Peveril noticed this piece of extravagance. ' My horse is my saint, and I dedicate a candle to him.'

' Without asking so great a favour for mine, which I see standing behind yonder old hen-coop,' replied Peveril, ' I will at least relieve him of his saddle and bridle.'

' Leave him to the lad of the inn,' said Smith ; ' he is not worthy of any other person's handling ; and I promise you, if you slip a single buckle, you will so flavour of that stable duty, that you might as well eat roast-beef as ragouts, for any relish you will have of them.'

' I love roast-beef as well as ragouts, at any time,' said Peveril, adjusting himself to a task which every young man should know how to perform when need is ; ' and my horse, though it be but a sorry jade, will champ better on hay and corn, than on an iron bit.'

While he was unsaddling his horse, and shaking down some litter for the poor wearied animal, he heard Smith observe to Ganlesse—' By my faith, Dick, thou hast fallen into poor Slender's blunder ; missed Anne Page, and brought us a great lubberly post-master's boy.'

' Hush, he will hear thee,' answered Ganlesse ; ' there are reasons for all things—it is well as it is. But, prithee, tell thy fellow to help the youngster.'

' What ! ' replied Smith, ' d'ye think I am mad ? Ask Tom Beacon—Tom of Newmarket—Tom of ten thousand, to touch such a four-legged brute as that ? Why, he would turn me away on the spot—discard me, i' faith. It was all he would do to take in hand your own, my good friend ; and if you consider him not the better, you are like to stand groom to him yourself to-morrow.'

' Well, Will,' answered Ganlesse, ' I will say that for thee, thou hast a set of the most useless, scoundrelly, insolent vermin about thee, that ever eat up a poor gentleman's revenues.'

' Useless ? I deny it,' replied Smith. ' Every one of my fellows does something or other so exquisitely, that it were sin to make him do anything else—it is your jacks-of-all-trades who are masters of none. But hark to Chaubert's signal. The coxcomb is twangling it on the lute, to the tune of *Eveillez-vous, belle endormie*. Come, Master What

T 2

d'ye call (addressing Peveril)—get ye some water, and
wash this filthy witness from your hand, as Betterton
says in the play; for Chaubert's cookery is like Friar
Bacon's Head—time is—time was—time will soon be no
more.'

So saying, and scarce allowing Julian time to dip his hands
in a bucket, and dry them on a horse-cloth, he hurried him
from the stable back to the supper-chamber.

Here all was prepared for their meal, with an epicurean
delicacy which rather belonged to the saloon of a palace
than the cabin in which it was displayed. Four dishes of
silver, with covers of the same metal, smoked on the table;
and three seats were placed for the company. Beside the
lower end of the board was a small side-table, to answer the
purpose of what is now called a dumb waiter; on which
several flasks reared their tall, stately, and swan-like crests,
above glasses and rummers. Clean covers were also placed
within reach; and a small travelling-case of morocco,
hooped with silver, displayed a number of bottles containing
the most approved sauces that culinary ingenuity had then
invented.

Smith, who occupied the lower seat, and seemed to act
as president of the feast, motioned the two travellers to
take their places and begin. ' I would not stay a grace-
time,' he said, ' to save a whole nation from perdition. We
could bring no chauffettes with any convenience; and even
Chaubert is nothing, unless his dishes are tasted in the very
moment of projection. Come, uncover, and let us see what
he has done for us. Hum!—ha!—aye—squab-pigeons—
wildfowl—young chickens—venison cutlets—and a space
in the centre, wet, alas! by a gentle tear from Chaubert's
eye, where should have been the *soupe aux ecrevisses*. The
zeal of that poor fellow is ill repaid by his paltry ten louis
per month.'

' A mere trifle,' said Ganlesse; ' but, like yourself, Will,
he serves a generous master.'

The repast now commenced; and Julian, though he had
seen his young friend the Earl of Derby, and other gallants,
affect a considerable degree of interest and skill in the
science of the kitchen, and was not himself either an enemy
or a stranger to the pleasures of a good table, found that,

on the present occasion, he was a mere novice. Both his
companions, but Smith in especial, seemed to consider that
they were now engaged in the only true and real business
of life ; and weighed all its minutiae with a proportional
degree of accuracy. To carve the morsel in the most
delicate manner—and to apportion the proper seasoning
with the accuracy of the chemist—to be aware, exactly,
of the order in which one dish should succeed another, and
to do plentiful justice to all—was a minuteness of science
to which Julian had hitherto been a stranger. Smith
accordingly treated him as a mere novice in epicurism,
cautioning him to eat his soup before the bouilli, and to
forget the Manx custom of bolting the boiled meat before the
broth, as if Cutlar MacCulloch [n] and all his whingers were
at the door. Peveril took the hint in good part, and the
entertainment proceeded with animation.

At length Ganlesse paused, and declared the supper
exquisite. ' But, my friend Smith,' he added, ' are your
wines curious ?   When you brought all that trash of plates
and trumpery into Derbyshire, I hope you did not leave us
at the mercy of the strong ale of the shire, as thick and
muddy as the squires who drink it ? '

' Did I not know that *you* were to meet me, Lick Ganlesse ? ' answered their host.   ' And can you suspect me of
such an omission ?   It is true, you must make champagne
and claret serve, for my burgundy would not bear travelling.
But if you have a fancy for sherry, or Vin de Cahors, I have
a notion Chaubert and Tom Beacon have brought some
for their own drinking.'

' Perhaps the gentlemen would not care to impart,' said
Ganlesse.

'Oh, fie!—anything in the way of civility'; replied Smith.
' They are, in truth, the best-natured lads alive, when treated
respectfully ;   so that if you would prefer '——

' By no means,' said Ganlesse—' a glass of champagne
will serve in a scarcity of better.'

' The cork shall start obsequious to my thumb,'

said Smith ;   and as he spoke, he untwisted the wire, and
the cork struck the roof of the cabin.   Each guest took
a large rummer glass of the sparkling beverage, which

Peveril had judgement and experience enough to pronounce exquisite.

'Give me your hand, sir,' said Smith ; 'it is the first word of sense you have spoken this evening.'

'Wisdom, sir,' replied Peveril, 'is like the best ware in the pedlar's pack, which he never produces till he knows his customer.'

'Sharp as mustard,' returned the *bon vivant* ; 'but be wise, most noble pedlar, and take another rummer of this same flask, which you see I have held in an oblique position for your service—not permitting it to retrograde to the perpendicular. Nay, take it off before the bubble bursts on the rim, and the zest is gone.'

'You do me honour, sir,' said Peveril, taking the second glass. 'I wish you a better office than that of my cup-bearer.'

'You cannot wish Will Smith one more congenial to his nature,' said Ganlesse. 'Others have a selfish delight in the objects of sense. Will thrives, and is happy by imparting them to his friends.'

'Better help men to pleasures than to pains, Master Ganlesse,' answered Smith, somewhat angrily.

'Nay, wrath thee not, Will,' said Ganlesse ; 'and speak no words in haste, lest you may have cause to repent at leisure. Do I blame thy social concern for the pleasures of others ? Why, man, thou dost therein most philosophically multiply thine own. A man has but one throat, and can but eat, with his best efforts, some five or six times a day ; but thou dinest with every friend that cuts up a capon, and art quaffing wine in other men's gullets from morning to night—*et sic de caeteris.*'

'Friend Ganlesse,' returned Smith, 'I prithee beware— thou knowest I can cut gullets as well as tickle them.'

'Aye, Will,' answered Ganlesse carelessly ; 'I think I have seen thee wave thy whinyard at the throat of a Hogan-Mogan—a Netherlandish weasand, which expanded only on thy natural and mortal objects of aversion—Dutch cheese, rye-bread, pickled herring, onions, and Geneva.'

'For pity's sake, forbear the description !' said Smith ; 'thy words overpower the perfumes, and flavour the apartment like a dish of salmagundi !'

'But for an epiglottis like mine,' continued Ganlesse, 'down which the most delicate morsels are washed by such claret as thou art now pouring out, thou couldst not, in thy bitterest mood, wish a worse fate than to be necklaced somewhat tight by a pair of white arms.'

'By a tenpenny cord,' answered Smith; 'but not till you were dead; that thereafter you be presently embowelled, you being yet alive; that your head be then severed from your body, and your body divided into quarters, to be disposed of at his Majesty's pleasure. How like you that, Master Richard Ganlesse?'

'E'en as you like the thoughts of dining on bran-bread and milk-porridge—an extremity which you trust never to be reduced to. But all this shall not prevent me from pledging you in a cup of sound claret.'

As the claret circulated, the glee of the company increased; and Smith, placing the dishes which had been made use of upon the side-table, stamped with his foot on the floor, and the table sinking down a trap, again rose, loaded with olives, sliced neat's tongue, caviare, and other provocatives, for the circulation of the bottle.

'Why, Will,' said Ganlesse, 'thou art a more complete mechanist than I suspected; thou hast brought thy scene-shifting inventions to Derbyshire in marvellously short time.'

'A rope and pulleys can be easily come by,' answered Will; 'and with a saw and a plane, I can manage that business in half a day. I love that knack of clean and secret conveyance—thou knowest it was the foundation of my fortunes.'

'It may be the wreck of them too, Will,' replied his friend.

'True, Diccon,' answered Will; 'but, *dum vivimus, vivamus*—that is my motto; and therewith I present you a brimmer to the health of the fair lady you wot of.'

'Let it come, Will,' replied his friend; and the flask circulated briskly from hand to hand.

Julian did not think it prudent to seem a check on their festivity, as he hoped in its progress something might occur to enable him to judge of the character and purposes of his companions. But he watched them in vain. Their conversation was animated and lively, and often bore reference to the literature of the period, in which the elder seemed particularly well skilled. They also talked freely of the court, and of that numerous class of gallants who were then described as ' men of wit and pleasure about town ' ; and to which it seemed probable they themselves appertained.

At length the universal topic of the Popish Plot was started ; upon which Ganlesse and Smith seemed to entertain the most opposite opinions. Ganlesse, if he did not maintain the authority of Oates in its utmost extent, contended, that at least it was confirmed in a great measure by the murder of Sir Edmondsbury Godfrey, and the letters written by Coleman to the confessor of the French King.[n]

With much more noise, and less power of reasoning, Will Smith hesitated not to ridicule and run down the whole discovery, as one of the wildest and most causeless alarms which had ever been sounded in the ears of a credulous public. ' I shall never forget,' he said, ' Sir Godfrey's most original funeral. Two bouncing parsons, well armed with sword and pistol, mounted the pulpit, to secure the third fellow who preached from being murdered in the face of the congregation. Three parsons in one pulpit—three suns in one hemisphere—no wonder men stood aghast at such a prodigy.' [n]

' What then, Will,' answered his companion, ' you are one of those who think the good knight murdered himself, in order to give credit to the Plot ? '

' By my faith, not I,' said the other ; ' but some true blue Protestant might do the job for him, in order to give the thing a better colour. I will be judged by our silent friend, whether that be not the most feasible solution of the whole.'

' I pray you, pardon me, gentlemen,' said Julian ; ' I am but just landed in England, and am a stranger to the particular circumstances which have thrown the nation into such a ferment. It would be the highest degree of assurance in me to give my opinion betwixt gentlemen who argue the matter so ably ; besides, to say truth, I confess weariness —your wine is more potent than I expected, or I have drank more of it than I meant to do.'

' Nay, if an hour's nap will refresh you,' said the elder of the strangers, ' make no ceremony with us. Your bed—

all we can offer as such—is that old-fashioned Dutch-built sofa, as the last new phrase calls it. We shall be early stirrers to-morrow morning.'

'And that we may be so,' said Smith, 'I propose that we do sit up all this night—I hate lying rough, and detest a pallet-bed. So have at another flask, and the newest lampoon to help it out—

> Now a plague of their votes
> Upon Papists and Plots,
> And be d—d Doctor Oates.
>   Tol de rol.'

'Nay, but our Puritanic host,' said Ganlesse.

'I have him in my pocket, man—his eyes, ears, nose, and tongue,' answered his boon companion, 'are all in my possession.'

'In that case, when you give him back his eyes and nose, I pray you keep his ears and tongue,' answered Ganlesse. 'Seeing and smelling are organs sufficient for such a knave —to hear and tell are things he should have no manner of pretensions to.'

'I grant you it were well done,' answered Smith; 'but it were a robbing of the hangman and the pillory; and I am an honest fellow, who would give Dun [1] and the devil his due. So,

> All joy to great Caesar,
> Long life, love, and pleasure;
> May the King live for ever,
>   'Tis no matter for us, boys.'

While this Bacchanalian scene proceeded, Julian had wrapt himself closely in his cloak, and stretched himself on the couch which they had shown to him. He looked towards the table he had left—the tapers seemed to become hazy and dim as he gazed—he heard the sound of voices, but they ceased to convey any impression to his understanding; and in a few minutes he was faster asleep than he had ever been in the whole course of his life.

---

[1] Dun was the hangman of the day at Tyburn. He was successor of Gregory Brunden, who was by many believed to be the same who dropped the axe upon Charles I, though others were suspected of being the actual regicide.

CHAPTER XXIII

The Gordon then his bugle blew,
  And said, awa, awa;
The House of Rhodes is all on flame,
  I hauld it time to ga'.
                    Old Ballad.

WHEN Julian awaked the next morning, all was still and
vacant in the apartment. The rising sun, which shone
through the half-closed shutters, showed some relics of the
last night's banquet, which his confused and throbbing head
assured him had been carried into a debauch.

Without being much of a boon companion, Julian, like
other young men of the time, was not in the habit of shunning wine, which was then used in considerable quantities ;
and he could not help being surprised that the few cups he
had drank over night had produced on his frame the effects
of excess. He rose up, adjusted his dress, and sought in
the apartment for water to perform his morning ablutions,
but without success. Wine there was on the table ; and
beside it one stool stood, and another lay, as if thrown down
in the heedless riot of the evening. 'Surely,' he thought
to himself, the ' wine must have been very powerful, which
rendered me insensible to the noise my companions must
have made ere they finished their carouse.'

With momentary suspicion he examined his weapons,
and the packet which he had received from the countess, and
kept in a secret pocket of his upper coat, bound close about
his person. All was safe ; and the very operation reminded
him of the duties which lay before him. He left the apartment where they had supped, and went into another,
wretched enough, where, in a truckle-bed, were stretched
two bodies, covered with a rug, the heads belonging to
which were amicably deposited upon the same truss of
hay. The one was the black shock-head of the groom ;
the other, graced with a long thrum nightcap, showed
a grizzled pate, and a grave caricatured countenance,
which the hook-nose and lantern-jaws proclaimed to belong

to the Gallic minister of good cheer, whose praises he had
heard sung forth on the preceding evening. These worthies
seemed to have slumbered in the arms of Bacchus as well
as of Morpheus, for there were broken flasks on the floor ;
and their deep snoring alone showed that they were alive.

Bent upon resuming his journey, as duty and expedience
alike dictated, Julian next descended the trap-stair, and
essayed a door at the bottom of the steps. It was fastened
within. He called—no answer was returned. It must be,
he thought, the apartment of the revellers, now probably
sleeping as soundly as their dependants still slumbered, and
as he himself had done a few minutes before. Should he
awake them ?—To what purpose ? They were men with
whom accident had involved him against his own will ;
and situated as he was, he thought it wise to take the earliest
opportunity of breaking off from society, which was suspicious, and might be perilous. Ruminating thus, he
essayed another door, which admitted him to a bedroom,
where lay another harmonious slumberer. The mean
utensils, pewter measures, empty cans and casks, with
which this room was lumbered, proclaimed it that of the
host, who slept surrounded by his professional implements
of hospitality and stock-in-trade.

This discovery relieved Peveril from some delicate embarrassment which he had formerly entertained. He put
upon the table a piece of money, sufficient, as he judged,
to pay his share of the preceding night's reckoning ; not
caring to be indebted for his entertainment to the strangers,
whom he was leaving without the formality of an adieu.

His conscience cleared of this gentlemanlike scruple,
Peveril proceeded with a light heart, though somewhat a
dizzy head, to the stable, which he easily recognized among
a few other paltry out-houses. His horse, refreshed with
rest, and perhaps not unmindful of his services the evening
before, neighed as his master entered the stable ; and Peveril
accepted the sound as an omen of a prosperous journey.
He paid the augury with a sieveful of corn ; and, while his
palfrey profited by his attention, walked into the fresh air
to cool his heated blood, and consider what course he should
pursue in order to reach the Castle of Martindale before
sunset. His acquaintance with the country in general, gave

him confidence that he could not have greatly deviated
from the nearest road ; and with his horse in good condition, he conceived he might easily reach Martindale before
nightfall.

Having adjusted his route in his mind, he returned into
the stable to prepare his steed for the journey, and soon led
him into the ruinous courtyard of the inn, bridled, saddled,
and ready to be mounted. But, as Peveril's hand was upon
the mane, and his left foot in the stirrup, a hand touched
his cloak, and the voice of Ganlesse said, ' What, Master
Peveril, is this your foreign breeding ? or have you learned
in France to take French leave of your friends ? '

Julian started like a guilty thing, although a moment's
reflection assured him that he was neither wrong nor in
danger. ' I cared not to disturb you,' he said, ' although
I did come as far as the door of your chamber. I supposed
your friend and you might require, after our last night's
revel, rather sleep than ceremony. I left my own bed,
though a rough one, with more reluctance than usual ; and
as my occasions oblige me to be an early traveller, I thought
it best to depart without leave-taking. I have left a token
for mine host, on the table of his apartment.'

' It was unnecessary,' said Ganlesse ; ' the rascal is already
overpaid. But are you not rather premature in your
purpose of departing ? My mind tells me that Master
Julian Peveril had better proceed with me to London, than
turn aside for any purpose whatever. You may see already,
that I am no ordinary person, but a master-spirit of the
time. For the cuckoo I travel with, and whom I indulge
in his prodigal follies, he also has his uses. But you are of
a different cast ; and I not only would serve you, but even
wish you to be my own.'

Julian gazed on this singular person when he spoke. We
have already said his figure was mean and slight, with very
ordinary and unmarked features, unless we were to distinguish the lightnings of a keen grey eye, which corresponded, in its careless and prideful glance, with the haughty
superiority which the stranger assumed in his conversation.
It was not till after a momentary pause, that Julian replied,
' Can you wonder, sir, that in my circumstances—if they are
indeed known to you so well as they seem—I should decline

unnecessary confidence on the affairs of moment which have called me hither, or refuse the company of a stranger, who assigns no reason for desiring mine ? '

' Be it as you list, young man,' answered Ganlesse ; ' only remember hereafter you had a fair offer—it is not every one to whom I would have made it. If we should meet here-after, on other, and on worse terms, impute it to yourself and not to me.'

' I understand not your threat,' answered Peveril, ' if a threat be indeed implied. I have done no evil—I feel no apprehension—and I cannot, in common sense, conceive why I should suffer for refusing my confidence to a stranger, who seems to require that I should submit me blindfold to his guidance.'

' Farewell, then, Sir Julian of the Peak—that may soon be,' said the stranger, removing the hand which he had as yet left carelessly on the horse's bridle.

' How mean you by that phrase ? ' said Julian ; ' and why apply such a title to me ? '

The stranger smiled, and only answered, ' Here our conference ends. The way is before you. You will find it longer and rougher than that by which I would have guided you.'

So saying, Ganlesse turned his back and walked toward the house. On the threshold he turned about once more, and seeing that Peveril had not yet moved from the spot, he again smiled and beckoned to him ; but Julian, recalled by that sign to recollection, spurred his horse and set forward on his journey.

It was not long ere his local acquaintance with the country enabled him to regain the road to Martindale, from which he had diverged on the preceding evening for about two miles. But the roads, or rather the paths, of this wild country, so much satirized by their native poet, Cotton, were so complicated in some places, so difficult to be traced in others, and so unfit for hasty travelling in almost all, that, in spite of Julian's utmost exertions, and though he made no longer delay upon the journey than was necessary to bait his horse at a small hamlet through which he passed at noon, it was nightfall ere he reached an eminence, from which, an hour sooner, the battlements of Martindale Castle

would have been visible ; and where, when they were hid in
night, their situation was indicated by a light constantly
maintained in a lofty tower, called the Warder's Turret ;
and which domestic beacon had acquired, through all the
neighbourhood, the name of Peveril's Pole-star.

This was regularly kindled at curfew toll, and supplied
with as much wood and charcoal as maintained the light
till sunrise ; and at no period was the ceremonial omitted,
saving during the space intervening between the death of
a lord of the castle and his interment. When this last
event had taken place, the nightly beacon was rekindled
with some ceremony, and continued till fate called the
successor to sleep with his fathers. It is not known from
what circumstance the practice of maintaining this light
originally sprung. Tradition spoke of it doubtfully. Some
thought it was the signal of general hospitality, which, in
ancient times, guided the wandering knight, or the weary
pilgrim, to rest and refreshment. Others spoke of it as
a ' love-lighted watchfire,' by which the provident anxiety
of a former lady of Martindale guided her husband homeward through the terrors of a midnight storm. The less
favourable construction of unfriendly neighbours of the
dissenting persuasion, ascribed the origin and continuance
of this practice, to the assuming pride of the family of
Peveril, who thereby chose to intimate their ancient *suzerainté* over the whole country, in the manner of the admiral,
who carries the lantern in the poop, for the guidance of the
fleet. And in the former times, our old friend, Master
Solsgrace, dealt from the pulpit many a hard hit against
Sir Geoffrey, as he that had raised his horn, and set up his
candlestick on high. Certain it is, that all the Peverils,
from father to son, had been especially attentive to the
maintenance of this custom, as something intimately
connected with the dignity of their family ; and in the hands
of Sir Geoffrey, the observance was not likely to be omitted.

Accordingly, the polar star of Peveril had continued to
beam more or less brightly during all the vicissitudes of
the Civil War ; and glimmered, however faintly, during the
subsequent period of Sir Geoffrey's depression. But he
was often heard to say, and sometimes to swear, that while
there was a perch of woodland left to the estate, the old

beacon-grate should not lack replenishing. All this his son Julian well knew ; and therefore it was with no ordinary feelings of surprise and anxiety, that, looking in the direction of the castle, he perceived that the light was not visible. He halted—rubbed his eyes—shifted his position—and endeavoured, in vain, to persuade himself that he had mistaken the point from which the polar star of his house was visible, or that some newly intervening obstacle, the growth of a plantation, perhaps, or the erection of some building, intercepted the light of the beacon. But a moment's reflection assured him that from the high and free situation which Martindale Castle bore in reference to the surrounding country, this could not have taken place ; and the inference necessarily forced itself upon his mind, that Sir Geoffrey, his father, was either deceased, or that the family must have been disturbed by some strange calamity, under the pressure of which their wonted custom and solemn usage had been neglected.

Under the influence of undefinable apprehension, young Peveril now struck the spurs into his jaded steed, and forcing him down the broken and steep path, at a pace which set safety at defiance, he arrived at the village of Martindale-Moultrassie, eagerly desirous to ascertain the cause of this ominous eclipse. The street, through which his tired horse paced slow and reluctantly, was now deserted and empty ; and scarcely a candle twinkled from a casement, except from the latticed window of the little inn, called the Peveril Arms, from which a broad light shone, and several voices were heard in rude festivity.

Before the door of this inn, the jaded palfrey, guided by the instinct or experience which makes a hackney well acquainted with the outside of a house of entertainment, made so sudden and determined a pause, that, notwithstanding his haste, the rider thought it best to dismount, expecting to be readily supplied with a fresh horse by Roger Raine, the landlord, the ancient dependant of his family. He also wished to relieve his anxiety by inquiring concerning the state of things at the castle, when he was surprised to hear, bursting from the tap-room of the loyal old host, a well-known song of the Commonwealth time, which some puritanical wag had written in reprehension of

the Cavaliers, and their dissolute courses, and in which his
father came in for a lash of the satirist.

> Ye thought in the world there was no power to tame ye,
> So you tippled and drabb'd till the saints overcame ye;
> 'Forsooth,' and 'Ne'er stir,' sir, have vanquish'd 'G— d—n me,'
>   Which nobody can deny.

> There was bluff old Sir Geoffrey loved brandy and mum well,
> And to see a beer-glass turned over the thumb well;
> But he fled like the wind, before Fairfax and Cromwell,
>   Which nobody can deny.

Some strange revolution, Julian was aware, must have
taken place, both in the village and in the castle, ere these
sounds of unseemly insult could have been poured forth in
the very inn which was decorated with the armorial bearings
of his family ; and not knowing how far it might be advisable to intrude on these unfriendly revellers, without the
power of repelling or chastising their insolence, he led his
horse to a back-door, which, as he recollected, communicated with the landlord's apartment, having determined to
make private inquiry of him concerning the state of matters
at the castle. He knocked repeatedly, and as often called
on Roger Raine with an earnest but stifled voice. At
length a female voice replied, by the usual inquiry, ' Who
is there ? '

'It is I, Dame Raine—I, Julian Peveril—tell your husband
to come to me presently.'

' Alack, and a-well-a-day, Master Julian, if it be really
you—you are to know my poor goodman has gone where
he can come to no one ; but, doubtless, we shall all go to
him, as Matthew Chamberlain says.'

' He is dead, then ? ' said Julian. ' I am extremely
sorry '——

' Dead six months and more, Master Julian ; and let me
tell you, it is a long time for a lone woman, as Matt Chamberlain says.'

' Well, do you or your chamberlain undo the door. I
want a fresh horse ; and I want to know how things are at
the castle.'

' The Castle — lack-a-day ! — Chamberlain — Matthew
Chamberlain—I say, Matt ! '

Matt Chamberlain apparently was at no great distance, for he presently answered her call ; and Peveril, as he stood close to the door, could hear them whispering to each other, and distinguish in a great measure what they said. And here it may be noticed, that Dame Raine, accustomed to submit to the authority of old Roger, who vindicated as well the husband's domestic prerogative, as that of the monarch in the state, had, when left a buxom widow, been so far incommoded by the exercise of her newly acquired independence, that she had recourse, upon all occasions, to the advice of Matt Chamberlain ; and as Matt began no longer to go slipshod, and in a red nightcap, but wore Spanish shoes, and a high-crowned beaver (at least of a Sunday), and moreover was called Master Matthew by his fellow servants, the neighbours in the village argued a speedy change of the name on the sign-post ; nay, perhaps, of the very sign itself, for Matthew was a bit of a Puritan, and no friend to Peveril of the Peak.

' Now counsel me, an you be a man, Matt Chamberlain,' said Widow Raine ; ' for never stir, if here be not Master Julian's own self, and he wants a horse, and what not, and all as if things were as they wont to be.'

' Why, dame, an ye will walk by my counsel,' said the Chamberlain, ' e'en shake him off—let him be jogging while his boots are green.   This is no world for folks to scald their fingers in other folk's broth.'

' And that is well spoken, truly,' answered Dame Raine ; ' but then look you, Matt, we have eaten their bread, and, as my poor goodman used to say '——

' Nay, nay, dame, they that walk by the counsel of the dead, shall have none of the living ; and so you may do as you list ; but if you will walk by mine, drop latch, and draw bolt, and bid him seek quarters further—that is my counsel.'

' I desire nothing of you, sirrah,' said Peveril, ' save but to know how Sir Geoffrey and his lady do ? '

' Lack-a-day !—lack-a-day ! ' in a tone of sympathy, was the only answer he received from the landlady ; and the conversation betwixt her and her chamberlain was resumed, but in a tone too low to be overheard.

At length Matt Chamberlain spoke aloud, and with a tone of authority : ' We undo no doors at this time of night, for it is against the justices' orders, and might cost us our licence ; and for the castle, the road up to it lies before you, and I think you know it as well as we do.'

'And I know you,' said Peveril, remounting his wearied horse, 'for an ungrateful churl, whom, on the first opportunity, I will assuredly cudgel to a mummy.'

To this menace Matthew made no reply, and Peveril presently heard him leave the apartment, after a few earnest words betwixt him and his mistress.

Impatient at this delay, and at the evil omen implied in these people's conversation and deportment, Peveril, after some vain spurring of his horse, which positively refused to move a step further, dismounted once more, and was about to pursue his journey on foot, notwithstanding the extreme disadvantage under which the high riding-boots of the period laid those who attempted to walk with such encumbrances, when he was stopped by a gentle call from the window.

Her counsellor was no sooner gone, than the good nature and habitual veneration of the dame for the house of Peveril, and perhaps some fear for her counsellor's bones, induced her to open the casement, and cry, but in a low and timid tone, 'Hist ! hist ! Master Julian—be you gone ? '

'Not yet, dame,' said Julian ; 'though it seems my stay is unwelcome.'

'Nay, but good young master, it is because men counsel so differently ; for here was my poor old Roger Raine would have thought the chimney corner too cold for you ; and here is Matt Chamberlain thinks the cold courtyard is warm enough.'

'Never mind that, dame,' said Julian ; 'do but only tell me what has happened at Martindale Castle ? I see the beacon is extinguished.'

'Is it in troth ?—aye, like enough—then good Sir Geoffrey has gone to heaven with my old Roger Raine ! '

'Sacred Heaven ! ' exclaimed Peveril ! 'when was my father taken ill ? '

'Never as I knows of,' said the dame ; 'but, about three hours since, arrived a party at the castle, with buff-coats and bandoleers, and one of the Parliament's folks, like in Oliver's time. My old Roger Raine would have shut the gates of the inn against them, but he is in the churchyard, and Matt says it is against law ; and so they came in and refreshed men and horses, and sent for Master Bridgenorth, that is at Moultrassie Hall even now ; and so they went up to the castle, and there was a fray, it is like, as the old knight was no man to take napping, as poor Roger Raine used to say.   Always the officers had the best on't ; and reason there is, since they had the law of their side, as our Matthew says.   But since the pole star of the castle is out, as your honour says, why, doubtless, the old gentleman is dead.'

'Gracious Heaven !   Dear dame, for love or gold, let me have a horse to make for the castle ! '

'The castle ? ' said the dame ; 'the Roundheads, as my poor Roger called them, will kill you as they have killed your father !   Better creep into the woodhouse, and I will send Bett with a blanket and some supper—Or stay—my old Dobbin stands in the little stable beside the hencoop—e'en take him, and make the best of your way out of the country, for there is no safety here for you.   Hear what songs some of them are singing at the tap !—so take Dobbin, and do not forget to leave your own horse instead.'

Peveril waited to hear no further, only, that just as he turned to go off to the stable, the compassionate female was heard to exclaim—' O Lord !   what will Matthew Chamberlain say ? ' but instantly added, ' Let him say what he will, I may dispose of what 's my own.'

With the haste of a double-fee'd ostler did Julian exchange the equipments of his jaded brute with poor Dobbin, who stood quietly tugging at his rackful of hay, without dreaming of the business which was that night destined for him. Notwithstanding the darkness of the place, Julian succeeded marvellous quickly in preparing for his journey ; and leaving his own horse to find its way to Dobbin's rack by instinct, he leaped upon his new acquisition, and spurred him sharply against the hill, which rises steeply from the village to the castle.   Dobbin, little accustomed to such exertions, snorted, panted, and trotted as briskly as he could, until at length he brought his rider before the entrance-gate of his father's ancient seat.

The moon was now rising, but the portal was hidden from

its beams, being situated, as we have mentioned elsewhere, in a deep recess betwixt two large flanking towers. Peveril dismounted, turned his horse loose, and advanced to the gate, which, contrary to his expectation, he found open. He entered the large courtyard; and could then perceive that lights yet twinkled in the lower part of the building, although he had not before observed them, owing to the height of the outward walls. The main door, or great hall-gate, as it was called, was, since the partially decayed state of the family, seldom opened, save on occasions of particular ceremony. A smaller postern door served the purpose of ordinary entrance; and to that Julian now repaired. This also was open—a circumstance which would of itself have alarmed him, had he not already had so many causes for apprehension. His heart sank within him as he turned to the left, through a small outward hall, towards the great parlour, which the family usually occupied as a sitting apartment; and his alarm became still greater when, on a nearer approach, he heard proceeding from thence the murmur of several voices. He threw the door of the apartment wide; and the sight which was thus displayed, warranted all the evil bodings which he had entertained.

In front of him stood the old knight, whose arms were strongly secured, over the elbows, by a leathern belt drawn tight round them, and made fast behind; two ruffianly-looking men, apparently his guards, had hold of his doublet. The scabbardless sword which lay on the floor, and the empty sheath which hung by Sir Geoffrey's side, showed the stout old Cavalier had not been reduced to this state of bondage without an attempt at resistance. Two or three persons, having their backs turned towards Julian, sat round a table, and appeared engaged in writing—the voices which he had heard were theirs, as they murmured to each other. Lady Peveril—the emblem of death, so pallid was her countenance—stood at the distance of a yard or two from her husband, upon whom her eyes were fixed with an intenseness of gaze, like that of one who looks her last on the object which she loves the best. She was the first to perceive Julian; and she exclaimed, ' Merciful Heaven!— my son!—the misery of our house is complete! '

' My son ! ' echoed Sir Geoffrey, starting from the sullen state of dejection, and swearing a deep oath—' thou art come in the right time, Julian.   Strike me one good blow —cleave me that traitorous thief from the crown to the brisket ! and that done, I care not what comes next.'

The sight of his father's situation made the son forget the inequality of the contest which he was about to provoke

' Villains,' he said, ' unhand him ! ' and rushing on the guards with his drawn sword, compelled them to let go Sir Geoffrey, and stand on their own defence.

Sir Geoffrey, thus far liberated, shouted to his lady. ' Undo the belt, dame, and we will have three good blows for it yet—they must fight well that beat both father and son.'

But one of those men who had started up from the writing-table when the fray commenced, prevented Lady Peveril from rendering her husband this assistance ; while another easily mastered the hampered knight, though not without receiving several severe kicks from his heavy boots —his condition permitting him no other mode of defence. A third, who saw that Julian, young, active, and animated with the fury of a son who fights for his parents, was compelling the two guards to give ground, seized on his collar, and attempted to master his sword.   Suddenly dropping that weapon, and snatching one of his pistols, Julian fired it at the head of the person by whom he was thus assailed. He did not drop, but, staggering back as if he had received a severe blow, showed Peveril, as he sank into a chair, the features of old Bridgenorth, blackened with the explosion, which had even set fire to a part of his grey hair.   A cry of astonishment escaped from Julian ; and in the alarm and horror of the moment, he was easily secured and disarmed by those with whom he had been at first engaged.

' Heed it not, Julian,' said Sir Geoffrey ; ' heed it not, my brave boy—that shot has balanced all accompts !—but how—what the devil—he lives ! Was your pistol loaded with chaff ? or has the foul fiend given him proof against lead ? '

There was some reason for Sir Geoffrey's surprise, since, as he spoke, Major Bridgenorth collected himself—sat up in the chair as one who recovers from a stunning blow— then rose, and wiping with his handkerchief the marks of the explosion from his face, he approached Julian, and said, in the same cold unaltered tone in which he usually expressed himself, ' Young man, you have reason to bless God, who has this day saved you from the commission of a great crime.'

' Bless the devil, ye crop-eared knave ! ' exclaimed Sir Geoffrey ; ' for nothing less than the father of all fanatics saved your brains from being blown about like the rinsings of Beelzebub's porridge pot ! '

' Sir Geoffrey,' said Major Bridgenorth, ' I have already told you, that with you I will hold no argument ; for to you I am not accountable for any of my actions.'

' Master Bridgenorth,' said the lady, making a strong effort to speak, and to speak with calmness, ' whatever revenge your Christian state of conscience may permit you to take on my husband—I—I, who have some right to experience compassion at your hand, for most sincerely did I compassionate you when the hand of Heaven was heavy on you—I implore you not to involve my son in our common ruin ! Let the destruction of the father and mother, with the ruin of our ancient house, satisfy your resentment for any wrong which you have ever received at my husband's hand.'

' Hold your peace, housewife,' said the knight, ' you speak like a fool, and meddle with what concerns you not. Wrong at *my* hand ? The cowardly knave has ever had but even too much right. Had I cudgelled the cur soundly when he first bayed at me, the cowardly mongrel had been now crouching at my feet, instead of flying at my throat. But if I get through this action, as I have got through worse weather, I will pay off old scores, as far as tough crab-tree and cold iron will bear me out.'

' Sir Geoffrey,' replied Bridgenorth, ' if the birth you boast of has made you blind to better principles, it might have at least taught you civility. What do you complain of ? I am a magistrate ; and I execute a warrant, addressed to me by the first authority in the State. I am a creditor also of yours ; and law arms me with powers to recover my own property from the hands of an improvident debtor.'

' You a magistrate ! ' said the knight ; ' much such a magistrate as Noll was a monarch. Your heart is up,

I warrant, because you have the king's pardon ; and are
replaced on the bench, forsooth, to persecute the poor Papist.
There was never turmoil in the State, but knaves had their
vantage by it—never pot boiled, but the scum was cast
uppermost.'

'For God's sake, my dearest husband,' said Lady Peveril,
'cease this wild talk ! It can but incense Master Bridgenorth, who might otherwise consider, that in common
charity '——

'Incense him !' said Sir Geoffrey, impatiently interrupting her ; 'God's death, madam, you will drive me mad !
Have you lived so long in this world, and yet expect consideration and charity from an old starved wolf like that ?
And if he had it, do you think that I, or you, madam, as
my wife, are subjects for his charity ?—Julian, my poor
fellow, I am sorry thou hast come so unluckily, since thy
petronel was not better loaded—but thy credit is lost for
ever as a marksman.'

This angry colloquy passed so rapidly on all sides, that
Julian, scarce recovered from the extremity of astonishment
with which he was overwhelmed at finding himself suddenly
plunged into a situation of such extremity, had no time to
consider in what way he could most effectually act for the
succour of his parents. To speak Bridgenorth fair, seemed
the more prudent course ; but to this his pride could hardly
stoop ; yet he forced himself to say, with as much calmness
as he could assume, 'Master Bridgenorth, since you act as
a magistrate, I desire to be treated according to the laws of
England ; and demand to know of what we are accused,
and by whose authority we are arrested ? '

'Here is another howlet for ye !' exclaimed the impetuous
old knight ; 'his mother speaks to a Puritan of charity ;
and thou must talk of law to a roundheaded rebel, with
a wannion to you ! What warrant hath he, think ye, beyond
the Parliament's or the devil's ? '

'Who speaks of the Parliament ? ' said a person entering,
whom Peveril recognized as the official person whom he had
before seen at the horse-dealer's, and who now bustled in
with all the conscious dignity of plenary authority,—'Who
talks of the Parliament ? ' he exclaimed. 'I promise you,
enough has been found in this house to convict twenty

plotters—Here be arms, and that good store.   Bring them
in, captain.'

'The very same,' exclaimed the captain, approaching,
'which I mention in my printed Narrative of Information,
lodged before the Honourable House of Commons ; they
were commissioned from old Vander Huys of Rotterdam, by
orders of Don John of Austria, for the service of the Jesuits.'

'Now, by this light,' said Sir Geoffrey, 'they are the
pikes, musketoons, and pistols that have been hidden in the
garret ever since Naseby fight ! '

'And here,' said the captain's yoke-fellow, Everett, 'are
proper priests' trappings—antiphoners, and missals, and
copes, I warrant you—aye, and proper pictures, too, for
Papists to mutter and bow over.'

'Now plague on thy snuffling whine,' said Sir Geoffrey ;
'here is a rascal will swear my grandmother's old farthingale
to be priest's vestments, and the story book of Owlen-
spiegel, a Popish missal ! '

'But how's this, Master Bridgenorth ? ' said Topham,
addressing the magistrate ; 'your honour has been as busy
as we have ; and you have caught another knave while we
recovered these toys.'

'I think, sir,' said Julian, 'if you look into your warrant,
which, if I mistake not, names the persons whom you are
directed to arrest, you will find you have no title to
apprehend me.'

'Sir,' said the officer, puffing with importance, 'I do not
know who you are ; but I would you were the best man in
England, that I might teach you the respect due to the
warrant of the House.   Sir, there steps not the man within
the British seas, but I will arrest him on authority of this
bit of parchment ; and I do arrest you accordingly.—What
do you accuse him of, gentlemen ? '

Dangerfield swaggered forward, and peeping under
Julian's hat, 'Stop my vital breath,' he exclaimed, 'but
I have seen you before, my friend, an I could but think
where ; but my memory is not worth a bean, since I have
been obliged to use it so much of late, in the behalf of the
poor State.   But I do know the fellow ; and I have seen
him amongst the Papists—I'll take that on my assured
damnation.'

'Why, Captain Dangerfield,' said the captain's smoother but more dangerous associate—'verily, it is the same youth whom we saw at the horse-merchant's yesterday; and we had matter against him then, only Master Topham did not desire us to bring it out.'

'Ye may bring out what ye will against him now,' said Topham, 'for he hath blasphemed the warrant of the House. I think ye said ye saw him somewhere.'

'Aye, verily,' said Everett, 'I have seen him amongst the seminary pupils at Saint Omer's—he was—who but he—with the regents there.'

'Nay, Master Everett, collect yourself,' said Topham; 'for, as I think, you said you saw him at a consult of the Jesuits in London.'

'It was I said so, Master Topham,' said the undaunted Dangerfield; 'and mine is the tongue that will swear it.'

'Good Master Topham,' said Bridgenorth, 'you may suspend further inquiry at present, as it doth but fatigue and perplex the memory of the king's witnesses.'

'You are wrong, Master Bridgenorth—clearly wrong. It doth but keep them in wind—only breathes them like greyhounds before a coursing match.'

'Be it so,' said Bridgenorth, with his usual indifference of manner; 'but at present this youth must stand committed upon a warrant, which I will presently sign, of having assaulted me while in discharge of my duty as a magistrate, for the rescue of a person legally attached. Did you not hear the report of a pistol?'

'I will swear to it,' said Everett.

'And I,' said Dangerfield. 'While we were making search in the cellar, I heard something very like a pistol-shot; but I conceived it to be the drawing of a long-corked bottle of sack, to see whether there were any Popish relics in the inside on't.'

'A pistol-shot!' exclaimed Topham; 'here might have been a second Sir Edmondsbury Godfrey's matter.—Oh, thou real spawn of the red old dragon! for he too would have resisted the House's warrant, had we not taken him something at unawares.—Master Bridgenorth, you are a judicious magistrate, and a worthy servant of the state— I would we had many such sound Protestant justices. Shall

I have this young fellow away with his parents—what think you ?—or will you keep him for re-examination ? '

' Master Bridgenorth,' said Lady Peveril, in spite of her husband's efforts to interrupt her, ' for God's sake, if ever you knew what it was to love one of the many children you have lost, or her who is now left to you, do not pursue your vengeance to the blood of my poor boy ! I will forgive you all the rest—all the distress you have wrought—all the yet greater misery with which you threaten us ; but do not be extreme with one who never can have offended you ! Believe, that if your ears are shut against the cry of a despairing mother, those which are open to the complaint of all who sorrow will hear my petition and your answer ! '

The agony of mind and of voice with which Lady Peveril uttered these words seemed to thrill through all present, though most of them were but too much inured to such scenes. Every one was silent, when, ceasing to speak, she fixed on Bridgenorth her eyes, glistening with tears, with the eager anxiety of one whose life or death seemed to depend upon the answer to be returned. Even Bridgenorth's inflexibility seemed to be shaken ; and his voice was tremulous, as he answered, ' Madam, I would to God I had the present means of relieving your great distress, otherwise than by recommending to you a reliance upon Providence ; and that you take heed to your spirit, that it murmur not under this crook in your lot. For me, I am but as a rod in the hand of the strong man, which smites not of itself, but because it is wielded by the arm of him who holds the same.'

' Even as I and my black rod are guided by the Commons of England,' said Master Topham, who seemed marvellously pleased with the illustration.

Julian now thought it time to say something in his own behalf ; and he endeavoured to temper it with as much composure as it was possible for him to assume. ' Master Bridgenorth,' he said, ' I neither dispute your authority nor this gentleman's warrant '——

' You do not ? ' said Topham. ' Oh, ho, master youngster, I thought we should bring you to your senses presently ! '

' Then, if you so will it, Master Topham,' said Bridgenorth, ' thus it shall be. You shall set out with early day, taking with you, towards London, the persons of Sir Geoffrey and

Lady Peveril ; and that they may travel according to their quality, you will allow them their coach, sufficiently guarded.'

'I will travel with them myself,' said Topham ; 'for these rough Derbyshire roads are no easy riding ; and my very eyes are weary with looking on these bleak hills. In the coach I can sleep as sound as if I were in the House and Master Bodderbrains on his legs.'

'It will become you so to take your ease, Master Topham,' answered Bridgenorth. 'For this youth, I will take him under my charge, and bring him up myself.'

'I may not be answerable for that, worthy Master Bridgenorth,' said Topham, 'since he comes within the warrant of the House.'

'Nay, but,' said Bridgenorth, 'he is only under custody for an assault, with the purpose of a rescue ; and I counsel you against meddling with him, unless you have stronger guard. Sir Geoffrey is now old and broken, but this young fellow is in the flower of his youth, and hath at his beck all the debauched young Cavaliers of the neighbourhood— You will scarce cross the country without a rescue.'

Topham eyed Julian wistfully, as a spider may be supposed to look upon a stray wasp which has got into his web, and which he longs to secure, though he fears the consequences of attempting him.

Julian himself replied, 'I know not if this separation be well or ill meant on your part, Master Bridgenorth ; but on mine, I am only desirous to share the fate of my parents ; and therefore I will give my word of honour to attempt neither rescue nor escape, on condition you do not separate me from them.'

'Do not say so, Julian,' said his mother ; 'abide with Master Bridgenorth—my mind tells me he cannot mean so ill by us as his rough conduct would now lead us to infer.'

'And I,' said Sir Geoffrey, 'know, that between the doors of my father's house and the gates of hell there steps not such a villain on the ground ! And if I wish my hands ever to be unbound again, it is because I hope for one downright blow at a grey head that has hatched more treason than the whole Long Parliament.'

'Away with thee,' said the zealous officer ; 'is Parliament a word for so foul a mouth as thine ?—Gentlemen,' he added, turning to Everett and Dangerfield, ' you will bear witness to this.'

' To his having reviled the House of Commons—by G—d, that I will ! ' said Dangerfield ; ' I will take it on my damnation.'

' And verily,' said Everett, ' as he spoke of Parliament generally, he hath contemned the House of Lords also.'

' Why, ye poor insignificant wretches,' said Sir Geoffrey, ' whose very life is a lie—and whose bread is perjury— would you pervert my innocent words almost as soon as they have quitted my lips ?   I tell you the country is well weary of you ; and should Englishmen come to their senses, the jail, the pillory, the whipping-post, and the gibbet will be too good preferment for such base blood-suckers.—And now, Master Bridgenorth, you and they may do your worst ; for I will not open my mouth to utter a single word while I am in the company of such knaves.'

' Perhaps, Sir Geoffrey,' answered Bridgenorth, ' you would better have consulted your own safety in adopting that resolution a little sooner—the tongue is a little member, but it causes much strife.—You, Master Julian, will please to follow me, and without remonstrance or resistance ; for you must be aware that I have the means of compelling.'

Julian was, indeed, but too sensible that he had no other course but that of submission to superior force ; but ere he left the apartment he kneeled down to receive his father's blessing, which the old man bestowed not without a tear in his eye, and in the emphatic words, ' God bless thee, my boy ; and keep thee good and true to Church and king, whatever wind shall bring foul weather ! '

His mother was only able to pass her hand over his head, and to implore him, in a low tone of voice, not to be rash or violent in any attempt to render them assistance.   ' We are innocent,' she said, ' my son—we are innocent—and we are in God's hands.   Be the thought our best comfort and protection.'

Bridgenorth now signed to Julian to follow him, which he did, accompanied, or rather conducted, by the two guards who had first disarmed him.   When they had passed from the apartment, and were at the door of the outward hall, Bridgenorth asked Julian whether he should consider him

as under parole ; in which case, he said, he would dispense
with all other security but his own promise.

Peveril, who could not help hoping somewhat from the
favourable and unresentful manner in which he was treated
by one whose life he had so recently attempted, replied,
without hesitation, that he would give his parole for twenty-
four hours, neither to attempt to escape by force nor by
flight.

' It is wisely said,' replied Bridgenorth ; ' for though you
might cause bloodshed, be assured that your utmost efforts
could do no service to your parents.—Horses there—horses
to the courtyard ! '

The trampling of horses was soon heard ; and in obedience
to Bridgenorth's signal, and in compliance with his promise,
Julian mounted one which was presented to him, and
prepared to leave the house of his fathers, in which his
parents were now prisoners, and to go, he knew not whither,
under the custody of one known to be the ancient enemy
of his family. He was rather surprised at observing that
Bridgenorth and he were about to travel without any other
attendants.

When they were mounted, and as they rode slowly towards
the outer gate of the courtyard, Bridgenorth said to him,
' It is not every one who would thus unreservedly commit
his safety by travelling at night, and unaided, with the
hot-brained youth who so lately attempted his life.'

' Master Bridgenorth,' said Julian, ' I might tell you
truly, that I knew you not at the time when I directed my
weapon against you ; but I must also add, that the cause in
which I used it might have rendered me, even had I known
you, a slight respecter of your person. At present, I do
know you ; and have neither malice against your person
nor the liberty of a parent to fight for. Besides, you have
my word ; and when was a Peveril known to break it ? '

' Aye,' replied his companion, ' a Peveril—a Peveril of
the Peak !—a name which has long sounded like a war-
trumpet in the land ; but which has now perhaps sounded
its last loud note. Look back, young man, on the darksome
turrets of your father's house, which uplift themselves as
proudly on the brow of the hill as their owners raised themselves above the sons of their people. Think upon your

father, a captive—yourself in some sort a fugitive—your
light quenched—your glory abased—your estate wrecked
and impoverished. Think that Providence has subjected
the destinies of the race of Peveril to one whom, in their
aristocratic pride, they held as a plebeian upstart. Think
of this ; and when you again boast of your ancestry,
remember that he who raiseth the lowly can also abase the
high in heart.'

Julian did indeed gaze for an instant, with a swelling
heart, upon the dimly seen turrets of his paternal mansion,
on which poured the moonlight, mixed with long shadows
of the towers and trees. But while he sadly acknowledged
the truth of Bridgenorth's observation, he felt indignant at
his ill-timed triumph. ' If fortune had followed worth,' he
said, ' the Castle of Martindale, and the name of Peveril,
had afforded no room for their enemy's vainglorious boast.
But those who have stood high on Fortune's wheel must
abide by the consequence of its revolutions. This much
I will at least say for my father's house, that it has not
stood unhonoured ; nor will it fall—if it is to fall—un-
lamented. Forbear, then, if you are indeed the Christian
you call yourself, to exult in the misfortunes of others, or
to confide in your own prosperity. If the light of our house
be now quenched, God can rekindle it in his own good time.'

Peveril broke off in extreme surprise ; for as he spake the
last words the bright red beams of the family beacon began
again to glimmer from its wonted watch-tower, checkering
the pale moonbeam with a ruddier glow. Bridgenorth
also gazed on this unexpected illumination with surprise,
and not, as it seemed, without disquietude. ' Young
man,' he resumed, ' it can scarcely be but that Heaven
intends to work great things by your hand, so singularly
has that augury followed on your words.'

So saying, he put his horse once more in motion ; and
looking back, from time to time, as if to assure himself that
the beacon of the castle was actually rekindled, he led
the way through the well-known paths and alleys to his
own house of Moultrassie, followed by Peveril, who although
sensible that the light might be altogether accidental, could
not but receive as a good omen an event so intimately
connected with the traditions and usages of his family.

They alighted at the hall-door, which was hastily opened by a female; and while the deep tone of Bridgenorth called on the groom to take their horses, the well-known voice of his daughter Alice was heard to exclaim in thanksgiving to God, who had restored her father in safety.

CHAPTER XXIV

We meet, as men see phantoms in a dream,
Which glide, and sigh, and sign, and move their lips,
But make no sound; or, if they utter voice,
'Tis but a low and undistinguish'd moaning,
Which has nor word nor sense of utter'd sound.
The Chieftain.

WE said, at the conclusion of the last chapter, that a female form appeared at the door of Moultrassie Hall; and that the well-known accents of Alice Bridgenorth were heard to hail the return of her father from what she naturally dreaded as a perilous visit to the Castle of Martindale.

Julian, who followed his conductor with a throbbing heart into the lighted hall, was therefore prepared to see her whom he best loved, with her arms thrown around her father. The instant she had quitted his paternal embrace she was aware of the unexpected guest who had returned in his company. A deep blush, rapidly succeeded by a deadly paleness, and again by a slighter suffusion, showed plainly to her lover that his sudden appearance was anything but indifferent to her. He bowed profoundly—a courtesy which she returned with equal formality, but did not venture to approach more nearly, feeling at once the delicacy of his own situation and of hers.

Major Bridgenorth turned his cold, fixed, grey, melancholy glance first on the one of them and then on the other. 'Some,' he said gravely, 'would, in my case, have avoided this meeting; but I have confidence in you both, although you are young, and beset with the snares incidental to your age. There are those within who should not know that ye have been acquainted. Wherefore, be wise, and be as strangers to each other.'

Julian and Alice exchanged glances as her father turned
from them, and, lifting a lamp which stood in the entrance-
hall, led the way to the interior apartment. There was
little of consolation in this exchange of looks ; for the sadness
of Alice's glance was mingled with fear, and that of Julian
clouded by an anxious sense of doubt. The look also was
but momentary ; for Alice, springing to her father, took
the light out of his hand, and, stepping before him, acted as
the usher of both into the large oaken parlour, which has been
already mentioned as the apartment in which Bridgenorth
had spent the hours of dejection which followed the death
of his consort and family. It was now lighted up as for
the reception of company ; and five or six persons sat in
it, in the plain, black, stiff dress which was affected by
the formal Puritans of the time, in evidence of their
contempt of the manners of the luxurious Court of
Charles II ; amongst whom excess of extravagance in
apparel, like excess of every other kind, was highly
fashionable.

Julian at first glanced his eyes but slightly along the
range of grave and severe faces which composed this society
—men sincere, perhaps, in their pretensions to a superior
purity of conduct and morals, but in whom that high praise
was somewhat chastened by an affected austerity in dress
and manners allied to those Pharisees of old, who made
broad their phylacteries, and would be seen of man to fast,
and to discharge with rigid punctuality the observances of
the law. Their dress was almost uniformly a black cloak
and doublet, cut straight and close, and undecorated with
lace or embroidery of any kind, black Flemish breeches and
hose, square-toed shoes, with large roses made of serge
ribbon. Two or three had large, loose boots of calf-leather,
and almost every one was begirt with a long rapier, which
was suspended by leathern thongs to a plain belt of buff
or of black leather. One or two of the elder guests, whose
hair had been thinned by time, had their heads covered
with a skull-cap of black silk or velvet, which, being drawn
down betwixt the ears and the skull, and permitting no
hair to escape, occasioned the former to project in the
ungraceful manner which may be remarked in old pictures,
and which procured for the Puritans the term of prickeared

Roundheads ', so unceremoniously applied to them by their contemporaries.

These worthies were ranged against the wall, each in his ancient high-backed, long-legged chair ; neither looking towards nor apparently discoursing with each other ; but plunged in their own reflections, or awaiting, like an assembly of Quakers, the quickening power of divine inspiration.

Major Bridgenorth glided along this formal society with noiseless step, and a composed severity of manner resembling their own. He paused before each in succession, and apparently communicated, as he passed, the transactions of the evening, and the circumstances under which the heir of Martindale Castle was now a guest at Moultrassie Hall. Each seemed to stir at his brief detail, like a range of statues in an enchanted hall, starting into something like life as a talisman is applied to them successively. Most of them, as they heard the narrative of their host, cast upon Julian a look of curiosity, blended with haughty scorn and the consciousness of spiritual superiority ; though, in one or two instances, the milder influences of compassion were sufficiently visible. Peveril would have undergone this gauntlet of eyes with more impatience had not his own been for the time engaged in following the motions of Alice, who glided through the apartment ; and only speaking very briefly, and in whispers, to one or two of the company who addressed her, took her place beside a treble-hooded old lady, the only female of the party, and addressed herself to her in such earnest conversation as might dispense with her raising her head or looking at any others in the company.

Her father put a question to which she was obliged to return an answer—' Where was Mistress Debbitch ? '

' She had gone out,' Alice replied, ' early after sunset, to visit some old acquaintances in the neighbourhood, and she was not yet returned.'

Major Bridgenorth made a gesture indicative of displeasure ; and, not content with that, expressed his determined resolution that Dame Deborah should no longer remain a member of his family. ' I will have those,' he said aloud, and without regarding the presence of his guests, ' and those only, around me, who know how to keep within the

sober and modest bounds of a Christian family. Who
pretends to more freedom must go out from among us, as
not being of us.'

A deep and emphatic humming noise, which was at that
time the mode in which the Puritans signified their applause,
as well of the doctrines expressed by a favourite divine
in the pulpit as of those delivered in private society, ratified
the approbation of the assessors, and seemed to secure
the dismission of the unfortunate governante, who stood
thus detected of having strayed out of bounds. Even
Peveril, although he had reaped considerable advantages,
in his early acquaintance with Alice, from the mercenary and
gossiping disposition of her governess, could not hear of her
dismissal without approbation, so much was he desirous
that, in the hour of difficulty, which might soon approach,
Alice might have the benefit of countenance and advice
from one of her own sex of better manners, and less suspicious probity, than Mistress Debbitch.

Almost immediately after this communication had taken
place, a servant in mourning showed his thin, pinched, and
wrinkled visage in the apartment, announcing, with a voice
more like a passing bell than the herald of a banquet, that
refreshments were provided in an adjoining apartment.
Gravely leading the way, with his daughter on one side and
the puritanical female whom we have distinguished on
the other, Bridgenorth himself ushered his company, who
followed, with little attention to order or ceremony, into the
eating-room, where a substantial supper was provided.

In this manner, Peveril, although entitled according to
ordinary ceremonial to some degree of precedence—a matter
at that time considered of much importance, although now
little regarded—was left among the last of those who quitted
the parlour ; and might indeed have brought up the rear
of all, had not one of the company who was himself late
in the retreat bowed and resigned to Julian the rank in the
company which had been usurped by others.

This act of politeness naturally induced Julian to examine
the features of the person who had offered him this civility ;
and he started to observe, under the pinched velvet cap,
and above the short band-strings, the countenance of
Ganlesse, as he called himself—his companion on the pre-

ceding evening. He looked again and again, especially
when all were placed at the supper board, and when,
consequently, he had frequent opportunities of observing
this person fixedly, without any breach of good manners.
At first he wavered in his belief, and was much inclined to
doubt the reality of his recollection ; for the difference of
dress was such as to effect a considerable change of appearance ; and the countenance itself, far from exhibiting
anything marked or memorable, was one of those ordinary
visages which we see almost without remarking them, and
which leave our memory so soon as the object is withdrawn
from our eyes. But the impression upon his mind returned,
and became stronger, until it induced him to watch with
peculiar attention the manners of the individual who had
thus attracted his notice.

During the time of a very prolonged grace before meat,
which was delivered by one of the company—who, from
his Geneva band and serge doublet, presided, as Julian
supposed, over some dissenting congregation—he noticed
that this man kept the same demure and severe cast of
countenance usually affected by the Puritans, and which
rather caricatured the reverence unquestionably due upon
such occasions.   His eyes were turned upward, and his huge
penthouse hat, with a high crown and broad brim, held in
both hands before him, rose and fell with the cadences of
the speaker's voice ; thus marking time, as it were, to the
periods of the benediction. Yet when the slight bustle
took place which attends the adjusting of chairs, &c., as
men sit down to table, Julian's eye encountered that of the
stranger ; and as their looks met there glanced from those
of the latter an expression of satirical humour and scorn
which seemed to intimate internal ridicule of the gravity of
his present demeanour.

Julian again sought to fix his eye, in order to ascertain
that he had not mistaken the tendency of this transient
expression, but the stranger did not allow him another
opportunity. He might have been discovered by the tone
of his voice ; but the individual in question spoke little, and
in whispers, which was indeed the fashion of the whole
company, whose demeanour at table resembled that of
mourners at a funeral feast.

The entertainment itself was coarse, though plentiful ; and must, according to Julian's opinion, be distasteful to one so exquisitely skilled in good cheer, and so capable of enjoying, critically and scientifically, the genial preparations of his companion, Smith, as Ganlesse had shown himself on the preceding evening. Accordingly, upon close observation, he remarked that the food which he took upon his plate remained there unconsumed ; and that his actual supper consisted only of a crust of bread, with a glass of wine.

The repast was hurried over with the haste of those who think it shame, if not sin, to make mere animal enjoyments the means of consuming time or of receiving pleasure ; and when men wiped their mouths and moustaches, Julian remarked that the object of his curiosity used a handkerchief of the finest cambric—an article rather inconsistent with the exterior plainness, not to say coarseness, of his appearance. He used also several of the more minute refinements then only observed at tables of the higher rank ; and Julian thought he could discern, at every turn, something of courtly manners and gestures under the precise and rustic simplicity of the character which he had assumed.[1]

But if this were indeed that same Ganlesse with whom Julian had met on the preceding evening, and who had boasted the facility with which he could assume any character which he pleased to represent for the time, what could be the purpose of his present disguise ? He was, if his own words could be credited, a person of some importance, who dared to defy the danger of those officers and informers before whom all ranks at that time trembled ; nor was he likely, as Julian conceived, without some strong purpose, to subject himself to such a masquerade as the present, which could not be otherwise than irksome to one whose conversation proclaimed him of light life and free opinions. Was his appearance here for good or for evil ? Did it respect his father's house, or his own person, or the family of Bridgenorth ? Was the real character of Ganlesse known to the master of the house, inflexible as he was

---

[1] A Scottish gentleman *in hiding*, as it was emphatically termed, for some concern in a Jacobite insurrection or plot, was discovered among a number of ordinary persons by the use of his toothpick.

in all which concerned morals as well as religion ?   If not,
might not the machinations of a brain so subtile affect the
peace and happiness of Alice Bridgenorth ?

These were questions which no reflection could enable
Peveril to answer. His eyes glanced from Alice to the
stranger ; and new fears, and undefined suspicions, in which
the safety of that beloved and lovely girl was implicated,
mingled with the deep anxiety which already occupied his
mind on account of his father and his father's house.

He was in this tumult of mind when, after a thanksgiving
as long as the grace, the company arose from table, and
were instantly summoned to the exercise of family worship.
A train of domestics, grave, sad, and melancholy as their
superiors, glided in to assist at this act of devotion, and
ranged themselves at the lower end of the apartment.
Most of these men were armed with long tucks, as the
straight stabbing swords, much used by Cromwell's soldiery,
were then called.   Several had large pistols also ; and the
corslets or cuirasses of some were heard to clank, as they
seated themselves to partake in this act of devotion.   The
ministry of him whom Julian had supposed a preacher was
not used on this occasion.   Major Bridgenorth himself read
and expounded a chapter of Scripture with much strength
and manliness of expression, although so as not to escape
the charge of fanaticism.   The nineteenth chapter of
Jeremiah was the portion of Scripture which he selected ;
in which, under the type of breaking a potter's vessel, the
prophet presages the desolation of the Jews.   The lecturer
was not naturally eloquent ; but a strong, deep, and sincere
conviction of the truth of what he said supplied him with
language of energy and fire, as he drew a parallel between
the abominations of the worship of Baal and the corruptions
of the Church of Rome—so favourite a topic with the
Puritans of that period ; and denounced against the
Catholics, and those who favoured them, that hissing and
desolation which the prophet directed against the city of
Jerusalem.   His hearers made a yet closer application than
the lecturer himself suggested ; and many a dark proud
eye intimated, by a glance on Julian, that on his father's
house were already, in some part, realized those dreadful
maledictions.

The lecture finished, Bridgenorth summoned them to unite with him in prayer ; and on a slight change of arrangements amongst the company, which took place as they were about to kneel down, Julian found his place next to the single-minded and beautiful object of his affection, as she knelt, in her loveliness, to adore her Creator. A short time was permitted for mental devotion ; during which Peveril could hear her half-breathed petition for the promised blessings of peace on earth and goodwill towards the children of men.

The prayer which ensued was in a different tone. It was poured forth by the same person who had officiated as chaplain at the table ; and was in the tone of a Boanerges, or Son of Thunder—a denouncer of crimes—an invoker of judgements—almost a prophet of evil and of destruction. The testimonies and the sins of the day were not forgotten —the mysterious murder of Sir Edmondsbury Godfrey was insisted upon—and thanks and praise were offered, that the very night on which they were assembled had not seen another offering of a Protestant magistrate to the bloodthirsty fury of the revengeful Catholics.

Never had Julian found it more difficult, during an act of devotion, to maintain his mind in a frame befitting the posture and the occasion ; and when he heard the speaker return thanks for the downfall and devastation of his family he was strongly tempted to have started upon his feet and charged him with offering a tribute, stained with falsehood and calumny, at the throne of truth itself. He resisted, however, an impulse which it would have been insanity to have yielded to, and his patience was not without its reward ; for when his fair neighbour arose from her knees, the lengthened and prolonged prayer being at last concluded, he observed that her eyes were streaming with tears ; and one glance with which she looked at him in that moment showed more of affectionate interest for him in his fallen fortunes and precarious condition than he had been able to obtain from her when his worldly estate seemed so much the more exalted of the two.

Cheered and fortified with the conviction that one bosom in the company, and that in which he most eagerly longed to secure an interest, sympathized with his distress, he felt strong to endure whatever was to follow, and shrank not from the stern still smile with which, one by one, the meeting regarded him, as, gliding to their several places of repose, they indulged themselves at parting with a look of triumph on one whom they considered as their captive enemy.

Alice also passed by her lover, her eyes fixed on the ground, and answered his low obeisance without raising them. The room was now empty, but for Bridgenorth and his guest, or prisoner ; for it is difficult to say in which capacity Peveril ought to regard himself. He took an old brazen lamp from the table, and, leading the way, said at the same time, ' I must be the uncourtly chamberlain who am to usher you to a place of repose, more rude, perhaps, than you have been accustomed to occupy.'

Julian followed him, in silence, up an old-fashioned winding staircase, within a turret.   At the landing-place on the top was a small apartment, where an ordinary pallet bed, two chairs, and a small stone table were the only furniture. ' Your bed,' continued Bridgenorth, as if desirous to prolong their interview, ' is not of the softest ; but innocence sleeps as sound upon straw as on down.'

' Sorrow, Major Bridgenorth, finds little rest on either,' replied Julian.   ' Tell me, for you seem to await some question from me, what is to be the fate of my parents, and why you separate me from them ? '

Bridgenorth, for answer, indicated with his finger the mark which his countenance still showed from the explosion of Julian's pistol.

' That,' replied Julian, ' is not the real cause of your proceedings against me.   It cannot be, that you, who have been a soldier, and are a man, can be surprised or displeased by my interference in the defence of my father. Above all, you cannot, and I must needs say you do not, believe that I would have raised my hand against you personally, had there been a moment's time for recognition.'

' I may grant all this,' said Bridgenorth ; ' but what the better are you for my good opinion, or for the ease with which I can forgive you the injury which you aimed at me ? You are in my custody as a magistrate, accused of abetting the foul, bloody, and heathenish plot for the establishment of Popery, the murder of the king, and the general massacre of all true Protestants.'

'And on what grounds, either of fact or suspicion, dare any one accuse me of such a crime?' said Julian. 'I have hardly heard of the plot, save by the mouth of common rumour, which, while it speaks of nothing else, takes care to say nothing distinctly even on that subject.'

'It may be enough for me to tell you,' replied Bridgenorth, 'and perhaps it is a word too much—that you are a discovered intriguer—a spied spy—who carries tokens and messages betwixt the Popish Countess of Derby and the Catholic party in London. You have not conducted your matters with such discretion but that this is well known, and can be sufficiently proved. To this charge, which you are well aware you cannot deny, these men, Everett and Dangerfield, are not unwilling to add, from the recollection of your face, other passages, which will certainly cost you your life when you come before a Protestant jury.'

'They lie like villains,' said Peveril, 'who hold me accessory to any plot either against the king, the nation, or the state of religion; and for the countess, her loyalty has been too long and too highly proved to permit her being implicated in such injurious suspicions.'

'What she has already done,' said Bridgenorth, his face darkening as he spoke, 'against the faithful champions of pure religion, hath sufficiently shown of what she is capable. She hath betaken herself to her rock, and sits, as she thinks, in security, like the eagle reposing after his bloody banquet. But the arrow of the fowler may yet reach her—the shaft is whetted—the bow is bended—and it will be soon seen whether Amalek or Israel shall prevail. But for thee, Julian Peveril—why should I conceal it from thee?—my heart yearns for thee as a woman's for her first-born. To thee I will give, at the expense of my own reputation— perhaps at the risk of personal suspicion—for who, in these days of doubt, shall be exempted from it?—to thee, I say, I will give means of escape which else were impossible to thee. The staircase of this turret descends to the gardens —the postern-gate is unlatched—on the right hand lie the stables, where you will find your own horse—take it, and make for Liverpool—I will give you credit with a friend

under the name of Simon Simonson, one persecuted by the
prelates ; and he will expedite your passage from the
kingdom.'

'Major Bridgenorth,' said Julian, ' I will not deceive you.
Were I to accept your offer of freedom, it would be to
attend to a higher call than that of mere self-preservation.
My father is in danger—my mother in sorrow—the voices
of religion and nature call me to their side. I am their
only child—their only hope—I will aid them, or perish
with them ! '

' Thou art mad,' said Bridgenorth—' aid them thou canst
not—perish with them thou well mayst, and even accelerate
their ruin ; for, in addition to the charges with which thy
unhappy father is loaded, it would be no slight aggravation,
that while he meditated arming and calling together the
Catholics and High Churchmen of Cheshire and Derbyshire,
his son should prove to be the confidential agent of the
Countess of Derby, who aided her in making good her
stronghold against the Protestant commissioners, and was
dispatched by her to open secret communication with the
Popish interest in London.'

' You have twice stated me as such an agent,' said Peveril,
resolved that his silence should not be construed into an
admission of the charge, though he felt that it was in some
degree well founded—' What reason have you for such an
allegation ? '

' Will it suffice for a proof of my intimate acquaintance
with your mystery,' replied Bridgenorth, ' if I should repeat
to you the last words which the countess used to you when
you left the castle of that Amalekitish woman ? Thus
she spoke : " I am now a forlorn widow," she said, " whom
sorrow has made selfish." '

Peveril started, for these were the very words the countess
had used ; but he instantly recovered himself, and replied,
' Be your information of what nature it will, I deny, and
I defy it, so far as it attaches aught like guilt to me. There
lives not a man more innocent of a disloyal thought, or of
a traitorous purpose. What I say for myself, I will, to the
best of my knowledge, say and maintain on account of the
noble countess to whom I am indebted for nurture.'

' Perish, then, in thy obstinacy ! ' said Bridgenorth ; and

turning hastily from him, he left the room, and Julian heard him hasten down the narrow staircase, as if distrusting his own resolution.

With a heavy heart, yet with that confidence in an over-ruling Providence which never forsakes a good and brave man, Peveril betook himself to his lowly place of repose.

CHAPTER XXV

The course of human life is changeful still,
As is the fickle wind and wandering rill ;
Or, like the light dance which the wild breeze weaves
Amidst the fated race of fallen leaves ;
Which now its breath bears down, now tosses high,
Beats to the earth, or wafts to middle sky,
Such, and so varied, the precarious play,
Of fate with man, frail tenant of a day !
                              ANONYMOUS.

WHILST, overcome with fatigue, and worn out by anxiety, Julian Peveril slumbered as a prisoner in the house of his hereditary enemy, Fortune was preparing his release by one of those sudden frolics with which she loves to confound the calculations and expectances of humanity ; and as she fixes on strange agents for such purposes, she condescended to employ, on the present occasion, no less a personage than Mistress Deborah Debbitch.

Instigated, doubtless, by the pristine reminiscences of former times, no sooner had that most prudent and con-siderate dame found herself in the vicinity of the scenes of her earlier days, than she bethought herself of a visit to the ancient housekeeper of Martindale Castle, Dame Ellesmere by name, who, long retired from active service, resided at the keeper's lodge in the west thicket, with her nephew, Lance Outram, subsisting upon the savings of her better days, and on a small pension allowed by Sir Geoffrey to her age and faithful services.

Now Dame Ellesmere and Mistress Deborah had not by any means been formerly on so friendly a footing as this haste to visit her might be supposed to intimate.   But years had taught Deborah to forget and forgive ; or perhaps she had no special objection, under cover of a visit to Dame Ellesmere, to take the chance of seeing what changes time had made on her old admirer the keeper. Both inhabitants were in the cottage, when, after having seen her master set forth on his expedition to the castle, Mistress Debbitch, dressed in her very best gown, footed it through gutter, and over stile, and by pathway green, to knock at their door, and to lift the latch at the hospitable invitation which bade her come in.

Dame Ellesmere's eyes were so often dim, that, even with the aid of spectacles, she failed to recognize, in the portly and mature personage who entered their cottage, the tight well-made lass, who, presuming on her good looks and flippant tongue, had so often provoked her by insubordination ; and her former lover, the redoubted Lance, not being conscious that ale had given rotundity to his own figure, which was formerly so slight and active, and that brandy had transferred to his nose the colour which had once occupied his cheeks, was unable to discover that Deborah's French cap, composed of sarsenet and Brussels lace, shaded the features which had so often procured him a rebuke from Dr. Dummerar, for suffering his eyes, during the time of prayers, to wander to the maid-servants' bench.

In brief, the blushing visitor was compelled to make herself known ; and when known, was received by aunt and nephew with the most sincere cordiality.

The home-brewed was produced ; and, in lieu of more vulgar food, a few slices of venison presently hissed in the frying-pan, giving strong room for inference that Lance Outram, in his capacity of keeper, neglected not his own cottage when he supplied the larder at the castle. A modest sip of the excellent Derbyshire ale, and a taste of the highly-seasoned hash, soon placed Deborah entirely at home with her old acquaintance.

Having put all necessary questions, and received all suitable answers, respecting the state of the neighbourhood, and such of her own friends as continued to reside there, the conversation began rather to flag, until Deborah found the art of again renewing its interest by communicating to her friends the dismal intelligence that they must soon

look for deadly bad news from the castle ; for that her
present master, Major Bridgenorth, had been summoned by
some great people from London to assist in taking her old
master, Sir Geoffrey ; and that all Master Bridgenorth's
servants, and several other persons, whom she named
friends and adherents of the same interest, had assembled
a force to surprise the castle ; and that as Sir Geoffrey was
now so old, and gouty withal, it could not be expected he
should make the defence he was wont ; and then he was
known to be so stout-hearted, that it was not to be supposed
that he would yield up without stroke of sword ; and then
if he was killed, as he was like to be, amongst them that
liked never a bone of his body, and now had him at their
mercy, why, in that case, she, Dame Deborah, would look
upon Lady Peveril as little better than a dead woman ;
and undoubtedly there would be a general mourning through
all that country, where they had such great kin ; and silks
were likely to rise on it, as Master Lutestring, the mercer
of Chesterfield, was like to feel in his purse bottom.   But
for her part, let matters wag how they would, an if Master
Julian Peveril was to come to his own, she could give as
near a guess as e'er another who was likely to be lady at
Martindale.

The text of this lecture, or, in other words, the fact that
Bridgenorth was gone with a party to attack Sir Geoffrey
Peveril in his own castle of Martindale, sounded so stun-
ningly strange in the ears of those old retainers of his family,
that they had no power either to attend to Mistress Deborah's
inferences, or to interrupt the velocity of speech with which
she poured them forth.   And when at length she made
a breathless pause, all that poor Dame Ellesmere could
reply was the emphatic question, ' Bridgenorth brave
Peveril of the Peak !   Is the woman mad ? '

' Come, come, dame,' said Deborah, ' woman me no more
than I woman you.   I have not been called mistress at
the head of the table for so many years to be womaned
here by you.   And for the news, it is as true as that you are
sitting there in a white hood, who will wear a black one
ere long.'

' Lance Outram,' said the old woman, ' make out, if thou
be'st a man, and listen about if aught stirs up at the castle.'

'If there should,' said Outram, ' I am even too long here;' and he caught up his crossbow and one or two arrows, and rushed out of the cottage.

'Welladay!' said Mistress Deborah, ' see if my news have not frightened away Lance Outram too, whom they used to say nothing could start. But do not take on so, dame ; for I dare say if the castle and the lands pass to my new master, Major Bridgenorth, as it is like they will— for I have heard that he has powerful debts over the estate —you shall have my good word with him, and I promise you he is no bad man ; something precise about preaching and praying, and about the dress which one should wear, which, I must own, beseems not a gentleman, as, to be sure, every woman knows best what becomes her. But for you, dame, that wear a prayer-book at your girdle, with your housewife-case, and never change the fashion of your white hood, I dare say he will not grudge you the little matter you need, and are not able to win.'

'Out, sordid jade ! ' exclaimed Dame Ellesmere, her very flesh quivering betwixt apprehension and anger, ' and hold your peace this instant, or I will find those that shall flay the very hide from thee with dog-whips. Hast thou ate thy noble master's bread, not only to betray his trust, and fly from his service, but wouldst thou come here, like an ill-omened bird as thou art, to triumph over his downfall ? '

'Nay, dame,' said Deborah, over whom the violence of the old woman had obtained a certain predominance ; ' it is not I that say it—only the warrant of the Parliament folks.'

'I thought we had done with their warrants ever since the blessed twenty-ninth of May,' said the old housekeeper of Martindale Castle ; ' but this I tell thee, sweetheart, that I have seen such warrants crammed, at the sword's point, down the throats of them that brought them ; and so shall this be, if there is one true man left to drink of the Dove.'

As she spoke, Lance Outram re-entered the cottage ' Naunt,' he said in dismay, ' I doubt it is true what she says. The beacon-tower is as black as my belt. No Pole-star of Peveril. What does that betoken ? '

'Death, ruin, and captivity,' exclaimed old Ellesmere.

'Make for the castle, thou knave. Thrust in thy great body. Strike for the house that bred thee and fed thee; and if thou art buried under the ruins, thou diest a man's death.'

'Nay, naunt, I shall not be slack,' answered Outram. 'But here come folks that I warrant can tell us more on 't.'

One or two of the female servants who had fled from the castle during the alarm now rushed in with various reports of the case; but all agreeing that a body of armed men were in possession of the castle, and that Major Bridgenorth had taken young Master Julian prisoner, and conveyed him down to Moultrassie Hall, with his feet tied under the belly of the nag—a shameful sight to be seen—and he so well born and so handsome.

Lance scratched his head; and though feeling the duty incumbent upon him as a faithful servant, which was indeed specially dinned into him by the cries and exclamations of his aunt, he seemed not a little dubious how to conduct himself. 'I would to God, naunt,' he said at last, 'that old Whitaker were alive now, with his long stories about Marston Moor and Edgehill, that made us all yawn our jaws off their hinges, in spite of broiled rashers and double beer! When a man is missed, he is moaned, as they say; and I would rather than a broad piece he had been here to have sorted this matter, for it is clean out of my way as a woodsman, that have no skill of war. But dang it, if old Sir Geoffrey go to the wall without a knock for it! Here you, Nell' (speaking to one of the fugitive maidens from the castle)—'but, no—you have not the heart of a cat, and are afraid of your own shadow by moonlight—But, Cis, you are a stout-hearted wench, and know a buck from a bullfinch. Hark thee, Cis, as you would wish to be married, get up to the castle again, and get thee in—thou best knowest where —for thou hast oft gotten out of postern to a dance or junketing, to my knowledge—Get thee back to the castle, as ye hope to be married—See my lady—they cannot hinder thee of that—my lady has a head worth twenty of ours—If I am to gather force, light up the beacon for a signal; and spare not a tar barrel on 't. Thou mayst do it safe enough. I warrant the Roundheads busy with drink and plunder. And, hark thee, say to my lady I am gone down to the miners' houses at Bonadventure. The rogues were mutinying for their wages but yesterday ; they will be all ready for good or bad. Let her send orders down to me ; or do you come yourself, your legs are long enough.'

' Whether they are or not, Master Lance (and you know nothing of the matter), they shall do your errand to-night for love of the old knight and his lady.'

So Cisly Sellok, a kind of Derbyshire Camilla, who had won the smock at the foot-race at Ashbourne, sprang forward towards the castle with a speed which few could have equalled.

' There goes a mettled wench,' said Lance ; ' and now, naunt, give me the old broadsword—it is above the bed-head—and my wood-knife ; and I shall do well enough.'

' And what is to become of me ? ' bleated the unfortunate Mistress Deborah Debbitch.

' You must remain here with my aunt, Mistress Deb ; and, for old acquaintance' sake, she will take care no harm befalls you ; but take heed how you attempt to break bounds.'

So saying, and pondering in his own mind the task which he had undertaken, the hardy forester strode down the moonlight glade, scarcely hearing the blessings and cautions which Dame Ellesmere kept showering after him. His thoughts were not altogether warlike. ' What a tight ankle the jade hath !—she trips it like a doe in summer over the dew. Well, but here are the huts—Let us to this gear. Are ye all asleep, ye dammers, sinkers, and drift-drivers ? turn out, ye subterranean badgers. Here is your master, Sir Geoffrey, dead, for aught ye know or care. Do not you see the beacon is unlit, and you sit there like so many asses ? '

' Why,' answered one of the miners, who now began to come out of their huts,

> ' An he be dead,
> He will eat no more bread.'

' And you are like to eat none neither,' said Lance ; ' for the works will be presently stopped, and all of you turned off.'

' Well, and what of it, Master Lance ? As good play for naught as work for naught. Here is four weeks we have scarce seen the colour of Sir Geoffrey's coin ; and you ask us to care whether he be dead or in life ? For you that goes about trotting upon your horse, and doing for work what all men do for pleasure, it may be well enough ; but it is another matter to be leaving God's light, and burrowing all day and night in darkness like a toad in a hole—that 's not to be done for naught, I trow ; and if Sir Geoffrey is dead, his soul will suffer for 't ; and if he 's alive, we'll have him in the Barmoot Court.'

' Hark ye, gaffer,' said Lance, ' and take notice, my mates, all of you,' for a considerable number of these rude and subterranean people had now assembled to hear the discussion—' Has Sir Geoffrey, think you, ever put a penny in his pouch out of this same Bonadventure mine ? '

' I cannot say as I think he has,' answered old Ditchley, the party who maintained the controversy.

' Answer on your conscience, though it be but a leaden one, do not you know that he hath lost a good penny ? '

' Why, I believe he may,' said Gaffer Ditchley. ' What then !—lose to-day, win to-morrow—the miner must eat in the meantime.'

' True ; but what will you eat when Master Bridgenorth gets the land, that will not hear of a mine being wrought on his own ground ? Will he work on at dead loss, think ye ? ' demanded trusty Lance.

' Bridgenorth ?—he of Moultrassie Hall, that stopped the great Felicity Work, on which his father laid out, some say, ten thousand pounds, and never got in a penny ? Why, what has he to do with Sir Geoffrey's property down here at Bonadventure ? It was never his, I trow.'

' Nay, what do I know ? ' answered Lance, who saw the impression he had made. ' Law and debt will give him half Derbyshire, I think, unless you stand by old Sir Geoffrey.'

' But if Sir Geoffrey be dead,' said Ditchley cautiously, ' what good will our standing by do to him ? '

' I did not say he was dead, but only as bad as dead ; in the hands of the Roundheads—a prisoner up yonder, at his own castle,' said Lance ; ' and will have his head cut off, like the good Earl of Derby's, at Bolton-le-Moors.'

' Nay, then, comrades,' said Gaffer Ditchley, ' an it be as Master Lance says, I think we should bear a hand for

stout old Sir Geoffrey, against a low-born mean-spirited
fellow like Bridgenorth, who shut up a shaft had cost
thousands, without getting a penny profit on't. So hurra
for Sir Geoffrey, and down with the Rump ! But hold ye
a blink—hold' (and the waving of his hand stopped the
commencing cheer)—' Hark ye, Master Lance, it must be all
over, for the beacon is as black as night ; and you know
yourself that marks the lord's death.'

' It will kindle again in an instant,' said Lance ; internally
adding, ' I pray to God it may ! It will kindle in an instant
—lack of fuel, and the confusion of the family.'

' Aye, like enow, like enow,' said Ditchley ; ' but I winna
budge till I see it blazing.'

' Why then, there a-goes ! ' said Lance. ' Thank thee,
Cis—thank thee, my good wench.—Believe your own eyes,
my lads, if you will not believe me ; and now hurra for
Peveril of the Peak—the king and his friends—and down
with Rumps and Roundheads ! '

The sudden rekindling of the beacon had all the effect
which Lance could have desired upon the minds of his rude
and ignorant hearers, who, in their superstitious humour,
had strongly associated the polar star of Peveril with the
fortunes of the family. Once moved, according to the
national character of their countrymen, they soon became
enthusiastic ; and Lance found himself at the head of thirty
stout fellows and upwards, armed with their pickaxes, and
ready to execute whatever task he should impose on them.

Trusting to enter the castle by the postern, which had
served to accommodate himself and other domestics upon
an emergency, his only anxiety was to keep his march silent ;
and he earnestly recommended to his followers to reserve
their shouts for the moment of the attack. They had not
advanced far on their road to the castle, when Cisly Sellok
met them, so breathless with haste, that the poor girl was
obliged to throw herself into Master Lance's arms.

' Stand up, my mettled wench,' said he, giving her a sly
kiss at the same time, ' and let us know what is going on up
at the castle.'

' My lady bids you, as you would serve God and your
master, not to come up to the castle, which can but make
bloodshed ; for she says Sir Geoffrey is lawfully in hand,

and that he must bide the issue ; and that he is innocent of
what he is charged with, and is going up to speak for himself
before king and council, and she goes up with him.
And besides, they have found out the postern, the Roundhead rogues ; for two of them saw me when I went out of
door, and chased me ; but I showed them a fair pair of heels.'

' As ever dashed dew from the cowslip,' said Lance.
' But what the foul fiend is to be done ? for if they have
secured the postern, I know not how the dickens we can
get in.'

' All is fastened with bolt and staple, and guarded with
gun and pistol, at the castle,' quoth Cisly ; ' and so sharp
are they, that they nigh caught me coming with my lady's
message, as I told you. But my lady says, if you could
deliver her son, Master Julian, from Bridgenorth, that she
would hold it good service.'

' What ! ' said Lance, ' is young master at the castle ?
I taught him to shoot his first shaft. But how to get in ! '

' He was at the castle in the midst of the ruffle, but old
Bridgenorth has carried him down prisoner to the Hall,'
answered Cisly. ' There was never faith nor courtesy in an
old Puritan who never had pipe and tabor in his house since
it was built.'

' Or who stopped a promising mine,' said Ditchley, ' to
save a few thousand pounds, when he might have made
himself as rich as the Lord of Chatsworth, and fed a hundred
good fellows all the whilst.'

' Why, then,' said Lance, ' since you are all of a mind, we
will go draw the cover for the old badger ; and I promise
you that the Hall is not like one of your real houses of
quality, where the walls are as thick as whinstone dikes,
but foolish brickwork, that your pickaxes will work through
as if it were cheese. Huzza once more for Peveril of the
Peak ! down with Bridgenorth, and all upstart cuckoldy
Roundheads ! '

Having indulged the throats of his followers with one
buxom huzza, Lance commanded them to cease their
clamours, and proceeded to conduct them, by such paths as
seemed the least likely to be watched, to the courtyard of
Moultrassie Hall. On the road they were joined by several
stout yeomen farmers, either followers of the Peveril family,

or friends to the High-Church and Cavalier party ; most of whom, alarmed by the news which began to fly fast through the neighbourhood, were armed with sword and pistol.

Lance Outram halted his party at the distance, as he himself described it, of a flight-shot from the house, and advanced alone, and in silence, to reconnoitre ; and having previously commanded Ditchley and his subterranean allies to come to his assistance whenever he should whistle, he crept cautiously forward, and soon found that those whom he came to surprise, true to the discipline which had gained their party such decided superiority during the Civil War, had posted a sentinel, who paced through the courtyard, piously chanting a psalm-tune, while his arms, crossed on his bosom, supported a gun of formidable length.

' Now, a true soldier,' said Lance Outram to himself, ' would put a stop to thy snivelling ditty, by making a broad arrow quiver in your heart, and no great alarm given. But, dang it, I have not the right spirit for a soldier —I cannot fight a man till my blood 's up ; and for shooting him from behind a wall, it is cruelly like to stalking a deer. I'll e'en face him, and try what to make of him.'

With this doughty resolution, and taking no further care to conceal himself, he entered the courtyard boldly, and was making forward to the front door of the hall, as a matter of course. But the old Cromwellian, who was on guard, had not so learned his duty. ' Who goes there ? Stand, friend—stand ; or, verily, I will shoot thee to death ! ' were challenges which followed each other quick, the last being enforced by the levelling and presenting the said long-barrelled gun with which he was armed.

' Why, what a murrain ! ' answered Lance. ' Is it your fashion to go a-shooting at this time o' night ? Why, this is but a time for bat-fowling.'

' Nay, but hark thee, friend,' said the experienced sentinel, ' I am none of those who do this work negligently. Thou canst not snare me with thy crafty speech, though thou wouldst make it to sound simple in mine ear. Of a verity I will shoot, unless thou tell thy name and business.'

' Name ! ' said Lance ; ' why, what a dickens should it be but Robin Round—honest Robin of Redham ; and for business, an you must needs know, I come on a message

Y 2

from some Parliament man, up yonder at the castle, with
letters for worshipful Master Bridgenorth of Moultrassie
Hall; and this be the place, as I think; though why ye
be marching up and down at his door, like the sign of
a Red Man, with your old firelock there, I cannot so well
guess.'

'Give me the letters, my friend,' said the sentinel, to
whom this explanation seemed very natural and probable,
'and I will cause them forthwith to be delivered into his
worship's own hand.'

Rummaging in his pockets, as if to pull out the letters
which never existed, Master Lance approached within the
sentinel's piece, and, before he was aware, suddenly seized
him by the collar, whistled sharp and shrill, and exerting
his skill as a wrestler, for which he had been distinguished
in his youth, he stretched his antagonist on his back—the
musket for which they struggled going off in the fall.

The miners rushed into the courtyard at Lance's signal;
and, hopeless any longer of prosecuting his design in silence,
Lance commanded two of them to secure the prisoner, and
the rest to cheer loudly, and attack the door of the house.
Instantly the courtyard of the mansion rang with the cry
of ' Peveril of the Peak for ever ! ' with all the abuse which
the Royalists had invented to cast upon the Roundheads
during so many years of contention ; and at the same time,
while some assailed the door with their mining implements,
others directed their attack against the angle, where a kind
of porch joined to the main front of the building ; and there,
in some degree protected by the projection of the wall, and
of a balcony which overhung the porch, wrought in more
security, as well as with more effect, than the others ; for
the doors being of oak, thickly studded with nails, offered
a more effectual resistance to violence than the brickwork.

The noise of this hubbub on the outside soon excited wild
alarm and tumult within. Lights flew from window to
window, and voices were heard demanding the cause of the
attack, to which the party cries of those who were in the
courtyard afforded a sufficient, or at least the only, answer
which was vouchsafed. At length the window of a projecting staircase opened, and the voice of Bridgenorth
himself demanded authoritatively what the tumult meant,

and commanded the rioters to desist, upon their own proper and immediate peril.

'We want our young master, you canting old thief,' was the reply; 'and if we have him not instantly, the topmost stone of your house shall lie as low as the foundation.'

'We will try that presently,' said Bridgenorth; 'for if there is another blow struck against the walls of my peaceful house, I will fire my carabine among you, and your blood be upon your own head. I have a score of friends, well armed with musket and pistol, to defend my house; and we have both the means and heart, with Heaven's assistance, to repay any violence you can offer.'

'Master Bridgenorth,' replied Lance, who, though no soldier, was sportsman enough to comprehend the advantage which those under cover, and using fire-arms, must necessarily have over his party, exposed to their aim, in a great measure, and without means of answering their fire,— 'Master Bridgenorth, let us crave parley with you, and fair conditions. We desire to do you no evil, but will have back our young master; it is enough that you have got our old one and his lady. It is foul chasing to kill hart, hind, and fawn; and we will give you some light on the subject in an instant.'

This speech was followed by a great crash amongst the lower windows of the house, according to a new species of attack which had been suggested by some of the assailants.

'I would take the honest fellow's word, and let young Peveril go,' said one of the garrison, who, carelessly yawning, approached on the inside the post at which Bridgenorth had stationed himself.

'Are you mad?' said Bridgenorth; 'or do you think me poor enough in spirit to give up the advantages I now possess over the family of Peveril, for the awe of a parcel of boors, whom the first discharge will scatter like chaff before the whirlwind?'

'Nay,' answered the speaker, who was the same individual that had struck Julian by his resemblance to the man who called himself Ganlesse, 'I love a dire revenge, but we shall buy it somewhat too dear if these rascals set the house on

fire, as they are like to do, while you are parleying from
the window.   They have thrown torches or firebrands
into the hall ; and it is all our friends can do to keep
the flame from catching the wainscoting, which is old
and dry.'

'Now, may Heaven judge thee for thy lightness of spirit,'
answered Bridgenorth ; 'one would think mischief was so
properly thy element, that to thee it was indifferent whether
friend or foe was the sufferer.'

So saying, he ran hastily down stairs towards the hall,
into which, through broken casements, and betwixt the iron
bars, which prevented human entrance, the assailants had
thrust lighted straw, sufficient to excite much smoke and
some fire, and to throw the defenders of the house into great
confusion ; insomuch, that of several shots fired hastily
from the windows, little or no damage followed to the
besiegers, who, getting warm in the onset, answered the
hostile charges with loud shouts of 'Peveril for ever !'
and had already made a practicable breach through the
brick wall of the tenement, through which Lance, Ditchley,
and several of the most adventurous among their followers,
made their way into the hall.

The complete capture of the house remained, however,
as far off as ever.   The defenders mixed with much coolness
and skill that solemn and deep spirit of enthusiasm which
sets life at less than nothing in comparison to real or
supposed duty.   From the half-opened doors which led into
the hall they maintained a fire which began to grow fatal.
One miner was shot dead ; three or four were wounded ;
and Lance scarce knew whether he should draw his forces
from the house, and leave it a prey to the flames, or, making
a desperate attack on the posts occupied by the defenders,
try to obtain unmolested possession of the place.   At this
moment his course of conduct was determined by an
unexpected occurrence, of which it is necessary to trace the
cause.

Julian Peveril had been, like other inhabitants of Moultrassie Hall on that momentous night, awakened by the
report of the sentinel's musket, followed by the shouts of his
father's vassals and followers ; of which he collected enough
to guess that Bridgenorth's house was attacked with a view

to his liberation. Very doubtful of the issue of such an attempt, dizzy with the slumber from which he had been so suddenly awakened, and confounded with the rapid succession of events to which he had been lately a witness, he speedily put on a part of his clothes, and hastened to the window of his apartment. From this he could see nothing to relieve his anxiety, for it looked towards a quarter different from that on which the attack was made. He attempted his door ; it was locked on the outside ; and his perplexity and anxiety became extreme, when suddenly the lock was turned, and in an undress, hastily assumed in the moment of alarm, her hair streaming on her shoulders, her eyes gleaming betwixt fear and resolution, Alice Bridgenorth rushed into his apartment, and seized his hand with the fervent exclamation, ' Julian, save my father ! '

The light which she bore in her hand served to show those features which could rarely have been viewed by any one without emotion, but which bore an expression irresistible to a lover.

' Alice,' he said, ' what means this ?   What is the danger ? Where is your father ? '

' Do not stay to question,' she answered ; ' but if you would save him, follow me ! '

At the same time she led the way, with great speed, halfway down the turret staircase which led to his room, thence turning through a side door, along a long gallery, to a larger and wider stair, at the bottom of which stood her father, surrounded by four or five of his friends, scarce discernible through the smoke of the fire which began to take hold in the hall, as well as that which arose from the repeated discharge of their own fire-arms.

Julian saw there was not a moment to be lost if he meant to be a successful mediator. He rushed through Bridgenorth's party ere they were aware of his approach, and throwing himself amongst the assailants who occupied the hall in considerable numbers, he assured them of his personal safety, and conjured them to depart.

' Not without a few more slices at the Rump, master,' answered Lance. ' I am principally glad to see you safe and well ; but here is Joe Rimegap shot as dead as a buck

in season, and more of us are hurt ; and we'll have revenge,
and roast the Puritans like apples for lambswool ! '

' Then you shall roast me along with them,' said Julian ;
' for I vow to God, I will not leave the hall, being bound
by parole of honour to abide with Major Bridgenorth till
lawfully dismissed.'

' Now out on you, an you were ten times a Peveril ! ' said
Ditchley ; ' to give so many honest fellows loss and labour
on your behalf, and to show them no kinder countenance.
I say, beat up the fire, and burn all together ! '

' Nay, nay ; but peace, my masters, and hearken to
reason,' said Julian ; ' we are all here in evil condition, and
you will only make it worse by contention. Do you help
to put out this same fire, which will else cost us all dear.
Keep yourselves under arms. Let Master Bridgenorth and
me settle some grounds of accommodation, and I trust all
will be favourably made up on both sides ; and if not, you
shall have my consent and countenance to fight it out ; and
come on it what will, I will never forget this night's good
service.'

He then drew Ditchley and Lance Outram aside, while
the rest stood suspended at his appearance and words, and
expressing the utmost thanks and gratitude for what they
had already done, urged them, as the greatest favour which
they could do towards him and his father's house, to permit
him to negotiate the terms of his emancipation from thral-
dom ; at the same time, forcing on Ditchley five or six gold
pieces, that the brave lads of Bonadventure might drink
his health ; whilst to Lance he expressed the warmest sense
of his active kindness, but protested he could only consider
it as good service to his house, if he was allowed to manage
the matter after his own fashion.

' Why,' answered Lance, ' I am well out on it, Master
Julian ; for it is matter beyond my mastery. All that I
stand to is, that I will see you safe out of this same Moultrassie Hall ; for our old Naunt Ellesmere will else give me
but cold comfort when I come home. Truth is, I began
unwillingly ; but when I saw the poor fellow Joe shot beside
me, why, I thought we should have some amends. But
I put it all in your honour's hands.'

During this colloquy both parties had been amicably

employed in extinguishing the fire, which might otherwise
have been fatal to all.   It required a general effort to get it
under ; and both parties agreed on the necessary labour,
with as much unanimity as if the water they brought in
leathern buckets from the well to throw upon the fire had
some effect in slaking their mutual hostility.

CHAPTER XXVI

Necessity—thou best of peacemakers,
As well as surest prompter of invention—
Help us to composition !

ANONYMOUS.

WHILE the fire continued the two parties laboured in
active union, like the jarring factions of the Jews during
the siege of Jerusalem when compelled to unite in resisting
an assault of the besiegers.   But when the last bucket of
water had hissed on the few embers that continued to glimmer—when the sense of mutual hostility, hitherto suspended
by a feeling of common danger, was in its turn rekindled
—the parties, mingled as they had hitherto been in one
common exertion, drew off from each other, and began to
arrange themselves at opposite sides of the hall, and handle
their weapons as if for a renewal of the fight.

Bridgenorth interrupted any further progress of this
menaced hostility. ' Julian Peveril,' he said, ' thou art
free to walk thine own path, since thou wilt not walk with
me that road which is more safe, as well as more honourable.
But if you do by my counsel, you will get soon beyond the
British seas.'

' Ralph Bridgenorth,' said one of his friends, ' this is but
evil and feeble conduct on thine own part.   Wilt thou withhold thy hand from the battle, to defend from these sons
of Belial the captive of thy bow and of thy spear ?   Surely
we are enow to deal with them in the security of our good
old cause ; nor should we part with this spawn of the old
serpent, until we essay whether the Lord will not give us
victory therein.'

A hum of stern assent followed ; and had not Ganlesse now interfered the combat would probably have been renewed. He took the advocate for war apart into one of the window recesses, and apparently satisfied his objections ; for as he returned to his companions he said to them, ' Our friend hath so well argued this matter, that, verily, since he is of the same mind with the worthy Major Bridgenorth, I think the youth may be set at liberty.'

As no further objection was offered, it only remained with Julian to thank and reward those who had been active in his assistance. Having first obtained from Bridgenorth a promise of indemnity to them for the riot they had committed, a few kind words conveyed his sense of their services ; and some broad pieces, thrust into the hand of Lance Outram, furnished the means for affording them a holiday. They would have remained to protect him, but, fearful of further disorder, and relying entirely on the good faith of Major Bridgenorth, he dismissed them all excepting Lance, whom he detained to attend upon him for a few minutes, till he should depart from Moultrassie. But ere leaving the Hall, he could not repress his desire to speak with Bridgenorth in secret ; and advancing towards him, he expressed such a desire.

Tacitly granting what was asked of him, Bridgenorth led the way to a small summer saloon adjoining to the Hall, where, with his usual gravity and indifference of manner, he seemed to await in silence what Peveril had to communicate.

Julian found it difficult, where so little opening was afforded him, to find a tone in which to open the subjects he had at heart, that should be at once dignified and conciliating. ' Major Bridgenorth,' he said at length, ' you have been a son, and an affectionate one—You may conceive my present anxiety—My father ! What has been designed for him ? '

' What the law will,' answered Bridgenorth. ' Had he walked by the counsels which I procured to be given to him, he might have dwelt safely in the house of his ancestors. His fate is now beyond my control—far beyond yours. It must be with him as his country shall decide.'

' And my mother ? ' said Peveril.

' Will consult, as she has ever done, her own duty ; and

create her own happiness by doing so,' replied Bridgenorth.
' Believe, my designs towards your family are better than
they may seem through the mist which adversity has spread
around your house. I may triumph as a man ; but as
a man I must also remember, in my hour, that mine enemies
have had theirs. Have you aught else to say ? ' he added,
after a momentary pause. ' You have rejected once, yea,
and again, the hand I stretched out to you. Methinks little
more remains between us.'

These words, which seemed to cut short further discussion,
were calmly spoken ; so that though they appeared to
discourage further question, they could not interrupt that
which still trembled on Julian's tongue. He made a step
or two towards the door ; then suddenly returned. ' Your
daughter ? ' he said—' Major Bridgenorth—I should ask
—I *do* ask forgiveness for mentioning her name—but may
I not inquire after her ? May I not express my wishes for
her future happiness ? '

' Your interest in her is but too flattering,' said Bridgenorth ; ' but you have already chosen your part ; and you
must be, in future, strangers to each other. I may have
wished it otherwise, but the hour of grace is passed during
which your compliance with my advice might—I will speak
it plainly—have led to your union. For her happiness—
if such a word belongs to mortal pilgrimage—I shall care
for it sufficiently. She leaves this place to-day, under the
guardianship of a sure friend.'

' Not of—— ? ' exclaimed Peveril, and stopped short ;
for he felt he had no right to pronounce the name which
came to his lips.

' Why do you pause ? ' said Bridgenorth ; ' a sudden
thought is often a wise, almost always an honest one. With
whom did you suppose I meant to entrust my child, that the
idea called forth so anxious an expression ? '

' Again I should ask your forgiveness,' said Julian, ' for
meddling where I have little right to interfere. But I saw
a face here that is known to me—the person calls himself
Ganlesse—Is it with him that you mean to entrust your
daughter ? '

' Even to the person who calls himself Ganlesse,' said
Bridgenorth, without expressing either anger or surprise.

'And do you know to whom you commit a charge so precious to all who know her, and so dear to yourself ? ' said Julian.

'Do *you* know, who ask me the question ? ' answered Bridgenorth.

'I own I do not,' answered Julian ; ' but I have seen him in a character so different from what he now wears, that I feel it my duty to warn you how you entrust the charge of your child to one who can alternately play the profligate or the hypocrite, as it suits his own interest or humour.'

Bridgenorth smiled contemptuously. 'I might be angry,' he said, ' with the officious zeal which supposes that its green conceptions can instruct my grey hairs ; but, good Julian, I do but only ask from you the liberal construction, that I, who have had much converse with mankind, know with whom I trust what is dearest to me. He of whom thou speakest hath one visage to his friends, though he may have others to the world, living amongst those before whom honest features should be concealed under a grotesque vizard ; even as in the sinful sports of the day, called maskings and mummeries, where the wise, if he show himself at all, must be contented to play the apish and fantastic fool.'

'I would only pray your wisdom to beware,' said Julian, ' of one who, as he has a vizard for others, may also have one which can disguise his real features from you yourself.'

'This is being over careful, young man,' replied Bridgenorth, more shortly than he had hitherto spoken ; ' if you would walk by my counsel, you will attend to your own affairs, which, credit me, deserve all your care, and leave others to the management of theirs.'

This was too plain to be misunderstood ; and Peveril was compelled to take his leave of Bridgenorth, and of Moultrassie Hall, without further parley or explanation. The reader may imagine how oft he looked back, and tried to guess, amongst the lights which continued to twinkle in various parts of the building, which sparkle it was that gleamed from the bower of Alice. When the road turned into another direction he sank into a deep reverie, from which he was at length roused by the voice of Lance, who demanded where he intended to quarter for the night.

He was unprepared to answer the question, but the honest keeper himself prompted a solution of the problem, by requesting that he would occupy a spare bed in the lodge ; to which Julian willingly agreed.   The rest of the inhabitants had retired to rest when they entered ; but Dame Elles-mere, apprised by a messenger of her nephew's hospitable intent, had everything in the best readiness she could for the son of her ancient patron.   Peveril betook himself to rest ;   and, notwithstanding so many subjects of anxiety, slept soundly till the morning was far advanced.

His slumbers were first broken by Lance, who had been long up, and already active in his service.   He informed him that his horse, arms, and small cloak-bag had been sent from the castle by one of Major Bridgenorth's servants, who brought a letter, discharging from the Major's service the unfortunate Deborah Debbitch and prohibiting her return to the Hall.   The officer of the House of Commons, escorted by a strong guard, had left Martindale Castle that morning early, travelling in Sir Geoffrey's carriage—his lady being also permitted to attend on him.   To this he had to add, that the property at the castle was taken possession of by Master Win-the-Fight, the attorney, from Chesterfield, with other officers of the law, in name of Major Bridgenorth, a large creditor of the unfortunate knight.

Having told these Job's tidings, Lance paused ;   and, after a moment's hesitation, declared he was resolved to quit the country, and go up to London along with his young master.   Julian argued the point with him ;   and insisted he had better stay to take charge of his aunt, in case she should be disturbed by these strangers.   Lance replied, ' She would have one with her who would protect her well enough ;   for there was wherewithal to buy protection amongst them.   But for himself, he was resolved to follow Master Julian to the death.'

Julian heartily thanked him for his love.

' Nay, it is not altogether out of love neither,' said Lance, ' though I am as loving as another ;   but it is, as it were, partly out of fear, lest I be called over the coals for last night's matter ;   for as for the miners, they will never trouble them, as the creatures only act after their kind.'

'I will write in your behalf to Major Bridgenorth, who is bound to afford you protection, if you have such fear,' said Julian.

'Nay, for that matter, it is not altogether fear, more than altogether love,' answered the enigmatical keeper, 'although it hath a tasting of both in it. And, to speak plain truth, thus it is—Dame Debbitch and Naunt Ellesmere have resolved to set up their horses together, and have made up all their quarrels. And of all ghosts in the world, the worst is when an old true-love comes back to haunt a poor fellow like me. Mistress Deborah, though distressed enow for the loss of her place, has been already speaking of a broken sixpence, or some such token, as if a man could remember such things for so many years, even if she had not gone over seas, like a woodcock, in the meanwhile.'

Julian could scarce forbear laughing. 'I thought you too much of a man, Lance, to fear a woman marrying you whether you would or no.'

'It has been many an honest man's luck, for all that,' said Lance ; 'and a woman in the very house has so many deuced opportunities. And then there would be two upon one ; for Naunt, though high enough when any of *your* folks are concerned, hath some look to the main chance ; and it seems Mistress Deb is as rich as a Jew.'

'And you, Lance,' said Julian, 'have no mind to marry for cake and pudding.'

'No, truly, master,' answered Lance, 'unless I knew of what dough they were baked. How the devil do I know how the jade came by so much ? And then if she speaks of tokens and love-passages, let her be the same tight lass I broke the sixpence with, and I will be the same true lad to her. But I never heard of true love lasting ten years ; and hers, if it lives at all, must be nearer twenty.'

'Well, then, Lance,' said Julian, 'since you are resolved on the thing, we will go to London together ; where, if I cannot retain you in my service, and if my father recovers not these misfortunes, I will endeavour to promote you elsewhere.'

'Nay, nay,' said Lance, 'I trust to be back to bonny Martindale before it is long, and to keep the greenwood, as I have been wont to do ; for, as to Dame Debbitch, when they have not me for their common butt, Naunt and she will soon bend bows on each other. So here comes old Dame Ellesmere with your breakfast. I will but give some directions about the deer to Rough Ralph, my helper, and saddle my forest pony, and your honour's horse, which is no prime one, and we will be ready to trot.'

Julian was not sorry for this addition to his establishment ; for Lance had shown himself, on the preceding evening, a shrewd and bold fellow, and attached to his master. He therefore set himself to reconcile his aunt to parting with her nephew for some time. Her unlimited devotion for ' the family ' readily induced the old lady to acquiesce in his proposal, though not without a gentle sigh over the ruins of a castle in the air, which was founded on the well-saved purse of Mistress Deborah Debbitch. ' At any rate,' she thought, ' it was as well that Lance should be out of the way of that bold, long-legged, beggarly trollop, Cis Sellok.' But to poor Deb herself, the expatriation of Lance, whom she had looked to as a sailor to a port under his lee, for which he can run if weather becomes foul, was a second severe blow, following close on her dismissal from the profitable service of Major Bridgenorth.

Julian visited the disconsolate damsel, in hopes of gaining some light upon Bridgenorth's projects regarding his daughter—the character of this Ganlesse—and other matters with which her residence in the family might have made her acquainted ; but he found her by far too much troubled in mind to afford him the least information. The name of Ganlesse she did not seem to recollect—that of Alice rendered her hysterical—that of Bridgenorth, furious. She numbered up the various services she had rendered in the family—and denounced the plague of swartness to the linen—of leanness to the poultry—of dearth and dishonour to the housekeeping—and of lingering sickness and early death to Alice ;—all which evils, she averred, had only been kept off by her continued, watchful, and incessant cares. Then again turning to the subject of the fugitive Lance, she expressed such a total contempt of that mean-spirited fellow, in a tone between laughing and crying, as

satisfied Julian it was not a topic likely to act as a sedative ;
and that, therefore, unless he made a longer stay than the
urgent state of his affairs permitted, he was not likely to
find Mistress Deborah in such a state of composure as might
enable him to obtain from her any rational or useful information.

Lance, who good-naturedly took upon himself the whole
burden of Dame Debbitch's mental alienation, or ' taking
on ', as such fits of *passio hysterica* are usually termed in
the country, had too much feeling to present himself before
the victim of her own sensibility and of his obduracy.
He therefore intimated to Julian, by his assistant Ralph,
that the horses stood saddled behind the lodge, and that all
was ready for their departure.

Julian took the hint, and they were soon mounted, and
clearing the road at a rapid trot in the direction of London ;
but not by the most usual route. Julian calculated that
the carriage in which his father was transported would
travel slowly ; and it was his purpose, if possible, to get
to London before it should arrive there, in order to have
time to consult with the friends of his family what measures
should be taken in his father's behalf.

In this manner they advanced a day's journey towards
London ; at the conclusion of which, Julian found his
resting-place in a small inn upon the road. No one came, at
the first call, to attend upon the guests and their horses,
although the house was well lighted up ; and there was
a prodigious chattering in the kitchen, such as can only be
produced by a French cook when his mystery is in the very
moment of projection. It instantly occurred to Julian—
so rare was the ministry of these Gallic artists at that time
—that the clamour he heard must necessarily be produced
by the Sieur Chaubert, on whose *plats* he had lately feasted
along with Smith and Ganlesse.

One or both of these were therefore probably in the
little inn ; and if so, he might have some opportunity to
discover their real purpose and character. How to avail
himself of such a meeting, he knew not ; but chance favoured
him more than he could have expected.

' I can scarce receive you, gentlefolks,' said the landlord,
who at length appeared at the door ; ' here be a sort of

quality in my house to-night whom less than all will not satisfy ; nor all neither, for that matter.'

' We are but plain fellows, landlord,' said Julian ; ' we are bound for Moseley market, and can get no further to-night. Any hole will serve us, no matter what.'

' Why,' said the honest host, ' if that be the case, I must e'en put one of you behind the bar, though the gentlemen have desired to be private ; the other must take heart of grace, and help me at the tap.'

' The tap for me,' said Lance, without waiting his master's decision. ' It is an element which I could live and die in.'

' The bar, then, for me,' said Peveril ; and stepping back, whispered to Lance to exchange cloaks with him, desirous, if possible, to avoid being recognized.

The exchange was made in an instant ; and presently afterwards the landlord brought a light ; and as he guided Julian into his hostelry, cautioned him to sit quiet in the place where he should stow him ; and if he was discovered, to say that he was one of the house, and leave him to make it good. ' You will hear what the gallants say,' he added ; ' but I think thou wilt carry away but little on it ; for when it is not French, it is court gibberish ; and that is as hard to construe.'

The bar, into which our hero was inducted on these conditions, seemed formed, with respect to the public room, upon the principle of a citadel, intended to observe and bridle a rebellious capital. Here sat the host on the Saturday evenings, screened from the observation of his guests, yet with the power of observing both their wants and their behaviour, and also that of overhearing their conversation—a practice which he was much addicted to, being one of that numerous class of philanthropists to whom their neighbours' business is of as much consequence, or rather more, than their own.

Here he planted his new guest, with a repeated caution not to disturb the gentlemen by speech or motion ; and a promise that he should be speedily accommodated with a cold buttock of beef and a tankard of home-brewed. And here he left him with no other light than that which glimmered from the well-illuminated apartment within,

through a sort of shuttle which accommodated the landlord
with a view into it.

This situation, inconvenient enough in itself, was, on the
present occasion, precisely what Julian would have selected.
He wrapped himself in the weather-beaten cloak of Lance
Outram, which had been stained by age and weather into
a thousand variations from its original Lincoln green; and
with as little noise as he could, set himself to observe the
two inmates, who had engrossed to themselves the whole of
the apartment, which was usually open to the public. They
sat by a table well covered with such costly rarities as
could only have been procured by much forecast, and prepared by the exquisite Monsieur Chaubert; to which both
seemed to do much justice.

Julian had little difficulty in ascertaining that one of the
travellers was, as he had anticipated, the master of the said
Chaubert, or, as he was called by Ganlesse, Smith; the
other, who faced him, he had never seen before. This last
was dressed like a gallant of the first order. His periwig,
indeed, as he travelled on horseback, did not much exceed
in size the bar-wig of a modern lawyer; but then the
essence which he shook from it with every motion, impreg-
nated a whole apartment which was usually only perfumed
by that vulgar herb, tobacco. His riding-coat was laced
in the newest and most courtly style; and Grammont
himself might have envied the embroidery of his waistcoat
and the peculiar cut of his breeches, which buttoned above
the knee, permitting the shape of a very handsome leg
to be completely seen. This, by the proprietor thereof,
had been stretched out upon a stool, and he contemplated its proportions, from time to time, with infinite
satisfaction.

The conversation between these worthies was so interesting that we propose to assign to it another chapter.

CHAPTER XXVII

This is some creature of the elements,
Most like your sea-gull. He can wheel and whistle
His screaming song, e'en when the storm is loudest—
Take for his sheeted couch the restless foam
Of the wild wave-crest—slumber in the calm,
And dally with the storm. Yet 'tis a gull,
An arrant gull, with all this.

The Chieftain.

'AND here is to thee,' said the fashionable gallant whom we have described, ' honest Tom ; and a cup of welcome to thee out of Looby-land. Why, thou hast been so long in the country, that thou hast got a bumpkinly clod-compelling sort of look thyself. That greasy doublet fits thee as if it were thy reserved Sunday's apparel ; and the points seem as if they were stay-laces bought for thy true-love Marjory. I marvel thou canst still relish a ragout. Methinks now, to a stomach bound in such a jacket, eggs and bacon were a diet more conforming.'

' Rally away, my good lord, while wit lasts,' answered his companion ; ' yours is not the sort of ammunition which will bear much expenditure. Or rather, tell me news from court, since we have met so opportunely.'

' You would have asked me these an hour ago,' said the lord, ' had not your very soul been under Chaubert's covered dishes. You remembered king's affairs will keep cool, and *entre-mets* must be eaten hot.'

' Not so, my lord ; I only kept common talk whilst that eaves-dropping rascal of a landlord was in the room ; so that, now the coast is clear once more, I pray you for news from court.'

' The plot is nonsuited,' answered the courtier—' Sir George Wakeman acquitted "—the witnesses discredited by the jury—Scroggs, who ranted on one side, is now ranting on t'other.'

' Rat the Plot, Wakeman, witnesses, Papists, and Protestants, all together ! Do you think I care for such trash as that ?—Till the Plot comes up the palace back-stair, and

z 2

gets possession of old Rowley's own imagination, I care not a farthing who believes or disbelieves. I hang by him will bear me out.'

'Well then,' said my lord, 'the next news is Rochester's disgrace.'

'Disgraced! How, and for what? The morning I came off, he stood as fair as any one.'

'That's over—the epitaph [1] has broken his neck—and now he may write one for his own court favour, for it is dead and buried.'

'The epitaph!' exclaimed Tom; 'why, I was by when it was made; and it passed for an excellent good jest with him whom it was made upon.'

'Aye, so it did amongst ourselves,' answered his companion; 'but it got abroad, and had a run like a mill-race. It was in every coffee-house, and in half the diurnals. Grammont translated it into French too; and there is no laughing at so sharp a jest, when it is dinned into your ears on all sides. So, disgraced is the author; and but for his Grace of Buckingham, the court would be as dull as my Lord Chancellor's wig.'

'Or as the head it covers. Well, my lord, the fewer at court, there is the more room for those that can bustle there. But there are two mainstrings of Shaftesbury's fiddle broken—the Popish Plot fallen into discredit—and Rochester disgraced. Changeful times—but here is to the little man who shall mend them.'

'I apprehend you,' replied his lordship; 'and meet your health with my love. Trust me, my lord loves you, and longs for you. Nay, I have done you reason. By your leave, the cup is with me. Here is to his buxom Grace of Bucks.'

'As blithe a peer,' said Smith, 'as ever turned night to day. Nay, it shall be an overflowing bumper, an you will;

---

[1] The epitaph alluded to is the celebrated epigram made by Rochester on Charles II. It was composed at the king's request, who nevertheless resented its poignancy.

The lines are well known:—

> Here lies our sovereign lord the King,
>   Whose word no man relies on,
> Who never said a foolish thing,
>   And never did a wise one.

and I will drink it *super naculum.*—And how stands the great Madam ? ' [1]

' Stoutly against all change,' answered my lord—' Little Anthony [2] can make naught of her.'

' Then he shall bring her influence to naught.   Hark in thine ear.   Thou knowest— ' (Here he whispered so low that Julian could not catch the sound.)

' Know him ? ' answered the other—' Know Ned of the Island ?   To be sure I do.'

' He is the man that shall knot the great fiddle-strings that have snapped.   Say I told you so ; and thereupon I give thee his health.'

' And thereupon I pledge thee,' said the young nobleman, ' which on any other argument I were loath to do—thinking of Ned as somewhat the cut of a villain.'

' Granted, man—granted,' said the other—' a very thorough-paced rascal ; but able, my lord, able and necessary ; and, in this plan, indispensable.   Pshaw !   This champagne turns stronger as it gets older, I think.'

' Hark, mine honest fellow,' said the courtier ; ' I would thou wouldst give me some item of all this mystery.   Thou hast it, I know ; for whom do men entrust but trusty Chiffinch ? '

' It is your pleasure to say so, my lord,' answered Smith (whom we shall hereafter call by his real name of Chiffinch) with much drunken gravity, for his speech had become a little altered by his copious libations in the course of the evening—' few men know more, or say less, than I do ; and it well becomes my station.   *Conticuere omnes,* as the grammar hath it—all men should learn to hold their tongue.'

' Except with a friend, Tom—except with a friend. Thou wilt never be such a dog-bolt as to refuse a hint to a friend ?   Come, you get too wise and statesmanlike for your office—The ligatures of thy most peasantly jacket there are like to burst with thy secret.   Come, undo a button, man ; it is for the health of thy constitution—Let

---

[1] The Duchess of Portsmouth, Charles II's favourite mistress ; very unpopular at the time of the Popish Plot, as well from her religion as her country, being a Frenchwoman and a Catholic.

[2] Anthony Ashley Cooper, Earl of Shaftesbury, the politician and intriguer of the period.

out a reef ; and let thy chosen friend know what is meditating. Thou knowest I am as true as thyself to little Anthony,
if he can but get uppermost.'

' *If*, thou lordly infidel ! ' said Chiffinch—' talk'st thou
to me of *ifs* ?—There is neither *if* nor *and* in the matter.
The great Madam shall be pulled a peg down—the great

CHIFFINCH

Plot screwed a peg or two up. Thou knowest Ned ?
Honest Ned had a brother's death to revenge.'

' I have heard so,' said the nobleman ; ' and that his
persevering resentment of that injury was one of the few
points which seemed to be a sort of heathenish virtue in
him.'

' Well,' continued Chiffinch, ' in manœuvring to bring
about this revenge, which he hath laboured at many a day,
he hath discovered a treasure·'

' What !   In the Isle of Man ? ' said his companion.

' Assure yourself of it.   She is a creature so lovely, that she needs but be seen to put down every one of the favourites, from Portsmouth and Cleveland down to that threepenny baggage, Mistress Nelly.'

' By my word, Chiffinch,' said my lord, ' that is a reinforcement after the fashion of thine own best tactics.   But bethink thee, man !   To make such a conquest, there wants more than a cherry cheek and a bright eye—there must be wit—wit, man, and manners, and a little sense besides, to keep influence when it is gotten.'

' Pshaw ! will you tell me what goes to this vocation ? ' said Chiffinch.   ' Here, pledge me her health in a brimmer. Nay, you shall do it on knees, too.   Never such a triumphant beauty was seen—I went to church on purpose, for the first time these ten years—Yet I lie, it was not to church neither —it was to chapel.'

' To chapel !—What the devil, is she a Puritan ? ' exclaimed the other courtier.

' To be sure she is.   Do you think I would be accessory to bringing a Papist into favour in these times, when, as my good lord said in the House, there should not be a Popish man-servant, nor a Popish maid-servant, not so much as dog or cat, left to bark or mew about the king ! ' [1]

' But consider, Chiffie, the dislikelihood of her pleasing,' said the noble courtier.—' What ! old Rowley, with his wit, and love of wit—his wildness, and love of wildness— he form a league with a silly, scrupulous, unidea'd Puritan ! Not if she were Venus.'

' Thou knowest naught of the matter,' answered Chiffinch. ' I tell thee, the fine contrast between the seeming saint and falling sinner will give zest to the old gentleman's inclinations.   If I do not know him, who does ?—Her health, my lord, on your bare knee, as you would live to be of the bed-chamber.'

' I pledge you most devoutly,' answered his friend.   ' But you have not told me how the acquaintance is to be made ; for you cannot, I think, carry her to Whitehall.'

' Aha, my dear lord, you would have the whole secret ! but that I cannot afford—I can spare a friend a peep at my

[1] Such was the extravagance of Shaftesbury's eloquence.

ends, but no one must look on the means by which they are achieved.' So saying, he shook his drunken head most wisely.

The villainous design which this discourse implied, and which his heart told him was designed against Alice Bridgenorth, stirred Julian so extremely, that he involuntarily shifted his posture and laid his hand on his sword-hilt.

Chiffinch heard a rustling, and broke off, exclaiming, ' Hark ! Zounds, something moved—I trust I have told the tale to no ears but thine.'

' I will cut off any which have drunk in but a syllable of thy words,' said the nobleman ; and raising a candle, he took a hasty survey of the apartment. Seeing nothing that could incur his menaced resentment, he replaced the light and continued :—' Well, suppose the Belle Louise de Querouaille [1] shoots from her high station in the firmament, how will you rear up the downfallen Plot again—for without that same Plot, think of it as thou wilt, we have no change of hands—and matters remain as they were, with a Protestant courtesan instead of a Papist—Little Anthony can but little speed without that Plot of his—I believe, in my conscience, he begot it himself.' [2]

' Whoever begot it,' said Chiffinch, ' he hath adopted it ; and a thriving babe it has been to him. Well, then, though it lies out of my way, I will play Saint Peter again—up with t'other key, and unlock t'other mystery.'

' Now thou speakest like a good fellow ; and I will, with my own hands, unwire this fresh flask, to begin a brimmer to the success of thy achievement.'

' Well, then,' continued the communicative Chiffinch, ' thou knowest that they have long had a nibbling at the old Countess of Derby. So Ned was sent down—he owes her an old accompt, thou knowest—with private instructions to possess himself of the island, if he could, by help of some of his old friends. He hath ever kept up spies upon her ; and happy man was he, to think his hour of vengeance was

---

[1] Charles's principal mistress *en titre*. She was created Duchess of Portsmouth.

[2] Shaftesbury himself is supposed to have said that he knew not who was the inventor of the Plot, but that he himself had all the advantage of the discovery.

come so nigh. But he missed his blow ; and the old girl
being placed on her guard, was soon in a condition to make
Ned smoke for it. Out of the island he came with little
advantage for having entered it ; when, by some means—
for the devil, I think, stands ever his friend—he obtained
information concerning a messenger whom her old Majesty
of Man had sent to London to make party in her behalf.
Ned stuck himself to this fellow—a raw, half-bred lad, son
of an old blundering Cavalier of the old stamp, down in
Derbyshire—and so managed the swain, that he brought
him to the place where I was waiting, in anxious expectation
of the pretty one I told you of. By Saint Anthony, for
I will swear by no meaner oath, I stared when I saw this
great lout—not that the fellow is so ill-looked neither—
I stared like—like—good now, help me to a simile.'

'Like Saint Anthony's pig, an it were sleek,' said the
young lord ; ' your eyes, Chiffie, have the very blink of one.
But what hath all this to do with the Plot ? Hold—I have
had wine enough.'

'You shall not balk me,' said Chiffinch ; and a jingling
was heard, as if he were filling his comrade's glass with
a very unsteady hand. 'Hey—what the devil is the
matter ? I used to carry my glass steady—very steady.'

'Well, but this stranger ? '

'Why, he swept at game and ragout as he would at
spring beef or summer mutton. Never saw so unnurtured
a cub—Knew no more what he ate than an infidel—I cursed
him by my gods when I saw Chaubert's chef-d'œuvres glutted
down so indifferent a throat. We took the freedom to spice
his goblet a little, and ease him of his packet of letters ; and
the fool went on his way the next morning with a budget
artificially filled with grey paper. Ned would have kept
him, in hopes to have made a witness of him, but the boy
was not of that mettle.'

'How will you prove your letters ? ' said the courtier.

'La you there, my lord,' said Chiffinch ; ' one may see
with half an eye, for all your laced doublet, that you have
been of the family of Furnival's, before your brother's death
sent you to court. How prove the letters ? Why, we have
but let the sparrow fly with a string round his foot—We
have him again so soon as we list.'

' Why, thou art turned a very Machiavel, Chiffinch,' said
his friend.   ' But how if the youth proved restive ?—I have
heard these Peak men have hot heads and hard hands.'

' Trouble not yourself—that was cared for, my lord,'
said Chiffinch—' his pistols might bark, but they could not
bite.'

' Most exquisite Chiffinch, thou art turned micher as well
at padder—Canst both rob a man and kidnap him ! '

' Micher and padder—what terms be these ? ' said
Chiffinch.   ' Methinks these are sounds to lug out upon.
You will have me angry to the degree of falling foul—robber
and kidnapper ! '

' You mistake verb for noun-substantive,' replied his
lordship ;   ' I said *rob* and *kidnap*—a man may do either
once and away without being professional.'

' But not without spilling a little foolish noble blood, or
some such red-coloured gear,' said Chiffinch, starting up.

' Oh yes,' said his lordship ;   ' all this may be without
these direful consequences, and as you will find to-morrow,
when you return to England ;   for at present you are in the
land of Champagne, Chiffie ;   and that you may continue so,
I drink thee this parting cup to line thy nightcap.'

' I do not refuse your pledge,' said Chiffinch ;   ' but I
drink to thee in dudgeon and in hostility—It is a cup of
wrath, and a gage of battle.   To-morrow, by dawn, I will
have thee at point of fox, wert thou the last of the Savilles.
—What the devil ! think you I fear you because you are
a lord ? '

' Not so, Chiffinch,' answered his companion.   ' I know
thou fearest nothing but beans and bacon, washed down
with bumpkin-like beer.   Adieu, sweet Chiffinch—to bed
—Chiffinch—to bed.'

So saying, he lifted a candle, and left the apartment.   And
Chiffinch, whom the last draught had nearly overpowered,
had just strength enough left to do the same, muttering,
as he staggered out, ' Yes, he shall answer it.—Dawn of
day ?   D—n me—It is come already—Yonder's the dawn
—No, d—n me, 'tis the fire glancing on the cursed red
lattice—I am whistled drunk, I think—This comes of
a country inn—It is the smell of the brandy in this cursed
room—It could not be the wine—Well, old Rowley shall

send me no more errands to the country again—Steady, steady.'

So saying, he reeled out of the apartment, leaving Peveril to think over the extraordinary conversation he had just heard.

The name of Chiffinch, the well-known minister of Charles's pleasures, was nearly allied to the part which he seemed about to play in the present intrigue ; but that Christian, whom he had always supposed a Puritan as strict as his brother-in-law, Bridgenorth, should be associated with him in a plot so infamous, seemed alike unnatural and monstrous. The near relationship might blind Bridgenorth, and warrant him in confiding his daughter to such a man's charge ; but what a wretch he must be, that could coolly meditate such an ignominious abuse of his trust ! In doubt whether he could credit for a moment the tale which Chiffinch had revealed, he hastily examined his packet, and found that the sealskin case in which it had been wrapped up, now only contained an equal quantity of waste paper. If he had wanted further confirmation, the failure of the shot which he had fired at Bridgenorth, and of which the wadding only struck him, showed that his arms had been tampered with. He examined the pistol which still remained charged, and found that the ball had been drawn. ' May I perish,' said he to himself, ' amid these villainous intrigues, but thou shalt be more surely loaded, and to better purpose ! The contents of these papers may undo my benefactress—their having been found on me, may ruin my father—that I have been the bearer of them, may cost, in these fiery times, my own life —that I care least for—they form a branch of the scheme laid against the honour and happiness of a creature so innocent that it is almost sin to think of her within the neighbourhood of such infamous knaves. I will recover the letters at all risks—But how ?—that is to be thought on. Lance is stout and trusty ; and when a bold deed is once resolved upon, there never yet lacked the means of executing it.'

His host now entered, with an apology for his long absence ; and after providing Peveril with some refreshments, invited him to accept, for his night-quarters, the accommodation of a remote hay-loft, which he was to share with his comrade ; professing, at the same time, he could hardly have afforded them this courtesy, but out of deference to the exquisite talents of Lance Outram, as assistant at the tap ; where, indeed, it seems probable that he, as well as the admiring landlord, did that evening contrive to drink nearly as much liquor as they drew.

But Lance was a seasoned vessel, on whom liquor made no lasting impression ; so that when Peveril awaked that trusty follower at dawn, he found him cool enough to comprehend and enter into the design which he expressed, of recovering the letters which had been abstracted from his person.

Having considered the whole matter with much attention, Lance shrugged, grinned, and scratched his head; and at length manfully expressed his resolution. ' Well, my naunt speaks truth in her old saw,—

> He that serves Peveril munna be slack,
> Neither for weather, nor yet for wrack.

And then again, my good dame was wont to say, that whenever Peveril was in a broil, Outram was in a stew ; so I will never bear a base mind, but even hold a part with you as my fathers have done with yours, for four generations, whatever more.'

' Spoken like a most gallant Outram,' said Julian ; ' and were we but rid of that puppy lord and his retinue, we two could easily deal with the other three.'

' Two Londoners and a Frenchman ? ' said Lance— ' I would take them in mine own hand. And as for my Lord Saville, as they call him, I heard word last night that he and all his men of gilded gingerbread—that looked at an honest fellow like me, as if they were the ore and I the dross—are all to be off this morning to some races, or such-like junketings, about Tutbury. It was that brought him down here, where he met this other civet-cat by accident.'

In truth, even as Lance spoke, a trampling was heard of horses in the yard ; and from the hatch of their hay-loft they beheld Lord Saville's attendants mustered, and ready to set out as soon as he should make his appearance.

' So ho, Master Jeremy,' said one of the fellows, to a sort

of principal attendant, who just came out of the house, 'methinks the wine has proved a sleeping-cup to my lord this morning.'

'No,' answered Jeremy, 'he hath been up before light, writing letters for London ; and to punish thy irreverence, thou, Jonathan, shalt be the man to ride back with them.'

'And so to miss the race ? ' said Jonathan sulkily ; 'I thank you for this good turn, good Master Jeremy ; and hang me if I forget it.'

Further discussion was cut short by the appearance of the young nobleman, who, as he came out of the inn, said to Jeremy, 'These be the letters. Let one of the knaves ride to London for life and death, and deliver them as directed ; and the rest of them get to horse and follow me.'

Jeremy gave Jonathan the packet with a malicious smile ; and the disappointed groom turned his horse's head sullenly towards London, while Lord Saville, and the rest of his retinue, rode briskly off in an opposite direction, pursued by the benedictions of the host and his family, who stood bowing and curtsying at the door, in gratitude, doubtless, for the receipt of an unconscionable reckoning.

It was full three hours after their departure, that Chiffinch lounged into the room in which they had supped, in a brocade nightgown, and green velvet cap, turned up with the most costly Brussels lace. He seemed but half awake ; and it was with drowsy voice that he called for a cup of cold small beer. His manner and appearance were those of a man who had wrestled hard with Bacchus on the preceding evening, and had scarce recovered the effects of his contest with the jolly god. Lance, instructed by his master to watch the motions of the courtier, officiously attended with the cooling beverage he called for, pleading, as an excuse to the landlord, his wish to see a Londoner in his morning gown and cap.

No sooner had Chiffinch taken his morning draught, than he inquired after Lord Saville.

'His lordship was mounted and away by peep of dawn,' was Lance's reply.

'What, the devil ! ' exclaimed Chiffinch ; 'why, this is scarce civil. What ! off for the races with his whole retinue ? '

'All but one,' replied Lance, 'whom his lordship sent back to London with letters.'

'To London with letters!' said Chiffinch. 'Why, I am for London, and could have saved his express a labour. But stop—hold—I begin to recollect—d——n, can I have blabbed? I have—I have—I remember it all now—I have blabbed; and to the very weazel of the court, who sucks the yelk out of every man's secret. Furies and fire—that my afternoons should ruin my mornings thus! I must turn boon companion and good fellow in my cups—and have my confidences and my quarrels—my friends and my enemies, with a plague to me, as if any one could do a man much good or harm but his own self. His messenger must be stopped, though—I will put a spoke in his wheel. Hark ye, drawer-fellow—call my groom hither—call Tom Beacon.'

Lance obeyed; but failed not, when he had introduced the domestic, to remain in the apartment, in order to hear what should pass betwixt him and his master.

'Hark ye, Tom,' said Chiffinch, 'here are five pieces for you.'

'What's to be done now, I trow?' said Tom, without even the ceremony of returning thanks, which he was probably well aware would not be received even in part payment of the debt he was incurring.

'Mount your fleet nag, Tom—ride like the devil—overtake the groom whom Lord Saville dispatched to London this morning—lame his horse—break his bones—fill him as drunk as the Baltic sea; or do whatever may best and most effectually stop his journey. Why does the lout stand there without answering me? Dost understand me?'

'Why, aye, Master Chiffinch,' said Tom; 'and so I am thinking doth this honest man here, who need not have heard quite so much of your counsel, an it had been your will.'

'I am bewitched this morning,' said Chiffinch to himself, 'or else the champagne runs in my head still. My brain has become the very lowlands of Holland—a gill-cup would inundate it—Hark thee, fellow,' he added, addressing Lance, 'keep my counsel—there is a wager betwixt Lord Saville and me, which of us shall first have a letter in

London.   Here is to drink my health, and bring luck on
my side.   Say nothing of it ; but help Tom to his nag.
Tom, ere thou startest, come for thy credentials—I will
give thee a letter to the Duke of Bucks, that may be evidence
thou wert first in town.'

Tom Beacon ducked and exit ; and Lance, after having
made some show of helping him to horse, ran back to tell
his master the joyful intelligence, that a lucky accident
had abated Chiffinch's party to their own number.

Peveril immediately ordered his horses to be got ready ;
and, so soon as Tom Beacon was dispatched towards London
on a rapid trot, had the satisfaction to observe Chiffinch,
with his favourite Chaubert, mount to pursue the same
journey, though at a more moderate rate.   He permitted
them to attain such a distance, that they might be dogged
without suspicion ; then paid his reckoning, mounted his
horse, and followed, keeping his men carefully in view,
until he should come to a place proper for the enterprise
which he meditated.

It had been Peveril's intention, that when they came to
some solitary part of the road, they should gradually mend
their pace, until they overtook Chaubert—that Lance
Outram should then drop behind, in order to assail the
man of spits and stoves, while he himself, spurring onwards,
should grapple with Chiffinch.   But this scheme presup-
posed that the master and servant should travel in the
usual manner—the latter riding a few yards behind the
former.   Whereas, such and so interesting were the subjects
of discussion betwixt Chiffinch and the French cook, that,
without heeding the rules of etiquette, they rode on together, amicably abreast, carrying on a conversation on the
mysteries of the table, which the ancient Comus, or a modern
gastronome, might have listened to with pleasure.   It was,
therefore, necessary to venture on them both at once.

For this purpose, when they saw a long tract of road
before them, unvaried by the least appearance of man,
beast, or human habitation, they began to mend their pace,
that they might come up to Chiffinch, without giving him
any alarm, by a sudden and suspicious increase of haste.
In this manner they lessened the distance which separated
them till they were within about twenty yards, when Peveril,

afraid that Chiffinch might recognize him at a nearer
approach, and so trust to his horse's heels, made Lance the
signal to charge.

At the sudden increase of their speed, and the noise with
which it was necessarily attended, Chiffinch looked around,
but had time to do no more, for Lance, who had pricked
his pony (which was much more speedy than Julian's horse)
into full gallop, pushed, without ceremony, betwixt the
courtier and his attendant; and ere Chaubert had time for
more than one exclamation, he upset both horse and
Frenchman,—*mortbleu!* thrilling from his tongue as he
rolled on the ground amongst the various articles of his
occupation, which, escaping from the budget in which he
bore them, lay tumbled upon the highway in strange
disorder; while Lance, springing from his palfrey, commanded his foeman to be still, under no less a penalty than
that of death, if he attempted to rise.

Before Chiffinch could avenge his trusty follower's downfall, his own bridle was seized by Julian, who presented
a pistol with the other hand, and commanded him to stand
or die.

Chiffinch, though effeminate, was no coward. He stood
still as commanded, and said, with firmness, ' Rogue, you
have taken me at surprise. If you are highwaymen, there
is my purse. Do us no bodily harm, and spare the budget
of spices and sauces.'

' Look you, Master Chiffinch,' said Peveril, ' this is no
time for dallying. I am no highwayman, but a man of
honour. Give me back that packet which you stole from
me the other night; or, by all that is good, I will send
a brace of balls through you, and search for it at leisure.'

' What night? what packet?' answered Chiffinch,
confused; yet willing to protract the time for the chance
of assistance, or to put Peveril off his guard. ' I know
nothing of what you mean. If you are a man of honour,
let me draw my sword, and I will do you right, as a gentleman should do to another.'

' Dishonourable rascal!' said Peveril, ' you escape not in
this manner. You plundered me when you had me at odds;
and I am not the fool to let my advantage escape, now
that my turn is come. Yield up the packet; and then, if

you will, I will fight you on equal terms. But first,' he reiterated, ' yield up the packet, or I will instantly send you where the tenor of your life will be hard to answer for.'

The tone of Peveril's voice, the fierceness of his eye, and the manner in which he held the loaded weapon, within a hand's-breadth of Chiffinch's head, convinced the last there was neither room for compromise nor time for trifling. He thrust his hand into a side-pocket of his cloak, and with visible reluctance, produced those papers and dispatches with which Julian had been entrusted by the Countess of Derby.

' They are five in number,' said Julian ; ' and you have given me only four. Your life depends on full restitution.'

' It escaped from my hand,' said Chiffinch, producing the missing document—' There it is. Now, sir, your pleasure is fulfilled, unless,' he added, sulkily, ' you design either murder or further robbery.'

' Base wretch ! ' said Peveril, withdrawing his pistol, yet keeping a watchful eye on Chiffinch's motions, ' thou art unworthy any honest man's sword ; and yet, if you dare draw your own, as you proposed but now, I am willing to give you a chance upon fair equality of terms.'

' Equality ! ' said Chiffinch sneeringly ; ' yes, a proper equality—sword and pistol against single rapier, and two men upon one, for Chaubert is no fighter. No, sir ; I shall seek amends upon some more fitting occasion, and with more equal weapons.'

' By backbiting, or by poison, base pander ! ' said Julian ; ' these are thy means of vengeance. But mark me—I know your vile purpose respecting a lady who is too worthy that her name should be uttered in such a worthless ear. Thou hast done me one injury, and thou see'st I have repaid it. But prosecute this further villany, and be assured I will put thee to death like a foul reptile, whose very slaver is fatal to humanity. Rely upon this, as if Machiavel had sworn it ; for so surely as you keep your purpose, so surely will I prosecute my revenge.—Follow me, Lance, and leave him to think on what I have told him.'

Lance had, after the first shock, sustained a very easy part in this rencontre ; for all he had to do was to point the butt of his whip, in the manner of a gun, at the intimidated

Frenchman, who, lying on his back, and gazing at random on the skies, had as little the power or purpose of resistance, as any pig which had ever come under his own slaughter-knife.

Summoned by his master from the easy duty of guarding such an unresisting prisoner, Lance remounted his horse, and they both rode off, leaving their discomfited antagonists to console themselves for their misadventure as they best could. But consolation was hard to come by in the circumstances. The French artist had to lament the dispersion of his spices, and the destruction of his magazine of sauces—an enchanter despoiled of his magic wand and talisman could scarce have been in more desperate extremity. Chiffinch had to mourn the downfall of his intrigue, and its premature discovery. ' To this fellow, at least,' he thought, ' I can have bragged none—here my evil genius alone has betrayed me. With this infernal discovery, which may cost me so dear on all hands, champagne had naught to do. If there be a flask left unbroken, I will drink it after dinner, and try if it may not even yet suggest some scheme of redemption and of revenge.'

With this manly resolution, he prosecuted his journey to London.

CHAPTER XXVIII

A man so various, that he seem'd to be
Not one, but all mankind's epitome ;
Stiff in opinions—always in the wrong—
Was every thing by starts, but nothing long ;
Who, in the course of one revolving moon,
Was chemist, fiddler, statesman, and buffoon ;
Then, all for women, painting, fiddling, drinking ;
Besides a thousand freaks that died in thinking.
DRYDEN.

WE must now transport the reader to the magnificent hotel in ——— Street, inhabited at this time by the celebrated George Villiers, Duke of Buckingham, whom Dryden has doomed to a painful immortality by the few lines which we have prefixed to this chapter. Amid the gay and the

GEORGE VILLIERS, DUKE OF BUCKINGHAM

licentious of the laughing court of Charles, the duke was
the most licentious and most gay ; yet, while expending
a princely fortune, a strong constitution, and excellent
talents, in pursuit of frivolous pleasures, he nevertheless
nourished deeper and more extensive designs ; in which
he only failed from want of that fixed purpose and regulated
perseverance essential to all important enterprises, but particularly in politics.

It was long past noon ; and the usual hour of the duke's
levée—if anything could be termed usual where all was
irregular—had been long past. His hall was filled with
lackeys and footmen, in the most splendid liveries ; the
interior apartments, with the gentlemen and pages of his
household, arrayed as persons of the first quality, and, in
that respect, rather exceeding than falling short of the duke
in personal splendour. But his antechamber, in particular,
might be compared to a gathering of eagles to the slaughter,
were not the simile too dignified to express that vile race,
who, by a hundred devices all tending to one common end,
live upon the wants of needy greatness, or administer to the
pleasures of summer-teeming luxury, or stimulate the wild
wishes of lavish and wasteful extravagance, by devising
new modes and fresh motives of profusion. There stood
the projector, with his mysterious brow, promising unbounded wealth to whomsoever might choose to furnish
the small preliminary sum necessary to change egg-shells
into the great *arcanum*. There was Captain Seagull,
undertaker for a foreign settlement, with the map under
his arm of Indian or American kingdoms, beautiful as the
primitive Eden, waiting the bold occupants, for whom
a generous patron should equip two brigantines and a fly-
boat. Thither came, fast and frequent, the gamesters, in
their different forms and calling. This, light, young, gay
in appearance, the thoughtless youth of wit and pleasure—
the pigeon rather than the rook—but at heart the same
sly, shrewd, cold-blooded calculator, as yonder old hard-
featured professor of the same science, whose eyes are grown
dim with watching the dice at midnight ; and whose
fingers are even now assisting his mental computation of
chances and of odds. The fine arts, too—I would it were
otherwise—have their professors amongst this sordid

train. The poor poet, half ashamed, in spite of habit, of the part which he is about to perform, and abashed by consciousness at once of his base motive and his shabby black coat, lurks in yonder corner for the favourable moment to offer his dedication. Much better attired, the architect presents his splendid vision of front and wings, and designs a palace, the expense of which may transfer his employer to a jail. But uppermost of all, the favourite musician, or singer, who waits on my lord to receive, in solid gold, the value of the dulcet sounds which solaced the banquet of the preceding evening.

Such, and many such-like, were the morning attendants of the Duke of Buckingham—all genuine descendants of the daughter of the horse-leech, whose cry is ' Give, give.'

But the levée of his Grace contained other and very different characters ; and was indeed as various as his own opinions and pursuits. Besides many of the young nobility and wealthy gentry of England, who made his Grace the glass at which they dressed themselves for the day, and who learned from him how to travel, with the newest and best grace, the general Road to Ruin ; there were others of a graver character—discarded statesmen, political spies, opposition orators, servile tools of administration, men who met not elsewhere, but who regarded the duke's mansion as a sort of neutral ground ; sure, that if he was not of their opinion to-day, this very circumstance rendered it most likely he should think with them to-morrow. The Puritans themselves did not shun intercourse with a man whose talents must have rendered him formidable, even if they had not been united with high rank and an immense fortune. Several grave personages, with black suits, short cloaks, and band-strings of a formal cut, were mingled, as we see their portraits in a gallery of paintings, among the gallants who ruffled in silk and embroidery. It is true, they escaped the scandal of being thought intimates of the duke, by their business being supposed to refer to money matters. Whether these grave and professing citizens mixed politics with money-lending, was not known ; but it had been long observed, that the Jews, who in general confine themselves to the latter department, had become for some time faithful attendants at the duke's levée.

It was high tide in the antechamber, and had been so for more than an hour, ere the duke's gentleman in ordinary ventured into his bedchamber, carefully darkened so as to make midnight at noonday, to know his Grace's pleasure. His soft and serene whisper, in which he asked whether it were his Grace's pleasure to rise, was briefly and sharply answered by the counter questions, ' Who waits ? What's o'clock ? '

' It is Jerningham, your Grace,' said the attendant. ' It is one, afternoon ; and your Grace appointed some of the people without at eleven.'

' Who are they ? What do they want ? '

' A message from Whitehall, your Grace.'

' Pshaw ! it will keep cold. Those who make all others wait, will be the better of waiting in their turn. Were I to be guilty of ill-breeding, it should rather be to a king than a beggar.'

' The gentlemen from the city.'

' I am tired of them—tired of their all cant, and no religion—all Protestantism, and no charity. Tell them to go to Shaftesbury—to Aldersgate Street with them—that's the best market for their wares.'

' Jockey, my lord, from Newmarket.'

' Let him ride to the devil—he has horse of mine, and spurs of his own. Any more ? '

' The whole antechamber is full, my lord—knights and squires, doctors and dicers.'

' The dicers, with their doctors [1] in their pockets, I presume.'

' Counts, captains, and clergymen.'

' You are alliterative, Jerningham,' said the duke ; ' and that is a proof you are poetical. Hand me my writing things.'

Getting half out of bed—thrusting one arm into a brocade nightgown deeply furred with sables, and one foot into a velvet slipper, while the other pressed in primitive nudity the rich carpet—his Grace, without thinking further on the assembly without, began to pen a few lines of a satirical poem ; then suddenly stopped—threw the pen into the chimney—exclaimed that the humour was past—and

---

[1] Doctor, a cant name for false dice.

asked his attendant if there were any letters.   Jerningham produced a huge packet.

'What the devil!' said his Grace, 'do you think I will read all these?   I am like Clarence, who asked a cup of wine, and was soused into a butt of sack.   I mean, is there anything which presses?'

'This letter, your Grace,' said Jerningham, 'concerning the Yorkshire mortgage.'

'Did I not bid thee carry it to old Gatheral, my steward?'

'I did, my lord,' answered the other; 'but Gatheral says there are difficulties.'

'Let the usurers foreclose, then—there is no difficulty in that; and out of a hundred manors I shall scarce miss one,' answered the duke.   'And hark ye, bring me my chocolate.'

'Nay, my lord, Gatheral does not say it is impossible— only difficult.'

'And what is the use of him, if he cannot make it easy? But you are all born to make difficulties,' replied the duke.

'Nay, if your Grace approves the terms in this schedule, and pleases to sign it, Gatheral will undertake for the matter,' answered Jerningham.

'And could you not have said so at first, you blockhead?' said the duke, signing the paper without looking at the contents—'What other letters?   And remember, I must be plagued with no more business.'

'Billets-doux, my lord—five or six of them.   This left at the porter's lodge by a vizard mask.'

'Pshaw!' answered the duke, tossing them over, while his attendant assisted in dressing him—'an acquaintance of a quarter's standing.'

'This given to one of the pages by my Lady ——'s waiting-woman.'

'Plague on it—a jeremiad on the subject of perjury and treachery, and not a single new line to the old tune,' said the duke, glancing over the billet.   'Here is the old cant —*cruel man—broken vows—Heaven's just revenge*.   Why, the woman is thinking of murder—not of love.   No one should pretend to write upon so threadbare a topic without having at least some novelty of expression.   *The despairing Araminta*—Lie there, fair desperate.   And this—how comes it?'

' Flung into the window of the hall by a fellow who ran off at full speed,' answered Jerningham.

' This is a better text,' said the duke ; ' and yet it is an old one too—three weeks old at least—The little countess with the jealous lord—I should not care a farthing for her save for that same jealous lord—Plague on 't, and he 's gone down to the country—*this evening—in silence and safety—written with a quill pulled from the wing of Cupid*—Your lady-ship has left him pen-feathers enough to fly away with—better clipped his wings when you had caught him, my lady—And *so confident of her Buckingham's faith,*—I hate confidence in a young person—She must be taught better—I will not go.'

' Your Grace will not be so cruel ! ' said Jerningham.

' Thou art a compassionate fellow, Jerningham ; but conceit must be punished.'

' But if your lordship should resume your fancy for her ? '

' Why, then, you must swear the billet-doux miscarried,' answered the duke. ' And stay, a thought strikes me—it shall miscarry in great style. Hark ye—Is—what is the fellow's name—the poet—is he yonder ? '

' There are six gentlemen, sir, who, from the reams of paper in their pocket, and the threadbare seams at their elbows, appear to wear the livery of the Muses.'

' Poetical once more, Jerningham. He, I mean, who wrote the last lampoon,' said the duke.

' To whom your Grace said you owed five pieces and a beating ! ' replied Jerningham.

' The money for his satire, and the cudgel for his praise—Good—find him—give him the five pieces, and thrust the countess's billet-doux—Hold—take Araminta's and the rest of them—thrust them all into his portfolio—All will come out at the Wit's Coffeehouse ; and if the promulgator be not cudgelled into all the colours of the rainbow, there is no spite in woman, no faith in crabtree, or pith in heart of oak—Araminta's wrath alone would overburden one pair of mortal shoulders.'

' But, my lord duke,' said his attendant, ' this Settle [1]

---

[1] Elkana Settle, the unworthy scribbler whom the envy of Rochester and others tried to raise to public estimation as a rival to Dryden ; a circumstance which has been the means of elevating him to a very painful species of immortality.

is so dull a rascal, that nothing he can write will take.'

'Then as we have given him steel to head the arrow,' said the duke, ' we will give him wings to waft it with—wood, he has enough of his own to make a shaft or bolt of. Hand me my own unfinished lampoon—give it to him with the letters—let him make what he can of them all.'

'My lord duke—I crave pardon—but your Grace's style will be discovered ; and though the ladies' names are not at the letters, yet they will be traced.'

'I would have it so, you blockhead. Have you lived with me so long, and cannot discover that the éclat of an intrigue is, with me, worth all the rest of it ? '

'But the danger, my lord duke ? ' replied Jerningham. ' There are husbands, brothers, friends, whose revenge may be awakened.'

'And beaten to sleep again,' said Buckingham haughtily. ' I have Black Will and his cudgel for plebeian grumblers ; and those of quality I can deal with myself. I lack breathing and exercise of late.'

'But yet your Grace '——

'Hold your peace, fool ! I tell you that your poor dwarfish spirit cannot measure the scope of mine. I tell thee I would have the course of my life a torrent—I am weary of easy achievements, and wish for obstacles, that I can sweep before my irresistible course.'

Another gentleman now entered the apartment. 'I humbly crave your Grace's pardon,' he said ; ' but Master Christian is so importunate for admission instantly, that I am obliged to take your Grace's pleasure.'

'Tell him to call three hours hence. Damn his politic pate, that would make all men dance after his pipe ! '

'I thank thee for the compliment, my lord duke,' said Christian, entering the apartment in somewhat a more courtly garb, but with the same unpretending and undistinguished mien, and in the same placid and indifferent manner with which he had accosted Julian Peveril upon different occasions during his journey to London. ' It is precisely my present object to pipe to you ; and you may dance to your own profit, if you will.'

'On my word, Master Christian,' said the duke haughtily,

'the affair should be weighty that removes ceremony so entirely from betwixt us. If it relates to the subject of our last conversation, I must request our interview be postponed to some further opportunity. I am engaged in an affair of some weight.' Then turning his back on Christian, he went on with his conversation with Jerningham. ' Find the person you wot of, and give him the papers ; and hark ye, give him this gold to pay for the shaft of his arrow—the steel-head and peacock's wing we have already provided.'

' This is all well, my lord,' said Christian calmly, and taking his seat at the same time in an easy chair at some distance ; ' but your Grace's levity is no match for my equanimity. It is necessary I should speak with you ; and I will await your Grace's leisure in the apartment.'

' *Very* well, sir,' said the duke peevishly ; ' if an evil is to be undergone, the sooner it is over the better—I can take measures to prevent its being renewed. So let me hear your errand without further delay.'

' I will wait till your Grace's toilette is completed,' said Christian, with the indifferent tone which was natural to him. ' What I have to say must be between ourselves.'

' Begone, Jerningham ; and remain without till I call. Leave my doublet on the couch. How now, I have worn this cloth of silver a hundred times.'

' Only twice, if it please your Grace,' replied Jerningham.

' As well twenty times—keep it for yourself, or give it to my valet, if you are too proud of your gentility.'

' Your Grace has made better men than me wear your cast clothes,' said Jerningham submissively.

' Thou art sharp, Jerningham,' said the duke—' in one sense I have, and I may again. So now, that pearl-coloured thing will do with the ribbon and George. Get away with thee.—And now that he is gone, Master Christian, may I once more crave your pleasure ? '

' My lord duke,' said Christian, ' you are a worshipper of difficulties in State affairs, as in love matters.'

' I trust you have been no eavesdropper, Master Christian,' replied the duke ; ' it scarce argues the respect due to me, or to my roof.'

' I know not what you mean, my lord,' replied Christian.

' Nay, I care not if the whole world heard what I said but

now to Jerningham.   But to the matter,' replied the Duke
of Buckingham.

' Your Grace is so much occupied with conquests over the
fair and over the witty, that you have perhaps forgotten
what a stake you have in the little Island of Man.'

' Not a whit, Master Christian.   I remember well enough
that my roundheaded father-in-law, Fairfax, had the island
from the Long Parliament ;   and was ass enough to quit hold
of it at the Restoration, when, if he had closed his clutches,
and held fast, like a true bird of prey, as he should have
done, he might have kept it for him and his.   It had been
a rare thing to have had a little kingdom—made laws of
my own—had my chamberlain with his white staff—I
would have taught Jerningham, in half a day, to look as
wise, walk as stiffly, and speak as sillily, as Harry Bennet.' [11]

' You might have done this, and more, if it had pleased
your Grace.'

' Aye, and if it had pleased my Grace, thou, Ned Christian,
shouldst have been the Jack Ketch of my dominions.'

' *I* your Jack Ketch, my lord ? ' said Christian, more in
a tone of surprise than of displeasure.

' Why, aye ;   thou hast been perpetually intriguing against
the life of yonder poor old woman.   It were a kingdom to
thee to gratify thy spleen with thy own hands.'

' I only seek justice against the countess,' said Christian.

' And the end of justice is always a gibbet,' said the duke.

' Be it so,' answered Christian.   ' Well, the countess is
in the Plot.'

' The devil confound the Plot, as I believe he first invented
it ! ' said the Duke of Buckingham ;   ' I have heard of
nothing else for months.   If one must go to hell, I would
it were by some new road, and in gentlemen's company.
I should not like to travel with Oates, Bedlow, and the rest
of that famous cloud of witnesses.'

' Your Grace is then resolved to forgo all the advantages
which may arise ?   If the house of Derby fall under forfeiture, the grant to Fairfax, now worthily represented by
your duchess, revives, and you become the Lord and
Sovereign of Man.'

' In right of a woman,' said the duke ;   ' but, in troth, my
godly dame owes me some advantage for having lived the

first year of our marriage with her and old Black Tom, her grim, fighting, puritanic father. A man might as well have married the Devil's daughter, and set up housekeeping with his father-in-law.' [1]

'I understand you are willing, then, to join your interest for a heave at the house of Derby, my lord duke?'

HENRY BENNETT, EARL OF ARLINGTON

'As they are unlawfully possessed of my wife's kingdom, they certainly can expect no favour at my hand. But thou knowest there is an interest at Whitehall predominant over mine.'

[1] Mary, daughter of Thomas, Lord Fairfax, was wedded to the Duke of Buckingham, whose versatility made him capable of rendering himself for a time as agreeable to his father-in-law, though a rigid Presbyterian, as to the gay Charles II.

' That is only by your Grace's sufferance,' said Christian.

' No, no ; I tell thee a hundred times, no,' said the duke, rousing himself to anger at the recollection. ' I tell thee that base courtesan, the Duchess of Portsmouth, hath impudently set herself to thwart and contradict me ; and Charles has given me both cloudy looks and hard words before the court. I would he could but guess what is the offence between her and me ! I would he knew but that ! But I will have her plumes picked, or my name is not Villiers. A worthless French *fille-de-joie* to brave me thus ! —Christian, thou art right ; there is no passion so spirit-stirring as revenge. I will patronize the Plot, if it be but to spite her, and make it impossible for the king to uphold her.'

As the duke spoke he gradually wrought himself into a passion, and traversed the apartment with as much vehemence as if the only object he had on earth was to deprive the duchess of her power and favour with the king. Christian smiled internally to see him approach the state of mind in which he was most easily worked upon, and judiciously kept silence, until the duke called out to him, in a pet, ' Well, Sir Oracle, you that have laid so many schemes to supplant this she-wolf of Gaul, where are all your con-trivances now ? Where is the exquisite beauty who was to catch the sovereign's eye at the first glance ? Chiffinch, hath he seen her ?—and what does he say, that exquisite critic in beauty and blanc-mange, women and wine ? '

' He has *seen* and approves, but has not yet heard her ; and her speech answers to all the rest. We came here yesterday ; and to-day I intend to introduce Chiffinch to her, the instant he arrives from the country ; and I expect him every hour. I am but afraid of the damsel's peevish virtue, for she hath been brought up after the fashion of our grandmothers—our mothers had better sense.'

' What ! so fair, so young, so quick-witted, and so difficult ? ' said the duke. ' By your leave, you shall introduce me as well as Chiffinch.'

' That your Grace may cure her of her intractable modesty ? ' said Christian.

' Why,' replied the duke, ' it will but teach her to stand in her own light. Kings do not love to court and sue ; they should have their game run down for them.'

' Under your Grace's favour,' said Christian, ' this cannot
be—*Non omnibus dormio*—Your Grace knows the classic
allusion. If this maiden become a prince's favourite,
rank gilds the shame and the sin. But to any under
Majesty she must not vail topsail.'

' Why, thou suspicious fool, I was but in jest,' said the
duke. ' Do you think I would interfere to spoil a plan so
much to my own advantage as that which you have laid
before me ? '

Christian smiled and shook his head. ' My lord,' he said,
' I know your Grace as well, or better perhaps, than you
know yourself. To spoil a well-concerted intrigue by some
cross-stroke of your own, would give you more pleasure
than to bring it to a successful termination according to
the plans of others. But Shaftesbury, and all concerned,
have determined that our scheme shall at least have fair
play. We reckon, therefore, on your help ; and—forgive
me when I say so—we will not permit ourselves to be
impeded by your levity and fickleness of purpose.'

' Who ? I light and fickle of purpose ? ' said the duke.
' You see me here as resolved as any of you to dispossess
the mistress, and to carry on the Plot ; these are the only
two things I live for in this world. No one can play the
man of business like me, when I please, to the very filing
and labelling of my letters. I am regular as a scrivener.'

' You have Chiffinch's letter from the country ; he told
me he had written to you about some passages betwixt him
and the young Lord Saville.'

' He did so—he did so,' said the duke, looking among his
letters ; ' but I see not his letter just now—I scarcely noted
the contents—I was busy when it came—but I have it
safely.'

' You should have acted on it,' answered Christian.
' The fool suffered himself to be choused out of his secret,
and prayed you to see that my lord's messenger got not to
the duchess with some dispatches which he sent up from
Derbyshire, betraying our mystery.'

The duke was now alarmed, and rang the bell hastily.
Jerningham appeared. ' Where is the letter I had from
Master Chiffinch some hours since ? '

' If it be not amongst those your Grace has before you,

I know nothing of it,' said Jerningham. 'I saw none such arrive.'

'You lie, you rascal,' said Buckingham; 'have you a right to remember better than I do?'

'If your Grace will forgive me reminding you, you have scarce opened a letter this week,' said his gentleman.

'Did you ever hear such a provoking rascal?' said the duke. 'He might be a witness in the Plot. He has knocked my character for regularity entirely on the head with his damned counter-evidence.'

'Your Grace's talent and capacity will at least remain unimpeached,' said Christian; 'and it is those that must serve yourself and your friends. If I might advise, you will hasten to court, and lay some foundation for the impression we wish to make. If your Grace can take the first word, and throw out a hint to crossbite Saville, it will be well. But above all, keep the king's ear employed, which no one can do so well as you. Leave Chiffinch to fill his heart with a proper object. Another thing is, there is a blockhead of an old Cavalier, who must needs be a bustler in the Countess of Derby's behalf—he is fast in hold, with the whole tribe of witnesses at his haunches.'

'Nay, then, take him, Topham.'

'Topham has taken him already, my lord,' said Christian; 'and there is, besides, a young gallant, a son of the said knight, who was bred in the household of the Countess of Derby, and who has brought letters from her to the Provincial of the Jesuits, and others in London.'

'What are their names?' said the duke dryly.

'Sir Geoffrey Peveril of Martindale Castle, in Derbyshire, and his son Julian.'

'What! Peveril of the Peak?' said the duke—'a stout old Cavalier as ever swore an oath—A Worcester man, too —and, in truth, a man of all work, when blows were going. I will not consent to his ruin, Christian. These fellows must be flogged off such false scents—flogged in every sense, they must and will be, when the nation comes to its eyesight again.'

'It is of more than the last importance, in the meantime, to the furtherance of our plan,' said Christian, 'that your Grace should stand for a space between them and the king's favour. The youth hath influence with the maiden, which we should find scarce favourable to our views ; besides, her father holds him as high as he can any one who is no such puritanic fool as himself.'

' Well, most Christian Christian,' said the duke, ' I have heard your commands at length. I will endeavour to stop the earths under the throne, that neither the lord, knight, nor squire in question shall find it possible to burrow there. For the fair one, I must leave Chiffinch and you to manage her introduction to her high destinies, since I am not to be trusted. Adieu, most Christian Christian.'

He fixed his eyes on him, and then exclaimed, as he shut the door of the apartment—' Most profligate and damnable villain ! And what provokes me most of all, is the knave's composed insolence. Your Grace will do this—and your Grace will condescend to do that—A pretty puppet I should be, to play the second part, or rather the third, in such a scheme ! No, they shall all walk according to my purpose, or I will cross them. I will find this girl out in spite of them, and judge if their scheme is likely to be successful. If so, she shall be mine—mine entirely, before she becomes the king's ; and I will command her who is to guide Charles. Jerningham ' [n] (his gentleman entered), ' cause Christian to be dogged wherever he goes, for the next four-and-twenty hours, and find out where he visits a female newly come to town. You smile, you knave ? '

' I did but suspect a fresh rival to Araminta and the little countess,' said Jerningham.

' Away to your business, knave,' said the duke, ' and let me think of mine. To subdue a Puritan *in esse*—a king's favourite *in posse*—the very muster of western beauties— that is point first. The impudence of this Manx mongrel to be corrected—the pride of Madame la Duchesse to be pulled down—an important State intrigue to be furthered, or baffled, as circumstances render most to my own honour and glory—I wished for business but now, and I have got enough of it. But Buckingham will keep his own steerage-way through shoal and through weather.'

CHAPTER XXIX

——Mark you this, Bassanio—
The devil can quote Scripture for his purpose.
                              Merchant of Venice.

AFTER leaving the proud mansion of the Duke of Buckingham, Christian, full of the deep and treacherous schemes
which he meditated, hastened to the city, where, in a decent
inn, kept by a person of his own persuasion, he had been
unexpectedly summoned to meet with Ralph Bridgenorth
of Moultrassie. He was not disappointed—the major had
arrived that morning, and anxiously expected him. The
usual gloom of his countenance was darkened into a yet
deeper shade of anxiety, which was scarcely relieved, even
while, in answer to his inquiry after his daughter, Christian
gave the most favourable account of her health and spirits,
naturally and unaffectedly intermingled with such praises
of her beauty and her disposition as were likely to be most
grateful to a father's ear.

But Christian had too much cunning to expatiate on this
theme, however soothing. He stopped short exactly at
the point where, as an affectionate relative, he might be
supposed to have said enough. ' The lady,' he said, ' with
whom he had placed Alice, was delighted with her aspect
and manners, and undertook to be responsible for her
health and happiness. He had not, he said, deserved so
little confidence at the hand of his brother, Bridgenorth, as
that the major should, contrary to his purpose, and to the
plan which they had adjusted together, have hurried up
from the country, as if his own presence were necessary for
Alice's protection.'

' Brother Christian,' said Bridgenorth in reply, ' I must
see my child—I must see this person with whom she is
entrusted.'

' To what purpose ? ' answered Christian. ' Have you
not often confessed that the over excess of the carnal
affection which you have entertained for your daughter
hath been a snare to you ? Have you not, more than once,
been on the point of resigning those great designs which

should place righteousness as a counsellor beside the throne, because you desired to gratify your daughter's girlish passion for this descendant of your old persecutor—this Julian Peveril ?'

'I own it,' said Bridgenorth ; 'and worlds would I have given, and would yet give, to clasp that youth to my bosom and call him my son. The spirit of his mother looks from his eye, and his stately step is as that of his father when he daily spoke comfort to me in my distress, and said, " The child liveth." '

'But the youth walks,' said Christian, 'after his own lights, and mistakes the meteor of the marsh for the polar star. Ralph Bridgenorth, I will speak to thee in friendly sincerity. Thou must not think to serve both the good cause and Baal. Obey, if thou wilt, thine own carnal affections, summon this Julian Peveril to thy house, and let him wed thy daughter—But mark the reception he will meet with from the proud old knight, whose spirit is now, even now, as little broken with his chains as after the sword of the saints had prevailed at Worcester. Thou wilt see thy daughter spurned from his feet like an outcast.'

'Christian,' said Bridgenorth, interrupting him, 'thou dost urge me hard ; but thou dost it in love, my brother, and I forgive thee—Alice shall never be spurned. But this friend of thine—this lady—thou art my child's uncle ; and after me, thou art next to her in love and affection—Still, thou art not her father—hast not her father's fears. Art thou sure of the character of this woman to whom my child is entrusted ?'

'Am I sure of my own ?—Am I sure that my name is Christian—yours Bridgenorth ?—Is it a thing I am likely to be insecure in ?—Have I not dwelt for many years in this city ?—Do I not know this court ?—And am I likely to be imposed upon ? For I will not think you can fear my imposing upon you.'

'Thou art my brother,' said Bridgenorth—'the blood and bone of my departed saint—and I am determined that I will trust thee in this matter.'

'Thou dost well,' said Christian ; 'and who knows what reward may be in store for thee ?   I cannot look upon Alice, but it is strongly borne in on my mind that there will be work for a creature so excellent beyond ordinary women. Courageous Judith freed Bethulia by her valour, and the comely features of Esther made her a safeguard and a defence to her people in the land of captivity, when she found favour in the sight of King Ahasuerus.'

'Be it with her as Heaven wills,' said Bridgenorth; 'and now tell me what progress there is in the great work.'

'The people are weary of the iniquity of this court,' said Christian; 'and if this man will continue to reign, it must be by calling to his councils men of another stamp. The alarm excited by the damnable practices of the Papists has called up men's souls, and awakened their eyes to the dangers of their State. He himself—for he will give up brother and wife to save himself—is not averse to a change of measures; and though we cannot at first see the court purged as with a winnowing fan, yet there will be enough of the good to control the bad—enough of the sober party to compel the grant of that universal toleration for which we have sighed so long, as a maiden for her beloved. Time and opportunity will lead the way to more thorough reformation; and that will be done without stroke of sword which our friends failed to establish on a sure foundation, even when their victorious blades were in their hands.'

'May God grant it!' said Bridgenorth; 'for I fear me I should scruple to do aught which should once more unsheath the civil sword; but welcome all that comes in a peaceful and parliamentary way.'

'Aye,' said Christian, 'and which will bring with it the bitter amends which our enemies have so long merited at our hands. How long hath our brother's blood cried for vengeance from the altar! Now shall that cruel French-woman find that neither lapse of years, nor her powerful friends, nor the name of Stanley, nor the sovereignty of Man, shall stop the stern course of the pursuer of blood. Her name shall be struck from the noble, and her heritage shall another take.'

'Nay, but, brother Christian,' said Bridgenorth, 'art thou not over eager in pursuing this thing?—It is thy duty as a Christian to forgive thine enemies.'

'Aye, but not the enemies of Heaven—not those who

shed the blood of the saints,' said Christian, his eyes kindling with that vehement and fiery expression which at times gave to his uninteresting countenance the only character of passion which it ever exhibited. 'No, Bridgenorth,' he continued, 'I esteem this purpose of revenge holy—I account it a propitiatory sacrifice for what may have been evil in my life. I have submitted to be spurned by the haughty—I have humbled myself to be as a servant ; but in my breast was the proud thought, I who do this—do it that I may avenge my brother's blood.'

'Still, my brother,' said Bridgenorth, 'although I participate thy purpose, and have aided thee against this Moabitish woman, I cannot but think thy revenge is more after the law of Moses than after the law of love.'

'This comes well from thee, Ralph Bridgenorth,' answered Christian ; 'from thee, who hast just smiled over the downfall of thine own enemy.'

'If you mean Sir Geoffrey Peveril,' said Bridgenorth, 'I smile not on his ruin. It is well he is abased ; but if it lies with me, I may humble his pride, but will never ruin his house.'

'You know your purpose best,' said Christian ; 'and I do justice, brother Bridgenorth, to the purity of your principles ; but men who see with but worldly eyes would discern little purpose of mercy in the strict magistrate and severe creditor—and such have you been to Peveril.'

'And, brother Christian,' said Bridgenorth, his colour rising as he spoke, 'neither do I doubt your purpose, nor deny the surprising address with which you have procured such perfect information concerning the purposes of yonder woman of Ammon. But it is free to me to think that in your intercourse with the court, and with courtiers, you may, in your carnal and worldly policy, sink the value of those spiritual gifts for which you were once so much celebrated among the brethren.'

'Do not apprehend it,' said Christian, recovering his temper, which had been a little ruffled by the previous discussion. 'Let us but work together as heretofore ; and I trust each of us shall be found doing the work of a faithful servant to that good old cause for which we have heretofore drawn the sword.'

So saying, he took his hat and, bidding Bridgenorth farewell, declared his intention of returning in the evening.

'Fare thee well!' said Bridgenorth; 'to that cause wilt thou find me ever a true and devoted adherent. I will act by that counsel of thine, and will not even ask thee—though it may grieve my heart as a parent—with whom, or where, thou hast entrusted my child. I will try to cut off, and cast from me, even my right hand, and my right eye; but for thee, Christian, if thou dost deal otherwise than prudently and honestly in this matter, it is what God and man will require at thy hand.'

'Fear not me,' said Christian hastily, and left the place, agitated by reflections of no pleasant kind.

'I ought to have persuaded him to return,' he said, as he stepped out into the street. 'Even his hovering in this neighbourhood may spoil the plan on which depends the rise of my fortunes—aye, and of his child's. Will men say I have ruined her, when I shall have raised her to the dazzling height of the Duchess of Portsmouth, and perhaps made her a mother to a long line of princes? Chiffinch hath vouched for opportunity; and the voluptuary's fortune depends upon his gratifying the taste of his master for variety. If she makes an impression, it must be a deep one; and once seated in his affections, I fear not her being supplanted. What will her father say? Will he, like a prudent man, put his shame in his pocket, because it is well gilded? or will he think it fitting to make a display of moral wrath and parental frenzy? I fear the latter—He has ever kept too strict a course to admit his conniving at such licence. But what will his anger avail? I need not be seen in the matter—those who are will care little for the resentment of a country Puritan. And after all, what I am labouring to bring about is best for himself, the wench, and above all, for me, Edward Christian.'

With such base opiates did this unhappy wretch stifle his own conscience, while anticipating the disgrace of his friend's family, and the ruin of a near relative, committed in confidence to his charge. The character of this man was of no common description; nor was it by an ordinary road that he had arrived at the present climax of unfeeling and infamous selfishness.

Edward Christian, as the reader is aware, was the brother of that William Christian, who was the principal instrument in delivering up the Isle of Man to the Republic, and who became the victim of the Countess of Derby's revenge on that account. Both had been educated as Puritans, but William was a soldier, which somewhat modified the strictness of his religious opinions ; Edward, a civilian, seemed to entertain these principles in the utmost rigour. But it was only seeming. The exactness of deportment, which procured him great honour and influence among the *sober party*, as they were wont to term themselves, covered a voluptuous disposition, the gratification of which was sweet to him as stolen waters, and pleasant as bread eaten in secret. While, therefore, his seeming godliness brought him worldly gain, his secret pleasures compensated for his outward austerity ; until the Restoration, and the countess's violent proceedings against his brother, interrupted the course of both. He then fled from his native island, burning with the desire of revenging his brother's death—the only passion foreign to his own gratification which he was ever known to cherish, and which was also, at least, partly selfish, since it concerned the restoration of his own fortunes.

He found easy access to Villiers, Duke of Buckingham, who, in right of his duchess, claimed such of the Derby estate as had been bestowed by the Parliament on his celebrated father-in-law, Lord Fairfax. His influence at the court of Charles, where a jest was a better plea than a long claim of faithful service, was so successfully exerted, as to contribute greatly to the depression of that loyal and ill-rewarded family. But Buckingham was incapable, even for his own interest, of pursuing the steady course which Christian suggested to him ; and his vacillation probably saved the remnant of the large estates of the Earl of Derby.

Meantime, Christian was too useful a follower to be dismissed. From Buckingham, and others of that stamp, he did not affect to conceal the laxity of his morals ; but, towards the numerous and powerful party to which he belonged, he was able to disguise them by a seeming gravity of exterior, which he never laid aside. Indeed, so wide and absolute was then the distinction betwixt the court and the city, that a man might have for some time played two several parts, as in two different spheres, without its being discovered in the one that he exhibited himself in a different light in the other. Besides, when a man of talent shows himself an able and useful partisan, his party will continue to protect and accredit him, in spite of conduct the most contradictory to their own principles. Some facts are, in such cases, denied—some are glossed over—and party zeal is permitted to cover at least as many defects as ever doth charity.

Edward Christian had often need of the partial indulgence of his friends ; but he experienced it, for he was eminently useful. Buckingham, and other courtiers of the same class, however dissolute in their lives, were desirous of keeping some connexion with the Dissenting or Puritanic party, as it was termed ; thereby to strengthen themselves against their opponents at court. In such intrigues, Christian was a notable agent ; and at one time had nearly procured an absolute union between a class which professed the most rigid principles of religion and morality, and the latitudinarian courtiers, who set all principle at defiance.

Amidst the vicissitudes of a life of intrigue, during which Buckingham's ambitious schemes, and his own, repeatedly sent him across the Atlantic, it was Edward Christian's boast that he never lost sight of his principal object—revenge on the Countess of Derby. He maintained a close and intimate correspondence with his native island, so as to be perfectly informed of whatever took place there ; and he stimulated, on every favourable opportunity, the cupidity of Buckingham to possess himself of this petty kingdom, by procuring the forfeiture of its present lord. It was not difficult to keep his patron's wild wishes alive on this topic, for his own mercurial imagination attached particular charms to the idea of becoming a sort of sovereign even in this little island ; and he was, like Catiline, as covetous of the property of others, as he was profuse of his own.

But it was not until the pretended discovery of the Papist Plot that the schemes of Christian could be brought to ripen ; and then, so odious were the Catholics in the eyes of the credulous people of England, that, upon the accusation of the most infamous of mankind, common informers, the

scourings of jails, and the refuse of the whipping-post, the
most atrocious charges against persons of the highest rank
and fairest character were readily received and credited.

This was a period which Christian did not fail to improve.
He drew close his intimacy with Bridgenorth, which had
indeed never been interrupted, and readily engaged him in
his schemes, which, in the eyes of his brother-in-law, were
alike honourable and patriotic. But, while he flattered
Bridgenorth with the achieving a complete reformation in
the State—checking the profligacy of the court—relieving
the consciences of the dissenters from the pressure of the
penal laws—amending, in fine, the crying grievances of the
time—while he showed him also, in prospect, revenge upon
the Countess of Derby, and a humbling dispensation on the
house of Peveril, from whom Bridgenorth had suffered such
indignity, Christian did not neglect, in the meanwhile, to
consider how he could best benefit himself by the confidence
reposed in him by his unsuspicious relation.

The extreme beauty of Alice Bridgenorth—the great
wealth which time and economy had accumulated on her
father—pointed her out as a most desirable match to repair
the wasted fortunes of some of the followers of the court;
and he flattered himself that he could conduct such a
negotiation so as to be in a high degree conducive to his own
advantage. He found there would be little difficulty in
prevailing on Major Bridgenorth to entrust him with the
guardianship of his daughter. That unfortunate gentleman
had accustomed himself, from the very period of her birth,
to regard the presence of his child as a worldly indulgence
too great to be allowed to him; and Christian had little
trouble in convincing him that the strong inclination which
he felt to bestow her on Julian Peveril, provided he could
be brought over to his own political opinions, was a blameable compromise with his more severe principles. Late
circumstances had taught him the incapacity and unfit-
ness of Dame Debbitch for the sole charge of so dear a
pledge; and he readily and thankfully embraced the kind
offer of her maternal uncle, Christian, to place Alice under
the protection of a lady of rank in London, whilst he himself
was to be engaged in the scenes of bustle and blood, which,
in common with all good Protestants, he expected was

speedily to take place on a general rising of the Papists, unless prevented by the active and energetic measures of the good people of England. He even confessed his fears, that his partial regard for Alice's happiness might enervate his efforts in behalf of his country ; and Christian had little trouble in eliciting from him a promise that he would forbear to inquire after her for some time.

Thus certain of being the temporary guardian of his niece for a space long enough, he flattered himself, for the execution of his purpose, Christian endeavoured to pave the way by consulting Chiffinch, whose known skill in court policy qualified him best as an adviser on this occasion. But this worthy person, being, in fact, a purveyor for his Majesty's pleasures, and on that account high in his good graces, thought it fell within the line of his duty to suggest another scheme than that on which Christian consulted him. A woman of such exquisite beauty as Alice was described, he deemed more worthy to be a partaker of the affections of the merry Monarch, whose taste in female beauty was so exquisite, than to be made the wife of some worn-out prodigal of quality. And then, doing perfect justice to his own character, he felt it would not be one whit impaired, while his fortune would be, in every respect, greatly amended, if, after sharing the short reign of the Gwyns, the Davises, the Robertses, and so forth, Alice Bridgenorth should retire from the state of a royal favourite into the humble condition of Mrs. Chiffinch.

After cautiously sounding Christian, and finding that the near prospect of interest to himself effectually prevented his starting at this iniquitous scheme, Chiffinch detailed it to him fully, carefully keeping the final termination out of sight, and talking of the favour to be acquired by the fair Alice as no passing caprice, but the commencement of a reign as long and absolute as that of the Duchess of Portsmouth, of whose avarice and domineering temper Charles was now understood to be much tired, though the force of habit rendered him unequal to free himself of her yoke.

Thus chalked out, the scene prepared was no longer the intrigue of a court pander, and a villainous resolution for the ruin of an innocent girl, but became a State intrigue for the removal of an obnoxious favourite, and the subsequent change of the king's sentiments upon various material points, in which he was at present influenced by the Duchess of Portsmouth. In this light it was exhibited to the Duke of Buckingham, who, either to sustain his character for daring gallantry, or in order to gratify some capricious fancy, had at one time made love to the reigning favourite, and experienced a repulse which he had never forgiven.

But one scheme was too little to occupy the active and enterprising spirit of the duke. An appendix of the Popish Plot was easily so contrived as to involve the Countess of Derby, who, from character and religion, was precisely the person whom the credulous part of the public were inclined to suppose the likely accomplice of such a conspiracy. Christian and Bridgenorth undertook the perilous commission of attacking her even in her own little kingdom of Man, and had commissions for this purpose, which were only to be produced in case of their scheme taking effect.

It miscarried, as the reader is aware, from the countess's alert preparations for defence ; and neither Christian nor Bridgenorth held it sound policy to practise openly, even under parliamentary authority, against a lady so little liable to hesitate upon the measures most likely to secure her feudal sovereignty ; wisely considering that even the omnipotence, as it has been somewhat too largely styled, of Parliament might fail to relieve them from the personal consequences of a failure.

On the continent of Britain, however, no opposition was to be feared ; and so well was Christian acquainted with all the motions in the interior of the countess's little court, or household, that Peveril would have been arrested the instant he set foot on shore, but for the gale of wind, which obliged the vessel, in which he was a passenger, to run for Liverpool. Here Christian, under the name of Ganlesse, unexpectedly met with him, and preserved him from the fangs of the well-breathed witnesses of the Plot, with the purpose of securing his dispatches, or, if necessary, his person also, in such a manner as to place him at his own discretion— a narrow and perilous game, which he thought it better, however, to undertake, than to permit these subordinate agents, who were always ready to mutiny against all in league with them, to obtain the credit which they must have done by the seizure of the Countess of Derby's dispatches. It was, besides, essential to Buckingham's schemes that these should not pass into the hands of a public officer like Topham, who, however pompous and stupid, was upright and well-intentioned, until they had undergone the revisal of a private committee, where something might have probably been suppressed, even supposing that nothing had been added. In short, Christian, in carrying on his own separate and peculiar intrigue, by the agency of the Great Popish Plot, as it was called, acted just like an engineer, who derives the principle of motion which turns his machinery, by means of a steam-engine, or large water-wheel, constructed to drive a separate and larger engine. Accordingly, he was determined that, while he took all the advantage he could from their supposed discoveries, no one should be admitted to tamper or interfere with his own plans of profit and revenge.

Chiffinch, who, desirous of satisfying himself with his own eyes of that excellent beauty which had been so highly extolled, had gone down to Derbyshire on purpose, was infinitely delighted, when, during the course of a two hours' sermon at the dissenting chapel in Liverpool, which afforded him ample leisure for a deliberate survey, he arrived at the conclusion that he had never seen a form or face more captivating. His eyes having confirmed what was told him, he hurried back to the little inn which formed their place of rendezvous, and there awaited Christian and his niece, with a degree of confidence in the success of their project which he had not before entertained ; and with an apparatus of luxury, calculated, as he thought, to make a favourable impression on the mind of a rustic girl. He was somewhat surprised, when, instead of Alice Bridgenorth, to whom he expected that night to have been introduced, he found that Christian was accompanied by Julian Peveril. It was indeed a severe disappointment, for he had prevailed on his own indolence to venture thus far from the court, in order that he might judge, with his own paramount taste, whether Alice was really the prodigy which her uncle's praises had bespoken her, and, as such, a victim worthy of the fate to which she was destined.

A few words betwixt the worthy confederates determined them on the plan of stripping Peveril of the countess's dispatches ; Chiffinch absolutely refusing to take any share in arresting him, as a matter of which his master's approbation might be very uncertain.

Christian had also his own reasons for abstaining from so decisive a step. It was by no means likely to be agreeable to Bridgenorth, whom it was necessary to keep in good humour ;—it was not necessary, for the countess's dispatches were of far more importance than the person of Julian. Lastly, it was superfluous in this respect also, that Julian was on the road to his father's castle, where it was likely he would be seized, as a matter of course, along with the other suspicious persons who fell under Topham's warrant, and the denunciations of his infamous companions. He, therefore, far from using any violence to Peveril, assumed towards him such a friendly tone, as might seem to warn him against receiving damage from others, and vindicate himself from having any share in depriving him of his charge. This last manœuvre was achieved by an infusion of a strong narcotic into Julian's wine ; under the influence of which he slumbered so soundly that the confederates were easily able to accomplish their inhospitable purpose.

The events of the succeeding days are already known to the reader. Chiffinch set forward to return to London, with the packet, which it was desirable should be in Buckingham's hands as soon as possible ; while Christian went to Moultrassie, to receive Alice from her father, and convey her safely to London—his accomplice agreeing to defer his curiosity to see more of her until they should have arrived in that city.

Before parting with Bridgenorth, Christian had exerted his utmost address to prevail on him to remain at Moultrassie ; he had even overstepped the bounds of prudence, and, by his urgency, awakened some suspicions of an indefinite nature, which he found it difficult to allay. Bridgenorth, therefore, followed his brother-in-law to London ; and the reader has already been made acquainted with the arts which Christian used to prevent his further interference with the destinies of his daughter, or the unhallowed schemes of her ill-chosen guardian. Still Christian, as he strode along the street in profound reflection, saw that his undertaking was attended with a thousand perils ; and the drops stood like beads on his brow when he thought of the presumptuous levity and fickle temper of Buckingham—the frivolity and intemperance of Chiffinch— the suspicions of the melancholy and bigoted, yet sagacious and honest Bridgenorth. ' Had I,' he thought, ' but tools fitted, each to their portion of the work, how easily could I heave asunder and disjoint the strength that opposes me ! But with these frail and insufficient implements, I am in daily, hourly, momentary danger, that one lever or other gives way, and that the whole ruin recoils on my own head. And yet, were it not for those failings I complain of, how were it possible for me to have acquired that power over them all which constitutes them my passive tools, even when they seem most to exert their own free will ? Yes, the bigots have some right when they affirm that all is for the best.'

It may seem strange, that, amidst the various subjects of Christian's apprehension, he was never visited by any long or permanent doubt that the virtue of his niece might prove the shoal on which his voyage should be wrecked. But he was an arrant rogue, as well as a hardened libertine ; and, in both characters, a professed disbeliever in the virtue of the fair sex.

CHAPTER XXX

As for John Dryden's Charles, I own that King
Was never any very mighty thing ;
And yet he was a devilish honest fellow—
Enjoy'd his friend and bottle, and got mellow.
                                        DR. WOLCOT.

LONDON, the grand central point of intrigues of every description, had now attracted within its dark and shadowy region the greater number of the personages whom we have had occasion to mention.

Julian Peveril, amongst others of the dramatis personae, had arrived, and taken up his abode in a remote inn in the suburbs. His business, he conceived, was to remain incognito until he should have communicated in private with the friends who were most likely to lend assistance to his parents, as well as to his patroness, in their present

THE DUKE OF ORMOND

situation of doubt and danger. Amongst these, the most powerful was the Duke of Ormond, whose faithful services, high rank, and acknowledged worth and virtue, still preserved an ascendancy in that very court, where, in general, he was regarded as out of favour. Indeed, so much con-

sciousness did Charles display in his demeanour towards
that celebrated noble, and servant of his father, that
Buckingham once took the freedom to ask the king whether
the Duke of Ormond had lost his Majesty's favour, or
his Majesty the duke's ? since, whenever they chanced to
meet, the king appeared the more embarrassed of the two.
But it was not Peveril's good fortune to obtain the advice
or countenance of this distinguished person. His Grace of
Ormond was not at that time in London.

The letter, about the delivery of which the countess had
seemed most anxious after that to the Duke of Ormond,
was addressed to Captain Barstow (a Jesuit, whose real
name was Fenwicke), to be found, or at least to be heard of,
in the house of one Martin Christal in the Savoy. To this
place hastened Peveril, upon learning the absence of the
Duke of Ormond. He was not ignorant of the danger
which he personally incurred, by thus becoming a medium
of communication betwixt a Popish priest and a suspected
Catholic. But when he undertook the perilous commission
of his patroness, he had done so frankly, and with the
unreserved resolution of serving her in the manner in which
she most desired her affairs to be conducted. Yet he could
not forbear some secret apprehension, when he felt himself
engaged in the labyrinth of passages and galleries, which
led to different obscure sets of apartments in the ancient
building termed the Savoy.

This antiquated and almost ruinous pile occupied a part
of the site of the public offices in the Strand, commonly
called Somerset House. The Savoy had been formerly
a palace, and took its name from an Earl of Savoy, by
whom it was founded. It had been the habitation of John
of Gaunt, and various persons of distinction—had become
a convent, an hospital, and finally, in Charles II's time,
a waste of dilapidated buildings and ruinous apartments,
inhabited chiefly by those who had some connexion with,
or dependence upon, the neighbouring palace of Somerset
House, which, more fortunate than the Savoy, had still
retained its royal title, and was the abode of a part of the
court, and occasionally of the king himself, who had apartments there.

It was not without several inquiries, and more than one

mistake, that, at the end of a long and dusky passage,
composed of boards so wasted by time that they threatened
to give way under his feet, Julian at length found the name
of Martin Christal, broker and appraiser, upon a shattered
door.   He was about to knock, when some one pulled
his cloak ; and looking round, to his great astonishment,
which indeed almost amounted to fear, he saw the little
mute damsel, who had accompanied him for a part of the
way on his voyage from the Isle of Man. ' Fenella ! ' he
exclaimed, forgetting that she could neither hear nor reply,
—' Fenella ! Can this be you ? '

Fenella, assuming the air of warning and authority,
which she had heretofore endeavoured to adopt towards
him, interposed betwixt Julian and the door at which he
was about to knock—pointed with her finger towards it in
a prohibiting manner, and at the same time bent her brows,
and shook her head sternly.

After a moment's consideration, Julian could place but
one interpretation upon Fenella's appearance and conduct,
and that was, by supposing her lady had come up to London,
and had dispatched this mute attendant, as a confidential
person, to apprise him of some change of her intended
operations, which might render the delivery of her letters
to Barstow, *alias* Fenwicke, superfluous, or perhaps dangerous.   He made signs to Fenella, demanding to know
whether she had any commission from the countess.   She
nodded. ' Had she any letter ? ' he continued, by the
same mode of inquiry.   She shook her head impatiently,
and, walking hastily along the passage, made a signal to
him to follow.   He did so, having little doubt that he was
about to be conducted into the countess's presence ; but
his surprise, at first excited by Fenella's appearance, was
increased by the rapidity and ease with which she seemed
to track the dusky and decayed mazes of the dilapidated
Savoy, equal to that with which he had seen her formerly
lead the way through the gloomy vaults of Castle Rushin,
in the Isle of Man.

When he recollected, however, that Fenella had accompanied the countess on a long visit to London, it appeared
not improbable that she might then have acquired this local
knowledge which seemed so accurate.   Many foreigners,

dependent on the queen or queen-dowager, had apartments
in the Savoy. Many Catholic priests also found refuge in
its recesses, under various disguises, and in defiance of
the severity of the laws against Popery. What was more
likely than that the Countess of Derby, a Catholic and
a Frenchwoman, should have had secret commissions
amongst such people ; and that the execution of such
should be entrusted, at least occasionally, to Fenella ?

Thus reflecting, Julian continued to follow her light
and active footsteps as she glided from the Strand to
Spring Garden, and thence into the Park.

It was still early in the morning, and the Mall was un-
tenanted, save by a few walkers, who frequented these
shades for the wholesome purposes of air and exercise.
Splendour, gaiety, and display, did not come forth, at that
period, until noon was approaching. All readers have
heard that the whole space where the Horse Guards are now
built, made, in the time of Charles II, a part of St. James's
Park ; and that the old building, now called the Treasury,
was a part of the ancient Palace of Whitehall, which was
thus immediately connected with the Park. The canal
had been constructed, by the celebrated Le Notre, for the
purpose of draining the Park ; and it communicated with
the Thames by a decoy, stocked with a quantity of the
rarer waterfowl. It was towards this decoy that Fenella
bent her way with unabated speed ; and they were approaching a group of two or three gentlemen, who sauntered by its
banks, when, on looking closely at him who appeared to be
the chief of the party, Julian felt his heart beat uncommonly
thick, as if conscious of approaching some one of the highest
consequence.

The person whom he looked upon was past the middle age
of life, of a dark complexion, corresponding with the long,
black, full-bottomed periwig, which he wore instead of his
own hair. His dress was plain black velvet, with a diamond
star, however, on his cloak, which hung carelessly over one
shoulder. His features, strongly lined, even to harshness,
had yet an expression of dignified good humour ; he was well
and strongly built, walked upright and yet easily, and had
upon the whole the air of a person of the highest consideration. He kept rather in advance of his companions, but

turned and spoke to them, from time to time, with much affability, and probably with some liveliness, judging by the smiles, and sometimes the scarce restrained laughter, by which some of his sallies were received by his attendants. They also wore only morning dresses ; but their looks and manner were those of men of rank, in presence of one in station still more elevated. They shared the attention of their principal in common with seven or eight little black curly-haired spaniels, or rather, as they are now called, cockers, which attended their master as closely, and perhaps with as deep sentiments of attachment, as the bipeds of the group ; and whose gambols, which seemed to afford him much amusement, he sometimes checked, and some-times encouraged. In addition to this pastime, a lackey, or groom, was also in attendance, with one or two little baskets and bags, from which the gentleman we have described took, from time to time, a handful of seeds, and amused himself with throwing them to the waterfowl.

This, the king's favourite occupation, together with his remarkable countenance, and the deportment of the rest of the company towards him, satisfied Julian Peveril that he was approaching, perhaps indecorously, near to the person of Charles Stuart, the second of that unhappy name.

While he hesitated to follow his dumb guide any nearer, and felt the embarrassment of being unable to communicate to her his repugnance to further intrusion, a person in the royal retinue touched a light and lively air on the flageolet, at a signal from the king, who desired to have some tune repeated which had struck him in the theatre on the pre-ceding evening. While the good-natured monarch marked time with his foot, and with the motion of his hand, Fenella continued to approach him, and threw into her manner the appearance of one who was attracted, as it were in spite of herself, by the sounds of the instrument.

Anxious to know how this was to end, and astonished to see the dumb girl imitate so accurately the manner of one who actually heard the musical notes, Peveril also drew near, though at somewhat greater distance

The king looked good-humouredly at both, as if he admitted their musical enthusiasm as an excuse for their intrusion ; but his eyes became riveted on Fenella, whose face and appearance, although rather singular than beautiful, had something in them wild, fantastic, and, as being so, even captivating, to an eye which had been gratified perhaps to satiety with the ordinary forms of female beauty. She did not appear to notice how closely she was observed ; but, as if acting under an irresistible impulse, derived from the sounds to which she seemed to listen, she undid the bodkin round which her long tresses were winded, and flinging them suddenly over her slender person, as if using them as a natural veil, she began to dance, with infinite grace and agility, to the tune which the flageolet played.

Peveril lost almost his sense of the king's presence, when he observed with what wonderful grace and agility Fenella kept time to notes, which could only be known to her by the motions of the musician's fingers. He had heard, indeed among other prodigies, of a person in Fenella's unhappy situation acquiring, by some unaccountable and mysterious tact, the power of acting as an instrumental musician, nay, becoming so accurate a performer as to be capable of lead- ing a musical band ; and he had also heard of deaf and dumb persons dancing with sufficient accuracy, by observing the motions of their partner. But Fenella's performance seemed more wonderful than either, since the musician was guided by his written notes, and the dancer by the motions of the others ; whereas Fenella had no intimation, save what she seemed to gather, with infinite accuracy, by observing the motion of the artist's fingers on his small instrument.

As for the king, who was ignorant of the particular circumstances which rendered Fenella's performance almost marvellous, he was contented, at her first commencement, to authorize what seemed to him the frolic of this singular- looking damsel, by a good-humoured smile ; but when he perceived the exquisite truth and justice, as well as the wonderful combination of grace and agility, with which she executed to his favourite air a dance which was perfectly new to him, Charles turned his mere acquiescence into something like enthusiastic applause. He bore time to her motions with the movement of his foot—applauded with head and with hand—and seemed, like herself, carried away by the enthusiasm of the gestic art.

After a rapid yet graceful succession of *entrechats*, Fenella introduced a slow movement, which terminated the dance ; then dropping a profound curtsy, she continued to stand motionless before the king, her arms folded on her bosom, her head stooped, and her eyes cast down, after the manner of an Oriental slave ; while, through the misty veil of her shadowy locks, it might be observed that the colour which exercise had called to her cheeks was dying fast away, and resigning them to their native dusky hue.

' By my honour,' exclaimed the king, ' she is like a fairy who trips it in moonlight. There must be more of air and fire than of earth in her composition. It is well poor Nelly Gwyn saw her not, or she would have died of grief and envy. —Come, gentlemen, which of you contrived this pretty piece of morning pastime ? '

The courtiers looked at each other, but none of them felt authorized to claim the merit of a service so agreeable.

' We must ask the quick-eyed nymph herself, then,' said the king ; and, looking at Fenella, he added, ' Tell us, my pretty one, to whom we owe the pleasure of seeing you ? —I suspect the Duke of Buckingham ; for this is exactly a *tour de son métier.*'

Fenella, on observing that the king addressed her, bowed low, and shook her head, in signal that she did not understand what he said. ' Odds-fish, that is true,' said the king ; ' she must perforce be a foreigner—her complexion and agility speak it. France or Italy has had the moulding of these elastic limbs, dark cheek, and eye of fire.' He then put to her in French, and again in Italian, the question, ' By whom she had been sent hither ? '

At the second repetition, Fenella threw back her veiling tresses, so as to show the melancholy which sat on her brow ; while she sadly shook her head, and intimated by imperfect muttering, but of the softest and most plaintive kind, her organic deficiency.

' Is it possible Nature can have made such a fault ? ' said Charles. ' Can she have left so curious a piece as thou art without the melody of voice, whilst she has made thee so exquisitely sensible to the beauty of sound ? Stay : what means this ? and what young fellow are you bringing up there ? Oh, the master of the show, I suppose.—Friend,'

he added, addressing himself to Peveril, who, on the signal
of Fenella, stepped forward almost instinctively, and kneeled
down, ' we thank thee for the pleasure of this morning.—
My lord marquis, you rooked me at piquet last night; for
which disloyal deed thou shalt now atone, by giving a couple
of pieces to this honest youth, and five to the girl.'

As the nobleman drew out his purse, and came forward
to perform the king's generous commission, Julian felt
some embarrassment ere he was able to explain that he had
no title to be benefited by the young person's performance,
and that his Majesty had mistaken his character.

' And who art thou, then, my friend ? ' said Charles ;
' but, above all, and particularly, who is this dancing
nymph, whom thou standest waiting on like an attendant
faun ? '

' The young person is a retainer of the Countess-Dowager
of Derby, so please your Majesty,' said Peveril, in a low
tone of voice ; ' and I am '——

' Hold, hold,' said the king ; ' this is a dance to another
tune, and not fit for a place so public. Hark thee, friend ;
do thou and the young woman follow Empson where he
will conduct thee.—Empson, carry them—hark in thy
ear.'

' May it please your Majesty, I ought to say,' said Peveril,
' that I am guiltless of any purpose of intrusion '——

' Now a plague on him who can take no hint,' said the
king, cutting short his apology. ' Oddsfish, man, there
are times when civility is the greatest impertinence in the
world. Do thou follow Empson, and amuse thyself for
a half-hour's space with the fairy's company, till we shall
send for you.'

Charles spoke this not without casting an anxious eye
around, and in a tone which intimated apprehension of
being overheard. Julian could only bow obedience, and
follow Empson, who was the same person that played so
rarely on the flageolet.

When they were out of sight of the king and his party,
the musician wished to enter into conversation with his
companions, and addressed himself first to Fenella, with
a broad compliment of, ' By the mass, ye dance rarely—
ne'er a slut on the boards shows such a shank ! I would

be content to play to you till my throat were as dry as my whistle. Come, be a little free—old Rowley will not quit the park till nine. I will carry you to Spring Gardens, and bestow sweet cakes and a quart of Rhenish on both of you ; and we'll be cameradoes. What the devil ? no answer ?—How's this, brother ?—Is this neat wench of yours deaf or dumb, or both ? I should laugh at that, and she trip it so well to the flageolet.'

To rid himself of this fellow's discourse, Peveril answered him in French, that he was a foreigner, and spoke no English ; glad to escape, though at the expense of a fiction, from the additional embarrassment of a fool, who was likely to ask more questions than his own wisdom might have enabled him to answer.

' *Étranger*—that means stranger,' muttered their guide ; ' more French dogs and jades come to lick the good English butter off our bread, or perhaps an Italian puppet-show. Well, if it were not that they have a mortal enmity to the whole *gamut,* this were enough to make any honest fellow turn Puritan. But if I am to play to her at the Duchess's, I'll be d—d but I put her out in the tune, just to teach her to have the impudence to come to England, and to speak no English.'

Having muttered to himself this truly British resolution, the musician walked briskly on towards a large house near the bottom of St. James's Street, and entered the court, by a grated door, from the Park, of which the mansion commanded an extensive prospect.

Peveril, finding himself in front of a handsome portico under which opened a stately pair of folding-doors, was about to ascend the steps that led to the main entrance, when his guide seized him by the arm, exclaiming, ' Hold, Mounseer ! What ! you'll lose nothing, I see, for want of courage ; but you must keep the back way, for all your fine doublet. Here it is not, knock and it shall be opened ; but may be instead, knock and you shall be knocked.'

Suffering himself to be guided by Empson, Julian deviated from the principal door, to one which opened, with less ostentation, in an angle of the courtyard. On a modest tap from the flute-player, admittance was afforded him and

his companions by a footman, who conducted them through
a variety of stone passages, to a very handsome summer
parlour, where a lady, or something resembling one, dressed
in a style of extra elegance, was trifling with a play-book
while she finished her chocolate. It would not be easy to
describe her, but by weighing her natural good qualities
against the affectations which counterbalanced them. She
would have been handsome, but for rouge and *minauderie*
—would have been civil, but for overstrained airs of patronage and condescension—would have had an agreeable
voice, had she spoken in her natural tone—and fine eyes,
had she not made such desperate hard use of them. She
could only spoil a pretty ankle by too liberal display ; but
her shape, though she could not yet be thirty years old, had
the *embonpoint* which might have suited better with ten
years more advanced. She pointed Empson to a seat with
the air of a duchess, and asked him, languidly, how he
did this age, that she had not seen him ? and what folks
these were he had brought with him ?

'Foreigners, madam; d——d foreigners,' answered Empson ; 'starving beggars, that our old friend has picked
up in the Park this morning—the wench dances, and the
fellow plays on the Jews' trump, I believe. On my life,
madam, I begin to be ashamed of old Rowley ; I must
discard him, unless he keeps better company in future.'

'Fie, Empson,' said the lady ; 'consider it is our duty
to countenance him, and keep him afloat ; and indeed I
always make a principle of it. Hark ye, he comes not
hither this morning ? '

'He will be here,' answered Empson, 'in the walking
of a minuet.'

'My God ! ' exclaimed the lady, with unaffected alarm ;
and starting up with utter neglect of her usual and graceful
languor, she tripped as swiftly as a milkmaid into an
adjoining apartment, where they heard presently a few
words of eager and animated discussion.

'Something to be put out of the way, I suppose,' said
Empson. 'Well for madam I gave her the hint. There
he goes, the happy swain.'

Julian was so situated, that he could, from the same
casement through which Empson was peeping, observe

a man in a laced roquelaure, and carrying his rapier under his arm, glide from the door by which he had himself entered, and out of the court, keeping as much as possible under the shade of the buildings.

The lady re-entered at this moment, and observing how Empson's eyes were directed, said with a slight appearance of hurry, ' A gentleman of the Duchess of Portsmouth's with a billet ; and so tiresomely pressing for an answer, that I was obliged to write without my diamond pen. I have daubed my fingers, I dare say,' she added, looking at a very pretty hand, and presently after dipping her fingers in a little silver vase of rose-water. ' But that little exotic monster of yours, Empson, I hope she really understands no English ?—On my life she coloured. Is she such a rare dancer ?—I must see her dance, and hear him play on the Jews' harp.'

' Dance ! ' replied Empson ; ' she danced well enough when I played to her. I can make anything dance. Old Counsellor Clubfoot danced when he had a fit of the gout ; you have seen no such *pas seul* in the theatre. I would engage to make the Archbishop of Canterbury dance the hays like a Frenchman. There is nothing in dancing ; it all lies in the music. Rowley does not know that now. He saw this poor wench dance ; and thought so much on't, when it was all along of me. I would have defied her to sit still. And Rowley gives her the credit of it, and five pieces to boot ; and I have only two for my morning's work ! '

' True, Master Empson,' said the lady ; ' but you are of the family, though in a lower station ; and you ought to consider '——

' By G—; madam,' answered Empson, ' all I consider is that I play the best flageolet in England ; and that they can no more supply my place, if they were to discard me, than they could fill Thames from Fleet Ditch.'

' Well, Master Empson, I do not dispute but you are a man of talents,' replied the lady ; ' still I say, mind the main chance—you please the ear to-day—another has the advantage of you to-morrow.'

' Never, mistress, while ears have the heavenly power of distinguishing one note from another.'

'Heavenly power, say you, Master Empson?' said
the lady.

'Aye, madam, heavenly; for some very neat verses
which we had at our festival say,

> What know we of the blest above,
> But that they sing and that they love?

It is Master Waller wrote them, as I think; who, upon my
word, ought to be encouraged.'

'And so should you, my dear Empson,' said the dame,
yawning, 'were it only for the honour you do to your own
profession. But in the meantime, will you ask these
people to have some refreshment?—and will you take some
yourself?—the chocolate is that which the ambassador
Portuguese fellow brought over to the queen.'

'If it be genuine,' said the musician.

'How, sir,' said the fair one, half rising from her pile of
cushions—'Not genuine, and in this house!—Let me
understand you, Master Empson—I think, when I first saw
you, you scarce knew chocolate from coffee.'

'By G—, madam,' answered the flageolet-player, 'you
are perfectly right. And how can I show better how much
I have profited by your ladyship's excellent cheer, except
by being critical?'

'You stand excused, Master Empson,' said the *petite
maitresse*, sinking gently back on the downy couch, from
which a momentary irritation had startled her—'I think
the chocolate will please you, though scarce equal to what
we had from the Spanish resident Mendoza.—But we must
offer these strange people something. Will you ask them
if they would have coffee and chocolate, or cold wild-fowl,
fruit, and wine? They must be treated so as to show them
where they are, since here they are.'

'Unquestionably, madam,' said Empson; 'but I have
just at this instant forgot the French for chocolate, hot
bread, coffee, game, and drinkables.'

'It is odd,' said the lady; 'and I have forgot my French
and Italian at the same moment. But it signifies little—
I will order the things to be brought, and they will remember
the names of them themselves.'

Empson laughed loudly at this jest, and pawned his soul

that the cold sirloin which entered immediately after, was
the best emblem of roast-beef all the world over. Plentiful
refreshments were offered to all the party, of which both
Fenella and Peveril partook.

In the meanwhile, the flageolet-player drew closer to
the side of the lady of the mansion—their intimacy was
cemented, and their spirits set afloat, by a glass of liqueur,
which gave them additional confidence in discussing the
characters, as well of the superior attendants of the court,
as of the inferior rank, to which they themselves might be
supposed to belong.

The lady, indeed, during this conversation, frequently
exerted her complete and absolute superiority over Master
Empson ; in which that musical gentleman humbly
acquiesced whenever the circumstance was recalled to his
attention, whether in the way of blunt contradiction,
sarcastic insinuation, downright assumption of higher importance, or in any of the other various modes by which
such superiority is usually asserted and maintained. But
the lady's obvious love of scandal was the lure which very
soon brought her again down from the dignified part which
for a moment she assumed, and placed her once more on
a gossiping level with her companion.

Their conversation was too trivial, and too much allied
to petty court intrigues, with which he was totally unacquainted, to be in the least interesting to Julian. As it
continued for more than an hour, he soon ceased to pay
the least attention to a discourse consisting of nicknames,
patchwork, and innuendo ; and employed himself in reflecting on his own complicated affairs, and the probable issue
of his approaching audience with the king, which had been
brought about by so singular an agent, and by means so
unexpected. He often looked to his guide, Fenella ; and
observed that she was, for the greater part of the time,
drowned in deep and abstracted meditation. But three or
four times—and it was when the assumed airs and affected
importance of the musician and their hostess rose to the
most extravagant excess—he observed that Fenella dealt
askance on them some of those bitter and almost blighting
elfin looks, which in the Isle of Man were held to imply
contemptuous execration. There was something in all her

manner so extraordinary, joined to her sudden appearance, and her demeanour in the king's presence, so oddly, yet so well contrived to procure him a private audience—which he might, by graver means, have sought in vain—that it almost justified the idea, though he smiled at it internally, that the little mute agent was aided in her machinations by the kindred imps, to whom, according to Manx superstition, her genealogy was to be traced.

Another idea sometimes occurred to Julian, though he rejected the question, as being equally wild with those doubts which referred Fenella to a race different from that of mortals—' Was she really afflicted with those organical imperfections which had always seemed to sever her from humanity ?—If not, what could be the motives of so young a creature practising so dreadful a penance for such an unremitted term of years ? And how formidable must be the strength of mind which could condemn itself to so terrific a sacrifice—How deep and strong the purpose for which it was undertaken ! '

But a brief recollection of past events enabled him to dismiss this conjecture as altogether wild and visionary. He had but to call to memory the various stratagems prac- tised by his light-hearted companion, the young Earl of Derby, upon this forlorn girl—the conversations held in her presence, in which the character of a creature so irritable and sensitive upon all occasions, was freely, and some- times satirically discussed, without her expressing the least acquaintance with what was going forward, to convince him that so deep a deception could never have been practised for so many years, by a being of a turn of mind so peculiarly jealous and irascible.

He renounced, therefore, the idea, and turned his thoughts to his own affairs, and his approaching interview with his sovereign ; in which meditation we propose to leave him, until we briefly review the changes which had taken place in the situation of Alice Bridgenorth.

CHAPTER XXXI

I fear the devil worst when gown and cassock,
Or, in the lack of them, old Calvin's cloak,
Conceals his cloven hoof.

ANONYMOUS.

JULIAN PEVERIL had scarce set sail for Whitehaven,
when Alice Bridgenorth and her governante, at the hasty
command of her father, were embarked with equal speed
and secrecy on board of a bark bound for Liverpool.
Christian accompanied them on their voyage, as the friend
to whose guardianship Alice was to be consigned during any
future separation from her father, and whose amusing
conversation, joined to his pleasing though cold manners,
as well as his near relationship, induced Alice, in her forlorn
situation, to consider her fate as fortunate in having such
a guardian.

At Liverpool, as the reader already knows, Christian took
the first overt step in the villany which he had contrived
against the innocent girl, by exposing her at a meeting-
house to the unhallowed gaze of Chiffinch, in order to convince him she was possessed of such uncommon beauty as
might well deserve the infamous promotion to which they
meditated to raise her.

Highly satisfied with her personal appearance, Chiffinch
was no less so with the sense and delicacy of her conversation,
when he met her in company with her uncle afterwards in
London. The simplicity, and at the same time the spirit of
her remarks, made him regard her as his scientific attendant
the cook might have done a newly invented sauce, sufficiently
piquante in its qualities to awaken the jaded appetite of
a cloyed and gorged epicure. She was, he said and swore,
the very corner-stone on which, with proper management,
and with his instructions, a few honest fellows might build
a court fortune.

That the necessary introduction might take place, the
confederates judged fit she should be put under the charge
of an experienced lady, whom some called Mistress Chiffinch, and others Chiffinch's mistress—one of those obliging

creatures who are willing to discharge all the duties of a wife, without the inconvenient and indissoluble ceremony.

It was one, and not perhaps the least prejudicial consequence of the licence of that ill-governed time, that the bounds betwixt virtue and vice were so far smoothed down and levelled, that the frail wife, or the tender friend who was no wife, did not necessarily lose their place in society ; but, on the contrary, if they moved in the higher circles, were permitted and encouraged to mingle with women whose rank was certain, and whose reputation was untainted.

A regular liaison, like that of Chiffinch and his fair one, inferred little scandal ; and such was his influence, as prime minister of his master's pleasures, that, as Charles himself expressed it, the lady whom we introduced to our readers in the last chapter had obtained a brevet commission to rank as a married woman. And to do the gentle dame justice, no wife could have been more attentive to forward his plans, or more liberal in disposing of his income.

She inhabited a set of apartments called Chiffinch's— the scene of many an intrigue, both of love and politics ; and where Charles often held his private parties for the evening, when, as frequently happened, the ill humour of the Duchess of Portsmouth, his reigning sultana, prevented his supping with her. The hold which such an arrangement gave a man like Chiffinch, used as he well knew how to use it, made him of too much consequence to be slighted even by the first persons in the State, unless they stood aloof from all manner of politics and court intrigue.

In the charge of Mistress Chiffinch, and of him whose name she bore, Edward Christian placed the daughter of his sister, and of his confiding friend, calmly contemplating her ruin as an event certain to follow ; and hoping to ground upon it his own chance of a more assured fortune than a life spent in intrigue had hitherto been able to procure for him.

The innocent Alice, without being able to discover what was wrong either in the scenes of unusual luxury with which she was surrounded, or in the manners of her hostess, which, both from nature and policy, were kind and caressing— felt nevertheless an instinctive apprehension that all was not right—a feeling in the human mind, allied, perhaps, to that sense of danger which animals exhibit when placed in the vicinity of the natural enemies of their race, and which makes birds cower when the hawk is in the air, and beasts tremble when the tiger is abroad in the desert. There was a heaviness at her heart which she could not dispel ; and the few hours which she had already spent at Chiffinch's were like those passed in prison by one unconscious of the cause or event of his captivity. It was the third morning after her arrival in London, that the scene took place which we now recur to.

The impertinence and vulgarity of Empson, which was permitted to him as an unrivalled performer upon his instrument, were exhausting themselves at the expense of all other musical professors, and Mrs. Chiffinch was listening with careless indifference, when some one was heard speaking loudly, and with animation, in the inner apartment.

' Oh, gemini and gilliflower water ! ' exclaimed the damsel, startled out of her fine airs into her natural vulgarity of exclamation, and running to the door of communication —' if he has not come back again after all !—and if old Rowley ' ——

A tap at the farther and opposite door here arrested her attention—she quitted the handle of that which she was about to open, as speedily as if it had burnt her fingers, and, moving back towards her couch, asked, ' Who is there ? '

' Old Rowley himself, madam,' said the king, entering the apartment with his usual air of easy composure.

' O crimini !—your Majesty !—I thought ' ——

' That I was out of hearing, doubtless,' said the king ; ' and spoke of me as folks speak of absent friends. Make no apology. I think I have heard ladies say of their lace, that a rent is better than a darn. Nay, be seated. Where is Chiffinch ? '

' He is down at York House, your Majesty,' said the dame, recovering, though with no small difficulty, the calm affectation of her usual demeanour. ' Shall I send your Majesty's commands ? '

' I will wait his return,' said the king. ' Permit me to taste your chocolate.'

' There is some fresh frothed in the office,' said the lady ; and using a little silver call, or whistle, a black boy, superbly

dressed, like an oriental page, with gold bracelets on his
naked arms, and a gold collar around his equally bare neck,
attended with the favourite beverage of the morning, in an
apparatus of the richest china.

While he sipped his cup of chocolate, the king looked
round the apartment, and observing Fenella, Peveril, and
the musician, who remained standing beside a large Indian
screen, he continued, addressing Mistress Chiffinch, though
with polite indifference, ' I sent you the fiddles this morning
—or rather the flute—Empson, and a fairy elf whom I met
in the Park, who dances divinely. She has brought us the
very newest saraband from the court of Queen Mab, and
I sent her here, that you may see it at leisure.'

' Your Majesty does me by far too much honour,' said
Chiffinch, her eyes properly cast down, and her accents
minced into becoming humility.

' Nay, little Chiffinch,' answered the king, in a tone of as
contemptuous familiarity as was consistent with his good-
breeding, ' it was not altogether for thine own private ear,
though quite deserving of all sweet sounds ; but I thought
Nelly had been with thee this morning.'

' I can send Bajazet for her, your Majesty,' answered the
lady.

' Nay, I will not trouble your little heathen sultan to go
so far. Still it strikes me that Chiffinch said you had
company—some country cousin, or such a matter—Is there
not such a person ? '

' There is a young person from the country,' said Mistress
Chiffinch, striving to conceal a considerable portion of embarrassment ; ' but she is unprepared for such an honour
as to be admitted into your Majesty's presence, and '——

' And therefore the fitter to receive it, Chiffinch. There
is nothing in nature so beautiful as the first blush of a little
rustic between joy and fear, and wonder and curiosity. It
is the down on the peach—pity it decays so soon !—the
fruit remains, but the first high colouring and exquisite
flavour are gone.—Never put up thy lip for the matter,
Chiffinch, for it is as I tell you ; so pray let us have *la belle
cousine.*'

Mistress Chiffinch, more embarrassed than ever, again
advanced towards the door of communication, which she

had been in the act of opening when his Majesty entered.
But just as she coughed pretty loudly, perhaps as a signal
to some one within, voices were again heard in a raised tone
of altercation—the door was flung open, and Alice rushed
out of the inner apartment, followed to the door of it by
the enterprising Duke of Buckingham, who stood fixed with
astonishment on finding his pursuit of the flying fair one had
hurried him into the presence of the king.

Alice Bridgenorth appeared too much transported with
anger to permit her to pay attention to the rank or character
of the company into which she had thus suddenly entered.
' I remain no longer here, madam,' she said to Mrs. Chiffinch,
in a tone of uncontrollable resolution ; ' I leave instantly
a house where I am exposed to company which I detest,
and to solicitations which I despise.'

The dismayed Mrs. Chiffinch could only implore her, in
broken whispers, to be silent ; adding, while she pointed
to Charles, who stood with his eyes fixed rather on his
audacious courtier than on the game which he pursued,
' The king—the king ! '

' If I am in the king's presence,' said Alice aloud, and in
the same torrent of passionate feeling, while her eyes
sparkled through tears of resentment and insulted modesty,
' it is the better—it is his Majesty's duty to protect me ;
and on his protection I throw myself.'

These words, which were spoken aloud, and boldly, at once
recalled Julian to himself, who had hitherto stood, as it
were, bewildered. He approached Alice, and, whispering
in her ear that she had beside her one who would defend her
with his life, implored her to trust to his guardianship in
this emergency.

Clinging to his arm in all the ecstasy of gratitude and
joy, the spirit which had so lately invigorated Alice in her
own defence, gave way in a flood of tears, when she saw
herself supported by him whom perhaps she most wished
to recognize as her protector. She permitted Peveril gently
to draw her back towards the screen before which he had
been standing ; where, holding by his arm, but at the same
time endeavouring to conceal herself behind him, they
waited the conclusion of a scene so singular.

The king seemed at first so much surprised at the unex-

pected apparition of the Duke of Buckingham, as to pay
little or no attention to Alice, who had been the means
of thus unceremoniously introducing his Grace into the
presence at a most unsuitable moment. In that intriguing
court, it had not been the first time that the duke had
ventured to enter the lists of gallantry in rivalry of his
sovereign, which made the present insult the more intoler-
able. His purpose of lying concealed in those private apartments was explained by the exclamations of Alice ; and
Charles, notwithstanding the placidity of his disposition,
and his habitual guard over his passions, resented the
attempt to seduce his destined mistress, as an Eastern
sultan would have done the insolence of a vizier, who
anticipated his intended purchases of captive beauty in the
slave-market. The swarthy features of Charles reddened,
and the strong lines on his dark visage seemed to become
inflated, as he said, in a voice which faltered with passion,
' Buckingham, you dared not have thus insulted your equal !
To your master you may securely offer any affront, since
his rank glues his sword to the scabbard.'

The haughty duke did not brook this taunt unanswered.
' My sword,' he said, with emphasis, ' was never in the
scabbard, when your Majesty's service required it should
be unsheathed.'

' Your Grace means, when its service was required for its
master's interest,' said the king ; ' for you could only gain
the coronet of a duke by fighting for the royal crown. But
it is over—I have treated you as a friend—a companion—
almost an equal—you have repaid me with insolence and
ingratitude.'

' Sire,' answered the duke firmly, but respectfully, ' I am
unhappy in your displeasure ; yet thus far fortunate, that
while your words can confer honour, they cannot impair
or take it away. It is hard,' he added, lowering his voice,
so as only to be heard by the king—' It is hard that the
squall of a peevish wench should cancel the services of so
many years ! '

' It is harder,' said the king, in the same subdued tone,
which both preserved through the rest of the conversation,
' that a wench's bright eyes can make a nobleman forget
the decencies due to his sovereign's privacy.'

'May I presume to ask your Majesty what decencies are those?' said the duke.

Charles bit his lip to keep himself from smiling. 'Buckingham,' he said, 'this is a foolish business; and we must not forget (as we have nearly done), that we have an audience to witness this scene, and should walk the stage with dignity. I will show you your fault in private.'

'It is enough that your Majesty has been displeased, and that I have unhappily been the occasion,' said the duke, kneeling; 'although quite ignorant of any purpose beyond a few words of gallantry; and I sue thus low for your Majesty's pardon.'

So saying, he kneeled gracefully down. 'Thou hast it, George,' said the placable prince. 'I believe thou wilt be sooner tired of offending than I of forgiving.'

'Long may your Majesty live to give the offence, with which it is your royal pleasure at present to charge my innocence,' said the duke.

'What mean you by that, my lord?' said Charles, the angry shade returning to his brow for a moment.

'My liege,' replied the duke, 'you are too honourable to deny your custom of shooting with Cupid's bird-bolts in other men's warrens. You have ta'en the royal right of free-forestry over every man's park. It is hard that you should be so much displeased at hearing a chance arrow whiz near your own pales.'

'No more on't,' said the king; 'but let us see where the dove has harboured.'

'The Helen has found a Paris while we were quarrelling,' replied the duke.

'Rather an Orpheus,' said the king; 'and what is worse, one that is already provided with a Eurydice—She is clinging to the fiddler.'

'It is mere fright,' said Buckingham, 'like Rochester's, when he crept into the bass-viol to hide himself from Sir Dermot O'Cleaver.'

'We must make the people show their talents,' said the king, 'and stop their mouths with money and civility, or we shall have this foolish encounter over half the town.'

The king then approached Julian, and desired him to

take his instrument, and cause his female companion to perform a saraband.

'I had already the honour to inform your Majesty,' said Julian, 'that I cannot contribute to your pleasure in the way you command me ; and that this young person is '——

'A retainer of the Lady Powis,' said the king, upon whose mind things not connected with his pleasures made a very slight impression. 'Poor lady, she is in trouble about the lords in the Tower.'

'Pardon me, sir,' said Julian, 'she is a dependant of the Countess of Derby.'

'True, true,' answered Charles ; 'it is indeed of Lady Derby, who hath also her own distresses in these times. Do you know who taught the young person to dance ? Some of her steps mightily resemble Le Jeune's of Paris.'

'I presume she was taught abroad, sir,' said Julian ; 'for myself, I am charged with some weighty business by the countess, which I would willingly communicate to your Majesty.'

'We will send you to our Secretary of State,' said the king. 'But this dancing envoy will oblige us once more, will she not ?—Empson, now that I remember, it was to your pipe that she danced—Strike up, man, and put mettle into her feet.'

Empson began to play a well-known measure ; and, as he had threatened, made more than one false note, until the king, whose ear was very accurate, rebuked him with, 'Sirrah, art thou drunk at this early hour, or must thou too be playing thy slippery tricks with me ? Thou thinkest thou art born to beat time, but I will have time beat into thee.'

The hint was sufficient, and Empson took good care so to perform his air as to merit his high and deserved reputation. But on Fenella it made not the slightest impression. She rather leant than stood against the wall of the apartment ; her countenance as pale as death, her arms and hands hanging down as if stiffened, and her existence only testified by the sobs which agitated her bosom, and the tears which flowed from her half-closed eyes.

'A plague on it,' said the king, 'some evil spirit is abroad this morning ; and the wenches are all bewitched, I think.

Cheer up, my girl. What, in the devil's name, has changed thee at once from a nymph to a Niobe ? If thou standest there longer, thou wilt grow to the very marble wall—Or—oddsfish, George, have you been bird-bolting in this quarter also ? '

Ere Buckingham could answer to this charge, Julian again kneeled down to the king, and prayed to be heard, were it only for five minutes. ' The young woman,' he said, ' had been long in attendance on the Countess of Derby. She was bereaved of the faculties of speech and hearing.'

' Oddsfish, man, and dances so well ? ' said the king. ' Nay, all Gresham College shall never make me believe that.'

' I would have thought it equally impossible, but for what I to-day witnessed,' said Julian ; ' but only permit me, sir, to deliver the petition of my lady the countess.'

' And who art thou thyself, man ? ' said the sovereign ; ' for though everything which wears bodice and breast-knot has a right to speak to a king, and be answered, I know not that they have a title to audience through an envoy extra-ordinary.'

' I am Julian Peveril of Derbyshire,' answered the suppli-cant, ' the son of Sir Geoffrey Peveril of Martindale Castle, who '——

' Body of me—the old Worcester man ? ' said the king. ' Oddsfish, I remember him well—some harm has happened to him, I think,—Is he not dead, or very sick at least ? ''

' Ill at ease, an' it please your Majesty, but not ill in health. He has been imprisoned on account of an alleged accession to this Plot.'

' Look you there,' said the king ; ' I knew he was in trouble ; and yet how to help the stout old knight, I can hardly tell. I can scarce escape suspicion of the Plot myself, though the principal object of it is to take away my own life. Were I to stir to save a plotter, I should certainly be brought in as an accessory. Buckingham, thou hast some interest with those who built this fin > State engine, or at least who have driven it on—be good-n tured for once, though it is scarcely thy wont, and interfere to shelter our old Worcester friend, Sir Godfrey. You have not forgot him ? '

' No, sir,' answered the duke ; ' for I never heard the name.'

' It is Sir Geoffrey his Majesty would say,' said Julian.

' And if his Majesty *did* say Sir Geoffrey, Master Peveril, I cannot see of what use I can be to your father,' replied the duke coldly. ' He is accused of a heavy crime ; and a British subject so accused can have no shelter either from prince or peer, but must stand to the award and deliverance of God and his country.'

' Now, Heaven forgive thee thy hypocrisy, George,' said the king hastily. ' I would rather hear the devil preach religion than thee teach patriotism. Thou knowest as well as I, that the nation is in a scarlet fever for fear of the poor Catholics, who are not two men to five hundred ; and that the public mind is so harassed with new narrations of conspiracy, and fresh horrors every day, that people have as little real sense of what is just or unjust, as men who talk in their sleep of what is sense or nonsense. I have borne, and borne with it—I have seen blood flow on the scaffold, fearing to thwart the nation in its fury—and I pray to God that I or mine be not called on to answer for it. I will no longer swim with the torrent, which honour and con-science call upon me to stem—I will act the part of a sovereign, and save my people from doing injustice, even in their own despite.'

Charles walked hastily up and down the room as he expressed these unwonted sentiments, with energy equally unwonted. After a momentary pause, the duke answered him gravely, ' Spoken like a royal king, sir, but—pardon me—not like a king of England.'

Charles paused, as the duke spoke, beside a window which looked full on Whitehall, and his eye was involuntarily attracted by the fatal window of the Banqueting House out of which his unhappy father was conducted to execu-tion. Charles was naturally, or, more properly, constitu-tionally brave ; but a life of pleasure, together with the habit of governing his course rather by what was expedient than by what was right, rendered him unapt to dare the same scene of danger or of martyrdom which had closed his father's life and reign ; and the thought came over his half-formed resolution like the rain upon a kindling beacon.

In another man, his perplexity would have seemed almost ludicrous ; but Charles would not lose, even under these circumstances, the dignity and grace which were as natural to him as his indifference and good humour. ' Our council must decide in this matter,' he said, looking to the duke ; ' and be assured, young man,' he added, addressing Julian, ' your father shall not want an intercessor in his king, so far as the laws will permit my interference in his behalf.'

Julian was about to retire, when Fenella, with a marked look, put into his hand a slip of paper on which she had hastily written, ' The packet—give him the packet.'

After a moment's hesitation, during which he reflected that Fenella was the organ of the countess's pleasure, Julian resolved to obey. ' Permit me, then, sire,' he said, ' to place in your royal hands this packet, entrusted to me by the Countess of Derby. The letters have already been once taken from me ; and I have little hope that I can now deliver them as they are addressed. I place them, therefore, in your royal hands, certain that they will evince the innocence of the writer.'

The king shook his head as he took the packet reluctantly. ' It is no safe office you have undertaken, young man. A messenger has sometimes his throat cut for the sake of his dispatches—But give them to me ; and, Chiffinch, give me wax and a taper.' He employed himself in folding the countess's packet in another envelope. ' Buckingham,' he said, ' you are evidence that I do not read them till the council shall see them.'

Buckingham approached, and offered his services in folding the parcel, but Charles rejected his assistance ; and having finished his task, he sealed the packet with his own signet-ring. The duke bit his lip and retired.

' And now, young man,' said the king, ' your errand is sped, so far as it can at present be forwarded.'

Julian bowed deeply, as to take leave at these words, which he rightly interpreted as a signal for his departure. Alice Bridgenorth still clung to his arm, and motioned to withdraw along with him. The king and Buckingham looked at each other in conscious astonishment, and yet not without a desire to smile, so strange did it seem to them that a prize for which, an instant before, they had been

mutually contending, should thus glide out of their
grasp, or rather be borne off by a third and very inferior
competitor.

' Mistress Chiffinch,' said the king, with a hesitation which
he could not disguise, ' I hope your fair charge is not about
to leave you ? '

' Certainly not, your Majesty,' answered Chiffinch. ' Alice,
my love—you mistake—that opposite door leads to your
apartments.'

' Pardon me, madam,' answered Alice ; ' I have indeed
mistaken my road, but it was when I came hither.'

' The errant damozel,' said Buckingham, looking at
Charles with as much intelligence as etiquette permitted
him to throw into his eye, and then turning it towards
Alice, as she still held by Julian's arm, ' is resolved not to
mistake her road a second time. She has chosen a sufficient
guide.'

' And yet stories tell that such guides have led maidens
astray,' said the king.

Alice blushed deeply, but instantly recovered her composure so soon as she saw that her liberty was likely to
depend upon the immediate exercise of resolution. She
quitted, from a sense of insulted delicacy, the arm of Julian,
to which she had hitherto clung ; but as she spoke, she
continued to retain a slight grasp of his cloak. ' I have
indeed mistaken my way,' she repeated, still addressing
Mrs. Chiffinch, ' but it was when I crossed this threshold.
The usage to which I have been exposed in your house has
determined me to quit it instantly.'

' I will not permit that, my young mistress,' answered
Mrs. Chiffinch, ' until your uncle, who placed you under my
care, shall relieve me of the charge of you.'

' I will answer for my conduct both to my uncle and,
what is of more importance, to my father,' said Alice. ' You
must permit me to depart, madam ; I am free-born, and
you have no right to detain me.'

' Pardon me, my young madam,' said Mistress Chiffinch,
' I have a right, and I will maintain it too.'

' I will know that before quitting this presence,' said
Alice firmly ; and, advancing a step or two, she dropped
on her knee before the king. ' Your Majesty,' said she, ' if

indeed I kneel before King Charles, is the father of your subjects.'

'Of a good many of them,' said the Duke of Buckingham, apart.

'I demand protection of you, in the name of God, and of the oath your Majesty swore when you placed on your head the crown of this kingdom !'

'You have my protection,' said the king, a little confused by an appeal so unexpected and so solemn. 'Do but remain quiet with this lady, with whom your parents have placed you ; neither Buckingham nor any one else shall intrude on you.'

'His Majesty,' added Buckingham, in the same tone, and speaking from the restless and mischief-making spirit of contradiction, which he never could restrain, even when indulging it was most contrary, not only to propriety, but to his own interest,—'His Majesty will protect you, fair lady, from all intrusion save what must not be termed such.'

Alice darted a keen look on the duke, as if to read his meaning ; another on Charles, to know whether she had guessed it rightly. There was a guilty confession on the king's brow, which confirmed Alice's determination to depart. 'Your Majesty will forgive me,' she said ; 'it is not here that I can enjoy the advantage of your royal protection. I am resolved to leave this house. If I am detained, it must be by violence, which I trust no one dare offer to me in your Majesty's presence. This gentleman, whom I have long known, will conduct me to my friends.'

'We make but an indifferent figure in this scene, me-thinks,' said the king, addressing the Duke of Buckingham, and speaking in a whisper ; 'but she must go—I neither will nor dare stop her from returning to her father.'

'And if she does,' swore the duke internally, 'I would, as Sir Andrew Smith saith, I might never touch fair lady's hand.' And stepping back, he spoke a few words with Empson the musician, who left the apartment for a few minutes, and presently returned.

The king seemed irresolute concerning the part he should act under circumstances so peculiar. To be foiled in a gallant intrigue, was to subject himself to the ridicule of his gay court ; to persist in it by any means which approached to constraint, would have been tyrannical ; and, what perhaps he might judge as severe an imputation, it would have been unbecoming a gentleman. 'Upon my honour, young lady,' he said, with an emphasis, ' you have nothing to fear in this house. But it is improper, for your own sake, that you should leave it in this abrupt manner. If you will have the goodness to wait but a quarter of an hour, Mistress Chiffinch's coach will be placed at your command, to transport you where you will. Spare yourself the ridicule, and me the pain, of seeing you leave the house of one of my servants as if you were escaping from a prison.'

The king spoke in good-natured sincerity, and Alice was inclined for an instant to listen to his advice ; but recollecting that she had to search for her father and uncle, or, failing them, for some suitable place of secure residence, it rushed on her mind that the attendants of Mrs. Chiffinch were not likely to prove trusty guides or assistants in such a purpose. Firmly and respectfully she announced her purpose of instant departure. She needed no other escort, she said, than what this gentleman, Master Julian Peveril, who was well known to her father, would willingly afford her ; nor did she need that further than until she had reached her father's residence.

' Farewell, then, lady, a God's name ! ' said the king ; ' I am sorry so much beauty should be wedded to so many shrewish suspicions. For you, Master Peveril, I should have thought you had enough to do with your own affairs without interfering with the humours of the fair sex. The duty of conducting all strayed damsels into the right path is, as matters go in this good city, rather too weighty an undertaking for your youth and inexperience.'

Julian, eager to conduct Alice from a place of which he began fully to appreciate the perils, answered nothing to this taunt, but, bowing reverently, led her from the apartment. Her sudden appearance, and the animated scene which followed, had entirely absorbed, for the moment, the recollection of his father and of the Countess of Derby ; and while the dumb attendant of the latter remained in the room, a silent and, as it were, stunned spectator of all that had happened, Peveril had become, in the predominating interest of Alice's critical situation, totally forgetful of her presence. But no sooner had he left the room, without noticing or attending to her, than Fenella, starting as from a trance, drew herself up, and looked wildly around, like one waking from a dream, as if to assure herself that her companion was gone, and gone without paying the slightest attention to her. She folded her hands together, and cast her eyes upwards with an expression of such agony as explained to Charles (as he thought) what painful ideas were passing in her mind. 'This Peveril is a perfect pattern of successful perfidy,' said the king; 'he has not only succeeded at first sight in carrying off this Queen of the Amazons, but he has left us, I think, a disconsolate Ariadne in her place. But weep not, my princess of pretty movements,' he said, addressing himself to Fenella; 'if we cannot call in Bacchus to console you, we will commit you to the care of Empson, who shall drink with *Liber Pater* for a thousand pounds, and I will say done first.'

As the king spoke these words, Fenella rushed past him with her wonted rapidity of step, and, with much less courtesy than was due to the royal presence, hurried down stairs and out of the house, without attempting to open any communication with the monarch. He saw her abrupt departure with more surprise than displeasure; and presently afterwards, bursting into a fit of laughter, he said to the duke, 'Oddsfish, George, this young spark might teach the best of us how to manage the wenches. I have had my own experience, but I could never yet contrive either to win or lose them with so little ceremony.'

'Experience, sir,' replied the duke, 'cannot be acquired without years.'

'True, George; and you would, I suppose, insinuate,' said Charles, 'that the gallant who acquires it, loses as much in youth as he gains in art? I defy your insinuation, George. You cannot overreach your master, old as you think him, either in love or politics. You have not the secret *plumer la poule sans la faire crier*, witness this morning's work. I will give you odds at all games—aye, and at the Mall, too, if thou darest accept my challenge.—Chiffinch, what for dost thou convulse thy pretty throat and face with sobbing and hatching tears, which seem rather unwilling to make their appearance?'

'It is for fear,' whined Chiffinch, ' that your Majesty should think—that you should expect '——

'That I should expect gratitude from a courtier, or faith from a woman ? ' answered the king, patting her at the same time under the chin, to make her raise her face— 'Tush ! chicken, I am not so superfluous.'

'There it is now,' said Chiffinch, continuing to sob the more bitterly as she felt herself unable to produce any tears ; 'I see your Majesty is determined to lay all the blame on me, when I am innocent as an unborn babe—I will be judged by his Grace.'

'No doubt, no doubt, Chiffie,' said the king. ' His Grace and you will be excellent judges in each other's cause, and as good witnesses in each other's favour. But to investigate the matter impartially, we must examine our evidence apart. My lord duke, we meet at the Mall at noon, if your Grace dare accept my challenge.'

His Grace of Buckingham bowed and retired.

CHAPTER XXXII

> But when the bully, with assuming pace,
> Cocks his broad hat, edged round with tarnish'd lace,
> Yield not the way—defy his strutting pride,
> And thrust him to the muddy kennel's side,
> Yet rather bear the shower and toils of mud,
> Than in the doubtful quarrel risk thy blood.
>   GAY's *Trivia*.

JULIAN PEVERIL, half leading, half supporting Alice Bridgenorth, had reached the middle of Saint James's Street ere the doubt occurred to him which way they should bend their course. He then asked Alice whither he should conduct her, and learned, to his surprise and embarrassment, that, far from knowing where her father was to be found, she had no certain knowledge that he was in London, and only hoped that he had arrived from the expressions which he had used at parting. She mentioned her uncle Christian's address, but it was with doubt and hesitation, arising from

the hands in which he had already placed her ; and her
reluctance to go again under his protection was strongly
confirmed by her youthful guide, when a few words had
established to his conviction the identity of Ganlesse and
Christian. What then was to be done ?

'Alice,' said Julian, after a moment's reflection, 'you
must seek your earliest and best friend—I mean my mother.
She has now no castle in which to receive you—she has but
a miserable lodging, so near the jail in which my father is
confined that it seems almost a cell of the same prison.
I have not seen her since my coming hither ; but thus much
have I learned by inquiry. We will now go to her apartment ; such as it is, I know she will share it with one so
innocent and so unprotected as you are.'

'Gracious Heaven !' said the poor girl, 'am I then so
totally deserted, that I must throw myself on the mercy
of her who, of all the world, has most reason to spurn me
from her ? Julian, can you advise me to this ? Is there
none else who will afford me a few hours' refuge, till I can
hear from my father ? No other protectress but her whose
ruin has, I fear, been accelerated by——Julian, I dare not
appear before your mother ! she must hate me for my
family, and despise me for my meanness. To be a second
time cast on her protection, when the first has been so evil
repaid—Julian, I dare not go with you.'

'She has never ceased to love you, Alice,' said her conductor, whose steps she continued to attend, even while
declaring her resolution not to go with him, 'she never
felt anything but kindness towards you, nay, towards your
father ; for though his dealings with us have been harsh,
she can allow much for the provocation which he has
received. Believe me, with her you will be safe as with
a mother—perhaps may be the means of reconciling the
divisions by which we have suffered so much.'

'Might God grant it !' said Alice. 'Yet how shall I face
your mother ? And will she be able to protect me against
these powerful men—against my uncle Christian ? Alas,
that I must call him my worst enemy !'

'She has the ascendancy which honour hath over infamy,
and virtue over vice,' said Julian ; 'and to no human power
but your father's will she resign you, if you consent to

choose her for your protectress. Come, then, with me,
Alice ; and '——

Julian was interrupted by some one who, laying an
unceremonious hold of his cloak, pulled it with so much
force as compelled him to stop and lay his hand on his
sword. He turned at the same time, and, when he turned,
beheld Fenella. The cheek of the mute glowed like fire ;
her eyes sparkled, and her lips were forcibly drawn together,
as if she had difficulty to repress those wild screams which
usually attended her agonies of passion, and which, uttered
in the open street, must instantly have collected a crowd.
As it was, her appearance was so singular, and her emotion
so evident, that men gazed as they came on, and looked
back after they had passed, at the singular vivacity of her
gestures ; while, holding Peveril's cloak with one hand,
she made, with the other, the most eager and imperious
signs that he should leave Alice Bridgenorth and follow her.
She touched the plume in her bonnet, to remind him of the
earl—pointed to her heart, to intimate the countess—
raised her closed hand, as if to command him in their name
—and next moment folded both, as if to supplicate him in
her own ; while, pointing to Alice with an expression at
once of angry and scornful derision, she waved her hand
repeatedly and disdainfully, to intimate that Peveril ought
to cast her off, as something undeserving his protection.

Frightened, she knew not why, at these wild gestures,
Alice clung closer to Julian's arm than she had at first dared
to do : and this mark of confidence in his protection seemed
to increase the passion of Fenella.

Julian was dreadfully embarrassed ; his situation was
sufficiently precarious, even before Fenella's ungovernable
passions threatened to ruin the only plan which he had been
able to suggest. What she wanted with him—how far the
fate of the earl and countess might depend on his following
her, he could not even conjecture ; but be the call how
peremptory soever, he resolved not to comply with it
until he had seen Alice placed in safety. In the meantime,
he determined not to lose sight of Fenella ; and disregarding
her repeated, disdainful, and impetuous rejection of the
hand which he offered her, he at length seemed so far to
have soothed her that she seized upon his right arm, and,

as if despairing of his following *her* path, appeared reconciled to attend him on that which he himself should choose.

Thus, with a youthful female clinging to each arm, and
both remarkably calculated to attract the public eye, though
from very different reasons, Julian resolved to make the
shortest road to the water-side, and there to take boat for
Blackfriars, as the nearest point of landing to Newgate,
where he concluded that Lance had already announced his
arrival in London to Sir Geoffrey, then inhabiting that
dismal region, and to his lady, who, so far as the jailer's
rigour permitted, shared and softened his imprisonment.

Julian's embarrassment in passing Charing Cross and
Northumberland House was so great as to excite the
attention of the passengers ; for he had to compose his steps
so as to moderate the unequal and rapid pace of Fenella to
the timid and faint progress of his left-hand companion ;
and while it would have been needless to address himself to
the former, who could not comprehend him, he dared not
speak himself to Alice, for fear of awakening into frenzy
the jealousy, or at least the impatience, of Fenella.

Many passengers looked at them with wonder, and some
with smiles ; but Julian remarked that there were two who
never lost sight of them, and to whom his situation, and
the demeanour of his companions, seemed to afford matter
of undisguised merriment. These were young men, such as
may be seen in the same precincts in the present day,
allowing for the difference in the fashion of their apparel.
They abounded in periwig, and fluttered with many hundred
yards of ribbon, disposed in bow-knots upon their sleeves,
their breeches, and their waistcoats, in the very extremity
of the existing mode. A quantity of lace and embroidery
made their habits rather fine than tasteful. In a word,
they were dressed in that caricature of the fashion which
sometimes denotes a hare-brained man of quality who has
a mind to be distinguished as a fop of the first order, but
is much more frequently the disguise of those who desire
to be esteemed men of rank on account of their dress,
having no other pretension to the distinction.

These two gallants passed Peveril more than once, linked
arm in arm, then sauntered, so as to oblige him to pass them
in turn, laughing and whispering during these manœuvres—

staring broadly at Peveril and his female companions—and
affording them, as they came into contact, none of those
facilities of giving place which are required on such occasions
by the ordinary rules of the *pavé*.

Peveril did not immediately observe their impertinence ;
but when it was too gross to escape his notice his gall
began to arise ; and, in addition to all the other embarrass-
ments of his situation, he had to combat the longing desire
which he felt to cudgel handsomely the two coxcombs who
seemed thus determined on insulting him. Patience and
sufferance were indeed strongly imposed on him by circumstances ; but at length it became scarcely possible to
observe their dictates any longer.

When, for the third time, Julian found himself obliged,
with his companions, to pass this troublesome brace of fops,
they kept walking close behind him, speaking so loud as
to be heard, and in a tone of perfect indifference whether
he listened to them or not.

' This is bumpkin's best luck,' said the taller of the two
(who was indeed a man of remarkable size, alluding to the
plainness of Peveril's dress, which was scarce fit for the
streets of London)—' Two such fine wenches, and under
guard of a grey frock and an oaken riding-rod ! '

' Nay, Puritan's luck rather, and more than enough of it,'
said his companion.   ' You may read Puritan in his pace
and in his patience.'

' Right as a pint bumper, Tom,' said his friend—' Issachar
is an ass that stoopeth between two burdens.'

' I have a mind to ease long-eared Laurence of one of his
encumbrances,' said the shorter fellow.   ' That black-eyed
sparkler looks as if she had a mind to run away from him.'

' Aye,' answered the taller, ' and the blue-eyed trembler
looks as if she would fall behind into my loving arms.'

At these words, Alice, holding still closer by Peveril's arm
than formerly, mended her pace almost to running, in order
to escape from men whose language was so alarming ; and
Fenella walked hastily forward in the same manner, having
perhaps caught, from the men's gestures and demeanour,
that apprehension which Alice had taken from their
language.

Fearful of the consequences of a fray in the streets, which

must necessarily separate him from these unprotected females, Peveril endeavoured to compound betwixt the prudence necessary for their protection and his own rising resentment; and as this troublesome pair of attendants endeavoured again to pass them close to Hungerford Stairs, he said to them with constrained calmness, 'Gentlemen, I owe you something for the attention you have bestowed on the affairs of a stranger. If you have any pretension to the name I have given you, you will tell me where you are to be found.'

'And with what purpose,' said the taller of the two, sneeringly, 'does your most rustic gravity, or your most grave rusticity, require of us such information?'

So saying, they both faced about, in such a manner as to make it impossible for Julian to advance any further.

'Make for the stairs, Alice,' he said; 'I will be with you in an instant.' Then freeing himself with difficulty from the grasp of his companions, he cast his cloak hastily round his left arm, and said, sternly, to his opponents, 'Will you give me your names, sirs; or will you be pleased to make way?'

'Not till we know for whom we are to give place,' said one of them.

'For one who will else teach you what you want—good manners,' said Peveril, and advanced, as if to push between them.

They separated, but one of them stretched forth his foot before Peveril, as if he meant to trip him. The blood of his ancestors was already boiling within him; he struck the man on the face with the oaken rod which he had just sneered at, and throwing it from him, instantly unsheathed his sword. Both the others drew, and pushed at once; but he caught the point of the one rapier in his cloak, and parried the other thrust with his own weapon. He might have been less lucky in the second close, but a cry arose among the watermen of 'Shame, shame! two upon one!'

'They are men of the Duke of Buckingham's,' said one fellow—'there's no safe meddling with them.'

'They may be the devil's men, if they will,' said an ancient Triton, flourishing his stretcher; 'but I say fair play, and old England for ever; and I say, knock the gold-laced

puppies down, unless they will fight turn-about with grey
jerkin, like honest fellows. One down—t'other come on.'

The lower orders of London have in all times been remarkable for the delight which they have taken in club law, or
fist law ; and for the equity and impartiality with which
they see it administered. The noble science of defence was
then so generally known that a bout at single rapier excited
at that time as much interest and as little wonder as a
boxing-match in our own days. The bystanders, experienced
in such affrays, presently formed a ring, within which Peveril
and the taller and more forward of his antagonists were soon
engaged in close combat with their swords, whilst the other,
overawed by the spectators, was prevented from interfering.

' Well done, the tall fellow ! '—' Well thrust, long-legs ! '—
' Huzza for two ells and a quarter ! ' were the sounds with
which the fray was at first cheered ; for Peveril's opponent
not only showed great activity and skill in fence, but had
also a decided advantage, from the anxiety with which
Julian looked out for Alice Bridgenorth ; the care for whose
safety diverted him in the beginning of the onset from that
which he ought to have exclusively bestowed on the defence
of his own life. A slight flesh-wound in the side at once
punished and warned him of his inadvertence ; when,
turning his whole thoughts on the business in which he was
engaged, and animated with anger against his impertinent
intruder, the rencontre speedily began to assume another
face, amidst cries of ' Well done, grey jerkin ! '—' Try the
metal of his gold doublet ! '—' Finely thrust ! '—' Curiously
parried ! '—' There went another eyelet-hole to his broidered
jerkin ! '—' Fairly pinked, by G—d ! ' In fact, the last
exclamation was uttered amid a general roar of applause,
accompanying a successful and conclusive lunge, by which
Peveril ran his gigantic antagonist through the body. He
looked at his prostrate foe for a moment ; then, recovering
himself, called loudly to know what had become of the lady.

' Never mind the lady, if you be wise,' said one of the
watermen ; ' the constable will be here in an instant. I'll
give your honour a cast across the water in a moment. It
may be as much as your neck's worth. Shall only charge
a Jacobus.'

' You be d—d ! ' said one of his rivals in profession, ' as

your father was before you ; for a Jacobus, I'll set the
gentleman into Alsatia, where neither bailiff nor constable
dare trespass.'

' The lady, you scoundrels, the lady ! ' exclaimed Peveril
—' Where is the lady ? '

' I'll carry your honour where you shall have enough of
ladies, if that be your want,' said the old Triton ; and as he
spoke, the clamour amongst the watermen was renewed,
each hoping to cut his own profit out of the emergency of
Julian's situation.

' A sculler will be least suspected, your honour,' said one
fellow.

' A pair of oars will carry you through the water like a
wild-duck,' said another.

' But you have got never a tilt, brother,' said a third.
' Now I can put the gentleman as snug as if he were under
hatches.'

In the midst of the oaths and clamour attending this
aquatic controversy for his custom, Peveril at length made
them understand that he would bestow a Jacobus, not on
him whose boat was first oars, but on whomsoever should
inform him of the fate of the lady.

' Of which lady ? ' said a sharp fellow ; ' for, to my
thought, there was a pair on them.'

' Of both, of both,' answered Peveril ; ' but first, of the
fair-haired lady ? '

' Aye, aye, that was she that shrieked so when gold-
jacket's companion handed her into No. 20.'

' Who—what—who dared to hand her ? ' exclaimed
Peveril.

' Nay, master, you have heard enough of my tale without
a fee,' said the waterman.

' Sordid rascal ! ' said Peveril, giving him a gold piece,
' speak out, or I'll run my sword through you ! '

' For the matter of that, master,' answered the fellow,
' not while I can handle this trunnion—but a bargain's a
bargain ; and so I'll tell you, for your gold piece, that the
comrade of the fellow forced one of your wenches, her with
the fair hair, will she nill she, into Tickling Tom's wherry ;
and they are far enough up Thames by this time, with wind
and tide.'

' Sacred Heaven, and I stand here ! ' exclaimed Julian.

' Why, that is because your honour will not take a boat.'

' You are right, my friend—a boat—a boat instantly ! '

' Follow me, then, squire. Here, Tom, bear a hand—the gentleman is our fare.'

A volley of water language was exchanged betwixt the successful candidate for Peveril's custom and his disappointed brethren, which concluded by the ancient Triton's bellowing out, in a tone above them all, ' that the gentleman was in a fair way to make a voyage to the isle of gulls, for that sly Jack was only bantering him—No. 20 had rowed for York Buildings.'

' To the isle of gallows,' cried another; ' for here comes one who will mar his trip up Thames, and carry him down to Execution Dock.'

In fact, as he spoke the word, a constable, with three or four of his assistants, armed with the old-fashioned brown-bills, which were still used for arming those guardians of the peace, cut off our hero's further progress to the water's edge by arresting him in the king's name. To attempt resistance would have been madness, as he was surrounded on all sides ; so Peveril was disarmed, and carried before the nearest justice of the peace for examination and committal.

The legal sage before whom Julian was taken was a man very honest in his intentions, very bounded in his talents, and rather timid in his disposition. Before the general alarm given to England, and to the city of London in particular, by the notable discovery of the Popish Plot, Master Maulstatute had taken serene and undisturbed pride and pleasure in the discharge of his duties as a justice of the peace, with the exercise of all its honorary privileges and awful authority. But the murder of Sir Edmondsbury Godfrey had made a strong, nay, an indelible impression on his mind ; and he walked the Courts of Themis with fear and trembling after that memorable and melancholy event.

Having a high idea of his official importance, and rather an exalted notion of his personal consequence, his honour saw nothing from that time but cords and daggers before his eyes, and never stepped out of his own house, which he fortified, and in some measure garrisoned, with half

a dozen tall watchmen and constables, without seeing
himself watched by a Papist in disguise with a drawn
sword under his cloak. It was even whispered that, in the
agonies of his fears, the worshipful Master Maulstatute
mistook the kitchen-wench with a tinder-box for a Jesuit
with a pistol; but if any one dared to laugh at such an
error, he would have done well to conceal his mirth, lest
he fell under the heavy inculpation of being a banterer and
stifler of the Plot—a crime almost as deep as that of being
himself a plotter. In fact, the fears of the honest justice,
however ridiculously exorbitant, were kept so much in
countenance by the outcry of the day, and the general
nervous fever which afflicted every good Protestant, that
Master Maulstatute was accounted the bolder man and the
better magistrate, while, under the terror of the air-drawn
dagger which fancy placed continually before his eyes, he
continued to dole forth justice in the recesses of his private
chamber, nay, occasionally to attend quarter-sessions, when
the hall was guarded by a sufficient body of the militia.
Such was the wight at whose door, well chained and doubly
bolted, the constable who had Julian in custody now gave
his important and well-known knock.

Notwithstanding this official signal, the party was not
admitted until the clerk, who acted the part of high-warder,
had reconnoitred them through a grated wicket; for who
could say whether the Papists might not have made themselves master of Master Constable's sign, and have prepared
a pseudo watch to burst in and murder the justice, under
pretence of bringing a criminal before him? Less hopeful
projects had figured in the Narrative of the Popish Plot.

All being found right, the key was turned, the bolts were
drawn, and the chain unhooked, so as to permit entrance
to the constable, the prisoner, and the assistants; and the
door was then as suddenly shut against the witnesses, who,
as less trustworthy persons, were requested (through the
wicket) to remain in the yard until they should be called in
their respective turns.

Had Julian been inclined for mirth, as was far from being
the case, he must have smiled at the incongruity of the
clerk's apparel, who had belted over his black buckram
suit a buff baldric, sustaining a broadsword and a pair of

huge horse-pistols ; and, instead of the low flat hat, which, coming in place of the city cap, completed the dress of a scrivener, had placed on his greasy locks a rusted steel-cap, which had seen Marston Moor ; across which projected his well-used quill, in the guise of a plume—the shape of the morion not admitting of its being stuck, as usual, behind his ear.

This whimsical figure conducted the constable, his assistants, and the prisoner, into the low hall, where his principal dealt forth justice ; who presented an appearance still more singular than that of his dependant.

Sundry good Protestants, who thought so highly of themselves as to suppose they were worthy to be distinguished as objects of Catholic cruelty, had taken to defensive arms on the occasion. But it was quickly found that a breastplate and backplate of proof, fastened together with iron clasps, was no convenient enclosure for a man who meant to eat venison and custard ; and that a buff-coat, or shirt of mail, was scarcely more accommodating to the exertions necessary on such active occasions. Besides, there were other objections, as the alarming and menacing aspects which such warlike habiliments gave to the Exchange, and other places, where merchants most do congregate ; and excoriations were bitterly complained of by many, who, not belonging to the artillery company, or trained bands, had no experience in bearing defensive armour.

To obviate these objections, and, at the same time, to secure the persons of all true Protestant citizens against open force or privy assassinations on the part of the Papists, some ingenious artist, belonging, we may presume, to the worshipful Mercers' Company, had contrived a species of armour, of which neither the horse-armoury in the Tower, nor Gwynnap's Gothic Hall, no, nor Dr. Meyrick's invaluable collection of ancient arms, has preserved any specimen. It was called silk-armour,[n] being composed of a doublet and breeches of quilted silk, so closely stitched, and of such thickness, as to be proof against either bullet or steel ; while a thick bonnet of the same materials, with ear-flaps attached to it, and, on the whole, much resembling a nightcap, completed the equipment, and ascertained the security of the wearer from the head to the knee.

Master Maulstatute, among other worthy citizens, had adopted this singular panoply, which had the advantage of being soft, and warm, and flexible, as well as safe. And he now sat in his judicial elbow-chair—a short, rotund figure, hung round, as it were, with cushions, for such was the appearance of the quilted garments; and with a nose protruded from under the silken casque, the size of which, together with the unwieldiness of the whole figure, gave his worship no indifferent resemblance to the sign of the Hog in Armour, which was considerably improved by the defensive garment being of a dusty orange-colour, not altogether unlike the hue of those half-wild swine which are to be found in the forests of Hampshire.

Secure in these invulnerable envelopments, his worship had rested content, although severed from his own death-doing weapons, of rapier, poniard, and pistols, which were placed, nevertheless, at no great distance from his chair. One offensive implement, indeed, he thought it prudent to keep on the table beside his huge Coke upon Lyttleton. This was a sort of pocket-flail, consisting of a piece of strong ash, about eighteen inches long, to which was attached a swinging club of *lignum-vitae*, nearly twice as long as the handle, but jointed so as to be easily folded up. This instrument, which bore at that time the singular name of the Protestant flail, might be concealed under the coat until circumstances demanded its public appearance. A better precaution against surprise than his arms, whether offensive or defensive, was a strong iron grating, which, crossing the room in front of the justice's table, and communicating by a grated door, which was usually kept locked, effectually separated the accused party from his judge.

Justice Maulstatute, such as we have described him, chose to hear the accusation of the witnesses before calling on Peveril for his defence. The detail of the affray was briefly given by the bystanders, and seemed deeply to touch the spirit of the examinator. He shook his silken casque emphatically, when he understood that, after some language betwixt the parties, which the witnesses did not quite understand, the young man in custody struck the first blow, and drew his sword before the wounded party had unsheathed his weapon. Again he shook his crested head yet more solemnly, when the result of the conflict was known ; and yet again, when one of the witnesses declared that, to the best of his knowledge, the sufferer in the fray was a gentle-man belonging to the household of his Grace the Duke of Buckingham.

'A worthy peer,' quoth the armed magistrate—'a true Protestant, and a friend to his country. Mercy on us, to what a height of audacity hath this age arisen ! We see well, and could, were we as blind as a mole, out of what quiver this shaft hath been drawn.'

He then put on his spectacles, and having desired Julian to be brought forward, he glared upon him awfully with those glazen eyes, from under the shade of his quilted turban.

'So young,' he said, 'and so hardened—lackaday !—and a Papist, I'll warrant.'

Peveril had time enough to recollect the necessity of his being at large, if he could possibly obtain his freedom, and interposed here a civil contradiction of his worship's gracious supposition. 'He was no Catholic,' he said, 'but an unworthy member of the Church of England.'

'Perhaps but a lukewarm Protestant, notwithstanding,' said the sage justice ; 'there are those amongst us who ride tantivy to Rome, and have already made out half the journey—ahem ! '

Peveril disowned his being any such.

'And who art thou, then ? ' said the justice ; 'for, friend, to tell you plainly, I like not your visage—ahem ! '

These short and emphatic coughs were accompanied each by a succinct nod, intimating the perfect conviction of the speaker that he had made the best, the wisest, and the most acute observation of which the premises admitted.

Julian, irritated by the whole circumstances of his deten-tion, answered the justice's interrogation in rather a lofty tone. 'My name is Julian Peveril.'

'Now, Heaven be around us ! ' said the terrified justice —'the son of that black-hearted Papist and traitor, Sir Geoffrey Peveril, now in hands, and on the verge of trial ! '

'How, sir ! ' exclaimed Julian, forgetting his situation,

and, stepping forward to the grating with a violence which made the bars clatter, he so startled the appalled justice, that snatching his Protestant flail, Master Maulstatute aimed a blow at his prisoner, to repel what he apprehended was a premeditated attack. But whether it was owing to the justice's hurry of mind, or inexperience in managing the weapon, he not only missed his aim, but brought the swinging part of the machine round his own skull, with such a severe counterbuff, as completely to try the efficacy of his cushioned helmet, and, in spite of its defence, to convey a stunning sensation, which he rather hastily imputed to the consequence of a blow received from Peveril.

His assistants did not directly confirm the opinion which the justice had so unwarrantably adopted ; but all with one voice agreed that, but for their own active and instantaneous interference, there was no knowing what mischief might have been done by a person so dangerous as the prisoner. The general opinion that he meant to proceed in the matter of his own rescue, *par voie du fait*, was indeed so deeply impressed on all present, that Julian saw it would be in vain to offer any defence, especially being but too conscious that the alarming, and probably the fatal consequences of his rencontre with the bully, rendered his commitment inevitable. He contented himself with asking into what prison he was to be thrown ; and when the formidable word Newgate was returned as full answer, he had at least the satisfaction to reflect, that, stern and dangerous as was the shelter of that roof, he should at least enjoy it in company with his father ; and that, by some means or other, they might perhaps obtain the satisfaction of a melancholy meeting, under the circumstances of mutual calamity, which seemed impending over their house.

Assuming the virtue of more patience than he actually possessed, Julian gave the magistrate (to whom all the mildness of his demeanour could not, however, reconcile him), the direction to the house where he lodged, together with a request that his servant, Lance Outram, might be permitted to send him his money and wearing apparel ; adding that all which might be in his possession, either of arms or writings,—the former amounting to a pair of

travelling pistols, and the last to a few memoranda of little
consequence—he willingly consented to place at the disposal of the magistrate. It was in that moment that
he entertained, with sincere satisfaction, the comforting
reflection that the important papers of Lady Derby were
already in the possession of the sovereign.

The justice promised attention to his requests ; but
reminded him, with great dignity, that his present com-
placent and submissive behaviour ought, for his own sake,
to have been adopted from the beginning, instead of disturbing the presence of magistracy with such atrocious
marks of the malignant, rebellious, and murderous spirit
of Popery as he had at first exhibited. ' Yet,' he said, ' as
he was a goodly young man, and of honourable quality, he
would not suffer him to be dragged through the streets as
a felon, but had ordered a coach for his accommodation.'

His honour, Master Maulstatute, uttered the word
' coach ' with the importance of one who, as Dr. Johnson
saith of later date, is conscious of the dignity of putting
horses to his chariot. The worshipful Master Maulstatute
did not, however, on this occasion, do Julian the honour of
yoking to his huge family caroche the two ' frampal jades '
(to use the term of the period) which were wont to drag
that ark to the meeting-house of pure and precious Master
Howlaglass on a Thursday's evening for lecture, and on
a Sunday for a four-hours' sermon. He had recourse to
a leathern convenience, then more rare, but just introduced,
with every prospect of the great facility which has since
been afforded by hackney coaches, to all manner of communication, honest and dishonest, legal and illegal. Our
friend Julian, hitherto much more accustomed to the saddle
than to any other conveyance, soon found himself in
a hackney carriage, with the constable and two assistants
for his companions, armed up to the teeth—the port of
destination being, as they had already intimated, the
ancient fortress of Newgate.

CHAPTER XXXIII

'Tis the black ban-dog of our jail—Pray look on him,
But at a wary distance—rouse him not—
He bays not till he worries.
The Black Dog of Newgate.

THE coach stopped before those tremendous gates, which resemble those of Tartarus, save only that they rather more frequently permit safe and honourable egress; although at the price of the same anxiety and labour with which Hercules, and one or two of the demi-gods, extricated themselves from the Hell of the ancient mythology, and sometimes, it is said, by the assistance of the golden boughs.

Julian stepped out of the vehicle, carefully supported on either side by his companions, and also by one or two turnkeys, whom the first summons of the deep bell at the gate had called to their assistance. That attention, it may be guessed, was not bestowed lest he should make a false step, so much as for fear of his attempting an escape, of which he had no intentions. A few prentices and straggling boys of the neighbouring market, which derived considerable advantage from increase of custom, in consequence of the numerous committals on account of the Popish Plot, and who therefore were zealous Protestants, saluted him on his descent with jubilee shouts of ' Whoop, Papist ! whoop, Papist ! D——n to the Pope, and all his adherents ! '

Under such auspices, Peveril was ushered in beneath that gloomy gateway, where so many bid adieu on their entrance at once to honour and to life. The dark and dismal arch under which he soon found himself opened upon a large courtyard, where a number of debtors were employed in playing at hand-ball, pitch-and-toss, hustle-cap, and other games ; for which relaxations the rigour of their creditors afforded them full leisure, while it debarred them the means of pursuing the honest labour by which they might have redeemed their affairs, and maintained their starving and beggared families.

But with this careless and desperate group Julian was not

to be numbered, being led, or rather forced, by his conductors, into a low arched door, which, carefully secured by bolts and bars, opened for his reception on one side of the archway, and closed, with all its fastenings, the moment after his hasty entrance. He was then conducted along two

NEWGATE, AS BUILT BY SIR RICHARD WHITTINGTON

or three gloomy passages, which, where they intersected each other, were guarded by as many strong wickets, one of iron gates, and the others of stout oak, clenched with plates, and studded with nails of the same metal. He was not allowed to pause until he found himself hurried into a little round vaulted room, which several of these passages opened into, and which seemed, with respect to the labyrinth through part of which he had passed, to resemble the central point of a spider's web, in which the main lines of that reptile's curious maze are always found to terminate.

The resemblance did not end here ; for in this small vaulted apartment, the walls of which were hung round with musketoons, pistols, cutlasses, and other weapons, as well as with many sets of fetters and irons of different construction, all disposed in great order, and ready for employment, a person sat, who might not unaptly be compared to a huge bloated and bottled spider, placed there to secure the prey which had fallen into his toils.

This official had originally been a very strong and square-built man, of large size, but was now so overgrown, from over-feeding, perhaps, and want of exercise, as to bear the same resemblance to his former self which a stall-fed ox still retains to a wild bull. The look of no man is so inauspicious as a fat man upon whose features ill nature has marked an habitual stamp. He seems to have reversed the old proverb of ' laugh and be fat,' and to have thriven under the influence of the worst affections of the mind. Passionate we can allow a jolly mortal to be ; but it seems unnatural to his goodly case to be sulky and brutal. Now this man's features, surly and tallow-coloured ; his limbs, swelled and disproportioned ; his huge paunch and unwieldy carcass suggested the idea that, having once found his way into this central recess, he had there fattened, like the weasel in the fable, and fed largely and foully, until he had become incapable of retreating through any of the narrow paths that terminated at his cell ; and was thus compelled to remain, like a toad under the cold stone, fattening amid the squalid airs of the dungeons by which he was surrounded, which would have proved pestiferous to any other than such a congenial inhabitant. Huge iron-clasped books lay before this ominous specimen of pinguitude—the records of the realm of misery, in which office he officiated as prime minister ; and had Peveril come thither as an unconcerned visitor, his heart would have sunk within him at considering the mass of human wretchedness which must needs be registered in these fatal volumes. But his own distresses sat too heavy on his mind to permit any general reflections of this nature.

The constable and this bulky official whispered together,

after the former had delivered to the latter the warrant of
Julian's commitment. The word *whispered* is not quite
accurate, for their communication was carried on less by
words than by looks and expressive signs ; by which, in all

JULIAN BEFORE THE WARDEN OF NEWGATE

such situations, men learn to supply the use of language,
and to add mystery to what is in itself sufficiently terrible
to the captive. The only words which could be heard were
those of the warden, or, as he was called then, the captain
of the jail, ' Another bird to the cage ? '——

' Who will whistle " Pretty Pope of Rome " with any starling in your knight's ward,' answered the constable, with a facetious air, checked, however, by the due respect to the superior presence in which he stood.

The Grim Feature relaxed into something like a smile as he heard the officer's observation ; but instantly composing himself into the stern solemnity which for an instant had been disturbed, he looked fiercely at his new guest, and pronounced with an awful and emphatic, yet rather an under-voice, the single and impressive word, ' *Garnish !* '

Julian Peveril replied with assumed composure ; for he had heard of the customs of such places, and was resolved to comply with them, so as if possible to obtain the favour of seeing his father, which he shrewdly guessed must depend on his gratifying the avarice of the keeper. ' I am quite ready,' he said, ' to accede to the customs of the place in which I unhappily find myself. You have but to name your demands, and I will satisfy them.'

So saying, he drew out his purse, thinking himself at the same time fortunate that he had retained about him a considerable sum of gold. The captain remarked its width, depth, its extension, and depression, with an involuntary smile, which had scarce contorted his hanging under-lip, and the wiry and greasy moustache which thatched the upper, when it was checked by the recollection that there were regulations which set bounds to his rapacity, and prevented him from pouncing on his prey like a kite, and swooping it all off at once.

This chilling reflection produced the following sullen reply to Peveril :—' There were sundry rates. Gentlemen must choose for themselves. He asked nothing but his fees. But civility,' he muttered, ' must be paid for.'

' And shall, if I can have it for payment,' said Peveril, ' but the price, my good sir, the price ? '

He spoke with some degree of scorn, which he was the less anxious to repress, that he saw, even in this jail, his purse gave him an indirect but powerful influence over his jailer.

The captain seemed to feel the same ; for, as he spoke, he plucked from his head, almost involuntarily, a sort of scalded fur-cap, which served it for covering. But his

fingers revolting from so unusual an act of complaisance,
began to indemnify themselves by scratching his grizzly
shock-head, as he muttered, in a tone resembling the
softened growling of a mastiff when he has ceased to bay
the intruder who shows no fear of him—' There are different
rates.   There is the Little Ease, for common fees of the
crown—rather dark, and the common-sewer runs below it ;
and some gentlemen object to the company, who are chiefly
padders and michers.   Then the master's side—the garnish
came to one piece—and none lay stowed there but who were
in for murder at the least.'

' Name your highest price, sir, and take it,' was Julian's
concise reply.

' Three pieces for the knight's ward,' answered the
governor of this terrestrial Tartarus.

' Take five, and place me with Sir Geoffrey,' was again
Julian's answer, throwing down the money upon the desk
before him.

' Sir Geoffrey ?—Hum !—aye, Sir Geoffrey,' said the
jailer, as if meditating what he ought to do.   ' Well, many
a man has paid money to see Sir Geoffrey—Scarce so much
as you have, though.   But then you are like to see the last
of him.   Ha, ha, ha ! '

These broken muttered exclamations, which terminated
somewhat like the joyous growl of a tiger over his meal,
Julian could not comprehend ;   and only replied to by
repeating his request to be placed in the same cell with
Sir Geoffrey.

' Aye, master,' said the jailer, ' never fear ;   I'll keep word
with you, as you seem to know something of what belongs
to your station and mine.   And hark ye, Jem Clink will
fetch you the darbies.'

' Derby ! '   interrupted Julian,—' Has the earl or coun
tess '——

' Earl or countess !   Ha, ha, ha ! '   again laughed, or
rather growled, the warden.   ' What is your head running
on ?   You are a high fellow belike !   but all is one here.   The
darbies are the fetlocks—the fast-keepers, my boy—the bail
for good behaviour, my darling ;   and if you are not the
more conforming, I can add you a steel nightcap, and
a curious bosom-friend, to keep you warm of a winter night.

But don't be disheartened ; you have behaved genteel ; and you shall not be put upon. And as for this here matter, ten to one it will turn out chance-medley, or manslaughter, at the worst on it ; and then it is but a singed thumb instead of a twisted neck—always if there be no Papistry about it, for then I warrant nothing. Take the gentleman's worship away, Clink.'

A turnkey, who was one of the party that had ushered Peveril into the presence of this Cerberus, now conveyed him out in silence ; and, under his guidance, the prisoner was carried through a second labyrinth of passages with cells opening on each side, to that which was destined for his reception.

On the road through this sad region, the turnkey more than once ejaculated, ' Why, the gentleman must be stark mad ! Could have had the best crown cell to himself for less than half the garnish, and must pay double to pig in with Sir Geoffrey ! Ha, ha ! Is Sir Geoffrey akin to you, if any one may make free to ask ? '

' I am his son,' answered Peveril sternly, in hopes to impose some curb on the fellow's impertinence ; but the man only laughed louder than before.

' His son ! Why, that's best of all—Why, you are a strapping youth—five feet ten, if you be an inch—and Sir Geoffrey's son ! Ha, ha, ha ! '

' Truce with your impertinence,' said Julian. ' My situation gives you no title to insult me ! '

' No more I do,' said the turnkey, smothering his mirth at the recollection, perhaps, that the prisoner's purse was not exhausted. ' I only laughed because you said you were Sir Geoffrey's son. But no matter—'tis a wise child that knows his own father. And here is Sir Geoffrey's cell ; so you and he may settle the fatherhood between you.'

So saying, he ushered his prisoner into a cell, or rather a strong room of the better order, in which there were four chairs, a truckle-bed, and one or two other articles of furniture.

Julian looked eagerly around for his father ; but to his surprise the room appeared totally empty. He turned with anger on the turnkey, and charged him with misleading

him ; but the fellow answered, ' No, no, master ; I have
kept faith with you. Your father, if you call him so, is only
tappiced in some corner. A small hole will hide him ; but
I'll rouse him out presently for you. Here, hoicks ! Turn
out, Sir Geoffrey ! Here is—ha, ha, ha !—your son—or
your wife's son—for I think you can have but little share in
him—come to wait on you.'

Peveril knew not how to resent the man's insolence ;
and indeed his anxiety, and apprehension of some strange
mistake, mingled with, and in some degree neutralized his
anger. He looked again and again, around and around the
room ; until at length he became aware of something rolled
up in a dark corner, which rather resembled a small bundle
of crimson cloth than any living creature. At the vocifera-
tion of the turnkey, however, the object seemed to acquire
life and motion, uncoiled itself in some degree, and, after
an effort or two, gained an erect posture ; still covered
from top to toe with the crimson drapery in which it was at
first wrapped. Julian, at the first glance, imagined from
the size that he saw a child of five years old ; but a shrill
and peculiar tone of voice soon assured him of his mistake.

' Warder,' said this unearthly sound, ' what is the meaning of this disturbance ? Have you more insults to heap
on the head of one who hath ever been the butt of fortune's
malice ? But I have a soul that can wrestle with all my
misfortunes ; it is as large as any of your bodies.'

' Nay, Sir Geoffrey, if this be the way you welcome your
own son ! '—said the turnkey ; ' but you quality folks
know your own ways best.'

' My son ! ' exclaimed the little figure. ' Audacious '——

' Here is some strange mistake,' said Peveril, in the same
breath. ' I sought Sir Geoffrey '——

' And you have him before you, young man,' said the
pygmy tenant of the cell, with an air of dignity ; at the same
time casting on the floor his crimson cloak, and standing
before them in his full dignity of three feet six inches of
height. ' I who was the favoured servant of three successive
sovereigns of the Crown of England, am now the tenant of
this dungeon, and the sport of its brutal keepers. I am
Sir Geoffrey Hudson.'

Julian, though he had never before seen this important

personage, had no difficulty in recognizing, from description, the celebrated dwarf of Henrietta Maria, who had survived the dangers of civil war and private quarrel—the murder of his royal master, Charles I, and the exile of his widow— to fall upon evil tongues and evil days, amidst the unsparing accusations connected with the Popish Plot. He bowed to the unhappy old man, and hastened to explain to him, and to the turnkey, that it was Sir Geoffrey Peveril, of Martin- dale Castle in Derbyshire, whose prison he had desired to share.

'You should have said that before you parted with the gold-dust, my master,' answered the turnkey ; ' for t' other Sir Geoffrey, that is the big, tall, grey-haired man, was sent to the Tower last night ; and the captain will think he has kept his word well enow with you, by lodging you with this here Sir Geoffrey Hudson, who is the better show of the two.'

'I pray you go to your master,' said Peveril ; ' explain the mistake ; and say to him I beg to be sent to the Tower.'

'The Tower ! Ha, ha, ha ! ' exclaimed the fellow. ' The Tower is for lords and knights, and not for squires of low degree—for high treason, and not for ruffling on the streets with rapier and dagger ; and there must go a secretary's warrant to send you there.'

'At least, let me not be a burden on this gentleman,' said Julian. 'There can be no use in quartering us together, since we are not even acquainted. Go tell your master of the mistake.'

'Why, so I should,' said Clink, still grinning, ' if I were not sure that he knew it already. You paid to be sent to Sir Geoffrey, and he sent you to Sir Geoffrey. You are so put down in the register, and he will blot it for no man. Come, come, be conformable, and you shall have light and easy irons—that 's all I can do for you.'

Resistance and expostulation being out of the question, Peveril submitted to have a light pair of fetters secured on his ankles, which allowed him, nevertheless, the power of traversing the apartment.

During this operation, he reflected that the jailer, who had taken the advantage of the equivoque betwixt the two Sir Geoffrey's, must have acted as his assistant had hinted, and cheated him from malice prepense, since the warrant of

committal described him as the son of Sir Geoffrey Peveril.
It was therefore in vain, as, well as degrading, to make
further application to such a man on the subject. Julian
determined to submit to his fate, as what could not be
averted by any effort of his own.

Even the turnkey was moved in some degree by his
youth, good mien, and the patience with which, after the
first effervescence of disappointment, the new prisoner

WILLIAM EVANS, PORTER TO CHARLES I, AND
SIR G. HUDSON, HIS DWARF

resigned himself to his situation. ' You seem a brave young
gentleman,' he said ; ' and shall at least have a good dinner,
and as good a pallet to sleep on, as is within the walls of
Newgate.—And, Master Sir Geoffrey, you ought to make
much of him, since you do not like tall fellows ; for I can
tell you that Master Peveril is in for pinking long Jack
Jenkins, that was the master of defence—as tall a man as
is in London, always excepting the king's porter, Master
Evans, that carried you about in his pocket, Sir Geoffrey,
as all the world has heard tell.'

' Begone, fellow ! ' answered the dwarf. ' Fellow, I scorn you ! '

The turnkey sneered, withdrew, and locked the door behind him.

CHAPTER XXXIV

Degenerate youth, and not of Tydeus' kind,
Whose little body lodged a mighty mind.
Iliad.

LEFT quiet at least, if not alone, for the first time after the events of this troubled and varied day, Julian threw himself on an old oaken seat, beside the embers of sea-coal fire, and began to muse on the miserable situation of anxiety and danger in which he was placed ; where, whether he contemplated the interests of his love, his family affections, or his friendships, all seemed such a prospect as that of a sailor who looks upon breakers on every hand, from the deck of a vessel which no longer obeys the helm.

As Peveril sat sunk in despondency, his companion in misfortune drew a chair to the opposite side of the chimney-corner, and began to gaze at him with a sort of solemn earnestness, which at length compelled him, though almost in spite of himself, to pay some attention to the singular figure who seemed so much engrossed with contemplating him.

Geoffrey Hudson (we drop occasionally the title of knighthood, which the king had bestowed on him in a frolic, but which might introduce some confusion into our history), although a dwarf of the least possible size, had nothing positively ugly in his countenance, or actually distorted in his limbs. His head, hands, and feet, were indeed large, and disproportioned to the height of his body, and his body itself much thicker than was consistent with symmetry, but in a degree which was rather ludicrous than disagreeable to look upon. His countenance, in particular, had he been a little taller, would have been accounted, in youth, handsome, and now, in age, striking and expressive ; it was but the uncommon disproportion betwixt the head and the

trunk which made the features seem whimsical and bizarre
—an effect which was considerably increased by the dwarf's
moustaches, which it was his pleasure to wear so large, that
they almost twisted back amongst, and mingled with, his
grizzled hair.

The dress of this singular wight announced that he was
not entirely free from the unhappy taste which frequently
induces those whom nature has marked by personal deformity, to distinguish, and at the same time to render
themselves ridiculous, by the use of showy colours, and

SIR GEOFFREY HUDSON

garments fantastically and extraordinarily fashioned. But
poor Geoffrey Hudson's laces, embroideries, and the rest of
his finery, were sorely worn and tarnished by the time which
he had spent in jail, under the vague and malicious accusation that he was somehow or other an accomplice in this
all-involving, all-devouring whirlpool of a Popish conspiracy
—an impeachment which, if pronounced by a mouth the
foulest and most malicious, was at that time sufficiently predominant to sully the fairest reputation. It will presently
appear that, in the poor man's manner of thinking and tone
of conversation, there was something analogous to his
absurd fashion of apparel ; for, as in the latter, good stuff
and valuable decorations were rendered ludicrous by the
fantastic fashion in which they were made up ; so, such

glimmerings of good sense and honourable feeling as the little man often evinced, were made ridiculous by a restless desire to assume certain airs of importance, and a great jealousy of being despised, on account of the peculiarity of his outward form.

After the fellow prisoners had looked at each other for some time in silence, the dwarf, conscious of his dignity as first owner of their joint apartment, thought it necessary to do the honours of it to the new-comer. 'Sir,' he said, modifying the alternate harsh and squeaking tones of his voice into accents as harmonious as they could attain, ' I understand you to be the son of my worthy namesake, and ancient acquaintance, the stout Sir Geoffrey Peveril of the Peak. I promise you, I have seen your father where blows have been going more plenty than gold pieces ; and for a tall heavy man, who lacked, as we martialists thought, some of the lightness and activity of our more slightly made Cavaliers, he performed his duty as a man might desire. I am happy to see you, his son ; and, though by a mistake, I am glad we are to share this comfortless cabin together.'

Julian bowed, and thanked his courtesy ; and Geoffrey Hudson having broken the ice, proceeded to question him without further ceremony. ' You are no courtier, I presume, young gentleman ? '

Julian replied in the negative.

' I thought so,' continued the dwarf ; ' for although I have now no official duty at court, the region in which my early years were spent, and where I once held a considerable office, yet I still, when I had my liberty, visited the presence from time to time, as in duty bound for former service ; and am wont, from old habit, to take some note of the courtly gallants, those choice spirits of the age, among whom I was once enrolled. You are, not to compliment you, a marked figure, Master Peveril—though something of the tallest, as was your father's case ; I think I could scarce have seen you anywhere without remembering you.'

Peveril thought he might, with great justice, have returned the compliment, but contented himself with saying, ' he had scarce seen the British court.'

' 'Tis pity,' said Hudson ; ' a gallant can hardly be

formed without frequenting it. But you have been perhaps
in a rougher school ; you have served, doubtless ? '

' My Maker, I hope,' said Julian.

' Fie on it, you mistake. I meant,' said Hudson, ' *à la
Française*—you have served in the army ? '

' No. I have not yet had that honour,' said Julian.

' What ! neither courtier nor soldier, Master Peveril ? '
said the important little man : ' Your father is to blame.
By cock and pie he is, Master Peveril ! How shall a man
be known, or distinguished, unless by his bearing in peace
and war ? I tell you, sir, that at Newbury, where I charged
with my troop abreast with Prince Rupert, and when, as
you may have heard, we were both beaten off by those
cuckoldly hinds the Trained Bands of London—we did
what men could ; and I think it was a matter of three or
four minutes after most of our gentlemen had been driven
off, that his highness and I continued to cut at their long
pikes with our swords ; and I think might have broken in,
but that I had a tall, long-legged brute of a horse, and my
sword was somewhat short—in fine, at last we were obliged
to make volte-face, and then, as I was going to say, the
fellows were so glad to get rid of us, that they set up a great
jubilee cry of " There goes Prince Robin and Cock Robin ! "
—Aye, aye, every scoundrel among them knew me well.
But those days are over. And where were you educated,
young gentleman ? '

Peveril named the household of the Countess of Derby.

' A most honourable lady, upon my word as a gentleman,'
said Hudson. ' I knew the noble countess well, when I was
about the person of my royal mistress, Henrietta Maria.
She was then the very muster of all that was noble, loyal,
and lovely. She was, indeed, one of the fifteen fair ones of
the court whom I permitted to call me Piccoluomini—
a foolish jest on my somewhat diminutive figure, which
always distinguished me from ordinary beings, even when
I was young—I have now lost much stature by stooping ;
but always the ladies had their jest at me. Perhaps, young
man, I had my own amends of some of them somewhere, and
somehow or other—I *say* nothing if I had or no ; far less
do I insinuate disrespect to the noble countess. She was
daughter of the Duc de la Tremouille, or, more correctly,

Des Thouars. But certainly to serve the ladies, and condescend to their humours, even when somewhat too free
or too fantastic, is the true decorum of gentle blood.'

Depressed as his spirits were, Peveril could scarce forbear
smiling when he looked at the pygmy creature, who told
these stories with infinite complacency, and appeared disposed to proclaim, as his own herald, that he had been
a very model of valour and gallantry, though love and arms
seemed to be pursuits totally irreconcilable to his shrivelled,
weatherbeaten countenance, and wasted limbs. Julian was,
however, so careful to avoid giving his companion pain,
that he endeavoured to humour him by saying that,
' Unquestionably, one bred up like Sir Geoffrey Hudson, in
courts and camps, knew exactly when to suffer personal
freedoms, and when to control them.'

The little knight, with great vivacity, though with some
difficulty, began to drag his seat from the side of the fire
opposite to that where Julian was seated, and at length
succeeded in bringing it near him, in token of increasing
cordiality.

' You say well, Master Peveril,' said the dwarf ; ' and
I have given proofs both of bearing and forbearing. Yes,
sir, there was not that thing which my most royal mistress,
Henrietta Maria, could have required of me, that I would
not have complied with, sir ; I was her sworn servant, both
in war and in festival, in battle and pageant, sir. At her
Majesty's particular request, I once condescended to
become—ladies, you know, have strange fancies—to become
the tenant, for a time, of the interior of a pie.'

' Of a pie ? ' said Julian, somewhat amazed.

' Yes, sir, of a pie. I hope you find nothing risible in my
complaisance?' replied his companion, something jealously.

' Not I, sir,' said Peveril ; ' I have other matters than
laughter in my head at present.'

' So had I,' said the dwarfish champion, ' when I found
myself imprisoned in a huge platter, of no ordinary dimensions you may be assured, since I could lie at length in it,
and when I was entombed, as it were, in walls of standing
crust, and a huge cover of pastry, the whole constituting
a sort of sarcophagus, of size enough to have recorded the
epitaph of a general officer or an archbishop on the lid. Sir,

notwithstanding the conveniences which were made to give
me air, it was more like being buried alive than aught else
which I could think of.' n

'I conceive it, sir,' said Julian.

'Moreover, sir,' continued the dwarf, 'there were few in
the secret, which was contrived for the queen's divertise-
ment; for advancing of which I would have crept into
a filbert nut, had it been possible; and few, as I said, being
private in the scheme, there was a risk of accidents. I
doubted, while in my darksome abode, whether some awk-
ward attendant might not have let me fall, as I have
seen happen to a venison pasty; or whether some hungry
guest might not anticipate the moment of my resurrection,
by sticking his knife into my upper crust. And though
I had my weapons about me, young man, as has been
my custom in every case of peril, yet, if such a rash
person had plunged deep into the bowels of the supposed
pasty, my sword and dagger could barely have served
me to avenge, assuredly not to prevent, either of these
catastrophes.'

'Certainly I do so understand it,' said Julian, who began,
however, to feel that the company of little Hudson, talkative
as he showed himself, was likely rather to aggravate than
to alleviate the inconveniences of a prison.

'Nay,' continued the little man, enlarging on his former
topic, 'I had other subjects of apprehension; for it pleased
my Lord of Buckingham, his Grace's father who now bears
the title, in his plenitude of court favour, to command the
pasty to be carried down to the office, and committed anew
to the oven, alleging preposterously that it was better to be
eaten warm than cold.'

'And did this, sir, not disturb your equanimity?' said
Julian.

'My young friend,' said Geoffrey Hudson, 'I cannot
deny it. Nature will claim her rights from the best and
boldest of us. I thought of Nebuchadnezzar and his fiery
furnace; and I waxed warm with apprehension. But, I
thank Heaven, I also thought of my sworn duty to my
royal mistress; and was thereby obliged and enabled to
resist all temptations to make myself prematurely known.
Nevertheless, the duke—if of malice, may Heaven forgive

him—followed down into the office himself, and urged the master-cook very hard that the pasty should be heated, were it but for five minutes. But the master-cook, being privy to the very different intentions of my royal mistress, did most manfully resist the order ; and I was again recon- veyed in safety to the royal table.'

' And in due time liberated from your confinement, I doubt not ? ' said Peveril.

' Yes, sir ; that happy and, I may say, glorious moment at length arrived,' continued the dwarf. ' The upper crust was removed—I started up to the sound of trumpet and clarion, like the soul of a warrior when the last summons shall sound—or rather (if that simile be over audacious), like a spell-bound champion relieved from his enchanted state. It was then that, with my buckler on my arm, and my trusty Bilboa in my hand, I executed a sort of warlike dance, in which my skill and agility then rendered me pre- eminent, displaying, at the same time, my postures, both of defence and offence, in a manner so totally inimitable, that I was almost deafened with the applause of all around me, and half-drowned by the scented waters with which the ladies of the court deluged me from their casting bottles. I had amends of his Grace of Buckingham also ; for as I tripped a hasty morris hither and thither upon the dining- table, now offering my blade, now recovering it, I made a blow at his nose—a sort of *estramaçon*—the dexterity of which consists in coming mighty near to the object you seem to aim at, yet not attaining it. You may have seen a barber make such a flourish with his razor. I promise you his Grace sprang back a half-yard at least. He was pleased to threaten to brain me with a chicken-bone, as he disdain- fully expressed it ; but the king said, " George, you have but a Rowland for an Oliver." And so I tripped on, showing a bold heedlessness of his displeasure, which few dared to have done at that time, albeit countenanced to the utmost like me by the smiles of the brave and the fair. But, welladay ! sir, youth, its fashions, its follies, its frolics, and all its pomp and pride, are as idle and transitory as the crackling of thorns under a pot.'

' The flower that is cast into the oven were a better simile,' thought Peveril. ' Good God, that a man should live to

regret not being young enough to be still treated as baked
meat, and served up in a pie ! '

His companion, whose tongue had for many days been as
closely imprisoned as his person, seemed resolved to indemnify his loquacity by continuing to indulge it on the
present occasion at his companion's expense. He proceeded,
therefore, in a solemn tone, to moralize on the adventure
which he had narrated.

'Young men will no doubt think one to be envied,' he
said, ' who was thus enabled to be the darling and admiration of the court ' (Julian internally stood self-exculpated
from the suspicion) ' and yet it is better to possess fewer
means of distinction, and remain free from the backbiting,
the slander, and the odium, which are always the share of
court favour. Men who had no other cause, cast reflections
upon me because my size varied somewhat from the common
proportion ; and jests were sometimes unthinkingly passed
upon me by those I was bound to, who did not in that case,
peradventure, sufficiently consider that the wren is made
by the same hand which formed the bustard, and that the
diamond, though small in size, outvalues ten thousandfold
the rude granite. Nevertheless, they proceeded in the vein
of humour ; and as I could not in duty or gratitude retort
upon nobles and princes, I was compelled to cast about in
my mind how to vindicate my honour towards those who,
being in the same rank with myself, as servants and courtiers, nevertheless bore themselves towards me as if they
were of a superior class in the rank of honour, as well as in
the accidental circumstance of stature. And as a lesson to
my own pride, and that of others, it so happened, that the
pageant which I have but just narrated—which I justly
reckon the most honourable moment of my life, excepting
perhaps my distinguished share in the battle of Roundway-
down—became the cause of a most tragic event in which
I acknowledge the greatest misfortune of my existence.'

The dwarf here paused, fetched a sigh, big at once with
regret and with the importance becoming the subject of
a tragic history ; then proceeded as follows :—

'You would have thought in your simplicity, young
gentleman, that the pretty pageant I have mentioned could
only have been quoted to my advantage, as a rare masking

frolic, prettily devised, and not less deftly executed ; and yet the malice of the courtiers, who maligned and envied me, made them strain their wit, and exhaust their ingenuity, in putting false and ridiculous constructions upon it. In short, my ears were so much offended with allusions to pies, puff-paste, ovens, and the like, that I was compelled to prohibit such subject of mirth, under penalty of my instant and severe displeasure. But it happ'd there was then a gallant about the court, a man of good quality, son to a knight baronet, and in high esteem with the best in that sphere, also a familiar friend of mine own, from whom, therefore, I had no reason to expect any of that species of gibing which I had intimated my purpose to treat as offensive. Howbeit, it pleased the Honourable Mr. Crofts, so was this youth called and designed, one night, at the groom porter's, being full of wine and waggery, to introduce this threadbare subject, and to say something concerning a goosepie, which I could not but consider as levelled at me. Nevertheless, I did but calmly and solidly pray him to choose a different subject ; failing which, I let him know I should be sudden in my resentment. Notwithstanding, he continued in the same tone, and even aggravated the offence, by speaking of a tomtit, and other unnecessary and obnoxious comparisons ; whereupon I was compelled to send him a cartel, and we met accordingly. Now, as I really loved the youth, it was my intention only to correct him by a flesh-wound or two ; and I would willingly that he had named the sword for his weapon. Nevertheless, he made pistols his election ; and being on horseback, he produced by way of his own weapon, a foolish engine, which children are wont, in their roguery, to use for spouting water ; a—a—in short I forget the name.'

' A squirt, doubtless,' said Peveril, who began to recollect having heard something of this adventure.

' You are right,' said the dwarf ; ' you have indeed the name of the little engine, of which I have had experience in passing the yards at Westminster. Well, sir, this token of slight regard compelled me to give the gentleman such language as soon rendered it necessary for him to take more serious arms. We fought on horseback—breaking ground, and advancing by signal ; and, as I never miss aim, I had the misadventure to kill the Honourable Master Crofts at the first shot. I would not wish my worst foe the pain which I felt, when I saw him reel on his saddle, and so fall down to the earth !—and, when I perceived that the life-blood was pouring fast, I could not but wish to Heaven that it had been my own instead of his. Thus fell youth, hopes, and bravery, a sacrifice to a silly and thoughtless jest ; yet, alas ! wherein had I choice, seeing that honour is, as it were, the very breath in our nostrils ; and that in no sense can we be said to live, if we permit ourselves to be deprived of it ? '

The tone of feeling in which the dwarfish hero concluded his story gave Julian a better opinion of his heart, and even of his understanding, than he had been able to form of one who gloried in having, upon a grand occasion, formed the contents of a pasty. He was indeed enabled to conjecture that the little champion was seduced into such exhibitions by the necessity attached to his condition, by his own vanity, and by the flattery bestowed on him by those who sought pleasure in practical jokes. The fate of the unlucky Master Crofts, however, as well as various exploits of this diminutive person during the Civil Wars, in which he actually, and with great gallantry, commanded a troop of horse, rendered most men cautious of openly rallying him, which was indeed the less necessary, as, when left alone, he seldom failed voluntarily to show himself on the ludicrous side.

At one hour after noon, the turnkey, true to his word, supplied the prisoners with a very tolerable dinner and a flask of well-flavoured though light claret ; which the old man, who was something of a bon-vivant, regretted to observe, was nearly as diminutive as himself. The evening also passed away, but not without continued symptoms of garrulity on the part of Geoffrey Hudson.

It is true these were of a graver character than he had hitherto exhibited, for when the flask was empty, he repeated a long Latin prayer. But the religious act in which he had been engaged only gave his discourse a more serious turn than belonged to his former themes of war, lady's love, and courtly splendour.

The little knight harangued, at first on polemical points

of divinity, and diverged from this thorny path into the neighbouring and twilight walk of mysticism. He talked of secret warnings—of the predictions of sad-eyed prophets —of the visits of monitory spirits, and the Rosicrucian secrets of the Cabala ; all which topics he treated of with such apparent conviction, nay, with so many appeals to personal experience, that one would have supposed him a member of the fraternity of gnomes, or fairies, whom he resembled so much in point of size.

In short, he persevered for a stricken hour in such a torrent of unnecessary tattle, as determined Peveril, at all events, to endeavour to procure a separate lodging. Having repeated his evening prayers in Latin, as formerly (for the old gentleman was a Catholic, which was the sole cause of his falling under suspicion), he set off on a new score, as they were undressing, and continued to prattle until he had fairly talked both himself and his companion to sleep.

CHAPTER XXXV

Of airy tongues that syllable men's names.
Comus.

JULIAN had fallen asleep with his brain rather filled with his own sad reflections than with the mystical lore of the little knight ; and yet it seemed as if in his visions the latter had been more present to his mind than the former.

He dreamed of gliding spirits, gibbering phantoms, bloody hands, which, dimly seen by twilight, seemed to beckon him forward like errant-knight on sad adventure bound. More than once he started from his sleep, so lively was the influence of these visions on his imagination ; and he always awaked under the impression that some one stood by his bedside. The chillness of his ankles, the weight and clatter of the fetters, as he turned himself on his pallet, reminded him on these occasions where he was, and under what circumstances. The extremity to which he saw all that was dear to him at present reduced, struck a deeper cold on his heart than the iron upon his limbs ; nor could he com-

pose himself again to rest without a mental prayer to
Heaven for protection. But when he had been for a third
time awakened from repose by these thick-stirring fancies,
his distress of mind vented itself in speech, and he was unable
to suppress the almost despairing ejaculation, ' God have
mercy upon us ! '

' Amen ! ' answered a voice as sweet and ' soft as honey
dew,' which sounded as if the words were spoken close by
his bedside.

The natural inference was that Geoffrey Hudson, his
companion in calamity, had echoed the prayer which was
so proper to the situation of both. But the tone of voice
was so different from the harsh and dissonant sounds of the
dwarf's enunciation, that Peveril was impressed with the
certainty it could not proceed from Hudson. He was
struck with involuntary terror, for which he could give
no sufficient reason ; and it was not without an effort that
he was able to utter the question, ' Sir Geoffrey, did you
speak ? '

No answer was returned. He repeated the question
louder ; and the same silver-toned voice, which had formerly
said ' *Amen* ' to his prayers, answered to his interrogatory,
' Your companion will not awake while I am here.'

' And who are you ?—What seek you ?—How came you
into this place ? ' said Peveril, huddling, eagerly, question
upon question.

' I am a wretched being, but one who loves you well—
I come for your good.—Concern yourself no further.'

It now rushed on Julian's mind that he had heard of
persons possessed of the wonderful talent of counterfeiting
sounds to such accuracy, that they could impose on their
hearers the belief that they proceeded from a point of the
apartment entirely opposite to that which the real speaker
occupied. Persuaded that he had now gained the depth
of the mystery, he replied, ' This trifling, Sir Geoffrey, is
unseasonable. Say what you have to say in your own
voice and manner. These apish pleasantries do not become
midnight in a Newgate dungeon.'

' But the being who speaks with you,' answered the voice,
' is fitted for the darkest hour, and the most melancholy
haunts.'

Impatient of suspense, and determined to satisfy his curiosity, Julian jumped at once from his pallet, hoping to secure the speaker, whose voice indicated he was so near. But he altogether failed in his attempt, and grasped nothing save thin air.

For a turn or two, Peveril shuffled at random about the room, with his arms extended ; and then at last recollected, that with the impediment of his shackles, and the noise which necessarily accompanied his motions, and announced where he was, it would be impossible for him to lay hands on any one who might be disposed to keep out of his reach. He therefore endeavoured to return to his bed ; but, in groping for his way, lighted first on that of his fellow prisoner. The little captive slept deep and heavy, as was evinced from his breathing ; and upon listening a moment, Julian became again certain, either that his companion was the most artful of ventriloquists and of dissemblers, or that there was actually within the precincts of that guarded chamber some third being, whose very presence there seemed to intimate that it belonged not to the ordinary line of humanity.

Julian was no ready believer in the supernatural ; but that age was very far from being so incredulous concerning ghostly occurrences as our own ; and it was no way derogatory to his good sense that he shared the prejudices of his time. His hair began to bristle, and the moisture to stand on his brow, as he called on his companion to awake, for Heaven's sake.

The dwarf answered—but he spoke without awaking,— ' The day may dawn and be d—d. Tell the master of the horse I will not go to the hunting, unless I have the little black jennet.'

' I tell you,' said Julian, ' there is some one in the apartment. Have you not a tinder-box to strike a light ? '

' I care not how slight my horse be,' replied the slumberer, pursuing his own train of ideas, which, doubtless, carried him back to the green woods of Windsor, and the royal deer-hunts which he had witnessed there. ' I am not overweight. I will not ride that great Holstein brute, that I must climb up to by a ladder, and then sit on his back like a pin-cushion on an elephant.'

Julian at length put his hand to the sleeper's shoulder, and shook him, so as to awake him from his dream ; when, after two or three snorts and groans, the dwarf asked peevishly, what the devil ailed him ?

' The devil himself, for what I know,' said Peveril, ' is at this very moment in the room here beside us.'

The dwarf on this information started up, crossed himself, and began to hammer a flint and steel with all dispatch, until he had lighted a little piece of candle, which he said was consecrated to Saint Bridget, and as powerful as the herb called *fuga daemonum*, or the liver of the fish burnt by Tobit in the house of Raguel, for chasing all goblins, and evil or dubious spirits, from the place of its radiance ; ' if, indeed,' as the dwarf carefully guarded his proposition, ' they existed anywhere, save in the imagination of his fellow prisoner.'

Accordingly, the apartment was no sooner enlightened by this holy candle's end, than Julian began to doubt the evidence of his own ears ; for not only was there no one in the room save Sir Geoffrey Hudson and himself, but all the fastenings of the door were so secure, that it seemed impossible that they could have been opened and again fixed, without a great deal of noise, which, on the last occasion at least, could not possibly have escaped his ears, seeing that he must have been on his feet, and employed in searching the chamber, when the unknown, if an earthly being was in the act of retreating from it.

Julian gazed for a moment with great earnestness, and no little perplexity, first on the bolted door, then on the grated window ; and began to accuse his own imagination of having played him an unpleasant trick. He answered little to the questions of Hudson, and, returning to his bed, heard, in silence, a long studied oration on the merits of Saint Bridget, which comprehended the greater part of her long-winded legend, and concluded with the assurance that, from all accounts preserved of her, that holy saint was the least of all possible women, except those of the pygmy kind.

By the time the dwarf had ceased to speak, Julian's desire of sleep had returned ; and after a few glances around the apartment, which was still illuminated by the expiring beams of the holy taper, his eyes were again closed in forgetfulness, and his repose was not again disturbed in the course of that night.

Morning dawns on Newgate, as well as on the freest mountain-turf which Welshman or wild goat ever trode ; but in so different a fashion, that the very beams of heaven's precious sun, when they penetrate into the recesses of the prison-house, have the air of being committed to jail. Still, with the light of day around him, Peveril easily persuaded himself of the vanity of his preceding night's visions ; and smiled when he reflected that fancies similar to those to which his ear was often exposed in the Isle of Man had been able to arrange themselves in a manner so impressive, when he heard them from the mouth of so singular a character as Hudson, and in the solitude of a prison.

Before Julian had awaked, the dwarf had already quitted his bed, and was seated in the chimney corner of the apartment, where, with his own hands, he had arranged a morsel of fire, partly attending to the simmering of a small pot, which he had placed on the flame, partly occupied with a huge folio volume which lay on the table before him, and seemed wellnigh as tall and bulky as himself. He was wrapped up in the dusky crimson cloak already mentioned, which served him for a morning-gown, as well as a mantle against the cold, and which corresponded with a large montero-cap, that enveloped his head. The singularity of his features, and of the eyes, armed with spectacles, which were now cast on the subject of his studies, now directed towards his little cauldron, would have tempted Rembrandt to exhibit him on canvas, either in the character of an alchemist, or of a necromancer, engaged in some strange experiment, under the direction of one of the huge manuals which treat of the theory of these mystic arts.

The attention of the dwarf was bent, however, upon a more domestic object. He was only preparing soup, of no unsavoury quality, for breakfast, which he invited Peveril to partake with him. ' I am an old soldier,' he said, ' and, I must add, an old prisoner ; and understand how to shift for myself better than you can do, young man.— Confusion to the scoundrel Clink, he has put the spice-box out of my reach !—Will you hand it me from the mantelpiece ? I will teach you, as the French have it, *faire la cuisine;* and then, if you please, we will divide, like brethren, the labours of our prison-house.'

Julian readily assented to the little man's friendly proposal, without interposing any doubt as to his continuing

JULIAN PEVERIL AND SIR GEOFFREY HUDSON
IN NEWGATE

an inmate of the same cell. Truth is, that although, upon the whole, he was inclined to regard the whispering voice of the preceding evening as the impression of his own excited fancy, he felt, nevertheless, curiosity to see how a second night was to pass over in the same cell ; and the tone of the invisible intruder, which at midnight had been heard by him with terror, now excited, on recollection, a gentle and not unpleasing species of agitation—the combined effect of awe and of awakened curiosity.

Days of captivity have little to mark them as they glide away. That which followed the night which we have described, afforded no circumstance of note. The dwarf imparted to his youthful companion a volume similar to that which formed his own studies, and which proved to be a tome of one of Scuderi's now forgotten romances, of which Geoffrey Hudson was a great admirer, and which were then very fashionable both at the French and English courts ; although they contrive to unite in their immense folios all the improbabilities and absurdities of the old romances of chivalry, without that tone of imagination which pervades them, and all the metaphysical absurdities which Cowley and the poets of the age had heaped upon the passion of love, like so many load of small-coal upon a slender fire, which it smothers instead of aiding.

But Julian had no alternative, saving only to muse over the sorrows of Artamenes and Mandane, or on the com-plicated distresses of his own situation ; and in these disagreeable divertisements, the morning crept through as it could.

Noon first, and thereafter nightfall, were successively marked by a brief visit from their stern turnkey, who, with noiseless step and sullen demeanour, did in silence the necessary offices about the meals of the prisoners, exchang-ing with them as few words as an official in the Spanish Inquisition might have permitted himself upon a similar occasion. With the same taciturn gravity, very different from the laughing humour into which he had been surprised on a former occasion, he struck their fetters with a small hammer, to ascertain, by the sound thus produced, whether they had been tampered with by file or otherwise. He next mounted on a table, to make the same experiment on the window-grating.

Julian's heart throbbed ; for might not one of those grates have been so tampered with as to give entrance to the nocturnal visitant ? But they returned to the experienced ear of Master Clink, when he struck them in turn with the hammer, a clear and ringing sound, which assured him of their security.

'It would be difficult for any one to get in through these defences,' said Julian, giving vent in words to his own feelings.

'Few wish that,' answered the surly groom, misconstruing what was passing in Peveril's mind ; 'and let me tell you, master, folks will find it quite as difficult to get out.' He retired, and night came on.

The dwarf, who took upon himself for the day the whole duties of the apartment, trundled about the room, making a most important clatter as he extinguished their fire, and put aside various matters which had been in use in the course of the day, talking to himself all the while in a tone of no little consequence, occasionally grounded on the dexterity with which an old soldier could turn his hand to everything ; and at other times, on the wonder that a courtier of the first rank should condescend to turn his hand to anything. Then came the repetition of his accustomed prayers ; but his disposition to converse did not, as on the former occasion, revive after his devotions. On the contrary, long before Julian had closed an eye, the heavy breathing from Sir Geoffrey Hudson's pallet declared that the dwarf was already in the arms of Morpheus.

Amid the total darkness of the apartment, and with a longing desire, and at the same time no small fear, for the recurrence of the mysterious address of the preceding evening, Julian lay long awake without his thoughts receiving any interruption save when the clock told the passing hour from the neighbouring steeple of St. Sepulchre. At length he sank into slumber ; but had not slept, to his judgement, above an hour, when he was roused by the sound which his waking ear had so long expected in vain.

'Can you sleep ? Will you sleep ? Dare you sleep ?' were the questions impressed on his ear, in the same clear, soft, and melodious voice, which had addressed him on the preceding night.

'Who is it asks me the question ?' answered Julian. 'But be the questioner good or evil, I reply that I am a guiltless prisoner ; and that innocence may wish and dare to sleep soundly.'

'Ask no questions of me,' said the voice ; 'neither attempt to discover who speaks to you ; and be assured that folly alone can sleep, with fraud around and danger before him.'

' Can you, who tell me of dangers, counsel me how to combat or how to avoid them ? ' said Julian.

' My power is limited,' said the voice ; ' yet something I can do, as the glow-worm can show a precipice. But you must confide in me.'

' Confidence must beget confidence,' answered Julian. ' I cannot repose trust in I know not what or whom.'

' Speak not so loud,' replied the voice, sinking almost into a whisper.

' Last night you said my companion would not awake,' said Julian.

' To-night I warrant not that he shall sleep,' said the voice. And as it spoke, the hoarse, snatching, discordant tones of the dwarf were heard, demanding of Julian why he talked in his sleep—wherefore he did not rest himself, and let other people rest—and, finally, whether his visions of last night were returned upon him again ?

' Say yes,' said the voice, in a whisper, so low, yet so distinct, that Julian almost doubted whether it was not an echo of his own thought,—' Say but yes—and I part to return no more ! '

In desperate circumstances men look to strange and unusual remedies ; and although unable to calculate the chances of advantage which this singular communication opened to him, Julian did not feel inclined to let them at once escape from him. He answered the dwarf, that he had been troubled by an alarming dream.

' I could have sworn it, from the sound of your voice,' said Hudson. ' It is strange, now, that you overgrown men never possess the extreme firmness of nerves proper to us who are cast in a more compact mould. My own voice retains its masculine sounds on all occasions. Dr. Cockerel was of opinion, that there was the same allowance of nerve and sinew to men of every size, and that nature spun the stock out thinner or stronger, according to the extent of surface which they were to cover. Hence, the least creatures are oftentimes the strongest. Place a beetle under a tall candlestick, and the insect will move it by its efforts to get out ; which is, in point of comparative strength, as

if one of us should shake his Majesty's prison of Newgate by
similar struggles.   Cats also, and weasels, are creatures of
greater exertion or endurance than dogs or sheep.   And
in general you may remark that little men dance better,
and are more unwearied under exertion of every kind, than
those to whom their own weight must necessarily be burden-
some.   I respect you, Master Peveril, because I am told
you have killed one of those gigantic fellows who go about
swaggering as if their souls were taller than ours, because
their noses are nearer to the clouds by a cubit or two.   But
do not value yourself on this, as anything very unusual.
I would have you to know it hath been always thus ; and
that, in the history of all ages, the clean, tight, dapper little
fellow hath proved an overmatch for his bulky antagonist.
I need only instance, out of Holy Writ, the celebrated downfall of Goliah, and of another lubbard, who had more fingers
to his hand, and more inches to his stature, than ought to
belong to an honest man, and who was slain by a nephew
of good King David ; and of many others whom I do
not remember ; nevertheless, they were all Philistines of
gigantic stature.   In the classics, also, you have Tydeus, and
other tight, compact heroes, whose diminutive bodies were
the abode of large minds.   And indeed you may observe,
in sacred as well as profane history, that your giants are
ever heretics and blasphemers, robbers and oppressors,
outragers of the female sex, and scoffers at regular authority.
Such were Gog and Magog, whom our authentic chronicles
vouch to have been slain near to Plymouth, by the good
little knight Corineus, who gave name to Cornwall.   Asca-
parte also was subdued by Bevis, and Colbrand by Guy, as
Southampton and Warwick can testify.   Like unto these
was the giant Hoel, slain in Bretagne by King Arthur.
And if Ryence, King of North Wales, who was done to death
by the same worthy champion of Christendom, be not
actually termed a giant, it is plain he was little better, since
he required twenty-four king's beards, which were then worn
full and long, to fur his gown ; whereby, computing each
beard at eighteen inches (and you cannot allow less for
a beard-royal), and supposing only the front of the gown
trimmed therewith, as we use ermine ; and that the back
was mounted and lined, instead of cat-skins and squirrels'

fur, with the beards of earls and dukes, and other inferior dignitaries—may amount to—But I will work the question to-morrow.'

Nothing is more soporific to any (save a philosopher or moneyed man) than the operation of figures ; and when in bed, the effect is irresistible. Sir Geoffrey fell asleep in the act of calculating King Ryence's height, from the supposed length of his mantle. Indeed, had he not stumbled on this abstruse subject of calculation, there is no guessing how long he might have held forth upon the superiority of men of little stature, which was so great a favourite with him, that, numerous as such narratives are, the dwarf had collected almost all the instances of their victories over giants, which history or romance afforded.

No sooner had unequivocal signs of the dwarf's sound slumbers reached Julian's ears, than he began again to listen eagerly for the renewal of that mysterious communication which was at once interesting and awful. Even whilst Hudson was speaking, he had, instead of bestowing his attention upon his eulogy on persons of low stature, kept his ears on watchful guard to mark, if possible, the lightest sounds of any sort which might occur in the apartment ; so that he thought it scarce possible that even a fly should have left it without its motion being overheard. If, therefore, his invisible monitor was indeed a creature of this world, —an opinion which Julian's sound sense rendered him unwilling to renounce—that being could not have left the apartment ; and he waited impatiently for a renewal of their communication. He was disappointed ; not the slightest sound reached his ear ; and the nocturnal visitor, if still in the room, appeared determined on silence.

It was in vain that Peveril coughed, hemmed, and gave other symptoms of being awake ; at length, such became his impatience, that he resolved, at any risk, to speak first, in hopes of renewing the communication betwixt them. ' Whoever thou art,' he said, in a voice loud enough to be heard by a waking person, but not so high as to disturb his sleeping companion—' Whoever, or whatever thou art, that hast shown some interest in the fate of such a castaway as Julian Peveril, speak once more, I conjure thee ; and be your communication for good or evil, believe me, I am equally prepared to abide the issue.'

No answer of any kind was returned to this invocation ; nor did the least sound intimate the presence of the being to whom it was so solemnly addressed.

'I speak in vain,' said Julian, 'and perhaps I am but invoking that which is insensible of human feeling, or which takes a malign pleasure in human suffering.'

There was a gentle and half-broken sigh from a corner of the apartment, which, answering to this exclamation, seemed to contradict the imputation which it conveyed.

Julian, naturally courageous, and familiarized by this time to his situation, raised himself in bed, and stretched out his arm, to repeat his adjuration, when the voice, as if alarmed at his action and energy, whispered, in a tone more hurried than that which it had hitherto used, 'Be still —move not—or I am mute for ever !'

'It is then a mortal being who is present with me,' was the natural inference of Julian, 'and one who is probably afraid of being detected ; I have then some power over my visitor, though I must be cautious how I use it. If your intents are friendly,' he proceeded, 'there was never a time in which I lacked friends more, or would be more grateful for kindness. The fate of all who are dear to me is weighed in the balance, and with worlds would I buy the tidings of their safety.'

'I have said my power is limited,' replied the voice. '*You* I may be able to preserve—the fate of your friends is beyond my control.'

'Let me at least know it,' said Julian ; 'and, be it as it may, I will not shun to share it.'

'For whom would you inquire ?' said the soft, sweet voice, not without a tremulousness of accent, as if the question was put with diffident reluctance.

'My parents,' said Julian, after a moment's hesitation, 'how fare they ? What will be their fate ?'

'They fare as the fort under which the enemy has dug a deadly mine. The work may have cost the labour of years, such were the impediments to the engineers ; but Time brings opportunity upon its wings.'

'And what will be the event ?' said Peveril.

'Can I read the future,' answered the voice, ' save by comparison with the past ? Who has been hunted on these stern and unmitigable accusations, but has been at last brought to bay ? Did high and noble birth, honoured age, and approved benevolence, save the unfortunate Lord Stafford ? Did learning, capacity of intrigue, or high Court favour, redeem Coleman, although the confidential servant of the heir presumptive of the Crown of England ? Did subtilty and genius, and the exertions of a numerous sect, save Fenwicke, or Whitbread, or any other of the accused priests ? Were Groves, Pickering, or the other humble wretches who have suffered, safe in their obscurity ? There is no condition in life, no degree of talent, no form of principle, which affords protection against an accusation, which levels conditions, confounds characters, renders men's virtues their sins, and rates them as dangerous in proportion as they have influence, though attained in the noblest manner, and used for the best purposes. Call such a one but an accessory to the Plot—let him be mouthed in the evidence of Oates or Dugdale—and the blindest shall foresee the issue of their trial.'

'Prophet of Evil ! ' said Julian, ' my father has a shield invulnerable to protect him. He is innocent.'

'Let him plead his innocence at the bar of Heaven,' said the voice ; ' it will serve him little where Scroggs presides.'

'Still I fear not,' said Julian, counterfeiting more confidence than he really possessed ; ' my father's cause will be pleaded before twelve Englishmen.'

'Better before twelve wild beasts,' answered the Invisible, ' than before Englishmen, influenced with party prejudice, passion, and the epidemic terror of an imaginary danger. They are bold in guilt in proportion to the number amongst whom the crime is divided.'

'Ill-omened speaker,' said Julian, ' thine is indeed a voice fitted only to sound with the midnight bell, and the screech-owl. Yet speak again. Tell me, if thou canst '—(he would have said of Alice Bridgenorth, but the word would not leave his tongue)—' Tell me,' he said, ' if the noble house of Derby '——

'Let them keep their rock like the sea-fowl in the tempest ; and it may so fall out,' answered the voice, ' that

their rock may be a safe refuge.   But there is blood on their
ermine ; and revenge has dogged them for many a year,
like a bloodhound that hath been distanced in the morning
chase, but may yet grapple the quarry ere the sun shall
set.   At present, however, they are safe.   Am I now to
speak further on your own affairs, which involve little
short of your life and honour ? or are there yet any whose
interests you prefer to your own ? '

' There is,' said Julian, ' one, from whom I was violently
parted yesterday ; if I knew but of her safety, I were little
anxious for my own.'

' One ! ' returned the voice, ' only *one* from whom you
were parted yesterday ? '

' But in parting from whom,' said Julian, ' I felt separated
from all happiness which the world can give me.'

' You mean Alice Bridgenorth,' said the Invisible, with
some bitterness of accent ; ' but her you will never see more.
Your own life and hers depend on your forgetting each
other.'

' I cannot purchase my own life at that price,' replied
Julian.

' Then DIE in your obstinacy,' returned the Invisible ; nor
to all the entreaties which he used was he able to obtain
another word in the course of that remarkable night.

CHAPTER XXXVI

A short-hough'd man, but full of pride.
                              ALLAN RAMSAY.

THE blood of Julian Peveril was so much fevered by the
state in which his invisible visitor left him, that he was
unable, for a length of time, to find repose.   He swore to
himself, that he would discover and expose the nocturnal
demon which stole on his hours of rest, only to add gall
to bitterness, and to pour poison into those wounds which
already smarted so severely.   There was nothing which his
power extended to, that, in his rage, he did not threaten.
He proposed a closer and a more rigorous survey of his cell,

so that he might discover the mode by which his tormentor entered, were it as unnoticeable as an auger-hole. If his diligence should prove unavailing, he determined to inform the jailers, to whom it could not be indifferent to know that their prison was open to such intrusions. He proposed to himself, to discover from their looks, whether they were already privy to these visits ; and if so, to denounce them to the magistrates, to the judges, to the House of Commons, was the least that his resentment proposed. Sleep surprised his worn-out frame in the midst of his projects of discovery and vengeance, and, as frequently happens, the light of the ensuing day proved favourable to calmer resolutions.

He now reflected that he had no ground to consider the motives of his visitor as positively malevolent, although he had afforded him little encouragement to hope for assistance on the points he had most at heart   Towards himself, there had been expressed a decided feeling, both of sympathy and interest ; if through means of these he could acquire his liberty, he might, when possessed of freedom, turn it to the benefit of those for whom he was more interested than for his own welfare.   ' I have behaved like a fool,' he said ; ' I ought to have temporized with this singular being, learned the motives of its interference, and availed myself of its succour, provided I could do so without any dishonourable conditions.   It would have been always time enough to reject such when they should have been proposed to me.'

So saying, he was forming projects for regulating his intercourse with the stranger more prudently, in case their communication should be renewed, when his meditations were interrupted by the peremptory summons of Sir Geoffrey Hudson, that he would, in his turn, be pleased to perform those domestic duties of their common habitation, which the dwarf had yesterday taken upon himself.

There was no resisting a request so reasonable, and Peveril accordingly rose and betook himself to the arrangement of their prison, while Sir Hudson, perched upon a stool from which his legs did not by halfway reach the ground, sat in a posture of elegant languor, twangling upon an old broken-winded guitar, and singing songs in Spanish, Moorish, and Lingua Franca, most detestably out of tune.   He failed not, at the conclusion of each ditty, to favour Julian with some account of what he had sung, either in the way of translation, or historical anecdote, or as the lay was connected with some peculiar part of his own eventful history, in the course of which the poor little man had chanced to have been taken by a Sallee rover, and carried captive into Morocco.

This part of his life Hudson used to make the era of many strange adventures ; and, if he could himself be believed, he had made wild work among the affections of the Emperor's seraglio. But, although few were in a situation to cross-examine him on gallantries and intrigues of which the scene was so remote, the officers of the garrison of Tangier had a report current amongst them that the only use to which the tyrannical Moors could convert a slave of such slender corporeal strength, was to employ him to lie a-bed all day and hatch turkey's eggs. The least allusion to this rumour used to drive him wellnigh frantic, and the fatal termination of his duel with young Crofts, which began in wanton mirth, and ended in bloodshed, made men more coy than they had formerly been, of making the fiery little hero the subject of their raillery.

While Peveril did the drudgery of the apartment, the dwarf remained much at his ease, carolling in the manner we have described ; but when he beheld Julian attempting the task of the cook, Sir Geoffrey Hudson sprang from the stool on which he sat *en Signor*, at the risk of breaking both his guitar and his neck, exclaiming, ' That he would rather prepare breakfast every morning betwixt this and the day of judgement, than commit a task of such consequence to an inexperienced bungler like his companion.'

The young man gladly resigned his task to the splenetic little knight, and only smiled at his resentment when he added, that, to be but a mortal of middle stature, Julian was as stupid as a giant. Leaving the dwarf to prepare the meal after his own pleasure, Peveril employed himself in measuring the room with his eyes on every side, and in endeavouring to discover some private entrance, such as might admit his midnight visitant, and perhaps could be employed in case of need for effecting his own escape.

The floor next engaged a scrutiny equally minute, but more successful.

Close by his own pallet, and dropped in such a manner that he must have seen it sooner but for the hurry with which he obeyed the summons of the impatient dwarf, lay a slip of paper, sealed, and directed with the initial letters J. P., which seemed to ascertain that it was addressed to himself. He took the opportunity of opening it while the soup was in the very moment of projection, and the full attention of his companion was occupied by what he, in common with wiser and taller men, considered as one of the principal occupations of life ; so that, without incurring his observation or awaking his curiosity, Julian had the opportunity to read as follows :—

'Rash and infatuated as you are, there is one who would forfeit much to stand betwixt you and your fate. You are to-morrow to be removed to the Tower, where your life cannot be assured for a single day ; for, during the few hours you have been in London, you have provoked a resentment which is not easily slaked. There is but one chance for you,—renounce A. B.—think no more of her. If that be impossible, think of her but as one whom you can never see again. If your heart can resolve to give up an attachment which it should never have entertained, and which it would be madness to cherish longer, make your acquiescence in this condition known by putting on your hat a white band, or white feather, or knot of ribbon of the same colour, whichever you may most easily come by. A boat will, in that case, run, as if by accident, on board of that which is to convey you to the Tower. Do you in the confusion jump overboard, and swim to the Southwark side of the Thames. Friends will attend there to secure your escape, and you will find yourself with one who will rather lose character and life, than that a hair of your head should fall to the ground : but who, if you reject the warning, can only think of you as of the fool who perishes in his folly. May Heaven guide you to a sound judgement of your condition ! So prays one who would be your friend, if you pleased,

'UNKNOWN'.

The Tower !—it was a word of terror, even more so than a civil prison ; for how many passages to death did that dark structure present ! The severe executions which it had witnessed in preceding reigns, were not perhaps more numerous than the secret murders which had taken place within its walls ; yet Peveril did not a moment hesitate on the part which he had to perform. ' I will share my father's fate,' he said ; ' I thought but of him when they brought me hither ; I will think of nothing else when they convey me to yonder still more dreadful place of confinement ; it is his, and it is but meet that it should be his son's. And thou, Alice Bridgenorth, the day that I renounce thee may I be held alike a traitor and a dastard ! Go, false adviser, and share the fate of seducers and heretical teachers ! '

He could not help uttering this last expression aloud, as he threw the billet into the fire, with a vehemence which made the dwarf start with surprise. ' What say you of burning heretics, young man ? ' he exclaimed ; ' by my faith, your zeal must be warmer than mine, if you talk on such a subject when the heretics are the prevailing number. May I measure six feet without my shoes, but the heretics would have the best of it if we came to that work. Beware of such words.'

' Too late to beware of words spoken and heard,' said the turnkey, who, opening the door with unusual precautions to avoid noise, had stolen unperceived into the room ; ' however, Master Peveril has behaved like a gentleman, and I am no tale-bearer, on condition he will consider I have had trouble in his matters.'

Julian had no alternative but to take the fellow's hint and administer a bribe, with which Master Clink was so well satisfied, that he exclaimed, ' It went to his heart to take leave of such a kind-natured gentleman, and that he could have turned the key on him for twenty years with pleasure. But the best friends must part.'

' I am to be removed, then ? ' said Julian.

' Aye, truly, master, the warrant is come from the Council.'

' To convey me to the Tower.'

' Whew ! ' exclaimed the officer of the law—' who the

devil told you that ? But since you do know it, there is no
harm to say aye. So make yourself ready to move immediately ; and first, hold out your dew-beaters till I take off
the darbies.'

'Is that usual ? ' said Peveril, stretching out his feet as
the fellow directed, while his fetters were unlocked.

'Why, aye, master, these fetters belong to the keeper ;
they are not a-going to send them to the Lieutenant, I trow.
No, no, the warders must bring their own gear with them ;
they get none here, I promise them. Nevertheless, if your
honour hath a fancy to go in fetters, as thinking it may
move compassion of your case'——

'I have no intention to make my case seem worse than
it is,' said Julian ; whilst at the same time it crossed his
mind that his anonymous correspondent must be well
acquainted both with his own personal habits, since the
letter proposed a plan of escape which could only be executed
by a bold swimmer, and with the fashions of the prison,
since it was foreseen that he would not be ironed on his
passage to the Tower. The turnkey's next speech made
him carry conjecture still further.

'There is nothing in life I would not do for so brave
a guest,' said Clink ; 'I would nab one of my wife's ribbons
for you, if your honour had the fancy to mount the white
flag in your beaver.'

'To what good purpose ? ' said Julian, shortly connecting,
as was natural, the man's proposed civility with the advice
given and the signal prescribed in the letter.

'Nay, to no good purpose I know of,' said the turnkey ;
'only it is the fashion to seem white and harmless—
a sort of token of not-guiltiness, as I may say, which
folks desire to show the world, whether they be truly
guilty or not ; but I cannot say that guiltiness or not-
guiltiness argufies much, saving they be words in the
verdict.'

'Strange,' thought Peveril, although the man seemed to
speak quite naturally, and without any double meaning,
'strange that all should apparently combine to realize the
plan of escape, could I but give my consent to it ! And
had I not better consent ? Whoever does so much for me
must wish me well, and a well-wisher would never enforce

H h

the unjust conditions on which I am required to consent
to my liberation.'

But this misgiving of his resolution was but for a moment.
He speedily recollected, that whoever aided him in escaping,
must be necessarily exposed to great risk, and had a right
to name the stipulation on which he was willing to incur
it. He also recollected that falsehood is equally base,
whether expressed in words or in dumb show ; and that
he should lie as flatly by using the signal agreed upon in
evidence of his renouncing Alice Bridgenorth, as he would
in direct terms if he made such renunciation without the
purpose of abiding by it.'

' If you would oblige me,' he said to the turnkey, ' let
me have a piece of black silk or crape for the purpose you
mention.'

' Of crape,' said the fellow ; ' what should that signify ?
Why, the bien morts, who bing out to tour at you [1] will
think you a chimney-sweeper on Mayday.'

' It will show my settled sorrow,' said Julian, ' as well as
my determined resolution.'

' As you will, sir,' answered the fellow ; ' I'll provide you
with a black rag of some kind or other. So, now ; let us
be moving.'

Julian intimated his readiness to attend him, and proceeded to bid farewell to his late companion, the stout
Geoffrey Hudson. The parting was not without emotion
on both sides, more particularly on that of the poor little
man, who had taken a particular liking to the companion
of whom he was now about to be deprived. ' Fare ye well,'
he said, ' my young friend,' taking Julian's hand in both
his own uplifted palms, in which action he somewhat
resembled the attitude of a sailor pulling a rope overhead,
—' Many in my situation would think himself wronged, as
a soldier and servant of the king's chamber, in seeing you
removed to a more honourable prison than that which I am
limited unto. But, I thank God, I grudge you not the
Tower, nor the rocks of Scilly, nor even Carisbrooke Castle,
though the latter was graced with the captivity of my
blessed and martyred master. Go where you will, I wish
you all the distinction of an honourable prison-house, and

---

[1] The smart girls, who turn out to look at you.

a safe and speedy deliverance in God's own time. For
myself, my race is near a close, and that because I fall a
martyr to the over-tenderness of my own heart. There is
a circumstance, good Master Julian Peveril, which should
have been yours, had Providence permitted our further
intimacy, but it fits not the present hour. Go, then, my
friend, and bear witness in life and death, that Geoffrey
Hudson scorns the insults and persecutions of fortune, as
he would despise, and has often despised, the mischievous
pranks of an overgrown schoolboy.'

So saying, he turned away, and hid his face with his little
handkerchief, while Julian felt towards him that tragi-
comic sensation which makes us pity the object which
excites it, not the less that we are somewhat inclined to
laugh amid our sympathy. The jailer made him a signal,
which Peveril obeyed, leaving the dwarf to disconsolate
solitude.

As Julian followed the keeper through the various wind-
ings of this penal labyrinth, the man observed, that ' he
was a rum fellow, that little Sir Geoffrey, and, for gallantry,
a perfect Cock of Bantam, for as old as he was. There was
a certain gay wench,' he said, ' that had hooked him ; but
what she could make of him, save she carried him to Smithfield, and took money for him, as for a motion of puppets,
it was,' he said, ' hard to gather.'

Encouraged by this opening, Julian asked if his attendant
knew why his prison was changed. ' To teach you to
become a King's post without commission,' answered the
fellow.

He stopped in his tattle as they approached that formidable central point, in which lay couched on his leathern
elbow-chair the fat commander of the fortress, stationed
apparently for ever in the midst of his citadel, as the huge
Boa is sometimes said to lie stretched as a guard upon the
subterranean treasures of Eastern Rajahs. This overgrown
man of authority eyed Julian wistfully and sullenly, as the
miser the guinea which he must part with, or the hungry
mastiff the food which is carried to another kennel. He
growled to himself as he turned the leaves of his ominous
register, in order to make the necessary entry respecting
the removal of his prisoner. ' To the Tower—to the Tower

—aye, aye, all must to the Tower—that's the fashion of it
—free Britons to a military prison, as if we had neither bolts
nor chains here ! I hope Parliament will have it up, this
Towering work, that's all. Well, the youngster will take no
good by the change, and that is one comfort.'

Having finished at once his official act of registration, and
his soliloquy, he made a signal to his assistants to remove
Julian, who was led along the same stern passages which
he had traversed upon his entrance, to the gate of the
prison, whence a coach, escorted by two officers of justice,
conveyed him to the water-side.

A boat here waited him, with four warders of the Tower,
to whose custody he was formally resigned by his late
attendants. Clink, however, the turnkey, with whom he
was more especially acquainted, did not take leave of him
without furnishing him with the piece of black crape which
he requested. Peveril fixed it on his hat amid the whispers
of his new guardians. ' The gentleman is in a hurry to go
into mourning,' said one ; ' mayhap he had better wait till
he has cause.'

' Perhaps others may wear mourning for him, ere he can
mourn for any one,' answered another of these functionaries.

Yet, notwithstanding the tenor of these whispers, their
behaviour to their prisoner was more respectful than he had
experienced from his former keepers, and might be termed
a sullen civility. The ordinary officers of the law were in
general rude, as having to do with felons of every description;
whereas these men were only employed with persons
accused of state crimes—men who were from birth and
circumstances usually entitled to expect, and able to
reward, decent usage.

The change of keepers passed unnoticed by Julian, as did
the gay and busy scene presented by the broad and beautiful
river on which he was now launched. A hundred boats
shot past them, bearing parties intent on business, or on
pleasure. Julian only viewed them with the stern hope,
that whoever had endeavoured to bribe him from his fidelity
by the hope of freedom, might see, from the colour of the
badge which he had assumed, how determined he was to
resist the temptation presented to him.

It was about high water, and a stout wherry came up the

river, with sail and oar, so directly upon that in which Julian was embarked, that it seemed as if likely to run her aboard. ' Get your carabines ready,' cried the principal warder to his assistants. ' What the devil can these scoundrels mean ? '

But the crew in the other boat seemed to have perceived their error, for they suddenly altered their course, and struck off into the middle stream, while a torrent of mutual abuse was exchanged betwixt them and the boat whose course they had threatened to impede.

' The Unknown has kept his faith,' said Julian to himself ; ' I too have kept mine.'

It even seemed to him, as the boats neared each other, that he heard, from the other wherry, something like a stifled scream or groan ; and when the momentary bustle was over, he asked the warder who sat next him, what boat that was.

' Men-of-war's-men, on a frolic, I suppose,' answered the warder. ' I know no one else would be so impudent as run foul of the King's boat ; for I am sure the fellow put the helm up on purpose. But mayhap you, sir, know more of the matter than I do.'

This insinuation effectually prevented Julian from putting further questions, and he remained silent until the boat came under the dusky bastions of the Tower. The tide carried them up under a dark and lowering arch, closed at the upper end by the well-known Traitor's Gate,[1] formed like a wicket of huge intersecting bars of wood, through which might be seen a dim and imperfect view of soldiers and warders upon duty, and of the steep ascending causeway which leads up from the river into the interior of the fortress. By this gate—and it is the well-known circumstance which assigned its name—those accused of state crimes were usually committed to the Tower. The Thames afforded a secret and silent mode of conveyance for transporting thither such whose fallen fortunes might move the commiseration, or whose popular qualities might excite the sympathy, of the public ; and even where no cause for especial secrecy existed, the peace of the city was undisturbed by the tumult attending the passage of the prisoner and his guards through the most frequented streets.

[1] See Note to *Fortunes of Nigel*, p. 419.

Yet this custom, however recommended by state policy, must have often struck chill upon the heart of the criminal, who thus, stolen, as it were, out of society, reached the place of his confinement, without encountering even one glance of compassion on the road ; and as, from under the dusky arch, he landed on those flinty steps, worn by many a footstep anxious as his own, against which the tide lapped fitfully with small successive waves, and thence looked forward to the steep ascent into a Gothic state prison, and backward to such part of the river as the low-brow'd vault suffered to become visible, he must often have felt that he was leaving daylight, hope, and life itself, behind him.

While the warder's challenge was made and answered, Peveril endeavoured to obtain information from his conductors where he was likely to be confined ; but the answer was brief and general—'Where the Lieutenant should direct.'

' Could he not be permitted to share the imprisonment of his father, Sir Geoffrey Peveril ? ' He forgot not, on this occasion, to add the surname of his house.

The warder, an old man of respectable appearance, stared, as if at the extravagance of the demand, and said bluntly, ' It is impossible.'

' At least,' said Peveril, ' show me where my father is confined, that I may look upon the walls which separate us.'

' Young gentleman,' said the senior warder, shaking his grey head, ' I am sorry for you ; but asking questions will do you no service. In this place we know nothing of fathers and sons.'

Yet chance seemed, in a few minutes afterwards, to offer Peveril that satisfaction which the rigour of his keepers was disposed to deny to him. As he was conveyed up the steep passage which leads under what is called the Wakefield Tower, a female voice, in a tone wherein grief and joy were indescribably mixed, exclaimed, ' My son !—My dear son ! '

Even those who guarded Julian seemed softened by a tone of such acute feeling. They slackened their pace. They almost paused to permit him to look up towards the casement from which the sounds of maternal agony proceeded ; but the aperture was so narrow, and so closely grated, that nothing was visible save a white female hand, which grasped one of those rusty barricadoes, as if for supporting the person within, while another streamed a white handkerchief, and then let it fall. The casement was instantly deserted.

'Give it me,' said Julian to the officer who lifted the handkerchief ; 'it is perhaps a mother's last gift.'

The old warder lifted the napkin, and looked at it with the jealous minuteness of one who is accustomed to detect secret correspondence in the most trifling acts of intercourse.

'There may be writing on it with invisible ink,' said one of his comrades.

'It is wetted, but I think it is only with tears,' answered the senior. 'I cannot keep it from the poor young gentleman.'

'Ah, Master Coleby,' said his comrade, in a gentle tone of reproach, 'you would have been wearing a better coat than a yeoman's to-day, had it not been for your tender heart.'

'It signifies little,' said old Coleby, 'while my heart is true to my king, what I feel in discharging my duty, or what coat keeps my old bosom from the cold weather.'

Peveril, meanwhile, folded in his breast the token of his mother's affection which chance had favoured him with ; and when placed in the small and solitary chamber which he was told to consider as his own during his residence in the Tower, he was soothed even to weeping by this trifling circumstance, which he could not help considering as an omen, that his unfortunate house was not entirely deserted by Providence.

But the thoughts and occurrences of a prison are too uniform for a narrative, and we must now convey our readers into a more bustling scene.

CHAPTER XXXVII

Henceforth 'tis done—Fortune and I are friends ;
And I must live, for Buckingham commends.

POPE.

THE spacious mansion of the Duke of Buckingham, with the demesne belonging to it, originally bore the name of York House, and occupied a large portion of the ground adjacent to the Savoy.

This had been laid out by the munificence of his father,
the favourite of Charles I, in a most splendid manner, so as
almost to rival Whitehall itself.   But during the increasing
rage for building new streets, and the creating of almost an
additional town, in order to connect London and Westminster, this ground had become of very great value ;   and
the second Duke of Buckingham, who was at once fond of
scheming, and needy of money, had agreed to a plan laid
before him by some adventurous architect, for converting
the extensive grounds around his palace into those streets,
lanes, and courts, which still perpetuate his name and
titles ;   though those who live in Buckingham Street,
Duke Street, Villiers Street, or in Of-alley (for even that
connecting particle is locally commemorated), probably
think seldom of the memory of the witty, eccentric, and
licentious George Villiers, Duke of Buckingham, whose
titles are preserved in the names of their residence and its
neighbourhood.

This building-plan the duke had entered upon with all the
eagerness which he usually attached to novelty.   His gardens were destroyed—his pavilions levelled—his splendid
stables demolished—the whole pomp of his suburban
demesne laid waste, cumbered with ruins, and intersected
with the foundations of new buildings and cellars, and the
process of levelling different lines for the intended streets.
But the undertaking, although it proved afterwards both
lucrative and successful, met with a check at the outset,
partly from want of the necessary funds, partly from the
impatient and mercurial temper of the duke, which soon
carried him off in pursuit of some more new object.   So
that, though much was demolished, very little, in comparison,
was reared up in the stead, and nothing was completed.
The principal part of the ducal mansion still remained
uninjured ;   but the demesne in which it stood bore a strange
analogy to the irregular mind of its noble owner.   Here
stood a beautiful group of exotic trees and shrubs, the
remnant of the garden, amid yawning common-sewers, and
heaps of rubbish.   In one place an old tower threatened
to fall upon the spectator ;   and in another, he ran the risk
of being swallowed up by a modern vault.   Grandeur of
conception could be discovered in the undertaking, but

was almost everywhere marred by poverty or negligence of execution. In short, the whole place was the true emblem of an understanding and talents run to waste, and become more dangerous than advantageous to society by the want of steady principle, and the improvidence of the possessor.

There were men who took a different view of the duke's purpose in permitting his mansion to be thus surrounded, and his demesne occupied by modern buildings which were incomplete, and ancient which were but half demolished. They alleged, that, engaged as he was in so many mysteries of love and of politics, and having the character of the most daring and dangerous intriguer of his time, his Grace found it convenient to surround himself with this ruinous arena, into which officers of justice could not penetrate without some difficulty and hazard ; and which might afford, upon occasion, a safe and secret shelter for such tools as were fit for desperate enterprises, and a private and unobserved mode of access to those whom he might have any special reason for receiving in secret.

Leaving Peveril in the Tower, we must once more convey our readers to the levée of the duke, who, on the morning of Julian's transference to that fortress, thus addressed his minister-in-chief, and principal attendant :—' I have been so pleased with your conduct in this matter, Jerningham, that if Old Nick were to arise in our presence, and offer me his best imp as a familiar in thy room, I would hold it but a poor compliment.'

' A legion of imps,' said Jerningham, bowing, ' could not have been more busy than I in your Grace's service ; but if your Grace will permit me to say so, your whole plan was wellnigh marred by your not returning home till last night, or rather this morning.'

' And why, I pray you, sage Master Jerningham,' said his Grace, ' should I have returned home an instant sooner than my pleasure and convenience served ? '

' Nay, my lord duke,' replied the attendant, ' I know not ; only, when you sent us word by Empson, in Chiffinch's apartment, to command us to make sure of the girl at any rate, and at all risks, you said you would be here so soon as you could get freed of the king.'

'Freed of the king, you rascal! What sort of phrase is that?' demanded the duke.

'It was Empson who used it, my lord, as coming from your Grace.'

'There is much very fit for my Grace to say, that misbecomes such mouths as Empson's or yours to repeat,' answered the duke haughtily, but instantly resumed his tone of familiarity, for his humour was as capricious as his pursuits. 'But I know what thou wouldst have; first, your wisdom would know what became of me since thou hadst my commands at Chiffinch's; and next, your valour would fain sound another flourish of trumpets on thine own most artificial retreat, leaving thy comrade in the hands of the Philistines.'

'May it please your Grace,' said Jerningham, 'I did but retreat for the preservation of the baggage.'

'What! do you play at crambo with me?' said the duke. 'I would have you to know that the common parish fool should be whipped, were he to attempt to pass pun or quodlibet as a genuine jest, even amongst ticket-porters and hackney chairmen.'

'And yet I have heard your Grace indulge in the *jeu de mots*,' answered the attendant.

'Sirrah Jerningham,' answered the patron, 'discard thy memory, or keep it under correction, else it will hamper thy rise in the world. Thou mayst perchance have seen me also have a fancy to play at trap-ball, or to kiss a serving-wench, or to guzzle ale and eat toasted cheese in a porterly whimsy; but is it fitting thou shouldst remember such follies? No more on't. Hark you; how came the long lubberly fool, Jenkins, being a master of the noble science of defence, to suffer himself to be run through the body so simply by a rustic swain like this same Peveril?'

'Please your Grace, this same Corydon is no such novice. I saw the onset; and, except in one hand, I never saw a sword managed with such life, grace, and facility.'

'Aye, indeed?' said the duke, taking his own sheathed rapier in his hand. 'I could not have thought that. I am somewhat rusted, and have need of breathing. Peveril is a name of note. As well go to the Barns-elms, or behind

Montagu House, with him as with another. His father a
rumoured plotter, too. The public would have noted it in
me as becoming a zealous Protestant. Needful I do something to maintain my good name in the city, to atone
for non-attendance on prayer and preaching. But your
Laertes is fast in the Fleet ; and I suppose his blundering
blockhead of an antagonist is dead or dying.'

'Recovering, my lord, on the contrary,' replied Jerningham; 'the blade fortunately avoided his vitals.'

'D—n his vitals !' answered the duke. 'Tell him to
postpone his recovery, or I will put him to death in earnest.'

'I will caution his surgeon,' said Jerningham, 'which
will answer equally well.'

'Do so ; and tell him he had better be on his own deathbed as cure his patient till I send him notice. That young
fellow must be let loose again at no rate.'

'There is little danger,' said the attendant. 'I hear some
of the witnesses have got their net flung over him on account
of some matters down in the north ; and that he is to be
translated to the Tower for that, and for some letters of the
Countess of Derby, as rumour goes.

'To the Tower let him go, and get out as he can,' replied
the duke ; 'and when you hear he is fast there, let the
fencing fellow recover as fast as the surgeon and he can
mutually settle it.'

The duke, having said this, took two or three turns in the
apartment, and appeared to be in deep thought. His
attendant waited the issue of his meditations with patience,
being well aware that such moods, during which his mind
was strongly directed in one point, were never of so long
duration with his patron as to prove a severe burden to his
own patience.

Accordingly, after the silence of seven or eight minutes,
the duke broke through it, taking from the toilette a large
silk purse, which seemed full of gold. 'Jerningham,' he
said, 'thou art a faithful fellow, and it would be sin not to
cherish thee. I beat the King at Mall on his bold defiance.
The honour is enough for me ; and thou, my boy, shalt have
the winnings.'

Jerningham pocketed the purse with due acknowledge-
ments.

' Jerningham,' his Grace continued, ' I know you blame me for changing my plans too often ; and on my soul I have heard you so learned on the subject, that I have become of your opinion, and have been vexed at myself for two or three hours together, for not sticking as constantly to one object, as doubtless I shall, when age ' (touching his forehead) ' shall make this same weathercock too rusty to turn with the changing breeze.   But as yet, while I have spirit and action, let it whirl like the vane at the masthead, which teaches the pilot how to steer his course ; and when I shift mine, think I am bound to follow fortune, and not to control her.'

' I can understand nothing from all this, please your Grace,' replied Jerningham, ' save that you have been pleased to change some purposed measures, and think that you have profited by doing so.'

' You shall judge yourself,' replied the duke.   ' I have seen the Duchess of Portsmouth.   You start.   It is true, by Heaven !   I have seen her, and from sworn enemies we have become sworn friends.   The treaty between such high and mighty powers had some weighty articles ; besides, I had a French negotiator to deal with ; so that you will allow a few hours' absence was but a necessary interval to make up our matters of diplomacy.'

' Your Grace astonishes me,' said Jerningham.   ' Christian's plan of supplanting the great lady is then entirely abandoned ?   I thought you had but desired to have the fair successor here, in order to carry it on under your own management.'

' I forget what I meant at the time,' said the duke ; ' unless that I was resolved she should not jilt me as she did the good-natured man of royalty ; and so I am still determined, since you put me in mind of the fair Dowsabelle. But I had a contrite note from the duchess while we were at the Mall.   I went to see her, and found her a perfect Niobe.   On my soul, in spite of red eyes and swelled features, and dishevelled hair, there are, after all, Jerningham, some women, who do, as the poets say, look lovely in affliction.   Out came the cause ; and with such humility, such penitence, such throwing herself on my mercy (she the proudest devil, too, in the whole court), that I must have had heart of steel to resist it all. In short, Chiffinch in a drunken fit had played the babbler, and let young Saville into our intrigue. Saville plays the rogue, and informs the duchess by a messenger, who luckily came a little late into the market. She learned, too, being a very devil for intelligence, that there had been some jarring between the master and me about this new Phillis ; and that I was most likely to catch the bird,—as any one may see who looks on us both. It must have been Empson who fluted all this into her Grace's ear ; and thinking she saw how her ladyship and I could hunt in couples, she entreats me to break Christian's scheme, and keep the wench out of the king's sight, especially if she were such a rare piece of perfection as fame has reported her.'

' And your Grace has promised her your hand to uphold the influence which you have so often threatened to ruin ? ' said Jerningham.

' Aye, Jerningham ; my turn was as much served when she seemed to own herself in my power, and cry me mercy. And observe, it is all one to me by which ladder I climb into the king's cabinet. That of Portsmouth is ready fixed —better ascend by it than fling it down to put up another— I hate all unnecessary trouble.'

' And Christian ? ' said Jerningham.

' May go to the devil for a self-conceited ass. One pleasure of this twist of intrigue is, to revenge me of that villain, who thought himself so essential, that, by Heaven ! he forced himself on my privacy and lectured me like a schoolboy. Hang the cold-blooded hypocritical vermin ! If he mutters, I will have his nose slit as wide as Coventry's.[1] Hark ye, is the colonel come ? '

' I expect him every moment, your Grace.'

' Send him up when he arrives,' said the duke. ' Why do you stand looking at me ? What would you have ? '

' Your Grace's direction respecting the young lady,' said Jerningham.

---

[1] The ill usage of Sir John Coventry by some of the Life Guardsmen, in revenge of something said in Parliament concerning the King's theatrical amours, gave rise to what was called Coventry's Act, against cutting and maiming the person.

' Odd zooks,' said the duke, ' I had totally forgotten her.
Is she very tearful ?   Exceedingly afflicted ? '

' She does not take on so violently as I have seen some
do,' said Jerningham ; ' but for a strong, firm, concentrated
indignation, I have seen none to match her.'

' Well, we will permit her to cool. I will not face the
affliction of a second fair one immediately. I am tired of
snivelling, and swelled eyes, and blubbered cheeks, for some
time ; and, moreover, must husband my powers of consolation.   Begone, and send the colonel.'

' Will your Grace permit me one other question ? '
demanded his confidant.

' Ask what thou wilt, Jerningham, and then be gone.'

' Your Grace has determined to give up Christian,' said
the attendant. ' May I ask what becomes of the kingdom
of Man ? '

' Forgotten, as I have a Christian soul ! ' said the duke ;
' as much forgotten as if I had never nourished that scheme
of royal ambition.   D—n it, we must knit up the ravelled
skein of that intrigue.   Yet it is but a miserable rock, not
worth the trouble I have been bestowing on it ; and for
a kingdom—it has a sound indeed ; but, in reality, I might
as well stick a cock-chicken's feather into my hat, and call
it a plume.   Besides, now I think upon it, it would scarce
be honourable to sweep that petty royalty out of Derby's
possession.   I won a thousand pieces of the young earl
when he was last here, and suffered him to hang about me
at court.   I question if the whole revenue of his kingdom is
worth twice as much.   Easily I could win it of him, were
he here, with less trouble than it would cost me to carry on
these troublesome intrigues of Christian's.'

' If I may be permitted to say so, please your Grace,'
answered Jerningham, ' although your Grace is perhaps
somewhat liable to change your mind, no man in England
can afford better reasons for doing so.'

' I think so myself, Jerningham,' said the duke ; ' and it
may be it is one reason for my changing.   One likes to
vindicate his own conduct, and to find out fine reasons for
doing what one has a mind to.   And now, once again, begone.
Or, hark ye—hark ye—I shall need some loose gold.   You
may leave the purse I gave you ; and I will give you an

order for as much, and two years' interest, on old Jacob
Doublefee.'

' As your Grace pleases,' said Jerningham, his whole stock
of complaisance scarcely able to conceal his mortification
at exchanging for a distant order, of a kind which of late
had not been very regularly honoured, the sunny contents of
the purse which had actually been in his pocket.   Secretly
but solemnly did he make a vow, that two years' interest
alone should not be the compensation for this involuntary
exchange in the form of his remuneration.

As the discontented dependant left the apartment, he
met, at the head of the grand staircase, Christian himself,
who, exercising the freedom of an ancient friend of the
house, was making his way, unannounced, to the duke's
dressing apartment.   Jerningham, conjecturing that his
visit at this crisis would be anything but well-timed, or well-
taken, endeavoured to avert his purpose, by asserting that
the duke was indisposed, and in his bed-chamber ; and
this he said so loud that his master might hear him, and,
if he pleased, realize the apology which he offered in his
name, by retreating into the bedroom as his last sanctuary,
and drawing the bolt against intrusion.

But, far from adopting a stratagem to which he had had
recourse on former occasions, in order to avoid those who
came upon him, though at an appointed hour, and upon
business of importance, Buckingham called, in a loud voice,
from his dressing apartment, commanding his chamberlain
instantly to introduce his good friend Master Christian, and
censuring him for hesitating for an instant to do so.

' Now,' thought Jerningham within himself, ' if Christian
knew the duke as well as I do, he would sooner stand the
leap of a lion, like the London 'prentice bold, than venture
on my master at this moment, who is even now in a humour
nearly as dangerous as the animal.'

He then ushered Christian into his master's presence,
taking care to post himself within earshot of the door.

CHAPTER XXXVIII

'Speak not of niceness, when there's chance of wreck,'
The captain said, as ladies writhed their neck
To see the dying dolphin flap the deck:
'If we go down, on us these gentry sup;
We dine upon them, if we haul them up.
Wise men applaud us when we eat the eaters,
As the devil laughs when keen folks cheat the cheaters.'

The Sea Voyage.

THERE was nothing in the duke's manner towards Christian which could have conveyed to that latter personage, experienced as he was in the worst possible ways of the world, that Buckingham would, at that particular moment, rather have seen the devil than himself; unless it was that Buckingham's reception of him, being rather extraordinarily courteous towards so old an acquaintance, might have excited some degree of suspicion.

Having escaped with some difficulty from the vague region of general compliments, which bears the same relation to that of business that Milton informs us the *Limbo Patrum* has to the sensible and material earth, Christian asked his Grace of Buckingham, with the same blunt plainness with which he usually veiled a very deep and artificial character, whether he had lately seen Chiffinch or his helpmate?

'Neither of them lately,' answered Buckingham. 'Have not you waited on them yourself? I thought you would have been more anxious about the great scheme.'

'I have called once and again,' said Christian, 'but I can gain no access to the sight of that important couple. I begin to be afraid they are paltering with me.'

'Which, by the welkin and its stars, you would not be slow in avenging, Master Christian. I know your puritanical principles on that point well,' said the duke. 'Revenge may be well said to be sweet, when so many grave and wise men are ready to exchange for it all the sugar-plums which pleasures offer to the poor sinful people of the world, besides the reversion of those which they talk of expecting in the way of *post obit.*'

' You may jest, my lord,' said Christian, ' but still '——

' But still you will be revenged on Chiffinch, and his little commodious companion. And yet the task may be difficult —Chiffinch has so many ways of obliging his master—his little woman is such a convenient pretty sort of a screen, and has such winning little ways of her own, that, in faith, in your case, I would not meddle with them. What is this refusing their door, man ? We all do it to our best friends now and then, as well as to duns and dull company.'

' If your Grace is in a humour of rambling thus wildly in your talk,' said Christian, ' you know my old faculty of patience—I can wait till it be your pleasure to talk more seriously.'

' Seriously ! ' said his Grace—' Wherefore not ? I only wait to know what your serious business may be.'

' In a word, my lord, from Chiffinch's refusal to see me, and some vain calls which I have made at your Grace's mansion, I am afraid either that our plan has miscarried, or that there is some intention to exclude me from the further conduct of the matter.' Christian pronounced these words with considerable emphasis.

' That were folly, as well as treachery,' returned the duke, ' to exclude from the spoil the very engineer who conducted the attack. But hark ye, Christian—I am sorry to tell bad news without preparation ; but as you insist on knowing the worst, and are not ashamed to suspect your best friends, out it must come. Your niece left Chiffinch's house the morning before yesterday.'

Christian staggered, as if he had received a severe blow ; and the blood ran to his face in such a current of passion, that the duke concluded he was struck with an apoplexy. But, exerting the extraordinary command which he could maintain under the most trying circumstances, he said, with a voice the composure of which had an unnatural contrast with the alteration of his countenance, ' Am I to conclude, that in leaving the protection of the roof in which I placed her, the girl has found shelter under that of your Grace ? '

' Sir,' replied Buckingham gravely, ' the supposition does my gallantry more credit than it deserves.'

' Oh, my lord duke,' answered Christian, ' I am not one

whom you can impose on by this species of courtly jargon.
I know of what your Grace is capable ; and that to gratify
the caprice of a moment, you would not hesitate to disappoint even the schemes at which you yourself have
laboured most busily. Suppose this jest played off. Take
your laugh at those simple precautions by which I intended
to protect your Grace's interest, as well as that of others.
Let us know the extent of your frolic, and consider how
far its consequences can be repaired.'

'On my word, Christian,' said the duke, laughing, ' you
are the most obliging of uncles and of guardians.   Let your
niece pass through as many adventures as Boccaccio's
bride of the King of Garba, you care not.   Pure or soiled,
she will still make the footstool of your fortune.'

An Indian proverb says that the dart of contempt will
even pierce through the shell of the tortoise ; but this is
more peculiarly the case when conscience tells the subject of
the sarcasm that it is justly merited.   Christian, stung with
Buckingham's reproach, at once assumed a haughty and
threatening mien, totally inconsistent with that in which
sufferance seemed to be as much his badge as that of Shy-
lock.   'You are a foul-mouthed and most unworthy lord,'
he said ; ' and as such I will proclaim you, unless you make
reparation for the injury you have done me.'

'And what,' said the Duke of Buckingham, ' shall I
proclaim *you*, that can give you the least title to notice
from such as I am ?   What name shall I bestow on the little
transaction which has given rise to such unexpected misunderstanding ? '

Christian was silent, either from rage or from mental
conviction.

'Come, come, Christian,' said the duke, smiling, ' we
know too much of each other to make a quarrel safe.   Hate
each other we may—circumvent each other—it is the way
of courts—but proclaim !—a fico for the phrase.'

'I used it not,' said Christian, ' till your Grace drove me
to extremity.   You know, my lord, I have fought both at
home and abroad ; and you should not rashly think that
I will endure any indignity which blood can wipe away.'

'On the contrary,' said the duke, with the same civil and
sneering manner, ' I can confidently assert that the life

of half a score of your friends would seem very light to
you, Christian, if their existence interfered, I do not say
with your character, as being a thing of much less consequence, but with any advantage which their existence might
intercept. Fie upon it, man, we have known each other
long. I never thought you a coward ; and am only glad
to see I could strike a few sparkles of heat out of your cold
and constant disposition. I will now, if you please, tell you
at once the fate of the young lady, in which I pray you to
believe that I am truly interested.'

'I hear you, my lord duke,' said Christian. 'The curl
of your upper lip, and your eyebrow, does not escape me.
Your Grace knows the French proverb, "He laughs best
who laughs last." But I hear you.'

'Thank Heaven you do,' said Buckingham ; 'for your
case requires haste, I promise you, and involves no laughing
matter. Well then, hear a simple truth, on which (if it
became me to offer any pledge for what I assert to be such)
I could pledge life, fortune, and honour. It was the morning before last, when meeting with the king at Chiffinch's
unexpectedly—in fact I had looked in to fool an hour away,
and to learn how your scheme advanced—I saw a singular
scene. Your niece terrified little Chiffinch—(the hen
Chiffinch, I mean)—bid the king defiance to his teeth, and
walked out of the presence triumphantly, under the guardianship of a young fellow of little mark or likelihood,
excepting a tolerable personal presence, and the advantage
of a most unconquerable impudence. Egad, I can hardly
help laughing to think how the king and I were both baffled ;
for I will not deny, that I had tried to trifle for a moment
with the fair Indamora. But, egad, the young fellow
swooped her off from under our noses, like my own Draw-
cansir clearing off the banquet from the two Kings of
Brentford. There was a dignity in the gallant's swaggering
retreat which I must try to teach Mohun ; [1] it will suit his
part admirably.'

'This is incomprehensible, my lord duke,' said Christian,
who by this time had recovered all his usual coolness ;
'you cannot expect me to believe this. Who dared be so
bold as to carry off my niece in such a manner, and from so

[1] Then a noted actor.

august a presence ? And with whom, a stranger as he must have been, would she, wise and cautious as I know her, have consented to depart in such a manner ? My lord, I cannot believe this.'

' One of your priests, my most devout Christian,' replied the duke, ' would only answer, Die, infidel, in thine unbelief ; but I am only a poor worldling sinner, and I will add what mite of information I can. The young fellow's name, as I am given to understand, is Julian, son of Sir Geoffrey, whom men call Peveril of the Peak.'

' Peveril of the Devil, who hath his cavern there ! ' said Christian warmly ; ' for I know that gallant, and believe him capable of anything bold and desperate. But how could he intrude himself into the royal presence ? Either Hell aids him, or Heaven looks nearer into mortal dealings than I have yet believed. If so, may God forgive us, who deemed He thought not on us at all ! '

' Amen, most Christian Christian,' replied the duke. ' I am glad to see thou hast yet some touch of grace that leads thee to augur so. But Empson, the hen Chiffinch, and half a dozen more, saw the swain's entrance and departure. Please examine these witnesses with your own wisdom, if you think your time may not be better employed in tracing the fugitives. I believe he gained entrance as one of some dancing or masking party. Rowley, you know, is accessible to all who will come forth to make him sport. So in stole this termagant tearing gallant, like Samson among the Philistines, to pull down our fine scheme about our ears.'

' I believe you, my lord,' said Christian ; ' I cannot but believe you ; and I forgive you, since it is your nature, for making sport of what is ruin and destruction. But which way did they take ? '

' To Derbyshire, I should presume, to seek her father,' said the duke. ' She spoke of going into the paternal protection, instead of yours, Master Christian. Something had chanced at Chiffinch's, to give her cause to suspect that you had not altogether provided for his daughter in the manner which her father was likely to approve of.'

' Now, Heaven be praised,' said Christian, ' she knows not her father is come to London ! and they must be gone down either to Martindale Castle, or to Moultrassie Hall ; in either case they are in my power—I must follow them close. I will return instantly to Derbyshire—I am undone if she meet her father until these errors are amended. Adieu, my lord. I forgive the part which I fear your Grace must have had in balking our enterprise—it is no time for mutual reproaches.'

'You speak truth, Master Christian,' said the duke, ' and I wish you all success. Can I help you with men, or horses, or money ? '

'I thank your Grace,' said Christian, and hastily left the apartment.

The duke watched his descending footsteps on the staircase, until they could be heard no longer, and then exclaimed to Jerningham, who entered, ' *Victoria ! victoria ! magna est veritas et praevalebit !* Had I told the villain a word of a lie, he is so familiar with all the regions of falsehood—his whole life has been such an absolute imposture, that I had stood detected in an instant; but I told him truth, and that was the only means of deceiving him. *Victoria !* my dear Jerningham, I am prouder of cheating Christian than I should have been of circumventing a minister of state.'

'Your Grace holds his wisdom very high,' said the attendant.

' His cunning, at least, I do, which, in court affairs, often takes the weather-gage of wisdom,—as in Yarmouth Roads a herring-buss will baffle a frigate. He shall not return to London, if I can help it, until all these intrigues are over.'

As his Grace spoke, the Colonel, after whom he had repeatedly made inquiry, was announced by a gentleman of his household. ' He met not Christian, did he ? ' said the duke hastily.

' No, my lord,' returned the domestic, ' the Colonel came by the old garden staircase.'

' I judged as much,' replied the duke ; ' 'tis an owl that will not take wing in daylight, when there is a thicket left to skulk under. Here he comes from threading lane, vault, and ruinous alley, very near as ominous a creature as the fowl of ill augury which he resembles.'

The Colonel, to whom no other appellation seemed to be given, than that which belonged to his military station, now entered the apartment. He was tall, strongly built, and past the middle period of life, and his countenance, but for the heavy cloud which dwelt upon it, might have been pronounced a handsome one. While the duke spoke

COLONEL BLOOD

to him, either from humility or some other cause, his large serious eye was cast down upon the ground; but he raised it when he answered, with a keen look of earnest observation. His dress was very plain, and more allied to that of the Puritans than of the Cavaliers of the time; a shadowy black hat, like the Spanish sombrero; a large black mantle or cloak, and a long rapier, gave him something the air of a Castilione, to which his gravity and stiffness of demeanour added considerable strength.

'Well, Colonel,' said the duke, 'we have been long strangers—how have matters gone with you ? '

'As with other men of action in quiet times,' answered the Colonel, ' or as a good war-caper [1] that lies high and dry in a muddy creek, till seams and planks are rent and riven.'

'Well, Colonel,' said the duke, ' I have used your valour before now, and I may again ; so that I shall speedily see that the vessel is careened, and undergoes a thorough repair.'

'I conjecture, then,' said the Colonel, ' that your Grace has some voyage in hand ? '

'No, but there is one which I want to interrupt,' replied the duke.

' 'Tis but another stave of the same tune. Well, my lord, I listen,' answered the stranger.

'Nay,' said the duke, ' it is but a trifling matter after all. —You know Ned Christian ? '

' Aye, surely, my lord,' replied the Colonel, ' we have been long known to each other.'

' He is about to go down to Derbyshire to seek a certain niece of his, whom he will scarcely find there. Now, I trust to your tried friendship to interrupt his return to London. Go with him, or meet him, cajole him, or assail him, or do what thou wilt with him—only keep him from London for a fortnight at least, and then I care little how soon he comes.'

' For by that time, I suppose,' replied the Colonel, ' any one may find the wench that thinks her worth the looking for.'

' Thou mayst think her worth the looking for thyself, Colonel,' rejoined the duke ; ' I promise you she hath many a thousand stitched to her petticoat ; such a wife would save thee from skeldering on the public.'

' My lord, I sell my blood and my sword, but not my honour,' answered the man sullenly ; ' if I marry, my bed may be a poor, but it shall be an honest one.'

' Then thy wife will be the only honest matter in thy possession, Colonel—at least since I have known you,' replied the duke.

' Why, truly, your Grace may speak your pleasure on

---

[1] A privateer.

that point. It is chiefly your business which I have done of late ; and if it were less strictly honest than I could have wished, the employer was to blame as well as the agent. But for marrying a cast-off mistress, the man (saving your Grace, to whom I am bound) lives not who dares propose it to me.'

The duke laughed loudly. 'Why, this is mine Ancient Pistol's vein,' he replied—

> ———'Shall I Sir Pandarus of Troy become,
> And by my side wear steel ? then, Lucifer take all !

'My breeding is too plain to understand ends of playhouse verse, my lord,' said the Colonel suddenly. 'Has your Grace no other service to command me ? '

'None—only I am told you have published a Narrative concerning the Plot.' [n]

'What should ail me, my lord ? ' said the Colonel ; 'I hope I am a witness as competent as any that has yet appeared ? '

'Truly, I think so to the full,' said the duke ; 'and it would have been hard, when so much profitable mischief was going, if so excellent a Protestant as yourself had not come in for a share.'

'I came to take your Grace's commands, not to be the object of your wit,' said the Colonel.

'Gallantly spoken, most resolute and most immaculate Colonel ! As you are to be on full pay in my service for a month to come, I pray your acceptance of this purse, for contingents and equipments, and you shall have my instructions from time to time.'

'They shall be punctually obeyed, my lord,' said the Colonel ; 'I know the duty of a subaltern officer. I wish your Grace a good morning.'

So saying, he pocketed the purse, without either affecting hesitation or expressing gratitude, but merely as a part of a transaction in the regular way of business, and stalked from the apartment with the same sullen gravity which marked his entrance. 'Now, there goes a scoundrel after my own heart,' said the duke ; 'a robber from his cradle, a murderer since he could hold a knife, a profound hypocrite in religion, and a worse and deeper hypocrite in honour,

—would sell his soul to the devil to accomplish any villany, and would cut the throat of his brother, did he dare to give the villany he had so acted its right name. Now, why stand you amazed, good Master Jerningham, and look on me as you would on some monster of Ind, when you had paid your shilling to see it, and were staring out your pennyworth with your eyes as round as a pair of spectacles ? Wink, man, and save them, and then let thy tongue untie the mystery.'

' On my word, my lord duke,' answered Jerningham, ' since I am compelled to speak, I can only say, that the longer I live with your Grace, I am the more at a loss to fathom your motives of action. Others lay plans, either to attain profit or pleasure by their execution ; but your Grace's delight is to counteract your own schemes, when in the very act of performance ; like a child—forgive me —that breaks its favourite toy, or a man who should set fire to the house he has half built.'

' And why not, if he wanted to warm his hands at the blaze ? ' said the duke.

' Aye, my lord,' replied his dependant ; ' but what if, in doing so, he should burn his fingers ? My lord, it is one of your noblest qualities, that you will sometimes listen to the truth without taking offence ; but were it otherwise, I could not, at this moment, help speaking out at every risk.'

' Well, say on, I can bear it,' said the duke, throwing himself into an easy-chair, and using his toothpick with graceful indifference and equanimity ; ' I love to hear what such potsherds as thou art, think of the proceedings of us who are of the pure porcelain clay of the earth.'

' In the name of Heaven, my lord, let me then ask you,' said Jerningham, ' what merit you claim, or what advantage you expect, from having embroiled everything in which you are concerned to a degree which equals the chaos of the blind old Roundhead's poem which your Grace is so fond of ? To begin with the king. In spite of good humour, he will be incensed at your repeated rivalry.'

' His Majesty defied me to it.'

' You have lost all hopes of the Isle, by quarrelling with Christian.'

' I have ceased to care a farthing about it,' replied the duke.

' In Christian himself, whom you have insulted, and to whose family you intend dishonour, you have lost a sagacious, artful, and cool-headed instrument and adherent,' said the monitor.

' Poor Jerningham ! ' answered the duke ; ' Christian would say as much for thee, I doubt not, wert thou discarded to-morrow. It is the common error of such tools as you and he to think themselves indispensable. As to his family, what was never honourable cannot be dishonoured by any connexion with my house.'

' I say nothing of Chiffinch,' said Jerningham, ' offended as he will be when he learns why, and by whom, his scheme has been ruined, and the lady spirited away—He and his wife, I say nothing of them.'

' You need not,' said the duke ; ' for were they even fit persons to speak to me about, the Duchess of Portsmouth has bargained for their disgrace.'

' Then this bloodhound of a Colonel, as he calls himself, your Grace cannot even lay *him* on a quest which is to do you service, but you must do him such indignity at the same time, as he will not fail to remember, and be sure to fly at your throat should he ever have an opportunity of turning on you.'

' I will take care he has none,' said the duke ; ' and yours, Jerningham, is a low-lived apprehension. Beat your spaniel heartily if you would have him under command. Ever let your agents see you know what they are, and prize them accordingly. A rogue, who must needs be treated as a man of honour, is apt to get above his work. Enough, therefore, of your advice and censure, Jerningham ; we differ in every particular. Were we both engineers, you would spend your life in watching some old woman's wheel, which spins flax by the ounce ; I must be in the midst of the most varied and counteracting machinery, regulating checks and counter-checks, balancing weights, proving springs and wheels, directing and controlling a hundred combined powers.'

' And your fortune, in the meanwhile ? ' said Jerningham ; ' pardon this last hint, my lord.'

' My fortune,' said the duke, ' is too vast to be hurt by a petty wound ; and I have, as thou knowest, a thousand

salves in store for the scratches and scars which it sometimes receives in greasing my machinery.'

'Your Grace does not mean Dr. Wilderhead's powder of
projection ? '

'Pshaw! he is a quacksalver, and mountebank, and beggar.'

'Or Solicitor Drowndland's plan for draining the fens ? '

'He is a cheat,—*videlicet*, an attorney.'

'Or the Laird of Lackpelf's sale of Highland woods ? '

'He is a Scotsman,' said the duke,—'*videlicet*, both
cheat and beggar.'

'These streets here, upon the site of your noble mansion-
house ? ' said Jerningham.

'The architect's a bite, and the plan's a bubble. I am
sick of the sight of this rubbish, and I will soon replace our
old alcoves, alleys, and flower-pots, by an Italian garden
and a new palace.'

'That, my lord, would be to waste, not to improve your
fortune,' said his domestic.

'Clodpate, and muddy spirit that thou art, thou hast
forgot the most hopeful scheme of all—the South Sea
Fisheries—their stock is up 50 per cent already. Post
down to the Alley, and tell old Manasses to buy £20,000 for
me. Forgive me, Plutus, I forgot to lay my sacrifice on thy
shrine, and yet expected thy favours !—Fly post haste,
Jerningham—for thy life, for thy life, for thy life ! ' [1]

With hands and eyes uplifted, Jerningham left the
apartment ; and the duke, without thinking a moment
further on old or new intrigues—on the friendship he had
formed, or the enmity he had provoked—on the beauty
whom he had carried off from her natural protectors, as well
as from her lover—or on the monarch against whom he
had placed himself in rivalship—sat down to calculate
chances with all the zeal of Demoivre, tired of the drudgery
in half an hour, and refused to see the zealous agent whom
he had employed in the city, because he was busily engaged
in writing a new lampoon.

---

[1] Stock-jobbing, as it is called, that is, dealing in shares of monopolies,
patent, and joint-stock companies of every description, was at least as
common in Charles II's time as our own ; and as the exercise of ingenuity
in this way promised a road to wealth without the necessity of industry,
it was then much pursued by dissolute courtiers.

CHAPTER XXXIX

Ah ! changeful head, and fickle heart !
Progress of Discontent.

No event is more ordinary in narratives of this nature,
than the abduction of the female on whose fate the interest
is supposed to turn ; but that of Alice Bridgenorth was
thus far particular, that she was spirited away by the Duke
of Buckingham more in contradiction than in the rivalry
of passion ; and that, as he made his first addresses to her
at Chiffinch's, rather in the spirit of rivalry to his sovereign,
than from any strong impression which her beauty had
made on his affections, so he had formed the sudden plan
of spiriting her away by means of his dependants, rather
to perplex Christian, the king, Chiffinch, and all concerned,
than because he had any particular desire for her society at
his own mansion. Indeed, so far was this from being the
case, that his Grace was rather surprised than delighted with
the success of the enterprise which had made her an inmate
there, although it is probable he might have thrown himself
into an uncontrollable passion, had he learned its miscarriage
instead of its success.

Twenty-four hours had passed over since he had returned
to his own roof, before, notwithstanding sundry hints from
Jerningham, he could even determine on the exertion
necessary to pay his fair captive a visit ; and then it was
with the internal reluctance of one who can only be stirred
from indolence by novelty.

' I wonder what made me plague myself about this wench,'
said he, ' and doom myself to encounter all the hysterical
rhapsodies of a country Phillis, with her head stuffed with
her grandmother's lessons about virtue and the Bible-book,
when the finest and best-bred women in town may be had
upon more easy terms. It is a pity one cannot mount the
victor's car of triumph without having a victory to boast
of ; yet, faith, it is what most of our modern gallants do,
though it would not become Buckingham. Well, I must see
her,' he concluded, ' though it were but to rid the house of

her. The Portsmouth will not hear of her being set at liberty near Charles, so much is she afraid of a new fair seducing the old sinner from his allegiance. So how the girl is to be disposed of—for I shall have little fancy to keep her here, and she is too wealthy to be sent down to Cliefden as a housekeeper—is a matter to be thought on.'

He then called for such a dress as might set off his natural good mien—a compliment which he considered as due to his own merit ; for as to anything further, he went to pay his respects to his fair prisoner with almost as little zeal in the cause, as a gallant to fight a duel in which he has no warmer interest than the maintenance of his reputation as a man of honour.

The set of apartments consecrated to the use of those favourites who occasionally made Buckingham's mansion their place of abode, and who were, so far as liberty was concerned, often required to observe the regulations of a convent, were separated from the rest of the duke's extensive mansion. He lived in the age when what was called gallantry warranted the most atrocious actions of deceit and violence ; as may be best illustrated by the catastrophe of an unfortunate actress, whose beauty attracted the attention of the last De Vere, Earl of Oxford. While her virtue defied his seductions, he ruined her under colour of a mock marriage, and was rewarded for a success which occasioned the death of his victim, by the general applause of the men of wit and gallantry who filled the drawing-room of Charles.

Buckingham had made provision in the interior of his ducal mansion for exploits of a similar nature ; and the set of apartments which he now visited were alternately used to confine the reluctant, and to accommodate the willing.

Being now destined for the former purpose, the key was delivered to the duke by a hooded and spectacled old lady, who sat reading a devout book in the outer hall which divided these apartments (usually called the Nunnery) from the rest of the house. This experienced dowager acted as mistress of the ceremonies on such occasions, and was the trusty depositary of more intrigues than were known to any dozen of her worshipful calling besides.

' As sweet a linnet,' she said, as she undid the outward
door, ' as ever sang in a cage.'

' I was afraid she might have been more for moping than
for singing, Dowlas,' said the duke.

' Till yesterday she was so, please your Grace,' answered
Dowlas ; ' or, to speak sooth, till early this morning, we
heard of nothing but Lachrymae. But the air of your
noble Grace's house is favourable to singing-birds ; and
to-day matters have been a-much mended.'

' 'Tis sudden, dame,' said the duke ; ' and 'tis something
strange, considering that I have never visited her, that the
pretty trembler should have been so soon reconciled to
her fate.'

' Ah, your Grace has such magic, that it communicates
itself to your very walls ; as wholesome Scripture says,
Exodus, first and seventh, " It cleaveth to the walls and
the door-posts." '

' You are too partial, Dame Dowlas,' said the Duke of
Buckingham.

' Not a word but truth,' said the dame ; ' and I wish
I may be an outcast from the fold of the lambs, but I think
this damsel's very frame has changed since she was under
your Grace's roof. Methinks she hath a lighter form, a
finer step, a more displayed ankle—I cannot tell, but I think
there is a change. But, lack-a-day, your Grace knows I
am as old as I am trusty, and that my eyes wax something
uncertain.'

' Especially when you wash them with a cup of canary,
Dame Dowlas,' answered the duke, who was aware that
temperance was not amongst the cardinal virtues which
were most familiar to the old lady's practice.

' Was it canary, your Grace said ? Was it indeed with
canary, that your Grace should have supposed me to have
washed my eyes ? ' said the offended matron. ' I am sorry
that your Grace should know me no better.'

' I crave your pardon, dame,' said the duke, shaking
aside, fastidiously, the grasp which, in the earnestness of
her exculpation, Madam Dowlas had clutched upon his
sleeve. ' I crave your pardon. Your nearer approach has
convinced me of my erroneous imputation—I should have
said nantz, not canary.'

So saying, he walked forward into the inner apartments, which were fitted up with an air of voluptuous magnificence.

' The dame said true, however,' said the proud deviser and proprietor of the splendid mansion—' A country Phillis might well reconcile herself to such a prison as this, even without a skilful bird-fancier to touch a bird-call. But I wonder where she can be, this rural Phidele. Is it possible she can have retreated, like a despairing commandant, into her bedchamber, the very citadel of the place, without even an attempt to defend the outworks ? '

As he made this reflection, he passed through an ante-chamber and little eating parlour, exquisitely furnished, and hung with excellent paintings of the Venetian school.

Beyond these lay a withdrawing-room, fitted up in a style of still more studied elegance. The windows were darkened with painted glass, of such a deep and rich colour, as made the midday beams, which found their way into the apartment, imitate the rich colours of sunset ; and, in the celebrated expression of the poet, ' taught light to counter-feit a gloom.'

Buckingham's feelings and taste had been too much, and too often, and too readily gratified, to permit him, in the general case, to be easily accessible even to those pleasures which it had been the business of his life to pursue. The hackneyed voluptuary is like the jaded epicure, the mere listlessness of whose appetite becomes at length a sufficient penalty for having made it the principal object of his enjoyment and cultivation. Yet novelty has always some charms, and uncertainty has more.

The doubt how he was to be received—the change of mood which his prisoner was said to have evinced—the curiosity to know how such a creature as Alice Bridgenorth had been described, was likely to bear herself under the circumstances in which she was so unexpectedly placed, had upon Buckingham the effect of exciting unusual interest. On his own part, he had none of those feelings of anxiety with which a man, even of the most vulgar mind, comes to the presence of the female whom he wishes to please, far less the more refined sentiments of love, respect, desire, and awe, with which the more refined lover approaches the beloved object. He had been, to use an expressive French

phrase, too completely *blasé* even from his earliest youth, to
permit him now to experience the animal eagerness of the
one, far less the more sentimental pleasure of the other.
It is no small aggravation of this jaded and uncomfortable
state of mind, that the voluptuary cannot renounce the
pursuits with which he is satiated, but must continue, for
his character's sake, or from the mere force of habit, to
take all the toil, fatigue, and danger of the chase, while he
has so little real interest in the termination.

Buckingham, therefore, felt it due to his reputation as
a successful hero of intrigue, to pay his addresses to Alice
Bridgenorth with dissembled eagerness ; and, as he opened
the door of the inner apartment, he paused to consider,
whether the tone of gallantry, or that of passion, was fittest
to use on the occasion. This delay enabled him to hear
a few notes of a lute touched with exquisite skill, and
accompanied by the still sweeter strains of a female voice,
which, without executing any complete melody, seemed to
sport itself in rivalship of the silver sound of the instrument.

' A creature so well educated,' said the duke, ' with the
sense she is said to possess, would, rustic as she is, laugh
at the assumed rants of Oroondates. It is the vein of
Dorimont—once, Buckingham, thine own—that must here
do the feat, besides that the part is easier.'

So thinking, he entered the room with that easy grace
which characterized the gay courtiers among whom he
flourished, and approached the fair tenant, whom he found
seated near a table covered with books and music, and
having on her left hand the large half-open casement, dim
with stained glass, admitting only a doubtful light into this
lordly retiring-room, which, hung with the richest tapestry
of the Gobelines, and ornamented with piles of china and
splendid mirrors, seemed like a bower built for a prince to
receive his bride.

The splendid dress of the inmate corresponded with the
taste of the apartment which she occupied, and partook of
the Oriental costume which the much-admired Roxalana
had then brought into fashion. A slender foot and ankle,
which escaped from the wide trouser of richly ornamented
and embroidered blue satin, was the only part of her person
distinctly seen ; the rest was enveloped, from head to foot,

in a long veil of silver gauze, which, like a feathery and light
mist on a beautiful landscape, suffered you to perceive
that what it concealed was rarely lovely, yet induced the
imagination even to enhance the charms it shaded. Such
part of the dress as could be discovered, was, like the veil
and the trousers, in the Oriental taste ; a rich turban, and
splendid caftan, were rather indicated than distinguished
through the folds of the former. The whole attire argued
at least coquetry on the part of a fair one, who must have
expected, from her situation, a visitor of some pretension ;
and induced Buckingham to smile internally at Christian's
account of the extreme simplicity and purity of his niece.

He approached the lady *en cavalier*, and addressed her
with the air of being conscious, while he acknowledged his
offences, that his condescending to do so formed a sufficient
apology for them. ' Fair Mistress Alice,' he said, ' I am
sensible how deeply I ought to sue for pardon for the mistaken zeal of my servants, who, seeing you deserted and
exposed without protection during an unlucky affray, took
it upon them to bring you under the roof of one who would
expose his life rather than suffer you to sustain a moment's
anxiety. Was it my fault that those around me should
have judged it necessary to interfere for your preservation ;
or that, aware of the interest I must take in you, they have
detained you till I could myself, in personal attendance,
receive your commands ? '

' That attendance has not been speedily rendered, my
lord,' answered the lady. ' I have been a prisoner for two
days—neglected, and left to the charge of menials.'

' How say you, lady ?—Neglected ? ' exclaimed the duke.
' By Heaven, if the best in my household has failed in his
duty, I will discard him on the instant ! '

' I complain of no lack of courtesy from your servants,
my lord,' she replied ; ' but methinks it had been but
complaisant in the duke himself to explain to me earlier
wherefore he has had the boldness to detain me as a state
prisoner.'

' And can the divine Alice doubt,' said Buckingham,
' that, had time and space, those cruel enemies to the flight
of passion, given permission, the instant in which you
crossed your vassal's threshold had seen its devoted master

at your feet, who hath thought, since he saw you, of nothing but the charms which that fatal morning placed before him at Chiffinch's ? '

THE DUKE OF BUCKINGHAM AND ZARAH

'I understand, then, my lord,' said the lady, 'that you have been absent, and have had no part in the restraint which has been exercised upon me ? '

'Absent on the king's command, lady, and employed in

the discharge of his duty,' answered Buckingham, without hesitation. 'What could I do?—The moment you left Chiffinch's, his Majesty commanded me to the saddle in such haste, that I had no time to change my satin buskins for riding-boots.[1]   If my absence has occasioned you a moment of inconvenience, blame the inconsiderate zeal of those, who, seeing me depart from London, half distracted at my separation from you, were willing to contribute their unmannered, though well-meant exertions, to preserve their master from despair, by retaining the fair Alice within his reach.   To whom, indeed, could they have restored you?   He whom you selected as your champion is in prison, or fled—your father absent from town—your uncle in the north.   To Chiffinch's house you had expressed your well-founded aversion; and what fitter asylum remained than that of your devoted slave, where you must ever reign a queen?'

'An imprisoned one,' said the lady.   'I desire not such royalty.'

'Alas! how wilfully you misconstrue me!' said the duke, kneeling on one knee; 'and what right can you have to complain of a few hours' gentle restraint—you, who destine so many to hopeless captivity?   Be merciful for once, and withdraw that envious veil; for the divinities are ever most cruel when they deliver their oracles from such clouded recesses.   Suffer at least my rash hand'——

'I will save your Grace that unworthy trouble,' said the lady haughtily; and rising up, she flung back over her shoulders the veil which shrouded her, saying, at the same time, 'Look on me, my lord duke, and see if these be indeed the charms which have made on your Grace an impression so powerful.'

Buckingham did look; and the effect produced on him by surprise was so strong, that he rose hastily from his knee, and remained for a few seconds as if he had been petrified.   The figure that stood before him had neither the

---

[1] This case is not without precedent.   Among the jealousies and fears expressed by the Long Parliament, they insisted much upon an agent for the king departing for the continent so abruptly, that he had not time to change his court dress—white buskins, to wit, and black silk pantaloons—for an equipment more suitable to travel with.

height nor the rich shape of Alice Bridgenorth; and, though
perfectly well made, was so slightly formed, as to seem almost
infantine. Her dress was three or four short vests of
embroidered satin, disposed one over the other, of different
colours, or rather different shades of similar colours ; for
strong contrast was carefully avoided. These opened in
front, so as to show part of the throat and neck, partially
obscured by an inner covering of the finest lace ; over the
uppermost vest was worn a sort of mantle, or coat of rich
fur.   A small but magnificent turban was carelessly placed
on her head, from under which flowed a profusion of coal-
black tresses, which Cleopatra might have envied.   The
taste and splendour of the Eastern dress corresponded with
the complexion of the lady's face, which was brunette,
of a shade so dark as might almost have served an
Indian.

   Amidst a set of features, in which rapid and keen expression made amends for the want of regular beauty, the
essential points of eyes as bright as diamonds, and teeth as
white as pearls, did not escape the Duke of Buckingham,
a professed connoisseur in female charms.   In a word,
the fanciful and singular female who thus unexpectedly
produced herself before him, had one of those faces which
are never seen without making an impression ; which, when
removed, are long after remembered ; and for which, in our
idleness, we are tempted to invent a hundred histories, that
we may please our fancy by supposing the features under
the influence of different kinds of emotion.   Every one
must have in recollection countenances of this kind, which,
from a captivating and stimulating originality of expression,
abide longer in the memory, and are more seductive to the
imagination, than even regular beauty.

   ' My lord duke,' said the lady, ' it seems the lifting of
my veil has done the work of magic upon your Grace.
Alas, for the captive princess, whose nod was to command
a vassal so costly as your Grace !   She runs, methinks, no
slight chance of being turned out of doors, like a second
Cinderella, to seek her fortune among lackeys and lighter-
men.'

   ' I am astonished ! ' said the duke.   ' That villain,
Jerningham—I will have the scoundrel's blood ! '

'Nay, never abuse Jerningham for the matter,' said the Unknown; 'but lament your own unhappy engagements. While you, my lord duke, were posting northward, in white satin buskins, to toil in the king's affairs, the right and lawful princess sat weeping in sables in the uncheered solitude to which your absence condemned her. Two days she was disconsolate in vain; on the third came an African enchantress to change the scene for her, and the person for your Grace. Methinks, my lord, this adventure will tell but ill, when some faithful squire shall recount or record the gallant adventures of the second Duke of Buckingham.'

"Fairly bit and bantered to boot,' said the duke—' the monkey has a turn for satire, too, by all that is *piquante*. Hark ye, fair princess, how dared you adventure on such a trick as you have been accomplice to ? '

'Dare, my lord ! ' answered the stranger ; ' put the question to others, not to one who fears nothing.'

'By my faith, I believe so ; for thy front is bronzed by nature. Hark ye, once more, mistress—What is your name and condition ? '

'My condition I have told you—I am a Mauritanian sorceress by profession, and my name is Zarah,' replied the Eastern maiden.

'But methinks that face, shape, and eyes '—said the duke —' when didst thou pass for a dancing fairy ?—Some such imp thou wert not many days since.'

'My sister you may have seen—my twin sister ; but not me, my lord,' answered Zarah.

'Indeed,' said the duke, ' that duplicate of thine, if it was not thy very self, was possessed with a dumb spirit, as thou with a talking one. I am still in the mind that you are the same ; and that Satan, always so powerful with your sex, had art enough, on our former meeting, to make thee hold thy tongue.'

'Believe what you will of it, my lord,' replied Zarah, ' it cannot change the truth.—And now, my lord, I bid you farewell. Have you any commands to Mauritania ? '

'Tarry a little, my princess,' said the duke ; ' and remember, that you have voluntarily entered yourself as pledge for another ; and are justly subjected to any penalty

which it is my pleasure to exact.   None must brave Buckingham with impunity.'

'I am in no hurry to depart, if your Grace hath any
commands for me.'

'What! are you neither afraid of my resentment, nor
of my love, fair Zarah ?' said the duke.

'Of neither, by this glove,' answered the lady.   'Your
resentment must be a petty passion indeed, if it could stoop
to such a helpless object as I am ; and for your love—good
lack! good lack!'

'And why good lack with such a tone of contempt, lady ?'
said the duke, piqued in spite of himself.   'Think you
Buckingham cannot love, or has never been beloved in
return ?'

'He may have thought himself beloved,' said the maiden ;
'but by what slight creatures !—things whose heads could
be rendered giddy by a playhouse rant—whose brains were
only filled with red-heeled shoes and satin buskins—and who
run altogether mad on the argument of a George and a star.'

'And are there no such frail fair ones in your climate,
most scornful princess ?' said the duke.

'There are,' said the lady ; 'but men rate them as
parrots and monkeys—things without either sense or soul,
head or heart.   The nearness we bear to the sun has purified,
while it strengthens, our passions.   The icicles of your
frozen climate shall as soon hammer hot bars into plough-
shares, as shall the foppery and folly of your pretended
gallantry make an instant's impression on a breast like mine.'

'You speak like one who knows what passion is,' said
the duke.   'Sit down, fair lady, and grieve not that I detain
you.   Who can consent to part with a tongue of so much
melody, or an eye of such expressive eloquence !—You
have known then what it is to love ?'

'I know—no matter if by experience, or through the
report of others—but I do know, that to love as I would
love, would be to yield not an iota to avarice, not one inch
to vanity, not to sacrifice the slightest feeling to interest
or to ambition ; but to give up all to fidelity of heart and
reciprocal affection.'

'And how many women, think you, are capable of feeling
such disinterested passion ?'

' More, by thousands, than there are men who merit it,'
answered Zarah. ' Alas ! how often do you see the female,
pale, and wretched, and degraded, still following with
patient constancy the footsteps of some predominating
tyrant, and submitting to all his injustice with the endurance
of a faithful and misused spaniel, which prizes a look from
his master, though the surliest groom that ever disgraced
humanity, more than all the pleasure which the world
besides can furnish him ? Think what such would be to one
who merited and repaid her devotion.'

' Perhaps the very reverse,' said the duke ; ' and for
your simile, I can see little resemblance. I cannot charge
my spaniel with any perfidy ; but for my mistresses—to
confess truth, I must always be in a cursed hurry if I would
have the credit of changing them before they leave me.'

' And they serve you but rightly, my lord,' answered the
lady ; ' for what are you ?—Nay, frown not ; for you must
hear the truth for once. Nature has done its part, and
made a fair outside, and courtly education hath added its
share. You are noble, it is the accident of birth—handsome, it is the caprice of Nature—generous, because to give
is more easy than to refuse—well-apparelled, it is to the
credit of your tailor—well-natured in the main, because you
have youth and health—brave, because to be otherwise were
to be degraded—and witty, because you cannot help it.'

The duke darted a glance on one of the large mirrors.
' Noble, and handsome, and court-like, generous, well-
attired, good-humoured, brave, and witty ! You allow me
more, madam, than I have the slightest pretension to, and
surely enough to make my way, at some point at least, to
female favour.'

' I have neither allowed you a heart nor a head,' said
Zarah calmly. ' Nay, never redden as if you would fly at
me. I say not but nature may have given you both ; but
folly has confounded the one, and selfishness perverted the
other. The man whom I call deserving the name, is one
whose thoughts and exertions are for others, rather than
himself,—whose high purpose is adopted on just principles,
and never abandoned while heaven or earth affords means
of accomplishing it. He is one who will neither seek an
indirect advantage by a specious road, nor take an evil path

to gain a real good purpose. Such a man were one for whom a woman's heart should beat constant while he breathes, and break when he dies.'

She spoke with so much energy that the water sparkled in her eyes, and her cheek coloured with the vehemence of her feelings.

'You speak,' said the duke, 'as if you had yourself a heart which could pay the full tribute to the merit which you describe so warmly.'

'And have I not?' said she, laying her hand on her bosom. 'Here beats one that would bear me out in what I have said, whether in life or in death.'

'Were it in my power,' said the duke, who began to get further interested in his visitor than he could at first have thought possible—'Were it in my power to deserve such faithful attachment, methinks it should be my care to requite it.'

'Your wealth, your titles, your reputation as a gallant— all you possess, were too little to merit such sincere affection.'

'Come, fair lady,' said the duke, a good deal piqued, 'do not be quite so disdainful. Bethink you, that if your love be as pure as coined gold, still a poor fellow like myself may offer you an equivalent in silver—The quantity of my affection must make up for its quality.'

'But I am not carrying my affection to market, my lord; and therefore I need none of the base coin you offer in change for it.'

'How do I know that, my fairest?' said the duke. This is the realm of Paphos—You have invaded it, with what purpose you best know; but I think with none consistent with your present assumption of cruelty. Come, come— eyes that are so intelligent can laugh with delight, as well as gleam with scorn and anger. You are here a waif on Cupid's manor, and I must seize on you in name of the deity.'

'Do not think of touching me, my lord,' said the lady. 'Approach me not, if you would hope to learn the purpose of my being here. Your Grace may suppose yourself a Solomon if you please; but I am no travelling princess, come from distant climes, either to flatter your pride, or wonder at your glory.'

'A defiance, by Jupiter!' said the duke.

'You mistake the signal,' said the 'dark ladye'; 'I came not here without taking sufficient precautions for my retreat.'

'You mouth it bravely,' said the duke; 'but never fortress so boasted its resources but the garrison had some thoughts of surrender. Thus I open the first parallel.'

They had been hitherto divided from each other by a long narrow table, which, placed in the recess of the large casement we have mentioned, had formed a sort of barrier on the lady's side, against the adventurous gallant. The duke went hastily to remove it as he spoke; but, attentive to all his motions, his visitor instantly darted through the half-open window. Buckingham uttered a cry of horror and surprise, having no doubt, at first, that she had precipitated herself from a height of at least fourteen feet; for so far the window was distant from the ground. But when he sprang to the spot, he perceived, to his astonishment, that she had effected her descent with equal agility and safety.

The outside of this stately mansion was decorated with a quantity of carving, in the mixed state, betwixt the Gothic and Grecian styles, which marks the age of Elizabeth and her successor; and though the feat seemed a surprising one, the projections of these ornaments were sufficient to afford footing to a creature so light and active, even in her hasty descent.

Inflamed alike by mortification and curiosity, Buckingham at first entertained some thought of following her by the same dangerous route, and had actually got upon the sill of the window for that purpose; and was contemplating what might be his next safe movement, when, from a neighbouring thicket of shrubs, amongst which his visitor had disappeared, he heard her chant a verse of a comic song, then much in fashion, concerning a despairing lover who had recourse to a precipice—

> But when he came near,
>   Beholding how steep
> The sides did appear,
>   And the bottom how deep;
> Though his suit was rejected,
>   He sadly reflected,
> That a lover forsaken
>   A new love may get;
> But a neck that's once broken
>   Can never be set.

The duke could not help laughing, though much against his will, at the resemblance which the verses bore to his own absurd situation, and, stepping back into the apartment, desisted from an attempt which might have proved dangerous as well as ridiculous. He called his attendants, and contented himself with watching the little thicket, . unwilling to think that a female, who had thrown herself in a great measure into his way, meant absolutely to mortify him by a retreat.

That question was determined in an instant. A form, wrapped in a mantle, with a slouched hat and shadowy plume, issued from the bushes, and was lost in a moment amongst the ruins of ancient and of modern buildings, with which, as we have already stated, the demesne formerly termed York House was now encumbered in all directions.

The duke's servants, who had obeyed his impatient summons, were hastily directed to search for this tantalizing siren in every direction. Their master, in the meantime, eager and vehement in every new pursuit, but especially when his vanity was piqued, encouraged their diligence by bribes, and threats, and commands. All was in vain. They found nothing of the Mauritanian princess, as she called herself, but the turban and the veil ; both of which she had left in the thicket, together with her satin slippers ; which articles, doubtless, she had thrown aside as she exchanged them for others less remarkable.

Finding all his search in vain, the Duke of Buckingham, after the example of spoiled children of all ages and stations, gave a loose to the frantic vehemence of passion ; and fiercely he swore vengeance on his late visitor, whom he termed by a thousand opprobrious epithets, of which the elegant phrase ' jilt ' was most frequently repeated.

Even Jerningham, who knew the depths and shallows of his master's mood, and was bold to fathom them at almost every state of his passions, kept out of his way on the present occasion ; and, cabineted with the pious old housekeeper, declared to her, over a bottle of ratafia, that, in his apprehension, if his Grace did not learn to put some control on his temper, chains, darkness, straw, and Bedlam, would be the final doom of the gifted and admired Duke of Buckingham.

CHAPTER XL

——Contentions fierce,
Ardent, and dire, spring from no petty cause.
Albion.

THE quarrels between man and wife are proverbial ; but let not these honest folks think that connexions of a less permanent nature are free from similar jars. The frolic of the Duke of Buckingham, and the subsequent escape of Alice Bridgenorth, had kindled fierce dissension in Chiffinch's family, when, on his arrival in town, he learned these two stunning events : ' I tell you,' he said to his obliging helpmate, who seemed but little moved by all that he could say on the subject, ' that your d——d carelessness has ruined the work of years.'

' I think it is the twentieth time you have said so,' replied the dame ; ' and without such frequent assurance, I was quite ready to believe that a very trifling matter would overset any scheme of yours, however long thought of.'

' How on earth could you have the folly to let the duke into the house when you expected the king ? ' said the irritated courtier.

' Lord, Chiffinch,' answered the lady, ' ought not you to ask the porter rather than me, that sort of question ?—I was putting on my cap to receive his Majesty.'

' With the address of a madge-howlet,' said Chiffinch, ' and in the meanwhile you gave the cat the cream to keep.'

' Indeed, Chiffinch,' said the lady, ' these jaunts to the country do render you excessively vulgar ! there is a brutality about your very boots ! nay, your muslin ruffles, being somewhat soiled, give to your knuckles a sort of rural rusticity, as I may call it.'

' It were a good deed,' muttered Chiffinch, ' to make both boots and knuckles bang the folly and affectation out of thee.' Then speaking aloud, he added, like a man who would fain break off an argument, by extorting from his adversary a confession that he has reason on his side, ' I am sure, Kate, you must be sensible that our all depends on his Majesty's pleasure.'

'Leave that to me,' said she ; 'I know how to pleasure his Majesty better than you can teach me. Do you think his Majesty is booby enough to cry like a schoolboy because his sparrow has flown away ? His Majesty has better taste. I am surprised at you, Chiffinch,' she added, drawing herself up, ' who were once thought to know the points of a fine woman, that you should have made such a roaring about this country wench. Why, she has not even the country quality of being plump as a barn-door fowl, but is more like a Dunstable lark, that one must crack bones and all if you would make a mouthful of it. What signifies whence she came, or where she goes ? There will be those behind that are much more worthy of his Majesty's condescending attention, even when the Duchess of Portsmouth takes the frumps.'

'You mean your neighbour, Mistress Nelly,' said her worthy helpmate ; ' but, Kate, her date is out. Wit she has, let her keep herself warm with it in worse company, for the cant of a gang of strollers is not language for a prince's chamber.' [1]

'It is no matter what I mean, or whom I mean,' said Mrs. Chiffinch ; ' but I tell you, Tom Chiffinch, that you will find your master quite consoled for loss of the piece of prudish puritanism that you would needs saddle him with ; as if the good man were not plagued enough with them in Parliament, but you must, forsooth, bring them into his very bedchamber.'

'Well, Kate,' said Chiffinch, ' if a man were to speak all the sense of the seven wise masters, a woman would find nonsense enough to overwhelm him with ; so I shall say no more, but that I would to Heaven I may find the King in no worse humour than you describe him. I am com-

---

[1] In Evelyn's *Memoirs* is the following curious passage respecting Nell Gwyn, who is hinted at in the text :—' I walked with him [King Charles II] through Saint James Park to the garden, where I both saw and heard a very familiar discourse between . . . [*the king*] and Mrs. Nelly, as they called her, an intimate comedian, she looking out of her garden on a terrace at the top of the wall, and [*the king*] standing on the green walk under it. I was heartily sorry at this scene.'—EVELYN'S *Memoirs*, vol. i, p. 413.

manded to attend him down the river to the Tower to-day, where he is to make some survey of arms and stores. They are clever fellows who contrive to keep Rowley from engaging in business, for, by my word, he has a turn for it.'

' I warrant you,' said Chiffinch the female, nodding, but rather to her own figure reflected from a mirror, than to her politic husband,—' I warrant you we will find means of occupying him that will sufficiently fill up his time.'

' On my honour, Kate,' said the male Chiffinch, ' I find you strangely altered, and, to speak truth, grown most extremely opinionative. I shall be happy if you have good reason for your confidence.'

The dame smiled superciliously, but deigned no other answer, unless this were one,—' I shall order a boat to go upon the Thames to-day with the royal party.'

' Take care what you do, Kate ; there are none dare presume so far but women of the first rank. Duchess of Bolton—of Buckingham—of '——

' Who cares for a list of names ? why may not I be as forward as the greatest B. amongst your string of them ? '

' Nay, faith, thou mayest match the greatest B. in Court already,' answered Chiffinch ; ' so e'en take thy own course of it. But do not let Chaubert forget to get some collation ready, and a *souper au petit couvert*, in case it should be commanded for the evening.'

' Aye, there your boasted knowledge of Court matters begins and ends. Chiffinch, Chaubert, and Company ;— dissolve that partnership, and you break Tom Chiffinch for a courtier.'

' Amen, Kate,' replied Chiffinch ; ' and let me tell you it is as safe to rely on another person's fingers as on our own wit. But I must give orders for the water. If you will take the pinnace, there are the cloth-of-gold cushions in the chapel may serve to cover the benches for the day. They are never wanted where they lie, so you may make free with them too.'

Madam Chiffinch accordingly mingled with the flotilla which attended the king on his voyage down the Thames, amongst whom was the queen, attended by some of the principal ladies of the Court. The little plump Cleopatra, dressed to as much advantage as her taste could devise, and

seated upon her embroidered cushions like Venus in her
shell, neglected nothing that effrontery and *minauderie*
could perform to draw upon herself some portion of the
king's observation ; but Charles was not in the vein, and
did not even pay her the slightest passing attention of any
kind, until her boatmen having ventured to approach nearer
to the queen's barge than etiquette permitted, received a
peremptory order to back their oars, and fall out of the
royal procession. Madam Chiffinch cried for spite, and
transgressed Solomon's warning, by cursing the king in
her heart ; but had no better course than to return to Westminster, and direct Chaubert's preparations for the evening.

In the meantime, the royal barge paused at the Tower ;
and, accompanied by a laughing train of ladies and of
courtiers, the gay monarch made the echoes of the old
prison-towers ring with the unwonted sounds of mirth and
revelry. As they ascended from the river-side to the centre
of the building, where the fine old keep of William the
Conqueror, called the White Tower, predominates over the
exterior defences, Heaven only knows how many gallant
jests, good or bad, were run on the comparison of his
Majesty's state-prison to that of Cupid, and what killing
similes were drawn between the ladies' eyes and the guns
of the fortress, which, spoken with a fashionable *congé*, and
listened to with a smile from a fair lady, formed the fine
conversation of the day.

This gay swarm of flutterers did not, however, attend
close on the king's person, though they had accompanied
him upon his party on the river. Charles, who often formed
manly and sensible resolutions, though he was too easily
diverted from them by indolence or pleasure, had some
desire to make himself personally acquainted with the
state of the military stores, arms, &c., of which the Tower
was then, as now, the magazine ; and, although he had
brought with him the usual number of his courtiers, only
three or four attended him on the scrutiny which he intended.
Whilst, therefore, the rest of the train amused themselves as
they might in other parts of the Tower, the king, accompanied by the Dukes of Buckingham, Ormond, and one or
two others, walked through the well-known hall, in which
is preserved the most splendid magazine of arms in the

world, and which, though far from exhibiting its present extraordinary state of perfection, was even then an arsenal worthy of the great nation to which it belonged.

The Duke of Ormond, well known for his services during the great Civil War, was, as we have elsewhere noticed, at present rather on cold terms with his sovereign, who never-

CATHERINE OF BRAGANZA, QUEEN OF CHARLES II

theless asked his advice on many occasions, and who required it on the present amongst others, when it was not a little feared that the Parliament, in their zeal for the Protestant religion, might desire to take the magazines of arms and ammunition under their own exclusive orders. While Charles sadly hinted at such a termination of the popular jealousies of the period, and discussed with Ormond the means of resisting or evading it, Buckingham, falling a little behind, amused himself with ridiculing the antiquated appearance and embarrassed demeanour of the old warder who attended on the occasion, and who chanced to be the very same that escorted Julian Peveril to his present place of confinement. The duke prosecuted his raillery with the greater activity, that he found the old man, though restrained by the place and presence, was rather upon the whole testy, and disposed to afford what sportsmen call *play* to his persecutor. The various pieces of ancient armour, with which the wall was covered, afforded the principal source of the duke's wit, as he insisted upon knowing from the old man, who, he said, could best remember matters from the days of King Arthur downwards at the least, the history of the different warlike weapons, and anecdotes of the battles in which they had been wielded. The old man obviously suffered, when he was obliged, by repeated questions, to tell the legends (often sufficiently absurd) which the tradition of the place had assigned to particular relics. Far from flourishing his partisan, and augmenting the emphasis of his voice, as was and is the prevailing fashion of these warlike *ciceroni*, it was scarcely possible to extort from him a single word concerning those topics on which their information is usually overflowing.

'Do you know, my friend,' said the duke to him at last, 'I begin to change my mind respecting you. I supposed you must have served as a Yeoman of the Guard since bluff King Henry's time, and expected to hear something from you about the Field of the Cloth of Gold,—and I thought of asking you the colour of Anne Bullen's breastknot, which cost the Pope three kingdoms ; but I am afraid you are but a novice in such recollections of love and chivalry. Art sure thou didst not creep into thy warlike office from some dark shop in the Tower Hamlets, and that thou hast not converted an unlawful measuring-yard into that glorious halberd ? I warrant thou canst not even tell one whom this piece of antique panoply pertained to ? '

The duke pointed at random to a cuirass which hung amongst others, but was rather remarkable from being better cleansed.

'I should know that piece of iron,' said the warder

bluntly, yet with some change in his voice ; ' for I have known a man within side of it who would not have endured half the impertinence I have heard spoken to-day.'

The tone of the old man, as well as the words, attracted the attention of Charles and the Duke of Ormond, who were only two steps before the speaker. They both stopped, and turned round ; the former saying at the same time,— ' How now, sirrah !—what answers are these ?—What man do you speak of ? '

' Of one who is none now,' said the warder, ' whatever he may have been.'

' The old man surely speaks of himself,' said the Duke of Ormond, closely examining the countenance of the warder, which he in vain endeavoured to turn away. ' I am sure I remember these features—Are not you my old friend, Major Coleby ? '

' I wish your Grace's memory had been less accurate,' said the old man, colouring deeply, and fixing his eyes on the ground.

The king was greatly shocked. ' Good God ! ' he said, ' the gallant Major Coleby, who joined us with his four sons and a hundred and fifty men at Warrington ! And is this all we could do for an old Worcester friend ? '

The tears rushed thick into the old man's eyes as he said in broken accents, ' Never mind me, sire ; I am well enough here—a worn-out soldier rusting among old armour. Where one old cavalier is better, there are twenty worse. I am sorry your Majesty should know anything of it, since it grieves you.'

With that kindness, which was a redeeming point of his character, Charles, while the old man was speaking, took the partisan from him with his own hand, and put it into that of Buckingham, saying, ' What Coleby's hand has borne, can disgrace neither yours nor mine,—and you owe him this atonement. Time has been with him, that, for less provocation, he would have laid it about your ears.'

The duke bowed deeply, but coloured with resentment, and took an immediate opportunity to place the weapon carelessly against a pile of arms. The king did not observe a contemptuous motion, which, perhaps, would not have pleased him, being at the moment occupied with the veteran, whom he exhorted to lean upon him, as he conveyed him to a seat, permitting no other person to assist him. 'Rest there,' he said, 'my brave old friend; and Charles Stuart must be poor indeed, if you wear that dress an hour longer.—You look very pale, my good Coleby, to have had so much colour a few minutes since. Be not vexed at what Buckingham says, no one minds his folly. You look worse and worse. Come, come, you are too much hurried by this meeting. Sit still—do not rise—do not attempt to kneel. I command you to repose yourself till I have made the round of these apartments.'

The old cavalier stooped his head in token of acquiescence in the command of his sovereign, but he raised it not again. The tumultuous agitation of the moment had been too much for spirits which had been long in a state of depression, and health which was much decayed. When the king and his attendants, after half an hour's absence, returned to the spot where they had left the veteran, they found him dead, and already cold, in the attitude of one who has fallen easily asleep. The king was dreadfully shocked; and it was with a low and faltering voice that he directed the body, in due time, to be honourably buried in the Chapel of the Tower.[1] He was then silent, until he attained the steps in front of the arsenal, where the party in attendance upon his person began to assemble at his approach, along with some other persons of respectable appearance, whom curiosity had attracted.

'This is dreadful,' said the king. 'We must find some means of relieving the distresses, and rewarding the fidelity of our suffering followers, or posterity will cry fie upon our memory.'

'Your Majesty has had often such plans agitated in your Council,' said Buckingham.

'True, George,' said the king. 'I can safely say it is not my fault. I have thought of it for years.'

'It cannot be too well considered,' said Buckingham; 'besides, every year makes the task of relief easier.'

---

[1] A story of this nature is current in the legends of the Tower. The affecting circumstances are, I believe, recorded in one of the little manuals which are put into the hands of visitors, but are not to be found in the later editions.

'True,' said the Duke of Ormond, ' by diminishing the number of sufferers. Here is poor old Coleby will no longer be a burden to the Crown.'

'You are too severe, my Lord of Ormond,' said the king, ' and should respect the feelings you trespass on. You cannot suppose that we would have permitted this poor man to hold such a situation, had we known of the circumstance ? '

'For God's sake, then, sire,' said the Duke of Ormond, ' turn your eyes, which have just rested on the corpse of one old friend, upon the distresses of others. Here is the valiant old Sir Geoffrey Peveril of the Peak, who fought through the whole war, wherever blows were going, and was the last man, I believe, in England, who laid down his arms—Here is his son, of whom I have the highest accounts, as a gallant of spirit, accomplishments, and courage—Here is the unfortunate House of Derby—for pity's sake, interfere in behalf of these victims, whom the folds of this hydra-plot have entangled, in order to crush them to death—rebuke the fiends that are seeking to devour their lives, and disappoint the harpies that are gaping for their property. This very day seven-night the unfortunate family, father and son, are to be brought upon trial for crimes of which they are as guiltless, I boldly pronounce, as any who stand in this presence. For God's sake, sire, let us hope that, should the prejudices of the people condemn them, as it has done others, you will at last step in between the blood-hunters and their prey.'

The king looked, as he really was, exceedingly perplexed.

Buckingham, between whom and Ormond there existed a constant and almost mortal quarrel, interfered to effect a diversion in Charles's favour. ' Your Majesty's royal benevolence,' he said, ' needs never want exercise, while the Duke of Ormond is near your person. He has his sleeve cut in the old and ample fashion, that he may always have store of ruined cavaliers stowed in it to produce at demand, rare old raw-boned boys, with Malmsey noses, bald heads, spindle shanks, and merciless histories of Edgehill and Naseby.'

'My sleeve is, I dare say, of an antique cut,' said Ormond, looking full at the duke ; ' but I pin neither bravoes nor ruffians upon it, my Lord of Buckingham, as I see fastened to coats of the new mode.'

' That is a little too sharp for our presence, my lord,' said the king.

' Not if I make my words good,' said Ormond. ' My Lord of Buckingham, will you name the man you spoke to as you left the boat ? '

' I spoke to no one,' said the duke hastily—' nay, I mistake, I remember a fellow whispered in my ear, that one, who I thought had left London, was still lingering in town. A person whom I had business with.'

' Was yon the messenger ? ' said Ormond, singling out from the crowd who stood in the court-yard a tall dark-looking man, muffled in a large cloak, wearing a broad shadowy black beaver hat, with a long sword of the Spanish fashion—the very Colonel, in short, whom Buckingham had dispatched in quest of Christian, with the intention of detaining him in the country.

When Buckingham's eyes had followed the direction of Ormond's finger, he could not help blushing so deeply as to attract the king's attention.[n]

' What new frolic is this, George ? ' he said. ' Gentlemen, bring that fellow forward. On my life, a truculent-looking caitiff—Hark ye, friend, who are you ? If an honest man, Nature has forgot to label it upon your countenance. Does none here know him ?

> With every symptom of a knave complete,
> If he be honest, he's a devilish cheat.'

' He is well known to many, sire,' replied Ormond ; ' and that he walks in this area with his neck safe, and his limbs unshackled, is an instance, amongst many, that we live under the sway of the most merciful prince of Europe.'

' Oddsfish ! who is the man, my lord duke ? ' said the king. ' Your Grace talks mysteries—Buckingham blushes —and the rogue himself is dumb.'

' That honest gentleman, please your Majesty,' replied the Duke of Ormond, ' whose modesty makes him mute, though it cannot make him blush, is the notorious Colonel Blood, as he calls himself, whose attempt to possess himself of your Majesty's royal crown took place at no very distant date, in this very Tower of London.'

' That exploit is not easily forgotten,' said the king ; ' but that the fellow lives, shows your Grace's clemency as well as mine.'

' I cannot deny that I was in his hands, sire,' said Ormond, ' and had certainly been murdered by him, had he chosen to take my life on the spot, instead of destining me— I thank him for the honour—to be hanged at Tyburn. I had certainly been sped, if he had thought me worth knife or pistol, or anything short of the cord. Look at him, sire ! If the rascal dared, he would say at this moment, like Caliban in the play, " Ho, ho, I would I had done it ! " '

' Why, oddsfish ! ' answered the king, ' he hath a villainous sneer, my lord, which seems to say as much ; but, my lord duke, we have pardoned him, and so has your Grace.'

' It would ill have become me,' said the Duke of Ormond, ' to have been severe in prosecuting an attempt on my poor life, when your Majesty was pleased to remit his more outrageous and insolent attempt upon your royal crown. But I must conceive it as a piece of supreme insolence on the part of this bloodthirsty bully, by whomsoever he may be now backed, to appear in the Tower, which was the theatre of one of his villanies, or before me, who was wellnigh the victim of another.'

' It shall be amended in future,' said the king. ' Hark ye, sirrah Blood, if you again presume to thrust yourself in the way you have done but now, I will have the hangman's knife and your knavish ears made acquainted.'

Blood bowed, and with a coolness of impudence which did his nerves great honour, he said he had only come to the Tower accidentally, to communicate with a particular friend on business of importance. ' My Lord Duke of Buckingham,' he said, ' knew he had no other intentions.'

' Get you gone, you scoundrelly cut-throat,' said the duke, as much impatient of Colonel Blood's claim of acquaintance, as a town-rake of the low and blackguard companions of his midnight rambles, when they accost him in daylight amidst better company ; ' if you dare to quote my name again, I will have you thrown into the Thames.'

Blood, thus repulsed, turned round with the most insolent composure, and walked away down from the parade, all men looking at him, as at some strange and monstrous prodigy, so much was he renowned for daring and desperate villany. Some even followed him, to have a better survey of the notorious Colonel Blood, like the smaller tribe of birds which keep fluttering round an owl when he appears in the light of the sun. But as, in the latter case, these thoughtless flutterers are careful to keep out of reach of the beak and claws of the bird of Minerva, so none of those who followed and gazed on Blood as something ominous, cared to bandy looks with him, or to endure and return the lowering and deadly glances, which he shot from time to time on those who pressed nearest to him. He stalked on in this manner, like a daunted, yet sullen wolf, afraid to stop, yet unwilling to fly, until he reached the Traitor's Gate, and getting on board a sculler which waited for him, he disappeared from their eyes.

Charles would fain have obliterated all recollection of his appearance, by the observation, ' It were shame that such a reprobate scoundrel should be the subject of discord between two noblemen of distinction ; ' and he recommended to the Dukes of Buckingham and Ormond to join hands, and forget a misunderstanding which rose on so unworthy a subject.

Buckingham answered carelessly, ' That the Duke of Ormond's honoured white hairs were a sufficient apology for his making the first overtures to a reconciliation,' and he held out his hand accordingly. But Ormond only bowed in return, and said, ' The king had no cause to expect that the Court would be disturbed by his personal resentments, since time would not yield him back twenty years, nor the grave restore his gallant son Ossory. As to the ruffian who had intruded himself there, he was obliged to him, since, by showing that his Majesty's clemency extended even to the very worst of criminals, he strengthened his hopes of obtaining the king's favour for such of his innocent friends as were now in prison, and in danger, from the odious charges brought against them on the score of the Popish Plot.'

The king made no other answer to this insinuation, than by directing that the company should embark for their return to Whitehall ; and thus took leave of the officers of the Tower who were in attendance, with one of those well-turned compliments to their discharge of duty, which no man knew better how to express ; and issued at the same time strict and anxious orders for protection and defence of the important fortress confided to them, and all which it contained.

Before he parted with Ormond on their arrival at White-hall, he turned round to him, as one who has made up his resolution, and said, ' Be satisfied, my lord duke—our friends' case shall be looked to.'

In the same evening the Attorney-General, and North, Lord Chief Justice of the Common Pleas, had orders with all secrecy, to meet his Majesty that evening on especial matters of state, at the apartments of Chiffinch, the centre of all affairs, whether of gallantry or business.

CHAPTER XLI

> Yet, Corah, thou shalt from oblivion pass ;
> Erect thyself, thou monumental brass,
> High as the serpent of thy metal made,
> While nations stand secure beneath thy shade.
> *Absalom and Achitophel.*

THE morning which Charles had spent in visiting the Tower had been very differently employed by those un-happy individuals, whom their bad fate, and the singular temper of the times, had made the innocent tenants of that state prison, and who had received official notice that they were to stand their trial in the Court of Queen's Bench at Westminster, on the seventh succeeding day. The stout old cavalier at first only railed at the officer for spoiling his breakfast with the news, but evinced great feeling when he was told that Julian was to be put under the same indict-ment.

We intend to dwell only very generally on the nature of their trial, which corresponded, in the outline, with almost all those which took place during the prevalence of the

Popish Plot. That is, one or two infamous and perjured
evidences, whose profession of common informers had
become frightfully lucrative, made oath to the prisoners'
having expressed themselves interested in the great con-
federacy of the Catholics. A number of others brought
forward facts or suspicions, affecting the character of the
parties as honest Protestants and good subjects; and
betwixt the direct and presumptive evidence, enough was
usually extracted for justifying, to a corrupted court and
perjured jury, the fatal verdict of Guilty.

The fury of the people had, however, now begun to pass
away, exhausted even by its own violence. The English
nation differ from all others, indeed even from those of the
sister kingdoms, in being very easily sated with punishment,
even when they suppose it most merited. Other nations
are like the tamed tiger, which, when once its native appetite
for slaughter is indulged in one instance, rushes on in
promiscuous ravages. But the English public have always
rather resembled what is told of the sleuth-dog, which,
eager, fierce, and clamorous in pursuit of his prey, desists
from it so soon as blood is sprinkled upon his path.

Men's minds were now beginning to cool—the character
of the witnesses was more closely sifted—their testimonies
did not in all cases tally—and a wholesome suspicion began
to be entertained of men, who would never say they had
made a full discovery of all they knew, but avowedly
reserved some points of evidence to bear on future trials.

The king also, who had lain passive during the first burst
of popular fury, was now beginning to bestir himself, which
produced a marked effect on the conduct of the Crown
Counsel, and even the Judges. Sir George Wakeman had
been acquitted in spite of Oates's direct testimony; and
public attention was strongly excited concerning the event
of the next trial; which chanced to be that of the Peverils,
father and son, with whom, I know not from what con-
catenation, little Hudson the dwarf was placed at the bar
of the Court of King's Bench.

It was a piteous sight to behold a father and son, who
had been so long separated, meet under circumstances so
melancholy; and many tears were shed, when the majestic
old man—for such he was, though now broken with years—

folded his son to his bosom, with a mixture of joy, affection, and a bitter anticipation of the event of the impending trial. There was a feeling in the court that for a moment overcame every prejudice and party feeling. Many spectators shed tears ; and there was even a low moaning, as of those who weep aloud.

Such as felt themselves sufficiently at ease to remark the conduct of poor little Geoffrey Hudson, who was scarcely observed amid the preponderating interest created by his companions in misfortune, could not but notice a strong degree of mortification on the part of that diminutive gentleman. He had soothed his great mind by the thoughts of playing the character which he was called on to sustain, in a manner which should be long remembered in that place ; and on his entrance, had saluted the numerous spectators, as well as the court, with a cavalier air, which he meant should express grace, high-breeding, perfect coolness, with a noble disregard to the issue of their proceedings. But his little person was so obscured and jostled aside, on the meeting of the father and son, who had been brought in different boats from the Tower, and placed at the bar at the same moment, that his distress and his dignity were alike thrown into the background, and attracted neither sympathy nor admiration.

The dwarf's wisest way to attract attention would have been to remain quiet, when so remarkable an exterior would certainly have received in its turn the share of public notice which he so eagerly coveted. But when did personal vanity listen to the suggestions of prudence ?—Our impatient friend scrambled, with some difficulty, on the top of the bench intended for his seat ; and there, ' paining himself to stand a-tiptoe,' like Chaucer's gallant Sir Chaunticlere, he challenged the notice of the audience as he stood bowing and claiming acquaintance of his namesake Sir Geoffrey the larger, with whose shoulders, notwithstanding his elevated situation, he was scarcely yet upon a level.

The taller knight, whose mind was occupied in a very different manner, took no notice of these advances upon the dwarf's part, but sat down with the determination rather to die on the spot than evince any symptoms of weakness before Roundheads and Presbyterians ; under which obnoxious epithets, being too old-fashioned to find out party designations of newer date, he comprehended all persons concerned in his present trouble.

By Sir Geoffrey the larger's change of position, his face was thus brought on a level with that of Sir Geoffrey the less, who had an opportunity of pulling him by the cloak. He of Martindale Castle, rather mechanically than consciously, turned his head towards the large wrinkled visage, which, struggling between an assumed air of easy importance, and an anxious desire to be noticed, was grimacing within a yard of him. But neither the singular physiognomy, the nods and smiles of greeting and recognition into which it was wreathed, nor the strange little form by which it was supported, had at that moment the power of exciting any recollections in the old knight's mind ; and having stared for a moment at the poor little man, his bulky namesake turned away his head without further notice.

Julian Peveril, the dwarf's more recent acquaintance, had, even amid his own anxious feelings, room for sympathy with those of his little fellow sufferer. As soon as he discovered that he was at the same terrible bar with himself, although he could not conceive how their causes came to be conjoined, he acknowledged him by a hearty shake of the hand, which the old man returned with affected dignity and real gratitude. ' Worthy youth,' he said, ' thy presence is restorative, like the nepenthe of Homer even in this syncopé of our mutual fate. I am concerned to see that your father hath not the same alacrity of soul as that of ours, which are lodged within smaller compass ; and that he hath forgotten an ancient comrade and fellow soldier, who now stands beside him to perform, perhaps, their last campaign.'

Julian briefly replied, that his father had much to occupy him. But the little man—who, to do him justice, cared no more (in his own phrase) for imminent danger or death, than he did for the puncture of a flea's proboscis—did not so easily renounce the secret object of his ambition, which was to acquire the notice of the large and lofty Sir Geoffrey Peveril, who, being at least three inches taller than his son, was in so far possessed of that superior excellence, which the poor dwarf, in his secret soul, valued before all other distinctions, although, in his conversation, he was con-

stantly depreciating it. 'Good comrade and namesake,' he
proceeded, stretching out his hand, so as again to reach the
elder Peveril's cloak, 'I forgive your want of reminiscence,
seeing it is long since I saw you at Naseby, fighting as if you
had as many arms as the fabled Briareus.'

The Knight of Martindale, who had again turned his head
towards the little man, and had listened, as if endeavouring
to make something out of his discourse, here interrupted
him with a peevish 'Pshaw!'

'Pshaw!' repeated Sir Geoffrey the less; '*Pshaw* is an
expression of slight esteem—nay, of contempt—in all
languages; and were this a befitting place '——

But the Judges had now taken their places, the criers
called silence, and the stern voice of the Lord Chief Justice
(the notorious Scroggs) demanded what the officers meant
by permitting the accused to communicate together in open
court.

It may here be observed, that this celebrated personage
was, upon the present occasion, at a great loss how to
proceed. A calm, dignified, judicial demeanour, was at no
time the characteristic of his official conduct. He always
ranted and roared either on the one side or the other; and
of late he had been much unsettled which side to take,
being totally incapable of anything resembling impartiality.
At the first trials for the Plot, when the whole stream of
popularity ran against the accused, no one had been so loud
as Scroggs;—to attempt to impeach the character of Oates
or Bedlowe, or any other leading witnesses, he treated as
a crime more heinous than it would have been to blaspheme
the Gospel on which they had been sworn—it was a stifling
of the Plot, or discrediting of the king's witnesses—a crime
not greatly, if at all, short of high treason against the king
himself.

But, of late, a new light had begun to glimmer upon the
understanding of this interpreter of the laws. Sagacious
in the signs of the times, he began to see that the tide was
turning; and that court favour at least, and probably
popular opinion also, were likely, in a short time, to declare
against the witnesses, and in favour of the accused.

The opinion which Scroggs had hitherto entertained of
the high respect in which Shaftesbury, the patron of the

Plot, was held by Charles, had been definitively shaken by
a whisper from his brother North to the following effect :
" His lordship has no more interest at court than your
footman.'

This notice, from a sure hand, and received but that
morning, had put the judge to a sore dilemma ; for, however indifferent to actual consistency, he was most anxious
to save appearances. He could not but recollect how violent
he had been on former occasions in favour of these prose¬
cutions ; and being sensible at the same time that the
credit of the witnesses, though shaken in the opinion of the
more judicious, was, amongst the bulk of the people out of
doors, as strong as ever, he had a difficult part to play. His
conduct, therefore, during the whole trial, resembled the
appearance of a vessel about to go upon another tack, when
her sails are shivering in the wind, ere they have yet caught
the impulse which is to send her forth in a new direction.
In a word, he was so uncertain which side it was his interest
to favour, that he might be said on that occasion to have
come nearer a state of total impartiality than he was ever
capable of attaining, whether before or afterwards. This
was shown by his bullying now the accused, and now the
witnesses, like a mastiff too much irritated to lie still
without baying, but uncertain whom he shall first bite.

The indictment was then read ; and Sir Geoffrey Peveril
heard, with some composure, the first part of it, which
stated him to have placed his son in the household of the
Countess of Derby, a recusant Papist, for the purpose of
aiding the horrible and bloodthirsty Popish Plot—with
having had arms and ammunition concealed in his house—
and with receiving a blank commission from the Lord
Stafford, who had suffered death on account of the Plot.
But when the charge went on to state that he had communicated for the same purpose with Geoffrey Hudson,
sometimes called Sir Geoffrey Hudson, now, or formerly,
in the domestic service of the Queen Dowager, he looked at
his companion as if he suddenly recalled him to remembrance, and broke out impatiently, ' These lies are too gross
to require a moment's consideration. I might have had
enough of intercourse, though in nothing but what was
loyal and innocent, with my noble kinsman, the late Lord

Stafford—I will call him so in spite of his misfortunes—
and with my wife's relation, the Honourable Countess of
Derby. But what likelihood can there be that I should
have colleagued with a decrepit buffoon, with whom I never
had an instant's communication, save once at an Easter
feast, when I whistled a hornpipe, as he danced on a trencher,
to amuse the company ? '

The rage of the poor dwarf brought tears in his eyes,
while, with an affected laugh, he said, that instead of those
juvenile and festive passages, Sir Geoffrey Peveril might
have remembered his charging along with him at Wiggan
Lane.

' On my word,' said Sir Geoffrey, after a moment's recollection, ' I will do you justice, Master Hudson—I believe
you were there—I think I heard you did good service. But
you will allow you might have been near one without his
seeing you.'

A sort of titter ran through the court at the simplicity
of the larger Sir Geoffrey's testimony, which the dwarf
endeavoured to control, by standing on his tiptoes, and
looking fiercely around, as if to admonish the laughers that
they indulged their mirth at their own peril. But perceiving
that this only excited further scorn, he composed himself
into a semblance of careless contempt, observing, with
a smile, that no one feared the glance of a chained lion ;
a magnificent simile, which rather increased than diminished
the mirth of those who heard it.

Against Julian Peveril there failed not to be charged the
aggravated fact, that he had been bearer of letters between
the Countess of Derby and other Papists and priests,
engaged in the universal treasonable conspiracy of the
Catholics ; and the attack of the house at Moultrassie Hall,
—with his skirmish with Chiffinch, and his assault, as it was
termed, on the person of John Jenkins, servant to the Duke
of Buckingham, were all narrated at length, as so many
open and overt acts of treasonable import. To this charge
Peveril contented himself with pleading—Not Guilty.

His little companion was not satisfied with so simple
a plea ; for when he heard it read, as a part of the charge
applying to him, that he had received from an agent of the
Plot a blank commission as colonel of a regiment of grena-

diers, he replied, in wrath and scorn, that if Goliath of Gath had come to him with such a proposal, and proffered him the command of the whole sons of Anak in a body, he should never have had occasion or opportunity to repeat the temptation to another. ' I would have slain him,' said the little man of loyalty, ' even where he stood.'

The charge was stated anew by the Counsel for the Crown ; and forth came the notorious Doctor Oates, rustling in the full silken canonicals of priesthood, for it was a time when he affected no small dignity of exterior decoration and deportment.

This singular man, who, aided by the obscure intrigues of the Catholics themselves, and the fortuitous circumstance of Godfrey's murder, had been able to cram down the public throat such a mass of absurdity as his evidence amounts to, had no other talent for imposture than an impudence which set conviction and shame alike at defiance. A man of sense or reflection, by trying to give his plot an appearance of more probability, would most likely have failed, as wise men often do in addressing the multitude, from not daring to calculate upon the prodigious extent of their credulity, especially where the figments presented to them involve the fearful and the terrible.

Oates was by nature choleric ; and the credit he had acquired made him insolent and conceited. Even his exterior was portentous. A fleece of white periwig showed a most uncouth visage, of great length, having the mouth, as the organ by use of which he was to rise to eminence, placed in the very centre of the countenance, and exhibiting to the astonished spectator as much chin below as there was nose and brow above the aperture. His pronunciation, too, was after a conceited fashion of his own, in which he accented the vowels in a manner altogether peculiar to himself.

This notorious personage, such as we have described him, stood forth on the present trial, and delivered his astonishing testimony concerning the existence of a Catholic Plot for the subversion of the government and murder of the king, in the same general outline in which it may be found in every English history. But as the doctor always had in reserve some special piece of evidence affecting those immediately on trial, he was pleased, on the present occasion, deeply to inculpate the Countess of Derby. ' He had seen,' as he said, ' that honourable lady when he was at the Jesuits' College at Saint Omer's. She had sent for him to an inn, or *auberge*, as it was there termed—the sign of the Golden

TITUS OATES

Lamb ; and had ordered him to breakfast in the same room with her ladyship ; and afterwards told him, that, knowing he was trusted by the fathers of the Society, she was determined that he should have a share of her secrets also ; and therewithal, that she drew from her bosom a broad sharp-pointed knife, such as butchers kill sheep with, and demanded of him what he thought of it for *the purpose* ; and when he, the witness, said for what purpose, she rapt him on the fingers with her fan, called him a dull fellow, and said it was designed to kill the king with.'

Here Sir Geoffrey Peveril could no longer refrain his indignation and surprise. ' Mercy of Heaven ! ' he said, ' did ever one hear of ladies of quality carrying butchering knives about them, and telling every scurvy companion she meant to kill the king with them ? Gentlemen of the jury, do but think if this is reasonable—though, if the villain could prove by any honest evidence, that my Lady of Derby ever let such a scum as himself come to speech of her, I would believe all he can say.'

' Sir Geoffrey,' said the judge, ' rest you quiet—You must not fly out—passion helps you not here—the Doctor must be suffered to proceed.'

Doctor Oates went on to state, how the lady complained of the wrongs the House of Derby had sustained from the king, and the oppression of her religion, and boasted of the schemes of the Jesuits and seminary priests ; and how they would be fathered by her noble kinsman of the House of Stanley. He finally averred that both the countess and the fathers of the seminary abroad, founded much upon the talents and courage of Sir Geoffrey Peveril and his son— the latter of whom was a member of her family. Of Hudson, he only recollected of having heard one of the fathers say, ' that although but a dwarf in stature, he would prove a giant in the cause of the Church.'

When he had ended his evidence, there was a pause, until the judge, as if the thought had suddenly occurred to him, demanded of Doctor Oates, whether he had ever mentioned the names of the Countess of Derby in any of the previous informations which he had lodged before the Privy Council, and elsewhere, upon this affair.

Oates seemed rather surprised at the question, and coloured with anger, as he answered, in his peculiar mode of pronunciation, ' Whoy, no, maay laard.'

' And pray, doctor,' said the judge, ' how came so great a revealer of mysteries as you have lately proved, to have suffered so material a circumstance as the accession of this powerful family to the Plot to have remained undiscovered ? '

'Maay laard,' said Oates, with much effrontery, 'aye do not come here to have my evidence questioned as touching the Plaat.'

'I do not question your evidence, doctor,' said Scroggs, for the time was not arrived that he dared treat him roughly; 'nor do I doubt the existence of the *Plaat*, since it is your pleasure to swear to it. I would only have you, for your own sake, and the satisfaction of all good Protestants, to explain why you have kept back such a weighty point of information from the king and country.'

'Maay laard,' said Oates, 'I will tell you a pretty fable.'

'I hope,' answered the judge, 'it may be the first and last which you shall tell in this place.'

'Maay laard,' continued Oates, 'there was once a faux, who having to carry a goose over a frazen river, and being afraid the aice would not bear him and his booty, did caarry aaver a staane, my laard, in the first instance, to prove the strength of the aice.'

'So your former evidence was but the stone, and now, for the first time, you have brought us the goose?' said Sir William Scroggs; 'to tell us this, doctor, is to make geese of the court and jury.'

'I desoire your laardship's honest construction,' said Oates, who saw the current changing against him, but was determined to pay the score with effrontery. 'All men knaw at what coast and praice I have given my evidence, which has been always, under Gaad, the means of awakening this poor naation to the dangerous state in which it staunds. Many here knaw that I have been obliged to faartify my ladging at Whitehall against the bloody Papists. It was not to be thought that I should have brought all the story out at aance. I think your wisdom would have advised me otherwise.' [1]

'Nay, doctor,' said the judge, 'it is not for me to direct you in this affair; and it is for the jury to believe you or

---

[1] It was on such terms that Dr. Oates was pleased to claim the extraordinary privilege of dealing out the information which he chose to communicate to a court of justice. The only sense in which his story of the fox, stone, and goose, could be applicable, is by supposing that he was determined to ascertain the extent of his countrymen's credulity before supplying it with a full meal.

not ; and as for myself, I sit here to do justice to both—
the jury have heard your answer to my question.'

Doctor Oates retired from the witness-box reddening
like a turkey-cock, as one totally unused to have such
accounts questioned as he chose to lay before the courts of
justice ; and there was, perhaps, for the first time, amongst
the counsel and solicitors, as well as the templars and
students of law there present, a murmur, distinct and
audible, unfavourable to the character of the great father
of the Popish Plot.

Everett and Dangerfield, with whom the reader is already
acquainted, were then called in succession to sustain the
accusation. They were subordinate informers—a sort of
under-spur-leathers, as the cant term went—who followed
the path of Oates, with all deference to his superior genius
and invention, and made their own fictions chime in and
harmonize with his, as well as their talents could devise. But
as their evidence had at no time received the full credence
into which the impudence of Oates had cajoled the public,
so they now began to fall into discredit rather more hastily
than their prototype, as the superadded turrets of an ill-
constructed building are naturally the first to give way.

It was in vain that Everett, with the precision of a
hypocrite, and Dangerfield, with the audacity of a bully,
narrated, with added circumstances of suspicion and crimi-
nality, their meeting with Julian Peveril in Liverpool,
and again at Martindale Castle. It was in vain they described the arms and accoutrements which they pretended
to have discovered in old Sir Geoffrey's possession ; and
that they gave a most dreadful account of the escape of
the younger Peveril from Moultrassie Hall, by means of an
armed force.

The jury listened coldly, and it was visible that they
were but little moved by the accusation ; especially as the
judge, always professing his belief in the Plot, and his zeal
for the Protestant religion, was ever and anon reminding
them that presumptions were no proofs—that hearsay was
no evidence—that those who made a trade of discovery were
likely to aid their researches by invention—and that without
doubting the guilt of the unfortunate persons at the bar, he
would gladly hear some evidence brought against them of

a different nature. 'Here we are told of a riot, and an escape achieved by the younger Peveril, at the house of a grave and worthy magistrate, known, I think, to most of us. Why, Master Attorney, bring ye not Master Bridgenorth himself to prove the fact, or all his household, if it be necessary?—A rising in arms is an affair over public to be left on the hearsay tale of these two men—though Heaven forbid that I should suppose they speak one word more than they believe! They are the witnesses for the king—and, what is equally dear to us, the Protestant religion—and witnesses against a most foul and heathenish Plot. On the other hand, here is a worshipful old knight, for such I must suppose him to be, since he has bled often in battle for the king,—such, I must say, I suppose him to be, until he is proved otherwise. And here is his son, a hopeful young gentleman—we must see that they have right, Master Attorney.'

'Unquestionably, my lord,' answered the Attorney. 'God forbid else! But we will make out these matters against these unhappy gentlemen in a manner more close, if your lordship will permit us to bring in our evidence.'

'Go on, Master Attorney,' said the judge, throwing himself back in his seat. 'Heaven forbid I hinder proving the king's accusation! I only say, what you know as well as I, that *de non apparentibus et non existendibus eadem est ratio.*'

'We shall then call Master Bridgenorth, as your lordship advises, who I think is in waiting.'

'No!' answered a voice from the crowd, apparently that of a female; 'he is too wise and too honest to be here.'

The voice was distinct as that of Lady Fairfax, when she expressed herself to a similar effect on the trial of Charles the First; but the researches which were made on the present occasion to discover the speaker were unsuccessful.

After the slight confusion occasioned by this circumstance was abated, the Attorney, who had been talking aside with the conductors of the prosecution, said, 'Whoever favoured us with that information, my lord, had good reason for what they said. Master Bridgenorth has become, I am told, suddenly invisible since this morning.'

'Look you there now, Master Attorney,' said the judge

—' This comes of not keeping the crown witnesses together and in readiness—I am sure I cannot help the
consequences.'

' Nor I either, my lord,' said the Attorney pettishly.
' I could have proved by this worshipful gentleman, Master
Justice Bridgenorth, the ancient friendship betwixt this
party, Sir Geoffrey Peveril, and the Countess of Derby, of
whose doings and intentions Doctor Oates has given such
a deliberate evidence. I could have proved his having
sheltered her in his castle against a process of law, and
rescued her, by force of arms, from this very Justice Bridgenorth, not without actual violence. Moreover, I could have
proved against young Peveril the whole affray charged upon
him by the same worshipful evidence.'

Here the judge stuck his thumbs into his girdle, which was
a favourite attitude of his on such occasions, and exclaimed,
' Pshaw, pshaw, Master Attorney!—Tell me not that you
could have proved this, and you *could* have proved that,
or that, or this—Prove what you will, but let it be through
the mouths of your evidence. Men are not to be licked out
of their lives by the rough side of a lawyer's tongue.'

' Nor is a foul Plot to be smothered,' said the Attorney,
' for all the haste your lordship is in. I cannot call Master
Chiffinch neither, as he is employed on the king's especial
affairs, as I am this instant certiorated from the Court at
Whitehall.'

' Produce the papers, then, Master Attorney, of which
this young man is said to be the bearer,' said the judge.

' They are before the Privy Council, my lord.'

' Then why do you found on them here ? ' said the judge
—' This is something like trifling with the court.'

' Since your lordship gives it that name,' said the Attorney,
sitting down in a huff, ' you may manage the cause as
you will.'

' If you do not bring more evidence, I pray you to charge
the jury,' said the judge.

' I shall not take the trouble to do so,' said the Crown
Counsel. ' I see plainly how the matter is to go.'

' Nay, but be better advised,' said Scroggs. ' Consider,
your case is but half proved respecting the two Peverils,
and doth not pinch on the little man at all, saving that

Doctor Oates said that he was in a certain case to prove
a giant, which seems no very probable Popish miracle.'

This sally occasioned a laugh in the court, which the
Attorney-General seemed to take in great dudgeon.

' Master Attorney,' said Oates, who always interfered in
the management of these law-suits, ' this is a plain and
absolute giving away of the cause—I must needs say it,
a mere stoifling of the Plaat.'

' Then the devil who bred it may blow wind into it again,
if he lists,' answered the Attorney-General ; and, flinging
down his brief, he left the court, as in a huff with all who
were concerned in the affair.

The judge having obtained silence,—for a murmur arose
in the court when the counsel for the prosecution threw
up his brief,—began to charge the jury, balancing, as he had
done throughout the whole day, the different opinions by
which he seemed alternately swayed. He protested on
his salvation that he had no more doubt of the existence
of the horrid and damnable conspiracy called the Popish
Plot, than he had of the treachery of Judas Iscariot ; and
that he considered Oates as the instrument under Providence
of preserving the nation from all the miseries of his Majesty's
assassination, and of a second Saint Bartholomew, acted
in the streets of London. But then he stated it was the
candid construction of the law of England, that the worse
the crime, the more strong should be the evidence. Here
was the case of accessories tried, whilst their principal—
for such he should call the Countess of Derby—was uncon-
victed and at large; and for Doctor Oates, he had but spoke
of matters which personally applied to that noble lady,
whose words, if she used such in passion, touching aid which
she expected in some treasonable matters from these Peverils,
and from her kinsmen, or her son's kinsmen, of the House
of Stanley, may have been but a burst of female resentment
—*dulcis Amaryllidis ira*, as the poet hath it. Who knoweth
but Doctor Oates did mistake—he being a gentleman of
a comely countenance and easy demeanour—this same rap
with the fan as a chastisement for lack of courage in the
Catholic cause, when, peradventure, it was otherwise meant,
as Popish ladies will put, it is said, such neophytes and
youthful candidates for orders, to many severe trials.

' I speak these things jocularly,' said the judge, ' having no wish to stain the reputation either of the Honourable Countess or the Reverend Doctor ; only I think the bearing between them may have related to something short of high treason. As for what the Attorney-General hath set forth of rescues and force, and I wot not what, sure I am, that in a civil country, when such things happen, such things may be proved ; and that you and I, gentlemen, are not to take them for granted gratuitously. Touching this other prisoner, this *Galfridus minimus*, he must needs say,' he continued, ' he could not discover even a shadow of suspicion against him. Was it to be thought so abortive a creature would thrust himself into depths of policy, far less into stratagems of war ? They had but to look at him to conclude the contrary—the creature was, from his age, fitter for the grave than a conspiracy—and by his size and appearance, for the inside of a raree-show, than the mysteries of a plot.'

The dwarf here broke in upon the judge by force of screaming, to assure him that he had been, simple as he sat there, engaged in seven plots in Cromwell's time; and, as he proudly added, with some of the tallest men of England. The matchless look and air with which Sir Geoffrey made this vaunt, set all a-laughing, and increased the ridicule with which the whole trial began to be received ; so that it was amidst shaking sides and watery eyes that a general verdict of Not Guilty was pronounced, and the prisoners dismissed from the bar.

But a warmer sentiment awakened among those who saw the father and son throw themselves into each other's arms, and, after a hearty embrace, extend their hands to their poor little companion in peril, who, like a dog, when present at a similar scene, had at last succeeded, by stretching himself up to them and whimpering at the same time, to secure to himself a portion of their sympathy and gratulation.

Such was the singular termination of this trial. Charles himself was desirous to have taken considerable credit with the Duke of Ormond for the evasion of the law, which had been thus effected by his private connivance ; and was both surprised and mortified at the coldness with which his Grace replied, that he was rejoiced at the poor gentle-

men's safety, but would rather have had the king redeem
them like a prince, by his royal prerogative of mercy, than
that his judge should convey them out of the power of
the law, like a juggler with his cups and balls.

CHAPTER XLII

———On fair ground
I could beat forty of them !
CORIOLANUS.

IT doubtless occurred to many that were present at the
trial we have described, that it was managed in a singular
manner, and that the quarrel, which had the appearance
of having taken place between the court and the Crown
Counsel, might proceed from some private understanding
betwixt them, the object of which was the miscarriage of
the accusation. Yet though such underhand dealing was
much suspected, the greater part of the audience, being
well educated and intelligent, had already suspected the
bubble of the Popish Plot, and were glad to see that accusations, founded on what had already cost so much blood,
could be evaded in any way. But the crowd, who waited
in the Court of Requests, and in the hall, and without doors,
viewed in a very different light the combination, as they
interpreted it, between the judge and the Attorney-General,
for the escape of the prisoners.

Oates, whom less provocation than he had that day
received often induced to behave like one frantic with
passion, threw himself amongst the crowd, and repeated
till he was hoarse, ' Theay are stoifling the Plaat ! theay
are straangling the Plaat ! My Laard Justice and Maaster
Attarney are in league to secure the escape of the plaaters
and Paapists ! '

' It is the device of the Papist whore of Portsmouth,'
said one.

' Of old Rowley himself,' said another.

' If he could be murdered by himself, why hang those
that would hinder it ! ' exclaimed a third.

'He should be tried,' said a fourth, 'for conspiring his own death, and hanged *in terrorem.*'

In the meanwhile, Sir Geoffrey, his son, and their little companion, left the hall, intending to go to Lady Peveril's lodgings, which had been removed to Fleet Street. She had been relieved from considerable inconvenience, as Sir Geoffrey gave Julian hastily to understand, by an angel, in the shape of a young friend, and she now expected them doubtless with impatience. Humanity, and some indistinct idea of having unintentionally hurt the feelings of the poor dwarf, induced the honest Cavalier to ask this unprotected being to go with them. 'He knew Lady Peveril's lodgings were but small,' he said ; 'but it would be strange, if there was not some cupboard large enough to accommodate the little gentleman.'

The dwarf registered this well-meant remark in his mind, to be the subject of a proper explanation, along with the unhappy reminiscence of the trencher-horn-pipe, whenever time should permit an argument of such nicety.

And thus they sallied from the hall, attracting general observation, both from the circumstances in which they had stood so lately, and from their resemblance, as a wag of the Inner Temple expressed it, to the three degrees of comparison, Large, Lesser, Least. But they had not passed far along the street, when Julian perceived that more malevolent passions than mere curiosity began to actuate the crowd, which followed, and, as it were, dogged their motions.

'There go the Papist cut-throats, tantivy for Rome !' said one fellow.

'Tantivy to Whitehall, you mean !' said another.

'Ah! the bloodthirsty villains !' cried a woman : 'Shame, one of them should be suffered to live, after poor Sir Edmondsbury's cruel murder.'

'Out upon the mealy-mouthed jury, that turned out the bloodhounds on an innocent town !' cried a fourth.

In short, the tumult thickened, and the word began to pass among the more desperate, 'Lambe them, lads ; lambe them !'—a cant phrase of the time, derived from the fate of Dr. Lambe, an astrologer and quack, who was

knocked on the head by the rabble in Charles the First's
time.

Julian began to be much alarmed at these symptoms of
violence, and regretted that they had not gone down to
the city by water. It was now too late to think of that
mode of retreating, and he therefore requested his father
in a whisper to walk steadily forward towards Charing
Cross, taking no notice of the insults which might be cast
upon them, while the steadiness of their pace and appearance might prevent the rabble from resorting to actual
violence. The execution of this prudent resolution was
prevented after they had passed the palace, by the hasty
disposition of the elder Sir Geoffrey, and the no less choleric
temper of Galfridus Minimus, who had a soul which spurned
all odds, as well of numbers as of size.

'Now a murrain take the knaves, with their halloing
and whooping,' said the larger knight ; ' by this day, if
I could but light on a weapon, I would cudgel reason and
loyalty into some of their carcasses ! '

'And I also,' said the dwarf, who was toiling to keep
up with the longer strides of his companions, and therefore
spoke in a very phthisical tone.—' I also will cudgel the
plebeian knaves beyond measure—he !—hem ! '

Among the crowd who thronged around them, impeded,
and did all but assault them, was a mischievous shoe-
maker's apprentice, who, hearing this unlucky vaunt of
the valorous dwarf, repaid it by flapping him on the head
with a boot which he was carrying home to the owner,
so as to knock the little gentleman's hat over his eyes.
The dwarf, thus rendered unable to discover the urchin
that had given him the offence, flew with instinctive ambition against the biggest fellow in the crowd, who received
the onset with a kick on the stomach, which made the
poor little champion reel back to his companions. They
were now assaulted on all sides ; but fortune, complying
with the wish of Sir Geoffrey the larger, ordained that the
scuffle should happen near the booth of a cutler, from
amongst whose wares, as they stood exposed to the public,
Sir Geoffrey Peveril snatched a broadsword, which he
brandished with the formidable address of one who had
for many a day been in the familiar practice of using such

a weapon. Julian, while at the same time he called loudly
for a peace-officer, and reminded the assailants that they
were attacking inoffensive passengers, saw nothing better
for it than to imitate his father's example, and seized also
one of the weapons thus opportunely offered.

When they displayed these demonstrations of defence,
the rush which the rabble at first made towards them
was so great as to throw down the unfortunate dwarf, who
would have been trampled to death in the scuffle, had not
his stout old namesake cleared the rascal crowd from about
him with a few flourishes of his weapon, and seizing on the
fallen champion, put him out of danger (except from
missiles) by suddenly placing him on the bulkhead, that
is to say, the flat wooden roof of the cutler's projecting
booth. From the rusty ironware which was displayed
there, the dwarf instantly snatched an old rapier and
target, and, covering himself with the one, stood making
passes with the other, at the faces and eyes of the people
in the street ; so much delighted with his post of vantage,
that he called loudly to his friends who were skirmishing
with the rioters on more equal terms as to position, to lose
no time in putting themselves under his protection. But
far from being in a situation to need his assistance, the
father and son might easily have extricated themselves
from the rabble by their own exertions, could they have
thought of leaving the mannikin in the forlorn situation
in which, to every eye but his own, he stood like a diminutive puppet, tricked out with sword and target as a fencing-
master's sign.

Stones and sticks began now to fly very thick, and the
crowd, notwithstanding the exertions of the Peverils to
disperse them with as little harm as possible, seemed
determined on mischief, when some gentlemen who had
been at the trial, understanding that the prisoners who
had been just acquitted were in danger of being murdered
by the populace, drew their swords, and made forward to
effect their rescue, which was completed by a small party
of the King's Life Guards, who had been dispatched from
their ordinary post of alarm, upon intelligence of what
was passing. When this unexpected reinforcement arrived,
the old jolly knight at once recognized, amidst the cries

of those who then entered upon action, some of the sounds which had animated his more active years.

'Where be these cuckoldly Roundheads,' cried some.

SIR GEOFFREY AND JULIAN PEVERIL ATTACKED
BY THE MOB

'Down with the sneaking knaves!' cried others. 'The king and his friends, and the devil a one else!' exclaimed a third set, with more oaths and d—n me's, than, in the present more correct age, it is necessary to commit to paper.

The old soldier, pricking up his ears like an ancient hunter at the cry of the hounds, would gladly have scoured the Strand, with the charitable purpose, now he saw himself so well supported, of knocking the London knaves, who had insulted him, into twiggen bottles ; but he was withheld by the prudence of Julian, who, though himself extremely irritated by the unprovoked ill usage which they had received, saw himself in a situation in which it was necessary to exercise more caution than vengeance. He prayed and pressed his father to seek some temporary place of retreat from the fury of the populace, while that prudent measure was yet in their power. The subaltern officer who commanded the party of the Life Guards exhorted the old Cavalier eagerly to the same sage counsel, using, as a spice of compulsion, the name of the king ; while Julian strongly urged that of his mother. The old knight looked at his blade, crimsoned with cross-cuts and slashes which he had given to the most forward of the assailants, with the eye of one not half sufficed.

'I would I had pinked one of the knaves at least— but I know not how it was, when I looked on their broad round English faces, I shunned to use my point, and only sliced the rogues a little.'

'But the king's pleasure,' said the officer, ' is, that no tumult be prosecuted.'

'My mother,' said Julian, ' will die with fright, if the rumour of this scuffle reaches her ere we see her.'

'Aye, aye,' said the knight, ' the king's Majesty, and my good dame—well, their pleasure be done, that's all I can say—kings and ladies must be obeyed. But which way to retreat, since retreat we needs must ? '

Julian would have been at some loss to advise what course to take, for everybody in the vicinity had shut up their shops, and chained their doors, upon observing the confusion become so formidable. The poor cutler, however, with whose goods they made so free, offered them an asylum on the part of his landlord, whose house served as a rest for his shop, and only intimated gently, he hoped the gentlemen would consider him for the use of his weapons.

Julian was hastily revolving whether they ought, in prudence, to accept this man's invitation, aware, by experience, how many trepans, as they were then termed, were used betwixt two contending factions, each too inveterate to be very scrupulous of the character of fair play to an enemy, when the dwarf, exerting his cracked voice to the uttermost, and shrieking like an exhausted herald, from the exalted station which he still occupied on the bulkhead, exhorted them to accept the offer of the worthy man of the mansion. ' He himself,' he said, as he reposed himself after the glorious conquest in which he had some share, ' had been favoured with a beatific vision, too splendid to be described to common and mere mortal ears, but which had commanded him, in a voice to which his heart had bounded as to a trumpet sound, to take refuge with the worthy person of the house, and cause his friends to do so.'

' Vision ! ' said the Knight of the Peak,—' sound of a trumpet !—the little man is stark mad.'

But the cutler, in great haste, intimated to them that their little friend had received an intimation from a gentlewoman of his acquaintance, who spoke to him from the window, while he stood on the bulkhead, that they would find a safe retreat in his landlord's ; and desiring them to attend to two or three deep though distant huzzas, made them aware that the rabble were up still, and would soon be upon them with renewed violence, and increased numbers.

The father and son, therefore, hastily thanked the officer and his party, as well as the other gentlemen who had volunteered in their assistance, lifted little Sir Geoffrey Hudson from the conspicuous post which he had so creditably occupied during the skirmish, and followed the footsteps of the tenant of the booth, who conducted them down a blind alley and through one or two courts, in case, as he said, any one might have watched where they burrowed, and so into a back-door. This entrance admitted them to a staircase carefully hung with straw mats to exclude damp, from the upper step of which they entered upon a tolerably large withdrawing-room, hung with coarse green serge edged with gilded leather, which the poorer or more economical citizens at that time used instead of tapestry or wainscoting.

Here the poor cutler received from Julian such a gratuity for the loan of the swords that he generously abandoned the property to the gentlemen who had used them so well; ' the rather,' he said, ' that he saw, by the way they handled their weapons, that they were men of mettle, and tall fellows.'

Here the dwarf smiled on him courteously, and bowed, thrusting, at the same time, his hand into his pocket, which, however, he withdrew carelessly, probably because he found he had not the means of making the small donation which he had meditated.

The cutler proceeded to say, as he bowed and was about to withdraw, that he saw there would be merry days yet in Old England, and that Bilboa blades would fetch as good a price as ever. ' I remember,' he said, ' gentlemen, though I was then but a prentice, the demand for weapons in the years forty-one and forty-two; sword-blades were more in request than toothpicks, and Old Ironsides, my master, took more for rascally Provant rapiers, than I dare ask nowadays for a Toledo. But, to be sure, a man's life then rested on the blade he carried; the Cavaliers and Roundheads fought every day at the gates of Whitehall, as it is like, gentlemen, by your good example, they may do again, when I shall be enabled to leave my pitiful booth, and open a shop of better quality. I hope you will recommend me, gentlemen, to your friends. I am always provided with ware which a gentleman may risk his life on.'

' Thank you, good friend,' said Julian, ' I prithee begone. I trust we shall need thy ware no more for some time at least.'

The cutler retired, while the dwarf hallooed after him down stairs, that he would call on him soon, and equip himself with a longer blade, and one more proper for action; although, he said, the little weapon he had did well enough for a walking-sword, or in a skirmish with such canaille as they had been engaged with.

The cutler returned at this summons, and agreed to pleasure the little man with a weapon more suitable to his magnanimity; then, as if the thought had suddenly occurred to him, he said, ' But gentlemen, it will be wild work to walk with your naked swords through the Strand, and it can scarce fail to raise the rabble again. If you please, while you repose yourselves here, I can fit the blades with sheaths.'

The proposal seemed so reasonable, that Julian and his father gave up their weapons to the friendly cutler, an example which the dwarf followed, after a moment's hesitation, not caring, as he magnificently expressed it, to part so soon with the trusty friend which fortune had but the moment before restored to his hand. The man retired with the weapons under his arm ; and, in shutting the door behind him they heard him turn the key.

' Did you hear that ? ' said Sir Geoffrey to his son—' and we are disarmed.'

Julian, without reply, examined the door, which was fast secured ; and then looked at the casements, which were at a story's height from the ground, and grated besides with iron. ' I cannot think,' he said, after a moment's pause, ' that the fellow means to trepan us ; and, in any event, I trust we should have no difficulty in forcing the door, or otherwise making an escape. But, before resorting to such violent measures, I think it is better to give the rabble leisure to disperse, by waiting this man's return with our weapons within a reasonable time, when, if he does not appear, I trust we shall find little difficulty in extricating ourselves.' As he spoke thus, the hangings were pulled aside, and from a small door which was concealed behind them, Major Bridgenorth entered the room.

CHAPTER XLIII

He came amongst them like a new raised spirit
To speak of dreadful judgements that impend,
And of the wrath to come.

The Reformer.

THE astonishment of Julian at the unexpected apparition of Bridgenorth, was instantly succeeded by apprehension of his father's violence, which he had every reason to believe would break forth against one whom he himself could not but reverence on account of his own merits, as well as because he was the father of Alice. The appearance of

Bridgenorth was not, however, such as to awaken resentment. His countenance was calm, his step slow and composed, his eye not without the indication of some deep-seated anxiety, but without any expression either of anger or of triumph. 'You are welcome,' he said, ' Sir Geoffrey Peveril, to the shelter and hospitality of this house ; as welcome as you would have been in other days, when we called each other neighbours and friends.'

' Odzooks,' said the old Cavalier, ' and had I known it was thy house, man, I would sooner had my heart's blood run down the kennel, than my foot should have crossed your threshold—in the way of seeking safety, that is.'

' I forgive your inveteracy,' said Major Bridgenorth, ' on account of your prejudices.'

' Keep your forgiveness,' answered the Cavalier, ' until you are pardoned yourself. By Saint George I have sworn, if ever I got my heels out of yon rascally prison, whither I was sent much through your means, Master Bridgenorth, —that you should pay the reckoning for my bad lodging. I will strike no man in his own house ; but if you will cause the fellow to bring back my weapon, and take a turn in that blind court there below, along with me, you shall soon see what chance a traitor hath with a true man, and a kennel-blooded Puritan with Peveril of the Peak.'

Bridgenorth smiled with much composure. ' When I was younger and more warm-blooded,' he replied, ' I refused your challenge, Sir Geoffrey ; it is not likely I should now accept it, when each is within a stride of the grave. I have not spared, and will not spare, my blood, when my country wants it.'

' That is when there is any chance of treason against the king,' said Sir Geoffrey.

' Nay, my father,' said Julian, ' let us hear Master Bridgenorth ! We have been sheltered in his house ; and although we now see him in London, we should remember that he did not appear against us this day, when perhaps his evidence might have given a fatal turn to our situation.'

' You are right, young man,' said Bridgenorth ; ' and it should be some pledge of my sincere good will, that I was this day absent from Westminster, when a few words from my mouth had ended the long line of Peveril of the Peak :

it needed but ten minutes to walk to Westminster Hall, to have ensured your condemnation.   But could I have done this, knowing, as I now know, that to thee, Julian Peveril, I owe the extrication of my daughter—of my dearest Alice —the memory of her departed mother—from the snares which hell and profligacy had opened around her ? '

' She is, I trust, safe,' said Peveril eagerly, and almost forgetting his father's presence ; ' she is, I trust, safe, and in your own wardship ? '

' Not in mine,' said the dejected father ; ' but in that of one in whose protection, next to that of Heaven, I can most fully confide.'

' Are you sure—are you very sure of that ? ' repeated Julian eagerly.   ' I found her under the charge of one to whom she had been trusted, and who yet '——

' And who yet was the basest of women,' answered Bridgenorth ; ' but he who selected her for the charge was deceived in her character.'

' Say rather you were deceived in his ; remember that when we parted at Moultrassie, I warned you of that Ganlesse—that '——

' I know your meaning,' said Bridgenorth ; ' nor did you err in describing him as a worldly-wise man.   But he has atoned for his error by recovering Alice from the dangers into which she was plunged when separated from you ; and besides, I have not thought meet again to entrust him with the charge that is dearest to me.'

' I thank God your eyes are thus far opened ! ' said Julian.

' This day will open them wide, or close them for ever,' answered Bridgenorth.

During this dialogue, which the speakers hurried through without attending to the others who were present, Sir Geoffrey listened with surprise and eagerness, endeavouring to catch something which should render their conversation intelligible ; but as he totally failed in gaining any such key to their meaning, he broke in with,—' 'Sblood and thunder, Julian, what unprofitable gossip is this ? What hast thou to do with this fellow, more than to bastinado him, if you should think it worth while to beat so old a rogue ? '

' My dearest father,' said Julian, ' you know not this gentleman—I am certain you do him injustice.   My own obligations to him are many ; and I am sure when you come to know them '——

'I hope I shall die ere that moment come,' said Sir Geoffrey ; and continued with increasing violence, ' I hope in the mercy of Heaven, that I shall be in the grave of my ancestors, ere I learn that my son—my only son—the last hope of my ancient house—the last remnant of the name of Peveril—hath consented to receive obligations from the man on earth I am most bound to hate, were I not still more bound to contemn him! Degenerate dog-whelp ! ' he repeated with great vehemence, ' you colour, without replying ! Speak, and disown such disgrace ; or, by the God of my fathers '——

The dwarf suddenly stepped forward, and called out, ' Forbear ! ' with a voice at once so discordant and commanding that it sounded supernatural. ' Man of sin and pride,' he said, ' forbear ; and call not the name of a holy God to witness thine unhallowed resentments.'

The rebuke so boldly and decidedly given, and the moral enthusiasm with which he spoke, gave the despised dwarf an ascendancy for the moment over the fiery spirit of his gigantic namesake. Sir Geoffrey Peveril eyed him for an instant askance and shyly, as he might have done a supernatural apparition, and then muttered, ' What knowest thou of my cause of wrath ? '

' Nothing,' said the dwarf ; ' nothing but this—that no cause can warrant the oath thou wert about to swear. Ungrateful man ! thou wert to-day rescued from the devouring wrath of the wicked, by a marvellous conjunction of circumstances—Is this a day, thinkest thou, on which to indulge thine own hasty resentments ? '

' I stand rebuked,' said Sir Geoffrey, ' and by a singular monitor—the grasshopper, as the prayer-book saith, hath become a burden to me. Julian, I will speak to thee of these matters hereafter ;—and for you, Master Bridgenorth, I desire to have no further communication with you, either in peace or in anger. Our time passes fast, and I would fain return to my family. Cause our weapons to be restored ; unbar the doors, and let us part without further altercation, which can but disturb and aggravate our spirits.'

' Sir Geoffrey Peveril,' said Bridgenorth, ' I have no

desire to vex your spirit or my own ; but, for thus soon dismissing you, that may hardly be, it being a course inconsistent with the work which I have on hand.'

'How, sir ! Do you mean that we should abide here, whether with or against our inclinations ? ' said the dwarf. ' Were it not that I am laid under charge to remain here, by one who hath the best right to command this poor microcosm, I would show thee that bolts and bars are unavailing restraints on such as I am.'

' Truly,' said Sir Geoffrey, ' I think, upon an emergency, the little man might make his escape through the keyhole.'

Bridgenorth's face was moved into something like a smile at the swaggering speech of the pygmy hero, and the contemptuous commentary of Sir Geoffrey Peveril ; but such an expression never dwelt on his features for two seconds together, and he replied in these words :—' Gentlemen, each and all of you must be fain to content yourselves. Believe me, no hurt is intended towards you ; on the contrary, your remaining here will be a means of securing your safety, which would be otherwise deeply endangered. It will be your own fault if a hair of your head is hurt. But the stronger force is on my side ; and, whatever harm you may meet with should you attempt to break forth by violence, the blame must rest with yourselves. If you will not believe me, I will permit Master Julian Peveril to accompany me, where he shall see that I am provided fully with the means of repressing violence.'

' Treason !—treason ! ' exclaimed the old knight— ' Treason against God and King Charles !—Oh, for one half hour of the broadsword which I parted with like an ass ! '

' Hold, my father, I conjure you ! ' said Julian. ' I will go with Master Bridgenorth, since he requests it. I will satisfy myself whether there be danger, and of what nature. It is possible I may prevail on him to desist from some desperate measure, if such be indeed in agitation. Should it be necessary, fear not that your son will behave as he ought to do.'

' Do your pleasure, Julian,' said his father ; ' I will confide in thee. But if you betray my confidence, a father's curse shall cleave to you.'

Bridgenorth now motioned to Peveril to follow him, and they passed through the small door by which he had entered.

The passage led to a vestibule or anteroom, in which several other doors and passages seemed to centre. Through one of these Julian was conducted by Bridgenorth, walking with silence and precaution, in obedience to a signal made by his guide to that effect. As they advanced, he heard sounds, like those of the human voice, engaged in urgent and emphatic declamation. With slow and light steps Bridgenorth conducted him through a door which terminated this passage; and as he entered a little gallery, having a curtain in front, the sound of the preacher's voice—for such it now seemed—became distinct and audible.

Julian now doubted not that he was in one of those conventicles, which, though contrary to the existing laws, still continued to be regularly held in different parts of London and the suburbs. Many of these, as frequented by persons of moderate political principles, though dissenters from the church for conscience' sake, were connived at by the prudence or timidity of the government. But some of them, in which assembled the fiercer and more exalted sects of Independents, Anabaptists, Fifth Monarchy men, and other sectaries, whose stern enthusiasm had contributed so greatly to effect the overthrow of the late king's throne, were sought after, suppressed, and dispersed, whenever they could be discovered.

Julian was soon satisfied that the meeting into which he was thus secretly introduced, was one of the latter class; and, to judge by the violence of the preacher, of the most desperate character. He was still more effectually convinced of this, when, at a sign from Bridgenorth, he cautiously unclosed a part of the curtain which hung before the gallery, and thus, unseen himself, looked down on the audience, and obtained a view of the preacher.

About two hundred persons were assembled beneath, in an area filled up with benches, as if for the exercise of worship; and they were all of the male sex, and well armed with pikes and muskets, as well as swords and pistols. Most of them had the appearance of veteran soldiers, now past the middle of life, yet retaining such an appearance of strength as might well supply the loss of youthful agility. They stood, or sat, in various attitudes of stern attention ; and, resting on their spears and muskets, kept their eyes firmly fixed on the preacher, who ended the violence of his declamation by displaying from the pulpit a banner, on which was represented a lion, with the motto, '*Vicit Leo ex tribu Judae.*'

The torrent of mystical yet animating eloquence of the preacher—an old grey-haired man, whom zeal seemed to supply with the powers of voice and action, of which years had deprived him—was suited to the taste of his audience, but could not be transferred to these pages without scandal and impropriety. He menaced the rulers of England with all the judgements denounced on those of Moab and Assyria—he called upon the saints to be strong, to be up and doing ; and promised those miracles which, in the campaigns of Joshua, and his successors, the valiant Judges of Israel, supplied all odds against the Amorites, Midianites, and Philistines. He sounded trumpets, opened vials, broke seals, and denounced approaching judgements under all the mystical signs of the Apocalypse. The end of the world was announced, accompanied with all its preliminary terrors.

Julian, with deep anxiety, soon heard enough to make him aware that the meeting was likely to terminate in open insurrection, like that of the Fifth Monarchy men, under Venner, at an earlier period of Charles's reign ; and he was not a little concerned at the probability of Bridgenorth being implicated in so criminal and desperate an undertaking. If he had retained any doubts of the issue of the meeting, they must have been removed when the preacher called on his hearers to renounce all expectation which had hitherto been entertained of safety to the nation, from the execution of the ordinary laws of the land. This, he said, was at best but a carnal seeking after earthly aid—a going down to Egypt for help, which the jealousy of their Divine Leader would resent as a fleeing to another rock, and a different banner, from that which was this day displayed over them. —And here he solemnly swung the bannered lion over their heads, as the only sign under which they ought to seek for life and safety. He then proceeded to insist, that recourse to ordinary justice was vain as well as sinful.

' The event of that day at Westminster,' he said, ' might teach them that the man at Whitehall was even as the man

his father ; ' and closed a long tirade against the vices of
the Court, with assurance ' that Tophet was ordained of
old—for the king it was made hot.'

As the preacher entered on a description of the approaching theocracy, which he dared to prophesy, Bridgenorth,
who appeared for a time to have forgotten the presence of
Julian, whilst with stern and fixed attention he drank in
the words of the preacher, seemed suddenly to collect
himself, and, taking Julian by the hand, led him out of the
gallery, of which he carefully closed the door, into an
apartment at no great distance.

When they arrived there, he anticipated the expostulations of Julian, by asking him, in a tone of severe triumph,
whether these men he had seen were likely to do their work
negligently, or whether it would not be perilous to attempt
to force their way from a house, when all the avenues were
guarded by such as he had now seen—men of war from their
childhood upwards.

' In the name of Heaven,' said Julian, without replying to
Bridgenorth's question, ' for what desperate purpose have
you assembled so many desperate men ?   I am well aware
that your sentiments of religion are peculiar ; but beware
how you deceive yourself—No views of religion can sanction
rebellion and murder ; and such are the natural and
necessary consequences of the doctrine we have just heard
poured into the ears of fanatical and violent enthusiasts.'

' My son,' said Bridgenorth calmly, ' in the days of my
nonage, I thought as you do. I deemed it sufficient to
pay my tithes of cummin and aniseed—my poor petty
moral observances of the old law ; and I thought I was
heaping up precious things, when they were in value no
more than the husks of the swine-trough. Praised be
Heaven, the scales are fallen from mine eyes ; and after
forty years' wandering in the desert of Sinai, I am at length
arrived in the Land of Promise—My corrupt human nature
has left me—I have cast my slough, and can now with some
conscience put my hand to the plough, certain that there
is no weakness left in me wherethrough I may look back.
The furrows,' he added, bending his brows, while a gloomy
fire filled his large eyes, ' must be drawn long and deep, and
watered by the blood of the mighty.'   .

There was a change in Bridgenorth's tone and manner, when he used these singular expressions, which convinced Julian that his mind, which had wavered for so many years between his natural good sense and the insane enthusiasm of the time, had finally given way to the latter ; and, sensible of the danger in which the unhappy man himself, the innocent and beautiful Alice, and his own father, were likely to be placed—to say nothing of the general risk of the community by a sudden insurrection, he at the same time felt that there was no chance of reasoning effectually with one who would oppose spiritual conviction to all arguments which reason could urge against his wild schemes. To touch his feelings seemed a more probable resource; and Julian therefore conjured Bridgenorth to think how much his daughter's honour and safety were concerned in his abstaining from the dangerous course which he meditated. 'If you fall,' he said, 'must she not pass under the power and guardianship of her uncle, whom you allow to have shown himself capable of the grossest mistake in the choice of her female protectress; and whom I believe, upon good grounds, to have made that infamous choice with his eyes open ? '

' Young man,' answered Bridgenorth, ' you make me feel like the poor bird, around whose wing some wanton boy has fixed a line, to pull the struggling wretch to earth at his pleasure. Know, since thou wilt play this cruel part, and drag me down from higher contemplations, that she with whom Alice is placed, and who hath in future full power to guide her motions, and decide her fate, despite of Christian and every one else, is—I will not tell thee who she is—Enough—no one—thou least of all, needs to fear for her safety.'

At this moment a side-door opened, and Christian himself came into the apartment. He started and coloured when he saw Julian Peveril ; then turning to Bridgenorth with an assumed air of indifference, asked, ' Is Saul among the prophets ?—Is a Peveril among the saints ? '

' No, brother,' replied Bridgenorth, ' his time is not come more than thine own—thou art too deep in the ambitious intrigues of manhood, and he in the giddy passions of youth, to hear the still calm voice—You will both hear it, as I trust and pray.'

'Master Ganlesse, or Christian, or by whatever name you are called,' said Julian, ' by whatever reasons you guide yourself in this most perilous matter, *you* at least are not influenced by any idea of an immediate divine command for commencing hostilities against the state. Leaving, therefore, for the present, whatever subjects of discussion may be between us, I implore you, as a man of shrewdness and sense, to join with me in dissuading Master Bridgenorth from the fatal enterprise which he now meditates.'

'Young gentleman,' said Christian, with great composure, ' when we met in the west, I was willing to have made a friend of you, but you rejected the overture. You might, however, even then have seen enough of me to be assured that I am not likely to rush too rashly on any desperate undertaking. As to this which lies before us, my brother Bridgenorth brings to it the simplicity, though not the harmlessness of the dove, and I the subtilty of the serpent. He hath the leading of saints who are moved by the spirit ; and I can add to their efforts a powerful body, who have for their instigators, the world, the devil, and the flesh.'

'And can you,' said Julian, looking at Bridgenorth, ' accede to such an unworthy union ? '

'I unite not with them,' said Bridgenorth ; ' but I may not, without guilt, reject the aid which Providence sends to assist his servants. We are ourselves few, though determined—Those whose swords come to help the cutting down of the harvest, must be welcome—When their work is wrought, they will be converted or scattered.—Have you been at York Place, brother, with that unstable epicure ? We must have his last resolution, and that within an hour.'

Christian looked at Julian, as if his presence prevented him from returning an answer ; upon which Bridgenorth arose, and taking the young man by the arm, led him out of the apartment, into that in which they had left his father ; assuring him by the way, that determined and vigilant guards were placed in every different quarter by which escape could be effected, and that he would do well to persuade his father to remain a quiet prisoner for a few hours.

Julian returned him no answer, and Bridgenorth presently retired, leaving him alone with his father and Hudson. To their questions he could only briefly reply, that he feared they were trepanned, since they were in the house with at least two hundred fanatics, completely armed, and apparently prepared for some desperate enterprise. Their own want of arms precluded the possibility of open violence; and however unpleasant it might be to remain in such a condition, it seemed difficult, from the strength of the fastenings at doors and windows, to attempt any secret escape without instantaneous detection.

The valiant dwarf alone nursed hopes, with which he in vain endeavoured to inspire his companions in affliction. 'The fair one, whose eyes,' he said, 'were like the twin stars of Leda '—for the little man was a great admirer of lofty language—' had not invited him, the most devoted, and, it might be, not the least favoured of her servants, into this place as a harbour, in order that he might therein suffer shipwreck ; and he generously assured his friends, that in his safety they also should be safe.'

Sir Geoffrey, little cheered by this intimation, expressed his despair at not being able to get the length of Whitehall, where he trusted to find as many jolly Cavaliers as would help him to stifle the whole nest of wasps in their hive ; while Julian was of opinion that the best service he could now render Bridgenorth, would be timeously to disclose his plot, and, if possible, to send him at the same time warning to save his person.

But we must leave them to meditate over their plans at leisure; no one of which, as they all depended on their previous escape from confinement, seemed in any great chance of being executed.

CHAPTER XLIV

And some for safety took the dreadful leap ;
Some for the voice of Heaven seem'd calling on them ;
Some for advancement, or for lucre's sake—
I leap'd in frolic.
                                        The Dream.

AFTER a private conversation with Bridgenorth, Christian hastened to the Duke of Buckingham's hotel, taking at the same time such a route as to avoid meeting with any acquaintance. He was ushered into the apartment of the

duke, whom he found cracking and eating filberts, with
a flask of excellent white wine at his elbow. 'Christian,'
said his Grace, 'come help me to laugh—I have bit Sir
Charles Sedley—flung him for a thousand, by the gods!'

'I am glad at your luck, my lord duke,' replied Christian;
'but I am come here on serious business.'

'Serious?—why, I shall hardly be serious in my life
again—ha, ha, ha!—and for luck, it was no such thing—
sheer wit, and excellent contrivance; and but that I don't
care to affront Fortune, like the old Greek general, I might
tell her to her face—In this thou hadst no share. You have
heard, Ned Christian, that Mother Cresswell is dead?'

'Yes, I did hear that the devil hath got his due,' answered
Christian.

'Well,' said the duke, 'you are ungrateful; for I know
you have been obliged to her, as well as others. Before
George, a most benevolent and helpful old lady; and that
she might not sleep in an unblest grave, I betted—do you
mark me—with Sedley, that I would write her funeral
sermon; that it should be every word in praise of her life
and conversation, that it should be all true, and yet that the
diocesan should be unable to lay his thumb on Quodling,
my little chaplain, who should preach it.'

'I perfectly see the difficulty, my lord,' said Christian,
who well knew that if he wished to secure attention from
this volatile nobleman, he must first suffer, nay, encourage
him, to exhaust the topic, whatever it might be, that had
got temporary possession of his pineal gland.

'Why,' said the duke, 'I had caused my little Quodling
to go through his oration thus—"That whatever evil
reports had passed current during the lifetime of the worthy
matron whom they had restored to dust that day, malice
herself could not deny that she was born well, married well,
lived well, and died well; since she was born in Shadwell,
married to Cresswell, lived in Camberwell, and died in Bride-
well." Here ended the oration, and with it Sedley's ambitious
hopes of overreaching Buckingham—ha, ha, ha!—And now,
Master Christian, what are your commands for me to-day?'

'First, to thank your Grace for being so attentive as to
send so formidable a person as Colonel Blood, to wait upon
your poor friend and servant. Faith, he took such an

interest in my leaving town, that he wanted to compel me to do it at point of fox, so I was obliged to spill a little of his malapert blood. Your Grace's swordsmen have had ill luck of late ; and it is hard, since you always choose the best hands, and such scrupleless knaves too.'

' Come now, Christian,' said the duke, ' do not thus exult over me ; a great man, if I may so call myself, is never greater than amid miscarriage. I only played this little trick on you, Christian, to impress on you a wholesome idea of the interest I take in your motions. The scoundrel's having dared to draw upon you, is a thing not to be forgiven. What ! injure my old friend Christian ? '

' And why not,' said Christian coolly, ' if your old friend was so stubborn as not to go out of town, like a good boy, when your Grace required him to do so, for the civil purpose of entertaining his niece in his absence ? '

' How—what !—how do you mean by *my* entertaining your niece, Master Christian ? ' said the duke. ' She was a personage far beyond my poor attentions, being destined, if I recollect aright, to something like royal favour.'

' It was her fate, however, to be the guest of your Grace's convent for a brace of days, or so. Marry, my lord, the father confessor was not at home, and—for convents have been scaled of late—returned not till the bird was flown.'

' Christian, thou art an old reynard—I see there is no doubling with thee. It was thou, then, stole away my pretty prize, but left me something so much prettier in my mind, that, had it not made itself wings to fly away with, I would have placed it in a cage of gold. Never be downcast, man ; I forgive thee—I forgive thee.'

' Your Grace is of a most merciful disposition, especially considering it is I who have had the wrong ; and sages have said, that he who doth the injury, is less apt to forgive than he who only sustains it.'

' True, true, Christian,' said the duke, ' which, as you say, is something quite new, and places my clemency in a striking point of view. Well, then, thou forgiven man, when shall I see my Mauritanian princess again ? '

' Whenever I am certain that a quibble, and a carwhichit, for a play or a sermon, will not banish her from your Grace's memory.'

'Not all the wit of South, or of Etherege,' said Buckingham hastily, 'to say nothing of my own, shall in future
make me oblivious of what I owe the Morisco princess.'

'Yet, to leave the fair lady out of thought for a little
while—a very little while,' said Christian, 'since I swear
that in due time your Grace shall see her, and know in her
the most extraordinary woman that the age has produced—
to leave her, I say, out of sight for a little while, has your
Grace had late notice of your duchess's health ?'

'Health,' said the duke. 'Umph—no—nothing particular. She has been ill—but '——

'She is no longer so,' subjoined Christian ; 'she died in
Yorkshire forty-eight hours since.'

'Thou must deal with the devil,' said the duke.

'It would ill become one of my name to do so,' replied
Christian. 'But in the brief interval, since your Grace hath
known of an event which hath not yet reached the public
ear, you have, I believe, made proposals to the king for the
hand of the Lady Anne, second daughter of the Duke of
York, and your Grace's proposals have been rejected.'

'Fiends and firebrands, villain !' said the duke, starting
up and seizing Christian by the collar ; 'who hath told thee
that ?'

'Take your hand from my cloak, my lord duke, and
I may answer you,' said Christian. 'I have a scurvy touch
of old puritanical humour about me. I abide not the
imposition of hands—take off your grasp from my cloak, or
I will find means to make you unloose it.'

The duke, who had kept his right hand on his dagger-hilt
while he held Christian's collar with his left, unloosed it as
he spoke, but slowly, and as one who rather suspends than
abandons the execution of some hasty impulse ; while
Christian, adjusting his cloak with perfect composure, said,
'Soh—my cloak being at liberty, we speak on equal terms.
I come not to insult your Grace, but to offer you vengeance
for the insult you have received.'

'Vengeance !' said the duke—'It is the dearest proffer
man can present to me in my present mood. I hunger for
vengeance—thirst for vengeance—could die to ensure
vengeance !—'Sdeath !' he continued, walking up and
down the large apartment with the most unrestrained and

violent agitation ; ' I have chased this repulse out of my brain with ten thousand trifles, because I thought no one knew it. But it is known, and to thee, the very common-sewer of Court secrets—the honour of Villiers is in thy keeping, Ned Christian ! Speak, thou man of wiles and of intrigue—on whom dost thou promise the vengeance ? Speak ! and if thy answers meet my desires, I will make a bargain with thee as willingly as with thy master, Satan himself.'

' I will not be,' said Christian, ' so unreasonable in my terms as stories tell of the old apostate ; I will offer your Grace, as he might do, temporal prosperity and revenge, which is his frequent recruiting money, but I leave it to yourself to provide, as you may be pleased, for your future salvation.'

The duke, gazing upon him fixedly and sadly, replied, ' I would to God, Christian, that I could read what purpose of damnable villany thou hast to propose to me in thy countenance, without the necessity of thy using words ! '

' Your Grace can but try a guess,' said Christian, calmly smiling.

' No,' replied the duke, after gazing at him again for the space of a minute ; ' thou art so deeply dyed a hypocrite, that thy mean features, and clear grey eye, are as likely to conceal treason, as any petty scheme of theft or larceny more corresponding to your degree.'

' Treason, my lord ! ' echoed Christian ; ' you may have guessed more nearly than you were aware of. I honour your Grace's penetration.'

' Treason ! ' echoed the duke. ' Who dare name such a crime to me ? '

' If a name startles your Grace, you may call it vengeance —vengeance on the cabal of councillors who have ever countermined you, in spite of your wit and your interest with the king. Vengeance on Arlington, Ormond—on Charles himself.'

' No, by Heaven,' said the duke, resuming his disordered walk through the apartment—' Vengeance on these rats of the Privy Council,—come at it as you will. But the king !—never, never. I have provoked him a hundred times, where he has stirred me once. I have crossed his path in state intrigue—rivalled him in love—had the advantage in both,—and, d—n it, he has forgiven me ! If treason would put me in his throne, I have no apology for it—it were worse than bestial ingratitude.'

'Nobly spoken, my lord,' said Christian ; 'and consistent alike with the obligations under which your Grace lies to Charles Stuart, and the sense you have ever shown of them. But it signifies not. If your Grace patronize not our enterprise, there is Shaftesbury—there is Monmouth '——

'Scoundrel ! ' exclaimed the duke, even more vehemently agitated than before, 'think you that you shall carry on with others an enterprise which I have refused ?—No, by every heathen and every Christian God !—Hark ye, Christian, I will arrest you on the spot—I will, by gods and devils, and carry you to unravel your plot at Whitehall.'

'Where the first words I speak,' answered the imperturbable Christian, ' will be to inform the Privy Council in what place they may find certain letters, wherewith your Grace has honoured your poor vassal, containing, as I think, particulars which his Majesty will read with more surprise than pleasure.'

''Sdeath, villain ! ' said the duke, once more laying his hand on his poniard-hilt, 'thou hast me again at advantage. I know not why I forbear to poniard you where you stand ! '

' I might fall, my lord duke,' said Christian, slightly colouring, and putting his right hand into his bosom, ' though not, I think, unavenged—for I have not put my person into this peril altogether without means of defence. I might fall, but, alas ! your Grace's correspondence is in hands which, by that very act, would be rendered sufficiently active in handing them to the king and the Privy Council. What say you to the Moorish princess, my lord duke ? What if I have left her executrix of my will, with certain instructions how to proceed if I return not unharmed from York Place ? Oh, my lord, though my head is in the wolf's mouth, I was not goose enough to place it there without settling how many carbines should be fired on the wolf, so soon as my dying cackle was heard. Pshaw, my lord duke, you deal with a man of sense and courage, yet you speak to him as a child and a coward.'

The duke threw himself into a chair, fixed his eyes on the

ground, and spoke without raising them. 'I am about to call Jerningham,' he said ; 'but fear nothing—it is only for a draught of wine—That stuff on the table may be a vehicle for filberts and walnuts, but not for such communications as yours. Bring me champagne,' he said to the attendant who answered on his summons.

The domestic returned, and brought a flask of champagne, with two large silver cups. One of them he filled for Buckingham, who, contrary to the usual etiquette, was always served first at home, and then offered the other to Christian, who declined to receive it.

The duke drank off the large goblet which was presented to him, and, for a moment, covered his forehead with the palm of his hand ; then instantly withdrew it, and said, ' Christian, speak your errand plainly. We know each other. If my reputation be in some degree in your hands, you are well aware that your life is in mine. Sit down,' he said, taking a pistol from his bosom and laying it on the table— ' Sit down, and let me hear your proposal.'

' My lord,' said Christian, smiling, ' I shall produce no such ultimate argument on my part, though possibly, in time of need, I may not be found destitute of them. But my defence is in the situation of things, and in the composed view which, doubtless, your Majesty will take of them.'

' Majesty ! ' repeated the duke —' My good friend Christian, you have kept company with the Puritans so long, that you confuse the ordinary titles of the Court.'

' I know not how to apologize,' said Christian, ' unless your Grace will suppose that I spoke by prophecy.'

' Such as the devil delivered to Macbeth,' said the duke— again paced the chamber, and again seated himself, and said, ' Be plain, Christian—speak out at once, and manfully, what is it you intend ? '

' I,' said Christian—' What should I do ? I can do nothing in such a matter ; but I thought it right that your Grace should know that the godly of this city ' (he spoke the word with a kind of ironical grin)—' are impatient of inactivity, and must needs be up and doing. My brother Bridgenorth is at the head of all old Weiver's congregation ; for you must know, that, after floundering from one faith to another, he hath now got beyond ordinances, and is become a Fifth Monarchy man. He has nigh two hundred of Weiver's people, fully equipped, and ready to fall on; and, with slight aid from your Grace's people, they must carry Whitehall, and make prisoners of all within it.'

' Rascal ! ' said the duke, ' and is it to a peer of England you make this communication ? '

' Nay,' answered Christian, ' I admit it would be extreme folly in your Grace to appear until all is over. But let me give Blood and the others a hint on your part. There are the four Germans also—right Knipperdolings and Ana-baptists—will be specially useful. You are wise, my lord, and know the value of a corps of domestic gladiators, as well as did Octavius, Lepidus, and Antony, when, by such family forces they divided the world by indenture tripartite.'

' Stay, stay,' said the duke. ' Even if these bloodhounds were to join with you—not that I would permit it without the most positive assurances for the king's personal safety— but say the villains were to join, what hope have you of carrying the court ? '

' Bully Tom Armstrong,[1] my lord, hath promised his interest with the Life Guards. Then there are my Lord Shaftesbury's brisk boys in the city—thirty thousand on the holding up a finger.'

' Let him hold up both hands, and if he count a hundred for each finger,' said the duke, ' it will be more than I expect. You have not spoken to him ? '

' Surely not till your Grace's pleasure was known. But, if he is not applied to, there is the Dutch train, Hans Snore-hout's congregation, in the Strand—there are the French Protestants in Piccadilly—there are the family of Levi in Lewkenor's Lane—the Muggletonians in Thames Street'——

' Ah, faugh ! Out upon them—out upon them ! How the knaves will stink of cheese and tobacco when they come upon action !—they will drown all the perfumes in White-hall. Spare me the detail ; and let me know, my dearest Ned, the sum total of thy most odoriferous forces.'

---

[1] Thomas, or Sir Thomas Armstrong, a person who had distinguished himself in youth by duels and drunken exploits. He was particularly connected with the Duke of Monmouth, and was said to be concerned in the Rye House Plot, for which he suffered capital punishment, June 20, 1684.

'Fifteen hundred men, well armed,' said Christian, ' besides the rabble that will rise to a certainty—they have already nearly torn to pieces the prisoners who were this day acquitted on account of the Plot.'

'All, then, I understand. And now, hark ye, most Christian Christian,' said he, wheeling his chair full in front of that on which his agent was seated, ' you have told me many things to-day—Shall I be equally communicative ? Shall I show you that my accuracy of information matches yours ? Shall I tell you, in a word, why you have at once resolved to push every one, from the Puritan to the free-thinker, upon a general attack of the Palace at Whitehall, without allowing me, a peer of the realm, time either to pause upon or to prepare for a step so desperate ? Shall I tell you why you would lead or drive, seduce or compel me, into countenancing your measures ? '

'My lord, if you please to form a guess,' said Christian, ' I will answer with all sincerity, if you have assigned the right cause.'

' The Countess of Derby is this day arrived, and attends the Court this evening, with hopes of the kindest reception. She may be surprised amid the *mêlée* ? Ha ! said I not right, Master Christian ? You, who pretend to offer me revenge, know yourself its exquisite sweetness.'

' I would not presume,' said Christian, half smiling, ' to offer your Grace a dish without acting as your taster as well as purveyor.'

' That 's honestly said,' said the duke. ' Away then, my friend. Give Blood this ring—he knows it, and knows how to obey him who bears it. Let him assemble my gladiators, as thou dost most wittily term my *coup jarrets*. The old scheme of the German music may be resorted to, for I think thou hast the instruments ready. But take notice, I know nothing on't ; and Rowley's person must be safe—I will hang and burn on all hands if a hair of his black periwig [1] be but singed. Then what is to follow—a Lord Protector

---

[1] Charles, to suit his dark complexion, always wore a black peruke. He used to say of the players, that if they wished to represent a villain on the stage, ' Odd's-fish, they always clapp'd on him a black periwig, whereas the greatest rogue in England [meaning, probably, Doctor Oates] wears a white one.'—*See* CIBBER'S *Apology*.

of the realm—or stay—Cromwell has made the word somewhat slovenly and unpopular—a Lord Lieutenant of the
Kingdom ?—The patriots, who take it on themselves to
avenge the injustice done to the country, and to remove
evil counsellors from before the king's throne, that it may be
henceforward established in righteousness—so I think the
rubric runs—cannot fail to make a fitting choice.'

'They cannot, my lord duke,' said Christian, 'since
there is but one man in the three kingdoms on whom that
choice can possibly fall.'

'I thank you, Christian,' said his Grace ; 'and I trust
you. Away, and make all ready. Be assured your services
shall not be forgot. We will have you near to us.'

'My lord duke,' said Christian, 'you bind me doubly
to you. But remember, that as your Grace is spared any
obnoxious proceedings which may befall in the way of
military execution, or otherwise, so it will be advisable that
you hold yourself in preparation, upon a moment's notice,
to put yourself at the head of a band of honourable friends
and allies, and come presently to the palace, where you will
be received by the victors as a commander, and by the
vanquished as a preserver.'

'I conceive you—I conceive you. I will be in prompt
readiness,' said the duke.

'Aye, my lord,' continued Christian ; 'and, for Heaven's
sake, let none of those toys, which are the very Delilahs of
your imagination, come across your Grace this evening, and
interfere with the execution of this sublime scheme.'

'Why, Christian, dost think me mad ? ' was his Grace's
emphatic reply. 'It is you who linger, when all should be
ordered for a deed so daring. Go then. But hark ye, Ned ;
ere you go, tell me when I shall again see yonder thing of
fire and air—yon Eastern Peri, that glides into apartments
by the keyhole, and leaves them through the casement—
yon black-eyed houri of the Mahometan paradise—when,
I say, shall I see her once more ? '

'When your Grace has the truncheon of Lord Lieutenant
of the Kingdom,' said Christian, and left the apartment.

Buckingham stood fixed in contemplation for a moment
after he was gone. 'Should I have done this ? ' he said,
arguing the matter with himself ; 'or had I the choice,

rather, of doing aught else ? Should I not hasten to the Court, and make Charles aware of the treason which besets him ? I will, by Heaven ! Here, Jerningham, my coach, with the dispatch of light ! I will throw myself at his feet, and tell him of all the follies which I have dreamed of with this Christian. And then he will laugh at me, and spurn me. No, I have kneeled to him to-day already, and my repulse was nothing gentle. To be spurned once in the sun's daily round is enough for Buckingham.'

Having made this reflection, he seated himself, and began hastily to mark down the young nobles and gentlemen of quality, and others, their very ignoble companions, who he supposed might be likely to assume him for their leader in any popular disturbance. He had nearly completed it, when Jerningham entered, to say the coach would be ready in an instant, and to bring his master's sword, hat, and cloak.

' Let the coachman draw off,' said the duke, ' but be in readiness. And send to the gentlemen thou wilt find named in this list ; say I am but ill at ease, and wish their company to a slight collation. Let instant expedition be made, and care not for expense ; you will find most of them at the Club House in Fuller's Rents.' [1]

The preparations for festivity were speedily made, and the intended guests, most of them persons who were at leisure for any call that promised pleasure, though sometimes more deaf to those of duty, began speedily to assemble. There were many youths of the highest rank, and with them, as is usual in those circles, many of a different class, whom talents, or impudence, or wit, or a turn for gambling, had reared up into companions for the great and the gay. The Duke of Buckingham was a general patron of persons of this description ; and a numerous attendance took place on the present occasion

---

[1] The place of meeting of the Green Ribbon Club. ' Their place of meeting,' says Roger North, ' was in a sort of Carrefour at Chancery Lane, in a centre of business and company most proper for such anglers of fools. The house was double balconied in front, as may yet be seen, for the clubbers to issue forth *in fresco*, with hats and no perukes, pipes in their mouths, merry faces, and dilated throats for vocal encouragement of the canaglia below on usual and unusual occasions.'

The festivity was pursued with the usual appliances of
wine, music, and games of hazard ; with which, however,
there mingled in that period much more wit, and a good
deal more gross profligacy of conversation, than the talents
of the present generation can supply, or their taste would
permit.

The duke himself proved the complete command which
he possessed over his versatile character, by maintaining
the frolic, the laugh, and the jest, while his ear caught up,
and with eagerness, the most distant sounds, as intimating
the commencement of Christian's revolutionary project.
Such sounds were heard from time to time, and from time
to time they died away, without any of those consequences
which Buckingham expected.

At length, and when it was late in the evening, Jerningham
announced Master Chiffinch from the Court ; and that
worthy personage followed the annunciation.

' Strange things have happened, my lord duke,' he said ;
' your presence at Court is instantly required by his Majesty.'

' You alarm me,' said Buckingham, standing up.   ' I hope
nothing has happened—I hope there is nothing wrong—
I hope his Majesty is well ? '

' Perfectly well,' said Chiffinch ;   ' and desirous to see
your Grace without a moment's delay.'

' This is sudden,' said the duke.   ' You see I have had
merry fellows about me, and am scarce in case to appear,
Chiffinch.'

' Your Grace seems to be in very handsome plight,' said
Chiffinch ;   ' and you know his Majesty is gracious enough
to make allowances.'

' True,' said the duke, not a little anxious in his mind
touching the cause of this unexpected summons—' True—
his Majesty is most gracious—I will order my coach.'

' Mine is below,' replied the royal messenger ;   ' it will
save time, if your Grace will condescend to use it.'

Forced from every evasion, Buckingham took a goblet
from the table, and requested his friends to remain at his
palace so long as they could find the means of amusement
there.   He expected, he said, to return almost immediately ;
if not, he would take farewell of them with his usual
toast, ' May all of us that are not hanged in the interval,

meet together again here on the first Monday of next month.'

This standing toast of the duke bore reference to the character of several of his guests ; but he did not drink it on the present occasion without some anticipation concerning his own fate, in case Christian had betrayed him. He hastily made some addition to his dress, and attended Chiffinch in the chariot to Whitehall.

CHAPTER XLV

High feasting was there there—the gilded roofs
Rung to the wassail-health—the dancer's step
Sprung to the chord responsive—the gay gamester
To fate's disposal flung his heap of gold,
And laugh'd alike when it increased or lessen'd :
Such virtue hath court-air to teach us patience
Which schoolmen preach in vain.
    Why come ye not to Court ?

UPON the afternoon of this eventful day, Charles held his Court in the queen's apartments, which were opened at a particular hour to invited guests of a certain lower degree, but accessible without restriction to the higher classes of nobility who had from birth, and to the courtiers who held by office, the privilege of the entrée.

It was one part of Charles's character, which unquestionably rendered him personally popular, and postponed to a subsequent reign the precipitation of his family from the throne, that he banished from his Court many of the formal restrictions with which it was in other reigns surrounded. He was conscious of the good-natured grace of his manners, and trusted to it, often not in vain, to remove evil impressions arising from actions which he was sensible could not be justified on the grounds of liberal or national policy.

In the daytime the king was commonly seen in the public walks alone, or only attended by one or two persons ; and his answer to the remonstrance of his brother, on the risk of thus exposing his person, is well known,—' Believe me, James,' he said, ' no one will murder *me*, to make *you* king.'

In the same manner, Charles's evenings, unless such as were destined to more secret pleasures, were frequently spent amongst all who had any pretence to approach a courtly circle ; and thus it was upon the night which we are treating of. Queen Catherine, reconciled or humbled to her fate, had long ceased to express any feelings of jealousy, nay, seemed so absolutely dead to such a passion, that she received at her drawing-room, without scruple, and even with encouragement, the Duchesses of Portsmouth and Cleveland, and others, who enjoyed, though in a less avowed character, the credit of having been royal favourites. Constraint of every kind was banished from a circle so composed, and which was frequented at the same time, if not by the wisest, at least by the wittiest courtiers, who ever assembled round a monarch, and who, as many of them had shared the wants, and shifts, and frolics of his exile, had then acquired a sort of prescriptive licence, which the good-natured prince, when he attained his period of prosperity, could hardly have restrained had it suited his temper to do so. This, however, was the least of Charles's thoughts. His manners were such as secured him from indelicate obtrusion ; and he sought no other protection from over-familiarity than what these and his ready wit afforded him.

On the present occasion, he was peculiarly disposed to enjoy the scene of pleasure which had been prepared. The singular death of Major Coleby, which, taking place in his own presence, had proclaimed, with the voice of a passing bell, the ungrateful neglect of the prince for whom he had sacrificed everything, had given Charles much pain. But, in his own opinion at least, he had completely atoned for this negligence by the trouble which he had taken for Sir Geoffrey Peveril and his son, whose liberation he looked upon not only as an excellent good deed in itself, but, in spite of the grave rebuke of Ormond, as achieved in a very pardonable manner; considering the difficulties with which he was surrounded. He even felt a degree of satisfaction on receiving intelligence from the city that there had been disturbances in the streets, and that some of the more violent fanatics had betaken themselves to their meeting-houses, upon sudden summons, to inquire, as their preachers phrased it, into the causes of Heaven's wrath, and into the backsliding of the Court, lawyers, and jury, by whom the false and bloody favourers of the Popish Plot were screened and cloaked from deserved punishment.

The king, we repeat, seemed to hear these accounts with pleasure, even when he was reminded of the dangerous and susceptible character of those with whom such suspicions originated. ' Will any one now assert,' he said, with self-complacence, ' that I am so utterly negligent of the interest of friends ? You see the peril in which I place myself, and even the risk to which I have exposed the public peace, to rescue a man whom I have scarce seen for twenty years, and then only in his buff-coat and bandoleers, with other Train-Band officers who kissed hands upon the Restoration. They say kings have long hands—I think they have as much occasion for long memories, since they are expected to watch over and reward every man in England, who hath but shown his goodwill by crying " God save the king ! " '

' Nay, the rogues are even more unreasonable still,' said Sedley ; ' for every knave of them thinks himself entitled to your Majesty's protection in a good cause, whether he has cried " God save the king " or no.'

The king smiled, and turned to another part of the stately hall, where everything was assembled which could, according to the taste of the age, make the time glide pleasantly away.

In one place, a group of the young nobility, and of the ladies of the Court, listened to the reader's acquaintance Empson, who was accompanying with his unrivalled breathings on the flute, a young siren, who, while her bosom palpitated with pride and with fear, warbled to the courtly and august presence the beautiful air beginning,

> Young I am, and yet unskill'd,
> How to make a lover yield, &c.

She performed her task in a manner so corresponding with the strains of the amatory poet, and the voluptuous air with which the words had been invested by the celebrated Purcell, that the men crowded around in ecstasies, while most of the ladies thought it proper either to look extremely indifferent to the words she sung, or to withdraw from the circle as quietly as possible. To the song succeeded a concerto, performed by a select band of most admirable musicians, which the king, whose taste was indisputable, had himself selected.

At other tables in the apartment, the elder courtiers worshipped Fortune, at the various fashionable games of ombre, quadrille, hazard, and the like ; while heaps of gold which lay before the players, augmented or dwindled with every turn of a card or cast of a die. Many a year's rent of fair estates was ventured upon the main or the odds ; which, spent in the old deserted manor-house, had repaired the ravages of Cromwell upon its walls, and replaced the sources of good housekeeping and hospitality, that, exhausted in the last age by fine and sequestration, were now in a fair way of being annihilated by careless prodigality. Elsewhere, under cover of observing the gamester, or listening to the music, the gallantries of that all licensed age were practised among the gay and fair, closely watched the whilst by the ugly or the old, who promised themselves at least the pleasure of observing, and it may be that of proclaiming, intrigues in which they could not be sharers.

From one table to another glided the Merry Monarch, exchanging now a glance with a Court beauty, now a jest with a Court wit, now beating time to the music, and anon losing or winning a few pieces of gold on the chance of the game to which he stood nearest ;—the most amiable of voluptuaries—the gayest and best-natured of companions— the man that would, of all others, have best sustained his character, had life been a continued banquet, and its only end to enjoy the passing hour, and send it away as pleasantly as might be.

But kings are least of all exempted from the ordinary lot of humanity ; and Seged of Ethiopia is, amongst monarchs, no solitary example of the vanity of reckoning on a day or an hour of undisturbed serenity. An attendant on the Court announced suddenly to their Majesties that a lady, who would only announce herself as a peeress of England, desired to be admitted into the presence.

The queen said, hastily, it was *impossible*. No peeress, without announcing her title, was entitled to the privilege of her rank.

' I could be sworn,' said a nobleman in attendance, ' that it is some whim of the Duchess of Newcastle.'

The attendant who brought the message, said that he did indeed believe it to be the Duchess, both from the singularity of the message, and that the lady spoke with somewhat a foreign accent.

'In the name of madness, then,' said the king, 'let us admit her. Her Grace is an entire raree-show in her own person—a universal masquerade—indeed a sort of private Bedlam-hospital, her whole ideas being like so many patients crazed upon the subjects of love and literature, who act nothing in their vagaries, save Minerva, Venus, and the nine Muses.'

'Your Majesty's pleasure must always supersede mine,' said the queen. 'I only hope I shall not be expected to entertain so fantastic a personage. The last time she came to Court, Isabella' (she spoke to one of her Portuguese ladies of honour)—'you had not returned from our lovely Lisbon!—her Grace had the assurance to assume a right to bring a train-bearer into my apartment ; and when this was not allowed, what then, think you, she did ?—even caused her train to be made so long, that three mortal yards of satin and silver remained in the antechamber, supported by four wenches, while the other end was attached to her Grace's person, as she paid her duty at the upper end of the p esence-room. Full thirty yards of the most beautiful silk did her Grace's madness employ in this manner.'

And most beautiful damsels they were who bore this portentous train,' said the king—'a train never equalled save by that of the great comet in sixty-six. Sedley and Etherege told us wonders of them ; for it is one advantage of this new fashion brought up by the duchess, that a matron may be totally unconscious of the coquetry of her train and its attendants.'

'Am I to understand, then, your Majesty's pleasure is, that the lady is to be admitted ? ' said the usher.

'Certainly,' said the king ; 'that is, if the incognita be really entitled to the honour. It may be as well to inquire her title—there are more mad women abroad than the Duchess of Newcastle. I will walk into the anteroom myself, and receive your answer.'

But ere Charles had reached the lower end of the apartment in his progress to the anteroom, the usher surprised the assembly by announcing a name which had not for many a year been heard in these courtly halls—' the Countess of Derby ! '

Stately and tall, and still, at an advanced period of life, having a person unbroken by years, the noble lady advanced towards her sovereign, with a step resembling that with which she might have met an equal. There was indeed nothing in her manner that indicated either haughtiness or assumption unbecoming that presence ; but her conscious-ness of wrongs, sustained from the administration of Charles, and of the superiority of the injured party over those from whom, or in whose name, the injury had been offered, gave her look dignity, and her step firmness. She was dressed in widow's weeds, of the same fashion which were worn at the time her husband was brought to the scaffold ; and which, in the thirty years subsequent to that event, she had never permitted her tire-woman to alter

The surprise was no pleasing one to the king ; and cursing in his heart the rashness which had allowed the lady entrance on the gay scene in which they were engaged, he saw at the same time the necessity of receiving her in a manner suitable to his own character, and her rank in the British Court. He approached her with an air of welcome, into which he threw all his natural grace, while he began, ' *Chère Comtesse de Derby, puissante Reine de Man, notre très auguste sœur* '——

' Speak English, sire, if I may presume to ask such a favour,' said the countess. ' I am a peeress of this nation— mother to one English earl, and widow, alas, to another ! In England I have spent my brief days of happiness, my long years of widowhood and sorrow. France and its language are but to me the dreams of an uninteresting childhood. I know no tongue save that of my husband and my son. Permit me, as the widow and mother of Derby, thus to render my homage.'

She would have kneeled, but the king gracefully prevented her, and, saluting her cheek, according to the form, led her towards the queen, and himself performed the ceremony of introduction. ' Your Majesty,' he said, ' must be informed that the countess has imposed a restriction on French— the language of gallantry and compliment. I trust your

Majesty will, though a foreigner, like herself, find enough of honest English to assure the Countess of Derby with what pleasure we see her at Court, after the absence of so many years.'

'I will endeavour to do so, at least,' said the queen, on whom the appearance of the Countess of Derby made a more favourable impression than that of many strangers, whom, at the king's request, she was in the habit of receiving with courtesy.

Charles himself again spoke. 'To any other lady of the same rank I might put the question, why she was so long absent from the circle? I fear I can only ask the Countess of Derby, what fortunate cause produces the pleasure of seeing her here?'

'No fortunate cause, my liege, though one most strong and urgent.'

The king augured nothing agreeable from this commencement; and in truth, from the countess's first entrance, he had anticipated some unpleasant explanation, which he therefore hastened to parry, having first composed his features into an expression of sympathy and interest.

'If,' said he, 'the cause is of a nature in which we can render assistance, we cannot expect your ladyship should enter upon it at the present time; but a memorial addressed to our secretary, or, if it is more satisfactory, to ourselves directly, will receive our immediate, and I trust I need not add, our favourable construction.'

The countess bowed with some state, and answered, 'My business, sire, is indeed important; but so brief, that it need not for more than a few minutes withdraw your ear from what is more pleasing; yet it is so urgent, that I am afraid to postpone it even for a moment.'

'This is unusual,' said Charles. 'But you, Countess of Derby, are an unwonted guest, and must command my time. Does the matter require my private ear?'

'For my part,' said the countess, 'the whole Court might listen; but your Majesty may prefer hearing me in the presence of one or two of your counsellors.'

'Ormond,' said the king, looking around, 'attend us for an instant,—and do you, Arlington, do the same.'

The king led the way into an adjoining cabinet, and,

seating himself, requested the countess would also take a chair. 'It needs not, sire,' she replied ; then pausing for a moment, as if to collect her spirits, she proceeded with firmness.

'Your Majesty well said that no light cause had drawn me from my lonely habitation. I came not hither when the property of my son—that property which descended to him from a father who died for your Majesty's rights—was conjured away from him under pretext of justice, that it might first feed the avarice of the rebel Fairfax, and then supply the prodigality of his son-in-law, Buckingham.'

'These are over-harsh terms, lady,' said the king. 'A legal penalty was, as we remember, incurred by an act of irregular violence—so our courts and our laws term it, though personally I have no objection to call it, with you, an honourable revenge. But admit it were such, in prosecution of the laws of honour, bitter legal consequences are often necessarily incurred.'

'I come not to argue for my son's wasted and forfeited inheritance, sire,' said the countess ; 'I only take credit for my patience, under that afflicting dispensation. I now come to redeem the honour of the House of Derby, more dear to me than all the treasures and lands which ever belonged to it.'

'And by whom is the honour of the House of Derby impeached ?' said the king ; 'for on my word you bring me the first news of it.'

'Has there one Narrative, as these wild fictions are termed, been printed with regard to the Popish Plot—this pretended Plot as I will call it—in which the honour of our house has not been touched and tainted ? And are there not two noble gentlemen, father and son, allies of the House of Stanley, about to be placed in jeopardy of their lives, on account of matters in which we are the parties first impeached ?'

The king looked around, and smiled to Arlington and Ormond. 'The countess's courage, methinks, shames ours. What lips dared have called the immaculate Plot *pretended*, or the Narrative of the witnesses, our preservers from Popish knives, a wild fiction ? But, madam,' he said, 'though I admire the generosity of your interference in

behalf of the two Peverils, I must acquaint you, that
your interference is unnecessary—they are this morning
acquitted.'

'Now may God be praised!' said the countess, folding
her hands. 'I have scarce slept since I heard the news of
their impeachment; and have arrived here to surrender
myself to your Majesty's justice, or to the prejudices of the
nation, in hopes, by so doing, I might at least save the lives
of my noble and generous friends, enveloped in suspicion
only, or chiefly, by their connexion with us. Are they
indeed acquitted?'

'They are, by my honour,' said the king. 'I marvel
you heard it not.'

'I arrived but last night, and remained in the strictest
seclusion,' said the countess, 'afraid to make any inquiries that might occasion discovery ere I saw your
Majesty.'

'And now that we *have* met,' said the king, taking her
hand kindly—'a meeting which gives me the greatest
pleasure—may I recommend to you speedily to return to
your royal island with as little éclat as you came hither?
The world, my dear countess, has changed since we were
young. Men fought in the Civil War with good swords and
muskets; but now we fight with indictments and oaths,
and such-like legal weapons. You are no adept in such
warfare; and though I am well aware you know how to
hold out a castle, I doubt much if you have the art to parry
off an impeachment. This Plot has come upon us like a land
storm—there is no steering the vessel in the teeth of the
tempest—we must run for the nearest haven, and happy
if we can reach one.'

'This is cowardice, my liege,' said the countess. 'Forgive the word! it is but a woman who speaks it. Call your
noble friends around you, and make a stand like your
royal father. There is but one right and one wrong—one
honourable and forward course; and all others which
deviate are oblique and unworthy.'

'Your language, my venerated friend,' said Ormond—
who saw the necessity of interfering betwixt the dignity of
the actual sovereign and the freedom of the countess, who
was generally accustomed to receive, not to pay observance

—' your language is strong and decided, but it applies not to the times. It might occasion a renewal of the Civil War, and of all its miseries, but could hardly be attended with the effects you sanguinely anticipate.'

'You are too rash, my lady countess,' said Arlington, 'not only to rush upon this danger yourself, but to desire to involve his Majesty. Let me say plainly, that, in this jealous time, you have done but ill to exchange the security of Castle Rushin for the chance of a lodging in the Tower of London.'

'And were I to kiss the block there,' said the countess, 'as did my husband at Bolton-on-the-Moors, I would do so willingly, rather than forsake a friend !—and one, too, whom, as in the case of the younger Peveril, I have thrust upon danger.'

'But have I not assured you that both of the Peverils, elder and younger, are freed from peril ? ' said the king ; 'and, my dear countess, what can else tempt you to thrust *yourself* on danger, from which, doubtless, you expect to be relieved by my intervention ? Methinks a lady of your judgement should not voluntarily throw herself into a river, merely that her friends might have the risk and merit of dragging her out.'

The countess reiterated her intention to claim a fair trial. The two counsellors again pressed their advice that she should withdraw, though under the charge of absconding from justice, and remain in her own feudal kingdom.

The king, seeing no termination to the debate, gently reminded the countess that her Majesty would be jealous if he detained her ladyship longer, and offered her his hand to conduct her back to the company. This she was under the necessity of accepting, and returned accordingly to the apartments of state, where an event occurred immediately afterwards, which must be transferred to the next chapter.

CHAPTER XLVI

Here stand I tight and trim,
Quick of eye, though little of limb ;
He who denieth the word I have spoken,
Betwixt him and me shall lances be broken.
          Lay of the Little John De Saintré.

WHEN Charles had re-conducted the Countess of Derby into the presence-chamber, before he parted with her, he entreated her, in a whisper, to be governed by good counsel, and to regard her own safety ; and then turned easily from her, as if to distribute his attentions equally among the other guests.

These were a good deal circumscribed at the instant, by the arrival of a party of five or six musicians ; one of whom, a German, under the patronage of the Duke of Buckingham, was particularly renowned for his performance on the violoncello, but had been detained in inactivity in the antechamber by the non-arrival of his instrument, which had now at length made its appearance.

The domestic who placed it before the owner, shrouded as it was within its wooden case, seemed heartily glad to be rid of his load, and lingered for a moment, as if interested in discovering what sort of instrument was to be produced that could weigh so heavily. His curiosity was satisfied, and in a most extraordinary manner ; for, while the musician was fumbling with the key, the case being for his greater convenience placed upright against the wall, the case and instrument itself at once flew open, and out started the dwarf, Geoffrey Hudson,—at sight of whose unearthly appearance, thus suddenly introduced, the ladies shrieked and ran backwards ; the gentlemen started, and the poor German, on seeing the portentous delivery of his fiddle-case, tumbled on the floor in an agony, supposing, it might be, that his instrument was metamorphosed into the strange figure which supplied its place. So soon, however, as he recovered, he glided out of the apartment, and was followed by most of his companions.

'Hudson !' said the king—'My little old friend, I am

not sorry to see you ; though Buckingham, who I suppose
is the purveyor of this jest, hath served us up but a stale
one.'

'Will your Majesty honour me with one moment's
attention ? ' said Hudson.

'Assuredly, my good friend,' said the king. 'Old
acquaintances are springing up in every quarter to-night ;
and our leisure can hardly be better employed than in
listening to them.   It was an idle trick of Buckingham,'
he added, in a whisper to Ormond, ' to send the poor thing
hither, especially as he was to-day tried for the affair of
the Plot.   At any rate he comes not to ask protection
from us, having had the rare fortune to come off *Plot-free.*
He is but fishing, I suppose, for some little present or
pension.'

The little man, precise in Court etiquette, yet impatient
of the king's delaying to attend to him, stood in the midst
of the floor, most valorously pawing and prancing, like
a Scots pony assuming the airs of a war-horse, waving
meanwhile his little hat with the tarnished feather, and
bowing from time to time, as if impatient to be heard.

'Speak on, then, my friend,' said Charles ; ' if thou hast
some poetical address penned for thee, out with it, that
thou mayst have time to repose these flourishing little
limbs of thine.'

'No poetical speech have I, most mighty sovereign,'
answered the dwarf ; ' but, in plain and most loyal prose,
I do accuse, before this company, the once noble Duke of
Buckingham of high treason ! '

'Well spoken, and manfully—Get on, man,' said the
king, who never doubted that this was the introduction to
something burlesque or witty, not conceiving that the charge
was made in solemn earnest.

A great laugh took place among such courtiers as heard,
and among many who did not hear what was uttered by
the dwarf ;   the former entertained by the extravagant
emphasis and gesticulation of the little champion, and the
others laughing not the less loud that they laughed for
example's sake, and upon trust.

'What matter is there for all this mirth ? ' said he, very
indignantly.   ' Is it fit subject for laughing, that I, Geoffrey

Hudson, knight, do, before king and nobles, impeach George Villiers, Duke of Buckingham, of high treason ? '

'No subject of mirth, certainly,' said Charles, composing his features ; 'but great matter of wonder. Come, cease this mouthing, and prancing, and mummery. If there be a jest, come out with it, man ; and if not, even get thee to the beauffet, and drink a cup of wine to refresh thee after thy close lodging.'

'I tell you, my liege,' said Hudson impatiently, yet in a whisper, intended only to be audible by the king, 'that if you spend over much time in trifling, you will be convinced by dire experience of Buckingham's treason. I tell you,—I asseverate to your Majesty,—two hundred armed fanatics will be here within the hour, to surprise the guards.'

'Stand back, ladies,' said the king, 'or you may hear more than you will care to listen to. My Lord of Buckingham's jests are not always, you know, quite fitted for female ears ; besides, we want a few words in private with our little friend. You, my Lord of Ormond—you, Arlington ' (and he named one or two others), 'may remain with us.'

The gay crowd bore back, and dispersed through the apartment—the men to conjecture what the end of this mummery, as they supposed it, was likely to prove ; and what jest, as Sedley said, the bass-fiddle had been brought to bed of—and the ladies to admire and criticize the antique dress, and richly embroidered ruff and hood of the Countess of Derby, to whom the queen was showing particular attention.

'And now, in the name of Heaven, and amongst friends,' said the king to the dwarf, 'what means all this ? '

'Treason, my lord the king ! Treason to his Majesty of England ! When I was chambered in yonder instrument, my lord, the High-Dutch fellows who bore me, carried me into a certain chapel, to see, as they said to each other, that all was ready. Sire, I went where bass-fiddle never went before, even into a conventicle of Fifth Monarchists ; and when they brought me away, the preacher was concluding his sermon, and was within a " Now to apply " of setting off like the bell-wether at the head of his flock, to surprise your Majesty in your royal Court ! I heard him through the sound-holes of my instrument, when the fellow set me down for a moment to profit by this precious doctrine.'

'It would be singular,' said Lord Arlington, 'were there some reality at the bottom of this buffoonery ; for we know these wild men have been consulting together to-day, and five conventicles have held a solemn fast.'

'Nay,' said the king, 'if that be the case, they are certainly determined on some villany.'

'Might I advise,' said the Duke of Ormond, 'I would summon the Duke of Buckingham to this presence. His connexions with the fanatics are well known, though he affects to conceal them.'

'You would not, my lord, do his Grace the injustice to treat him as a criminal on such a charge as this ?' said the king. 'However,' he added, after a moment's consideration, 'Buckingham is accessible to every sort of temptation, from the flightiness of his genius. I should not be surprised if he nourished hopes of an aspiring kind—I think we had some proof of it but lately.—Hark ye, Chiffinch ; go to him instantly, and bring him here on any fair pretext thou canst devise. I would fain save him from what lawyers call an overt act. The Court would be dull as a dead horse, were Buckingham to miscarry.'

'Will not your Majesty order the Horse Guards to turn out ?' said young Selby, who was present, and an officer.

'No, Selby,' said the king, 'I like not horse-play. But let them be prepared ; and let the High Bailiff collect his civil officers, and command the Sheriffs to summon their worshipful attendants from javelin-men to hangmen,[n] and have them in readiness, in case of any sudden tumult— double the sentinels on the doors of the palace—and see no strangers get in.'

'Or *out*,' said the Duke of Ormond. 'Where are the foreign fellows who brought in the dwarf ?'

They were sought for, but they were not to be found. They had retreated, leaving their instruments—a circumstance which seemed to bear hard on the Duke of Buckingham, their patron.

Hasty preparations were made to provide resistance to any effort of despair which the supposed conspirators might be driven to ; and in the meanwhile, the king, withdrawing

with Arlington, Ormond, and a few other counsellors, into
the cabinet where the Countess of Derby had had her
audience, resumed the examination of the little discoverer.
His declaration, though singular, was quite coherent ; the
strain of romance intermingled with it, being in fact a part
of his character, which often gained him the fate of being
laughed at, when he would otherwise have been pitied, or
even esteemed.

He commenced with a flourish about his sufferings for
the Plot, which the impatience of Ormond would have cut
short, had not the king reminded his Grace, that a top,
when it is not flogged, must needs go down of itself at the
end of a definite time, while the application of the whip
may keep it up for hours.

Geoffrey Hudson was, therefore, allowed to exhaust himself on the subject of his prison-house, which he informed
the king was not without a beam of light—an emanation
of loveliness—a mortal angel—quick of step and beautiful
of eye, who had more than once visited his confinement
with words of cheering and comfort.

' By my faith,' said the king, ' they fare better in Newgate
than I was aware of.   Who would have thought of the little
gentleman being solaced with female society in such a
place ? '

' I pray your Majesty,' said the dwarf, after the manner
of a solemn protest, ' to understand nothing amiss.   My
devotion to this fair creature is rather like what we poor
Catholics pay to the blessed saints, than mixed with any
grosser quality.   Indeed, she seems rather a sylphid of
the Rosicrucian system, than aught more carnal ; being
slighter, lighter, and less than the females of common life,
who have something of that coarseness of make which
is doubtless derived from the sinful and gigantic race of the
antediluvians.'

' Well, say on, man,' quoth Charles.   ' Didst thou not
discover this sylph to be a mere mortal wench after all ? '

' Who ?—I, my liege ?—Oh, fie ! '

' Nay, little gentleman, do not be so particularly scan-
dalized,' said the king ; ' I promise you I suspect you of no
audacity of gallantry.'

' Time wears fast,' said the Duke of Ormond impatiently,

and looking at his watch. ' Chiffinch hath been gone ten
minutes, and ten minutes will bring him back.'

' True,' said Charles gravely. 'Come to the point, Hudson;
and tell us what this female has to do with your coming
hither in this extraordinary manner.'

' Everything, my lord,' said little Hudson. ' I saw her
twice during my confinement in Newgate, and, in my
thought, she is the very angel who guards my life and welfare ; for, after my acquittal, as I walked towards the city
with two tall gentlemen, who had been in trouble along with
me, and just while we stood to our defence against a rascally
mob, and just as I had taken possession of an elevated
situation, to have some vantage against the great odds of
numbers, I heard a heavenly voice sound, as it were, from
a window behind me, counselling me to take refuge in a
certain house ; to which measure I readily persuaded my
gallant friends the Peverils, who have always shown themselves willing to be counselled by me.'

' Showing therein their wisdom at once and modesty,'
said the king. ' But what chanced next ? Be brief—be like
thyself, man.'

' For a time, sire,' said the dwarf, ' it seemed as if I were
not the principal object of attention. First, the younger
Peveril was withdrawn from us by a gentleman of venerable
appearance, though something smacking of a Puritan, having
boots of neat's leather, and wearing his weapon without a
sword-knot. When Master Julian returned, he informed
us, for the first time, that we were in the power of a body of
armed fanatics, who were, as the poet says, prompt for
direful act. And your Majesty will remark, that both
father and son were in some measure desperate, and dis-
regardful from that moment of the assurances which I gave
them, that the star which I was bound to worship would,
in her own time, shine forth in signal of our safety. May
it please your Majesty, in answer to my hilarious exhortations to confidence, the father did but say *tush*, and the
son *pshaw*, which showed how men's prudence and manners are disturbed by affliction. Nevertheless, these two
gentlemen, the Peverils, forming a strong opinion of the
necessity there was to break forth, were it only to convey
a knowledge of these dangerous passages to your Majesty,

commenced an assault on the door of the apartment, I also assisting with the strength which Heaven hath given, and some threescore years have left me. We could not, as it unhappily proved, manage our attempt so silently, but that our guards overheard us, and, entering in numbers, separated us from each other, and compelled my companions, at point of pike and poniard, to go to some other and more distant apartment, thus separating our fair society. I was again enclosed in the now solitary chamber, and I will own that I felt a certain depression of soul. But when bale is at highest, as the poet singeth, boot is at nighest, for a door of hope was suddenly opened '——

'In the name of God, my liege,' said the Duke of Ormond, ' let this poor creature's story be translated into the language of common sense by some of the scribblers of romances about Court, and we may be able to make meaning of it.'

Geoffrey Hudson looked with a frowning countenance of reproof upon the impatient old Irish nobleman, and said, with a very dignified air, ' That one duke upon a poor gentleman's hand was enough at a time, and that, but for his present engagement and dependency with the Duke of Buckingham, he would have endured no such terms from the Duke of Ormond.'

'Abate your valour, and diminish your choler, at our request, most puissant Sir Geoffrey Hudson,' said the king ; ' and forgive the Duke of Ormond for my sake ; but at all events go on with your story.'

Geoffrey Hudson laid his hand on his bosom, and bowed in proud and dignified submission to his sovereign ; then waved his forgiveness gracefully to Ormond, accompanied with a horrible grin, which he designed for a smile of gracious forgiveness and conciliation. ' Under the duke's favour, then,' he proceeded, ' when I said a door of hope was opened to me, I meant a door behind the tapestry, from whence issued that fair vision—yet not so fair as lustrously dark, like the beauty of a continental night, where the cloudless azure sky shrouds us in a veil more lovely than that of day !—but I note your Majesty's impatience ;— enough. I followed my beautiful guide into an apartment, where there lay, strangely intermingled, warlike arms and musical instruments. Amongst these I saw my own late

place of temporary obscurity—a violoncello. To my astonishment, she turned around the instrument, and opening it behind by pressure of a spring, showed that it was
filled with pistols, daggers, and ammunition made up in
bandoleers. "These," she said, "are this night destined
to surprise the Court of the unwary Charles"—your
Majesty must pardon my using her own words; "but if
thou darest go in their stead, thou mayst be the saviour
of king and kingdoms; if thou art afraid, keep secret, I will
myself try the adventure." Now may Heaven forbid that
Geoffrey Hudson were craven enough, said I, to let thee
run such a risk! You know not—you cannot know, what
belongs to such ambuscades and concealments—I am accustomed to them—have lurked in the pocket of a giant, and
have formed the contents of a pasty. "Get in then," she
said, "and lose no time." Nevertheless, while I prepared
to obey, I will not deny that some cold apprehensions came
over my hot valour, and I confessed to her, if it might be
so, I would rather find my way to the palace on my own feet.
But she would not listen to me, saying hastily, "I would
be intercepted, or refused admittance, and that I must
embrace the means she offered me of introduction into the
presence, and when there, tell the king to be on his guard—
little more is necessary; for once the scheme is known, it
becomes desperate." Rashly and boldly, I bade adieu to
the daylight which was then fading away. She withdrew
the contents of the instrument destined for my concealment, and having put them behind the chimney-board,
introduced me in their room. As she clasped me in, I implored her to warn the men who were to be intrusted with
me, to take heed and keep the neck of the violoncello uppermost; but ere I had completed my request, I found I was
left alone, and in darkness. Presently, two or three fellows
entered, whom, by their language, which I in some sort
understood, I perceived to be Germans, and under the influence of the Duke of Buckingham. I heard them receive
from the leader a charge how they were to deport themselves, when they should assume the concealed arms—and—
for I will do the duke no wrong—I understood their orders
were precise, not only to spare the person of the king, but
also those of the courtiers, and to protect all who might be

in the presence against an irruption of the fanatics. In other respects, they had charge to disarm the Gentlemen Pensioners in the guard-room, and, in fine, to obtain the command of the Court.'

The king looked disconcerted and thoughtful at this communication, and bade Lord Arlington see that Selby quietly made search into the contents of the other cases which had been brought as containing musical instruments. He then signed to the dwarf to proceed in his story, asking him again and again, and very solemnly, whether he was sure that he heard the duke's name mentioned, as commanding or approving this action.

The dwarf answered in the affirmative.

' This,' said the king, ' is carrying the frolic somewhat far.'

The dwarf proceeded to state that he was carried after his metamorphosis into the chapel, where he heard the preacher seemingly about the close of his harangue, the tenor of which he also mentioned. Words, he said, could not express the agony which he felt when he found that his bearer, in placing the instrument in a corner, was about to invert its position, in which case, he said, human frailty might have proved too great for love, for loyalty, for true obedience, nay, for the fear of death, which was like to ensue on discovery ; and he concluded, that he greatly doubted he could not have stood on his head for many minutes without screaming aloud.

' I could not have blamed you,' said the king ; ' placed in such a posture in the royal oak, I must needs have roared myself. Is this all you have to tell us of this strange conspiracy ? ' Sir Geoffrey Hudson replied in the affirmative, and the king presently subjoined—' Go, my little friend, your services shall not be forgotten. Since thou hast crept into the bowels of a fiddle for our service, we are bound, in duty and conscience, to find you a more roomy dwelling in future.'

' It was a violoncello, if your Majesty is pleased to remember,'· said the little jealous man, ' not a common fiddle ; though, for your Majesty's service, I would have crept even into a kit.'

' Whatever of that nature could have been performed by any subject of ours, thou wouldst have enacted in our behalf —of that we hold ourselves certain. Withdraw for a little ;

and hark ye, for the present, beware what you say about this matter. Let your appearance be considered—do you mark me—as a frolic of the Duke of Buckingham ; and not a word of conspiracy.'

'Were it not better to put him under some restraint, sire ? ' said the Duke of Ormond, when Hudson had left the room.

'It is unnecessary,' said the king. 'I remember the little wretch of old. Fortune, to make him the model of absurdity, has closed a most lofty soul within that little miserable carcass. For wielding his sword and keeping his word, he is a perfect Don Quixote in decimo-octavo. He shall be taken care of.—But, oddsfish, my lords, is not this freak of Buckingham too villanous and ungrateful ? '

' He had not had the means of being so, had your Majesty,' said the Duke of Ormond, 'been less lenient on other occasions.'

' My lord, my lord,' said Charles hastily—' your lordship is Buckingham's known enemy—we will take other and more impartial counsel—Arlington, what think you of all this ? '

' May it please your Majesty,' said Arlington, ' I think the thing is absolutely impossible, unless the duke has had some quarrel with your Majesty, of which we know nothing. His Grace is very flighty, doubtless, but this seems actual insanity.'

' Why, faith,' said the king, ' some words passed betwixt us this morning—his duchess it seems is dead—and to lose no time, his Grace had cast his eyes about for means of repairing the loss, and had the assurance to ask our consent to woo my niece Lady Anne.'

' Which your Majesty of course rejected ? ' said the statesman.

' And not without rebuking his assurance,' added the king.

' In private, sire, or before any witnesses ? ' said the Duke of Ormond.

' Before no one,' said the king,—' excepting, indeed, little Chiffinch ; and he, you know, is no one.'

' *Hinc illae lachrymae*,' said Ormond. ' I know his Grace well. While the rebuke of his aspiring petulance was a matter betwixt your Majesty and him, he might have let it pass by ; but a check before a fellow from whom it was likely enough to travel through the Court, was a matter to be revenged.'

Here Selby came hastily from the other room, to say that his Grace of Buckingham had just entered the presence-chamber.

The king rose. 'Let a boat be in readiness, with a party of the yeomen,' said he. 'It may be necessary to attach him of treason, and send him to the Tower.'

'Should not a secretary of state's warrant be prepared ?' said Ormond.

'No, my lord duke,' said the king sharply. 'I still hope that the necessity may be avoided.'

CHAPTER XLVII

High-reaching Buckingham grows circumspect.
Richard III.

BEFORE giving the reader an account of the meeting be-twixt Buckingham and his injured sovereign, we may mention a trifling circumstance or two which took place betwixt his Grace and Chiffinch, in the short drive betwixt York Place and Whitehall.

In the outset, the duke endeavoured to learn from the courtier the special cause of his being summoned so hastily to the court. Chiffinch answered, cautiously, that he believed there were some gambols going forward, at which the king desired the duke's presence.

This did not quite satisfy Buckingham, for, conscious of his own rash purpose, he could not but apprehend discovery. After a moment's silence, 'Chiffinch,' he said, abruptly, 'did you mention to any one what the king said to me this morning touching the Lady Anne ?'

'My lord duke,' said Chiffinch, hesitating, 'surely my duty to the king—my respect to your Grace '——

'You mentioned it to no one, then ?' said the duke sternly.

'To no one,' replied Chiffinch faintly, for he was intimidated by the duke's increasing severity of manner.

' Ye lie, like a scoundrel ! ' said the duke—' You told Christian ! '

' Your Grace,' said Chiffinch—' your Grace—your Grace ought to remember that I told you Christian's secret ; that the Countess of Derby was come up.'

' And you think the one point of treachery may balance for the other ?   But no.   I must have a better atonement. Be assured I will blow your brains out, ere you leave this carriage, unless you tell me the truth of this message from Court.'

As Chiffinch hesitated what reply to make, a man, who, by the blaze of the torches, then always borne, as well by the lackeys who hung behind the carriage, as by the foot-men who ran by the side, might easily see who sat in the coach, approached, and sang in a deep manly voice the burden of an old French song on the battle of Marignan, in which is imitated the German French of the defeated Swiss.

> ' Tout est verlore
> La tintelore,
> Tout est verlore
>   Bei Got.'

' I am betrayed,' said the duke, who instantly conceived that this chorus, expressing ' all is lost,' was sung by one of his faithful agents, as a hint to him that their machinations were discovered.

He attempted to throw himself from the carriage, but Chiffinch held him with a firm, though respectful grasp. ' Do not destroy yourself, my lord,' he said, in a tone of deep humility—' there are soldiers and officers of the peace around the carriage, to enforce your Grace's coming to Whitehall, and to prevent your escape.   To attempt it would be to confess guilt ; and I advise you strongly against that—the king is your friend—be your own.'

The duke, after a moment's consideration, said sullenly, ' I believe you are right.   Why should I fly, when I am guilty of nothing but sending some fireworks to entertain the Court, instead of a concert of music ? '

' And the dwarf, who came so unexpectedly out of the bass-viol '——

' Was a masking device of my own, Chiffinch,' said the

duke, though the circumstance was then first known to him. ' Chiffinch, you will bind me for ever, if you will permit me to have a minute's conversation with Christian.'

' With Christian, my lord ? Where could you find him ? You are aware we must go straight on to the Court.'

' True,' said the duke, ' but I think I cannot miss finding him ; and you, Master Chiffinch, are no officer, and have no warrant either to detain me prisoner, or prevent my speaking to whom I please.'

Chiffinch replied, ' My lord duke, your genius is so great, and your escapes so numerous, that it will be from no wish of my own if I am forced to hurt a man so skilful and so popular.'

' Nay, then, there is life in it yet,' said the duke, and whistled ; when, from beside the little cutler's booth, with which the reader is acquainted, appeared, suddenly, Master Christian, and was in a moment at the side of the coach. ' *Ganz ist verloren*,' said the duke.

' I know it,' said Christian ; ' and all our godly friends are dispersed upon the news. Lucky the colonel and these German rascals gave a hint. All is safe—You go to Court —Hark ye, I will follow.'

' You, Christian ? that would be more friendly than wise.'

' Why, what is there against me ? ' said Christian. ' I am innocent as the child unborn—so is your Grace. There is but one creature who can bear witness to our guilt ; but I trust to bring her on the stage in our favour—besides, if I went not, I should presently be sent for.'

'The familiar of whom I have heard you speak, I warrant ? '

' Hark in your ear again.'

' I understand,' said the duke, ' and will delay Master Chiffinch,—for he, you must know, is my conductor,—no longer.—Well, Chiffinch, let them drive on.—*Vogue la galère !* ' he exclaimed, as the carriage went onward ; ' I have sailed through worse perils than this yet.'

' It is not for me to judge,' said Chiffinch ; ' your Grace is a bold commander ; and Christian hath the cunning of the devil for a pilot ; but——However, I remain your Grace's poor friend, and will heartily rejoice in your extrication.'

' Give me a proof of your friendship,' said the duke.

'Tell me what you know of Christian's familiar, as he calls her.'

'I believe it to be the same dancing wench who came with Empson to my house on the morning that Mistress Alice made her escape from us. But you have seen her, my lord ?'

'I ?' said the duke ; 'when did I see her ?'

'She was employed by Christian, I believe, to set his niece at liberty, when he found himself obliged to gratify his fanatical brother-in-law by restoring his child ; besides being prompted by a private desire, as I think, of bantering your Grace.'

'Umph ! I suspected so much. I will repay it,' said the duke. 'But first to get out of this dilemma. That little Numidian witch, then, was his familiar ; and she joined in the plot to tantalize me ? But here we reach Whitehall. Now, Chiffinch, be no worse than thy word, and—now, Buckingham, be thyself !'

But ere we follow Buckingham into the presence, where he had so difficult a part to sustain, it may not be amiss to follow Christian after his brief conversation with him. On re-entering the house, which he did by a circuitous passage, leading from a distant alley, and through several courts, Christian hastened to a low matted apartment, in which Bridgenorth sat alone, reading the Bible by the light of a small brazen lamp, with the utmost serenity of countenance.

'Have you dismissed the Peverils ?' said Christian hastily.

'I have,' said the major.

'And upon what pledge—that they will not carry information against you to Whitehall ?'

'They gave me their promise voluntarily, when I showed them our armed friends were dismissed. To-morrow, I believe, it is their purpose to lodge informations.'

'And why not to-night, I pray you ?' said Christian.

'Because they allow us that time for escape.'

'Why, then, do you not avail yourself of it ? Wherefore are you here ?' said Christian.

'Nay, rather, why do *you* not fly ?' said Bridgenorth. 'Of a surety, you are as deeply engaged as I.'

' Brother Bridgenorth, I am the fox, who knows a hundred modes of deceiving the hounds ; you are the deer, whose sole resource is in hasty flight. Therefore lose no time— begone to the country—or rather, Zedekiah Fish's vessel, the *Good Hope*, lies in the river, bound for Massachusetts —take the wings of the morning, and begone—she can fall down to Gravesend with the tide.'

' And leave to thee, brother Christian,' said Bridgenorth, ' the charge of my fortune and my daughter ?   No, brother ; my opinion of your good faith must be re-established ere I again trust thee.'

' Go thy ways, then, for a suspicious fool,' said Christian, suppressing his strong desire to use language more offensive ; ' or rather stay where thou art, and take thy chance of the gallows ! '

' It is appointed to all men to die once,' said Bridgenorth ; ' my life hath been a living death.   My fairest boughs have been stripped by the axe of the forester—that which survives must, if it shall blossom, be grafted elsewhere, and at a distance from my aged trunk.   The sooner, then, the root feels the axe, the stroke is more welcome.   I had been pleased, indeed, had I been called to bringing yonder licentious Court to a purer character, and relieving the yoke of the suffering people of God.   That youth too— son to that precious woman, to whom I owe the last tie that feebly links my wearied spirit to humanity—could I have travailed with *him* in the good cause !—But that, with all my other hopes, is broken for ever ; and since I am not worthy to be an instrument in so great a work, I have little desire to abide longer in this vale of sorrow.'

' Farewell, then, desponding fool ! ' said Christian, unable, with all his calmness, any longer to suppress his contempt for the resigned and hopeless predestinarian.   ' That fate should have clogged me with such confederates ! ' he muttered, as he left the apartment—' this bigoted fool is now nearly irreclaimable—I must to Zarah ; for she, or no one, must carry us through these straits.   If I can but soothe her sullen temper, and excite her vanity to action, —betwixt her address, the king's partiality for the duke, Buckingham's matchless effrontery, and my own hand upon the helm, we may yet weather the tempest that darkens around us. But what we do must be hastily done.'

In another apartment he found the person he sought—the same who visited the Duke of Buckingham's harem, and, having relieved Alice Bridgenorth from her confinement there, had occupied her place as has been already narrated, or rather intimated. She was now much more plainly attired than when she had tantalized the duke with her presence ; but her dress had still something of the Oriental character, which corresponded with the dark complexion and quick eye of the wearer. She had the kerchief at her eyes as Christian entered the apartment, but suddenly withdrew it, and, flashing on him a glance of scorn and indignation, asked him what he meant by intruding where his company was alike unsought for and undesired.

' A proper question,' said Christian, ' from a slave to her master ! '

' Rather say, a proper question, and of all questions the most proper, from a mistress to her slave ! Know you not, that from the hour in which you discovered your ineffable baseness, you have made me mistress of your lot ? While you seemed but a demon of vengeance, you commanded terror, and to good purpose ; but such a foul fiend as thou hast of late shown thyself—such a very worthless, base trickster of the devil—such a sordid grovelling imp of perdition, can gain nothing but scorn from a soul like mine.'

' Gallantly mouthed,' said Christian, ' and with good emphasis.'

' Yes,' answered Zarah, ' I can speak—sometimes—I can also be mute ; and that no one knows better than thou.'

' Thou art a spoiled child, Zarah, and dost but abuse the indulgence I entertain for your freakish humour,' replied Christian ; ' thy wits have been disturbed since ever you landed in England, and all for the sake of one who cares for thee no more than for the most worthless object who walks the streets, amongst whom he left you to engage in a brawl for one he loved better.'

' It is no matter,' said Zarah, obviously repressing very bitter emotion ; ' it signifies not that he loves another better ; there is none—no, none—that ever did, or can, love him so well.'

' I pity you, Zarah ! ' said Christian, with some scorn.

' I deserve your pity,' she replied, ' were your pity worth my accepting. Whom have I to thank for my wretchedness but you ? You bred me up in thirst of vengeance, ere I knew that good and evil were anything better than names ; —to gain your applause, and to gratify the vanity you had excited, I have for years undergone a penance, from which a thousand would have shrunk.'

' A thousand, Zarah ! ' answered Christian ; ' aye, a hundred thousand, and a million to boot; the creature is not on earth, being mere mortal woman, that would have undergone the thirtieth part of thy self-denial.'

' I believe it,' said Zarah, drawing up her slight but elegant figure ; ' I believe it—I have gone through a trial that few indeed could have sustained. I have renounced the dear intercourse of my kind ; compelled my tongue only to utter, like that of a spy, the knowledge which my ear had only collected as a base eavesdropper. This I have done for years—for years—and all for the sake of your private applause—and the hope of vengeance on a woman, who, if she did ill in murdering my father, has been bitterly repaid by nourishing a serpent in her bosom, that had the tooth, but not the deafened ear, of the adder.'

' Well—well—well,' reiterated Christian ; ' and had you not your reward in my approbation—in the consciousness of your own unequalled dexterity—by which, superior to anything of thy sex that history has ever known, you endured what woman never before endured, insolence without notice, admiration without answer, and sarcasm without reply ? '

' Not without reply ! ' said Zarah fiercely. ' Gave not Nature to my feelings a course of expression more impressive than words ? and did not those tremble at my shrieks, who would have little minded my entreaties or my complaints ? And my proud lady, who sauced her charities with the taunts she thought I heard not—she was justly paid by the passing of her dearest and most secret concerns into the hands of her mortal enemy ; and the vain earl—yet he was a thing as insignificant as the plume that nodded in his cap ;—and the maidens and ladies who taunted me—I had, or can easily have, my revenge upon them. But there is *one*,' she added, looking upward, ' who never taunted me ; one whose generous feelings could treat the poor dumb girl even as his sister ; who never spoke word of her but it was to excuse or defend—and you tell me I must not love him, and that it is madness to love him !—I *will* be mad then, for I will love him till the latest breath of my life ! '

' Think but an instant, silly girl—silly but in one respect, since in all others thou mayest brave the world of women. Think what I have proposed to thee, for the loss of this hopeless affection, a career so brilliant !—Think only that it rests with thyself to be the wife—the wedded wife—of the princely Buckingham ! With my talents—with thy wit and beauty—with his passionate love of these attributes—a short space might rank you among England's princesses. Be but guided by me—he is now at deadly pass—needs every assistance to retrieve his fortunes—above all, that which we alone can render him. Put yourself under my conduct, and not fate itself shall prevent your wearing a duchess's coronet.'

' A coronet of thistle-down, entwined with thistle-leaves,' said Zarah. ' I know not a slighter thing than your Bucking ham ! I saw him at your request—saw him when, as a man, he should have shown himself generous and noble —I stood the proof at your desire, for I laugh at those dangers from which the poor blushing wailers of my sex shrink and withdraw themselves. What did I find him ? —a poor wavering voluptuary—his nearest attempt to passion like the fire on a wretched stubble-field, that may singe, indeed, or smoke, but can neither warm nor devour. Christian ! were his coronet at my feet this moment, I would sooner take up a crown of gilded gingerbread, than extend my hand to raise it.'

' You are mad, Zarah—with all your taste and talent, you are utterly mad ! But let Buckingham pass—Do you owe *me* nothing on this emergency ?—Nothing to one who rescued you from the cruelty of your owner, the posture-master, to place you in ease and affluence ? '

' Christian,' she replied, ' I owe you much. Had I not felt I did so, I would, as I have been often tempted to do, have denounced thee to the fierce countess, who would have gibbeted you on her feudal walls of Castle Rushin, and bid your family seek redress from the eagles, that would long since have thatched their nest with your hair, and fed their young ospreys with your flesh.'

'I am truly glad you have had so much forbearance for me,' answered Christian.

'I have it, in truth, and in sincerity,' replied Zarah. 'Not for your benefits to me—such as they were, they were every one interested, and conferred from the most selfish considerations. I have overpaid them a thousand times by the devotion to your will which I have displayed at the greatest personal risk. But till of late, I respected your powers of mind—your inimitable command of passion—the force of intellect which I have ever seen you exercise over all others, from the bigot Bridgenorth to the debauched Buckingham—in that, indeed, I have recognized my master.'

'And those powers,' said Christian, 'are unlimited as ever ; and with thy assistance, thou shalt see the strongest meshes that the laws of civil society ever wove to limit the natural dignity of man, broke asunder like a spider's web.'

She paused, and answered, 'While a noble motive fired thee—aye, a noble motive, though irregular—for I was born to gaze on the sun which the pale daughters of Europe shrink from—I could serve thee—I could have followed, while revenge or ambition had guided thee—but love of *wealth*, and by what means acquired ! What sympathy can I hold with that ? Wouldst thou not have pandered to the lust of the king, though the object was thine own orphan niece ? You smile ? Smile again when I ask you whether you meant not my own prostitution, when you charged me to remain in the house of that wretched Buckingham ? Smile at that question, and by Heaven I stab you to the heart !' And she thrust her hand into her bosom, and partly showed the hilt of a small poniard.

'And if I smile,' said Christian, 'it is but in scorn of so odious an accusation. Girl, I will not tell thee the reason, but there exists not on earth the living thing over whose safety and honour I would keep watch as over thine. Buckingham's wife, indeed, I wished thee ; and, through thy own beauty and thy wit, I doubted not to bring the match to pass.'

' Vain flatterer,' said Zarah, yet seeming soothed even by
the flattery which she scoffed at, ' you would persuade me
that it was honourable love which you expected the duke
was to have offered me. How durst you urge so gross
a deception, to which time, place, and circumstance, gave
the lie ? How dare you now again mention it, when you
well know, that at the time you mention, the duchess was
still in life ? '

' In life, but on her deathbed,' said Christian ; ' and for
time, place, and circumstance, had your virtue, my Zarah,
depended on these, how couldst thou have been the creature
thou art ? I knew thee all-sufficient to bid him defiance—
else—for thou art dearer to me than thou thinkest—I had
not risked thee to win the Duke of Buckingham ; aye, and
the kingdom of England to boot. So now, wilt thou be
ruled, and go on with me ? '

Zarah, or Fenella, for our readers must have been long
aware of the identity of these two personages, cast down
her eyes, and was silent for a long time. ' Christian,' she
said at last, in a solemn voice, ' if my ideas of right and of
wrong be wild and incoherent, I owe it, first, to the wild
fever which my native sun communicated to my veins ;
next, to my childhood, trained amidst the shifts, tricks,
and feats of jugglers and mountebanks ; and then, to a youth
of fraud and deception, through the course thou didst
prescribe me, in which I might, indeed, hear everything,
but communicate with no one. The last cause of my wild
errors, if such they are, originates, O Christian, with you
alone ; by whose intrigues I was placed with yonder lady,
and who taught me that to revenge my father's death was
my first great duty on earth, and that I was bound by
nature to hate and injure her by whom I was fed and
fostered, though as she would have fed and caressed a dog,
or any other mute animal. I also think—for I will deal
fairly with you—that you had not so easily detected your
niece in the child whose surprising agility was making
yonder brutal mountebank's fortune ; nor so readily
induced him to part with his bondslave, had you not, for
your own purposes, placed me under his charge, and reserved
the privilege of claiming me when you pleased. I could
not, under any other tuition, have identified myself with

the personage of a mute, which it has been your desire that
I should perform through life.'

' You do me injustice, Zarah,' said Christian. ' I found
you capable of discharging, to an uncommon degree, a task
necessary to the avenging of your father's death—I consecrated you to it, as I consecrated my own life and hopes ;
and you held the duty sacred, till these mad feelings towards
a youth who loves your cousin '——

' Who—loves—my—cousin,' repeated Zarah (for we will
continue to call her by her real name), slowly, and as if the
words dropped unconsciously from her lips. ' Well—be it
so !—Man of many wiles, I will follow thy course for a little,
a very little farther ; but take heed—tease me not with
remonstrances against the treasure of my secret thoughts—
I mean my most hopeless affection to Julian Peveril—and
bring me not as an assistant to any snare which you may
design to cast around him. You and your duke shall rue
the hour most bitterly, in which you provoke me. You may
suppose you have me in your power ; but remember, the
snakes of my burning climate are never so fatal as when
you grasp them.'

' I care not for these Peverils,' said Christian—' I care
not for their fate a poor straw, unless where it bears on that
of the destined woman, whose hands are red in your father's
blood. Believe me, I can divide her fate and theirs. I will
explain to you how. And for the duke, he may pass among
men of the town for wit, and among soldiers for valour,
among courtiers for manners and for form ; and why,
with his high rank and immense fortune, you should
throw away an opportunity, which, as I could now improve it '——

' Speak not of it,' said Zarah, ' if thou wouldst have our
truce—remember it is no peace—if, I say, thou wouldst
have our truce grow to be an hour old ! '

' This, then,' said Christian, with a last effort to work
upon the vanity of this singular being, ' is she who pretended
such superiority to human passion that she could walk
indifferently and unmoved through the halls of the prosperous, and the prison cells of the captive, unknowing and
unknown, sympathizing neither with the pleasures of the
one, nor the woes of the other, but advancing with sure,

though silent steps, her own plans, in despite and regardless of either ! '

' My own plans ! ' said Zarah—' *Thy* plans, Christian—thy plans of extorting from the surprised prisoners, means whereby to convict them—thine own plans, formed with those more powerful than thyself, to sound men's secrets, and, by using them as a matter of accusation, to keep up the great delusion of the nation.'

' Such access was indeed given you as my agent,' said Christian, ' and for advancing a great national change. But how did you use it ?—to advance your insane passion.'

' Insane ! ' said Zarah. ' Had he been less than insane whom I addressed, he and I had ere now been far from the toils which you have pitched for us both. I had means prepared for everything ; and ere this, the shores of Britain had been lost to our sight for ever.'

' The dwarf, too,' said Christian. ' Was it worthy of you to delude that poor creature with flattering visions—lull him asleep with drugs ! Was *that* my doing ? '

' He was my destined tool,' said Zarah haughtily. ' I remembered your lessons too well not to use him as such. Yet scorn him not too much. I tell you, that yon very miserable dwarf, whom I made my sport in the prison—yon wretched abortion of nature, I would select for a husband, ere I would marry your Buckingham ;—the vain and imbecile pygmy has yet the warm heart and noble feelings that a man should hold his highest honour.'

' In God's name, then, take your own way,' said Christian ; ' and, for my sake, let never man hereafter limit a woman in the use of her tongue, since he must make it amply up to her, in allowing her the privilege of her own will. Who would have thought it ? But the colt has slipped the bridle, and I must needs follow, since I cannot guide her.'

Our narrative returns to the Court of King Charles, at Whitehall.

CHAPTER XLVIII

——But oh !
What shall I say to thee, Lord Scroop ; thou cruel,
Ingrateful, savage, and inhuman creature !
Thou that didst bear the key of all my counsels,
That knew'st the very bottom of my soul,
That almost mightst have coin'd me into gold,
Wouldst thou have practised on me for thy use ?
                                            Henry V.

AT no period of his life, not even when that life was in imminent danger, did the constitutional gaiety of Charles seem more overclouded, than when waiting for the return of Chiffinch with the Duke of Buckingham. His mind revolted at the idea that the person to whom he had been so particularly indulgent, and whom he had selected as the friend of his lighter hours and amusements, should prove capable of having tampered with a plot apparently directed against his liberty and life. He more than once examined the dwarf anew, but could extract nothing more than his first narrative contained. The apparition of the female to him in the cell of Newgate, he described in such fanciful and romantic colours, that the king could not help thinking the poor man's head a little turned ; and, as nothing was found in the kettledrum, and other musical instruments brought for the use of the duke's band of foreigners, he nourished some slight hope that the whole plan might be either a mere jest, or that the idea of an actual conspiracy was founded in mistake.

The persons who had been dispatched to watch the motions of Mr. Weiver's congregation brought back word that they had quietly dispersed. It was known, at the same time, that they had met in arms, but this augured no particular design of aggression, at a time when all true Protestants conceived themselves in danger of immediate massacre ; when the fathers of the city had repeatedly called out the Train Bands, and alarmed the citizens of London, under the idea of an instant insurrection of the Catholics ; and when, to sum the whole up, in the emphatic

words of an alderman of the day, there was a general belief
that they would all waken some unhappy morning with
their throats cut.   Who was to do these dire deeds, it was
more difficult to suppose ; but all admitted the possibility
that they might be achieved, since one justice of the peace
was already murdered.   There was, therefore, no inference
of hostile intentions against the state, to be decidedly
derived from a congregation of Protestants *par excellence*,
military from old associations, bringing their arms with them
to a place of worship, in the midst of a panic so universal.

Neither did the violent language of the minister, supposing that to be proved, absolutely infer meditated violence.
The favourite parables of the preachers, and the metaphors
and ornaments which they selected, were at all times of a
military cast ; and the taking the kingdom of heaven by
storm, a strong and beautiful metaphor, when used generally,
as in Scripture, was detailed in their sermons in all the
technical language of the attack and defence of a fortified
place.   The danger, in short, whatever might have been
its actual degree, had disappeared as suddenly as a bubble
upon the water, when broken by a casual touch, and had
left as little trace behind it.   It became, therefore, matter
of much doubt whether it had ever actually existed.

While various reports were making from without, and
while their tenor was discussed by the king, and such nobles
and statesmen as he thought proper to consult on the
occasion, a gradual sadness and anxiety mingled with, and
finally silenced, the mirth of the evening.   All became
sensible that something unusual was going forward ; and
the unwonted distance which Charles maintained from his
guests, while it added greatly to the dullness that began to
predominate in the presence-chamber, gave intimation that
something unusual was labouring in the king's mind.

Thus play was neglected—the music was silent, or played
without being heard—gallants ceased to make compliments,
and ladies to expect them ; and a sort of apprehensive
curiosity pervaded the circle.   Each asked the others why
they were grave ; and no answer was returned, any more
than could have been rendered by a herd of cattle instinctively disturbed by the approach of a thunderstorm.

To add to the general apprehension, it began to be

whispered that one or two of the guests, who were desirous
of leaving the palace, had been informed no one could be
permitted to retire until the general hour of dismissal.
And these, gliding back into the hall, communicated in
whispers that the sentinels at the gates were doubled, and
that there was a troop of the Horse Guards drawn up in the
court—circumstances so unusual as to excite the most
anxious curiosity.

Such was the state of the Court, when wheels were heard
without, and the bustle which took place denoted the arrival
of some person of consequence.

'Here comes Chiffinch,' said the king, ' with his prey in
his clutch.'

It was indeed the Duke of Buckingham ; nor did he
approach the royal presence without emotion.   On entering
the court, the flambeaux which were borne around the
carriage gleamed on the scarlet coats, laced hats, and drawn
broadswords of the Horse Guards—a sight unusual, and
calculated to strike terror into a conscience which was none
of the clearest.

The duke alighted from the carriage, and only said to the
officer, whom he saw upon duty, ' You are late under arms
to-night, Captain Carleton.'

' Such are our orders, sir,' answered Carleton, with military brevity ; and then commanded the four dismounted
sentinels at the under gate to make way for the Duke of
Buckingham.   His Grace had no sooner entered, than he
heard behind him the command, ' Move close up, sentinels—
closer yet to the gate.'   And he felt as if all chance of
rescue were excluded by the sound.

As he advanced up the grand staircase there were other
symptoms of alarm and precaution.   The Yeomen of the
Guard were mustered in unusual numbers, and carried
carabines instead of their halberds ; and the Gentlemen
Pensioners, with their partisans, appeared also in proportional force.   In short, all that sort of defence which the
royal household possesses within itself, seemed, for some
hasty and urgent reason, to have been placed under arms,
and upon duty.

Buckingham ascended the royal staircase with an eye
attentive to these preparations, and a step steady and slow,

as if he counted each step on which he trod. 'Who,' he
asked himself, shall ensure Christian's fidelity ? Let him
but stand fast and we are secure.   Otherwise '——

As he shaped the alternative, he entered the presence-
chamber.

The king stood in the midst of the apartment, surrounded
by the personages with whom he had been consulting.   The
rest of the brilliant assembly, scattered into groups, looked
on at some distance.   All were silent when Buckingham
entered, in hopes of receiving some explanation of the
mysteries of the evening.   All bent forward, though etiquette
forbade them to advance, to catch, if possible, something
of what was about to pass betwixt the king and his intriguing
statesman.   At the same time, those counsellors who stood
around Charles drew back on either side, so as to permit
the duke to pay his respects to his Majesty in the usual form.
He went through the ceremonial with his accustomed grace,
but was received by Charles with much unwonted gravity.

'We have waited for you for some time, my lord duke.
It is long since Chiffinch left us, to request your attendance
here.   I see you are elaborately dressed.   Your toilette
was needless on the present occasion.'

'Needless to the splendour of your Majesty's Court,' said
the duke, 'but not needless on my part.   This chanced to
be Black Monday at York Place, and my club of *Pendables*
were in full glee when your Majesty's summons arrived.
I could not be in the company of Ogle, Maniduc, Dawson,
and so forth, but what I must needs make some preparation,
and some ablution, ere entering the circle here.'

'I trust the purification will be complete,' said the king,
without any tendency to the smile which always softened
features, that, ungilded by its influence, were dark, harsh,
and even severe.   'We wished to ask your Grace concerning
the import of a sort of musical mask which you designed us
here, but which miscarried, as we are given to understand.'

'It must have been a great miscarriage indeed,' said the
duke, 'since your Majesty looks so serious on it.   I thought
to have done your Majesty a pleasure (as I have seen you
condescend to be pleased with such passages) by sending
the contents of that bass-viol ; but I fear the jest has been
unacceptable—I fear the fireworks may have done mischief.'

Charles II

'Not the mischief they were designed for, perhaps,' said the king gravely ; ' you see, my lord, we are all alive, and unsinged.'

'Long may your Majesty remain so,' said the duke ; ' yet I see there is something misconstrued on my part— it must be a matter unpardonable, however little intended, since it hath displeased so indulgent a master.'

'Too indulgent a master, indeed, Buckingham,' replied the king ; ' and the fruit of my indulgence has been to change loyal men into traitors.'

'May it please your Majesty, I cannot understand this,' said the duke.

'Follow us, my lord,' answered Charles, ' and we will endeavour to explain our meaning.'

Attended by the same lords who stood around him, and followed by the Duke of Buckingham, on whom all eyes were fixed, Charles retired into the same cabinet which had been the scene of repeated consultations in the course of the evening. There, leaning with his arms crossed on the back of an easy chair, Charles proceeded to interrogate the suspected nobleman.

'Let us be plain with each other. Speak out, Buckingham. What, in one word, was to have been the regale intended for us this evening ? '

'A petty mask, my lord. I had destined a little dancing girl to come out of that instrument, who, I thought, would have performed to your Majesty's liking—a few Chinese fireworks there were, which, thinking the entertainment was to have taken place in the marble hall, might, I hoped, have been discharged with good effect, and without the slightest alarm, at the first appearance of my little sorceress, and were designed to have masked, as it were, her entrance upon the stage. I hope there have been no perukes singed— no ladies frightened—no hopes of noble descent interrupted by my ill-fancied jest.'

'We have seen no such fireworks, my lord ; and your female dancer, of whom we now hear for the first time, came forth in the form of our old acquaintance Geoffrey Hudson, whose dancing days are surely ended.'

'Your Majesty surprises me ! I beseech you, let Christian be sent for—Edward Christian—he will be found lodging in

a large old house near Sharper the cutler's, in the Strand.
As I live by bread, sire, I trusted him with the arrangement
of this matter, as indeed the dancing girl was his property.
If he has done aught to dishonour my concert, or disparage
my character, he shall die under the baton.'

'It is singular,' said the king, ' and I have often observed
it, that this fellow Christian bears the blame of all men's
enormities—he performs the part which, in a great family,
is usually assigned to that mischief-doing personage, Nobody. When Chiffinch blunders, he always quotes Christian.
When Sheffield writes a lampoon, I am sure to hear of
Christian having corrected, or copied, or dispersed it—he is
the *âme damnée* of every one about my Court—the scape-
goat, who is to carry away all their iniquities ; and he will
have a cruel load to bear into the wilderness. But for
Buckingham's sins, in particular, he is the regular and
uniform sponsor ; and I am convinced his Grace expects
Christian should suffer every penalty he has incurred, in
this world or the next.'

'Not so,' with the deepest reverence replied the duke.
'I have no hope of being either hanged or damned by
proxy ; but it is clear some one hath tampered with and
altered my device. If I am accused of aught, let me at
least hear the charge, and see my accuser.'

'That is but fair,' said the king. 'Bring our little friend
from behind the chimney-board.' Hudson being accordingly produced, he continued. 'There stands the Duke of
Buckingham. Repeat before him the tale you told us.
Let him hear what were those contents of the bass-viol
which were removed that you might enter it. Be not afraid
of any one, but speak the truth boldly.'

'May it please your Majesty,' said Hudson, ' fear is a
thing unknown to me.'

'His body has no room to hold such a passion ; or there
is too little of it to be worth fearing for,' said Buckingham.
'But let him speak.'

Ere Hudson had completed his tale, Buckingham interrupted him by exclaiming, ' Is it possible that I can be
suspected by your Majesty on the word of this pitiful
variety of the baboon tribe ? '

'Villain lord, I appeal thee to the combat ! ' said the

little man, highly offended at the appellation thus bestowed
on him.

'La you there now!' said the duke. 'The little animal
is quite crazed, and defies a man who need ask no other
weapon than a corking-pin to run him through the lungs,
and whose single kick could hoist him from Dover to
Calais without yacht or wherry. And what can you expect
from an idiot, who is *engoué* of a common rope-dancing girl,
.that capered on a pack-thread at Ghent in Flanders, unless
they were to club their talents to set up a booth at Bartholomew Fair? Is it not plain, that supposing the little
animal is not malicious, as indeed his whole kind bear a
general and most cankered malice against those who have
the ordinary proportions of humanity—Grant, I say, that
this were not a malicious falsehood of his, why, what does
it amount to? That he has mistaken squibs and Chinese
crackers for arms! He says not he himself touched or
handled them; and judging by the sight alone, I question
if the infirm old creature, when any whim or preconception
hath possession of his noddle, can distinguish betwixt
a blunderbuss and a black-pudding.'

The horrible clamour which the dwarf made so soon as
he heard this disparagement of his military skill—the haste
with which he blundered out a detail of his warlike ex-
periences—and the absurd grimaces which he made in order
to enforce his story, provoked not only the risibility of
Charles, but even of the statesmen around him, and added
absurdity to the motley complexion of the scene. The king
terminated this dispute, by commanding the dwarf to
withdraw.

A more regular discussion of his evidence was then resumed, and Ormond was the first who pointed out, that it
went further than had been noticed, since the little man
had mentioned a certain extraordinary and treasonable
conversation held by the duke's dependants, by whom he
had been conveyed to the palace.

'I am sure not to lack my Lord of Ormond's good word,'
said the duke scornfully; 'but I defy him alike, and all
my other enemies, and shall find it easy to show that this
alleged conspiracy, if any grounds for it at all exist, is a
mere sham-plot, got up to turn the odium justly attached

to the Papists upon the Protestants. Here is a half-hanged
creature, who, on the very day he escapes from the gallows,
which many believe was his most deserved destiny, comes
to take away the reputation of a Protestant peer—and, on
what ?—on the treasonable conversation of three or four
German fiddlers, heard through the sound-holes of a violoncello, and that, too, when the creature was incased in it, and
mounted on a man's shoulders ! The urchin, too, in repeating their language, shows he understands German as
little as my horse does ; and if he did rightly hear, truly
comprehend, and accurately report what they said, still, is
my honour to be touched by the language held by such persons as these are, with whom I have never communicated,
otherwise than men of my rank do with those of their calling
and capacity? Pardon me, sire, if I presume to say, that the
profound statesmen who endeavoured to stifle the Popish
conspiracy by the pretended Meal-tub Plot, will take little
more credit by their figments about fiddles and concertos.'

The assistant counsellors looked at each other ; and
Charles turned on his heel, and walked through the room
with long steps.

At this period the Peverils, father and son, were announced
to have reached the palace, and were ordered into the royal
presence.

These gentlemen had received the royal mandate at a
moment of great interest. After being dismissed from
their confinement by the elder Bridgenorth, in the manner
and upon the terms which the reader must have gathered
from the conversation of the latter with Christian, they
reached the lodgings of Lady Peveril, who awaited them
with joy, mingled with terror and uncertainty. The news of
the acquittal had reached her by the exertions of the faithful
Lance Outram, but her mind had been since harassed by
the long delay of their appearance, and rumours of disturbances which had taken place in Fleet Street and in the Strand.

When the first rapturous meeting was over, Lady Peveril,
with an anxious look towards her son, as if recommending
caution, said she was now about to present to him the
daughter of an old friend, whom he had *never* (there was an
emphasis on the word) seen before. ' This young lady,'
she continued, ' was the only child of Colonel Mitford, in

North Wales, who had sent her to remain under her guardianship for an interval, finding himself unequal to attempt the task of her education.'

'Aye, aye,' said Sir Geoffrey, 'Dick Mitford must be old now—beyond the threescore and ten, I think. He was no chicken, though a cock of the game, when he joined the Marquis of Hertford at Namptwich with two hundred wild Welshmen.—Before George, Julian, I love that girl as if she was my own flesh and blood! Lady Peveril would never have got through this work without her; and Dick Mitford sent me a thousand pieces, too, in excellent time, when there was scarce a cross to keep the devil from dancing in our pockets, much more for these law-doings. I used it without scruple, for there is wood ready to be cut at Martindale when we get down there, and Dick Mitford knows I would have done the like for him. Strange that he should have been the only one of my friends to reflect I might want a few pieces.'

Whilst Sir Geoffrey thus ran on, the meeting betwixt Alice and Julian Peveril was accomplished, without any particular notice on his side, except to say, 'Kiss her, Julian —kiss her. What the devil! is that the way you learned to accost a lady at the Isle of Man, as if her lips were a red-hot horseshoe?—And do not you be offended, my pretty one; Julian is naturally bashful, and has been bred by an old lady, but you will find him, by and by, as gallant as thou hast found me, my princess.—And now, Dame Peveril, to dinner, to dinner! the old fox must have his belly-timber, though the hounds have been after him the whole day.'

Lance, whose joyous congratulations were next to be undergone, had the consideration to cut them short, in order to provide a plain but hearty meal from the next cook's shop, at which Julian sat like one enchanted, betwixt his mistress and his mother. He easily conceived that the last was the confidential friend to whom Bridgenorth had finally committed the charge of his daughter, and his only anxiety now was, to anticipate the confusion that was likely to arise when her real parentage was made known to his father. Wisely, however, he suffered not these anticipations to interfere with the delight of his present

situation, in the course of which, many slight but delightful
tokens of recognition were exchanged, without censure,
under the eye of Lady Peveril, under cover of the boisterous
mirth of the old baronet, who spoke for two, ate for four,
and drank wine for half a dozen.   His progress in the latter
exercise might have proceeded rather too far, had he not
been interrupted by a gentleman bearing the king's orders,
that he should instantly attend upon the presence at
Whitehall, and bring his son along with him.

Lady Peveril was alarmed, and Alice grew pale with
sympathetic anxiety; but the old knight, who never saw
more than what lay straight before him, set it down to the
king's hasty anxiety to congratulate him on his escape; an
interest on his Majesty's part which he considered by no
means extravagant, conscious that it was reciprocal on his
own side.   It came upon him, indeed, with the more joyful
surprise that he had received a previous hint, ere he left the
court of justice, that it would be prudent in him to go
down to Martindale before presenting himself at Court—a
restriction which he supposed as repugnant to his Majesty's
feelings as it was to his own.

While he consulted with Lance Outram about cleaning his
buff-belt and sword-hilt, as well as time admitted, Lady
Peveril had the means to give Julian more distinct information that Alice was under her protection by her father's
authority, and with his consent to their union, if it could be
accomplished.   She added that it was her determination to
employ the mediation of the Countess of Derby, to overcome the obstacles which might be foreseen on the part of
Sir Geoffrey.

CHAPTER XLIX

> In the king's name,
> Let fall your swords and daggers!
> *Critic.*

WHEN the father and son entered the cabinet of audience,
it was easily visible that Sir Geoffrey had obeyed the
summons as he would have done the trumpet's call to
horse ; and his dishevelled grey locks and half-arranged

dress, though they showed zeal and haste, such as he would have used when Charles I called him to attend a council of war, seemed rather indecorous in a pacific drawing-room. He paused at the door of the cabinet, but when the king called on him to advance, came hastily forward, with every feeling of his earlier and later life afloat and contending in his memory, threw himself on his knees before the king, seized his hand, and, without even an effort to speak, wept aloud. Charles, who generally felt deeply so long as an impressive object was before his eyes, indulged for a moment the old man's rapture. ' My good Sir Geoffrey,' he said, ' you have had some hard measure ; we owe you amends, and will find time to pay our debt.'

' No suffering—no debt,' said the old man ; ' I cared not what the rogues said of me—I knew they could never get twelve honest fellows to believe a word of their most damnable lies. I did long to beat them when they called me traitor to your Majesty—that I confess—But to have such an early opportunity of paying my duty to your Majesty, overpays it all. The villains would have persuaded me I ought not to come to Court—aha ! '

The Duke of Ormond perceived that the king coloured much ; for in truth it was from the Court that the private intimation had been given to Sir Geoffrey to go down to the country, without appearing at Whitehall ; and he, moreover, suspected that the jolly old knight had not risen from his dinner altogether dry-lipped, after the fatigues of a day so agitating. ' My old friend,' he whispered, ' you forget that your son is to be presented—permit me to have that honour.'

' I crave your Grace's pardon humbly,' said Sir Geoffrey, ' but it is an honour I design for myself, as I apprehend no one can so utterly surrender and deliver him up to his Majesty's service as the father that begot him is entitled to do.—Julian, come forward, and kneel.—Here he is, please your Majesty—Julian Peveril—a chip of the old block— as stout, though scarce so tall a tree, as the old trunk when at the freshest. Take him to you, sir, for a faithful servant, *à vendre et à pendre*, as the French say ; if he fears fire or steel, axe or gallows, in your Majesty's service, I renounce him—he is no son of mine—I disown him, and he may go to the Isle of Man, the Isle of Dogs, or the Isle of Devils, for what I care.'

Charles winked to Ormond, and having, with his wonted courtesy, expressed his thorough conviction that Julian would imitate the loyalty of his ancestors, and especially of his father, added, that he believed his Grace of Ormond had something to communicate which was of consequence to his service. Sir Geoffrey made his military reverence at this hint, and marched off in the rear of the duke, who proceeded to inquire of him concerning the events of the day. Charles, in the meanwhile, having, in the first place, ascertained that the son was not in the same genial condition with the father, demanded and received from him a precise account of all the proceedings subsequent to the trial.

Julian, with the plainness and precision which such a subject demanded, when treated in such a presence, narrated all that had happened, down to the entrance of Bridgenorth ; and his Majesty was so much pleased with his manner, that he congratulated Arlington on their having gained the evidence of at least one man of sense to these dark and mysterious events. But when Bridgenorth was brought upon the scene, Julian hesitated to bestow a name upon him ; and although he mentioned the chapel which he had seen filled with men in arms, and the violent language of the preacher, he added, with earnestness, that notwith-standing all this, the men departed without coming to any extremity, and had all left the place before his father and he were set at liberty.

'And you retired quietly to your dinner in Fleet Street, young man,' said the king severely, 'without giving a magistrate notice of the dangerous meeting which was held in the vicinity of our palace, and who did not conceal their intention of proceeding to extremities ?'

Peveril blushed, and was silent. The king frowned, and stepped aside to communicate with Ormond, who reported that the father seemed to have known nothing of the matter.

'And the son, I am sorry to say,' said the king, 'seems more unwilling to speak the truth than I should have expected. We have all variety of evidence in this singular investigation—a mad witness like the dwarf, a drunken witness like the father, and now a dumb witness.—Young

man,' he continued, addressing Julian, ' your behaviour is
less frank than I expected from your father's son. I must
know who this person is with whom you held such familiar
intercourse—you know him, I presume ? '

Julian acknowledged that he did, but, kneeling on one
knee, entreated his Majesty's forgiveness for concealing his
name ; ' he had been freed,' he said, ' from his confinement,
on promising to that effect.'

' That was a promise made, by your own account, under
compulsion,' answered the king, ' and I cannot authorize
your keeping it ; it is your duty to speak the truth—if you
are afraid of Buckingham, the duke shall withdraw.'

' I have no reason to fear the Duke of Buckingham,' said
Peveril ; ' that I had an affair with one of his household,
was the man's own fault, and not mine.'

' Oddsfish ! ' said the king, ' the light begins to break in
on me—I thought I remembered thy physiognomy. Wert
thou not the very fellow whom I met at Chiffinch's yonder
morning ? The matter escaped me since ; but now I recollect thou saidst then, that thou wert the son of that jolly
old three-bottle baronet yonder.'

' It is true,' said Julian, ' that I met your Majesty at
Master Chiffinch's, and I am afraid had the misfortune to
displease you ; but '——

' No more of that, young man—no more of that—But
I recollect you had with you that beautiful dancing siren.
Buckingham, I will hold you gold to silver, that she was
the intended tenant of that bass-fiddle ? '

' Your Majesty has rightly guessed it,' said the duke ;
' and I suspect she has put a trick upon me, by substituting
the dwarf in her place ; for Christian thinks '——

' Damn Christian ! ' said the king hastily—' I wish they
would bring him hither, that universal referee.' And as the
wish was uttered, Christian's arrival was announced. ' Let
him attend,' said the king : ' But hark—a thought strikes
me.—Here, Master Peveril—yonder dancing maiden, that
introduced you to us by the singular agility of her performance, is she not, by your account, a dependant on the
Countess of Derby ? '

' I have known her such for years,' answered Julian.

' Then will we call the countess hither,' said the king :

'It is fit we should learn who this little fairy really is ; and if she be now so absolutely at the beck of Buckingham, and this Master Christian of his—why I think it would be but charity to let her ladyship know so much, since I question if she will wish, in that case, to retain her in her service. Besides,' he continued, speaking apart, 'this Julian, to whom suspicion attaches in these matters from his obstinate silence, is also of the countess's household. We will sift this matter to the bottom, and do justice to all.'

The Countess of Derby, hastily summoned, entered the royal closet at one door, just as Christian and Zarah, or Fenella, were ushered in by the other. The old Knight of Martindale, who had ere this returned to the presence, was scarce controlled, even by the signs which she made, so much was he desirous of greeting his old friend ; but as Ormond laid a kind restraining hand upon his arm, he was prevailed on to sit still.

The countess, after a deep reverence to the king, acknowledged the rest of the nobility present by a slighter reverence, smiled to Julian Peveril, and looked with surprise at the unexpected apparition of Fenella. Buckingham bit his lip, for he saw the introduction of Lady Derby was likely to confuse and embroil every preparation which he had arranged for his defence ; and he stole a glance at Christian, whose eye, when fixed on the countess, assumed the deadly sharpness which sparkles in the adder's, while his cheek grew almost black under the influence of strong emotion.

'Is there any one in this presence whom your ladyship recognizes,' said the king, graciously, 'besides your old friends of Ormond and Arlington ? '

'I see, my liege, two worthy friends of my husband's house,' replied the countess ; 'Sir Geoffrey Peveril and his son—the latter a distinguished member of my son's household.'

'Any one else ? ' continued the king.

'An unfortunate female of my family, who disappeared from the Island of Man at the same time when Julian Peveril left it upon business of importance. She was thought to have fallen from the cliff into the sea.'

'Had your ladyship any reason to suspect—pardon me,' said the king, 'for putting such a question, any improper intimacy between Master Peveril and this same female attendant ? '

' My liege,' said the countess, colouring indignantly, ' my household is of reputation.'

' Nay, my lady, be not angry,' said the king ; ' I did but ask—such things will befall in the best regulated families.'

' Not in mine, sire,' said the countess.   ' Besides that, in common pride and in common honesty, Julian Peveril is incapable of intriguing with an unhappy creature, removed by her misfortune almost beyond the limits of humanity.'

Zarah looked at her, and compressed her lips, as if to keep in the words that would fain break from them.

' I know not how it is,' said the king—' What your ladyship says may be true in the main, yet men's tastes have strange vagaries.   This girl is lost in Man as soon as the youth leaves it, and is found in Saint James's Park, bouncing and dancing like a fairy so soon as he appears in London.'

' Impossible ! ' said the countess ;   ' she cannot dance.'

' I believe,' said the king, ' she can do more feats than your ladyship either suspects or would approve of.'

The countess drew up, and was indignantly silent.

The king proceeded—' No sooner is Peveril in Newgate, than, by the account of the venerable little gentleman, this merry maiden is even there also for company.   Now, without inquiring how she got in, I think charitably that she had better taste than to come there on the dwarf's account. Ah ha ! I think Master Julian is touched in conscience ! '

Julian did indeed start as the king spoke, for it reminded him of the midnight visit in his cell.

The king looked fixedly at him, and then proceeded— ' Well, gentlemen, Peveril is carried to his trial, and is no sooner at liberty, than we find him in the house where the Duke of Buckingham was arranging what he calls a musical mask.   Egad, I hold it next to certain, that this wench put the change on his Grace, and popped the poor dwarf into the bass-viol, reserving her own more precious hours to be spent with Master Julian Peveril.—Think you not so, Sir Christian, you, the universal referee ?   Is there any truth in this conjecture ? '

Christian stole a glance at Zarah, and read that in her eye which embarrassed him.   ' He did not know,' he said ;

' he had indeed engaged this unrivalled performer to take the proposed part in the mask ; and she was to have come forth in the midst of a shower of lambent fire, very artificially prepared with perfumes, to overcome the smell of the powder ; but he knew not why—excepting that she was wilful and capricious, like all great geniuses,—she had certainly spoiled the concert by cramming in that more bulky dwarf.'

' I should like,' said the king, ' to see this little maiden stand forth, and bear witness, in such manner as she can express herself, on this mysterious matter. Can any one here understand her mode of communication ? '

Christian said he knew something of it since he had become acquainted with her in London. The countess spoke not till the king asked her, and then owned, dryly, that she had necessarily some habitual means of intercourse with one who had been immediately about her person for so many years.

' I should think,' said Charles, ' that this same Master Peveril has the more direct key to her language, after all we have heard.'

The king looked first at Peveril, who blushed like a maiden at the inference which the king's remark implied, and then suddenly turned his eyes on the supposed mute, on whose cheek a faint colour was dying away. A moment afterwards, at a signal from the countess, Fenella, or Zarah, stepped forward, and having kissed her lady's hand, stood with her arms folded on her breast, with a humble air, as different from that which she wore in the harem of the Duke of Buckingham, as that of a Magdalene from a Judith. Yet this was the least show of her talent of versatility, for so well did she play the part of the dumb girl, that Buckingham, sharp as his discernment was, remained undecided whether the creature which stood before him could possibly be the same with her, who had, in a different dress, made such an impression on his imagination, or indeed was the imperfect creature she now represented. She had at once all that could mark the imperfection of hearing, and all that could show the wonderful address by which nature so often makes up for the deficiency. There was the lip that trembled not at any sound—the seeming insensibility to the conversation that passed around ; while, on the other hand, was the quick and vivid glance, that seemed anxious to devour the meaning of those sounds, which she could gather no otherwise than by the motion of the lips.

Examined after her own fashion, Zarah confirmed the tale of Christian in all its points, and admitted that she had deranged the project laid for a mask, by placing the dwarf in her own stead ; the cause of her doing so she declined to assign, and the countess pressed her no further.

' Everything tells to exculpate my Lord of Buckingham,' said Charles, ' from so absurd an accusation : the dwarf's testimony is too fantastic, that of the two Peverils does not in the least affect the duke ; that of the dumb damsel completely contradicts the possibility of his guilt. Methinks, my lords, we should acquaint him that he stands acquitted of a complaint, too ridiculous to have been subjected to a more serious scrutiny than we have hastily made upon this occasion.'

Arlington bowed in acquiescence, but Ormond spoke plainly. ' I should suffer, sire, in the opinion of the Duke of Buckingham, brilliant as his talents are known to be, should I say that I am satisfied in my own mind on this occasion. But I subscribe to the spirit of the times ; and I agree it would be highly dangerous, on such accusations as we have been able to collect, to impeach the character of a zealous Protestant like his Grace—Had he been a Catholic, under such circumstances of suspicion, the Tower had been too good a prison for him.'

Buckingham bowed to the Duke of Ormond, with a meaning which even his triumph could not disguise.—' *Tu me la pagherai!* ' he muttered, in a tone of deep and abiding esentment ; but the stout old Irishman, who had long since braved his utmost wrath, cared little for this expression of his displeasure.

The king then, signing to the other nobles to pass into the public apartments, stopped Buckingham as he was about to follow them ; and when they were alone, asked, with a significant tone, which brought all the blood in the duke's veins into his countenance, ' When was it, George, that your useful friend Colonel Blood[n] became a musician ?—You are silent,' he said ; ' do not deny the charge, for yonder villain, once seen, is remembered for ever. Down, down on your knees, George, and acknowledge that you have abused my easy temper. Seek for no apology—none will serve your turn. I saw the man myself, among your Germans as you call them ; and you know what I must needs believe from such a circumstance.'

' Believe that I have been guilty—most guilty, my liege and king,' said the duke, conscience-stricken, and kneeling down ;—' believe that I was misguided—that I was mad— Believe anything but that I was capable of harming, or being accessory to harm, your person.'

' I do not believe it,' said the king ; ' I think of you, Villiers, as the companion of my dangers and my exile, and am so far from supposing you mean worse than you say, that I am convinced you acknowledge more than ever you meant to attempt.'

' By all that is sacred,' said the duke, still kneeling, ' had I not been involved to the extent of life and fortune with the villain Christian '——

' Nay, if you bring Christian on the stage again,' said the king, smiling, ' it is time for me to withdraw. Come, Villiers, rise—I forgive thee, and only recommend one act of penance—the curse you yourself bestowed on the dog who bit you—marriage, and retirement to your country-seat.'

The duke rose abashed, and followed the king into the circle, which Charles entered, leaning on the shoulder of his repentant peer ; to whom he showed so much countenance, as led the most acute observers present to doubt the possibility of there existing any real cause for the surmises to the duke's prejudice.

The Countess of Derby had in the meanwhile consulted with the Duke of Ormond, with the Peverils, and with her other friends ; and, by their unanimous advice, though with considerable difficulty, became satisfied, that to have thus shown herself at Court, was sufficient to vindicate the honour of her house ; and that it was her wisest course, after having done so, to retire to her insular dominions, without further provoking the resentment of a powerful faction. She took farewell of the king in form, and demanded his permission to carry back with her the helpless creature who had so strangely escaped from her protection, into a world where her condition rendered her so subject to every species of misfortune.

'Will your ladyship forgive me?' said Charles. 'I have studied your sex long—I am mistaken if your little maiden is not as capable of caring for herself as any of us.'

'Impossible!' said the countess.

'Possible, and most true,' whispered the king. 'I will instantly convince you of the fact, though the experiment is too delicate to be made by any but your ladyship. Yonder she stands, looking as if she heard no more than the marble pillar against which she leans. Now, if Lady Derby will contrive either to place her hand near the region of the damsel's heart, or at least on her arm, so that she can feel the sensation of the blood when the pulse increases, then do you, my Lord of Ormond, beckon Julian Peveril out of sight—I will show you in a moment that it can stir at sounds spoken.'

The countess, much surprised, afraid of some embarrassing pleasantry on the part of Charles, yet unable to repress her curiosity, placed herself near Fenella, as she called her little mute; and, while making signs to her, contrived to place her hand on her wrist.

At this moment the king, passing near them, said, 'This is a horrid deed—the villain Christian has stabbed young Peveril!'

The mute evidence of the pulse, which bounded as if a cannon had been discharged close by the poor girl's ear, was accompanied by such a loud scream of agony, as distressed, while it startled, the good-natured monarch himself. 'I did but jest,' he said; 'Julian is well, my pretty maiden. I only used the wand of a certain blind deity, called Cupid, to bring a deaf and dumb vassal of his to the exercise of her faculties.' [n]

'I am betrayed!' she said, with her eyes fixed on the ground—'I am betrayed!—and it is fit that she, whose life has been spent in practising treason on others, should be caught in her own snare. But where is my tutor in iniquity? —where is Christian, who taught me to play the part of spy on this unsuspicious lady, until I had wellnigh delivered her into his bloody hands?'

'This,' said the king, 'craves more secret examination.

Let all leave the apartment who are not immediately connected with these proceedings, and let this Christian be
again brought before us.—Wretched man,' he continued,
addressing Christian, ' what wiles are these you have practised, and by what extraordinary means ? '

' She has betrayed me, then ! ' said Christian—' Betrayed
me to bonds and death, merely for an idle passion, which
can never be successful !—But know, Zarah,' he added,
addressing her sternly, ' when my life is forfeited through
thy evidence, the daughter has murdered the father ! '

The unfortunate girl stared on him in astonishment.
' You said,' at length she stammered forth, ' that I was
the daughter of your slaughtered brother ? '

' That was partly to reconcile thee to the part thou wert
to play in my destined drama of vengeance—partly to hide
what men call the infamy of thy birth.   But *my* daughter
thou art ! and from the eastern clime, in which thy mother
was born, you derive that fierce torrent of passion which
I laboured to train to my purposes, but which, turned into
another channel, has become the cause of your father's
destruction,—my destiny is the Tower, I suppose ? '

He spoke these words with great composure, and scarce
seemed to regard the agonies of his daughter, who, throwing
herself at his feet, sobbed and wept most bitterly.

' This must not be,' said the king, moved with compassion
at this scene of misery.   ' If you consent, Christian, to leave
this country, there is a vessel in the river bound for New
England—Go, carry your dark intrigues to other lands.'

' I might dispute the sentence,' said Christian boldly ;
' and if I submit to it, it is a matter of my own choice.   One
half hour had made me even with that proud woman, but
fortune hath cast the balance against me.—Rise, Zarah,
Fenella no more ! Tell the Lady of Derby, that, if the daughter of Edward Christian, the niece of her murdered victim,
served her as a menial, it was but for the purpose of vengeance—miserably, miserably frustrated ! Thou seest thy
folly now—thou wouldst follow yonder ungrateful stripling
—thou wouldst forsake all other thoughts to gain his
slightest notice ; and now, thou art a forlorn outcast, ridi-
culed and insulted by those on whose necks you might have
trod, had you governed yourself with more wisdom ! But

come, thou art still my daughter—there are other skies than that which canopies Britain.'

' Stop him,' said the king ; ' we must know by what means this maiden found access to those confined in our prisons.'

' I refer your Majesty to your most Protestant jailer, and to the most Protestant peers, who, in order to obtain perfect knowledge of the depth of the Popish Plot, have contrived these ingenious apertures for visiting them in their cells by night or day. His Grace of Buckingham can assist your Majesty, if you are inclined to make the inquiry.'[1]

' Christian,' said the duke, ' thou art the most barefaced villain who ever breathed.'

' Of a commoner, I may,' answered Christian, and led his daughter out of the presence.

' See after him, Selby,' said the king ; ' lose not sight of him till the ship sail ; if he dare return to Britain, it shall be at his peril. Would to God we had as good riddance of others as dangerous ! And I would also,' he added, after a moment's pause, ' that all our political intrigues and feverish alarms could terminate as harmlessly as now. Here is a plot without a drop of blood ; and all the elements of a romance, without its conclusion. Here we have a wandering island princess (I pray my Lady of Derby's pardon), a dwarf, a Moorish sorceress, an impenitent rogue, and a repentant man of rank, and yet all ends without either hanging or marriage.'

' Not altogether without the latter,' said the countess, who had an opportunity, during the evening, of much private conversation with Julian Peveril. ' There is a certain Major Bridgenorth, who, since your Majesty relinquishes further inquiry into these proceedings, which he had otherwise intended to abide, designs, as we are informed, to leave England for ever. Now, this Bridgenorth, by dint of the law, hath acquired strong possession over the domains of Peveril, which he is desirous to restore to the ancient owners, with much fair land besides, conditionally, that our young Julian will receive them as the dowry of his only child and heir.'

' By my faith,' said the king, ' she must be a foul-favoured

---

[1] It was said that very unfair means were used to compel the prisoners, committed on account of the Popish Plot, to make disclosures, and that several of them were privately put to the torture.

wench, indeed, if Julian requires to be pressed to accept her on such fair conditions.'

'They love each other like lovers of the last age,' said the countess ; 'but the stout old knight likes not the round-headed alliance.'

'Our royal recommendation shall put that to rights,' said the king ; 'Sir Geoffrey Peveril has not suffered hardship so often at our command, that he will refuse our recommendation when it comes to make him amends for all his losses.'

It may be supposed the king did not speak without being fully aware of the unlimited ascendancy which he possessed over the old Tory ; for within four weeks afterwards, the bells of Martindale-Moultrassie were ringing for the union of the families, from whose estates it takes its compound name, and the beacon-light of the castle blazed high over hill and dale, and summoned all to rejoice who were within twenty miles of its gleam.

THE BEACON OF MARTINDALE-MOULTRASSIE

NOTES

The attempt to contrast the manners of the jovial cavaliers, and enthusiastic, yet firm and courageous, Puritans, was partly taken from a hint of Shadwell, who sketched several scenes of humour with great force, although they hung heavy on his pencil when he attempted to finish them for the stage.

In a dull play named *The Volunteers, or the Stock-Jobbers*, the dramatis personae present ' Major-General Blunt, an old cavalier officer, somewhat rough in speech, but very brave and honest, and of good understanding, and a good patriot '. A contrast to the General is ' Colonel Hackwell, senior, an old Anabaptist Colonel of Cromwell's, very stout and godly, but somewhat immoral '.

These worthies, so characterized, hold a dialogue together, which will form a good example of Shadwell's power of dramatizing. The stage is filled by Major-General Blunt and some of his old acquaintance cavaliers, and Hackwell, the ancient parliamentarian.

' *Major-General Blunt.* Fear not, my old cavaliers. According to your laudable customs, you shall be drunk, swagger, and fight over all your battles, from Edgehill to Brentford. You have not forgotten how this gentleman (*points to Colonel Hackwell*) and his demure psalm-singing fellows used to drub us ?

' *1st Cavalier.* No, 'gad ! I felt 'em once to purpose.

' *M.-G. Blunt.* Ah ! a-dod, in high-crowned hats, collared bands, great loose coats, long tucks under 'em, and calves-leather boots, they used to sing a psalm, fall on, and beat us to the devil !

' *Hackwell, senior.* In that day we stood up to the cause ; and the cause, the spiritual cause, did not suffer under our carnal weapons, but the enemy was discomfited, and lo ! they used to flee before us.

' *1st Cavalier.* Who would think such a snivelling, psalm-singing puppy would fight ? But these godly fellows would lay about them as if the devil were in 'em.

' *Sir Nicholas.* What a filthy slovenly army was this ! I warrant you not a well-dressed man among the Roundheads.

' *M.-G. Blunt.* But these plain fellows would so thrash your swearing, drinking, fine fellows in laced coats—just such as you of the drawing-room and Locket's fellows are now—and so strip them, by the Lord Harry, that after a battle those saints looked like the Israelites loaden with the Egyptian baggage.

' *Hackwell.* Verily, we did take the spoil ; and it served us to turn the penny, and advanced the cause thereby ; we fought upon a principle that carried us through.

' *M.-G. Blunt.* Prithee, Colonel, we know thy principle—'twas not right : thou foughtest against children's baptism, and not for liberty, but who should be your tyrant ; none so zealous for Cromwell as thou wert then, nor such a furious agitator and test-man as thou hast been lately.

' *Hackwell, senior.* Look you, Colonel, we but proceeded in the way of liberty of worship.

' *M.-G. Blunt.* A-dod, there is something more in it. This was thy principle, Colonel—*Dominion is founded in grace, and the righteous shall inherit the earth.* And, by the Lord Harry, thou didst so ; thou gottest three thousand pound a-year by fighting against the Court, and I lost a thousand by fighting for it.'—See *The Volunteers, or Stock-Jobbers*, Shadwell's *Works*, vol. iv, p. 437.

In a former scene, Hackwell, the old fanatic officer, conceiving himself offended by one of the dramatis personae, says, with great *naïveté*—' I prithee, friend, put me not to use the carnal weapon in my own defence.' Such are the traits of phraseology with which Shadwell painted the old Puritan officers, many of whom he—no mean observer of human nature—must have known familiarly.

Note 2.—Concealment of the Countess of Derby, p. 49

The concealment and discovery of the Countess of Derby is taken from a picturesque account of a similar event, described to me by the person by whom it was witnessed in childhood. This lady, by name Mrs. Margaret Swinton, and a daughter of that ancient house, was a sister of my maternal grandmother, and of course my grand-aunt. She was, as often happens on such occasions, our constant resource in sickness, or when we tired of noisy play, and closed around her to listen to her tales. As she might be supposed to look back to the beginning of the last century, the fund which supplied us with amusement often related to events of that period. I may here notice that she told me the unhappy story of the *Bride of Lammermoor*, being nearly related to the Lord President, whose daughter was the heroine of that melancholy tragedy.

The present tale, though of a different character, was also sufficiently striking, when told by an eyewitness. Aunt Margaret was, I suppose, seven or eight years old, when residing in the old mansion-house of Swinton, and already displayed the firmness and sagacity which distinguished her through life. Being one of a large family, she was, owing to slight indisposition, left at home one day when the rest of the family went to church, with Sir John and Lady Swinton, their parents. Before leaving the little invalid, she was strictly enjoined not to go into the parlour where the elder party had breakfasted. But when she found herself alone in the upper part of the house, the spirit of her great ancestress Eve took possession of my Aunt Margaret, and forth she went to examine the parlour in question. She was struck with admiration and fear at what she saw there. A lady, ' beautiful exceedingly,' was seated by the breakfast-table, and employed in washing the dishes which had been used. Little Margaret would have had no doubt in accounting this singular vision an emanation from the angelical world, but for her employment, which she could not so easily reconcile to her ideas of angels.

The lady, with great presence of mind, called the astonished child to her, fondled her with much tenderness, and judiciously avoiding to render the necessity of secrecy too severe, she told the girl she must not let any one except her mother know that she had seen her. Having allowed this escape-valve for the benefit of her curiosity, the mysterious stranger desired the little girl to look from the window of the parlour to see if her mother was returning from church. When she turned her head again, the fair vision had vanished, but by what means Miss Margaret was unable to form a conjecture.

Long watched, and eagerly waited for, the Lady Swinton at last returned from church, and her daughter lost no time in telling her extraordinary tale. ' You are a very sensible girl, Peggy,' answered her mother, ' for if you had spoken of that poor lady to any one but me, it might have cost her her life. But now I will not be afraid of trusting you with any secret, and I will show you where the poor lady lives.' In fact, she introduced her to a concealed apartment opening by a sliding panel from the parlour, and showed her the lady in the hiding-place which she inhabited. It may be said, in passing, that there were few Scottish houses belonging to families of rank which had not such contrivances, the political incidents of the times often calling them into occupation.

The history of the lady of the closet was both melancholy and bloody, and though I have seen various accounts of the story, I do not pretend to distinguish the right edition. She was a young woman of extreme beauty, who had been married to an old man, a writer, named MacFarlane. Her situation, and perhaps her manners, gave courage to some who desired to be accounted her suitors. Among them was a young Englishman, named Cayley, who was a commissioner of Government upon the estates forfeited in the Rebellion of 1715. In 1716, Mr. Cayley visited this lady in her lodgings, when they quarrelled, either on account of his having offered her some violence, or, as another account said, because she reproached him with having boasted of former favours. It ended in her seizing upon a pair of pistols, which lay loaded in a closet, her husband intending to take them with him on a journey. The gallant commissioner approached with an air of drollery, saying, ' What, madam, do you intend to perform a comedy ? '—' You shall find it a tragedy,' answered the lady ; and fired both pistols, by which Commissioner Cayley fell dead.

She fled, and remained concealed for a certain time. Her claim of refuge in Swinton House I do not know—it arose probably from some of the indescribable genealogical filaments which connect Scottish families. A very small cause would even at any time have been a reason for interfering between an individual and the law.

Whatever were the circumstances of Mrs. MacFarlane's case, it is certain that she returned, and lived and died in Edinburgh, without being brought to trial. Indeed, considering the times, there was no great wonder ; for, to one strong party, the death of an English commissioner was not a circumstance to require much apology. The Swintons, however, could not be of that opinion, the family being of Presbyterian and Whig principles.

NOTE 3.—EXECUTION OF CHRISTIAN, p. 61

The reader will find, in an Appendix to the Introduction (p. xiii), an account of this tragedy, as related by one who may be said to favour the sufferer. It must be admitted, on the other hand, that Captain Christian's trial and execution were conducted according to the laws of the island. He was tried in all due form, by the Dempster, or chief judge, then named Norris, the Keys of the island, and other constituted authorities, making what is called a Tinwald court. This word, yet retained in many parts of Scotland, signifies *Vallis Negotii*, and is applied to those artificial mounds which were in ancient times assigned to the meeting of the inhabitants for holding their *Comitia*. It was pleaded that the articles of accusation against Christian were found fully relevant, and, as he refused to plead at the bar, that he was, according to the Laws of Man, most justly sentenced to death. It was also stated that full time was left for appeal to England, as he was apprehended about the end of September, and not executed until the 2nd January, 1662. These defences were made for the various officers of the Isle of Man, called before the Privy Council, on account of Christian's death, and supported with many quotations from the Laws of the Island, and appear to have been received as a sufficient defence for their share in those proceedings.

I am obliged to the present reverend Vicar of Malew, for a certified extract to the following effect :—' Malew Burials. A.D. 1662. Mr. William Christian of Ronalds-wing, late receiver, was shot to death at Hange Hall, the 2d January. He died most penitently and couradgeously, made a good end, prayed earnestly, made an excellent speech, and the next day was buried in the chancell of Kirk Malew.'

It is certain that the death of William Christian made a very deep impression upon the minds of the islanders, and a Mr. Calcell or Colquit was much blamed on the occasion. Two lesser incidents are worth preservation as occurring at his execution. The place on which he stood was covered with white blankets, that his blood might not fall on the ground ; and, secondly, the precaution proved unnecessary, for, the musket wounds bleeding internally, there was no outward effusion of blood.

Many on the island deny Christian's guilt altogether, like his respectable descendant, the present Dempster; but there are others, and those men of judgement and respectability, who are so far of a different opinion, that they only allow the execution to have been wrong in so far as the culprit died by a military rather than a civil death. I willingly drop the veil over a transaction which took place *flagrantibus odiis* at the conclusion of a civil war, when Revenge at least was awake if Justice slept.

NOTE 4.—PAGES, p. 72

Even down to a later period than that in which the tale is laid, the ladies of distinction had for their pages young gentlemen of distinguished rank, whose education proceeded within the family of their patroness. Anne, Duchess of Buccleuch and Monmouth, who in several respects laid claim to the honour due to royal blood, was, I believe, the last person of rank who kept up this old custom. A general officer distinguished in the American war was bred up as a page in her family. At present the youths whom we sometimes see in the capacity of pages of great ladies, are, I believe, mere lackeys.

NOTE 5.—EJECTION OF THE PRESBYTERIAN CLERGY, p. 98

The ejection of the Presbyterian clergy took place on Saint Bartholomew's day, thence called Black Bartholomew. Two thousand Presbyterian pastors were on that day displaced and silenced throughout England. The preachers indeed had only the alternative to renounce their principles, or subscribe certain articles of uniformity. And to their great honour, Calamy, Baxter, and Reynolds refused bishoprics, and many other Presbyterian ministers declined deaneries and other preferments, and submitted to deprivation in preference.

NOTE 6.—PERSECUTION OF THE PURITANS, p. 125

It is naturally to be supposed, that the twenty years' triumph of the Puritans, and the violence towards the malignants, as they were wont to call the Cavaliers, had generated many grudges and feuds in almost every neighbourhood, which the victorious royalists failed not to act upon, so soon as the Restoration gave them a superiority. Captain Hodgson, a parliamentary officer who wrote his own memoirs, gives us many instances of this. I shall somewhat compress his long-winded account of his sufferings.

'It was after the King's return to London, one night a parcel of armed men comes to my house at Coalley Hall, near Halifax, and in an unseasonable hour in the night demands entrance, and my servants having some discourse with them on the outside, they gave threatening language, and put their pistols in at the window. My wife being with child, I ordered the doors to be opened, and they came in. After they had presented a pistol to my breast, they shewed me their authority to apprehend me under the hands and seals of two knights and deputy-lieutenants, "for speaking treasonable words against the King."' The ci-devant captain was conveyed to prison at Bradford, and bail refused. His prosecutor proved to be one Daniel Lyster, brother to the peace-officer who headed the troop for his apprehension. It seems that the prisoner Hodgson had once in former days bound over to his good behaviour this Daniel Lyster, then accused of adultery and other debauched habits. 'After the King came in,' says Hodgson, 'this man meets me, and demands the names of those that informed against him, and a copy of their information. I told him that the business was over, and that it was not reasonable to rip up old troubles, on which he threatened me, and said he would have them. "The sun," he said, "now shines on our side of the hedge."' Such being his accuser, Hodgson was tried for having said, 'There is a crown provided, but the King will never wear it'; to which was added, that he alleged he had 'never been a turncoat,' —never took the oath of allegiance, and never would do.' Little or no part of the charge was proved, while, on the contrary, it was shown that the prosecutor had been heard to say, that if times ever changed, he would sit on Hodgson's skirts. In fine, Hodgson escaped for five months' imprisonment, about thirty pounds expenses, and the necessity of swallowing the oath of allegiance, which seems to have been a bitter pill.

About the middle of June, 1662, Captain Hodgson was again arrested in a summary manner by one Peebles, an attorney, quarter-master to Sir John Armytage's troop of horse-militia, with about twelve other Cavaliers, who used him rudely, called him rebel and traitor, and seemed to wish to pick a quarrel with him, upon which he demanded to see their authority. Peebles laid his hand on his sword, and told him it was better authority than any ever granted by Cromwell. They suffered him, however, to depart, which he partly owed to the valour of his landlady, who sat down at the table-end betwixt him and danger, and kept his antagonist at some distance.

He was afterwards accused of having assembled some troopers, from his having been accidentally seen riding with a soldier, from which accusation he also escaped. Finally, he fell under suspicion of being concerned in a plot, of which the scene is called Sowerby. On this charge he is not explicit, but the grand jury found the bill ignoramus.

After this the poor Roundhead was again repeatedly accused and arrested; and the last occasion we shall notice occurred on 11th September, 1662, when he was disarmed by his old friend Mr. Peebles, at the head of a party. He demanded to see the warrant; on which he was answered as formerly by the quarter-master laying his hand on his sword-hilt, saying it was a better order than Oliver used to give. At length a warrant was produced, and Hodgson submitting to the search, they took from his dwelling-house better than £20 value in fowling-pieces, pistols, muskets, carbines, and such like. A quarrel ensued about his buff-coat, which Hodgson refused to deliver, alleging they had no authority to take his wearing-apparel. To this he remained constant, even upon the personal threats of Sir John Armytage, who called him rebel and traitor, and said, ' if I did not send the buff-coat with all speed, he would commit me to jail. I told him,' says Hodgson, ' I was no rebel, and he did not well to call me so before these soldiers and gentlemen, to make me the mark for every one to shoot at.' The buff-coat was then peremptorily demanded, and at length seized by open force. One of Sir John Armytage's brethren wore it for many years after, making good Prince Henry's observation, that a buff-jerkin is a most sweet robe of durance. An agent of Sir John's came to compound for this garment of proof. Hodgson says he would not have taken ten pounds for it. Sir John would have given about four, but insisting on the owner's receipt for the money, which its former possessor was unwilling to grant, the Tory magistrate kept both sides, and Hodgson never received satisfaction.

We will not prosecute Mr. Hodgson's tale of petty grievances any further. Enough has been said to display the melancholy picture of the country after the civil war, and to show the state of irritability and oppression which must have extended itself over the face of England, since there was scarcely a county in which battles had not been fought, and deep injuries sustained, during the ascendancy of the Roundheads, which were not afterwards retaliated by the vengeance of the Cavaliers.

NOTE 7.—FESTIVITIES IN THE ISLE OF MAN, p. 128

Waldron mentions the two popular festivities in the Isle of Man which are alluded to in the text, and vestiges of them are, I believe, still to be traced in this singular island. The Contest of Winter and Summer seems directly derived from the Scandinavians, long the masters in Man, as Olaus Magnus mentions a similar festival among the northern nations. On the first of May, he says, ' the country is divided into two bands, the captain of one of which hath the name and appearance of Winter, is clothed in skins of beasts, and he and his band armed with fire-forks. They fling about ashes, by way of prolonging the reign of Winter; while another band, whose captain is called Florro, represents Spring, with green boughs, such as the season offers. These parties skirmish in sport, and the mimic contest concludes with a general feast.' —*History of the Northern Nations*, by Olaus, book xv, chap. 2.

Waldron gives an account of a festival in Wales, exactly similar :

' In almost all the great parishes, they choose from among the daughters of the most wealthy farmers, a young maid, for the Queen of May. She is drest in the gayest and best manner they can, and is attended by about twenty others, who are called maids of honour. She has also a young man, who is her captain, and has under his command a good number of inferior officers. In opposition to her is the Queen of Winter, who is a man drest in woman's clothes, with woollen hoods, fur tippets, and loaded with the warmest and heaviest habits, one upon another; in the same manner are those, who represent her attendants, drest; nor is she without a captain and troop for her defence. Both being equipt as proper emblems of the beauty of the spring, and the deformity of the winter, they set forth from their respective quarters, the one preceded by violins and flutes, the other with the rough music of the tongs and cleavers. Both companies march till they meet on a common, and then their trains engage in a mock battle. If the Queen of Winter's forces get the better, so far as to take the Queen of May prisoner, she is ransomed for as much as pays the expenses of the day. After this ceremony, Winter and her company retire, and divert themselves in a barn, and the others remain on the green, where having danced a considerable time, they conclude the evening with a feast; the queen at one table with her maids, the captain with his troop at another. There are seldom less than fifty or sixty persons at each board, but not more than three or four knives. Christmas is ushered in with a form much less meaning, and infinitely more fatiguing. On the 24th of December, towards evening, all the servants in general have a holiday; they go not to bed all night, but ramble about till the bells ring in all the churches, which is at twelve o'clock; prayers being over, they go to hunt the wren, and after having found one of these poor birds, they kill her, and lay her on a bier with the utmost solemnity, bringing her to the parish church, and burying her with a whimsical kind of solemnity, singing dirges over her in the Manx language, which they call her knell; after which Christmas begins. There is not a barn unoccupied the whole twelve days, every parish hiring fiddlers at the public charge; and all the youth, nay, sometimes people well advanced in years, making no scruple to be among these nocturnal dancers.'—Waldron's *Description of the Isle of Man*, folio, 1731.

With regard to horse-racing in the Isle of Man, I am furnished with a certified copy of the rules on which that sport was conducted, under the permission of the Earl of Derby, in which the curious may see that a descendant of the unfortunate Christian entered a horse for the prize. I am indebted for this curiosity to my kind friend the learned Dr. Dibdin.

INSULA MONÆ. } *Articles for the plate which is to be run for in the said island, being of the value of five pounds sterling, (the fashion included,) given by the Right Honourable William Earl of Derby, Lord of the said Isle, &c.*

' 1*st*. The said plate is to be run for upon the 28th day of July, in euery year, whiles his honour is pleased to allow the same, (being the day of the nativity of the Honourable James Lord Strange,) except it happen upon a Sunday, and if soe, the said plate is to be run for upon the day following.

' 2*d*. That noe horse, gelding, or mair, shall be admitted to run for the said plate, but such as was foaled within the said island, or in the Calfe of Mann.

3*d.* That euery horse, gelding, or mair, that is designed to run, shall be entred at or before the viiijth day of July, with his master's name and his owne, if he be generally knowne by any, or els his collour, and whether horse, mair, or gelding, and that to be done at the x comprs. office, by the cleark of the rolls for the time being.

' 4*th.* That euery person that puts in either horse, mair, or gelding, shall, at the time of their entring, depositt the sume of fiue shill. apiece into the hands of the said cleark of the rolls, which is to goe towards the augmenting of the plate for the year following, besides one shill. apiece to be giuen by them to the said cleark of the rolls, for entring their names and engrossing these articles.

5*th.* That euery horse, mair, or gelding, shall carry horseman's weight, that is to say, ten stone weight, at fourteen pounds to each stone, besides sadle and bridle.

6*th.* That euery horse, mair, or gelding, shall haue a person for its tryer, to be named by the owner of the said horse, mair, or gelding, which tryers are to have the comand of the scales and weights, and to see that euery rider doe carry full weight, according as is mencioned in the foregoing article, and especially that the wining rider be soe with the usuall allowance of one pound for———.

' 7*th.* That a person be assigned by the tryers to start the runinge horses, who are to run for the said plate, betwixt the howers of one and three of the clock in the afternoon.

8*th.* That euery rider shall leave the two first powles which are sett upp in Macybreas close, in this maner following, that is to say, the first of the said two powles upon his right hand, and the other upon his left hand ; and the two powles by the rockes are to be left upon the left hand likewise ; and the fifth powle, which is sett up at the lower end of the Conney-warren, to be left alsoe upon the left hand, and soe the turning powle next to Wm. Looreyes house to be left in like maner upon the left hand, and the other two powles, leading to the ending powle, to be left upon the right hand ; all which powles are to be left by the riders as aforesaid, excepting only the distance-powle, which may be rid on either hand, at the discrecion of the rider,' &c. &c. &c.

July 14*th,* 1687.

' The names of the persons who have entered their horses to run for the within plate for this present year, 1687.

' Ro. Heywood, Esq., Governor of this Isle, hath entered ane bay-gelding, called by the name of Loggerhead, and hath deposited towards the augmenting of the plate for the next year, . . £00 05 00

' Captain Tho. Hudlston hath entred one white gelding, called Snowball, and hath depositted, ... 00 05 00

' Mr. William Faigler hath entred his gray gelding, called the Gray-Carraine, and depositted, ... 00 05 00

' Mr. Nicho. Williams hath entred one gray stone horse, called the Yorkshire gray, and depositted, ... 00 05 00

' Mr. Demster Christian hath entred one gelding, called the Dapple-gray, and hath depossitted, ... 00 05 00

' MEMORANDUM,   ' 28*th July,* 1687.

' That this day the above plate was rûn for by the fore-mencioned horse, and the same was fairly won by the right worshipful governor's horse at the two first heates.

' 17*th August,* 1688.

' Received this day the above   , which I am to pay to my
master to augment yᵉ plate, by me,
                                    ' JOHN WOOD.

'It is my good-will and pleasure y^t ye 2 prizes formerly granted (by me) for hors runing and shouting, shall continue as they did, to be run, or shot for, and soe to continue dureing my good-will and pleasure. Given under my hand att Lathom, ye 12 of July, 1669.

'DERBY.

'To my governor's deputy-governor, and y^e
rest of my officers in my Isle of Man.'

NOTE 8.—RICHARD WHALLEY, p. 176

There is a common tradition in America that this person, who was never heard of after the Restoration, fled to Massachusetts, and, living for some years concealed in that province, finally closed his days there. The remarkable and beautiful story of his having suddenly emerged from his place of concealment, and, placing himself at the head of a party of settlers, shown them the mode of acquiring a victory, which they were on the point of yielding to the Indians, is also told ; and in all probability truly. I have seen the whole tradition commented upon at large in a late North American publication, which goes so far as to ascertain the obscure grave to which the remains of Whalley were secretly committed. This singular story has lately afforded the justly celebrated American novelist, Mr. Cooper, the materials from which he has compiled one of those impressive narratives of the aboriginal inhabitants of the Transatlantic woods and the hardy Europeans by whom they were invaded and dispossessed.

NOTE 9.—HOLM PEEL, p. 179

The author has never seen this ancient fortress, which has in its circuit so much that is fascinating to the antiquary. Waldron has given the following description, which is perhaps somewhat exaggerated :—

'Peel, or Pile Town, is so called from its garrison and castle ; though in effect the castle cannot properly be said to be in the town, an arm of the sea running between them, which in high tides would be deep enough to bear a ship of forty or fifty ton, though sometimes quite drained of salt water ; but then it is supplied with fresh by a river which runs from Kirk Jarmyn Mountains, and empties itself into the sea. This castle for its situation, antiquity, strength, and beauty, might justly come in for one of the wonders of the world. Art and nature seem to have vied with each other in the model, nor ought the most minute particular to escape observation. As to its situation, it is built upon the top of a huge rock, which rears itself a stupendous height above the sea, with which, as I said before, it is surrounded. And also by natural fortifications of other lesser rocks, which render it inaccessible but by passing that little arm of the sea which divides it from the town ; this you may do in a small boat ; and the natives, tucking up their clothes under their arms, and plucking off their shoes and stockings, frequently wade it in low tides. When you arrive at the foot of the rock, you ascend about some threescore steps, which are cut out of it to the first wall, which is immensely thick and high, and built of a very durable and bright stone, though not of the same sort with that of Castle Russin in Castle Town ; and has on it four little houses, or watch-towers, which overlook the sea. The gates are wood, but most curiously arched, carved, and adorned with pilasters. Having passed the first, you have other stairs of near half the number with the former to mount, before you come at the second wall, which, as well as the other, is full of port-holes, for cannon, which are planted on stone crosses on a third wall. Being entered, you find yourself in a wide plain, in the midst of which stands the castle, encompassed by four churches, three of which time has so much decayed, that there is little remaining besides the walls, and some few tombs, which seem to have been erected with so much care, as to perpetuate the memory of those buried in them till the final dissolution of all things. The fourth is kept a little better in repair ; but not so much for its own sake, though it has been the most magnificent of them all, as for a chapel within it ; which is appropriated to the use of the bishop, and has under it a prison, or rather dungeon, for those offenders who are so miserable as to incur the spiritual censure. This is certainly one of the most dreadful places that imagination can form. The sea runs under it through the hollows of the rock with such a continual roar, that you would think it were every moment breaking in upon you, and over it are the vaults for burying the dead. The stairs descending to this place of terrors are not above thirty, but so steep and narrow, that they are very difficult to go down, a child of eight or nine years old not being able to pass them but sideways. Within it are thirteen pillars, on which the whole chapel is supported. They have a superstition that whatsoever stranger goes to see this cavern out of curiosity, and omits to count the pillars, shall do something to occasion being confined there. There are places for penance also under all the other churches, containing several very dark and horrid cells ; some have nothing in them either to sit or lie down on, others a small piece of brick work ; some are lower and more dark than others, but all of them, in my opinion, dreadful enough for almost any crime humanity is capable of being guilty of ; though 'tis supposed they were built with different degrees of horror, that the punishment might be proportionate to the faults of those wretches who were to be confined in them. These have never been made use of since the times of popery ; but that under the bishop's chapel is the common and only prison for all offences in the spiritual court, and to that the delinquents are sentenced. But the soldiers of the garrison permit them to suffer their confinement in the castle, it being morally impossible for the strongest constitution to sustain the damps and noisomeness of the cavern even for a few hours, much less for months and years, as is the punishment sometimes allotted. But I shall speak hereafter more fully of the severity of the ecclesiastical jurisdiction. 'Tis certain that here have been very great architects in this island ; for the noble monuments in this church, which is kept in repair, and indeed the ruins of the others also, show the builders to be masters of all the orders in that art, though the great number of Doric pillars prove them to be chiefly admirers of that. Nor are the epitaphs and inscriptions on the tombstones less worthy of remark ; the various languages in which they are engraved testify by what a diversity of nations this little spot of earth has been possessed. Though time has defaced too many of the letters to render the remainder intelligible, yet you may easily perceive fragments of the Hebrew, Greek, Latin, Arabian, Saxon, Scotch, and Irish characters ; some dates yet visible declare they were written before the coming of Christ ; and, indeed, if one considers the walls, the thickness of them, and the durableness of the stone of which they are composed, one must be sensible that a great number of centuries must pass before such strong workmanship could be reduced to the condition it now is. These churches, therefore, were doubtless once the temples of Pagan deities, though since consecrated to the worship of the true divinity ; and what confirms me more strongly in this conjecture is, that there is still a part of one remaining, where stands a large stone directly in form and manner like the Triposes, which in those days of ignorance the priests stood upon, to deliver their fabulous oracles. Through one of these old churches, there was formerly a passage to the apartment belonging to the captain of the guard, but is now closed up. The reason they give you for it is a pretty odd one ; but as I think it not sufficient satisfaction to my curious reader, to acquaint him with what sort of buildings this island affords, without letting him know also what traditions are concerning them, I shall have little regard to the censure of those critics who find fault with everything out of the common road ; and in this, as well as in all other places where it falls in my way, shall make it my endeavour to lead him into the humours and very souls of the Manx people. They say that an apparition, called in their language the Mauthe Doog, in the shape of a large black spaniel with curled shaggy hair, was used to haunt Peel Castle, and has been frequently seen in every room, but particularly in the guard-chamber, where, as soon as candles were lighted, it came and lay down before the fire, in presence of all the soldiers, who at length, by being so much accustomed to the sight of it, lost great part of the terror they were seized with at its first appearance. They still, however, retained a certain awe, as believing it was an evil spirit which only waited permission to do them hurt, and for that reason forbore swearing and all profane discourse while in its company. But though they endured the shock of such a guest when altogether in a body, none cared to be left alone with it. It being the custom, therefore, for one of the soldiers to lock the gates of the castle at a certain hour, and carry the keys to the captain, to whose apartment, as I said before, the way led through a church, they agreed among themselves, that whoever was to succeed the ensuing night his fellow in this errand should accompany him that went first, and by this means no man would be exposed singly to the danger; for I forgot to mention that the Mauthe Doog was always seen to come out from that passage at the close of day, and return to it again as soon as the morning dawned, which made them look on this place as its peculiar residence. One night a fellow being drunk, and by the strength of his liquor rendered more daring than ordinary, laughed at the simplicity of his companions, and though it was not his turn to go with the keys, would needs take that office upon him to testify his courage. All the soldiers endeavoured to dissuade him, but the more they said the more resolute he seemed, and swore that he desired nothing more than that Mauthe Doog would follow him, as it had done the others, for he would try if it were dog or devil. After having talked in a very reprobate manner for some time, he snatched up the keys, and went out of the guard-room; in some time after his departure a great noise was heard, but nobody had the boldness to see what occasioned it, till, the adventurer returning, they demanded the knowledge of him; but as loud and noisy as he had been at leaving them, he was now become sober and silent enough, for he was never heard to speak more; and though all the time he lived, which was three days, he was entreated by all who came near him, either to speak, or, if he could not do that, to make some signs, by which they might understand what had happened to him, yet nothing intelligible could be got from him, only that by the distortion of his limbs and features it might be guessed that he died in agonies more than is common in a natural death. The Mauthe Doog was, however, never seen after in the castle, nor would any one attempt to go through that passage, for which reason it was closed up, and another way made. This accident happened about threescore years since, and I heard it attested by several, but especially by an old soldier, who assured me he had seen it oftener than he had then hairs on his head. Having taken notice of everything remarkable in the churches, I believe my reader will be impatient to come to the castle itself, which, in spite of the magnificence the pride of modern ages has adorned the palaces of princes with, exceeds not only everything I have seen, but also read of, in nobleness of structure. Though now no more than a garrison for soldiers, you cannot enter it without being struck with a veneration which the most beautiful buildings of later years cannot inspire you with; the largeness and loftiness of the rooms, the vast echo resounding through them, the many winding galleries, the prospect of the sea, and the ships, which, by reason of the height of the place, seem but like buoys floating on the waves, make you fancy yourself in a superior orb to what the rest of mankind inhabit, and fill you with contemplations the most refined and pure that the soul is capable of conceiving.'— Waldron's *Description of the Isle of Man*, folio, 1731, p. 103.

In this description, the account of the inscriptions in so many Oriental languages, and bearing date before the Christian era, is certainly as much exaggerated as the story of the *Mauthe Doog* itself. It would be very desirable to find out the meaning of the word *Mauthe* in the Manx language, which is a dialect of the Gaelic. I observe that Maithe in Gaelic, amongst other significations, has that of *active* or *speedy*; and also that a dog of Richard II, mentioned by Froissart, and supposed to intimate the fall of his master's authority by leaving him and fawning on Bolingbroke, was termed Mauthe; but neither of these particulars tends to explain the very impressive story of the fiendish hound of Peel Castle.

NOTE 10.—MANX SUPERSTITIONS, p. 196

The story often alludes to the various superstitions which are, or at least were, received by the inhabitants of the Isle of Man, an ancient Celtic race, still speaking the language of their fathers. They retained a plentiful stock of those wild legends which overawed the reason of a dark age, and in our own time annoy the imagination of those who listen to the fascination of the tale, while they despise its claims to belief. The following curious legendary traditions are extracted from Waldron, a huge mine, in which I have attempted to discover some specimens of spar, if I cannot find treasure.

' 'Tis this ignorance,' meaning that of the islanders, ' which is the occasion of the excessive superstition which reigns among them. I have already given some hints of it, but not enough to show the world what a Manksman truly is, and what power the prejudice of education has over weak minds. If books were of any use among them, one would swear the Count of Gabalis had been not only translated into the Manks tongue, but that it was a sort of rule of faith to them, since there is no fictitious being mentioned by him in his book of absurdities, which they would not readily give credit to. I know not, idolizers as they are of the clergy, whether they would not be even refractory to them, were they to preach against the existence of fairies, or even against their being commonly seen; for though the priesthood are a kind of gods among them, yet still tradition is a greater god than they; and as they confidently assert that the first inhabitants of their island were fairies, so do they maintain that these little people have still their residence among them. They call them the Good People, and say they live in wilds and forests, and on mountains, and shun great cities because of the wickedness acted therein; all the houses are blessed where they visit, for they fly vice. A person would be thought impudently profane, who should suffer his family to go to bed without having first set a tub, or pail, full of clean water, for these guests to bathe themselves in, which the natives aver they constantly do, as soon as ever the eyes of the family are closed, wherever they vouchsafe to come. If anything happen to be mislaid, and found again in some place where it was not expected, they presently tell you a fairy took it and returned it; if you chance to get a fall and hurt yourself, a fairy laid something in your way to throw you down, as a punishment for some sin you have committed. I have heard many of them protest they have been carried insensibly great distances from home, and, without knowing how they came there, found themselves on the top of a mountain. One story in particular was told me of a man who had been led by invisible musicians for several miles together; and not being able to resist the harmony, followed till it conducted him to a large common, where were a great number of little people sitting round a table, and eating and drinking in a very jovial manner. Among them were some faces whom he thought he had formerly seen, but forbore taking any notice, or they of him, till the little people, offering him drink, one of them, whose features seemed not unknown to him, plucked him by the coat, and forbade him, whatever he did, to taste anything he saw before him; for if you do, added he, you will be as I am, and return no more to your family. The poor man was much affrighted, but resolved to obey the injunction; accordingly a large silver cup, filled with some sort of liquor, being put into his hand, he found an opportunity to throw what it contained on the ground. Soon after the music ceasing, all the company disappeared, leaving the cup in his hand, and he returned home, though much wearied and fatigued.

He went the next day and communicated to the minister of the parish all that had happened, and asked his advice how he should dispose of the cup, to which the parson replied, he could not do better than devote it to the service of the church ; and this very cup, they tell me, is that which is now used for the consecrated wine in Kirk-Merlugh.

'Another instance they gave me to prove the reality of fairies, was of a fiddler, who having agreed with a person, who was a stranger, for so much money, to play to some company he should bring him to, all the twelve days of Christmas, and received earnest for it, saw his new master vanish into the earth the moment he had made the bargain. Nothing could be more terrified than was the poor fiddler ; he found he had entered himself into the devil's service, and looked on himself as already damned ; but having recourse also to a clergyman, he received some hope ; he ordered him, however, as he had taken earnest, to go when he should be called : but that whatever tune should be called for, to play none but psalms. On the day appointed, the same person appeared, with whom he went, though with what inward reluctance 'tis easy to guess ; but punctually obeying the minister's directions, the company to whom he played were so angry, that they all vanished at once, leaving him at the top of a high hill, and so bruised and hurt, though he was not sensible when, or from what hand, he received the blows, that he got not home without the utmost difficulty. The old story of infants being changed in their cradles is here in such credit, that mothers are in continual terror at the thoughts of it. I was prevailed upon myself to go and see a child, who they told me was one of these changelings ; and, indeed, must own was not a little surprised, as well as shocked, at the sight : nothing under heaven could have a more beautiful face ; but though between five and six years old, and seemingly healthy, he was so far from being able to walk or stand, that he could not so much as move any one joint ; his limbs were vastly long for his age, but smaller than an infant's of six months ; his complexion was perfectly delicate, and he had the finest hair in the world ; he never spoke nor cried, eat scarce anything, and was very seldom seen to smile ; but if any one called him a fairy-elf, he would frown and fix his eyes so earnestly on those who said it, as if he would look them through. His mother, or at least his supposed mother, being very poor, frequently went out a-chairing, and left him a whole day together ; the neighbours, out of curiosity, have often looked in at the window to see how he behaved when alone ; which, whenever they did, they were sure to find him laughing, and in the utmost delight. This made them judge that he was not without company more pleasing to him than any mortals could be ; and what made this conjecture seem the more reasonable, was, that if he were left ever so dirty, the woman, at her return, saw him with a clean face, and his hair combed with the utmost exactness and nicety.

'A second account of this nature I had from a woman to whose offspring the fairies seemed to have taken a particular fancy. The fourth or fifth night after she was delivered of her first child, the family were alarmed with a most terrible cry of fire, on which everybody ran out of the house to see whence it proceeded, not excepting the nurse, who, being as much frighted as the others, made one of the number. The poor woman lay trembling in her bed alone, unable to help herself, and her back being turned to the infant, saw not that it was taken away by an invisible hand. Those who had left her having inquired about the neighbourhood, and finding there was no cause for the outcry they had heard, laughed at each other for the mistake ; but as they were going to re-enter the house, the poor babe lay on the threshold, and by its cries preserved itself from being trod upon. This exceedingly amazed all that saw it, and the mother being still in bed, they could ascribe no reason for finding it there, but having been removed by fairies, who, by their sudden return, had been prevented from carrying it any farther. About a year after, the same woman was brought to bed of a second child, which had not been born many nights before a great noise was heard in the house where they kept their cattle ; (for in this island, where there is no shelter in the fields from the excessive cold and damps, they put all their milch-kine into a barn, which they call a cattle-house). Everybody that was stirring ran to see what was the matter, believing that the cows had got loose; the nurse was as ready as the rest, but, finding all safe, and the barn door close, immediately returned, but not so suddenly but that the new-born babe was taken out of the bed, as the former had been, and dropped on their coming, in the middle of the entry. This was enough to prove the fairies had made a second attempt; and the parents sending for a minister, joined with him in thanksgiving to God, who had twice delivered their children from being taken from them. But in the time of her third lying-in, everybody seemed to have forgot what had happened in the first and second, and on a noise in the cattle-house, ran out to know what had occasioned it. The nurse was the only person, excepting the woman in the straw, who stayed in the house, nor was she detained through care or want of curiosity, but by the bonds of sleep, having drank a little too plentifully the preceding day. The mother, who was broad awake, saw her child lifted out of the bed, and carried out of the chamber, though she could not see any person touch it; on which she cried out as loud as she could, "Nurse, nurse! my child, my child is taken away!" but the old woman was too fast to be awakened by the noise she made, and the infant was irretrievably gone. When her husband, and those who had accompanied him, returned, they found her wringing her hands, and uttering the most piteous lamentations for the loss of her child; on which, said the husband, looking into the bed, The woman is mad, do not you see the child lies by you? On which she turned, and saw indeed something like a child, but far different from her own, who was a very beautiful, fat, well-featured babe; whereas, what was now in the room of it, was a poor, lean, withered, deformed creature. It lay quite naked, but the clothes belonging to the child that was exchanged for it lay wrapped up altogether on the bed. This creature lived with them near the space of nine years, in all which time it eat nothing except a few herbs, nor was ever seen to void any other excrement than water. It neither spoke, nor could stand or go, but seemed enervate in every joint, like the changeling I mentioned before, and in all its actions showed itself to be of the same nature.

'A woman, who lived about two miles distant from Ballasalli, and used to serve my family with butter, made me once very merry with a story she told me of her daughter, a girl of about ten years old, who being sent over the fields to the town, for a pennyworth of tobacco for her father, was on the top of a mountain surrounded by a great number of little men, who would not suffer her to pass any farther. Some of them said she should go with them, and accordingly laid hold of her; but one seeming more pitiful, desired they would let her alone; which they refusing, there ensued a quarrel, and the person who took her part fought bravely in her defence. This so incensed the others, that to be revenged on her for being her cause, two or three of them seized her, and pulling up her clothes, whipped her heartily; after which, it seems, they had no further power over her, and she run home directly, telling what had befallen her, and showing her buttocks, on which were the prints of several small hands. Several of the townspeople went with her to the mountain, and she conducting them to the spot, the little antagonists were gone, but had left behind them proofs (as the good woman said) that what the girl had informed them was true, for there was a great deal of blood to be seen on the stones. This did she aver with all the solemnity imaginable.

'Another woman, equally superstitious and fanciful as the former, told me, that being great with child, and expecting every moment the good hour, as she lay awake one night in her bed, she saw seven or eight little women come into her chamber, one of whom had an infant in her arms; they were followed by a man of the same size with themselves, but in the habit of a minister. One of them went to the pail, and finding no water in it, cried out to the others, what must they do to christen the child? On which they replied, it should be done in beer. With that the seeming parson took the child in his arms, and performed the ceremony of baptism, dipping his hand into a great tub of strong beer, which the woman had brewed the day before to be ready for her lying-in. She told me that they baptized the infant by the name of Joan, which made her know she was pregnant of a girl, as it proved a few days after, when she was delivered. She added also, that it was common for the fairies to make a mock christening when any person was near her time, and that according to what child, male or female, they brought, such should the woman bring into the world.

' But I cannot give over this subject without mentioning what they say befell a young sailor, who, coming off a long voyage, though it was late at night, chose to land rather than be another night in the vessel ; being permitted to do so, he was set on shore at Douglas. It happened to be a fine moonlight night, and very dry, being a small frost ; he therefore forbore going into any house to refresh himself, but made the best of his way to the house of a sister he had at Kirk-Merlugh. As he was going over a pretty high mountain, he heard the noise of horses, the hollow of a huntsman, and the finest horn in the world. He was a little surprised that anybody pursued those kinds of sports in the night, but he had not time for much reflection before they all passed by him, so near, that he was able to count what number there was of them, which, he said, was thirteen, and that they were all dressed in green, and gallantly mounted. He was so well pleased with the sight, that he would gladly have followed, could he have kept pace with them ; he crossed the footway, however, that he might see them again, which he did more than once, and lost not the sound of the horn for some miles. At length, being arrived at his sister's, he tells her the story, who presently clapped her hands for joy that he was come home safe ; for, said she, those you saw were fairies, and 'tis well they did not take you away with them. There is no persuading them but that these huntings are frequent in the island, and that these little gentry, being too proud to ride on Manks horses, which they might find in the field, make use of the English and Irish ones, which are brought over and kept by gentlemen. They say that nothing is more common than to find these poor beasts, in a morning, all over in a sweat and foam, and tired almost to death, when their owners have believed they have never been out of the stable. A gentleman of Ballafletcher assured me, he had three or four of his best horses killed with these nocturnal journeys.

' At my first coming into the island, and hearing these sort of stories, I imputed the giving credit to them merely to the simplicity of the poor creatures who related them ; but was strangely surprised when I heard other narratives of this kind, and altogether as absurd, attested by men who passed for persons of sound judgement. Among this number was a gentleman, my near neighbour, who affirmed, with the most solemn asseverations, that being of my opinion, and entirely averse to the belief that any such beings were permitted to wander for the purposes related of them, he had been at last convinced by the appearance of several little figures playing and leaping over some stones in a field, whom at a few yards' distance he imagined were schoolboys, and intended, when he came near enough, to reprimand for being absent from their exercises at that time of the day, it being then, he said, between three and four of the clock ; but when he approached, as near as he could guess, within twenty paces, they all immediately disappeared, though he had never taken his eye off them from the first moment he beheld them ; nor was there any place where they could so suddenly retreat, it being an open field without hedge or bush, and, as I said before, broad day.

' Another instance, which might serve to strengthen the credit of the other, was told me by a person who had the reputation of the utmost integrity. This man being desirous of disposing of a horse he had at that time no great occasion for, and riding him to market for that purpose, was accosted, in passing over the mountains, by a little man in a plain dress, who asked him if he would sell his horse. 'Tis the design I am going on, replied the person who told me the story. On which the other desired to know the price. Eight pounds, said he. No, resumed the purchaser, I will give no more than seven; which, if you will take, here is your money. The owner, thinking he had bid pretty fair, agreed with him; and the money being told out, the one dismounted, and the other got on the back of the horse, which he had no sooner done, than both beast and rider sunk into the earth immediately, leaving the person who had made the bargain in the utmost terror and consternation. As soon as he had a little recovered himself, he went directly to the parson of the parish, and related what had passed, desiring he would give his opinion whether he ought to make use of the money he had received or not. To which he replied, that as he had made a fair bargain, and no way circumvented, nor endeavoured to circumvent, the buyer, he saw no reason to believe, in case it was an evil spirit, it could have any power over him. On this assurance, he went home well satisfied, and nothing afterward happened to give him any disquiet concerning this affair.

' A second account of the same nature I had from a clergyman, and a person of more sanctity than the generality of his function in this island. It was his custom to pass some hours every evening in a field near his house, indulging meditation, and calling himself to an account for the transactions of the past day. As he was in this place one night, more than ordinarily wrapped in contemplation, he wandered, without thinking where he was, a considerable way farther than it was usual for him to do; and, as he told me, he knew not how far the deep musing he was in might have carried him, if it had not been suddenly interrupted by a noise, which, at first, he took to be the distant bellowing of a bull; but as he listened more heedfully to it, found there was something more terrible in the sound than could proceed from that creature. He confessed to me, that he was no less affrighted than surprised, especially when, the noise coming still nearer, he imagined, whatever it was that it proceeded from, it must pass him. He had, however, presence enough of mind to place himself with his back to a hedge, where he fell on his knees, and began to pray to God with all the vehemence so dreadful an occasion required. He had not been long in that position, before he beheld something in the form of a bull, but infinitely larger than ever he had seen in England, much less in Man, where the cattle are very small in general. The eyes, he said, seemed to shoot forth flames, and the running of it was with such a force, that the ground shook under it as an earthquake. It made directly toward a little cottage, and thereafter most horribly disappeared. The moon being then at the full, and shining in her utmost splendour, all these passages were visible to our amazed divine, who, having finished his ejaculation, and given thanks to God for his preservation, went to the cottage, the owner of which, they told him, was that moment dead. The good old gentleman was loath to pass a censure which might be judged an uncharitable one; but the deceased having the character of a very ill liver, most people who heard the story were apt to imagine this terrible apparition came to attend his last moments.

' A mighty bustle they also make of an apparition, which, they say, haunts Castle Russin, in the form of a woman who was some years since executed for the murder of her child. I have heard not only persons who have been confined there for debt, but also the soldiers of the garrison, affirm they have seen it various times; but what I took most notice of, was the report of a gentleman, of whose good understanding, as well as veracity, I have a very great opinion. He told me, that happening to be abroad late one night, and catched in an excessive storm of wind and rain, he saw a woman stand before the castle gate, where, being not the least shelter, it something surprised him that anybody, much less one of that sex, should not rather run to some little porch, or shed, of which there are several in Castle Town, than choose to stand still, exposed and alone, to such a dreadful tempest. His curiosity exciting him to draw nearer, that he might discover who it was that seemed so little to regard the fury of the elements, he perceived she retreated on his approach, and at last, he thought, went into the Castle, though the gates were shut. This obliging him to think he had seen a spirit, sent him home very much terrified ; but the next day, relating his adventure to some people who lived in the Castle, and describing, as near as he could, the garb and stature of the apparition, they told him it was that of the woman above-mentioned, who had been frequently seen by the soldiers on guard, to pass in and out of the gates, as well as to walk through the rooms, though there was no visible means to enter. Though so familiar to the eye, no person has yet, however, had the courage to speak to it, and, as they say a spirit has no power to reveal its mind without being conjured to do so in a proper manner, the reason of its being permitted to wander is unknown.

' Another story of the like nature I have heard concerning an apparition, which has frequently been seen on a wild common near Kirk Jarmyn mountains, which, they say, assumes the shape of a wolf, and fills the air with most terrible howlings. But having run on so far in the account of supernatural appearances, I cannot forget what was told me by an English gentleman, and my particular friend. He was about passing over Douglas Bridge before it was broken down, but the tide being high, he was obliged to take the river, having an excellent horse under him, and one accustomed to swim. As he was in the middle of it, he heard, or imagined he heard, the finest symphony, I will not say in the world, for nothing human ever came up to it. The horse was no less sensible of the harmony than himself, and kept in an immovable posture all the time it lasted ; which, he said, could not be less than three-quarters of an hour, according to the most exact calculation he could make, when he arrived at the end of his little journey, and found how long he had been coming. He, who before laughed at all the stories told of fairies, now became a convert, and believed as much as ever a Manksman of them all. As to circles in the grass, and the impression of small feet among the snow, I cannot deny but I have seen them frequently, and once thought I heard a whistle, as though in my ear, when nobody that could make it was near me. For my part, I shall not pretend to determine if such appearances have any reality, or are only the effect of the imagination ; but as I had much rather give credit to them, than be convinced by ocular demonstration, I shall leave the point to be discussed by those who have made it more their study, and only say, that whatever belief we ought to give to some accounts of this kind, there are others, and those much more numerous, which merit only to be laughed at—it not being at all consonant to reason, or the idea religion gives us of the fallen angels, to suppose spirits, so eminent in wisdom and knowledge as to be exceeded by nothing but their Creator, should visit the earth for such trifling purposes as to throw bottles and glasses about a room, and a thousand other as ridiculous gambols mentioned in those voluminous treatises of apparitions.

' The natives of this island tell you also, that before any person dies, the procession of the funeral is acted by a sort of beings, which for that end render themselves visible. I know several that have offered to make oath, that as they have been passing the road one of these funerals has come behind them, and even laid the bier on their shoulders, as though to assist the bearers. One person, who assured me he had been served so, told me that the flesh of his shoulder had been very much bruised, and was black for many weeks after. There are few or none of them who pretend not to have seen or heard these imaginary obsequies (for I must not omit that they sing psalms in the same manner as those do who accompany the corpse of a dead friend), which so little differ from real ones, that they are not to be known till both coffin and mourners are seen to vanish at the church doors. These they take to be a sort of friendly demons, and their business, they say, is to warn people of what is to befall them ; accordingly, they give notice of any stranger's approach, by the trampling of horses at the gate of the house where they are to arrive. As difficult as I found it to bring myself to give any faith to this, I have frequently been very much surprised, when, on visiting a friend, I have found the table ready spread, and everything in order to receive me, and being told by the person to whom I went, that he had knowledge of my coming, or some other guest, by these good-natured intelligencers ; nay, when obliged to be absent some time from home, my own servants have assured me they were informed by these means of my return, and expected me the very hour I came, though perhaps it was some days before I hoped it myself at my going abroad. That this is fact, I am positively convinced by many proofs ; but how or wherefore it should be so, has frequently given me much matter of reflection, yet left me in the same uncertainty as before. Here, therefore, I will quit the subject, and proceed to things much easier to be accounted for.'—Waldron's *Description of the Isle of Man*, folio, 1731, p. 125.

This long quotation is extremely curious, as containing an account of those very superstitions in the Isle of Man which are frequently collected both in Ireland and in the Highlands of Scotland, and which have employed the attention of Mr. Crofton Croker, and of the author of the *Fairy Mythology*. The superstitions are in every respect so like each other, that they may be referred to one common source ; unless we conclude that they are natural to the human mind, and, like the common orders of vegetables, which naturally spring up in every climate, these naturally arise in every bosom ; as the best philologists are of opinion that fragments of an original speech are to be discovered in almost all languages in the globe.

NOTE 11.—SALE OF A DANCING GIRL, p. 246

An instance of such a sale of an unfortunate dancing girl occurred in Edinburgh in the end of the seventeenth century.

' 13th January, 1687.—Reid the mountebank pursues Scott of Harden and his lady, for stealing away from him a little girl called *The tumbling lassie*, that danced upon a stage, and he claimed damages, and produced a contract, by which he bought her from her mother for thirty pounds Scots [£2 10s. sterling]. But we have no slaves in Scotland,' continues the liberal reporter, ' and mothers cannot sell their bairns; and physicians attested that the employment of tumbling would kill her, and her joints were now grown stiff, and she declined to return, though she was at least an apprentice, and could not run away from her master. Yet some quoted Moses's Law, that if a servant shelter himself with thee, against his master's cruelty, thou shalt surely not deliver him up. The Lords, *renitente cancellario*, assoilzied [i. e. acquitted] Harden.'—Fountainhall's *Decisions*, vol. i, p. 441.

A man may entertain some vanity in being connected with a patron of the cause of humanity ; so the author may be pardoned mentioning, that he derives his own direct descent from the father of this champion of humanity.

Reid the mountebank apparently knew well how to set the sails of his own interest to whatever wind proved most likely to turn them. He failed not to avail himself of King James's rage for the conversion of heretics, on which subject Fountainhall has this sarcastic memorandum :—

' Reid the mountebank is received into the Popish church, and one of his blackamoors was persuaded to accept of baptism from the Popish priests, and to turn Christian Papist, which was a great trophy. He was christened James after the King, and Chancellor, and the Apostle James ! '—Ibid., p. 440.

NOTE 12.—THE POPISH PLOT, p. 253

The infamous character of those who contrived and carried on the pretended Popish Plot may be best estimated by the account given in North's *Examen*, who describes Oates himself with considerable power of colouring. ' He was now in his trine exaltation, his plot in full force, efficacy, and virtue ; he walked about with his guards [assigned for fear of the Papists murdering him]. He had lodgings in Whitehall, and 1,200*l.* per annum pension : and no wonder, after he had the impudence to say to the House of Lords, in plain terms, that, if they would not help him to more money, he must be forced to help himself. He put on an Episcopal garb (except the lawn sleeves), silk gown and cassock, great hat, satin hatband and rose, long scarf, and was called, or most blasphemously called himself, the Saviour of the nation ; whoever he pointed at, was taken up and committed ; so that many people got out of his way, as from a blast, and glad they could prove their two last years' conversation. The very breath of him was pestilential, and, if it brought not imprisonment, or death, over such on whom it fell, it surely poisoned reputation, and left good Protestants arrant Papists, and something worse than that—in danger of being put in the plot as traitors. Upon his examination before the Commons, the Lord Chief Justice Scroggs was sent for to the House, and there signed warrants for the imprisonment of five Roman Catholic peers, upon which they were laid up in the Tower. The votes of the Houses seemed to confirm the whole. A solemn form of prayer was desired upon the subject of the plot, and when one was prepared, it was found faulty, because the Papists were not named as authors of it ; God surely knew whether it were so or not : however, it was yielded to, that omniscience might not want information. The queen herself was accused at the Commons' bar. The city, for fear of the Papists, put up their posts and chains ; and the chamberlain, Sir Thomas Player, in the Court of Aldermen, gave his reason for the city's using that caution, which was, that he did not know but the next morning they might all rise with their throats cut. The trials, convictions, and executions of the priests, Jesuits, and others, were had, and attended with vast mob and noise. Nothing ordinary or moderate was to be heard in people's communication ; but every debate and action was high-flown and tumultuous. All freedom of speech was taken away ; and not to believe the plot, was worse than being Turk, Jew, or infidel. For this fact of Godfrey's murder, the three poor men of Somerset House were, as was said, convicted. The most pitiful circumstance was that of their trial, under the popular prejudice against them. The Lord Chief Justice Scroggs took in with the tide, and ranted for the plot, hewing down Popery, as Scanderbeg hewed the Turk ; which was but little propitious to them. The other judges were passive, and meddled little, except some that were takers in also ; and particularly the good Recorder Terby, who eased the Attorney-General, for he seldom asked a question, but one might guess he foresaw the answer. Some may blame the (at best) passive behaviour of the judges ; but really, considering it was impossible to stem such a current, the appearing to do it in vain had been more unprofitable, because it had inflamed the great and small rout, drawn scandal on themselves, and disabled them from taking in, when opportunity should be more favourable. The prisoners, under these hardships, had enough to do to make any defence ; for where the testimony was positive, it was conclusive ; for no reasoning *ab improbabili* would serve the turn ; it must be *ab impossibili*, or not at all. Whoever doth not well observe the power of judging, may think many things, in the course of justice, very strange. If one side is held to demonstration, and the other allowed presumptions for proofs, any cause may be carried. In a word, anger, policy, inhumanity, and prejudice, had, at this time, a planetary possession of the minds of most men, and destroyed in them that golden rule, of doing as they would be done unto.'

In another passage Oates's personal appearance is thus described.—' He was a low man, of an ill cut, very short neck, and his visage and features were most particular. His mouth was the centre of his face ; and a compass there would sweep his nose, forehead, and chin, within the perimeter. *Cave quos ipse Deus notavit.* In a word, he was a most consummate cheat, blasphemer, vicious, perjured, impudent, and saucy, foul-mouth'd wretch ; and were it not for the truth of history, and the great emotions in the public he was the cause of, not fit (so little deserving) to be remembered.'

NOTE 13.—NARRATIVES OF THE PLOT, p. 269.

There is no more odious feature of this detestable plot than that the forsworn witnesses by whose oaths the fraud was supported, claimed a sort of literary interest in their own fabrications by publications under such titles as the following : ' A narrative and impartial discovery of the horrid Popish Plot, carried on for burning and destroying the cities of London and Westminster, with their suburbs, setting forth the several councils, orders, and resolutions of the Jesuits, concerning the same, by (a person so and so named), lately engaged in that horrid design, and one of the Popish committee for carrying on such fires.'

At any other period, it would have appeared equally unjust and illegal to poison the public mind with stuff of this kind, before the witnesses had made their depositions in open court. But in this moment of frenzy, everything which could confirm the existence of these senseless delusions was eagerly listened to ; and whatever seemed to infer doubt of the witnesses, or hesitation concerning the existence of the plot, was a stifling, strangling, or undervaluing the discovery of the grand conspiracy. In short, as expressed by Dryden,

'Twas worse than plotting, to suspect the plot.'

NOTE 14.—RICHARD GANLESSE, p. 272

It will be afterwards found that in the supposed Richard Ganlesse is first introduced into the story the detestable Edward Christian, a character with as few redeeming good qualities as the author's too prolific pencil has ever attempted to draw. He is a mere creature of the imagination ; and although he may receive some dignity of character from his talents, energy, and influence over others, he is, in other respects, a moral monster, since even his affection for his brother, and resentment of his death, are grounded on vindictive feelings, which scruple at no means, even the foulest, for their gratification. The author will be readily believed when he affirms that no original of the present times, or those which preceded them, has given the outline for a character so odious. The personage is a mere fancy piece. In particular, the author disclaims all allusion to a gentleman named Edward Christian, who actually existed during those troublesome times, was brother of William Christian, the Dempster, and died in prison in the Isle of Man. With this unfortunate gentleman the character in the novel has not the slightest connexion, nor do the incidents of their lives in any respect agree. There existed, as already stated, an Edward Christian of the period, who was capable of very bad things, since he was a companion and associate of the robber Thomas Blood, and convicted along with him of a conspiracy against the celebrated Duke of Buckingham. This character was probably not unlike that of his namesake in the novel, at least the feats ascribed to him are *haud aliena a Scaevolae studiis*. But Mr. Christian of Unwin, if there existed a rogue of his name during that period of general corruption, has the more right to have him distinguished from his unfortunate relative, who died in prison before the period mentioned.

NOTE 15.—CUTLAR MacCULLOCH, p. 277

This alludes to a singular custom of the inhabitants of the northern coast of the Isle of Man, who used of old to eat the sodden meat before they supped the broth, lest, it is said, they should be deprived of the more substantial part of the meal, if they waited to eat it at the second course.

They account for this anomaly in the following manner :—About the commencement of the sixteenth century, the Earl of Derby, being a fiery young chief, fond of war and honour, made a furious inroad, with all his forces, into the Stewartry of Kirkcudbright, and committed great ravages, still remembered in Manx song. Mr. Train, with his usual kindness, sent me the following literal translation of the verses :

> ' There came Thomas Derby, born king,
> He it was who wore the golden crupper ;
> There was not one lord in wide England itself,
> With so many vassals as he had.

> ' On Scottishmen he avenged himself ;
> He went over to Kirkcudbright,
> And there made such havoc of houses,
> That some are uninhabitable to this day.

> ' Was not that fair in a youth,
> To avenge himself on his foe while he was so young,
> Before his beard had grown around his mouth,
> And to bring home his men in safety ? '

This incursion of the Earl with the golden crupper was severely revenged. The gentlemen of the name of MacCulloch, a clan then and now powerful in Galloway, had at their head, at the time, a chief of courage and activity, named Cutlar MacCulloch. He was an excellent seaman, and speedily equipped a predatory flotilla, with which he made repeated descents on the northern shores of the Isle of Man, the dominions of the Earl of Derby, carrying off all that was not, in the border phrase, too hot or too heavy.

The following is the deposition of John Machariotic concerning the losses he had suffered by this sea-king and his Galloway men. It is dated at Peel Castle : —' Taken by Collard MacCulloch and his men by wrongous spoliation, Twa box beddes and aykin burdes, i c lathe, a feder bouster, a cote of Mailzie, a mete burde, two kystis, five barrels, a gyle-fat, xx pipes, twa gunys, three bolls of malt, a querne of rosate of vi stane, certain petes, [peats,] extending to i c load, viii bolls of threschit corn, xii unthraschin, and xl knowte.'—Challerson, p. 47, edit. London, 1653.

This active rover rendered his name so formidable, that the custom of eating the meat before the broth was introduced by the islanders whose festivals he often interrupted. They also remembered him in their prayers and graces ; as

> ' God keep the house and all within,
> From Cut MacCulloch and his kin '

or, as I have heard it recited,

> ' God keep the good corn, and the sheep, and the bullock,
> From Satan, from sin, and from Cutlar MacCulloch.'

It is said to have chanced, as the master of the house had uttered one of these popular benisons, that Cutlar in person entered the habitation with this reply :

> ' Gudeman, gudeman, ye pray too late,
> MacCulloch's ships are at the Yaite.'

The *Yaite* is a well-known landing-place on the north side of the Isle of Man. This redoubted corsair is, I believe, now represented by the chief of the name, James MacCulloch, Esq., of Ardwall, the author's friend and near connexion.

NOTE 16.—COLEMAN, p. 280

The unfortunate Coleman, executed for the Popish Plot, was secretary to the late Duchess of York, and had been a correspondent of the French King's confessor, Père la Chaise. Their correspondence was seized, and although the papers contained nothing to confirm the monstrous fictions of the accusers, yet there was a great deal to show that he and other zealous Catholics anxiously sought for and desired to find the means to bring back England to the faith of

Rome. 'It is certain,' says Hume, 'that the restless and enterprising spirit of the Catholic Church, particularly of the Jesuits, merits attention, and is in some degree dangerous to every other communion. Such zeal of proselytism actuates that sect, that its missionaries have penetrated into every region of the globe, and in one sense there is a Popish plot continually carrying on against all states, Protestant, Pagan, and Mahometan.'—*History of England*, vol. vii, p. 72, edit. 1797.

Note 17.—Funeral of Sir Edmondsbury Godfrey, p. 280

This solemnity is specially mentioned by North. 'The crowd was prodigious, both at the procession and in and about the church, and so heated, that any thing called Papist, were it a cat or a dog, had probably gone to pieces in a moment. The Catholics all kept close in their houses and lodgings, thinking it a good compensation to be safe there, so far were they from acting violently at that time. But there was all that which upheld among the common people an artificial fright, so that every one almost fancied a Popish knife just at his throat ; and at the sermon, beside the preacher, two thumping divines stood upright in the pulpit, to guard him from being killed, while he was preaching, by the Papists. I did not see this spectre, but was credibly told by some that affirmed that they did see it, and I never met with any that did contradict it. A most portentous spectacle, sure, three parsons in one pulpit ! Enough of itself, on a less occasion, to excite terror in the audience. The like, I guess, was never seen before, and probably will never be seen again ; and it had not been so now, as is most evident, but for some stratagem founded upon the impetuosity of the mob.'—*Examen*, p. 104.

It may be, however, remarked, that the singular circumstance of Sir Edmondsbury Godfrey, the justice before whom Oates had made his deposition, being found murdered, was the incident upon which most men relied as complete proof of the existence of the plot. As he was believed to have lost his life by the Papists, for having taken Oates's deposition, the panic spread with inconceivable rapidity, and every species of horror was apprehended—every report, the more absurd the better, eagerly listened to and believed. Whether this unfortunate gentleman lost his life by Papist or Protestant, by private enemies, or by his own hand (for he was a low-spirited and melancholy man), will probably never be discovered.

Note 18.—First Check to the Plot, p. 339

The first check received by Doctor Oates and his colleagues in the task of supporting the Plot by their testimony, was in this manner :—After a good deal of prevarication, the prime witness at length made a direct charge against Sir George Wakeman, the queen's physician, of an attempt to poison the king, and even connected the queen with this accusation, whom he represented as Wakeman's accomplice. This last piece of effrontery recalled the king to some generous sentiments. 'The villains,' said Charles, 'think I am tired of my wife ; but they shall find I will not permit an innocent woman to be persecuted.' Scroggs, the Lord Chief Justice, accordingly received instructions to be favourable to the accused ; and, for the first time, he was so. Wakeman was acquitted, but thought it more for his safety to retire abroad. His acquittal, however, indicated a turn of the tide, which had so long set in favour of the Plot, and of the witnesses by whom it had hitherto been supported.

Note 19.—Employment of Bravoes, p. 362

It was the unworthy distinction of men of wit and honour about town, to revenge their own quarrels with inferior persons by the hands of bravoes. Even in the days of chivalry, the knights, as may be learned from *Don Quixote*, turned over to the chastisement of their squires such adversaries as were not dubbed ;

and thus it was not unusual for men of quality in Charles II's time, to avenge their wrongs by means of private assassination. Rochester writes composedly concerning a satire imputed to Dryden, but in reality composed by Mulgrave: 'If he falls upon me with the blunt, which is his very good weapon in wit, I will forgive him, if you please, and leave the repartee to Black Will with a cudgel.' And, in conformity with this cowardly and brutal intimation, that distinguished poet was waylaid and beaten severely in Rose Street, Covent Garden, by ruffians who could not be discovered, but whom all concluded to be the agents of Rochester's mean revenge.

Note 20.—Bennet, Earl of Arlington, p. 364

Bennet, Earl of Arlington, was one of Charles's most attached courtiers during his exile. After the Restoration, he was employed in the ministry, and the name of Bennet supplies its initial B to the celebrated word Cabal. But the King was supposed to have lost respect for him; and several persons at court took the liberty to mimic his person and behaviour, which was stiff and formal. Thus it was a common jest for some courtier to put a black patch on his nose, and strut about with a white staff in his hand, to make the king merry. But, notwithstanding, he retained his office of Lord Chamberlain and his seat in the Privy Council, till his death in 1685.

Note 21.—Letter from the Dead, p. 369

The application of the very respectable old English name of Jerningham to the valet-de-chambre of the Duke of Buckingham has proved of force sufficient to wake the resentment of the dead, who had in early days won that illustrious surname,—for the author received by post the following expostulation on the subject:—

'To the learned Clerk and Worshipful Knight, Sir Walter Scott, give these:

'Mye mortal frame has long since mouldered into dust, and the young saplinge that was planted on the daye of mye funeral, is now a doddered oak, standinge hard bye the mansion of the familie. The windes doe whistle thro' its leaves, moaninge among its moss-covered branches, and awakeninge in the soules of my descendants, that pensive melancholy which leads back to the contemplating those that are gone!—I, who was once the courtly dame, that held high revelry in these gaye bowers, am now light as the blast!

'If I essaye, from vain affection, to make my name be thought of by producing the noise of rustlinge silkes, or the slow tread of a midnight foot along the chapel floor, alas! I only scare the simple maidens, and my wearie efforts (how wearie none alive can tell) are derided and jeered at by my knightlie descendants. Once indeed—but it boots not to burthen your ear with this particular, nor why I am still sad and aching, between earth and heaven! Know only, that I still walk this place (as mye playmate, your great-grandmother, does hers). I sit in my wonted chair, tho' now it stands in a dusty garret. I frequent my ladye's room, and I have hushed her wailinge babes, when all the cunning of the nurse has failed. I sit at the window where so long a succession of honorable dames have presided their daye, and are passed away! But in the change that centuries brought, honour and truth have remained; and, as adherents to King Harry's eldest daughter, as true subjects to her successors, as faithful followers of the unfortunate Charles and his posteritie, and as loyal and attached servauntes of the present royal stock, the name of Jerningham has ever remained unsullied in honor, and uncontaminated in aught unfitting its ancient knightlie origin. You, noble and learned sir, whose quill is as the trumpet arousinge the slumberinge soule to feelings of loftie chivalrie,—you, Sir Knight, who feel and doe honor to your noble lineage, wherefore did you say, in your chronicle or historie of the brave knight, Peveril of the Peake, that my Lord of Buckingham's servaunte was a Jerningham ! ! ! a vile varlet to a viler noble ! Many honorable families have, indeed, shot and spread from the parent stock into wilde entangled mazes, and reached perchance beyond the confines of gentle blood : but it so pleased Providence, that mye worshipful husband, good Sir Harry's line, has flowed in one confined, but clear deep stream, down to my well-beloued son, the present Sir George Jerningham (by just claim Lorde Stafforde) ; and if any of your courtly ancestors that hover round your bed, could speak, they would tell you that the Duke's valet was not Jerningham, but Sayer or Sims.—Act as you shall think mete hereon, but defend the honored names of those whose champion you so well deserve to be.

' J. JERNINGHAM.'

Having no mode of knowing how to reply to this ancient dignitary, I am compelled to lay the blame of my error upon wicked example, which has misled me ; and to plead that I should never have been guilty of so great a misnomer, but for the authority of one Oliver Goldsmith, who, in an elegant dialogue between the Lady Blarney and Miss Carolina Wilhelmina Amelia Skeggs, makes the former assure Miss Skeggs as a fact, that the next morning my lord called out three times to his valet-de-chambre, ' Jernigan, Jernigan, Jernigan ! bring me my garters ! ' Some inaccurate recollection of this passage has occasioned the offence rendered, for which I make this imperfect, yet respectful apology.

NOTE 22.—SILK ARMOUR, p. 422

Roger North gives us a ridiculous description of these warlike habiliments, when talking of the Whig Club in Fuller's Rents : ' The conversation and ordinary discourse of the club was chiefly on the subject of bravery in defending the cause of liberty and property, and what every Protestant Englishman ought to venture and do, rather than be overrun with Popery and slavery. There was much recommendation of silk armour, and the prudence of being provided with it, against the time that Protestants were to be massacred ; and accordingly there were abundance of these silken backs, breasts, and pots [i. e. head pieces], made and sold, which were pretended to be pistol-proof, in which any man dressed up was as safe as in a house ; for it was impossible any one could go to strike him for laughing, so ridiculous was the figure, as they say, of hogs in armour—an image of derision insensible but to the view, as I have had it [viz. that none can imagine without seeing it as I have]. This was armour of defence, but our sparks were not altogether so tame as to carry their provisions no farther ; for truly they intended to be assailants upon fair occasion, and had for that end recommended to them a certain pocket-weapon, which, for its design and efficacy, had the honour to be called a Protestant flail. It was for street and crowd work, and the instrument, lurking *perdue* in a coat-pocket, might readily sally out to execution, and by clearing a great hall, piazza, or so, carry an election, by a choice way of polling called " knocking down ". The handle resembled a farrier's blood-stick, and the fall was joined to the end by a strong nervous ligature, that in its swing fell short of the hand, and was made of *lignum-vitae*, or rather, as the poet termed it, *mortis*.'—*Examen*, p. 173.

This last weapon will remind the reader of the blood-stick so cruelly used, as was alleged, in a murder committed in England some years ago, and for a participation in which two persons were tried and acquitted at the assizes of autumn, 1830.

NOTE 23.—GEOFFREY HUDSON, p. 442

Geoffrey or Jeffrey Hudson is often mentioned in anecdotes of Charles I's time. His first appearance at court was his being presented, as mentioned in the text, in a pie at an entertainment given by the Duke of Buckingham to Charles I and Henrietta Maria. Upon the same occasion, the duke presented the tenant of the pasty to the queen, who retained him as her page. When about eight years of age, he was but eighteen or twenty inches high; and remained stationary at that stature till he was thirty years old, when he grew to the height of three feet nine inches, and there stopped.

This singular *lusus naturae* was trusted in some negotiations of consequence. He went to France to fetch over a midwife to his mistress, Henrietta Maria. On his return, he was taken by Dunkirk privateers, when he lost many valuable presents sent to the queen from France, and about £2,500 of his own. Sir William Davenant makes a real or supposed combat between the dwarf and a turkey-cock the subject of a poem called Jeffreidos. The scene is laid at Dunkirk, where, as the satire concludes—

> 'Jeffrey strait was thrown, when, faint and weak,
> The cruel fowl assaults him with his beak.
> A lady midwife now he there by chance
> Espied, that came along with him from France.

> ' "A heart brought up in war, that ne'er before
> This time could bow," he said, " doth now implore
> Thou, that *delivered* hast so many, be
> So kind of nature as deliver me." '

We are not acquainted how far Jeffrey resented this lampoon. But we are assured he was a consequential personage, and endured with little temper the teasing of the domestics and courtiers, and had many squabbles with the king's gigantic porter.

The fatal duel with Mr. Crofts actually took place, as mentioned in the text. It happened in France. The poor dwarf had also the misfortune to be taken prisoner by a Turkish pirate. He was, however, probably soon set at liberty, for Hudson was a captain for the king during the civil war. In 1644, the dwarf attended his royal mistress to France. The Restoration recalled him, with other royalists, to England. But this poor being, who received, it would seem, hard measure both from nature and fortune, was not doomed to close his days in peace. Poor Jeffrey, upon some suspicion respecting the Popish Plot, was taken up in 1682, and confined in the Gate-house prison, Westminster, where he ended his life in the sixty-third year of his age.

Jeffrey Hudson has been immortalized by the brush of Vandyke, and his clothes are said to be preserved as articles of curiosity in Sir Hans Sloane's Museum.

NOTE 24.—COLONEL BLOOD'S NARRATIVE, p. 488

Of Blood's Narrative, Roger North takes the following notice :—' There was another sham plot of one Netterville.——And here the good Colonel Blood, that stole the Duke of Ormond, and, if a timely rescue had not come in, had hanged him at Tyburn, and afterwards stole the crown, though he was not so happy as to carry it off; no player at small games, he, even he, the virtuous Colonel, as this sham plot says, was to have been destroyed by the Papists. It seems these Papists would let no eminent Protestant be safe. But some amends were made to the Colonel by sale of the narrative licensed Thomas Blood. It would have been strange if so much mischief were stirring, and he had not come in for a snack.'—*Examen*, edit. 1711, p. 311.

NOTE 25.—COLONEL BLOOD, p. 516

The conspirator Blood even fought or made his way into good society, and sat at good men's feasts. Evelyn's *Diary* bears, 10th May, 1671,—' Dined at Mr. Treasurer's, where dined Monsieur de Grammont and several French noblemen, and one Blood, that impudent, bold fellow, that had not long ago attempted to steal the Imperial crown itself out of the Tower, pretending curiosity of seeing the Regalia, when, stabbing the keeper, though not mortally, he boldly went away with it through all the guards, taken only by the accident of his horse falling down. How he came to be pardoned, and even received into favour, not only after this, but several other exploits almost as daring, both in Ireland and here, I could never come to understand. Some believed he became a spy of several parties, being well with the sectaries and enthusiasts, and did his Majesty service that way, which none alive could do so well as he. But it was certainly, as the boldest attempt, so the only treason of the sort that was ever pardoned. The man had not only a daring, but a villainous unmerciful look, a false countenance, but very well spoken and dangerously insinuating.' Evelyn's *Memoirs*, vol. i, p. 413.

This is one of the many occasions on which we might make curious remarks on the disregard of our forefathers for appearances, even in the regulation of society. What should we think of a Lord of the Treasury, who, to make up a party of French nobles and English gentlemen of condition, should invite as a guest Barrington or Major Semple, or any well-known *chevalier d'industrie*? Yet Evelyn does not seem to have been shocked at the man being brought into society, but only at his remaining unhanged.

NOTE 26.—THE SHERIFFS, p. 578

It can hardly be forgotten that one of the great difficulties of Charles II's reign was to obtain for the crown the power of choosing the sheriffs of London. Roger North gives a lively account of his brother, Sir Dudley North, who agreed to serve for the court. ' I omit the share he had in composing the tumults about burning the Pope, because that is accounted for in the *Examen*, and the *Life of the Lord Keeper North*. Neither is there occasion to say anything of the rise and discovery of the Rye Plot, for the same reason. Nor is my subject much concerned with this latter, further than that the conspirators had taken especial care of Sir Dudley North. For he was one of those who, if they had succeeded, was to have been knocked on the head, and his skin to be stuffed, and hung up in Guildhall. But, all that apart, he reckoned it a great unhappiness, that so many trials for high treason, and executions, should happen in his year. However, in these affairs, the sheriffs were passive ; for all returns of panels, and other dispatches of the law, were issued and done by under-officers ; which was a fair screen for them. They attended at the trials and executions, to coerce the crowds, and keep order, which was enough for them to do. I have heard Sir Dudley North say, that, striking with his cane, he wondered to see what blows his countrymen would take upon their bare heads, and never look up at it. And indeed, nothing can match the zeal of the common people to see executions. The worst grievance was the executioner coming to him for orders, touching the abscinded members, and to know where to dispose of them. Once, while he was abroad, a cart, with some of them, came into the court-yard of his house, and frighted his lady almost out of her wits ; and she could never be reconciled to the dog hangman's saying he came to speak with his master. These are inconveniences that attend the stations of public magistracy, and are necessary to be borne with, as magistracy itself is necessary. I have now no more to say of any incidents during the shrievalty ; but that, at the year's end, he delivered up his charges to his successors in like manner as he had received them from his predecessor ; and, having reinstated his family, he lived well and easy at his own house, as he did before these disturbances put him out of order.'

NOTE 27.—LIFE OF COLONEL BLOOD, p. 615

This person, who was capable of framing and carrying into execution the most desperate enterprises, was one of those extraordinary characters who can only arise amid the bloodshed, confusion, destruction of morality, and wide-spreading violence, which take place during civil war. We cannot, perhaps, enter upon a subject more extraordinary or entertaining than the history of this notorious desperado, who exhibited all the elements of a most accomplished ruffian. As the account of these adventures is scattered in various and scarce publications, it will probably be a service to the reader to bring the most remarkable of them under his eye, in a simultaneous point of view.

Blood's father is reported to have been a blacksmith; but this was only a disparaging mode of describing a person who had a concern in iron-works, and had thus acquired independence. He entered early in life into the Civil War, served as a lieutenant in the Parliament forces, and was put by Henry Cromwell, Lord Deputy of Ireland, into the commission of the peace, when he was scarcely two-and-twenty. This outset in life decided his political party for ever; and however unfit the principles of such a man rendered him for the society of those who professed a rigidity of religion and morals, so useful was Blood's rapidity of invention, and so well was he known, that he was held capable of framing with sagacity, and conducting with skill, the most desperate undertakings, and in a turbulent time was allowed to associate with the non-jurors, who affected a peculiar austerity of conduct and sentiments. In 1663, the Act of Settlement in Ireland, and the proceedings thereupon, affected Blood deeply in his fortune, and from that moment he appears to have nourished the most inveterate hatred to the Duke of Ormond, the Lord Lieutenant of Ireland, whom he considered as the author of the measures under which he suffered. There were at this time many malcontents of the same party with himself, so that Lieutenant Blood, as the most daring among them, was able to put himself at the head of a conspiracy which had for its purpose the exciting a general insurrection, and, as a preliminary step, the surprising of the Castle of Dublin. The means proposed for the last purpose, which was to be the prelude to the rising, augured the desperation of the person by whom it was contrived, and yet might probably have succeeded from its very boldness. A declaration was drawn up by the hand of Blood himself, calling upon all persons to take arms for the liberty of the subject, and the restoration of the Solemn League and Covenant. For the surprise of the castle, it was provided that several persons with petitions in their hands were to wait within the walls, as if they stayed to present them to the Lord Lieutenant, while about fourscore of the old daring disbanded soldiers were to remain on the outside, dressed like carpenters, smiths, shoemakers, and other ordinary mechanics. As soon as the Lord Lieutenant went in, a baker was to pass by the main guard with a large basket of white bread on his back. By making a false step he was to throw down his burden, which might create a scramble among the soldiers, and offer the fourscore men before mentioned an opportunity of disarming them, while the others with petitions in their hands secured all within; and being once master of the castle and the Duke of Ormond's person, they were to publish their declaration. But some of the principal conspirators were apprehended about twelve hours before the time appointed for the execution of the design, in which no less than seven members of the House of Commons (for the Parliament of Ireland was then sitting) were concerned. Leckie, a minister, the brother-in-law of Blood, was with several others tried, condemned, and executed. Blood effected his escape, but was still so much the object of public apprehension, that a rumour having arisen during Leckie's execution, that Major Blood was at hand with a party to rescue the prisoner, every one of the guards, and the executioner himself, shifted for themselves, leaving Leckie, with the halter about his neck, standing alone under the gallows: but as no rescue appeared, the sheriff-officers returned to their duty, and the criminal was executed. Meantime Blood retired among the mountains of Ireland, where he herded alternately with fanatics and Papists, provided only they were discontented with the government. There were few persons better acquainted with the intrigues of the time than this active partisan, who was alternately Quaker, Anabaptist, or Catholic, but always a rebel and revolutionist; he shifted from place to place, and from kingdom to kingdom;

became known to the Admiral de Ruyter, and was the soul of every desperate plot.

In particular, about 1665, Mr. Blood was one of a revolutionary committee, or secret council, which continued its sittings, notwithstanding that government knew of its meetings. For their security, they had about thirty stout fellows posted around the place where they met in the nature of a *corps de garde*. It fell out, that two of the members of the council, to save themselves, and perhaps for the sake of a reward, betrayed all their transactions to the ministry, which Mr. Blood soon suspected, and in a short time got to the bottom of the whole affair. He appointed these two persons to meet him at a tavern in the city, where he had his guard ready, who secured them without any noise, and carried them to a private place provided for the purpose, where he called a kind of court-martial, before whom they were tried, found guilty, and sentenced to be shot two days after in the same place. When the time appointed came, they were brought out, and all the necessary preparations made for putting the sentence in execution ; and the poor men, seeing no hopes of escape, disposed themselves to suffer as well as they could. At this critical juncture, Mr. Blood was graciously pleased to grant them his pardon, and at the same time advised them to go to their new master, tell him all that had happened, and request him, in the name of their old confederates, to be as favourable to such of them as should at any time stand in need of his mercy. Whether these unfortunate people carried Mr. Blood's message to the king, does not anywhere appear. It is, however, certain that not long after the whole conspiracy was discovered ; in consequence of which, on the 26th of April, 1666, Col. John Rathbone, and some other officers of the late disbanded army, were tried and convicted at the Old Bailey for a plot to surprise the Tower, and to kill General Monk.

After his concern with this desperate conclave, who were chiefly fanatics and Fifth-Monarchy men, Blood exchanged the scene for Scotland, where he mingled among the Cameronians, and must have been a most acceptable associate to John Balfour of Burley, or any other who joined the insurgents more out of spleen or desire of plunder than from religious motives. The writers of the sect seem to have thought his name a discredit, or perhaps did not know it ; nevertheless, it is affirmed in a pamphlet written by a person who seems to have been well acquainted with the incidents of his life, that he shared the dangers of the defeat at Pentland Hills, November 27, 1666, in which the Cameronians were totally routed. After the engagement, he found his way again to Ireland, but was hunted out of Ulster by Lord Dungannon, who pursued him very closely. On his return to England, he made himself again notorious by an exploit, of which the very singular particulars are contained in the pamphlet already mentioned.[1] The narrative runs as follows :—' Among the persons apprehended for the late fanatic conspiracy, was one Captain Mason, a person for whom Mr. Blood had a particular affection and friendship. This person was to be removed from London to one of the northern counties, in order to his trial at the assizes ; and to that intent was sent down with eight of the Duke's troop to guard him, being reckoned to be a person bold and courageous. Mr. Blood having notice of this journey, resolves by the way to rescue his friend. The prisoner and his guard went away in the morning, and Mr. Blood having made choice of three more of his acquaintance, set forward the same day at night, without boots, upon small horses, and their pistols in their trousers, to prevent suspicion. But opportunities are not so easily had, neither were all places convenient, so that the convoy and their prisoner were gone a good way beyond Newark, before Mr. Blood and his friends had any scent of their prisoner. At one place, they set a sentinel to watch his coming by ; but whether it was out of fear, or that the person was tired with a tedious expectation, the sentinel brought them no tidings either of the prisoner or his guard, insomuch that

[1] *Remarks on the Life of the famed Mr. Blood.* London, 1680. Folio.

Mr. Blood and his companions began to think their friend so far before them upon the road, that it would be in vain to follow him. Yet not willing to give over an enterprise so generously undertaken, upon Mr. Blood's encouragement, they rode on, though despairing of success, till finding it grow towards evening, and meeting with a convenient inn upon the road in a small village not far from Doncaster, they resolved to lie there all night, and return for London the next morning. In that inn they had not sat long in a room next the street, condoling among themselves the ill success of such a tedious journey, and the misfortune of their friend, before the convoy came thundering up to the door of the said inn with their prisoner, Captain Mason having made choice of that inn, as being the best known to him, to give his guardians the refreshment of a dozen of drink. There Mr. Blood, unseen, had a full view of his friend, and of the persons he had to deal with. He had bespoke a small supper, which was at the fire, so that he had but very little time for consultation, finding that Captain Mason's party did not intend to alight. On this account he only gave general directions to his associates to follow his example in whatever they saw him do. In haste, therefore, they called for their horses, and threw down their money for their reckoning, telling the woman of the house that, since they had met with such good company, they were resolved to go forward. Captain Mason went off first upon a sorry beast, and with him the commander of the party, and four more ; the rest stayed behind to make an end of their liquor. Then away marched one more single, and in a very small time after, the last two. By this time, Mr. Blood and one of his friends being horsed, followed the two that were hindmost, and soon overtook them. These four rode some little time together, Mr. Blood on the right hand of the two soldiers, and his friend on the left. But upon a sudden, Mr. Blood laid hold of the reins of the horse next him, while his friend, in observation to his directions, did the same on the other hand ; and having presently by surprise dismounted the soldiers, pulled off their bridles, and sent their horses to pick their grass where they pleased. These two being thus made sure of, Mr. Blood pursues his game, intending to have reached the single trooper ; but he being got to the rest of his fellows, now reduced to six, and a barber of York, that travelled in their company, Mr. Blood made up, heads the whole party, and stops them ; of which some of the foremost, looking upon him to be either drunk or mad, thought the rebuke of a switch to be a sufficient chastisement of such a rash presumption, which they exercised with more contempt than fury, till, by the rudeness of his compliments in return, he gave them to understand he was not in jest, but in very good earnest. He was soon seconded by his friend that was with him in his first exploit ; but there had been several rough blows dealt between the unequal number of six to two, before Mr. Blood's two other friends came up to their assistance ; nay, I may safely say six to two ; for the barber of York, whether out of his natural propensity to the sport, or that his pot-valiantness had made him so generous as to help his fellow travellers, would needs show his valour at the beginning of the fray ; but better had he been at the latter end of a feast ; for though he showed his prudence to take the stronger side, as he guessed by the number, yet because he would take no warning, which was often given him, not to put himself to the hazard of losing a guitar-finger by meddling in a business that nothing concerned him, he lost his life, as they were forced to dispatch him, in the first place, for giving them a needless trouble. The barber, being become a useless instrument, and the other of Mr. Blood's friends being come up, the skirmish began to be very smart, the four assailants having singled out their champions as fairly and equally as they could. All this while, Captain Mason, being rode before upon his thirty-shilling steed, wondering his guard came not with him, looked back, and observing a combustion, and that they were altogether by the ears, knew not what to think. He conjectured it at first to have been some intrigue upon him, as if the troopers had a design to tempt him to an escape, which might afterwards prove more to his prejudice ;

just like cats, that, with regardless scorn, seem to give the distressed mouse all the liberty in the world to get away out of their paws, but soon recover their prey again at one jump. Thereupon, unwilling to undergo the hazard of such a trial, he comes back, at which time Mr. Blood cried out to him, "Horse, horse, quickly!" an alarm so amazing at first, that he could not believe it to be his friend's voice when he heard it; but as the thoughts of military men are soon summoned together, and never hold Spanish councils, the Captain presently settled his resolution, mounts the next horse that wanted a rider, and puts it in for a share of his own self-preservation. In this bloody conflict, Mr. Blood was three times unhorsed, occasioned by his forgetfulness, as having omitted to new girt his saddle, which the ostler had unloosed upon the wadding at his first coming into the inn. Being then so often dismounted, and not knowing the reason, which the occasion would not give him leave to consider, he resolved to fight it out on foot; of which two of the soldiers taking the advantage, singled him out, and drove him into a court-yard, where he made a stand with a full body, his sword in one hand, and his pistol in the other. One of the soldiers taking that advantage of his open body, shot him near the shoulder-blade of his pistol-arm, at which time he had four other bullets in his body, that he had received before; which the soldier observing, flung his discharged pistol at him with that good aim and violence, that he hit him a stunning blow just under the forehead, upon the upper part of the nose between the eyes, which for the present so amazed him, that he gave himself over for a dead man; yet resolving to give one sparring blow before he expired, such is the strange provocation and success of despair, with one vigorous stroke of his sword he brought his adversary with a vengeance from his horse, and laid him in a far worse condition than himself at his horse's feet. At that time, full of anger and revenge, he was just going to make an end of his conquest, by giving him the fatal stab, but that in the very nick of time, Captain Mason, having, by the help of his friends, done his business where they had fought, by the death of some, and the disabling of others that opposed him, came in, and bid him hold and spare the life of one that had been the civilest person to him upon the road—a fortunate piece of kindness in the one, and of gratitude in the other; which Mr. Blood easily condescending to, by the joint assistance of the captain the other soldier was soon mastered, and the victory, after a sharp fight, that lasted above two hours, was at length completed. You may be sure the fight was well maintained on both sides, while two of the soldiers, besides the barber, were slain upon the place, three unhorsed, and the rest wounded. And it was observable, that though the encounter happened in a village, where a great number of people were spectators of the combat, yet none would adventure the rescue of either party, as not knowing which was in the wrong, or which in the right, and were therefore wary of being arbitrators in such a desperate contest, where they saw the reward of assistance to be nothing but present death. After the combat was over, Mr. Blood and his friends divided themselves, and parted several ways.'

Before he had engaged in this adventure, Blood had placed his wife and son in an apothecary's shop at Rumford, under the name of Weston. He himself afterwards affected to practise as a physician under that of Ayliffe, under which guise he remained concealed until his wounds were cured, and the hue and cry against him and his accomplices was somewhat abated.

In the meantime, this extraordinary man, whose spirits toiled in framing the most daring enterprises, had devised a plot which, as it respected the person at whom it was aimed, was of a much more ambitious character than that for the delivery of Mason. It had for its object the seizure of the person of the Duke of Ormond, his ancient enemy, in the streets of London. In this some have thought he only meant to gratify his resentment, while others suppose that he might hope to extort some important advantages by detaining his grace in his hands as a prisoner. The duke's historian, Carte, gives the following account of this extraordinary enterprise :—' The Prince of Orange came this year (1670) into England, and being invited, on Dec. 6, to an entertainment in the City of London, his Grace attended him thither. As he was returning homewards in a dark night, and going up St. James's Street, at the end of which, facing the palace, stood Clarendon House, where he then lived, he was attacked by Blood and five of his accomplices. The Duke always used to go attended with six footmen ; but as they were too heavy a load to ride upon a coach, he always had iron spikes behind it to keep them from getting up ; and continued this practice to his dying day, even after this attempt of assassination. These six footmen used to walk on both sides of the street, over against the coach ; but by some contrivance or other, they were all stopped and out of the way, when the Duke was taken out of his coach by Blood and his son, and mounted on horseback behind one of the horsemen in his company. The coachman drove on to Clarendon House, and told the porter that the Duke had been seized by two men, who had carried him down Pickadilly. The porter immediately ran that way, and Mr. James Clarke chancing to be at that time in the court of the house, followed with all possible haste, having first alarmed the family, and ordered the servants to come after him as fast as they could. Blood, it seems, either to gratify the humour of his patron, who had set him upon this work, or to glut his own revenge by putting his Grace to the same ignominious death, which his accomplices in the treasonable design upon Dublin Castle had suffered, had taken a strong fancy into his head to hang the Duke at Tyburn. Nothing could have saved his Grace's life, but that extravagant imagination and passion of the villain, who, leaving the Duke mounted and buckled to one of his comrades, rode on before, and (as is said) actually tied a rope to the gallows, and then rode back to see what was become of his accomplices, whom he met riding off in a great hurry. The horseman to whom the Duke was tied, was a person of great strength, but being embarrassed by his Grace's struggling, could not advance as fast as he desired. He was, however, got a good way beyond Berkeley (now Devonshire) House, towards Knightsbridge, when the Duke, having got his foot under the man's, unhorsed him, and they both fell down together in the mud, where they were struggling, when the porter and Mr. Clarke came up. The villain then disengaged himself, and seeing the neighbourhood alarmed, and numbers of people running towards them, got on horseback, and having, with one of his comrades, fired their pistols at the Duke (but missed him, as taking their aim in the dark, and in a hurry), rode off as fast as they could to save themselves. The Duke (now sixty years of age) was quite spent with struggling, so that when Mr. Clarke and the porter came up, they knew him rather by feeling his star, than by any sound of voice he could utter ; and they were forced to carry him home, and lay him on a bed to recover his spirits. He received some wounds and bruises in the struggle, which confined him within doors for some days. The king, when he heard of this intended assassination of the Duke of Ormond, expressed a great resentment on that occasion, and issued out a proclamation for the discovery and apprehension of the miscreants concerned in the attempt.'

Blood, however, lay concealed, and, with his usual success, escaped apprehension. While thus lurking, he entertained and digested an exploit evincing the same atrocity which had characterized the undertakings he had formerly been engaged in ; there was also to be traced in his new device something of that peculiar disposition which inclined him to be desirous of adding to the murder of the Duke of Ormond, the singular infamy of putting him to death at Tyburn. With something of the same spirit, he now resolved to show his contempt of monarchy, and all its symbols, by stealing the crown, sceptre, and other articles of the regalia out of the office in which they were deposited, and enriching himself and his needy associates with the produce of the spoils. This feat, by which Blood is now chiefly remembered, is, like all his transactions, marked with a daring strain of courage and duplicity, and like most of his undertakings, was very likely to have proved successful. John Bayley, Esq., in his *History and Antiquities of the Tower of London*, gives the following distinct account of this curious exploit. At this period, Sir Gilbert Talbot was Keeper, as it was called, of the Jewel House.

' It was soon after the appointment of Sir Gilbert Talbot that the Regalia in the Tower first became objects of public inspection, which King Charles allowed in consequence of the reduction in the emoluments of the master's office. The profits which arose from showing the jewels to strangers, Sir Gilbert assigned in lieu of a salary, to the person whom he had appointed to the care of them. This was an old confidential servant of his father's, one Talbot Edwards, whose name is handed down to posterity as keeper of the regalia when the notorious attempt to steal the crown was made in the year 1673 ; the following account of which is chiefly derived from a relation which Mr. Edwards himself made of the transaction.

' About three weeks before this audacious villain Blood made his attempt upon the crown, he came to the Tower in the habit of a parson, with a long cloak, cassock, and canonical girdle, accompanied by a woman, whom he called his wife. They desired to see the regalia, and, just as their wishes had been gratified, the lady feigned sudden indisposition ; this called forth the kind offices of Mrs. Edwards, the keeper's wife, who, having courteously invited her into their house to repose herself, she soon recovered, and on their departure, professed themselves thankful for this civility. A few days after, Blood came again, bringing a present to Mrs. Edwards, of four pairs of white gloves from his pretended wife ; and having thus begun the acquaintance, they made frequent visits to improve it. After a short respite of their compliments, the disguised ruffian returned again ; and in conversation with Mrs. Edwards, said that his wife could discourse of nothing but the kindness of those good people in the Tower—that she had long studied, and at length bethought herself of a handsome way of requital. You have, quoth he, a pretty young gentlewoman for your daughter, and I have a young nephew, who has two or three hundred a year in land, and is at my disposal. If your daughter be free, and you approve it, I'll bring him here to see her, and we will endeavour to make it a match. This was easily assented to by old Mr. Edwards, who invited the parson to dine with him on that day ; he readily accepted the invitation ; and taking upon him to say grace, performed it with great seeming devotion, and casting up his eyes, concluded it with a prayer for the king, queen, and royal family. After dinner, he went up to see the rooms, and observing a handsome case of pistols hang there, expressed a great desire to buy them, to present to a young lord, who was his neighbour ; a pretence by which he thought of disarming the house against the period intended for the execution of his design. At his departure, which was a canonical benediction of the good company, he appointed a day and hour to bring his nephew to see his mistress, which was the very day that he made his daring attempt. The good old gentleman had got up ready to receive his guest, and the daughter was in her best dress to entertain her expected lover ; when, behold, Parson Blood, with three more, came to the jewel-house, all armed with rapier-blades in their canes, and every one a dagger, and a brace of pocket pistols. Two of his companions entered in with him, on pretence of seeing the crown, and the third stayed at the door, as if to look after the young lady, a jewel of a more charming description, but in reality as a watch. The daughter, who thought it not modest to come down till she was called, sent the maid to take a view of the company, and bring a description of her gallant ; and the servant, conceiving that he was the intended bridegroom who stayed at the door, being the youngest of the party, returned to soothe the anxiety of her young mistress with the idea she had formed of his person. Blood told Mr. Edwards that they would not go upstairs till his wife came, and desired him to show his friends the crown to pass the time till then ; and they had no sooner entered the room, and the door, as usual, shut, than a cloak was thrown over the old man's head, and a gag put in his mouth. Thus secured, they told him that their resolution was to have the crown, globe, and sceptre; and, if he would quietly submit to it, they would spare his life; otherwise he was to expect no mercy. He thereupon endeavoured to make all the noise he possibly could, to be heard above; they then knocked him down with a wooden mallet, and told him, that, if yet he would lie quietly, they would spare his life; but if not, upon his next attempt to discover them, they would kill him. Mr. Edwards, however, according to his own account, was not intimidated by this threat, but strained himself to make the greater noise, and in consequence, received several more blows on the head with the mallet, and was stabbed in the belly; this again brought the poor old man to the ground, where he lay for some time in so senseless a state, that one of the villains pronounced him dead. Edwards had come a little to himself, and hearing this, lay quietly, conceiving it best to be thought so. The booty was now to be disposed of, and one of them, named Parrot, secreted the orb. Blood held the crown under his cloak, and the third was about to file the sceptre in two, in order that it might be placed in a bag, brought for that purpose; but, fortunately, the son of Mr. Edwards, who had been in Flanders with Sir John Talbot, and on his landing in England had obtained leave to come away post to visit his father, happened to arrive whilst this scene was acting; and on coming to the door, the person that stood sentinel asked with whom he would speak; to which he answered, that he belonged to the house; and, perceiving the person to be a stranger, told him that if he had any business with his father, that he would acquaint him with it, and so hastened upstairs to salute his friends. This unexpected accident spread confusion amongst the party, and they instantly decamped with the crown and orb, leaving the sceptre yet unfiled. The aged keeper now raised himself upon his legs, forced the gag from his mouth, and cried, "Treason! murder!" which being heard by his daughter, who was, perhaps, anxiously expecting far other sounds, ran out and reiterated the cry. The alarm now became general, and young Edwards and his brother-in-law, Captain Beckman, ran after the conspirators, whom a warder put himself in a position to stop, but Blood discharged a pistol at him, and he fell, although unhurt, and the thieves proceeded safely to the next post, where one Sill, who had been a soldier under Cromwell, stood sentinel; but he offered no opposition, and they accordingly passed the drawbridge. Horses were waiting for them at St. Catherine's gate; and as they ran that way along the Tower wharf, they themselves cried out, "Stop the rogues!" by which they passed on unsuspected, till Captain Beckman overtook them. At his head Blood fired another pistol, but missed him, and was seized. Under the cloak of this daring villain was found the crown, and, although he saw himself a prisoner, he had yet the impudence to struggle for his prey; and when it was finally wrested from him, said, "It was a gallant attempt, however unsuccessful; it was for a crown!" Parrot, who had formerly served under General Harrison, was also taken; but Hunt, Blood's son-in-law, reached his horse and rode off, as did two other of the thieves; but he was soon afterwards stopped, and likewise committed to custody. In this struggle and confusion, the great pearl, a large diamond, and several smaller stones, were lost from the crown; but the two former, and some of the latter, were afterwards found and restored; and the Ballas ruby, broken off the sceptre, being found in Parrot's pocket, nothing considerable was eventually missing.

'As soon as the prisoners were secured, young Edwards hastened to Sir Gilbert Talbot, who was then master and treasurer of the Jewel House, and gave him an account of the transaction. Sir Gilbert instantly went to the king, and acquainted his Majesty with it; and his Majesty commanded him to proceed forthwith to the Tower, to see how matters stood; to take the examination of Blood and the others; and to return and report it to him. Sir Gilbert accordingly went; but the king in the meantime was persuaded by some about him, to hear the examination himself, and the prisoners were in consequence sent for to Whitehall; a circumstance which is supposed to have saved these daring wretches from the gallows.'

On his examination under such an atrocious charge, Blood audaciously replied, ' that he would never betray an associate, or defend himself at the expense of uttering a falsehood.' He even averred, perhaps, more than was true against himself, when he confessed that he had lain concealed among the reeds for the purpose of killing the king with a carabine, while Charles was bathing; but he pretended that on this occasion his purpose was disconcerted by a secret awe,—appearing to verify the allegation in Shakespeare, ' There 's such divinity doth hedge a king, that treason can but peep to what it would, acts little of its will.' To this story, true or false, Blood added a declaration that he was at the head of a numerous following, disbanded soldiers and others, who, from motives of religion, were determined to take the life of the king, as the only obstacle to their obtaining freedom of worship and liberty of conscience. These men, he said, would be determined, by his execution, to persist in the resolution of putting Charles to death; whereas, he averred that, by sparing his life, the king might disarm a hundred poniards directed against his own. This view of the case made a strong impression on Charles, whose selfishness was uncommonly acute: yet he felt the impropriety of pardoning the attempt upon the life of the Duke of Ormond, and condescended to ask that faithful servant's permission, before he would exert his authority, to spare the assassin. Ormond answered, that if the king chose to pardon the attempt to steal his crown, he himself might easily consent, that the attempt upon his life, as a crime of much less importance, should also be forgiven. Charles, accordingly, not only gave Blood a pardon, but endowed him with a pension of £500 a year; which led many persons to infer, not only that the king wished to preserve himself from the future attempts of this desperate man, but that he had it also in view to secure the services of so determined a ruffian, in case he should have an opportunity of employing him in his own line of business. There is a striking contrast between the fate of Blood, pensioned and rewarded for this audacious attempt, and that of the faithful Edwards, who may be safely said to have sacrificed his life in defence of the property entrusted to him! In remuneration for his fidelity and his sufferings, Edwards only obtained a grant of £200 from the Exchequer, with £100 to his son; but so little pains were taken about the regular discharge of these donatives, that the parties entitled to them were glad to sell them for half the sum. After this wonderful escape from justice, Blood seems to have affected the airs of a person in favour, and was known to solicit the suits of many of the old republican party, for whom he is said to have gained considerable indulgences, when the old cavaliers, who had ruined themselves in the cause of Charles the First, could obtain neither countenance nor restitution. During the ministry called the Cabal, he was high in favour with the Duke of Buckingham; till upon their declension, his favour began also to fail, and we find him again engaged in opposition to the Court. Blood was not likely to lie idle amid the busy intrigues and factions which succeeded the celebrated discovery of Oates. He appears to have passed again into violent opposition to the Court, but his steps were no longer so sounding as to be heard above his contemporaries. North hints at his being involved in a plot against his former friend and patron the Duke of Buckingham. The passage is quoted at length in Note 24, p. 644.

The Plot, it appears, consisted in an attempt to throw some scandalous imputation upon the Duke of Buckingham, for a conspiracy to effect which Edward Christian, Arthur O'Brien, and Thomas Blood were indicted in the King's Bench, and found guilty, June 25, 1680. The damages sued for were laid as high as ten thousand pounds, for which Colonel Blood found bail. But he appears to have been severely affected in health, as, August 24, 1680, he departed this life in a species of lethargy. It is remarkable enough that the story of his death and funeral was generally regarded as fabricated, preparative to some exploit of his own ; nay, so general was this report, that the coroner caused his body to be raised, and a jury to sit upon it, for the purpose of ensuring that the celebrated Blood had at length undergone the common fate of mankind. There was found unexpected difficulty in proving that the miserable corpse before the jury was that of the celebrated conspirator. It was at length recognized by some of his acquaintants, who swore to the preternatural size of the thumb, so that the coroner, convinced of the identity, remanded this once active, and now quiet person, to his final rest in Tothill Fields.

Such were the adventures of an individual, whose real exploits, whether the motive, the danger, or the character of the enterprises be considered, equal, or rather surpass, those fictions of violence and peril which we love to peruse in romance. They cannot, therefore, be deemed foreign to a work dedicated, like the present, to the preservation of extraordinary occurrences, whether real or fictitious.

NOTE 28.—TEST OF THE SENSES, p. 617

This little piece of superstition was suggested by the following incident. The author of *Waverley* happened to be standing by with other gentlemen, while the captain of the Selkirk Yeomanry was purchasing a horse for the use of his trumpeter. The animal offered was a handsome one, and neither the officer, who was an excellent jockey, nor any one present, could see any imperfection in wind or limb. But a person happened to pass, who was asked to give an opinion. This man was called Blind Willie, who drove a small trade in cattle and horses, and what seemed as extraordinary, in watches, notwithstanding his having been born blind. He was accounted to possess a rare judgement in these subjects of traffic. So soon as he had examined the horse in question, he immediately pronounced it to have something of his own complaint, and in plain words stated it to be blind, or verging upon that imperfection, which was found to be the case on close examination. None present had suspected this fault in the animal ; which is not wonderful, considering that it may frequently exist without any appearance in the organ affected. Blind Willie, being asked how he made a discovery imperceptible to so many gentlemen who had their eyesight, explained, that after feeling the horse's limbs, he laid one hand on its heart, and drew the other briskly across the animal's eyes, when, finding no increase of pulsation, in consequence of the latter motion, he had come to the conclusion that the horse must be blind.

GLOSSARY

abiit—evasit—erupit, he has gone —he has slipped away—he has broken forth.

ad valorem, according to the value.

aîné, elder brother.

à la Française, in the French use.

à la mort, overcome.

alias, otherwise.

allons, forward.

âme damnée, a cat's paw.

amo, I love.

arcanum, the secret (of transmuting base metal into gold).

Archbishop of Granada's apoplexy, Gil Blas was dismissed from the Archbishop's service for adverse criticism of sermons composed by his master after suffering from a fit of apoplexy (*Gil Blas* vii. 4).

auberge, tavern, inn.

à vendre et à pendre, to sell or to hang, i. e. to do as you like with.

Barmoot Court, a local court amongst miners.

barnacles, spectacles.

bâton, rod.

beauffet, sideboard.

black-jack, a leather beer-jug coated externally with tar.

blasé, wearied-out, bored.

bolt, arrow.

bon vivant, a gourmand.

boot, to the, into the bargain.

bouilli, boiled meat.

brisket, breast.

buskins, half-boots.

Cabala, a secret system of magic.

cameradoes, comrades.

carder, one who cards (combs out the impurities and straightens) wool for spinning.

carwitchet, a pun, conundrum.

Catiline, a noted conspirator against the government and state of Rome.

cave, &c. (p. 638), beware of those whom God has marked.

caviare, the roe of the sturgeon, pressed and salted.

cedant arma togae, let the soldier give place to the man of peace.

Century White, John White, author of *The First Century of scandalous, malignant Priests, made and admitted into Benefices by the Prelates*, 1643.

certiorated, certified, informed authoritatively.

chauffette, a chafing-dish (vessel containing charcoal, for heating anything placed upon it).

chef-d'œuvres, masterpieces.

Chère Comtesse, &c. (p. 570), dear Countess of Derby, powerful Queen of Man, our very august sister.

ciceroni, guides who show and explain the antiquities or curiosities of a place to strangers.

ci-devant, former.

comitia, the assembly of the people.

congée, bow.

conticuere omnes, all were silent.

coupe-jarrets, paid assassins.

couranto, a dance.

cuckoldy, a term of abuse.

cum privilegio parliamenti, with the privilege of parliament.

dammer, one who constructs dams.

darbies, handcuffs, fetters.

decimo-octavo, size of a book-page, about 6 × 3¾ inches.

Demoivre, a French mathematician, 1667–1754.

dempster, a judge.

de non apparentibus, &c. (p. 531), the same account is taken of things that do not appear as of things that do not exist.

divertissement, amusement.

dog-bolt, lit. a blunt-headed arrow (used as a term of contempt or reproach).

Dove, a river in Derbyshire.

dramatis personae, persons of the drama.

drift-drivers, those who drive in piles.

dulcis Amaryllidis ira, the anger of sweet Amaryllis.

dum vivimus, vivamus, while we live, let us enjoy life.

éclat, magnificence, noise.

eidolon, an unsubstantial image, spectre, phantom.

ein, a.

embonpoint, plumpness.

en cavalier, like a gallant.

engoué, infatuated with.

ennui, weariness, boredom.

en signor, like a nobleman.

entrechats, dancing-movements.

entrée, admittance.

entremets, side-dishes.

epiglottis, the cartilage at the root of the tongue.

estramaçon, a term in sword-play.

étranger, stranger.

et sic de caeteris, and so of other matters.

Éveillez-vous, belle endormie, awake, fair sleeper !

faire la cuisine, to do the cooking.

faitour, impostor, cheat.

fief, an estate in land held on condition of homage and service to a superior lord.

fille-de-joie, a prostitute.

flagrantibus odiis, amid the burning hate.

fox, a sword.

frampal jades, fiery, mettlesome, spirited horses.

frumps, sulks, ill humour.

fuga daemonum, the flight of the devils.

fuoruscito, outlaw.

Galfridus minimus, smallest of all Geoffreys.

ganz ist verloren, all is lost.

gastronome, a judge of good eating.

gear, affair, business.

Gobelines, the state-factory of tapestry in Paris, so named after its founders.

governante, housekeeper.

Governor of Tilbury. The reference is to Sheridan's *Critic* ii. 2.

Gulielmus Bastardus, William the Bastard.

haud aliena, &c. (p. 639), lit. :—' not very different from the works of Scaevola', similar in kind.

haud equidem, &c. (p. xxxvii). I am not envious but rather wonder at it.

hays, a country dance having a winding or serpentine movement.

herring-buss, a two- or three-masted vessel used in the herring-fishery.

hinc illae lachrymae, hence those tears.

hough, the hollow part behind the knee-joint.

howlet, owl, owlet.

hundsfoot, rascal.

ignoramus, not a true bill.

immodicum surgit, &c. (p. xl), his enormous nose stands out like a spear.

incognito, incognita, unknown.

in esse, in being.

in posse, possible.

Insula Monae, the Isle of Man.

in terrorem, as a warning, to terrify.

intra parietes, between house-walls.

jacobus, a gold coin, value 25*s.*, struck in the reign of James I.
jeu de mots, play upon words.
jocose hoc, this for a jest.

la belle cousine, the fair cousin.
lachrymae Christi, red wine from the slopes of Vesuvius.
laus propria sordet, self-praise is worthless.
leaguer, an investing force; a siege.
Le Notre, a French architect, the planner of St. James's Park.
Lehrjahre, apprenticeship.
le prix juste, the fair price.
liaison, illicit intimacy between a man and a woman.
Liber Pater, the god of wine.
licentia exeundi, leave to go out.
lignum vitae, an exceedingly hard close-grained wood.
Limbo Patrum, the fools' paradise of *Paradise Lost*, Book III, 495.
Lingua Franca, mixed language spoken by Europeans in the East.
Looby-land, lubberland, an imaginary land of plenty without labour.
lymph, liquid.

madge-howlet, the barn-owl.
mains, a home farm.
maire de palais, mayor of the palace.
malice prepense, premeditated malice.
malum in se, evil in itself.
Martello towers, a small circular fort with massive walls, usually erected on a coast to repel invasion.
mauthe dog, a spectral hound, in Welsh and Manx superstition.
mauvaise plaisanterie, bad joke.
mein Gott, my God.
mêlée, a mixed or irregular fight.
mercer, one who deals in textile fabrics.
micher, a secret or petty thief.

minauderie, mincing manners.
montero-cap, a Spanish hunter's cap, having a spherical crown and a flap capable of being drawn over the ears.
mortbleu, an oath.
Morte D'Arthur, the collection of Arthurian legends.

naïveté, innocence, frankness.
naunt, aunt.
nepenthe, a drug supposed to banish grief or trouble from the mind.
non omnibus dormio, I am not asleep to all matters.

obstupui, steteruntque comae, I was astounded, and my hair stood on end.

Palmerin of England, a famous knight in the tales of chivalry.
par excellence, pre-eminently.
par voie du fait, by force of arms.
pas seul, dance by a single performer.
passio hysterica, hysteria.
pavé, pavement.
peccadillo, a small or venial fault or sin.
pendables, men liable to be hanged.
penthouse, shelter, porch.
petite-maitresse, a female dandy.
Piccoluomini, little man.
pinguitude, fatness.
pink, a sailing vessel with a narrow stern.
pinners, a coif or woman's cap) with two long flaps.
piquante, tasty
plats, dishes.
plumer la poule sans la faire crier, to pluck the fowl without causing it to cry out.
porterly, porter-like.
posse comitatus, the force of men at the disposal of the sheriff.
posso tirare, I can shoot.
post obit, interest after death.
powle, pole.

PEVERIL U u

projection, powder of, powder of the philosopher's stone cast upon a metal to effect its transmutation into gold.

properare in mediam rem, to hasten to the very midst of the matter.

pursuivant, a warrant-officer.

quem ego, whom I . . .

quodlibet, any question in philosophy or theology proposed as an exercise in disputation.

ragout, a dish of meat cut in small pieces, stewed with vegetables, and highly seasoned.

rede, to advise or counsel.

renitente cancellario, the chancellor opposing.

ridge-and-furrow, knitted stockings with ridges.

roi fainéant, lazy king.

Rosicrucian, appertaining to a supposed society whose members were said to claim various forms of secret and magic knowledge.

rummer, a large drinking-glass.

salmagundi, a mixture of chopped meat and various ingredients with seasonings.

saraband, a slow Spanish dance.

sarsenet, a fine, thin woven silk.

Schelm, rogue.

Sequestrations, the taking possession of others' property till some claim is paid.

sieur, master.

sinkers, men who sink shafts.

solus, alone.

soupe d'écrivisses, lobster soup.

souper au petit couvert, supper without ceremony.

stingo, a strong pungent beer or liquor.

super naculum, to the very bottom (alluding to the custom of draining the glass upon the thumbnail, to show that all the wine has been drunk).

suzerainté, suzerainty, feudal lordship.

swartness, a dark hue.

tabak, tobacco.

tandem triumphans, at length triumphant.

tantivy, with great speed.

thrift, household work.

Tinwald, the parliament of the Isle of Man.

tour de son métier, a trick after his fashion.

trepans, traps ; *to trepan,* to entrap.

triposes, tripods.

trollop, a slattern.

trowl, to push.

trunnion, a ring fixed to the shank of an anchor.

tu me la pagherai, you shall pay me for it.

Tutbury-running, a fair at Tutbury, in Staffs.

vallis negotii, the valley of business.

verjuice, sour (from the liquor expressed from sour apples, sour grapes, &c.).

vicinage, neighbourhood.

Vicit Leo ex tribu Judae, the Lion of the tribe of Judah has conquered.

victoria ! &c. (p. 485), victory ! victory ! great is truth and it shall prevail.

videlicet, namely.

vin de Cahors, Cahors wine.

vogue la galère, come what may.

volte-face, right about face.

wannion, vengeance.

weasand, windpipe.

welkin, the sky.

whimsy, a whim, freak.

whinyard, sword.

wrack, wreck, ruin.

zecchin, gold Byzantine or Venetian coin, about 9s. 4d.

OXFORD: HORACE HART
PRINTER TO THE UNIVERSITY